Ivailo Petrov

WOLF HUNT

Translated from the Bulgarian
by Angela Rodel

archipelago books

Archipelago Books
232 Third Street #A111
Brooklyn, NY 11215

www.archipelagobooks.org

Library of Congress Cataloging-in-Publication Data
Wolf hunt / Ivailo Petrov ; translated from the Bulgarian by Angela Rodel.
Other titles: Hayka za valtsi. English
LCCN 2016051928 | ISBN 9780914671701 (paperback)
BISAC: FICTION / Literary.
LCC PG1038.26.E8 K43313 2017 | DDC 891.8/133--dc23
LC record available at https://lccn.loc.gov/2016051928

Cover art: Marta Rayhel

Distributed by Penguin Random House
www.penguinrandomhouse.com

Archipelago Books gratefully acknowledges the generous support from
the *National Book Centre* program of the Bulgarian National Palace of Culture,
Sofia Municipality Culture Programme, the Lannan Foundation, the National
Endowment for the Arts,
the New York City Department of Cultural Affairs,
and the New York State Council on the Arts, a state agency.

PRINTED IN CANADA

WOLF HUNT

INTRODUCTION

AT THAT TIME, the so-called process of industrial migration had success-fully come to an end, and in my village only aging and elderly people were left to live out their lives. The youngest were past fifty, so the process of giving birth had successfully come to an end as well. In seven years, only one child had been born in the village, to the tractor driver, and he was a transplant. In the fall the child had gone to school in the main village on the local cooperative farm's bus, which would come by in the morning to pick up kids from the neighboring two villages as well. But since the big cold snap had taken hold, the bus hadn't stopped to get the boy, as there was still no paved road to the main village, and no vehicle could get down the dirt road, piled as it was with snow and iced over. Incidentally, for this same reason I, too, wasn't able to slip away from the village for ten whole days.

The case of the tractor driver's boy had become a village-wide topic of conversation, so when I went down to the *horemag* (you likely recall that years ago, all our villages had one of these highly propitious, righteous establishments – a combination of a hotel, restaurant, and store – which eventually reverted to your average, ordinary tavern), the men were dis-cussing it yet again. They had told me about the child Lord knows how many times, yet I still had to listen to the whole story from beginning to end and, of course, weigh in on the question. I said what everyone had been saying for months already, namely that, on the one hand, the school authorities in the main village were to blame for not sending the bus to pick the boy up, while on the other, they weren't to blame at all, since the bus couldn't get through the icebound road.

"I understand that it's a complex business," the tractor driver shouted heatedly, "but that's cold comfort for me! I want my kid to study, I want to make a decent man out of him, no ifs, ands, or buts about it!"

Meanwhile, the Holy Communion I had been invited to partake in had begun. In late December, the homemade wine started clearing up, so the locals here had established the ritual of taking a bottle down to the tavern to hear opinions on their "domestic production." Bay* Trendo Two-Bits set out glasses on the table quick as a flash and with a professional flick of the wrist divvied up the first bottle. He had run a tavern for as long as I could remember and would keep running one despite the vicissitudes of the times. When the co-op was founded, some teetotaling wave to close down the pubs had gathered steam, so they tried to stick him with some other job, but he gave them the slip and disappeared for a few years. He went to a different village, and from there to the city, where he opened up a tavern right across from the city slaughterhouse. His best and most loyal clients were the butchers – swaggering, dyed-in-the-wool boozers, every one of them. There were seven of them and they would arrive early in the morning, before dawn. Bellied up to the bar, they would toss back a shot or two and roar: "Mmmm-hmm, that devil's piss set my soul on fire!" In the evening, Two-Bits would leave the shot glasses out, filled with water to freshen them up a bit, then in the morning he'd fill them with brandy and line them up on the bar to save the butchers time. One morning he was held up a bit in the storeroom, and when he got back, what did he see? – there they were, lined up at the bar, raising the shot glasses full of pure water, shaking their heads and praising the brandy: "This time you gave us your strongest stuff!" After that, Two-Bits never once served them brandy again, and never once, over the course of a whole year, did they realize that they were drinking pure water.

While recounting this incident from his life and times as a tavern keeper, Bay Trendo Two-Bits took the first sip and declared: "Bravo, Kalcho, your wine is *très magnifique!*"

The others accepted this judgment stoically, because they knew that due to long years of alcohol consumption, the tavern keeper had lost any sense of taste for drink, just like the butchers he had just told them about. Everyone turned to Stoyan "Man of Steel" Kralev, who passed as the best taster among them. He raised his glass to his lips, took a large swig and stared at the slogan – likely thought up by the tavern keeper, but written out in a calligraphic hand by Ivan "Painkiller" Shibilev:

Socialism and alcohol are like cats and dogs, yet they live under the same roof.

The other men were staring at him, watching silently as he squinted his eyes slightly and froze up, as if sunk in the magic of some mystery. His gray moustache, cut short and placed like a square rug between his nose and mouth, flinched and puckered, his windpipe shuddered as well, showing that he had let the sip wash over his palate. He opened his eyes, smacked his lips, and finally offered his weighty pronouncement: "Here's to your health – may you drink it with pleasure on television! Three flavors stand out: our local vine, Muscat, and a hint of Pamid. Intertwined like the three strands of a rope…"

"You hit the nail on the head!" Zhendo "the Bandit" said, impressed. "He even picked up on the hint of Pamid."

They all took sips of the wine – some more impatiently, others with the dignity that the situation demanded – and unanimously confirmed Stoyan Kralev's authoritative opinion. Next they tried wines made by Nikolin "Little Horn" Miyalkov and Kiro "Up Yours" Dzhelebov, which both received the same high praise. Incidentally, you have probably noticed that everyone has nicknames, and rather disconcerting ones at that, but let us not get ahead of ourselves – it will later become clear why, how, and under what circumstances each man got his nickname. For the time being, I will merely note that there were a few wiseacres in our village whose vocation for thinking up nicknames was passed on from father to son, such that no one was left without a nickname, while others had even two or three, for everyday use and for special occasions, as it were. Even domestic animals bore the nicknames of their owners, so if some dog was barking or some cow was mooing, everybody'd say: "Petko the Kibitzer's barking" or "Dobri the Spaz is mooing again." The local wiseacres not only lacked a sense of collegial solidarity – indeed, on the contrary, driven by artistic envy, it seems, they were so merciless toward one another that some of their very own nicknames were used only by a tight circle, while those meant for general usage were uttered by all without the slightest hint of embarrassment: Yanko the Motherkiller, Green Apple Gancho, Pissant Georgi, Snotnosed Ivan, and so on.

In any case, only twenty or so people in the village had vineyards, so it was no secret which sorts each man grew, how many liters he'd made, and what his bouquet entailed, yet this Holy Communion had the irresistible charm of mutual magnanimity. Everyone enjoyed running a swig of another man's wine over his palate, giving his blessing and receiving one in return. After the solemn tasting ritual concluded, each man would drink his wine at home "on television," as Stoyan Kralev put it – that is, not in front of a television set, but from a bowl or a shallow cup. At that time, there was already one television set in the village, the local folks had filed past it to take a look, and by-the-by had noticed that their images were reflected in bowls of wine just like on television when they raised them up to take a drink.

From time to time, there was a pounding on the door, somebody would come in, wrapped in a fur cloak or an overcoat, and along with him a whole cloud of fine, hard snow would bluster inside, showering a good half of the tavern like sand. The newcomer would stamp his feet one last time behind the door, and if he was carrying wine, would leave it on the table and sit down wherever he could find a seat. The enormous oval barrel stove, dark as a buffalo's belly, crackled and strained to redness, while the air around it shimmered like summer haze, and the room swayed in the sweet daze brought on by the scent of new wine and wet furs. The fantastical designs on the nearby windowpane turned to murky moisture, now and again someone would wipe the lowest pane with his sleeve, and you could see the branches of a tree twisting nearby, black as coal, forlorn and cheerless; you could also see the ghostly outlines of the closest houses, veiled in the impressionistic white of the snowflakes, behind which the head of the old well jutted up into the sky like a cabalistic sign, while everything else around it, swathed in grayish-white invisibility, hinted at mysteriousness and enchantment. Inside the tavern as well reigned a mood unusual for the occasion. The men had been sipping wine for a whole hour already and a slight flush filled their cheeks, but strangely, they did not raise their voices, but rather with a ritualistic solemnity spoke quietly and courteously about the finer points of the art of viniculture. Even the youngest, the tractor driver, who had been on the lookout the whole time for a suitable moment to once again raise the unsettled question of his child's education, carefully set his emptied glass down on the table and said, as if uttering an incantation: "I came here over hill and dale to earn a buck or two and get my child an education. And what of it? They tell me to rent the kid an apartment in town – but how can I put up a seven-year-old in an apartment? My wife and I would have to go with him. And that's damn well what I intend to do. Once the weather breaks, I'm going to find a new job in a village that has a school. The only thing I care about is making a decent man out of him..."

"Yeah, well, we all made decent folks out of our kids, and we haven't seen hide or hair of them since," said Grandpa Radi, also known as Grandpa Saggy Pants. "If you shook a stick around this whole village, you wouldn't hit a single young person. Last summer my oldest boy came to visit with his wife. We hadn't seen them or the grandkids in three years.

Now, my son might think to drop a line every now and then, but her, the wife, she never gives us the time of day. She slurps up brandy and puffs on cigarettes like a regular floozy, while spewing out such hogwash that it makes your ears burn to hear it! So Grandma and I said to ourselves, well, they finally thought to come see us, while those two, by-the-by, started wheedling me to sell half the yard and give them the money. Said they wanted to buy themselves a place to build a villa. A while back I'd given them three grand to buy a car, and now they're nagging at me for a villa. The jig is up, I said. I'm not going to give your brother a red cent either, as long as I live, since he hasn't bothered to show his face here for years. You get married without us, I said, you have children without us, you baptize them without us, you can build your villa without us as well. And they whined: You're not thinking about us at all, you're getting on in years already, while we've still got our whole lives in front of us. Damn right, I tell 'em, since I'm getting on in years, that's exactly why I need a house and a yard and some money tucked away for rainy days, so when I fall, there'll be someone to look after me. Then I sent them packing with a sack of potatoes and nothing more."

"The Pangarovs didn't even come to bury their father," someone from the same table chimed in. "Two sons and two daughters, and not a single one of them came to toss a handful of dirt on his grave. One didn't get the telegram in time, the other was on a business trip… But when it came time to split up the house and the land, all four of them showed up lightning-fast. They fought like cats and dogs, splitting up everything down to the last brick…"

The blizzard pounded at the windows, showering them with snow, the stovepipes howled ominously like sirens, while the buffalo-belly of a stove choked, coughed, spit fire from its mouth, and seemed to rise toward the ceiling a bit. It had come time to try Zhendo "the Bandit" Ivanov's wine. The tavern keeper pulled the corncob out of the neck of the bottle and was just about to pour a round when the door opened, hitting the wall with a bang. Amidst the white surge of the blizzard, a dog yellow as a flame appeared, standing in the middle of the tavern on three legs. Everyone stared at it, as if some evil spirit had come inside, incarnated as that lame yellow dog. It began turning its head, looking over all the men first with its left, then with its right eye, as if looking for someone to deliver a message to or to hex with an evil omen. No one dared to flinch, so as not to attract its attention.

"Noseless Anani!" the tavern keeper cried. He was Anani's neighbor and saw the dog in his yard every day. "He keeps it hungry, so that's why the no-good mutt roams around the whole village! Now, git, Anani, shoo, shoo!"

The tavern keeper waved to chase the dog off and knocked one of the glasses from the table onto the floor. The dog, seeming to sense that the men in the pub were nonplussed by its visit, turned around and disappeared into the blizzard. The superstitious old men saw this as a bad omen. Dogs presage earthquakes, bad weather, and impending death. Anani was a night owl, if, God forbid, he had gotten into trouble, nobody'd be the wiser. However, Stoyan Kralev said that only an hour earlier he had seen Anani coming back from the well with his shoulder pole, others seconded this, and the Holy Communion continued. It had come time to taste Zhendo "the Bandit" Ivanov's wine as well. He took off his cap and tucked it under his arm. He had only recently gotten his vineyard, this was his first time making homemade wine, so while he was awaiting the other men's blessings, he stood at attention as if at an exam. It turned out that the tavern keeper had knocked Salty Kalcho's glass off the table. He looked for another glass but couldn't find one, so he poured wine into a soda bottle. It was now Kalcho's turn to take a sip of wine and give his blessing, so he grabbed the bottle but didn't lift it to his lips. His fingers pulled away from the bottle and like five little dwarves from a fairy tale, they put their heads together conspiratorially, as if plotting something and cooking up a plan of action. The men at the table fell silent and stared at these little dwarves, as if trying to overhear their whispers and puzzle out their plans. I can't say how long it went on, but it must have been too long, because it felt awkward and painful. But I, like all the others, didn't dare move, so as not to disturb what I thought might be some ritual of theirs. I merely allowed myself to look them over and noticed that Zhendo's balding forehead was very white, while Salty Kalcho's eyes were moist. Overexcited by the Holy Communion, it seemed, he couldn't stand the tension, which was growing ever more agonizing, he covered his eyes with his hands and some wild, heart-wrenching groan tore from his lips: "Mmaaah!"

The tavern fell silent, the men from the neighboring tables set down their glasses and turned toward Salty Kalcho's table. Several seconds passed in heavy silence. Zhendo's face turned from white to beet-red, he wiped his sweaty forehead with a cap and again tucked it under his arm. His hands were shaking, and he started rubbing them together. And then Ivan Shibilev leapt to his feet, as if he had just remembered something very important, cheerfully took a sip from his glass, and said with a smile: "Hey, people! Well now, I came here to tell you about the wolves, but wouldn't you know it, this wine has addled my brain. Did you know that three wolves showed up in our common pasture? This morning Keran the shepherd came to my place to borrow my rifle. They felled a dozen sheep just like that, he says, but since we don't have any guns, we can't get rid of them. We chase them out of one pen, they rush into the other one. With all the hunters we've got in this village, he says, you'll blow them away in no time. Their tracks lead all the way to the quarry, they prowl around there by day. I didn't give him my gun, because I said to myself, if we leave now, we'll have knocked them off by evening. Who's in? We'll have a wolf hunt."

As we shall see, Ivan Shibilev, also known as the "Painkiller" for his ability to remedy all ills, has since time out of mind showed all sorts of eccentricities, so his suggestion to go out into the woods in this blizzard to hunt wolves did not stun, but rather amused the men in the tavern who were not hunters. And he had started talking about this wolf hunt with the cheerful enthusiasm of a person who's suddenly gotten an idea that was unexpected even to himself, which was absolutely in keeping with his character. The strangest part was that the other five members of the village hunting club happened to be at that same table and all of them – as if they had planned it in advance – got up and went to get their rifles. Once they were outside, Ivan Shibilev tried to backpedal, saying the blizzard had gotten worse so they had better leave the hunt for the next day, but the other five replied that putting it off was unthinkable and even reproached him for stringing them along. They agreed to meet half an hour later in front of his gate and went to get their rifles.

When he got home, Ivan Shibilev saw a pot on the stove and felt hungry. He took off his fur wrap, served himself a plate of food, and sat down to eat. He was convinced that the others wouldn't come get him, so after he finished eating, he lay down for a nap. But wouldn't you know – he heard shouts and whistles from outside, soon followed by knocks on the window. Ivan Shibilev jumped out of bed, opened the door a crack, and saw them standing in his yard with rifles on their shoulders. *These people are nuts*, he thought to himself, *but what could he do?* He put on his fur coat and grabbed his rifle off the wall. He hadn't gone out hunting for a long time; out of habit he looked around for his cartridge belt, and not finding it, he left without bullets.

"Come on, you lead!" somebody called.

"Damn right I'll lead!" Ivan Shibilev smiled to show that he'd let them play out their prank to the very end.

He suspected and could see that his friends were still in a pleasant mood after the wine tasting and had decided with this joke to get back at him for all the jokes he had played on them. At the same time, he was pleased that they had "taken up" the wolf hunt, which showed that they, too, had anticipated some clash between Salty Kalcho and Zhendo and had left the tavern without a second thought so as to prevent it. Ivan Shibilev was further convinced of their mischievous intentions, since a short while earlier he had said that the wolves' tracks led to the quarry, and not toward the woods where they were headed now, and besides that, anyone could see that they would never find any tracks in a howler like this. This was why he expected that as soon as they reached the edge of the village, they would burst out laughing and say that was the end of the wolf hunt. It also crossed his mind that they could have planned to drop away one by one and go back home, leaving him to trudge toward the woods by himself. At one point it even seemed like he could only hear his own footsteps, so he stopped ostensibly to tighten his shoelace, and glanced back. They were all behind him single file, and as far as he could tell, no one showed any signs of stopping and turning back. He turned his rifle so the barrel was facing downward, tossed it over his shoulder, and pushed on ahead. It was half an hour's walk to the woods, and during that time, no one spoke. Ivan Shibilev cleared the path, hearing the crunch of his own footsteps; from time to time he again thought the others were lagging behind, so he always found some excuse to look back.

And so they reached the Dogwoods, the only grove in these parts. Once it had been a big oak forest and only one end of it, nearest to the village, had any dogwoods. But little by little they had cleared the trees to give land to the indigent and to settlers, first the dogwood grove, then half the oak forest as well. Right in the middle of it there is a large, steep ravine, which opens to the south and which is known by the frightening name "the Inferno." That's what it had been dubbed by some holy roller from the neighboring village who had come to worship at our church. During one harsh winter, the holy roller fell into the ravine at night, and after he crawled out more dead than alive, he told our folks here: "I've come from the Inferno."

Actually, the Inferno was our local slice of paradise – its slopes, now as then, were grown over with oak foliage and shrubs, while down on its floor, a finger-thin spring spurted forth. In the spring, summer, and fall, it was always warm and sheltered, the first crocuses and snowdrops bloomed there, followed by the first strawberries; May Day, Saint George's Day, and Easter were celebrated there, it was also pastureland for our livestock in seasons when the crops hadn't yet been harvested from the fields.

Ivan Shibilev took a hundred or so steps into the woods and stopped beneath an enormous oak.

"Well, I'll be damned, we ended up right here at our oak!"

"We sure did!" the others said.

After having been silent all the way from the village, everyone now livened up, as if taking the oak as some kind of sign. They started talking anxiously, unclearly, as their lips were blue from the cold, while their moustaches and eyebrows were white with frost. Ivan Shibilev could not recognize their faces but saw in them a crushing and wild ugliness; he glanced toward the forest and tried to smile: "So what now?"

"What do you mean, 'what now'? Let's draw lots!"

Ivan Shibilev, obeying somehow mechanically, took out a matchbox and explained which end meant beaters and which meant shooters. Nikolin Miyalkov was standing closest to him and drew the first lot – shooter. Kiro Dzhelebov and Salty Kalcho drew the same, leaving the other three to be beaters.

"I'm going to the blind," Kiro Dzhelebov said, and stepped first into the forest.

PART ONE:

KALCHO STATEV,
AKA SALTY KALCHO OR TROTSKY

I'LL TRY TO INTRODUCE to you the six hunters individually and I'll start with him, since he was the reason they set off in that miserable weather to track wolves.

Years ago, Salty Kalcho was the syndicated watchman for the village vineyards. He wore a tan military uniform and a peaked cap minus the cockade, pulled down low over his brow year-round, he also had a cartridge pouch on a strap, white gaiters, and a rifle slung over his shoulder. He had gotten the uniform itself from the soldiers at the border post, while the gaiters with their goat-hair laces were his own domestic production. Ivan Shibilev had read somewhere – albeit with considerable delay – that the Russian defense minister after the revolution was some Trotsky or other, and thus had dubbed the uniformed watchman "Trotsky."

We were related to the Trotsky family along a couple of lines (my grandmother and his wife were the daughters of two sisters), so we did most of our farmwork together. We would hoe or reap one of their fields, then one of ours – this collective work was called *medzhiya*. Trotsky had about a dozen acres of land, left completely to the womenfolk, as he had a strong aversion to agricultural labor. His wife and three daughters worked the fields and also raised livestock, since the land alone could hardly keep four mouths fed. On rare occasions during hoeing or reaping time, Trotsky would come down to the field to demonstrate his speed and skill at such work. People from the nearby fields would stand up in their rows to watch him, while he, in his peaked cap and uniform jacket buttoned up to the very top, with his cartridge pouches at his waist and his rifle over his shoulder, would take up a swath as wide as half the field and start hoeing or reaping away. He would work so fast that even ten men couldn't keep up with him, without stopping for a minute from morning until noon, then in the afternoon he would toss down his hoe or scythe and head back to the vineyard.

He had a spacious and comfortable shack there thatched with a thick layer of hay, with a fireplace and a bed, he even built a two-story veranda on the front of it. Our vineyard was right next to his, and when I'd go with my grandfather to pick cherries or grapes, I was always in awe of the watchman, perched like a vulture on the upper level of the veranda, ready to blow his whistle or shout as soon as he spotted some suspicious character pottering around the vineyard, while the veranda itself seemed to rise to the heavens. My grandfather would often stop by to shoot the breeze and then I would have the good fortune to climb up first to the lower level, then to the upper level of his veranda, which offered a bird's-eye view of the vineyard and the two neighboring villages. Trotsky spent his best years on that veranda. In his hours on duty, he scanned the vineyard from one end to the other like a hawk, ready like Gyuro Mihaylov* to sacrifice himself for our constitutionally sanctified and inviolable property. The only ones who unlawfully encroached on our property were local kids herding flocks nearby and dogs, thus in his years-long employ as watchman, Trotsky did not chalk up a single heroic deed besides the killing of several strays.

In his hours off duty, he would sit on the lower level of the veranda, eating or dozing in the cool shade, bareheaded and in his shirtsleeves. Only here, far from prying eyes, did he remove his uniform and munitions, but as soon as the dog caught scent of a person, he would pull them back on in an instant, even if that person was one of his own daughters. Like a knight stripped of his armor, he seemed to lose his self-confidence as a formidable personality, thus he never appeared to anyone without his uniform. Beneath his shirt, unbuttoned to the waist and yellowish-green with sweat, his chicken-like chest could be seen, hairless, white and swollen like dough; his arms, naked to the elbow, were thin as sticks, and he looked somehow yellow, like a turtle without a shell or a hedgehog without quills.

Trotsky didn't go home to eat, instead his wife brought food to him at the shack every midday and evening. Once his daughters grew up a bit, the eldest took her mother's place, and when she was married off, she was replaced by the middle girl, Radka. At that time, the local authorities started building a paved road from the neighboring village to ours. For four years, they dug stones out of the quarry, trucked them over, smashed them into gravel, and during all those years, Radka crossed those two trenches at one and the same place every day. By the time the road was finished, she'd grown up, a young woman ripe for the picking, and wouldn't you know – one day Zhendo "the Bandit" Ivanov sent his matchmakers calling on her father at his shack. Trotsky went down to the yard and met his guests there. He heard them out, reeled off a lengthy fit of smoker's cough, and sent them away: "I've got no daughters to marry off!"

His land had been in wretched shape since time immemorial, and now he figured that if he married off Radka as well, he would find himself face-to-face with complete economic ruin.

Not only was Zhendo not fazed by Trotsky's categorical response, he even announced that he would go himself to arrange the match. Everyone was surprised by his eagerness to have Radka as a daughter-in-law at any cost, especially since her father enjoyed a reputation as the biggest sluggard in the village, while she herself did not shine with any particular virtues. A few days later, he went to visit Trotsky at his thatched residence by night, when he had lit the fire and was sitting down to dinner.

"I'll cut right to the chase, my friend!" Zhendo started in after they'd said their hellos and sat down face-to-face across the fire. "It might vex you to hear it, but since you've got a daughter, and I've got a son, we need to talk. You're the seller, and I'm the buyer, as it were. That's how it's been since the days of yore, and that's how it'll be as long as there are young-sters to marry off. If it suits you, you'll give us your daughter, if not – so be it." As he said this, Zhendo pulled a bottle of brandy, a hunk of cheese, and a few tomatoes out of a bag and set them on the broad stump that served as a table. "Let's drink a snort and talk man-to-man. You know very well, my friend, that I'm not here to browbeat you, but rather to hear your final word with my own two ears. Whatever you say – that's how it'll be."

"Well, now, I don't rightly know what to tell you. It's all happened so sudden-like…" Trotsky coughed, lit a cigarette from the fire, and fell silent.

He was flattered and flustered by Zhendo's opening speech; he had been expecting arrogance and reproaches but heard only goodwill and respect, so he truly did not know what to say.

"There's no law that says you've got to give your final word right this minute. Tomorrow's another day. Don't you go thinking that if they came asking for my son that I'd tell 'em yes or no right off the bat. I'd think it over, I'd do my reckoning. To be frank, my friend, I could choose me another daughter-in-law. Why the hell not? I'm not feebleminded or poor as a church mouse, now am I?" Zhendo went on, lifting the bottle a third time. "But Koycho has taken a shine to Radka, he won't hear of any other girl, and that's that. Well, I could make him change his tune right quick if I put my mind to it, but he's my only son, now, so I says to myself – why take the wind out of his sails? And besides, Radka's a hard-working girl, haven't I seen her out slogging in the fields since she was a kid? But I know what's eating at you, friend. You're saying to yourself: Well now, if I give her away, who'll be left to work at my place? That's how it is, raising a daughter is like watering your neighbor's garden. But there's a cure for that ill, too. We'll be in-laws, friend, we'll look after each other. Till now you've done *medzhiya* with other folks, from now on you'll do it with us. One day our field, the next day yours, like we're working common land."

Trotsky was staring into the fire, smoking one cigarette after another and listening carefully. Once Zhendo promised to help him with the field-work, which meant that in the future he could continue lounging on his veranda, he himself reached for the bottle, took a swig, and passed it to his guest.

"Well, lemme drink to your health as well! I got nothing against your offer, but it's just that we ain't ready yet, Zhendo. We ain't ready. If this business is gonna happen, it'll happen next year at the earliest. You can't send a girl off empty-handed."

"Are you hinting at a dowry? Forget all that hogwash, for the love of Pete! What, you think I came here to ask for your daughter because of some dowry, mate? If I can't dress my daughter-in-law, then my name's not Zhendo! When it comes to the kids, I'm no tightwad and I'm not greedy after land. Fifteen acres, a house, livestock, I won't take 'em with me to the grave. It'll all be left to them, let them make dowries to their heart's content, let them live their lives."

Trotsky was touched by his future in-law's generosity and most of all by his frankness. He had been isolated from people throughout his adult years, he hadn't come into conflict with anyone, so to him everyone was honest and good. Now he had to raise his final objection as well, but purely out of courtesy at this point, as had been the custom since time immemorial in such situations.

"All that's well and good, Zhendo, but you know… Radka's still a bit too young. She ain't even turned eighteen yet."

"Too young, my eye!" Zhendo cried. "Didn't our mothers get married at that age? You know what they say: Stick a woman in a kerosene tin and if her head pops out, that means she's ready for you-know-what. She's like a rubber band."

Trotsky could think of no objection to this worldly truism and smirked in affirmation. Only one formality remained – when to hold the wedding.

"On Saint Dimitar's Day," Zhendo said. "If you leave it any longer, you get into the Advent fast, so then we've got to wait all the way to the new year. Since we've started this thing, let's finish it, and not drag it out like entrails at slaughtering time."

And so it was. The local folks were rather shocked by the harmony between the in-laws, since they'd gotten used to noisy prenuptial haggling, but what shocked them most was that they had rejected the depraved aristocratic tradition of using their children's marriage to gain some advantage for themselves. I was back to the village for a few days, so I was at the wedding too. On Sunday morning, Saint Dimitar's Day itself, the bagpipe squealed at Trotsky's place and the neighborhood youngsters started up a round dance in the yard. In Radka's dingy, stuffy room, her girlfriends were dressing her in her wedding clothes, slathering her with various ointments, and singing songs. Ivan Shibilev also showed up to announce that the groom would soon arrive to take the bride to the church. In one hand he was carrying three honey cakes with sprigs of boxwood stuck into them, while in the other hand he was clutching an enormous rooster by the feet. Around the rooster's neck hung an embroidered bag filled with grain and dried fruit. The rooster symbolized the groom's menacing masculinity, and the full bag – the future couple's prosperity. Ivan Shibilev was the "hostage" from the young man's side. If the latter rejected the bride, the hostage would have to remain in the girl's home as a slave to make up for the groom's perfidy. In actuality, the hostage played the role of master of ceremonies at the wedding, directing what should be done when. When the bride was finally dressed, he sent word for the groom to come. At the same time, a messenger came running from Zhendo's place and whispered in his ear that there was no one to officiate at the wedding. By tradition, the godfather Stoyan Kralev was supposed to arrange for a priest, but Stoyan Kralev was a staunch communist and had refused to enter into any dealings with men of the cloth. So Zhendo had taken this task upon himself and the previous evening had gone to remind the priest about the wedding. Father Encho had said he knew well enough how to do his job, but now Zhendo had found him lying as stiff as a board. At first Zhendo thought the old man had overdone it with brandy the night before, so he snapped at him from the doorway: "Come on now, Father, the whole wedding is waiting on you, and you're still in bed!"

"I'm lying here, my son, I'm lying here and I can't move an inch. I threw out my back and it's like I've been split in two with an axe."

"You mean you can't get up at all?"

"Not at all! I can't move anything but my eyes and my hands. I can't even heed nature's call, if you pardon my saying so, my dear wife has to help me wee in a bedpan like a little child."

Goddamn Buffalo (our folks hadn't shied from giving the priest a nickname too), *who knows what's gotten into him to pull a stunt like this on me now*, Zhendo thought, and his temper flared again: "I don't care if you're dead as a doornail, you've got to get to that church. Otherwise you'll spoil this wedding of mine, and who's going to foot the bill? Since you can't move, we'll carry you over there. You'll sing a few words and that's that."

"The Lord is watching from above, my child! It hurts even to breathe, getting up is out of the question – but you go to Vladimirovo and get Father Tanas to perform the wedding. Today we'd agreed that I'd go to their village fair, but you tell him I'm sick, so he has to come stand in for me."

Zhendo leapt into the cart he'd prepared for the bride and whipped his horses all the way to Vladimirovo, making it there in only fifteen minutes. The village was having a fair, so it took him another fifteen minutes to find the priest's house, and when he found it, they told him that the priest had gone to the neighboring village for a funeral and would be back late in the afternoon. Zhendo was at his wits' end. He decided to go to that village and grab the priest right out of the graveyard, but when he stopped to think that they were waiting for him back at the wedding not knowing what had happened, he cracked his whip again and headed back toward home. The godparents, Stoyan Kralev and his wife, were waiting in front of his house.

"Well now, my kinsman, you've been gone a long time, what's happening with the priest?"

"May God strike him dead!" Zhendo spit as he jumped out of the cart. "Last night his back started hurting something fierce, now he can't budge from his bed. I went to Vladimirovo to get Father Tanas, but he was gone to a funeral, they may as well bury him, too, for all I care! This place is crawling with priests when you don't need 'em, but now there's not a single cassock to be seen."

Stoyan Kralev tactlessly laughed out loud. "Well, then, we'll hold the wedding Soviet-style."

"What do you mean, 'Soviet-style'?"

"Well, just like that, without a priest. In Soviet Russia, they have civil weddings without a priest."

"You communists may get married without a priest, but we can't!" Zhendo snapped at him, but then realized he was talking to his godfather, so he gave a sour smile. "Go ahead and joke around, Godfather, you haven't got a care in the world while my ass is on the line here."

"Since there's no priest, we'll have to put off the wedding!"

"Out of the question! They'll elope if they have to, but I'm not going to wait till the new year, I'm not gonna shell out for this twice."

Zhendo led the horses into the shed, and Stoyan Kralev started pacing around the yard. He saw weddings – and all folk traditions – as bourgeois prejudice and thus did not feel an ounce of sympathy for Zhendo. He had wanted to refuse the role of godfather as well, but his wife would have none of it. She kicked up a fuss to the rafters and declared that she would sooner serve as godmother without him than become the laughingstock of the village. Their family had been godparents to Zhendo's family since time immemorial – that made them practically related and to dishonor those ties would be tantamount to a blood feud. After long squabbles, Stoyan Kralev agreed to act as godfather, but on the condition that he would not enter the church, so as not to compromise his ideals. He would feign a sudden attack of kidney stones and only in the evening would he reappear at the wedding as custom required. His wife would have to ask her brother to stand in for him at the church, but as she didn't dare warn him about her husband's impending kidney stones, she was on tenterhooks the whole time to make sure her brother didn't slip away to the fair in Vladimirovo or wander off somewhere. When they found out there was no priest, they both breathed a sigh of relief that they could finally go back home. But then Stoyan Kralev turned around abruptly and called to Zhendo: "Kinsman, c'mere for a second! Something just popped into my head."

Zhendo left the horses and went over to him.

"I can see, kinsman, that you've got your heart set on this wedding, so I'm wondering whether Ivan Shibilev couldn't do the job in place of the priest?"

"Godfather!" Zhendo cried, his face blazing. "Forgive me for saying so, but now you're downright mocking me! Fine, I can take a joke as well as the next person, but I would never have expected you to go this far."

Stoyan Kralev threw a friendly arm around his shoulder and whispered: "I'm dead serious, kinsman. Don't get angry, but listen carefully to what I'm saying. Why do they call Ivan Shibilev "the Painkiller"? Because he's got all sorts of tricks up his sleeve. On top of everything, he's a cantor, the priest's right-hand man, he knows that church stuff better than the priest himself. He'll pull on his stole, sing a few words, and that'll be that. You went to get the priest from Vladimirovo but couldn't find him, so after that you went to Mogilarovo and found the one there. It's three villages away, the folks here haven't so much as caught sight of his beard, let alone heard his voice. Plus, there's nobody here in the village today, they're all at the fair. There'll be all of a dozen people in the church at most, and even if more do show up, they'll be nothing but a bunch of blue-hairs."

Zhendo could see that his godfather was looking at the humorous side of things, because he was a communist and didn't respect the old-fashioned rituals. His tongue was itching to tell him that communists were good-for-nothing idlers as he had told him many times before, but right now he was in a tight spot, so he patiently heard out his advice to the end. And while he was hearing him out, it occurred to him that Ivan Shibilev, as sly and shrewd as he was, really could make short work of the wedding in place of the priest.

"But who's going to sign the certificate? If Father Encho refuses to sign it, it's like the marriage never happened."

"He'll sign it, what else can he do?" Stoyan Kralev said, clutching at his lower back. "My kidneys are aching something fierce, I think I'm going to follow the priest's lead and lie down awhile. It hits me every year right at this time. In any case, that priest might be bedridden for a year, who's going to marry folks then? He's got to find himself a replacement."

"That's all well and good, but Ivan Shibilev might not agree to it, and even if he does, you can't trust him further than you can throw him. He'll get up to some stunt faster than you can say Jack Robinson…"

"Ivan Shibilev and the priest are thick as thieves. The one always does what the other says. Plus, if he opens his big mouth, he's the one who'll be in hot water."

Zhendo took off his cap and scratched his head. Steam rose off his hair.

"Hell, I don't know what to do. It's either the frying pan or the fire."

He went into the house, while Stoyan Kralev sat down on the chopping block. He hadn't even finished his cigarette when what do you know? The "hostage" came into sight, heading toward the yard carrying the rooster, adorned like a peacock with tinseled bouquets, strings of popcorn, and various trinkets. He clearly had been informed as to why he was being called and immediately got into character. He stood in front of Stoyan Kralev, made the sign of the cross, and submissively said: "May God bless you, my child!"

"Huh?"

"By the grace of God, everything will be fine. I'll be ready in an hour and will be waiting for you in the church."

As before every new caper, Ivan Shibilev was seized by a rush of inspiration, so he ran home, stuffed the rooster under a tub, grabbed what he needed, and went to see Father Encho.

I had just gotten to Radka's house when the groom arrived. Zhendo lived only three houses away, but he had decided to come for the bride with a cart. The horses were decked out with braided tails and blue collars, while Koycho, in spite of the heat, was dressed in a black fur coat and an Astrakhan hat. His brother-in-law strutted beside him with a scarlet banner, while the godmother's brother was sitting beside her instead of Stoyan Kralev. In short, the groom arrived with such pomp and fanfare as if he had come for the bride from the back of beyond – and in the dead of winter, at that. They led Radka out onto the porch so the people could get a look at her. As Stoyan Kralev had suspected, only a few elderly neighbors had stayed around for the wedding, the young people had snuck off to the fair in Vladimirovo. Radka's girlfriends had started singing, and she was crying, her whole body was shaking with sobs beneath her veil and it was all she could do to keep from bawling out loud. Her mother, Auntie Gruda – a dry woman with a big, flattened nose that was always moist like a slug – was scurrying across the porch from one room to another, looking as if she would step on the hem of her dress at any moment and fall flat on her nose. The bride's crying was also part of the wedding scenario. A bride who doesn't cry when leaving her parents, who doesn't experience a sense of filial attachment to them, is clearly not a good and grateful daughter, hence the grannies were enraptured by Radka.

"*Mashallah*, now there's some pretty crying for you!"

Koycho descended from the cart with his suite – his brother-in-law, the godmother, and the godfather – while Auntie Gruda and Trotsky went out to meet them. Trotsky was in full uniform minus munitions, like a soldier on day leave, and held out his hand for the groom to kiss. As would later become clear, he had invited an important guest and had been sitting with him in the one room the whole time, keeping his spirits high and his cup full. This guest was the former Sergeant Major Chakov, whom we will hear more about shortly.

Koycho stepped up next to his future wife as if stopping next to a tree, without deigning to greet her, puffed himself up under his fur coat, and froze to the spot. The curious grannies barged up right under his nose, trying to chitchat with him, but he just glanced at them with the whites of his eyes and kept silent as a clam. Radka's girlfriends started shrieking out the traditional song "A Girl Takes Leave of Her Mother," the bagpipe started squealing as well, while Radka kept shaking with sobs. The grannies started exchanging glances and whispering. Back in the day, they, too, had cried beneath their veils, as was proper, but now they felt that Radka was taking it too far and thus insulting her husband.

"That's enough now, girl, you've cried for your father and mother, that's enough!"

"Look here, you're snotting up your veil!"

"You're getting hitched, not hanged!"

But the more insistently the grannies advised her to quiet down, the sadder Radka became and the harder she cried. She seemed to have fallen into hysterics and could not get ahold of herself. My throat choked up, so I went over to her to give her my wedding present. Every time I came back home for vacation, I would bring her some trifle – a ring, a necklace, or a colorful handkerchief. We were the same age and had gone to school together until fourth grade. She had spent two years in first grade, two years in third grade, and two years in fourth, and so her seven mandatory years of schooling had passed in primary education. During the summers, our families would work the fields together, and Radka and I would hoe or reap next to each other. She was constantly asking me about the city, where she had never been, what it was like to live there, what kinds of people I met, and most of all about the city's fashionable coquettes. Like every village girl, she felt an innate antagonism toward urban women and believed that they lived in perfect bliss, they didn't work so as not to soil their delicate white hands, and spent their days strolling daintily around the city streets. Try as I might to dispel her naïve ideas of city life, she simply could not believe that people there also worked, that most were poorer than she was and were barely scraping by. You're only saying that because you've become a city slicker too, she would say. Once you're done studying, you'll bring home some fine lady, her face all painted white and rouged, with a gaudy little parasol to shade her from the sun. And as she imagined this city girl clumsily bending down to reap or hoe with her parasol in her hand, Radka would straighten up in her row and laugh wildly and ingenuously with all her heart.

But now she was crying inconsolably under her veil, so I decided to give her the simple brass bracelet I had bought for her in the city. Gifts are usually given to the bride late in the evening at her new house, but I violated this custom so as to snap her out of her hysteria, which I assumed was due to overexcitement. I congratulated her on her marriage, and congratulated Koycho as well. Our houses were right next door to each other, separated only by a wattle fence, we had grown up and gone to school together too. Like Radka, he had only reached fourth grade; he shied away from middle school like barbed wire in wartime, refusing to attack. I told him to comfort his bride, so he turned, without glancing at me, and said: "If she wants to cwy, let her cwy!"

He couldn't say the letter r and a perfectly natural consequence of this impediment was his nickname, Koycho the Wawa. To hide this defect, he didn't talk much, and when he did, he tried to avoid the letter r. In any other situation, he would have said "bawl," but he wasn't in his right mind at the moment. By the looks of it, he had no clear idea of why he was standing there in front of everyone, decked out in a heavy fur coat and an Astrakhan hat, who this sniveling girl next to him was, or what he was supposed to do next.

I took Radka's hand and struggled to shove the bracelet over her large palm with its strong, stubby fingers. I told her I was happy that she was marrying Koycho, because from now on, besides being relatives, we would also be neighbors. I promised to bring her an even nicer present during the Christmas holidays and wished her all the best. She quieted down for a moment, just as a child distracted by something stops crying, only her shoulders continued shuddering. Perhaps it was because I was looking at her face in the aureole of the celebration and through the veil, but it seemed beautiful and sweet to me, bathed in tears like the face of a weeping child. I murmured something more to her, she squeezed my hand, leaned over and kissed it, and burst into tears again. Auntie Gruda was forced to console her.

"That's enough now, my girl!" she said, bursting into tears herself. "Why are you bawling as if for the dead?"

"Mooooommmy!" Radka gave a piercing shriek and collapsed onto her mother's shoulder. "My dearest mooooooother!"

After this shriek, she seemed to calm down, straightened herself up, and headed toward the cart on her own, with Koycho following after her. They climbed into the cart, the godparents climbed in as well. When they reached the gate, Koycho pulled a pistol out of the pocket of his fur coat, fired it, and the horses galloped off toward the church.

A few minutes later, we, the young people, were already at the church, while the older folks straggled along behind us. The bride and groom had just come inside and were standing in the corner in front of a little table. The doors of the iconostasis were closed, the embroidered curtain was drawn shut, giving the church the look of an office not yet open for business. In the sand-filled candle boxes in front of the sanctuary, two candles were burning, long and thick as shepherd's flutes, while not a single candle had been lit in the chandelier. The old folks, who were trickling in one by one, were saying that the marriage would be performed by the priest from Mogilarovo, and at every noise they turned toward the door. But suddenly, the curtain split in two, shuddered for a moment, then opened up. The royal doors opened as well, and the Mogilarovo priest stepped over the threshold, glanced at the young couple, and rushed over to them. His gait made it clear that he was a young man and that he had come to perform the wedding as quickly as possible. His hair, unlike that of other priests, was cut short, but his face was so thickly covered by a black beard that only his nose was visible. He held a censer in one hand and two candles in the other; he lit them from the thick candles in the candle boxes and hurried over to the couple. He pulled the rings off their fingers, handed each of them a candle, and waved the censer. Thin blue streams of smoke wafted toward the ceiling, spreading the sweet, sad scent of incense and wax. And then in the empty, echoing church, a sonorous falsetto boomed out, as if some mariachi had broken into song: "O Lord, hallowed be Thy holy name, now and forever, world without end!"

That almost female voice, so incongruous with his orangutan-like beard, sounded pleasantly exotic, yet at the same time somehow blasphemous. The old folks, accustomed for years to Father Encho's hoarse and feeble mumbling, started exchanging bewildered glances. But the priest won them over as soon as he sang the first prayer as a drawling, melodious rendition of a folk tune.

"O great and eternal God, Who in creating the human race willed that man and wife should be one, just as Thou blessed Isaac and Rebekah and made them the true heirs of Thy covenant, bless these Thy servants, Koycho and Radka, that what they receive in faith they may live out in deeds." He took the two rings off the table, made the sign of the cross over the couple with them, declared that with this ring, God's servant Koycho weds God's servant Radka, just as Radka weds him, and shoved the rings on their fingers. After that, he led them over to the lectern, put the crowns on their heads, and announced that the two humble servants of God were now man and wife.

He was clearly following the fast-track procedure, because the old folks started grumbling that he hadn't read a single troparion, not even the parable of the Wedding at Cana in Galilee, where the young Jesus turned water into wine, thus beginning his string of miracles. The priest made the couple drink from the cup and circle the lectern three times, and there was nothing more to be done. But the old folks' grumbling that in his haste he had given short shrift to the sacrament of holy matrimony seemed to cut him to the quick, so instead of leaving the newlyweds to be congratulated by their nearest and dearest, he instead opened up the missal and read one more prayer. "O Father, Lord of Mercies, Who existed before the ages and surpasses all good, we beseech Thee to accept all those who call upon Thy holy name, through the love of Thy Child, Jesus Christ, the Holy One, and Thine all-powerful Spirit. Cast away from our souls every malady, all disbelief, spare us from the furious attacks of unclean, infernal, subterranean, fiery, putrid, lustful spirits, the love of gold and silver, conceit, fornication, every shameless, unseemly, dark, and profane demon. O God, expel from Thy servants Koycho and Radka every energy of the devil, every poison, all voluptuousness, carnality, lustfulness, adultery, licentiousness, and shamelessness. Yea, O Lord our God, watch over them and us, and guard our hearts; for all things are possible to Thee, O Lord. We give glory to the Father, and to the Son, and to the Holy Spirit, now and ever and unto the ages of ages. Amen."

Later, when word of this hoax got around the village, Ivan Shibilev told me in great detail how everything had happened, and it was only then that I recalled that he had performed several roles on the local community center stage in that same beard and Asiatic moustache, long and thin as the whiskers of the monarchs from the First Bulgarian Kingdom. He had meant to perform the whole ceremony, but at one point saw that Grandpa Christaki, another cantor, had come into the narthex of the church and stopped there. He had been told the day before that there wouldn't be a Sunday service due to Father Encho's illness, but the ringing of the bells had likely surprised him, so he had come to see what was going on in the church. But since he hadn't been warned about the arrival of the priest from Mogilarovo, whom he knew very well, he would surely throw a wrench in the whole works. As it turned out, the old man was someone else entirely and hadn't even come into the sanctuary, but Ivan Shibilev was flustered and instead of chanting, say, Saint Paul's Letter to the Ephesians or a parable from the Gospel of Mark, he instead had sung a prayer for those tormented by unclean spirits.

That evening, most folks stopped by the wedding on their way home from the fair, and Zhendo's house more or less filled up with people. Some had stopped by to "pay their respects" to the wedding party, while others merely wanted a bite to eat and a pint after the fair. Zhendo, who seemed to have foreseen this onslaught, had put two lambs and a pig under the knife right after the church service. He had set a thirty-gallon keg in the middle of the yard, as well as another one next to the porch stairs, and the guests, especially the boozers among them, were gathered around them, filling their bowls and toasting the newlyweds. Zhendo had thrown a wedding in grand style and he wanted everyone to see that. From time to time, he'd come out to the guests in the yard, pour them a round, and invite them to sit down at the table, shouting: "Come on, people, eat and drink up! I'll only marry off a son once!"

Inside one of the rooms, the inner circle had gathered: the godparents, the new in-laws, relatives, and, of course, former Sergeant Major Chakov. A bagpiper was sitting at the end of the table, his face red as molten steel from all the blowing; next to him, some woman was singing in a creaking, goat-like voice, some tried to join in with her, others tried to outshout her or got up to dance. The sweating windowpanes rattled from the dancers' stomps, the two lamps flickered and sputtered from the smoke and dust. Radka also appeared several times, with her veil thrown back over her shoulders, to refill the dishes or cups. Her mother-in-law, Auntie Kita, affectionately advised her as to what to put where, and Radka did so with smooth, unconscious movements. If someone said something to her, she would look at him somehow astonished, smile with her lips alone, and leave the room. Zhendo, by now heated up and with his shirt hanging open, frequently raised his glass and shouted at the top of his voice to Trotsky: "Here's to you, kinsman!"

"Long life to you, kinsman!" Trotsky would reply, as he sat at former Sergeant Major Chakov's right knee, seeming to fear that the latter would be offended if he spoke to anyone else.

At one point, Zhendo pulled a small-barrel revolver out of his pocket, aimed it at the ceiling, and fired three shots. The women screamed, the bagpipe hiccupped and fell silent, and chunks of plaster fell onto the table from the ceiling, where three holes had appeared. Outside, faces pressed up against the windowpane and a hush fell over the whole house. Smiling, Zhendo pulled the spent shells out of the barrel and tucked them back in his pocket, along with the revolver. An awkward silence overtook the room. The women began to trade knowing glances, while guilty expressions crept over their faces, as if somewhere nearby a deed was being done that was mysterious and shameful, yet as inevitable as a ritual sacrifice, which could be shared with a glance alone.

"What, cat got your tongue, people? Come on, Veliko, puff up that goatskin of yours again, 'cause this time me and my kinsman are gonna rattle the floorboards!" Zhendo said, pouring wine into the glasses.

The bagpiper had gone outside, as had Ivan Shibilev, who always found a way to keep everyone entertained. So Trotsky decided that his hour had finally come. The whole evening, he had been utterly devoted to his honored guest, seeming to have forgotten that he was at his daughter's wedding. The silence that had fallen suddenly snapped him out of the sergeant major's spell, or rather, precisely under the influence of that spell, he enthusiastically began telling his soldierly *Iliad*. They were all long since familiar with this *Iliad*, but now they gratefully turned their eyes toward him and readied themselves to listen. This solitary soul, who spent his life clamped in the rigid mold of his military uniform and in the company of a near-feral dog, had only a single social ace up his sleeve – his years-long and lasting friendship with Sergeant Major Chakov, which raised him to dizzying heights in his own eyes, and – as he believed – in the eyes of the whole village as well.

After retiring to the reserves, the former sergeant major had been living in a nearby hamlet, where his wife had inherited a bit of land. It was abundantly clear that some unpleasant circumstances had forced him to hole up in that distant and godforsaken little spot, because even the sergeant major himself liked to say that life had given him the orders: "About-face!" Trotsky was the only one of his former soldiers in the vicinity, so they had met and gotten to know each other, and since then the sergeant major had been a regular guest on all major holidays. He was past seventy, with a face squashed flat like a wine flask, healthy as a horse, and energetic for his years. He walked with an even, heavy step, as if marking out the rhythm to some regimental march, except that his soldierly charm was somehow absurdly marred by a nervous tic – he would bring together the three middle fingers on his right hand and spit on them several times. This spitting on his fingers could also have been a habit, of course, acquired after long years of maternal care for his soldiers. He wore a dark jacket of dyed military cloth, tan jodhpurs, and tall boots, whose waxy scent profaned the cozy aroma of home cooking and joyous celebration. He had kept his military habits not only where his clothes and behavior were concerned, but in his speech as well. When he started to eat, he would call out as if in the company canteen: "Hup!" When he got up: "At attention!" And when leaving: "Forward, march!" There could never be a higher-ranking guest in the village. He was worth more than all the illustrious personages in the region put together, thus all major holidays came and went graced by his imperial visitations. Radka had told me that her father had made the whole family rehearse for the sergeant major's visits, that he had taught them how to sit obediently before him, how to answer him, how to "sashay" gracefully, and how not to affront his dignity with so much as a gaze, how no one was to sit down until he sat down, what culinary delicacies they should lavish upon him, and what gifts they should send him away with.

Trotsky writhed in the throes of a criminal generosity, tearing away at his humble prosperity as if tearing living flesh from the bone, just so he could prepare for his idol a feast that would assuage even the insatiable Lucullus's hunger. However, these holidays were never a close family affair – Trotsky always invited the neighbors, because he wanted witnesses to his triumph. The standard guests from our side included my grandmother, my grandfather, and me. If Trotsky's social "ace up his sleeve" was the former sergeant major, then I was my grandfather's ace. I could recite several poems from the school primers, and my grandfather was so proud of my talent that he took me with him everywhere.

Everyone would be sitting on the floor, only the eminent guest would loom over us on a three-legged stool in front of a trunk specially prepared for him, which rose like a pulpit over the common table. His flattened visage hung over this pulpit like a moon over the heads of the people, illuminating them with its cold benevolence. No one dared to snicker – not even inwardly – when he spit on his fingers as if possessed, because everyone considered these apish gestures not a flaw, but a sign of nobility. They waited for him to reach for the food first, and only then would they break the bread. The sergeant major was not a gourmand and despite his hosts' insistence that he try everything, he would carefully mind his mouthfuls, sparingly sip his brandy, and very soon say "enough." Then he would wipe his mouth with a napkin and remain at his pulpit, as immobile and impenetrable as the Dalai Lama. Then my grandfather would gently nudge my shoulder and I would stand up in front of the table. It was not hard to guess the sergeant major's literary predilections and already at our second meeting I had started reciting for him an excerpt of Vazov's "The Defenders of Shipka Pass." The generals' commands, the volunteer fighters' "hooray," the din of the desperate battle, all inflamed his hollow imagination, his nostrils caught a whiff of gunpowder, his squashed face swelled with heroic emotions, and when I would recite how every one of our men was

> ... *in his own way*
> *Striving to be in the front of the fray*
> *Each, like a hero, death bravely defying*
> *Determined to leave one more enemy dying*

a cry of approval would burst from the sergeant major's lips loudly and ecstatically like a bullet from the barrel of a rifle: "Bravo, young hero!" The scales of his imperial benevolence would tip in my direction, he would pull a lev from the breast pocket of his jacket and hand it to me – after making me stand at attention, salute, and shout, "Thank you, sir!" He noted with satisfaction that each time I showed an ever greater mastery of military protocol, while I noted to myself that I showed an ever greater interest in the lev he gave me, and hence all the more doggedly worked at perfecting my rhetorical talent.

Trotsky was sitting cross-legged at his fetish's booted feet, tortured by jealousy and slavish devotion, looking him over from head to toe and waiting for the moment to turn the great man's attention toward himself.

"Well, I, for one, remember the nummer of my carbine," he would say at the first convenient moment. "Two thousan' eight hundert an' niney-five."

The sergeant major would turn to him, gratified by the lasting results of his educational activities, which had taken such deep root in the consciousness of his former soldiers and had stood the tests of time. Trotsky would gaze at him, his eyes blazing with devotion, and that was the sign that the moment had come for him to once again repay his former commander with kind words for the attention he had deigned to honor him with during his army days. Indeed, he subjected himself and his offspring to the sergeant major's tyranny solely so that he would have the chance to retell how this flat-faced person had "thrashed" him in the army every time he caught sight of him, so that no one would be left with any doubts that his patron was anything less than an exceptional individual. The patron himself would sit imperturbable behind his flattened mask and from time to time, clearly under the strain of his most delectable memories, would spit on the fingers of his right hand, as if with this sinister pantomime wanting to visually confirm his indisputable contribution to the shaping of Bulgarian spirituality.

Trotsky would begin by telling how, on the very first day, their solicitous "battalion mother" inspected the greenhorns' clothes, found lice on several men, and served them up such a "welcome-to-the-army" thrashing that their faces were black and blue. They were given vats to boil their clothes in, but wouldn't you know – the next day the battalion mother again found lice on two men, one of whom was Trotsky. The sergeant major took off his belt and laid into them in front of the whole company. They boiled their clothes again, but you know how it is with lice – where there's one, there's a thousand. Our local lice – raised for "breeding," as they say – they could pass through fire and be none the worse for it. "Well now, since a good thrashing didn't shake you up, the sergeant major declared, stand still and open your mouth! So I stand there with my mouth open, and he takes the little critters from the open collar of my shirt one by one an' shoves 'em in my mouth. Riiiight here, on my eyetooth. Chew! So I chewed. I must've scarfed down a dozen of 'em…"

Trotsky remembered the number of his carbine and that number had been deeply etched into his memory for all time like the Ten Commandments carved in stone, thanks to his punishments, which far exceeded that actual number. With the greatest relish and masochistic voluptuousness, he recounted one epic beating, which the sergeant major had doled out to him during his second year of service: "I was on barracks duty that day. The company'd gone outside o' town for shootin' drills. At some point the platoon commander came back and headed straight for mista sarjin mare's office. Turns out they didn't have no bullets for the drill. That morning mista sarjin mare'd been busy with somethin 'r other, so he'd given me the keys to the storeroom and tol' me to hand out blanks to the whole company, but I'd done gone and forgotten. Mista sarjin mare gave the commander the bullets and came over to me all bluish green, glarin' at me and shakin' from head to toe. Private Statev, did I order you to hand out bullets to the company? Yes, sir, I say, but it just slipped my mind. Well, now, he says, I'm going to jog your memory. When he wasn't mad, he'd affectionately call his soldiers turdbag, lowlife, or twerp. But when he called you Private So-and-so, you knew nothin' good was in store for you. He lashed out with his left hand, I ducked left, an' he caught me with a right hook. And bam! again, with the right, then pow! again with the left. My head starts squealing like a bagpipe, I can hardly stay on my feet. I cover my face with my hands and spin around like a top, and all the while he's like: Attention! I said, attention, don't move! At one point I'm thinkin' to run out of the room and onto the parade grounds, reckonin' he might just leave me alone. That's all well and good, but he beats me to it and shuts the door. Since there's no other escape, I take off runnin' down the aisle between the beds, he's at my heels shoutin': Halt! If only I'd had the good sense to stop, I would've gotten off easier, 'cause the man was shoutin' that if I didn't stop I'd earn myself another punishment for failin' to obey an order. But the scareder I got, the more his temper flared. So dunderhead that I am, I start jumping from bed to bed. He's waiting for me at the end, so I leap over to the other row. We kicked up quite a dust cloud in them barracks, and there was me and mista sarjin mare playin' tag in that dust cloud. I finally got my chance and darted out into the corridor. I'm just about to run down the stairs when gotcha! He grabs me by the neck. He sticks his arm through my belt and starts draggin' me down that corridor like a bundle of wheat. I grab on to the trunk where we stored wood for the stove. So he's lugging me, and I'm lugging the trunk, with all the wood to boot. He drags me over to the storeroom and tries to shove me in, but the trunk's too wide, it won't go in. Let go of the trunk! I don't let go. He stomps my fingers with his boot, I let go of the trunk. He hauls me into the storeroom, locks the door, and starts workin' me over. Inside there's nothing but junk, it's all dim and dank, the whole base is empty, even if I yelled for help, no one'd hear me. I says to myself, this man don't just want to hurt me, he wants to kill me. I get so scared that I dive under a shelf like a dog under a barn when it knows it's up shit creek. Mista sarjin mare is pullin' on my legs. I hang on to the shelf till it crashes down on me, buryin' me in blankets, sheets and boots, cartridge boxes and what-have-you. I'm suffocatin', I can't scream or worm my way out. At long last, mista sarjin mare pulls me out. Get up! Yes, sir! He'll take pity on me, I'm thinkin' to myself, and let me go, since I almost suffocated. I somehow scramble to my feet and I'm waitin' for him to dismiss me, but instead, 'You've just made more work for me,' he says. He pushes me to the ground, presses his knee into my back so I can't budge, and starts layin' into me again. He's wailin' on me with his belt, and it's like he's cuttin' me with a knife, I'm screamin' myself hoarse, while he's like: Shut up! One more peep outta you and I'll rip your tongue out! If you'd obeyed my order to stand still, this beating would already be history. But you go and play hide-and-seek on me. Screw you and your goddamn shelves, even if you crawled up your mother's ass, I'd yank you out and tan your hide again! And you can imagine what happened then…"

Trotsky didn't reach the culmination of his inspired tale and had to break it off at "mista sarjin mare's" obstetrical fantasy. The door opened and two women came into the room. The one was carrying a white chemise or cloth in her outstretched arms, and the other a plastic soda bottle with a red bow tied around the neck. The two of them stepped up to Trotsky with guilty, frightened expressions, and the one holding the bottle handed it to him: "Cheers, kinsman!"

Trotsky lifted the bottle to take a deep swig, but the bottle whistled, leaving his mouth empty. He shook it, sucked on it again, and the bottle again whistled emptily. He turned it upside down, saw that the bottom was punctured, and laughed, thinking this was some kind of joke. His wife let out a frantic shriek, pounded herself on the forehead with both hands, and froze.

"What are you screamin' about, woman?" Trotsky chided her, and was about to say something more when the woman who had handed him the bottle swallowed hard, closed her eyes, and said:

"If she wants to scream, let her scream. Because there's no sweet brandy!"

A sinister silence reigned over the table.

"You lie!" Auntie Gruda shrieked again. "You want to besmirch my daughter's honor. To cover my house in shame!"

They showed her the unstained chemise once again, she pushed it away, wriggled through the crowd that had pressed into the room, and ran out. Zhendo's wife jumped up after her. Then they brought the chemise over to the godparents so they, too, could confirm the bride's disgrace. The godmother glanced at it and lowered her eyes, while Stoyan Kralev waved it away and turned his face toward the wall in disgust. He had arrived shortly before Trotsky had begun the tale of his army days and was glaring at the former sergeant major with undisguised contempt, not missing the chance to snipe at him: "It's the tsarist army, what do you expect? Any idiot with epaulettes can torture his soldiers to his heart's content!"

Stoyan Kralev never missed such convenient opportunities to discredit the fascist government and to emphasize the advantages of Soviet rule, even though his fellow villagers listened to him indifferently and even made fun of him. The German Army had reached the Caucasus, the supreme command had fixed mid-November as the final deadline for taking Stalingrad, and no one believed there could be a turn in the tide of the war. Even the "powers-that-be" in the village were not annoyed by his propaganda; on the contrary, they relished arguments with him so they could corner him with indisputable facts and laugh at his political blindness. Empty-handed, Stoyan Kralev nevertheless stood his ground against them, constantly repeating that sooner or later the Germans would lose the war. He seemed so unshakable in his faith even when the end of the war was clear to everyone that his opponents did not consider him a true communist, but rather a long-winded crackpot, who was always harping on the same old tune. Indeed, Stoyan Kralev "harped away" every chance he got and more or less managed to draw from every fact of life some conclusion in communism's favor. That evening, everyone was shocked by the bride's unstained chemise, he was shocked as well, yet he remained true to his beliefs. His role as godfather demanded that the young couple's parents listen to him, so he started talking about the equality between the sexes that had been achieved in a great country that was now battling a fascist incursion. What had happened here tonight could never happen there, because there the young woman would never be humiliated in such a way. She had the right to mix with whomever she chose, to pick her comrade in life on her own, and to decide for herself with whom and how to live. In the end, Stoyan Kralev reached the conclusion that rituals such as this one with the bride's chemise were thought up by the bourgeoisie to deprive a woman of her rights. When she slaves in the fields alongside her husband, when she cooks, cleans, and looks after the children, no one gives a flying fig about her plight, but when she dares to love someone and he deceives her, then she becomes bad and dishonorable. How do you know that the girl has been with a man, anyway? This sort of·thing can happen on its own, there've been cases like that. Besides, maybe the groom (here Stoyan Kralev hesitated as to whether to say this or not), maybe the groom didn't do the deed properly, he's still a boy, after all…

"The deed has been done, Godfather, just not now," said the woman who had brought the bottle of sweet brandy. "But let's hear it from Sissy Dona as well."

Sissy Dona was the neighborhood midwife and had been entrusted with the task of confirming the bride's disgrace.

"'Tis true!" she said, and folded her arms over her belly.

"Well, even if it is true, for crying out loud, so what of it? Should something like that ruin the girl? The old folks say – and you women know better than anyone – that a woman's honor isn't between her legs, but between her ears."

"We did what was asked of us," Sissy Dona said with the indifference of a surgeon. "From here on out, let the groom and his parents decide."

The groom and his mother were not in the room, while his father was sitting with his head bowed, staring into the empty cup in front of him. When he felt that all eyes were on him, he waved his hand and this gesture of desperation was so expressive that everyone realized what he was going through and were filled with sincere sympathy for him. The whole village knew that he had swallowed his pride and gone to make the match with Trotsky in person, he had cast aside age-old tradition, and only his nobility and magnanimity had saved his dignity from public censure and ridicule – he hadn't demanded a dowry or even a trousseau from his future daughter-in-law. Now she repaid his kindness by putting him through this terrible and shameful ordeal – would he accept her, disgraced as she was, or send her away after she had already come into his house? Everyone waited with bated breath to see how Zhendo would solve this dilemma; as for Trotsky, he didn't seem to have fully grasped what had happened or else had grasped it so clearly and tragically that he was in no condition to move or talk. He was sitting there white as a sheet, only his eyes flitted restlessly from one end of the table to another, while his arm lay as if severed on the sergeant major's knee. For his part, the sergeant major was staring at the wall across from him, looking more than ever like the Dalai Lama. Only his right hand, true to its habit no matter what the circumstances, rose toward his lips and in the deathly silence the sound of him spitting on his fingers could be heard: *ptui, ptui, ptui!*

"That's how it goes!" Zhendo sighed at last. "When you've really got your heart set on something, it never works out."

The crowd outside surged through the door and the room was filled to bursting. Everyone wanted to hear what more Zhendo would say, but he fell silent.

"But it's already worked out, kinsman!" Stoyan Kralev called out. "You've got a good, hardworking daughter-in-law, that's the most important thing. All the rest is poppycock."

"Godfather!" Zhendo replied. "You're always going on about Russia as if you just arrived from there yesterday. But let me tell you this: Russia is Russia, but our folks here are our folks here. There, people might walk on their heads, they might not get married in church, they might eat from common bowls and share their women. That's their business. We're simple Bulgarians, so we'll do things the Bulgarian way."

"It's not the Bulgarian way, but the bourgeois way..."

"I'm no bourgeoisian, nor am I a communist. But I know that a woman should go to her wedding bed virtuous. A woman who's let some other man rock on top of her isn't fit to be a mother or a homemaker."

"Pardon me for saying so, kinsman, but you're talking like a fool!"

"Well, maybe I am a fool," Zhendo said, "and as my godfather, you'll pardon me for saying so, but since you're so smart, then you tell me: Did your wife come to you popped, or if she did, would you have taken her? Answer me that!"

A titter swept through the crowd, Stoyan Kralev's wife lowered her eyes in shame, while he just shrugged: You can't argue with an imbecile.

"There's an easy cure for everything in this world," Sissy Dona spoke up when the giggling had died down. "Whoever's made their bed must lie in it. Five acres and let bygones be bygones."

What was said in the room was instantly transmitted from mouth to mouth to the porch, and from there into the yard, because from all the way out in the yard many voices exclaimed: Whoa, a whole estate!

Zhendo didn't second – but nor did he reject – Sissy Dona's idea either with a word or a glance. Disappointment seemed to have snuffed out all emotions within him, such that it was all the same to him.

"It's easy to strut in borrowed plumes, Dona!" someone called out. "If you were in Radka's place, you think your father would've given a square inch of land for you?! Why are you sticking your nose in other people's business? Let Zhendo have his say."

"Zhendo's had a bad shock, he might make a blunder now and end up beating himself up for it forever afterward," Sissy Dona retorted. "He's my aunt's son, I won't just stand here and let them pull a fast one on him. If they don't like it, they can take her back. A woman's honor is worth even more than that."

Now everyone's attention was fixed on Trotsky. He was still sitting there pale as death, silent. His idol was silent as well, staring at the wall in front of him, from time to time spitting on the fingers of his right hand. Everyone was silent and it lasted so long that the silence became unbearable and ominous. Then Auntie Gruda appeared. No one saw how she had come, it was as if she had wriggled through the crowd's legs, she was disheveled, her kerchief hung down around her shoulders, she looked strained to the last nerve and pathetic. She stood next to her husband and told him calmly, the way only something with endless despair can be said: "Give it to them, give them all the land they want, may it lie barren and parched!"

She had gone to speak to her daughter in the other room and with these words confirmed her disgrace. The crowd fired off a new volley of exclamations. And so one of the mysteries of the evening had been solved. Two more remained. Who in the village had sullied Radka's honor, was it a married man or a bachelor (the village would rack its brains over this mystery later), and whether her father would give any land, and if so, how much. Former Sergeant Major Chakov carefully removed Trotsky's arm from his knee, said "Hup!" and got up. The crowd parted to make way for him and he left. Zhendo clutched his brow, got up, and followed him out.

"Well?" Sissy Dona asked, with the tone of a repossession agent, as she stood there with her arms crossed over her belly.

Trotsky started making some signs with his hands. He had been struck dumb, but none of us realized it and many people burst out laughing. He opened his mouth to say something, some garbled sounds spilled out of his mouth, while his eyes bulged from the strain. He finally pointed at Sissy Dona, grabbed a spoon, and started scribbling on the table cloth with it.

"He wants to write," someone realized.

"I see," Sissy Dona said, and darted into the other room, coming back a minute later with a piece of paper, a dip pen, and a bottle of ink. "Where is Ivan Shibilev to write for him?"

The hostage had disappeared somewhere and Trotsky grabbed at the pen himself. Sissy Dona flipped over an empty tray, placed the paper on top of it, and handed him the pen. He wrote for a long time, spattering his fingers with ink, and when he was done, Sissy Dona looked over what he had written.

"Write the day and the year!"

Trotsky added the day and year, she handed the paper to her husband, and he read it aloud, with the help of those more literate than he was:

I sine over to my dauter Ratka five akers of feelds, Kalchu Stetef, St dimiturs day 1942.

"Now that's what I call rubbing salt in his wound!" someone said.

I presume that his new nickname was born right that very minute, because by the next day they were already calling him Salty Kalcho. So that's what I'll have to call him from now on as well.

The blizzard was gathering strength, blustering down in the Inferno. Salty Kalcho had lost his left glove along the way and kept sticking his hand either under the collar of his sheepskin coat or in his pocket. Ten minutes hadn't even passed since he had taken up his post in the blind, yet his legs were already going numb with cold. *Let's hope the beaters come sooner rather than later, so we can go home, there's no sense in sitting out here freezing our tails off for nothing,* he thought to himself, and for the thousandth time since they had left the village felt guilty for this pointless wolf hunt. *Why didn't*

I just drink Zhendo's wine, may God strike me down! Would it have stuck in my throat and choked me? It all started with that bottle, just like that, all at once. It's as if it was the same bottle they gave me at Radka's wedding. As soon as I reached for it, my hand just froze. Take a sip, I told myself, folks are waitin' on you, you've come to a comradely gathering. Fine, but my hand doesn't want to grab that bottle and that's that. My heart starts pounding, I started gettin' all hottish, I don't know what to say, and I can't budge my tongue in any case. I thought I'd forgotten all that business, but there it was buried in my head like a thorn. Many times at night I've gone over it and over everything that happened after that, and my heart's ached with anguish. Many times I've thought to rub out Zhendo or do something that would fill his heart with anguish too, but I always told myself: Nope, that's not right. Even if I were to kill him, that wouldn't undo the wrong he's done me. He won't take that wrong to the grave with him, it'd only be redoubling the wrongs. But still, that thorn, for twenty years now I can't get it out of my head. How many things I've forgotten in that time, both good and bad, yet I still remember that business. I remember as if it were yesterday. It's never ceased to amaze me what a thing human memory is. You want to forget something, to cleanse your soul, but your memory hangs onto it your whole life, may it thrice be damned! If a man didn't have a memory, he'd live in this world like an angel. Memory's at the root of all this evil. Ivan Shibilev did right in luring us out into these woods. He's got a heart of gold, and is a sly dog to boot. So he, too, remembers that night with the empty bottle. And the others remember it too, or else they wouldn't have gotten up as one and gone out into this blizzard. And since they've up and gone out, they mean to say: Let bygones be bygones. We're not gonna take this bad blood to the grave with us...

But while he was vowing to forget the past, he recalled another blizzard that had buried his shack and practically suffocated him. The night of Radka's wedding, he had gone back to his shack and begun living there all alone. If earlier he had rarely sought company, after being struck dumb he didn't even want to see his wife. When Auntie Gruda brought him food the next day, he bellowed angrily, making it clear that she needn't bother trudging out to the vineyard. He would go to the village once a week – and then only at night, so as to avoid running into people – and would bring back a bag of bread, beans, and potatoes and would cook up a little soup over the fire. The vineyards were deserted, there wasn't a soul in sight, and he was left alone with his muteness like an ancient Hesychast. He wanted to give himself over to full unity with nature, just as he had done for years on end, but an emptiness had opened up in his soul, dark and impenetrable, and he couldn't experience the sweet and mystical harmony with life around him as before. He had cultivated senses and an inner sight for that life, he could see, hear, and sense the vines, trees, and grasses growing, blossoming, bearing fruit, and dying, only to be born again. Not only by day, but by night in his dreams he would witness the mystery of growth, and he knew that the mute plants were living creatures, divinely noble, the most noble creatures in this world, who grew, came into being, and died in unrepining silence, not complaining about the elements, not affronting anyone, not devouring their own fruit, immobile and drinking life from the depths of the earth, so as to pass it on to other living creatures. He knew people ridiculed him for living like an outcast, but in his every encounter with them he felt insignificant and helpless in the face of their vanity and vehemence and hurried back to his lair. Solitude and inactivity replenished his strength, balance, and peace; from the heights of his veranda the world looked majestic and calm, there were no wars, no brawls, no feuds, there were no lies and dishonor. His one passion was his military uniform, yet even it was not actually a passion, but a necessity. Like armor, his uniform hid his unfitness for life and lent him a certain authority in people's eyes, even if it was the authority of an official functionary of the lowest rank. For the same reason, he had built a cult around a paltry individual like the former Sergeant Major Chakov. His memories of his harsh life in the army and his personal relations with the sergeant major fed his feelings of manliness, strength, and physical stamina. And so he had managed to create or imagine a harmonic coexistence – albeit "in absentia" – with people and the world.

He often dreamed about goodness, which appeared in his dreams as the cherry tree growing next to his shack, weighted down with blossoms and fruit, reaching up toward the clear blue sky. A tiny white bird would alight at the very top of the tree, open its little beak toward the sky, and start singing, only instead of a birdsong, the sound of bells, clear and melodious as children's voices, would ring out. Usually he happened to be sitting on the veranda, and every time he would be amazed by the little white bird and every time he would discover that it was not the bird, but rather the leaves of the cherry tree fluttering gently in the breeze, brushing together and ringing out like tiny bells. Little by little, he himself would transform into the sound of a bell, flying through the open expanse, weightless and light as a soul, and he would see how everything on earth had fallen mute with bliss. Evil, on the other hand, even though he dreamed about it only rarely, inevitably appeared to him as a *karakondzhul*, the mythical bogeyman of his childhood, an indescribable, terrifying creature, a combination of all rapacious beasts and birds of prey, with its enormous, bloodthirsty mouth and sharp teeth, sometimes with a beak and wings. It would stand before him, ready to pounce, while he never thought to grab his rifle and kill it, but instead kept retreating until he fell to the bottom of some abyss, where evil would be looking down on him from above, laughing with a human laugh. The night of the wedding, when he had learned of his daughter's disgrace and had been forced into paying for it with land, evil had appeared before him, standing across the feast table from him. It crossed his mind that he was not dreaming and that evil was standing before him while wide awake, ready to tear him apart, yet he wasn't frightened as he was in his dreams. He only wanted to ask: "Why?" He gathered the air in his lungs, opened his mouth, yet couldn't utter the word. Since then the word had been constantly on the tip of his tongue, but he could never utter it. Why had Radka been ruined so young and green, why had Zhendo blackmailed him, why had he lost his words? Why had God punished him with three misfortunes at once, what harm had he ever done to anyone? This question weighed on his heart like a stone, he wanted to scream it at the top of his lungs before the whole world and couldn't. Until one night in early December when a sudden snowstorm raged and buried the shack, he broke a hole in the roof and slipped out.

He went home and didn't leave the yard the whole winter, and, for the first time since he had become watchman at the vineyard, set about working around the homestead. During the first few days, he started shoveling snow off the barn, to stay as far away from his family as possible so as not to torture them with his muteness, and then he simply fell into the habit of puttering about the yard. He split wood, fed the chickens and animals, and especially liked taking care of the two oxen and the cow, which had grown emaciated and splattered with piss stains. He groomed them with the metal comb, stirred up warm mash for them, stayed in the barn by night to feed them, and had them back in shape in two months. At nightfall, when they needed to be given water, Auntie Gruda or Mitka, his youngest daughter, would drive them to the well, because he didn't want to show his face in public. He was also forced to remove his military uniform, so as not to ruin it. He first took off the shoulder strap, followed a few days later by the belt, the jodhpurs, the jacket, and finally his snow-white gaiters. In their place he pulled on old clothes left over from his bachelor days, which made him look like an apprentice in his own home. Auntie Gruda wove homespun cloth, Stoyan Kralev sewed him a suit of clothes without bothering to take his measurements, and thus Salty Kalcho met the new year as a civilian.

He hadn't seen Radka since her wedding. Auntie Gruda would lie in wait for her by the well or the grocer's shop but never managed to detain her for more than a minute. "I'm fine, how else could I be," Radka would say, hurrying on her way. At these short meetings, she never once looked her mother in the eye and never once said anything about herself. Her face and figure had grown so thin that she could hardly carry the full pails of water on her shoulders. Auntie Gruda would come home in tears, telling her husband that Radka was not in a good way. He gave no sign of having heard or understood what she said. He would turn away or go outside. Yet Auntie Gruda would not leave him in peace, she would follow at his heels, lamenting: "Those people are going to work her to the bone, Kalcho, they'll ruin her health! Nothing left of her face but two big eyes, she's thin as a rail! Go get her and bring her home!"

Once as she was going on like this to him, he grabbed her by the arm and pointed at the door.

"No need to shout!" Auntie Gruda said out of habit. "Ooof, Good Lord, I'm going off the deep end myself. What do you want?"

"Boobooboo all vuhh!" he jabbered, and started making some kind of signs with his hands, his eyes filling with tears.

"You want me to go?"

"Mmm! Aha!"

Auntie Gruda tossed her shawl over her shoulders and set off, while he went to get corn from the crib for the chickens. He put a few cobs in the little trough, but before he got back to the house, the church bell began to toll. The peals echoed off the wall of the granary and faded away in the distance. Salty Kalcho looked toward the church and saw a large flock of pigeons soaring high in the sky. They were making wide circles over the village and at every turn their wings gleamed with the rays of the sunset. Salty Kalcho took off his hat and thought: *I wonder who passed away, may God have mercy on their soul!* The bell tolled once again, he went into the house, sat down by the stove, and set about shucking corn. Outside, in the vestibule, he heard a sort of whimpering, the door opened slowly, and on the threshold stood Auntie Gruda with her shawl in her hands.

"Kalcho, we've lost our daughter! Radka's passed away, Kalcho!"

The sun had set by the time the two of them arrived at Zhendo's house. Zhendo's wife met them teary-eyed in the yard. She was alone in the house and didn't dare go into the room with the dead girl. Zhendo wasn't home, while Koycho had been away in the army for several months already.

Radka was lying on her side, her hair scattered loose, in a corner of the room, where she had crawled from the bed in her final throes of agony. Salty Kalcho went over to her, picked her up in his arms, but instead of placing her in the bed, he carried her toward the door. Both women stared at him in silence and only when he kicked open the door and went out into the yard did Zhendo's wife start howling like a she-wolf: "Kinsmannnn, why are you taking our little daughter-in-law, why are you making a vampire of her soul?"

She's never been yours, neither alive nor dead, Salty Kalcho wanted to tell her, but couldn't. A man on horseback was blocking the gate, looming like a black monument against the glow of the sunset. Salty Kalcho slipped between the horse's head and the gatepost. He wouldn't have even noticed the rider if the latter hadn't called out to him: "What the hell are you doing?"

Salty Kalcho set off down the street as if he hadn't heard. As soon as she saw her husband, Zhendo's wife grabbed his leg and began screaming hysterically: "They took her! They took her! Get her back, they've brought shame upon us!"

Zhendo kicked her in the chest and urged the horse into the yard. Then he suddenly jumped to the ground, went back, grasped his wife by the hand and dragged her toward the house. At the same moment, my grandmother, who was carrying an armful of kindling, heard a cry and rushed over to the gate. "I look and what do I see? Kalcho carrying a child in his arms, and Gruda next to 'im, crying herself hoarse" – she later recounted. "So I go over there and crikey! I can't believe my eyes. Kalcho's carrying Radka like a little child. Her face is resting on his shoulder, her hair all hangin' loose, reaching all the way down to his waist. I'd been over to Zhendo's the day before to return a pan, but also so I could check on Radka. Ever since that bad blood at the wedding, her folks never came callin', but Gruda was always sendin' me over to Radka's place to report back what I heard and saw. But even if I hadn't gone over there, I would've known everything anyway – our houses are right next door, if anyone of us sneezes, they hear it, if anyone of them yawns, we hear it. So I'd see our Radka, she was always lying around, curled up like a kitten under a blanket, not moving, not sayin' a word. What's wrong, child, I'd ask her, but she'd just look away, wouldn't answer. Always one and the same thing..."

My grandmother dropped the kindling straight on the ground and just as she was, in the robe she'd gone out into the yard with, she set off with Auntie Gruda, both of them bawling in unison. A few more elderly women joined them, adding their voices to the lament. Salty Kalcho was walking in front of them, holding his dead daughter as if she were alive, the fragile layer of ice covering the ground shattered beneath his heavy footsteps, while the sinister tolling of the church bell rang out over the hushed village. Once they arrived home, the women lit the fireplace in the inner room, filled a cauldron with water, and set it over the fire. The others soon left, leaving only Grandma and Auntie Gruda by the hearth. Once the water was warm, the two women picked up the dead girl, placed her in a large tub, and began undressing her. Her body was tawny and supple as if still alive, yet so withered that she looked like a sleeping ten-year-old child. From her waist all the way down to her calves, she was spattered in thick black blood, her tunic was also soaked with blood. Grief-stricken, the two women exchanged glances, then finally Grandma said: "She miscarried, the poor thing..."

Auntie Gruda let out such a piercing, sinister shriek that Grandma jumped and, not knowing what to do, she started crossing herself and pounding her head with her fists. The dead girl's terrible, shameful past should not have been mentioned, and Grandma was cursing herself for this blasphemy. They didn't say a word while bathing the body, dressing it in clean clothes, and carrying it into the room. Still silent, communicating by glances alone, they placed the dead girl on the bed, lifted her head onto the pillow, and fixed a lighted candle in her hands. The scent of wax, incense, and dried basil filled the room, where the stiff, stark, soothing mystery of death reigned.

After leaving the dead girl to the women, Salty Kalcho went out into the yard, and from there into the garden. He felt like going somewhere far away, so he started walking and walked until late in the evening. It was nearly the end of February and winter had softened its grip, during the day the sun shined, melting the snow, while in the evenings the puddles formed a thin crust of ice. The night was bluishly light, cold, and deathly deserted, not a single lighted window could be seen, nor could any sound be heard. Salty Kalcho kept walking and walking with an ease he had never felt before, as if his feet weren't touching the ground, but rather moving through the air like the wings of a bird. Someone took him by the hand, pulled him back, and then he saw Mitka, his youngest daughter, standing next to him, looking at him with tears in her eyes.

"Daddy, I've been calling you for ages! Mom says you should come home. There's no one to watch over Radka." She led him toward the yard, and before going inside the house, she glanced toward the door of the barn and said: "Looks like the cow's going to calve any day now. She's just lying there, huffing and puffing…"

They spent the night keeping vigil over the dead girl, he on one side, Auntie Gruda on the other. Mitka fell asleep before midnight. She had spent the whole evening rushing back and forth, looking after the livestock, going to the well for water and to the carpenter's to order the coffin, and fell asleep as soon as she sat down by the stove. Auntie Gruda pulled her over to the bed, tucked her in, and sat back down across from her husband. As yellow as jasmine, he was sitting on a three-legged stool with his elbows on his knees, not moving and not taking his eyes off the dead girl's face. And so a whole hour passed, Auntie Gruda grew alarmed at his unmoving gaze and so as to distract him, started chattering about household business, saying it was time the onions and garlic were planted, that the sheep had already started giving birth, so they needed to fence off a special space in the barn for the mothers. He gave no sign with his hand or head to show that he had heard or understood her, and since he had gone mute at Radka's wedding, Auntie Gruda was afraid that he had now lost his mind upon her death. She found his cigarettes and matches on the windowsill and handed them to him, trying to get him to take his eyes off the dead girl, so she could peer into them and see whether he was still in his right mind.

"You usually smoke like a chimney, but now you won't even light up. Come on, now, have a smoke! Come on, husband, light up!"

He turned his eyes toward her and Auntie Gruda, leaning close to his face as she was, saw in his pupils a warm, resigned anguish, and not cold emptiness and madness. Her heart unclenched, and when he took a cigarette and lit up, she sat down at his knee, put her arms around him, and started to cry.

"Don't look at her like that!" she said through her tears. "God is watching her now. Her soul is pure, that's why he called her home so early. Come, go to bed now, you're tired."

Auntie Gruda led him to the other room, settled him in the bed, and as she pulled the covers over him he had already fallen asleep. They woke him up the next afternoon when they were leaving for the graveyard. The burial was quick and quiet, old Father Encho read the final prayer in his hoarse voice and they lowered the coffin into the grave. Several women began wailing loudly, as was the custom when taking final leave of the deceased, while Auntie Gruda, her voice and strength gone, collapsed onto the fresh grave. They pulled her to her feet, loaded her into the oxcart they had brought the coffin on, and the small funeral procession headed back toward the village. On their way to the cemetery, Salty Kalcho had been staring at the coffin, just as during the night he had stared at the dead girl's face, while now his gaze was fixed on the tracks from the cart's rear wheels. Wherever the tracks turned, he turned as well, and so he made his way home.

On the fourth day after Radka's funeral, Auntie Gruda forced him to hoe some space for the summer garlic. Even though the sun was shining, the earth was still cold and they could've waited, but she wanted to distract him with work. If he wasn't doing anything, he would sit frozen, staring into space, not wanting to "talk" to anyone. He looked after the livestock as before and worked around the yard, except now he needed to be reminded of everything. Auntie Gruda handed him the spade, showed him where to dig, and went back into the house. He went into the garden, swung the spade down off his shoulder, and froze. He turned around in a full circle, staring at the ground, and again froze to the spot. He suddenly felt how he was standing on the earth with his full weight, he caught the scent of newly sprouting corn and smoke, he heard the polyphonic sounds of the village, he saw the fruit trees stretching their budding branches toward the sky, thirsty for warmth and space, he saw the circle he had trampled down with his feet the night when he had left the house to go somewhere far away. He remembered, as if awakened from a heavy sleep, that he hadn't gone anywhere, but rather had walked around in that endless circle for hours, like a horse hitched to a post, he remembered how Mitka had come to bring him home, how he had stared at the dead girl's face the whole night, without feeling grief or pain, how he had watched her burial, without tossing even a handful of dirt on her coffin. "How did all of this happen," he asked himself, and realized that he had spent those four days in some quiet, oblivious world, from which he had looked upon everything around him without thought or conscience. Inconsolable tears burst from his eyes, and the question that had been tormenting him for months on end once again settled on his heart like a stone: "Why has God punished me with so much anguish, is it because I'm guilty, and if so, of what?"

After supper, Auntie Gruda sent him to check on the cow. He went into the barn, raised the lantern above his head, and saw the cow lying on one side, her belly distended and her head flopped back. He hung the lantern on the beam, and as he stepped toward the cow, he saw that she was drenched with sweat and that the calf's front legs were already showing. He knew that after the front legs, the little head would follow, so he knelt down and slowly started pulling the legs toward him. When the knees appeared, he realized that these were the back legs and fear seized him. The calf was breech and perhaps stillborn, and the cow might die as well. *What should I do now?* he wondered, not thinking to call Auntie Gruda or one of the neighbors. And so the night passed.

The calf was born safe and sound at dawn, all pinkish-red, with only one white patch on its head. The cow immediately got to her feet and started licking it. Drained from stress and exhaustion, Kalcho sat down on a pile of straw to rest and fell asleep. He dreamed that he was sitting on the upper veranda in the vineyard and that a little white bird had landed at the top of the cherry tree, which was in leaf, and started singing, yet instead of its song, the tinkling of little bells filled the space around him. Now, as always, he was amazed to discover that it was not the bird, but the leaves of the tree that were fluttering in the wind, brushing against one another and ringing like tiny bells, and everything had frozen in joyful repose and bliss…

I saw him in the autumn of '47, when I had just come back to the village after my army service. The drive to get folks to join the cooperative farm was at its height. Like most young people, I, too, took part in the agitprop brigades. The local party secretary Stoyan Kralev had assigned me the task of canvassing my relatives, friends, and neighbors, so I started with Salty Kalcho. Auntie Gruda was working away at something in the garden, so I hopped over the fence and went up to her.

"My man has started talking again!" she said as soon as she had greeted me.

I knew that he had gotten his speech back, but I pretended that I was hearing it for the first time to give her the pleasure of telling the story yet again. She was pulling up leeks, stacking the thicker and thinner stalks into little piles, so I leaned down to help her. And she told me how one night she had sent him out to check on the cow: "He lit a lantern, went out, and was gone a good long while, so long that I fell asleep. When I woke up, it was dawn, and he still wasn't there. I remembered that I'd sent him out to the barn the night before, so I tore over there, opened up the door, and what did I see? He's lying on his back in the straw, his arms stretched out as if stone-cold dead. Scared the living daylights out of me! 'Kalcho, Kalcho,' I cried, because I was afraid to go over to him, but he sprang to his feet, opened his eyes and said: 'We got ourselves a calf!' And ever since then he's been talking again. There he is now up on the roof of the sheep pen, resetting the tiles…"

He had seen me talking to her and had come down the ladder to greet me. He seemed like a completely different person, and not only because I was seeing him in civilian clothes for the first time. In the expression on his face, which was aged slightly and weather-beaten, in his eyes, and in his gait, there was a surprising change, as if along with his military uniform he had also tossed aside that unfitness for life that had caused him for years to live far from people in contemplative isolation, only to give himself over now to work and caring for his land like all the other villagers. He wiped his palms, which were stained with the red dust of the roof tiles, on his pants, then we shook hands and started chatting about who had been where during the four or five years we hadn't seen each other.

"I figgered I oughta fix the roof tiles on the sheep pen, 'cause ever since the first rain fell the other day, the sheep've been lying around wet, their fleece's gotten spattered with mud."

"But won't the sheep be spending the winter in the cooperative pen?" I tried to say this jokingly and by-the-by, to somehow start in on my canvassing. He looked at me just like everyone would look at me from then on when I tried to persuade them to join the new co-op – with astonishment and reproach, with mockery and a patronizing air reserved for someone who clearly believes the moon is made of green cheese. And they wouldn't tell me with their eyes alone, but at the top of their lungs: "You don't have any land, and even if you did, you wouldn't have to make your living from it, that's why you make free and easy with everyone else's." Salty Kalcho would later tell me this as well, but now he had no inkling that I had come to work him over, yet he still gave as good as he got: "You hintin' at the co-op? Leave off with that business already, they've been breathin' down my neck about it for six months now. Soon as you stick your nose out the door, they glom right on to you, then it's come on, sign up, sign up for membership in the co-op, that's the place for you. I thought membership was voluntary, for cryin' out loud, so then why're you always on my back, pressin' me about it, I ask 'em. I got nothin' against it, I tell 'em, you go ahead and do what you've got a mind to do, we'll see how far you get with it, and if it's all well and good, then we'll join up too. 'Cause what fool runs from a good thing? So they got together and decided to do it, but they ain't got enough people. They got eighty communists, but even they aren't keen on it, most of 'em have taken to their heels."

While instructing me as to how to propagandize the locals, Party Secretary Stoyan Kralev had told me that "Salty Kalcho" had "signed on with the opposition" and demanded that we find out by hook or by crook whether he'd done so of his own volition or whether someone else had put that bee in his bonnet, and if so, who. Stoyan Kralev wasn't just interested in idle gossip, he wanted to find out who had managed to turn this solitary, lily-livered fellow, who wouldn't know politics if it bit him on the nose, into our political enemy, and how they had done it.

"Uncle Kalcho," I said, "I hear you've cast your lot with the opposition. I didn't know you knew all that much about politics."

"What's there to know about politics!" He laughed ingenuously. "Politics – it's whatever suits you best. The opposition doesn't give me nothing, but they don't want nothing from me either. Whereas the communists don't give you nothing, but they want everything. Grain and milk and wool and land. The way things are headed, they're gonna strip off our underpants, too, before long! What kind of government keeps wantin', wantin', wantin', but never givin' anything?"

That's what he kept saying every time we met, yet at the constituent meeting to found the co-op, he surprised his ideological brethren from the opposition. Shortly before the meeting, Stoyan Kralev spoke to him one-on-one gently and politely, as he could when he wanted to, and by-the-by promised to appoint him as watchman of the future farm. Salty Kalcho signed the declaration of membership right there and then in front of him and from that moment on became one of the most zealous champions of the cooperative farm. That very same day, he got his old Mannlicher rifle back, which had been confiscated on September 9, the day of the Communist coup; he took it apart, cleaned it down to the last screw, put two bullets in his cartridge pouch, and in the morning appeared before Stoyan Kralev fully accoutered. He wanted to don his military uniform as well, but Stoyan Kralev forbade him.

"No militarism now! From this moment on, the village's land is in your hands, guard it with your life! The kulaks never sleep and are always on the lookout for a way to sabotage the people's property. If you catch one of them, arrest him; if he tries to run, shoot him to ribbons!"

"Yes, sir!" Salty Kalcho replied, army-style.

He tossed his rifle over his shoulder, cocked his cap, and took up his beloved post, for which he had nursed a hidden, yet vivid, nostalgia deep in his heart for years. And while the boundary markers on the land were being plowed up and the people were gasping like fish on dry land, he would first make the rounds of the fields with his rifle on his shoulder, then sit under a tree and give himself over to contemplation. There, amidst a natural landscape sunk in sumptuous greenery, ablaze with the bright hues of autumn, or desolate and melancholy with its black fallow fields, Salty Kalcho found refuge from the harsh and cruel ways of men. As always, he felt a constant and inexplicable dread of them, yet he didn't have the strength to stand up to them and quickly fell under their influence. Despite this, he didn't harbor hatred or any other hard feelings toward anyone, because in his view all people were good. When he was younger, he had demonstrated a certain shrewdness (albeit solely so as to be able to spend his time in seclusion in the vineyard, leaving all the farmwork to his female offspring) or he might have gotten miffed with someone over something, but in the past few years he had been devoid of even these small passions, such that Auntie Gruda would sometimes chide and rebuke him. She pitied him for his weak character, but when she saw how easily he became putty in others' hands, she still tried to talk some sense into him and preserve his dignity.

"Don't get in cahoots with Zhendo, he's a bad man!" she would tell him.

"What's so bad about him?"

"He drove your daughter to an early grave and plundered your land, and now you're gonna go get mixed up in politics with him!"

"He's not a bad man, it's just life that's bad."

"And who makes it bad? Folks like him, that's who. You're not going to say that Chakov is a good man too?!"

"Well, he's good too. Everybody's good, it's just like I told you, life makes them do all sorts o' things."

"Good God!" Auntie Gruda looked at him pityingly. "You were born into this world to drudge and toil!"

Indeed, Salty Kalcho was not capable of self-sacrifice, but rather of suffering, all because of his pliant, gullible character. But this suffering, which he had grown accustomed to like a constant and tolerable illness, did not drive him to despair. In his long hours of reflection and contemplation amidst nature, he always arrived at one and the same thought: that people would set themselves right if they would only "make way for the truth." But he had never thought about just what this truth was, just as he never stopped to think that perhaps every person had his own truth. This was why he trustingly accepted as his own the truth of whoever most persuasively impressed this truth upon him, and thus found himself in the paradoxical position of serving his own truth while at the same time serving many others' truths as well. And so he lurched between truths and this was precisely the source of his suffering.

At harvesttime, the communist authorities ordered that all sheaves of grain be stored at the edge of the village and threshed there, so that the state delivery quotas could be requisitioned on time. Most people stole sheaves by night and made "underground" threshing floors in secluded spots around the fields, they nicked corn, potatoes, and all kinds of food. Salty Kalcho caught some of the thieves, but he didn't shoot anybody to ribbons as Stoyan Kralev had ordered, nor did he even arrest them, because they begged him to keep the whole business hushed up. "You can see for yourself that the government takes everything, what's more, they're saying they'll pay us only twenty cents a day, all the way to the end of the year, so we'll starve to death this winter!" "Well, heck, that's how it is," Salty Kalcho would say, filled with sincere sympathy, and would advise them not to do such things again, because it was against the law, and would promise not to give them away. But the very next morning, he would appear before Stoyan Kralev or the chairman to give his report and with a clean conscience would tell them the truth: whom he had caught stealing and where.

The villagers were surprised to discover in him such a treacherous nature, which he had kept cleverly hidden until he had finally gotten his hands on that slothful little post of his, after which, so as to keep it, he would turn "his own people" over to the authorities without batting an eye. Arrests, investigations, and fines soon followed, while one local, whom the authorities had long had it in for as a notorious opponent of the co-op, was sent to a labor camp. Most people turned against the watchman and lost no time in taking their revenge. He was ambushed several times at night and given a sound thrashing, his pig was poisoned, and an attempt was even made to burn down his house. The police asked him if he recognized any of those who had jumped him, and if he'd accused anyone, even mistakenly, the suspect would've been punished or at least put under investigation, but Salty Kalcho could never name anyone. He had his suspicions about certain people, "but since I haven't heard his voice or seen the whites of his eyes, I can't bring down a load of troubles on a man. The truth is the truth, and that's that!"

He didn't forget the former Sergeant Major Chakov, either. No matter how busy he was, he always found time to drop in on him every month or two, if only for a few hours. He went to see him with his rifle on his shoulder and his cartridge pouch strapped to his waist, in which, along with the two bullets, there was always some little treat as well. The sergeant major was as hale and hardy as ever, but senility had sunk its claws deeply into him, and every time he would ask his guest who he was and where he was coming from.

"It's me, Mista Sarjin Mare, Kalcho Statev, from the second company."

"Sit! Where'd you get that rifle?"

While Salty Kalcho explained for perhaps the fifteenth time where he had gotten it and why, the sergeant major would take the rifle in his trembling, feeble hands, slide back the breechblock, take aim at some target, and pull the trigger. Then he would set the rifle between his knees and ask again: "Who gave you permission to carry a weapon?"

"I'm the watchman at the co-op, Mista Sarjin Mare."

"Well then! Carry out your duties down to the letter, or the birch switch will be dancing on your backside! Do you remember, Private Statev, how I once gave you the drubbing of your life in that barracks storeroom?"

Senility still had not managed to erase those sweet recollections of the past from the sergeant major's memory; his squashed, wrinkle-ridden face livened up, two weak flames flared up amidst the yellowish crust on his eyelids, while the trembling fingers of his right hand rose toward his mouth and instead of spitting on them, he merely beslobbered them.

"I remember, how could I forget, Mista Sarjin Mare? We were young, servin' out our army time."

The sergeant major's wife had passed away a few years earlier, yet he spoke about her as if she were alive, called to her by name from time to time, telling her to come serve their guest refreshments, or prattled on so incoherently that Salty Kalcho was ashamed to listen and would get up to go. What a man he had been, he would think about the former sergeant major on the way back to the village. He needed only yell, "Coooompany, hup!" and the soldiers' blood would run cold. But that's just how it is, some are rich, others poor, some dole out beatings, others take them, and in the end they all go to the grave and are made as pure as the day they were born. And with this humble philosophy, filled with compassion and empathy for the doddering sergeant major, he would make his way home.

After a year and a half, the co-op fell apart and Salty Kalcho once again came under the influence of the opposition. Just as earlier he had believed that the truth lay in the collective farm and equality, now with the same conviction he argued that leaving a man without land of his own was like taking away his soul and his hands. "If it ain't yours, it ain't dear to you," he would say, "and if it ain't dear to you, just think how much you'll work it. Well now, they made us form that co-op, and when we did, what came of it? A big fat nothing. The people don't want no co-op and that's that, and if they don't want it, they shouldn't force 'em. 'Cause when something's done by force, nothin' good'll come of it. Your own land, now that's another thing entirely, your umbil'cal cord is tossed there,* even if you have to slave away night 'n' day, you don't mind."

However, his "umbil'cal cord" was not tossed on his land, but somewhere else. Like every contemplative person, especially one who was scrawny to boot, for him physical labor was torture, he disliked agricultural work and did not feel any love for his land. Unlike his fellow villagers, for whom ownership over the land was sanctified by a living, age-old, primordial right, he felt the jolt of the revolution for completely different reasons. To him, collectivization was a kind of formal change to people's landowning status and didn't affect him, since the sense of ownership had not set down roots in his soul. Yet the turbulence of the revolution had dragged him out of the den of his solitude, thrown him together with people, and imposed their concerns and troubles upon him. Battered roughly from all sides, he was at a loss, and like any person with no social experience, pure and uncorrupted, he could not find balance on his own, and hence looked for it in others and believed that he had found it in them.

A year later, the co-op was reformed, and Salty Kalcho was once again appointed as watchman and stayed at that post until the age of fifty-five. During that time, his youngest daughter, Mitka, got married, while his wife passed away and his son-in-law came to live with them. He turned out to be a very hardworking and handy young man. He was one of the first two tractor drivers in the village and enjoyed widespread respect. He fixed up the old house, built on two more rooms, planted a new vineyard, and then turned his attention to the yard, the garden, and whatever private lands were left to them. Salty Kalcho was proud of him and never missed a chance to brag about his "golden boy" of a son-in-law. The young man understood perhaps better than anyone his father-in-law's character and left him to live his life as he saw fit. After retiring from his post, Salty Kalcho would go out at any time of the day or night and disappear for hours on end. He would go to the vineyard or stroll around the fields, coming back after dark. His son-in-law could see that his soul felt stifled at home, yearning for the old Mannlicher rifle that he had carried on his shoulder for more or less his whole life, so he brought a double-barreled Izhmash shotgun back for him from the USSR, where he'd gone for some training courses. He got his father-in-law a hunting license as well, and made a hunter out of him, so he could go out into the fields a few days a week. Little by little, Salty Kalcho fell in with the local hunting club, started going to the tavern and drinking a pint with the other men.

And so it was until that day and hour when he found himself standing in that hunting blind in the forest, thinking back over his life from Radka's wedding until the tasting of new wines at the tavern. His legs were starting to go numb with cold, he stamped his feet and from time to time called out to the beaters to hurry. No reply came from the woods in front of him, nor from Kiro Dzhelebov, who should have been standing a hundred or so feet from him; from the ravine, which was filled with a white, impenetrable slag, he could hear a loud blustering. *Down there, where it's sheltered, the snowdrifts must be over a man's head*, Salty Kalcho thought to himself, *the beaters must have sunk into it and can't get out*. To his left he could still see the tracks he'd made coming into the blind, so he decided to go over to Kiro Dzhelebov to see what they could do to help the beaters if they were stuck down in the ravine. And just then he thought he saw the foliage above him shudder, shaking off a cloud of snowy dust. He also thought he caught a glimpse of a human silhouette, so he called out: "Come on now, people, let's get this over right quick or we'll come to grief here in this…"

Something slammed into his chest and knocked him onto his back. His head sank into the snow and he felt a warmth on his face that immediately spread over his body. *My legs are frozen stiff and can't hold me*, he thought, trying to get up. He rolled over onto one side, dug at the snow, and managed to prop himself up on his elbows. The snow kept warming his face more and more, slipping into his nostrils and mouth and suffocating him. With his last ounce of strength, he rose to his knees, took a deep breath, and recalled that before he had fallen, he had heard a faint crack, like the snapping of a branch. *The blizzard must've broken it, just like it's broken me,* he thought, struggling to get to his feet before finally standing. But his legs wouldn't hold him, he fell to his knees again, and it was only then that he saw that the snowy pit where he had been rolling around was completely spattered with red. A sharp, burning spasm tore through his chest, he cried out, thick red blood spewed from his mouth, running down his chin onto the snow. He slumped to the ground slowly, just as he had gotten up – first on his elbows, then on his belly – crawled toward the snowdrift and slipped under it. Only his legs were left in the open, in their rubber boots, and their kicking, ever slower and flagging, showed his heart's final beat.

PART TWO:

ZHENDO "THE BANDIT" IVANOV

So you were asking where I got this here revolver. I'll tell you, but first let's raise another toast. Stoyan Kralev took a revolver from me back in the day, but he didn't know I had another one. I got scared they might find it if they came to search my place, so I went and buried it under the barn. It's been what, fifteen, sixteen years now, just look how the rust has eaten away at it. I found it this fall, when I tore down the barn. It was a nice little revolver. Ivan Pehlivanov gave it to me when I was just eighteen. As you know, I'm from the villages up in the highlands, in the Deliorman. My father was killed in the First Balkan War, I had a brother and sister as well, both younger than me.

One day I'd gone into the forest to gather some wood. I loaded up the cart and was just about to head back when I see this pair coming toward me. Two men, looked to be around thirtyish, one in a fur cap, the other bareheaded. They stopped next to me, sat down, lit up cigarettes. Where're you from, boy? Such-and-such village. Well, are you going to be coming back for more wood? Sure I will, I say. Then why don't you bring us some cigarettes, matches, and a little something to eat? A loaf of bread and this and that. The guy in the cap dug into his pocket and gave me some cash. I took it and set off for the village. It looked like a fair bit of money, so when I got out of the woods, I stopped to count it. Twenty-some leva, which was no mean sum back in those days. While I unloaded the wood, mama went to the shop, bought a dozen packs of cigarettes, a couple of pounds of olives, matches, plus bread, cheese, and a few other things tossed in from us. She also gave me the change so I could give it back to them.

So I brought them what I brought them, they ate their fill, and the one with the cap asked me if I knew where the village of Pisarovo was. I told them I'd heard of it but had never been there. They questioned me a little more about this and that, then said: "Boy, you brought back what was left of the money we gave you, exactly as much as you should have, so that means you're an honest lad. So we'd like to do you a good deed. Go to the village of Pisarovo and find the mosque. It's covered in stone slabs. Count the third slab to the right from the door along the wall. Pry it up with your pocketknife and underneath you'll find a bag of gold."

They gave me a little silver coin and went on their way. I didn't believe them for a second about the gold. If they knew where a bag of gold was hidden, they'd go and get it themselves, they wouldn't go leaving it to me. Decent folks, I said to myself, since they didn't have anything else, they repaid me with a silver coin and a kind word. That's all well and good, but in another day or two word got around the village that the police had smashed Karademirev's gang. Those were dark times after the war, troubled times. Robberies and burglaries galore all through the Deliorman and Dobruja. Lots of men from the villages would go around in twos or threes, thieving in Karademirev's name. His fame as a bandit and thief spread far and wide throughout these parts.

When I heard about that business, I got to thinking that that pair in the woods were from Karademirev's gang, one of them might've even been Karademirev himself. The police at their heels, looking to save their skins, why not do a good turn for a poor boy? So they met me and did me that good turn. One day Ivan Pehlivanov told me they'd found a man murdered in a shack out in the vineyard in Gevrekler, two villages away from ours. The man was Pasko Naumov from Karademirev's gang. The police didn't find anything on him, but they later reckoned he'd been killed by his crony Shevket. Once he fell asleep, Shevket killed him, took his gold, and fled to Turkey. He's still there, alive and well, with two hotels and a big store in Stamboul. Or so wrote our local Turks who settled there.

What Ivan Pehlivanov told me turned out to be true and I realized I'd seen the very same people. But I didn't tell him, 'cause I was afraid of him. He was bigger than me, already had two children. I chummed around with his little brother, so Ivan counted me as his kid brother too. He was a hot-tempered guy and was mixed up in some shady business. Rumor had it that he would go around to the villages here and there, stealing horses and running them across the border. If I told him about the mosque, he could go there himself and swipe the gold. But I didn't dare tell anyone else about all that, lest they think I was in cahoots with the bandits. Fine, but how could I go to Pisarovo and get into the mosque by myself! And so the winter passed, spring rolled around, but I just kept thinking about that mosque, kept seeing that bag of gold in front of my eyes. What else could I do? I had no choice but to turn to Ivan Pehlivanov. So by-the-by, I says, I know where some gold is – and I told him what had happened in the woods. It was them, he said, his eyes flashing. The very next day he hitched up his cart and the two of us took off for Pisarovo. It was four villages from ours, so we got there after midday. We stopped in front of the tavern and went inside. Ivan Pehlivanov had an old army buddy in that village and starting asking about him. Delcho was his name. They sent somebody to call for him and a little later he showed up. He and Ivan Pehlivanov drank a few rounds, shot the breeze, and Delcho invited us to stay at his place.

Around midnight we went to the mosque. Before going inside, Ivan Pehlivanov gave me this revolver, just like that, in case. We pried up two slabs – nothing. I dug around under the third one. My hand sank deep down, I felt something, and when we held it up to the candle, it was a gold coin, sure enough. We looked for more – nothing. The rest had been swiped by someone. Either Shevket had come by to get it before fleeing to Turkey, or one of their other henchmen. They gave me the gold coin. "It's your lucky charm," they said, "take it." Ivan Pehlivanov didn't want his revolver back, either. "You keep it," he said, "it might come in handy."

And very soon that revolver did come in handy. One night Ivan Pehlivanov found me and said we had a job to do. We went over to the common pasture near the village of Potok and found Delcho and another guy waiting there. I took a good look at him – Krustyo Marinov from our village. I realized that this was going to be dirty business, but what could I do? I went with them. It was threshing time, during the day folks flailed the grain, then in the evening left their horses to graze the stubble fields. At dawn, when the herdsmen were deepest asleep, Ivan Pehlivanov pulled aside four pairs of horses and slipped off their fetterlocks. We hopped on the horses and galloped for the border, a half an hour's ride away. There, four men were waiting for us, one spoke Bulgarian, the others spoke Vlach. They took the horses and disappeared across the border, while we headed back to the woods on our side. We sat down, Ivan Pehlivanov took out the money and handed us each a wad.

Word of the horse raid got around the very next day, the villages were swarming with cops and agents, they questioned suspicious characters and held them down at the station. I hid the money in a safe place and went about my business at the stackyard. Ivan Pehlivanov had given the three of us strict orders not to meet, and if we happened to run into each other somewhere, we were not to stop and talk. He also ordered us not to get any wise ideas on our own; if need be, he would decide what we should do. Fine, but Krustyo busted down the door of the general store one night and swiped a thousand leva from the till. He bungled the job, they caught him and sent him down to prison for three years. Ivan Pehlivanov got scared, he couldn't sit still for a second. He was afraid that Krustyo would squeal on us under interrogation. If he admits he was working with us and they bring us in, you deny everything, he said, otherwise we're done for. We only breathed easier once they'd finally sentenced Krustyo and tossed him in prison. Only, he didn't wait to serve out his time but escaped from jail with one other kid. The authorities were on their trail and they roamed around the forests in the Deliorman for a month or two on the run. One time they came near a village and saw a couple of girls hoeing a vegetable garden. They were mountain girls, day laborers. They kidnapped one of the girls, had their fun with her, then killed her and left the body near the woods. After that incident they found themselves in really hot water. The other kid disappeared somewhere, Krustyo was left alone, and for lack of anywhere else to go, he came back to the village. He went to Marko Doynov, who hid him at their place.

Around that time Ivan Pehlivanov had gotten a little gang together. We skittered around Inner Dobruja, robbing the wealthier folks. One night Doynov went to Ivan Pehlivanov and asked him to slip Krustyo across the border. Doynov had been the schoolteacher in the village for many years, he did all kinds of favors for people and everybody held him in high respect. Krustyo was his neighbor and he was very fond of him. On one of our raids across the border, we took Krustyo with us and set him up as a shepherd for a fellow from the village of Punduklii. This fellow promised to get him a passport from the Romanians. We continued on toward Silistra. The last time we'd gone by there, one of our boys had gotten lost. We had stopped to rest by the side of a highway in the middle of the night. After we'd gotten up and walked a mile or so, we saw that we were a man down. There was no way we could go back, so we fired off two shots, waited a bit, and when no one answered, we continued on our way. The kid had fallen asleep, and when he woke up and saw he was alone, he got scared. He thought it was the Romanians shooting, so he stayed by the roadside until dawn. Finally he tossed down his gun and started wandering every which way. The Romanians caught him the next day, arrested him, and after that we lost track of him. A month later we decided to make the rounds of the villages near Silistra and if we found him, we'd try to spring him. We spent a few days in a cave near Silistra. A Romanian spotted us and so as to head off disaster, we left the cave and pulled back toward the border. Along the way, we found out that the Romanians had punished our boy by letting a police dog have at him on the village square in Karapelit. After that they sent him into the interior and he was never seen or heard from again.

Not a week had passed since we were back in the village when one night Krustyo showed up most unexpectedly. The fellow we'd left him with hadn't been able to get him a passport, so he'd come back. While he'd been sitting in Punduklii, it was all over the papers that there was a ten-thousand-leva reward for anyone who killed or captured him. He even showed the newspaper to Ivan Pehlivanov, who laughed and said we'd missed our lucky chance. What are you saying, I told him, he's our comrade, after all! Come on, now, I'm just spouting off, he answered. Krustyo was afraid to go home, so he stayed at our place. He wanted us to take him across the border to Serbia. We mulled it over this way and that, and finally Ivan Pehlivanov told him that to clear him a channel all the way to Serbia, we'd need cash, and to get our hands on it, we'd have to rob the *hodja* in Gevrekler. The *hodja* was a rich man, we'd go just the three of us, so whatever we got we wouldn't have to split with too many people. Krustyo agreed. We set out for the border one night and we hadn't even gotten to the edge of the vineyard when Ivan Pehlivanov shot Krustyo in the back. When he fired, he got so scared that he took off running and screaming. I was barely able to catch up with him and calm him down. We dragged Krustyo's corpse toward the road and went back to the village. In the morning, Ivan Pehlivanov turned himself in at the town hall. They took him to the city, gave him the ten thousand leva, and made him a watchman. He didn't give me a red cent of that money. Later as watchman, he stole a gun from the police storehouse and landed himself in prison.

After him, I became head of the gang and we kept roaming around on this and that side of the border like before. Our gang was five men in all, and so as to find ourselves local backers, we told folks we were working for Karademirev. The police had caught some of his people, but they couldn't catch the man himself and he'd started running rampant again. The September Uprising* had been stamped out, the times were more troubled than ever, there was lots of unrest. Karademirev strung folks along, saying he was fighting Tsankov's government, so lots of communists and agrarians became his backers. He had backers in Romanian territory as well, so he was free to go about his business there, too. Alongside him, they hid us as well, told us who the rich folks in each village were and how many guards they had.

One time we decided to hit the mayor of Eni Cheshme. He was an Aromanian and a real son of a bitch. He tortured our Bulgarians, robbed them, and forced them to turn Romanian. There were plenty of types like him all around Dobruja, our backers told us where crimes had been committed and who was behind them. There were folks beaten and killed, others sent to prison. There was also a case like this: A Bulgarian bloke's horses got into a Romanian's field and trampled down the edges a bit. So the Romanian raised his rifle and shot both horses on the spot. We found him in that very same field at harvesttime. At dusk his wife had gone back to the village, while he'd stayed to graze his horses. We gagged his mouth with a rag and hung him up on a pear tree by his feet. Finally, we slaughtered his horses and set his wheat on fire. All the colonists' land was gathered in a single spot – summer and winter crops all in one. It was called *kadastra*. His wheat burned down to the very last ear, and he was hanging from the pear tree all the while. They cut him down alive, but nice and roasted.

Some time later we found out that the tax collector in a village had raped one of our girls for singing Stefan Karadzha's song. "Karadzha Told Rusanka," there's a song like that. The girl took her own life, drowned herself in a well. And wouldn't you know, that girl was a cousin of one of our boys. His name was Zhelyo, he'd fled from the Romanians a few years before. So the kid got fired up, we couldn't hold him back. If you don't come with me, he said, I'll go by myself and get even with that dirty Vlach oxherd! So one night we went to Zhelyo's village. We stopped by his folks' house, chatted a bit with his mother and father, had a bite to eat and took a rest. They told us that the taxman was guarded at night by the gendarmerie. The original owners of the house had fled to Bulgaria. Zhelyo knew the place like the back of his hand, because as a kid he'd played with the family's children and had often slept at their place. There was no moon, but it was light – the sky was one star next to another. A window was lit up on the lower floor, that was where the sentries slept. We had to hit them quietly, with no shooting, because it was a big village, a whole squadron of gendarmerie was posted there, twenty men strong. The taxman wasn't married, an old woman looked after the house and slept there too. It went without saying that the man would be armed, with his door bolted from the inside, and if he found himself in a tight spot, he'd shoot and yell for help. We also took half a can of gas, so if we didn't manage to get our hands on him we could at least torch his house.

At midnight we crept toward the house and lay down along the fence. The sentry was nowhere to be seen, nor did we catch a glimpse of anybody through the window on the lower floor. We lay there like that for an hour. The sentry stepped out of the shadow of the veranda, quickly made his rounds, and went into the lit-up room. Zhelyo and one other guy jumped up and headed straight for the place they'd first seen the sentry. There was a chair there where the sentry had been sitting. A few minutes later he came back. Whether it was the same sentry or a relief shift, we never did find out. He hit the ground out cold and couldn't utter a word. Then the three of us ran into the guardroom. There were two men inside, one was asleep on the bed with his back to us, the other was awake. Before he could even open his mouth, I pressed a revolver to his chest. We gagged him and tied his hands and made him lie facedown. The other fellow was still asleep. I don't know what was with him, whether he was tired or drunk or what, but he was sleeping like the dead, without budging. He only woke up when we rolled him over facedown. Plenty of time had passed, or so it seemed to me, and still there was no sound from up in the house, yet Zhelyo still hadn't come back. I sent one of our men to see what was going on there and he didn't come back either. Delcho was keeping watch out in the yard. I was left on my own in the guardroom and started thinking that somebody up there had laid a trap for my men and was catching them one by one. I got scared that maybe the head sentry would come to relieve them. If the head sentry came to oversee the shift change like back on our side, then we'd have to shoot. The two guards were lying facedown with their mouths gagged, and besides, I didn't know any Romanian to be able to ask them in any case. ·

At long last they came down and signaled for us to take off. Only when we were already out of the village did we realize that we'd forgotten to take the sentry's gun, and we were really fuming over that. We spent the day in the woods, and Zhelyo told us how he'd taken his revenge on the taxman. He first tried the door to the middle room, it wasn't locked from the inside. He switched on his pocket flashlight – a woman was asleep on the ottoman. Knowing that the sentry was on guard outside, she surely didn't bother to lock her door at night. Zhelyo grabbed her by the throat and asked her which room the taxman slept in. The woman's eyes bulged, she could hardly breathe. Let go of her throat, you'll strangle her, one of our boys whispered to him. He let her go and the poor woman pointed to the closet door. Zhelyo had been inside that closet many times and knew that there was a little door in it that led to the big room.

The Romanians took revenge for the tax collector. They killed a dozen folks from Zhelyo's village and as many again from the nearby villages. Those killings made the newspapers, our government protested to the

Romanian government. There were also other gangs that slipped into Dobruja to punish outrages committed against the Bulgarians there. It was a downright mess, nobody knew who was paying the piper or calling the tune. One night, we were just about to cross the border when we got caught in an ambush. We hit the ground and got ready for a firefight. We decided if they were Romanians, we'd shoot our way out, come what may. Because we'd seen cases like that: The gendarmerie would set up an ambush and take Bulgarians with them to fool you. Who are you, I yelled. Bulgarians, who are you? We're Bulgarians too, one of you come over here where we can get a good look at you. As soon as I said it, one of them got up and came over to us. I recognized him right away – the Doctor. Dimitar "the Doctor" Donchev. They were communists, their leader was Docho Mihaylov. You must've heard of Docho, they sang songs about him all throughout Dobruja. He led the DRO – the Dobrujan Revolutionary Organization. There was also the IDRO – the Internal Dobrujan Revolutionary Organization. The two organizations had started out as one, but then they split and started fighting amongst themselves. Docho was struggling against capitalism in league with the Romanian communists, while the others were fighting against the Romanian enslavement.

In any case, we chatted a bit with the Doctor, then he led us over to his band. Docho Mihaylov was there, too. I told him I knew both him and the Doctor. Their headquarters were in Dzhivel, one village over from ours. There was a whole neighborhood from Northern Dobruja there and they were all Docho's people. I'd heard him speak a couple of times at meetings in the villages. Well, how nice that we're acquainted, Docho said. He asked me whose side we were on, the IDRO's or Karademirev's and what we were after here in Romanian territory. I told him that we'd come to rub out a big landowner who'd killed a Bulgarian kid. Docho got really furious. So, did you rub him out? And so with plenty of hemming and hawing, we admitted it. Lay out the money, right here in front of me!

What else could we do, we set the money in front of him. There were only five of us and twelve of them, rigged out like regular troops with carbines and grenades. They wanted to take our weapons, too, but Dimitar Donchev protested. They might run across some Vlach patrol, he said, they'll slaughter them like lambs if we let them go bare-handed. Docho backed down. This time, he said, I'll let you off easy, but if I catch you here again, we settle things very differently. Because of the likes of you, he said, the Romanians torment the people, for every one of theirs killed, they kill ten of ours. Whichever of you wants to work for national liberation, we'll welcome him with open arms. But whichever of you wants to kill and plunder, we'll sweep him out of our path, because the government chalks up all your killing and thieving to our name. We promised to think over what we would do from then on and went our separate ways.

From then on we kept on doing things as we always had. But we made sure to steer clear of Docho's band, but it turned out we didn't have to watch our step for very long. Four months later Docho was killed and his band fell apart. The other leader, the Doctor, was killed later. He would've fallen then and there as well, if I hadn't saved his life. A month or two after our run-in with them, we got ambushed again. We thought it was Docho's men and said to ourselves: "This is it for us, this time they won't let us off the hook." But they turned out to be from the IDRO. They told us we were good boys because like them, we were fighting to free Dobruja from Romanian slavery, only they didn't like our guns much. They gave us five new carbines, bombs, bullets, and as we were leaving, they told us if we ever needed anything to go see so-and-so in such-and-such a village. In early August we ran across them again. They promised not to bother us in the future if we agreed to help liquidate a band of communists. Russian agents, or so they said, they killed rich people and wanted to overthrow the current government. The Romanian government had sent a diplomatic note to ours, demanding that they pull the communist detachments out of Dobruja or they couldn't be responsible for the consequences.

I realized they were talking about Docho Mihaylov. During our run-in with him as well as at those village meetings, he had said the exact opposite – that we wouldn't get anywhere with personal vendettas and banditry. We would liberate Dobruja only if we worked together and organized the population to rise up in revolt. Some folks say one thing, others – the exact opposite, so just go and try to figure out who's telling the truth. Besides, what did I care about their truth, let them gouge each other's eyes out, as long as they don't drag us into their squabbles. But stabbing Docho and the Doctor in the back – I didn't like that business one bit. No matter what they might have been, they were Bulgarians. And they were strong to boot. If they found out afterward that we were in cahoots with the police against them, they wouldn't forgive us. I tried to talk them out of it, but those folks from the IDRO didn't stand on ceremony at all. They told us flat out that if we didn't help, they'd turn us over to authorities. I was between a rock and a hard place, with no way forward and no way back.

In the end, I accepted the IDRO's conditions. First, because a person thinks above all about himself, and second, because I didn't believe they would catch Docho and the Doctor. They were seasoned fighters and wouldn't let themselves get caught so easily by the police. In late August the IDRO sent word for us to report to the village of Gyulleri. They put us up in a house there and told us to wait until they called us. As we later learned, around that time Docho's band had come back from Dobruja and had stopped to rest in Dzhivel. The forester gave them away. I remember him, he was the IDRO's man, but I've forgotten his name. Fifty policemen arrived that very same day and attacked. The band retreated to the woods. That's when they called the five of us in as backup. They wanted to take us down to the chief of police so he could assign us positions along the cordon, but I refused. The police were also after Karademirev, and we often hid under his name, so along with this raid they could very well catch us in a trap too. I told them that we knew the woods better than the police and we would take up positions there ourselves.

We kept watch for two days and two nights, the police scoured the woods – nothing. On the third day, a man came by and told us to lift the watch at dusk and to wait for further orders. They had information that the band had retreated to the neighboring village of Beshtepe, so at night we should lie in wait for them at the border. The five of us gathered together to figure out what we should do when we heard rifles crackling behind us. About five hundred yards away was a small stand of trees, surrounded by fields. It seemed that Docho and the Doctor, realizing that they would be discovered in the big forest, had gone into that little grove. They wouldn't have been found if Petko Mutafa hadn't betrayed them. He was from Dzhivel, I knew him, too. He had been cutting corn that day, and around noontime the Doctor had come to him asking for water. They had known each other a long time. The Doctor took a drink of water, brought the flask to his comrades so they could drink as well, and went back to Petko. He asked him to go back to the village right away and tell their man to meet them later that evening. Mutafa hitched up his cart, went to the village, found the man and gave him the message, then went to the police sergeant and told him some people were hiding in the little grove.

The shoot-out lasted two hours. We were standing on the edge of the big forest and had no idea what was going on. At one point we caught a glimpse of a man in the corn. He was barreling straight down the row, making a beeline for us without seeing us at all. He came out of the corn-field and ran right into us. The Doctor. Bareheaded, his shirt bloodied, with a grenade in one hand, a rifle in the other, white as a sheet. When he saw us five feet in front of him, he went to set off the grenade, but I shouted out to him: "Doctor, our rifles are on our shoulders, we're not going to shoot. Don't you recognize me?" He looked at me and kept silent.

He didn't recognize me, and even if he did, would he trust me at a moment like that? Go on your way, I told him, as if we're not here. He kept silent, not moving. He was holding the grenade's fuse in his hand, all he needed to do was pull it and he was done for, we were done for too. Since you don't believe us, I said, we'll leave our guns here on the ground and go with you, we'll escort you wherever you want. We took off our guns and grenades and hid them in the underbrush. Now, he said, you go on ahead of me. We walked half a mile or so, then he stopped us and said: "I recognized you, how could I not! After all, I came over to see who you were. We thought you were Romanian gendarmes, so we caught you in a trap. But now you're free. You have our comrades' gratitude, now farewell!" He went on ahead, while we turned back to get our weapons. It would've been a cinch to put a bullet in him, but I didn't have the heart. I remember how Docho had wanted to disarm us that night, but the Doctor told him: "Docho, we've scolded these boys enough, let them decide for themselves whether they want to work with us or go back home. And we can't let them go bare-handed, the Vlachs might slaughter them." The man did us a good deed and we repaid him with goodness in turn. That very same night we learned that Docho and one other member of the band had been killed, while the other two had surrendered.

So anyway, I had started telling you how we robbed the mayor of Eni Cheshmė. We knew that he'd be at his brother's son's wedding that night. We caught the village patrols, then went up to the house. The windows barred, two padlocks on each of the doors. Delcho was a big, husky fellow, first he rammed one door, then the other, and tore them off their hinges. We went inside and started ransacking the place. Two men went into the living rooms, another two went up to the attic, while the bedroom fell to me. I dug around, searching and searching – nothing. I felt something hard inside one of the pillows, sliced it open with a knife and pulled out a thick stack of bills. How much it was exactly, we couldn't tell, but it had to be at least twenty thousand.

It took all of half an hour, we regrouped and were on our way out of the village. As we passed the last house, someone shouted: "Halt, put your hands up!" We hit the deck, trying to figure out if we'd been ambushed. Zhelyo knew Romanian, he asked who was there, nobody answered. Later we found out what had happened and who was hollering at us. While we were ransacking the mayor's house, one of the patrolmen had gotten loose and had run to tell him. And wouldn't you know, that very same night Karademirev had come to visit the mayor and he had taken him along to the wedding. Karademirev jumped up from the banquet table fit to be tied and ordered all the men at the wedding to make a cordon around the village immediately. If we had known we were dealing with Karademirev, we would've tried to sneak out of the village some other way and give him the slip, but no, we jumped up and stormed ahead, firing away and making a run for the fields. Whoever had hollered at us to stop didn't pipe up again. Only when we got two or three hundred feet further on and rifles started crackling at us did we realize that we were surrounded by plenty of people. They came after us hot on our trail and chased us rat-a-tat-tat for a good half an hour before falling silent. We took to the woods, walking twenty feet apart. As soon as we got to the other side, we regrouped and took off straight through the fields. We walked for about an hour and suddenly another forest was blocking our way. We went into it, now taking this path, now that one, till we found ourselves stuck in some thick undergrowth. We thought we'd been following the stars, but here we were walking around in a circle. When we finally made it into the clear, the stars were fading and it was getting light over in the east. It was only a little ways to the border, the two posts were gleaming up on the hill, ours and the Romanians'. We split into two groups. Delcho and me would pass by on one side of the post, while the other three would go around the other.

We were tired, so when we crossed the border, we stopped by a sun-flower field to rest. Delcho ducked into the sunflowers to heed the call of nature, while I took off my coat, spread it on the ground, and lay down. And then I heard heavy footsteps, so I sat up and what did I see – a man on horseback galloping through the sunflowers straight at me. When he came closer I saw he was holding a rifle, so I jumped to my feet. I noticed he had a moustache and a black Vlach-style bowler on his head. His horse was black too. As I reached for my rifle, something burned through my chest, knocked me down hard, and I fell flat on my back. I remember as if in a dream how he leaned down over me and I felt a terrible pain in my left side. He was struggling to free the bag of money I'd slung over my left shoulder. Delcho heard the shot but by the time he came back, the horseman had already galloped back across the border. He saw the wound to my heart and ran to the village for a cart. Along the way I came to and told him to go straight to the city for a doctor.

We reached Varna after midday. Delcho asked around and they told him about some Dr. Stamatov or other, a real expert surgeon. He had a private hospital. They cleaned my wound, bandaged me up, and said I had to stay in the hospital. I spent a whole month there. Doc, I'd ask every time he examined me, can you patch me up good as new? I'll shower you with gold, if only you heal me. He kept silent. Finally on the twentieth day he said: "Young man, you've got a strong soul. The bullet passed just half an inch below your heart, without touching anything else. In all my years as a doctor, I tell you, I've never seen anything like it." At the end of the month, they discharged me fit as a fiddle, as if nothing had ever happened. I repaid him hand over fist and then some. I gave him pure gold from what I'd stashed away. And every year I made a blood sacrifice on that day. I would bring him a slaughtered lamb or piglet. No matter where I found myself at that time of year, I hitched up my horses and went straight to him. Until the day he died.

For a long time we racked our brains trying to figure out who'd shot me and taken the money. We finally found out that it was Karademirev.

He himself admitted it, so all folks like us would know and stay out of his way. That night, as soon as he realized that we'd slipped out of the village on him, he took the Aromanian's horse and headed straight for the border with a dozen men to lie in wait for us. He left his men near the border posts where he expected us to cross, on the other side, our side, no less. Once a man has crossed the border, he gets as careless as if he's in his own home, which is what we did too. Karademirev had given his word to that mayor to catch all of us sooner or later. I'll slaughter them down to the last man, he said, so I know who my true comrades and backers are. And he was right. That Aromanian would've lost faith in him and his cronies. He comes to visit you, eats and drinks at your table, while his men ransack your house in the meantime. So that's why Karademirev was foaming at the mouth with rage that night. And he was a man who always settled the score. Once he'd fixed someone in his sights, there was no stopping him. One time one of his men got a little greedy, helped himself to the common cache, and then disappeared somewhere in Bulgaria or Romania. Karademirev looked for him under hill and dale for three years and finally found him all the way in Sofia. The fellow had bought himself a big house, set up a store on the town square, and started trading to beat the band. One day at noon there was a knock on his door, he opened up and that was the last thing he ever did. One of Karademirev's men put a bullet in him and that was it for him.

When I was fully recovered, I bought an *intizap* from the town hall. An *intizap* is a tax paid to town hall when cattle are bought and sold. If the buyer or the seller dodges the tax or tries to cover up the sale, I would hit them with a fine three times the *intizap* itself, then I'd hit them with another fine in town hall's name. Around that time they caught Karademirev. Who gave him away and how they caught him, I don't know. One day they were taking him through our village on the way to the city. I had gone down to town hall to look for the mayor. I went into his office, he wasn't there, only his assistant and some old man. I sat down with them, we chatted a bit when all of a sudden a cart came clattering down the street. Soon the door opened, a head guardsman came in and said they were bringing Karademirev through. They hadn't told the local mayors in advance, as they were afraid his backers in the villages might organize an attack on the convoy. When I heard that, my blood ran cold and I was thinking to slip out, but two guards brought in Karademirev. We had all jumped to our feet. He came in and said: "Good day, people," and sat down in a chair. His hands were tied, heavy shackles hung from one leg. Grandfather, take a seat, why are you standing up, he told the old man, and chatted with him a bit. Finally he looked at the deputy mayor and asked him who he was and let out a laugh. He turned to me as well, looked at me and didn't say a thing. At one point he seemed to smile, and my legs all but gave out. If he were to up and say that he recognized me, that he'd shot me and taken the mayor of Eni Cheshme's money from me, they would've arrested me on the spot and carted me off along with him. But instead he said: "Boy, go get me some water!"

I took the empty bottle off the table and went out. There was a fountain behind town hall, I looked around – a dozen or so guards lapping at the spout. So I waited for them to drink their fill, trying to reckon what to do all the while. If I ran for it, I'd give myself away, if I went back to him, he could give me away. Both regular folks and the authorities knew what we'd been up to, only they didn't have any proof. Word had gotten around of a man killed near the border, but no one had figured out it was me. No, I told myself, I'm not going to run. I rose up from the grave, if I take to my heels and run now, everything will crumble to pieces, it'll all be shot to hell. If he's recognized me and gives me away, I'll deny it. They won't easily believe a man like him. I set the bottle on the table, but since his hands were tied, right, he said: "Lift it up, boy, to my lips." I pressed the bottle to his lips, he drank and kept looking at me. Looking from my face to my chest and back again. He gave me a sign, I pulled the bottle away, water spilled down his beard and chest. Boy, he said, your hand's shaking so badly you nearly broke my teeth. Don't worry, my hands are tied now. When he said "My hands are tied now," I knew that he'd recognized me.

A short while later they made him get up, the shackles rattled and he left. The others went out into the yard, I stayed in the room and watched the guards helping him into the cart through the window. After the cart took off, the guards and the other folks stayed in the yard watching after it, while I thought to myself that in life things happen that you couldn't imagine even in your wildest dreams. Karademirev had well nigh killed me, and it worked out that we met again and I gave him water to drink like a little child. He didn't give me away, but when I went home, I thought it over and got scared again. In court they would accuse him of a murder he had committed on this side of the border, in Bulgarian territory, because he himself had admitted to that murder. They would ask him who the dead man was, where the body was, and he would say there was no dead man. Only a wounded one, but he had recovered and is now living in such-and-such a village. He might even demand a face-to-face meeting.

I spent the whole month on tenterhooks, always waiting to be arrested and taken to the city. I had a mind to leave our village and move to another, farther-off one. I'd thought this up already back in the hospital, when my life was hanging by a thread. When I went around to the villages looking for a place, I came by here as well. They told me there was an empty house. It was an inherited place, the heirs were looking to sell. I looked it over and put down a deposit there and then. This very house here. That's all well and good, but my brother started carping at me. Go wherever you like, he said, just don't leave me empty-handed. It's true when they say your nearest cost you dearest. When I was out roaming around here and there, I would always give him something, I didn't leave him high and dry. He was a bachelor then, so I let him choose for himself – whether he'd live in the old house or build himself a new one when he got married. He got married and decided to stay in the old house, but he also wanted the money I'd promised him for a new one. Said he wanted to buy himself a little land. I gave it to him, but right when I was ready to up and move, he started bellyaching for more. You'll haul off all your hidden gold, he said, you'll buy yourself some nice big chunk of land somewhere, while I'll be here sweating over these measly five acres. You may have risked your life, but I took plenty of risks too, that whole time I lived in fear and shame on your account, I took care of your family. If they'd ratted you out, who would've looked after your wife and child? If I let just one word slip, you'll be sent to keep Karademirev company, so we'll split everything fair and square. Lord knows I didn't have all that much hidden away. I'd given to my backers, to my mates, to doctors. I had enough left to patch things up and buy myself a small place. So I gave some of it to my brother and moved here with your auntie Kita. You don't remember, how could you remember? Koycho was four, you were three. You were always playing together, heck, you even slept in the same bed. One night at our place, the next at yours. I fixed up the house, bought a dozen acres of land, livestock, this and that, and that's how I got started.

Say what you will, those were good times. What've we got now? Justice, order, freedom – horsefeathers. Again, there's freedom for one man, but not for the others. Let slip a single word and it's either the cudgel or the clink. Whatever so-and-so tells you, that's what you'll do. You've got a voice, but you'll say whatever suits him best. You don't have your own eyes, your own mouth, your own mind. You're just like everybody else. Fine, so maybe you're not like them on the surface, but you are. You know your place – in the pond with all the other frogs. Back in the day, I was my own lord, my own master. I slip my own neck in the noose and I'm off. I don't know what's going to happen to me an hour from now, but I keep going straight ahead. Whatever happens, I've made it happen. The important thing is that the world is mine. Maybe only for one day or one night, but it's mine. It might cost you your life, but the important thing is you're going someplace where you don't know what awaits you, what you'll see there, or how you'll get out of that jam. "But it's not legal," they say. Come on now, everything in this world is legal and nothing is legal. It all depends on how you look at it. If it suits you, then it's legal, if it doesn't suit you, then it's illegal. Life's such that every man has his own law. And every man robs every other. The stronger robs the weaker, the richer robs the poorer, the smarter robs the dumber. And the handsomer robs the uglier, even though he may not want to. 'Cause people aren't made alike. If they were to become exactly alike, there'd be no life, there'd be nobody to bake you a loaf of bread to eat.

Back in the day, there was this big landowner, Bliznakov, he held more than two thousand acres. One time we were coming back from an excursion, so to speak. We saw a bunch of people in a field, not working, just standing there. We passed by them and stopped to rest. And what do we see – the whole field bristling with leeks. It was springtime, what's with these leeks here, we ask the workers, and they told us that the boss man had given them a dozen leeks and a hunk of bread apiece. They hadn't eaten the leeks, but stuck them in the field as a protest, as it were. And by-the-by, the boss man himself showed up in his carriage, saw all those leeks stuck in the ground, and ordered his coachman to pull them all up. Tomorrow, he said, you're going to eat them, I'm not going to feed you with milk and honey. He went to get in his carriage, but I caught him by the coattails. *Chorbadzhi*, I said, hungry bellies have no ears. Since you've called these folks here to work for you, you'll feed them just like you feed yourself at home. Just who the hell do you think you are, he says, you good-for-nothing scoundrel, to tell me how to feed my workers! I grabbed him by the collar, pitched him to the ground, and pressed my knife to his throat. I might be a scoundrel, I says, but if you don't feed these people,

I'll fix you so you won't know which way is up. I sent two of our boys in the carriage with the coachman to bring food from the farm. I told them, you take everything you find to eat in the pantry and be back here in half an hour. The carriage took off, and the farmer was shouting: I'm going to sue you for pulling a knife on me. There are laws in this country. Who are you to give orders here? I'm nobody, I tell him, and yes, there's a law, and not just one but thousands. Only now, the law is in my hands. A minute ago it was in your hands, now it's in mine. Whoever holds it in his hands, to him that law's fair and just. So we go on talking like that and his workers, around thirty folks in all, are standing there silent, listening. Leaning on their hoes, they just keep quiet and listen, they submit to the law. The carriage comes back loaded with food: cheese, butter, yogurt, sausage, and all sorts of stuff. The workers sat down, and we sat down right along with them to have a bite to eat. The landowner was sitting with his back to us all, smoking and not saying a word. See, *chorbadzhi*, I tell him, see how my law feeds people, while tonight, when you take the law back in your hands, it'll leave them hungry?

Back in the day, when I didn't want to join the cooperative farm, Stoyan Kralev accused me of being a lawbreaker. He called me a murderer, too – meaning I'd murdered Salty Kalcho's daughter, my own daughter-in-law, as it were. You were at the wedding, you know what happened. I didn't kill her, but things just got all tangled up like I never expected them to. You remember when they built that highway, right? Then you remember the foreman Kuncho, too. The guy who lived in that little house on wheels at the edge of the village. A caravan, they called it. A month before the highway was done, I passed by the caravan. The door was open, but the foreman wasn't inside. Every other time I went past there, he was always sitting at the door. His legs hanging down over the edge, leaning on the door frame and playing his harmonica. He didn't have any work, so what else was he supposed to do? He'd nap a bit, play a bit. I'd given him watermelons and grapes, 'cause the path to the vineyard passed by him, I'd also given him sweet corn to grill. We'd shoot the breeze a bit, then I'd go on my way, and he'd start puffing on his harmonica again. He was from the villages around Shumen, had a wife and two kids. He'd go home to them in the winters, but spent the summers on the roadways.

So, when I didn't see him that time, I kept going down the path through the cornfields. I must've gone a hundred steps when I see him – standing there in the middle of the path, and some woman's next to him. He must've heard me coming from a ways off, 'cause he came striding up to meet me, while the woman ran off ahead and disappeared. We chitchatted a bit, I promised to leave him a watermelon on my way back. I pretended I hadn't seen the woman, but once I went around the bend, I cut straight through the cornfields. I stopped at the edge of the vineyard, waited a bit, and then Radka came by on the path. She went out to the vineyard every day to bring food to her father. What should I care who's meeting who and why, but hell, it's human nature. I was itching to find out whether Radka and the foreman had met up by chance or on purpose. The next day I headed that way again when Radka set out to bring her father his food. I took the long way around, stopped by the path, and hid. I waited a little, Radka passed by, then the foreman right after her. He caught up with her, they talked a bit, then headed straight into the corn. And so every few days I kept catching them in one and the same spot. One time I heard Radka crying, telling him: "You're just leading me on, then afterward I won't ever see you again." From then on, I kept an eye on Radka. We're in the same neighborhood, wherever she went – out to the fields, to the fountain, out in the yard, I always kept watch on her. The foreman left and she took to looking real crestfallen. I was the only one who noticed it, because I was the only one in the village who knew her secret. The foreman must've lied to her that he was a bachelor and that he'd come back to marry her. Maybe he really was a bachelor, who knows? The world is full of those types, shysters. They're always the smoothest talkers with the women, they can bamboozle them easy as pie. And Radka, as young and foolish as she was, I'm sure it didn't take much to reel her in. Her mother's out slogging in the fields by herself, her father doesn't set foot in the house to see his children, to keep them in line, to harangue them. While a woman on her own is like a horse set loose in a field – it'll gallop off wherever it wants. So when I saw her floundering like a fish on dry land, I decided to go and arrange a match with her father.

Salty Kalcho had repulsed me as long as I can remember. He'd never done me any harm, but still he struck me as downright repulsive. I don't know why folks like him make me so sick to my stomach. They don't walk upright on their own two feet, but slither around, leaving a trail of slime behind them. Makes me want to stomp on him good and hard, and if I can't squash him flat under my sole, at least I'll rip his tail off. He's nothing but entrails, food goes in one end, shit comes out the other. And other people are putting that food in his mouth. His father was a hardworking man and left him a nice bit of land, and he made a hash of it, turned it into a shambles. A dozen acres, that's a whole farm. We had three fields side by side. I never once saw him set foot in those fields to spread manure, plow, or sow. His wife would be out there digging around like a mole, sometimes on her own, sometimes with her daughters. I'm plowing or sowing on one side of the boundary, she's there on the other. There were years when even she didn't go to work those fields, they got grown clean over with thistles and thorns. And those weeds jumped right over onto my land, the wind spread the seeds. I had half a mind to plow right over that boundary, to plow them up and clean those fields, but no can do. It's not like going and swiping something and carrying it off. For years on end those fields were like a thorn in my side and I tried to buy them off him many times, but he was having none of it. I ain't got any land for sale, he would say. Just lying there on his veranda, smoking his cigarettes and listening to the birds sing. The man was having himself a real fine spa vacation, while I was out there busting my ass to yank up the weeds that spread from his field to mine like an infectious disease. But I finally found a way to stick it to him. As soon as the foreman had left, the very next day I went to make a match with his daughter. You may not believe it, but if he'd dug in his heels at the wedding, if he'd said: Nope, I ain't giving a square inch of land, I wouldn't have asked him for those five acres. Nor would I have sent his daughter packing. I was sure that after the wedding I would work that empty land as if it were my own. Fine, but when I saw how he swallowed his tongue and went dumb, I said to myself, take it, take as much as you want, even if you were to take the life of a slug like him you wouldn't lose a wink of sleep, 'cause the world's got no use for him.

During '46 or '47, they started talking up the cooperative farm, Stoyan Kralev and his people started going door to door, canvassing. They went to Salty Kalcho's, too, and he promised that as soon as they formed the co-op, he'd join up, too. Stoyan Kralev had found his soft spot, he'd promised to make him watchman over the co-op's vineyard and he was game, just so long as he could strut around in his army uniform and lie around on his veranda like before. I found out about that business and decided to have a little chat with him. We hadn't spoken a word to each other in five years, I thought he was angry with me and wouldn't even give me the time of day. I met him once on the road and stopped him. I'm talking away, he's listening. You voted for the republic in the elections, I told him, but that business is going to come back to haunt you when the Americans and the English roll in here. What, he says, they're coming? Just like the Russians came. Since one side came, why can't the other? Russia limped out of the war just skin and bones, while those folks are still strong. And the opposition's strong too. We got more or less half the votes in the elections, and when they press the people for more deliveries to the state, it'll get even stronger. All the Americans and Englishmen need to do is show up at the border, and the people'll welcome them with open arms. So over the course of our chat, I convinced him to come over to the opposition. You'll just stand aside, I told him, and keep your mouth shut. If they pressure you, you'll just tell them you're waiting to see how things are with the co-op, and if all's well and good, you'll join.

The cooperative farm was set up in the fall with sixty families. I checked the list of members and lo and behold! Salty Kalcho was there too. By the next fall, the co-op had fallen apart. They'd snatched back all their livestock and equipment, squabbled over the land, since the field boundaries had to be redrawn – in short, all hell had broken loose. Well, well, I said to Salty Kalcho, you all scampered away right quick! You went for wool and came home shorn. Don't get me started, he said, I got burned bad, now I've learned my lesson. The next year, they started talking about setting up a new co-op, and there he was again – all ready to sign up. The campaigners would corner him, he'd promise to join. We'd pull him aside, and he'd swear he wanted nothing to do with the co-op. He kept flip-flopping – going over to their side, then coming back to ours, as if he didn't have brains enough to decide on his own which side to join. And back then, they fought tooth and nail for every person. The co-op had fallen apart once and it would fall apart again unless more people joined the second time around. I told Salty Kalcho I'd give him back those five acres he'd given me as dowry if he promised not to join the co-op. They were mine by law, but his by honor and conscience since the bride had passed away so soon after the wedding. Besides, giving it back would mean a decrease in the deliveries I owed the state. I'd worked that land for five years as only I know how, and it had become one hell of a plot – sow one seed and two shoots sprout up. Salty Kalcho kept his promise, so I gave him the land on the condition that I would take it back if he failed to keep his word.

The new co-op did have more members, but no livestock to speak of. Anybody who had two cows butchered one of them. Anybody who had two pigs butchered one of them, and so on and so forth with sheep and poultry, so as not to put their animals in the common pot and get their state quotas upped. Hunger raged in the city, people were ready to tear you apart for a pound of meat, lard, or flour. The village turned into one giant slaughterhouse, every yard stank of rotting flesh. The authorities went sniffing around, but for every person they caught, ten others got away. They ordered that all threshing be done in one spot so that they could seize the grain right from the threshing machine. So folks started threshing on the sly. They'd reap during the day, sneak into the fields in the evening to steal sheaves, and thresh them at night. Some made threshing floors in the woods, down in the meadows or around the pastures, and did their threshing there. I never threshed on the sly myself. I knew Stoyan Kralev was watching me like a hawk, so I didn't dare pluck even a single ear of wheat from the fields. I'd trade meat for flour, cart stuff to town now and then, I somehow managed to get by. Yet they still found something to pin on me. One evening, as they were making the rounds of the village, snooping on the houses, they heard thumping sounds coming from Salty Kalcho's place. They burst in – and there was Gruda, Kalcho's wife, flailing wheat on the floor. She'd swiped three sheaves from the field and dragged them home. Just enough to land her in hot water. They pressed Salty Kalcho, even threatened to lock him up, so he – gutless wonder that he is – told them about our agreement and under what conditions I'd given him the five acres back. In short, I'd put him up to it. They forced him into the cooperative farm the following day, and grabbed hold of the five acres to boot. So he not only broke his word, but also left me holding the bag.

That whole business was a welcome turn for Stoyan Kralev, who made lots of hay from it, and it was then that we really locked horns. Before the Ninth, we'd never seen eye to eye on politics, but even after the Ninth we hadn't gotten into wrangles about anything. When we'd meet somewhere, he'd say: Kinsman, how 'bout me and you join forces in a collective farm? But he'd say it just like that, as a joke, 'cause he knew I was having none of it. But now he came to my place. I was by myself, the wife had gone out somewhere. Give me your revolver, he said. What revolver? The one you shot with at the wedding. I dug around in a little trunk under the bed that was full of all sorts of paraphernalia and gave it to him. I had another revolver, this one here you're looking at right now. That other one was all rusted out, I hadn't used it in years, at the wedding I'd fired the other one. What do you want with this old hunk of junk, I asked, can't you see the barrel's all plugged up, no bullet's gonna get through there. A gun's a gun, he says, it could be cleaned up and put to good use. A man like you can't be trusted, he says. You're with the opposition, who knows? You could take up arms against the government. If I wanted to take up arms against the government, I said, I would've hidden this here gun. I'm not taking up arms against anyone, I'm just protecting myself. That's why I'm in the opposition. If you catch me taking up arms against the government, you have the right to put me on trial. Before the Ninth, you were the opposition, going on and on about Russia to anybody who'd listen. Nobody did a thing to you. That's how you saw things, so that's what you prattled on about. Hard words break no bones. If they'd caught you with a gun in your hand or helping out those subversives, they would've sent you where you belong, and you would've dragged me down right along with you...

Those weren't just empty words. Back in '43, he'd again come to my house one evening. He had found out that I'd be going to the city the next day, so he gave me a sack of homespun cloth to take there for him. You can sit right on top of it, he said, it's just wool, you can't hurt it. He told me the street and the house I needed to deliver it to ten times, I even remember it to this day. Twenty-one Chataldzha Street. As soon as he told me to sit on that sack, I knew what this business was about so I set off. Along the way I opened up the sack – there were clothes inside. Ten sets of homespun woolens, jackets and pants. It was plain as day to me that he was a greenhorn who didn't know the first thing about conspiracies, so when I got close to the city I pulled off the road and hid the bag in a hole in the stone quarry. I pounded a stick into the ground as a sign and continued down the main road. And good thing that I did what I did. On the edge of the city, three policemen stopped me and searched me. I found the street and the house, I stopped and went into the courtyard. A woman came out to meet me. You were wanting to buy some meat, I said, so I brought it. The woman stared at me as if I weren't speaking Bulgarian. I sat down on a bench in front of the house, she sat down, too. I told her I had brought a sack of clothes for them, she ran into the house and brought a man out. I told him where he could find me in two hours and he found me. On my way back to the village, I left him by the quarry, told him where I'd hidden the bag, and continued on my way. I hadn't even unhitched the horses yet when Stoyan Kralev turned up. Kinsman, did you deliver the bag? Nope, I couldn't, I said. The police stopped me on my way into town, opened it up, saw what was inside, and took it. They wanted to arrest me, but I told them who'd given it to me, where I was taking it, and they let me go. They ordered me to tell you that I delivered the bag where it was supposed to go, or I'd be in the soup. I trust you won't give me away for telling you. That godfather of mine turned so yellow I could hardly recognize him. You better thank this old rebel, I told him, if it were up to you, you would've sent two houses up in flames. And I told him what had really happened. He calmed down, got ahold of himself. Kinsman, he said, long life to you, you've taken a heavy load off my shoulders.

I reminded him of that incident, he was none too pleased, started hemming and hawing. True, you did a great service to the party, I can't deny it, but the harm you're doing to the people's government is even greater still. And without saying another word, he took the revolver and left. It didn't cross my mind then to hand it over to him in front of witnesses so they could see it wasn't any weapon to speak of, and that turned out to be a huge mistake. The summer came and went, the campaign to get new members to join the co-op gathered steam. Stoyan Kralev started calling private farmers down to the party office and posed the question to them this way: either – or. Some of them signed the membership declaration, others put it off, while still others went into hiding. Stoyan Kralev lumped all the private farmers into one barrel – opposition supporters, and the opposition had been outlawed. If you were with the opposition, that meant you were an enemy of the people, so it turned out that half the people were enemies of the people. He called me in, too, and gave me the choice of either joining the co-op in a week's time or hitting the road. Since you're breaking with the people, he says, and adding fuel to the enemies' fire, we're going to start playing hardball too. We found a weapon at your place and that's no coincidence. We've got intelligence that says you're one of the leaders of the opposition, so just keep that in mind if you don't come to your senses. I didn't say anything, I just left. After that, I didn't meet up with anyone; as soon as dusk fell, I would go home. I was afraid they would try to set me up. I know my own nature, if somebody takes a swing at me, I'm not just going to stand there with my hands in my pockets. And if I so much as lifted a finger against one of his men, my goose would be cooked. Word got around the village that a hidden weapon had been found at my place, that I'd been organizing the opposition to rise up in armed resistance. Stoyan Kralev started that rumor so he'd have an ace up his sleeve against me and all the other private farmers.

The week passed and again I was called down to the village soviet. Stoyan Kralev was alone in the office, he met me at the door, gave me a chair to sit down on, while he stayed standing. He was pacing back and forth, keeping silent. His cap was pure Stalin, all he was missing were the boots. So, kinsman, what did you decide? I've got nothing to decide. So, that's it, you're refusing to join us? Listen, my man, don't you realize, he said, that we're struggling for the good of all? We want to make the land common land, to work it together, so there won't be rich and poor anymore. Don't you pin your hopes on any Americans or Englishmen. Fascism was defeated, the victors divvied everything up into zones of influences – this is for you, that's for us, end of story. Are you stupid enough to believe that America and England are going to take up arms again? You do realize, right, that if they're going to declare war on the Soviet Union over Bulgaria, then they're going to have to declare war over Yugoslavia and Albania, too, over Czechoslovakia and Poland, over Romania, Hungary, and East Germany, over half of Europe. How do you think that's going to work? Come on now, folks, declare World War Three, sacrifice another however many million men to pander to our opposition here, is that it? Even if they wanted to do it, they couldn't. There's no going back, and since there's not, why lose time, why not lay the foundations of the cooperative farm sooner rather than later? There's no socialism without the kolkhoz. The people want it.

Come on now, I say, the people aren't chomping at the bit for that kolkhoz, if they really wanted it, you wouldn't have to force them into it, they'd do it on their own. And when something's done by force, nothing good'll come of it, that's clear even now. Aren't most folks in the collective farm already? So why are they getting twenty cents a day? Because they're not working like farmers, but like petty clerks. Some brigadier or warden has to come and goad them into doing what they've always done without anyone breathing down their necks. And this whole business won't get anywhere without that constant goading, because people aren't ants or bees. Greed guides the fez best, as the saying goes, that's how it's been, and that's how it'll always be.

He talks, I listen. Then I talk, he listens, and so on for an hour or so. At one point he interrupts me and starts yelling. I've long seen you for what you really are, he says, but I've always reckoned you clung to your private property out of ignorance or stubbornness. But now I see that you're an enemy of socialism down to the marrow of your bones and your proper place is alongside your ideological leader Nikola Petkov.* This very minute, he says, I'm arresting you and turning you over to the people's militia because of the weapon I found at your house. He called the policeman who was waiting outside and the two of them shoved me down in the cellar. You're a killer, he said. You killed Kalcho Statev's daughter and now you're trying to wash your hands of it by giving him back his land. They locked me up and left the policeman standing outside by the little window, while Stoyan Kralev went back up to the office.

I could let the other business slide, but when he called me a killer, that really cut me to the quick. In my younger years I had gotten up to all kinds of mischief, sometimes with good reason, sometimes without, but I never stained my hands with blood. We had condemned two men to death, and only then Romanian colonists in Inner Dobruja who'd killed some of our folks. Both times someone else in the group did the dirty work. And I didn't kill my daughter-in-law. To this day I haven't told a living soul about her secret meetings with the foreman. You're the first person I've ever told. The very next day after the wedding I started spreading the rumor that she'd been meeting Koycho, and I just kept mum at the wedding so as to fleece her ninny of a father out of five acres. I did it to spare her people's wagging tongues. To Koycho and my wife, I told them that these things happen to some girls just like that. That's what I told the girl, too. Like every one-day wonder, it would blow over too. And that's exactly what happened. No man from the village boasted that he'd made love to her, and nobody had seen her with the foreman. Everyone believed what I'd said and even started congratulating me for being sly enough to get my hands on such a hefty dowry. Koycho didn't take the whole business to heart, either, and grew very fond of his young bride. And we were fond of her too, treated her like our own daughter. She hadn't thrust herself on our family, she wasn't to blame for anything. If she'd been any other girl, she wouldn't have batted an eye, she would've gotten on with her life as if nothing had happened. But she was cut from a different cloth. She felt guilty, her conscience kept gnawing at her. She withdrew, she didn't dare look anyone in the eye. If you didn't invite her to the table, she wouldn't eat, if you didn't tell her to go to bed, she wouldn't lie down. She was the first up in the morning, the last to bed in the evening, never stopping to rest even for a minute. And always silent. If you asked her something, she'd answer, but if you didn't talk to her, she'd keep quiet, her eyes could see what you were trying to tell her. We prodded her to go out and about, to go visit her mother, to take her mind off things, she didn't want to. In the evenings I could hear her and Koycho talking in the other room, but what they talked about, I couldn't tell you. Around the winter holidays Koycho and I went to the city, we bought her fancy shoes, a fur coat, a silk shawl. She tried them on once and never so much as glanced at them again. She spent the holidays at home, wouldn't poke her nose outside.

In the first few days of February, Koycho got called up for army duty. They took him early, put him on labor service, and trucked him all over the new territories, building roads. The girl completely sank into her own world, her eyes always red, crying whenever she was alone. The wife and I wondered what to do, how to console her. Once Koycho was gone, we got even more attached to her. The poor child was plainly suffering, and you couldn't do a thing to help her. We tried our damnedest to distract her, to cheer her up, sometimes she'd smile, but her eyes were full of misery, it was enough to break your heart. She's not a person, she's a little angel, my wife said, and that's exactly how it was. I cursed myself a thousand times for getting greedy over her father's land, but what's done is done. I've gone through plenty of hardships, my life has been hanging by a thread more than once, but believe you me, I never had a worse time of it than I did then. To watch a child melting away like a candle before your eyes and you can't do a damn thing to help her! I wanted to take her to a doctor, she was having none of it, crying as if I were trying to skin her alive. I'm fine, she'd say, there's nothing wrong with me. Nothing wrong, my eye; she was thin as a wraith. She got a letter from Koycho. The postman gave it to me, I read it. The army, he wrote, well, what can I say, I'll be out someday, but most of all I miss you. He told her a hundred times over to eat well, dress warmly, and be careful of the cold, because in the summer, fingers crossed, he would be coming home on leave. Look after your health, little darling, he wrote, because if something happens to you, that'll be the end of me, too, I'll have you know. I gave her the letter, she shut herself up in the other room and didn't come out till dark. I thought to myself, *when she sees how much Koycho adores her, she'll get up her courage, she'll pull herself together.* Dinnertime rolled around, come on now, come and eat, I'll be there in a minute, I'll be there in a minute, but still she didn't come. I sent the wife to call her and she was gone a good long while, came back half an hour later. She found her writhing in the bed, asked her what was wrong – nothing, she just felt a little sick. When she pulled off the cover – bathed in sweat from head to toe. The wife wanted to change her shift, she curled up in a ball, wouldn't let her. She made her undress and what did she see? The girl was pregnant. As if in her sixth month, my wife said, that's how big her belly was.

Now that's something I hadn't expected. When I went to make the match, who knows why but it never even crossed my mind that she might've been in a family way from the foreman. Those were wartimes, we were expecting Koycho to get called up any day or even for me to get mobilized, so I was only thinking about how to have the wedding as soon as possible. The old folks have a saying – a child belongs not to those who bore him, but to those who raise him. That's a nice little saying, but I must admit when I heard the girl was six months pregnant the first thing that popped into my head was that it'd better be stillborn. To think of my son raising another man's child, my grandchild a bastard – it made me sick. But the girl denied she was pregnant, said she'd had stomach problems since she was a kid and got bloated up now and again. I hope that's it, I said to myself. Fine, but women have a sense for these things. She's with child, my wife said, and in her sixth month at that, only she won't admit it, she's ashamed, I was ashamed in front of my mother-in-law too. And it's true, when my wife was carrying Koycho, she hid it from my mother up until her eighth month. My mother had been ashamed in front of her in-laws too, and my father was away in the army, so she all but had me right out there in the field. That's a holdover from the olden days, young brides are ashamed and hide their bellies from the old folks. My wife started worrying that only four months had passed since the wedding, while the bride was in her sixth month. I told her that Koycho and Radka had made love before getting married and that's why I'd rushed the whole wedding along, so as not to disgrace the girl. She believed it, and I had no choice but to believe it too. Since the child would be born in our house, it would be ours, and that was that.

And that's how it would've been, but the girl never got up out of bed again. She'd only get up to come to the table, eat two bites, and go back to the other room. The wife didn't let her lift a finger around the house. Once when she was cleaning up around her bed, she found two little bottles under her pillow. Girl, she said, what's in these bottles? Medicine, my mother sent it to me. My wife took a whiff of the bottles, one smelled like geranium, the other like onion. A thought flashed through her mind, she took the bottles. That night she met me worried, crying and carrying on that the girl had taken medicine to get rid of the child – geranium and boiled peels of red onion. Are you sure you're not mistaken, I said, why would she want to get rid of it? How should I know? But I knew, so I told her not to let the girl out of her sight. She stayed in her room a whole week, sleeping by her, feeding her like a child. One evening we went out for a bit – we were godparents to these folks, Iliya Dobrev's family, they'd invited us to a christening, so there was no way we could refuse. Just for a short while, just for a short while, but before we knew it, it was midnight. We came back home, what did we see? – the light was on in the girl's room, and Granny Kerka was there with her. You know her, she was the midwife when you were born too. As soon as she heard us coming, she took to her heels. I grabbed her scrawny arm and led her back to the house. What were you doing here at this time of night and who called you? Well, your daughter-in-law Radka called me. Did she go on her own to your place to call you? On her own. Is she with child? No, her stomach's just hurting, she'll be burning holes in the chamber pot these next few days. I'll burn so many holes in you, I told her, that you won't be able to put your raggedy old bones back together! If you ever set foot in my house again, you won't leave it alive. If I'd known what she'd done to the girl, I really wouldn't have let her leave the house. I chased her out and went to the girl's room. Why, my girl, why did you get out of bed to go out in the dark all the way to the other end of the village? In your condition, should you be going out at all, you might catch cold. I wanted to take you to the doctor, I told her, but you wouldn't hear of it, now here you went on your own to call that old hag. But you'd have better luck getting a word out of this chair here. She was like a wounded animal. Wants help from you, but scared at the same time.

The wife stayed with her to sleep, while I went back to the other room. I fell asleep at dawn and dreamed of Koycho naked. He was supposedly there somewhere at his army base, but it was really here in our yard, right over there, by the fence. The other soldiers all dressed, and he's naked as a jaybird, digging with a pickaxe and laughing. Why don't you get dressed, I tell him, aren't you ashamed to stand around like that, everybody else dressed and you naked? I'm not ashamed, he says, why should I be ashamed? And he starts laughing again. Right then, some big bird flies in from somewhere, its belly is torn open, you can see its guts, blood's dripping from it. Whether it was a raven or an eagle, I couldn't say. It swoops down on Koycho, picks him up under the arms with its talons, and caw-caw – carries him up toward the sky, and he's still laughing and laughing. I got scared that it would drop him from so high up, so I cried out and woke up. Dreaming of nakedness is a bad sign. I got up and went quick to ask how the girl was. When she saw me in the corridor, my wife came out of the room in tears and said our bride was writhing in pain, she'd passed out and was babbling deliriously. Talking now about Koycho, now about some Kuncho? Who's this Kuncho? How should I know, I told her, a sick person talks all kinds of nonsense. But Kuncho was the foreman. Just a bit earlier she had come to and said: "I'm going to have the baby and die. Last night Granny Kerka tore up my belly with a spindle. She didn't want to do it, but I gave her one of the gold coins and she gave in." After the wedding I'd given her four gold coins, and here she went and gave one to that witch. Run and get a doctor, my wife said, find a doctor from somewhere and bring him here. But where could you find a doctor out in the villages back in those days? I could only find a doctor in Dobrich, and who knows whether he'd be willing to come right away?

While we were dithering over what to do, we heard a scream from the room. My wife ran inside, I went to hitch up the horses. I'd just gone into the barn when my wife called from the house, telling me to wait and not go anywhere just yet. The girl was howling as if being skinned alive, I was waiting outside, not daring to peek in there and see what's going on. At one point the wife came out and said she'd lost the baby. I dug a little grave behind the house and we buried the child. In the meantime the girl had fallen asleep. My wife went in every hour to check on her, I looked in on her too. Her face pale as death, her lips bluish and bloodied from where she'd bitten them, crazed with pain. Let's hope she survives, we said to ourselves. We hadn't eaten a bite in two days, there wasn't any bread.

The wife sat down by the trough to knead a loaf and fell asleep, her hands covered in dough, that's how exhausted she was. I let her doze awhile and looked in on the girl. I checked on her three times – still sleeping. I looked in on her a fourth time, and she'd gotten out of bed and was crawling around the floor. Little bride, I said, why are you up, why don't you lie down? Her eyes yea big, looking at me as if she wanted to say something but didn't. Go to bed, I tell her, and see that you get a good rest, once you're rested up you'll get better. I leaned down to pick her up, but she fell on her face and went rigid. I could see she was giving up the ghost, so I went over to the wife, woke her up, and headed straight to the barn. I hopped on my horse and galloped straight for Vladimirovo. There was a medic there, he would come around to the village on horseback every now and then. So I rode over there, praying to God to find him at home, he'd be able to give some help in any case. I couldn't find him. I searched the whole village, house by house, he wasn't there. His horse was there, but he was nowhere to be found.

I came back at dusk and ran into Salty Kalcho at the gate. I looked at him and couldn't believe my eyes – he was carrying the girl in his arms. I thought he'd come over to take her back to their place. They hadn't set foot in our house since the wedding, not him or his wife. Only his youngest daughter, Mitka, stopped by every so often, she'd chat a bit with her sister then go on her way. Salty Kalcho knew Radka wasn't in a good way, but he never even came once to see her. Angry with me, and with his daughter as well. Shoot, even if my child was dragged down to hell, I'd fight the devil himself with my bare hands, I'd risk my own life just to see what kind of jam he was in. So at first I thought he'd been biding his time, waiting till I was far away from the village to take her back to their place. This ticked me off, but since I knew her life was hanging by a thread, I didn't dare yank her out of his arms. Since he wants her, I told myself, let him have her. She might get better faster over at their place, and when Koycho comes home from the army, she'll come back here, she can't play the widow as long as her husband's alive. It's only when I went into the yard that the wife told me he'd carried our bride off dead. I flew into a rage and decided to kill him. And I would've caught up with him on the street and killed him, I would've spattered my hands with blood over one big nothing if my wife hadn't stopped me. What, are two deaths in one day at your home not enough for you, she said, that you want a third one, too?

I didn't go to the funeral and I didn't let my wife go either. We didn't go because I knew I'd kill Salty Kalcho, either at the cemetery or on the way back. Nobody had ever insulted me like that, no one had twisted a knife in my heart like that before. Later on, when I thought it all over with a clear head, I realized that he wasn't having an easy time of it either, and he might not have known what he was doing. After all, he's a gutless softie, all he knows is to lie around and count the stars, so if he went and carried his dead daughter from one house to another, that means he wasn't in his right mind. That very same night I went down to town hall and pounded out a telegram to Koycho. He came four days later, looking like a wreck, crushed by grief and exhaustion. We went to the cemetery, when he saw his bride's grave he hurled himself down on it, we couldn't console him. He stayed with us for six days, I never left him alone for a second, I was afraid he might try to take his own life, he was that miserable. When he left I went with him on the train all the way to Shumen. I kept telling him, the dead are the dead, and the living are the living, time heals all wounds, one day he'd get married again and have a wife and children. But him, he was young, his heart was pure, he thought life began and ended with one woman. He left downcast, until his first leave we didn't eat a square meal or get a good night's sleep, our minds were always on him.

So that's how Salty Kalcho dodged the bullet. The second time I almost killed him was when Stoyan Kralev stuck me down in the cellar of the village soviet. The first night no one came down to check on me, they didn't even give me bread or water. Koycho came looking for me, but they told him they'd taken me to the city. There wasn't even anywhere to lie down. I don't know if you remember Captain Bardarov, the head of the border post. He was a big boozer and kept lots of wine and brandy down in the cellar. He also had the greasiest palms around. He made folks bring him wine and brandy to turn a blind eye to all sorts of border violations. He also gave his soldiers leave in exchange for wine and brandy, so the cellar of the border post was filled with barrels and kegs. In the '40s, when Southern Dobruja was liberated from the Romanians, the border post was abandoned, then after the Ninth they made it the village soviet. I spent the first night sitting on a barrel. In the morning they stuffed a hunk of bread, a jug of water, and a declaration for membership in the co-op through the little window. When I decided to sign it, I should knock on the door and they'd let me out. At dusk it started thundering, lightning was flashing, a strong storm whipped up and rain came pouring down. All summer not a single drop had fallen, now it had rained itself out all at once, as if the sky had bottomed out. Water started leaking in under the window jamb, running down the wall, and from there a puddle went creeping across the floor. I was dog-tired but didn't have anywhere to lie down. In the corner there was a big barrel, a good hundred and fifty gallons or so. I looked, its top head was dried up, so I pulled out the boards and climbed inside. I curled up in a ball and fell asleep like that. At one point I heard voices – he's escaped out the window. No, I called out, I haven't escaped.

Someone came over to the barrel and I see Stoyan Kralev's mug looking down through the opening. He's trying hard not to laugh, he can barely keep a straight face. You've never slept in a barrel before, he says, but let's hope it's knocked some sense into you. Get out of there so we can see what you've thought up! My whole body was numb, I got up, my legs were shaking, I couldn't get out of the barrel. I was standing there like a snail in its shell, Stoyan Kralev right in front of me. Just look what we've come to, he says! We're from one and the same village, we grew up together, we're godfathers and godsons to each other, and we've gotten to the point of arrests and squabbles. And again he starts haranguing me about how he and his comrades are slaving away for our good, they don't want anything for themselves, just for the people. 'Cause if we all work together, it won't be like the olden days, man exploiting man, there won't be rich and poor, we'll all be equal in the eyes of the law and so on. I listen to him, waiting for him to finish his song and dance, getting ready for him to show his true stripes. 'Cause at first he starts all gentle-like, listening to him you'd think there isn't and there couldn't be a nicer guy. But only if you dance to his tune. Otherwise he'll take off his kid gloves. And that's what happened then. So what have you thought up?

So I says: As the story goes, a little ducky thought and thought and by-the-by thought itself to death. What the hell am I supposed to think up, for Christ's sake? Whatever I come up with, you never like it anyway. For as long as I've known you, you've always been going on about "tomorrow." Before the Ninth you were always saying how great it'll be when the workers and villagers take power, how democratic it'll be, how we're all going to live high on the hog. It's been five years since the Ninth, and you're still going on about the future. You wanted a co-op, you made a co-op, so what more do you want? Get to work, end of story! But somehow things can't quite get rolling. "We don't have enough machines" – you'll get them eventually, the state will deliver them to you. "We don't have enough experience" – you'll get experience, too. "Every start is tough" – that's true. "The best lies ahead" – well now, that's something I'm not so sure about. When I look around at what's going on today, tomorrow looks dark to me. I don't see a thing. So why am I blind? Most of the people are with you, so they must have sharp eyes, what do you want with blind folks like me? We'll open your eyes, he says. Since you can't open them yourself, we'll open them so that you'll be seeing stars at high noon. Finally, will you sign the membership declaration or not? No, I say. Fine!

He turned around, went over to the door, opened it up, and who do you think came in? Salty Kalcho. Stoyan Kralev took him by the arm and led him over to me. He was staring at the ground like a bashful maiden, not daring to lift his eyes. I realized they'd dragged him in as a witness. Now tell us, Bay Kalcho, did he make you vote for the monarchy? Yes, he made me. Was he the one who forced you into the opposition? Hang on a minute, I said, just hang on! Don't waste your time questioning this twerp! I'll tell you everything myself. I made him vote for the monarchy and I also made him join the opposition, I even gave him land not to join the co-op. I gave it to him to get off with fewer deliveries to the state. But ask him whether I threatened him? No. I just told him those folks from the West would be coming. And I'll tell it to you, too – they'll come. If they don't come in our time, then they'll come in our children's or our grandchildren's time. This world wasn't created yesterday, it has its way of doing things. What was again will be. I was trying to win him over, because I have the right to try to win him over, just like you have the right to try to win me over. You say I've brainwashed him? Poppycock! So why don't I brainwash you, too? If I had told him to go jump in a well, would he have done it? He goes along with whoever suits him best at the moment. And now he's come to sell me down the river, 'cause that's the best way to save his own hide.

I pushed up on my arms and jumped out of the barrel. The boards from the upper head were lying on the floor, where I'd tossed them the night before. I grabbed one and swung it right at his head. As luck would have it, Stoyan Kralev dashed forward in time and knocked my arm away. With a nice hard swing like that I would've splattered his brains right there and then. Stoyan Kralev pushed me back, but I still managed to land a boot right in that nincompoop's groin, well near gelded him. He doubled over, the wind knocked clean out of him. Stoyan Kralev whipped out his pistol and pressed it to my chest. If you so much as flinch, he says, I'll shoot. I've got other folks, too, who will testify that you've been egging them on to fight the people's government. You killed his daughter, now it looks like you want to kill him, too. Because he told the truth about you. I'm sending you to court. Go ahead and send me to court, I'll pay him for a kick to the crotch. I'm ready to pay for the heads of the likes of him!

Late in the afternoon of the fourth day, a husky man with a worker's cap came in to see me. I didn't know him, I asked where he was from – that was none of my business. He tied my hands, led me out of the cellar, and shoved me into a covered truck. We sat down in the back across from each other and the truck took off. We passed through Vladimirovo and the truck turned right. I thought they were taking me to Dobrich, but once we were a mile or so past the village, the truck turned right again and headed down a dirt road. Ten minutes later we stopped, the guy with the cap got out, lugging me along with him. The truck turned around and took off the way we'd come. Full moon, as bright as day. I look around, we're at the Crag, up on the hill. The water's glittering down below. If you recall, after some heavy rains lots of water spilled over into that dry ravine, filled it up, then later they made it into a reservoir. Me and that guy are standing there face-to-face, neither of us saying a word. He's got one hand in his pocket, smoking a cigarette with the other one. We stand there like that for almost an hour, silent. Some headlights light up the highway, a motor is rumbling, and the truck comes back. They cut the headlights and the guy in the cap starts shoving me toward the truck. There's a barrel in front of it. I take a look – the same barrel I spent three nights in, the boards for the head are lying next to it. There's no one in sight near the truck. Get in, the guy in the cap says, grabbing me under the arms. He's a mountain of a man, lifts me right up and plants me in that barrel. Sit down – so I sit down on the bottom. I hear some coughing coming from the truck, so

I realize there's people inside it, but who they are I can't tell in the dark. I hear footsteps coming toward the barrel. Now everything's up to you, someone says, and I recognize Stoyan Kralev's voice. You've got a lot of sins to your name, he says, but if you've finally come to your senses, the people will forgive you. If not – you'll go where all the stooges of capitalism and filthy reactionism have gone. I'm giving you three more minutes to think it over. Either you're with the people, or you say your prayers.

No, I tell him, you've met your match this time, Comrade Kralev. You can't scare me in the name of the people, because if it were up to the people, they wouldn't lay a finger on me. The people don't know the first thing about power, if they really had power, they wouldn't allow you to torment the people themselves in their own name. If it were really that great in the co-op, you wouldn't have to strong-arm everybody in the village to join, no, you'd set up a cop at the door and only let your own people in with special passes. The power lies only with you and folks like you, neither Bulgarians nor Turks, who've never so much as touched the land with a ten-foot pole. So I'm not the least bit scared of you. You're scared of me. If you weren't, you wouldn't be standing there holding a gun to my head. I've got my hands tied, I'm sitting here in this barrel, but still you're scared.

While I was going on like that, the guy with the cap started putting the head on the barrel and tightening it up. He slipped a hoop on it and rolled the barrel over on one side. I figured out what they were up to. They would let the barrel roll down the hill and if I yelled that I would sign the membership form for the co-op, they'd stop the barrel and take me out. If I didn't scream, they would let it roll right into the swamp. As you know, the hill has a gentle slope, about three hundred yards long and covered with rocks. They shoved the barrel and – bumpity-bump – it started rolling down the hill. I hunkered down with all my might, clutching my head with my hands – come on, now, Bay Zhendo, let's see how brave you really are! While the barrel was rolling across the smooth part of the hill, I could take it. I was spinning around inside like a top, trying to protect my head. But whenever I hit a rock, it would shake me so hard that I thought it would rattle my bones clean apart. If the rock was smaller, the barrel would jump right over it, but if it got stuck on a bigger one, somebody nudged it on downward. And the one nudging it had to be Stoyan Kralev. He was waiting for me to yell, to give in. No, I told myself, you're not going to cry out! What're those teeth for anyway? Grit them as long as they're still in your head! You've passed through the eyes of needles before in this lifetime, you'll slip through again. If you don't hold out, if you give in, you won't live to tell about it, 'cause I'll shoot you down like a dog. So make your choice – either you die now, or a little later. Stoyan Kralev won't have the heart to drown you. He's only trying to scare you, he thinks he's dealing with a yellow-belly.

So that's what I'm thinking, to buck myself up. And that barrel, it's all dried out, right, rattling as if it'll fall to pieces any second. Finally it hits soft soil and splashes into the water. Water rushes in through the cracks right away, getting me wet and little by little covering me up. It reaches my mouth, I swallow a bit and started choking. Come on, now, I tell myself, you're not gonna yell, Zhendo, you're not gonna be the village laughing-stock. Show Stoyan "Man of Steel" Kralev that he's more scared than you are. If he's not scared, he'll shove the barrel in the deep water and drown you. He's not going to drown you, he's just going to torture you. Cowards always torture other people. Spit right in his face, so if he drowns you, at least he'll drown you spit-stained like the scoundrel he is. Chin up! Well and good, but my chin's already as far up as it can go. I suck in water again, choke again. The barrel rolls back and is hoisted onto dry land. Somebody hits it with a hammer, the hoop jangles and the boards of the head fall in. I can hear it – squish, squish – two pairs of footsteps walking away. The water drains out, I wait a bit to catch my breath, then wriggle out, wet as a drowned rat. Up on the hill the truck lights up, bellows, and disappears.

I shake myself off, pull myself together as best I can, and slowly but surely drag myself back home around midnight.

After that business, they left me alone. No one came to browbeat me about the co-op, so I kept doing my thing for another year. The co-op grew, there were only a dozen or so of us left outside it – me, Kiro "Up Yours" Dzhelebov, Ivan Swaphook, and a few others. The co-op kept growing, taking over the best land, and little by little pushing us out to the fringes of the fields. They gave us the worst land, loaded us with taxes and state delivery quotas, but we still eked out more than the co-opers. Things there were one big muddle, while they were paid mere pennies for a day's work. Some folks ditched their houses and land and headed to the cities to work for cold, hard cash. The factories and mills were looking for workers and took all comers. My Koycho started looking toward the city too. I kept stopping him, but when they traded our land for worse fields, he just threw up his hands at the whole business. You're not going to get the upper hand over the co-op, he kept saying, let's sell what we can and head to the city, there's no future for us here. I listened to him and couldn't believe my ears. That very same Koycho who had worked away on the land from morning till night and who'd been ready to fight to defend even a single furrow, now he was talking like he'd landed in this village from the moon. Aren't this house and yard dear to you, I'd say, aren't your mother and father dear to you, you're the reason we've broken our backs working our whole lives. If you leave us, you're no longer our son, even if you're starving, I won't give you a crust of bread. What, me starve? he'd say. I spent three years in the army labor corps, I picked up two trades, there's no way I'll be left hungry now. This here is family business, I told him, not just yours. Whatever the family decides, that's what you'll do. Nobody, he said, has the right to meddle in my life, I'll work wherever I want, and that's where I'll live.

Before he'd never so much as talked back, now here he was saying this straight to my face without batting an eye. For every one thing I'd say, he'd come back at me with two more. *I ought to give him a good smack*, I thought to myself, but I didn't dare – this wasn't the same Koycho who was wet behind the ears. He'd served his army time, he was strong as a bull, he could squeeze water from a stone. If I took a swing at him, he wouldn't take it lying down, he might even slap me around. I'm not going to give you a red cent, I told him. If you want to go off wandering, find your own money and wander to your heart's content. I'll get by without your money, he said, I've got army buddies in the city, they won't leave me high and dry. We wrangled like that for a month or two, until one day he finally ran away from home. He took a little bundle of clothes and told his mother he was going to visit a friend in Dobrich for a day or two. A month passed, we didn't hear anything from him, he was still angry. We learned he was working on a construction site. I hitched up the horses and went to Dobrich. I found the site, found his friend, too, but he wasn't there. He hadn't liked the work and had left for Varna. Lots of our folks were working in Varna, at Koralovag, the ship and train building yard. They told me that Koycho had joined up there as a woodworker. I went there, too, and found him. We chatted a bit and made up, but he wouldn't even hear of returning to the village. A year later he sent word that he'd gotten married. He didn't invite us to the wedding or even bring his wife around so we could get a look at her. They didn't have any time off, they said, so me and the wife had to go visit them. We were just about to set out to see them when they sent a letter saying they were off to some reservoir. From the reservoir they moved to Plovdiv, from Plovdiv to Karlovo. They're living there till this day. He's still in woodworking, head of a workshop or some such thing, she's a teacher. She took a correspondence course and became a teacher.

It's been sixteen years since he left the village, and he's only come back three times. Me and the wife have gone to visit them three or four times, so for all that time we've seen them once every three years or so. Fine, so

Karlovo's far away, but the truth is he doesn't want to come back. If they had told me that a man could lose all love for his birthplace like that, I never would've believed it. He walks around the place as if on eggshells, his eyes don't stop on anything, as if he hadn't been born here, as if he'd never plowed or worked this land. I tell him what's going on here with us, and he listens, but with half an ear, I can tell his mind is elsewhere. His wife and kids came to visit us twice as well. They got the fidgets too, always asking when they would be leaving, but for them it's different, it's not home. We've got two grandkids, a girl and a boy. The boy's name is Solveig. Named after his other grandfather, Slavi, or so they say. And the girl is Kate, named after her grandma Kita. I always gave Bulgarian names even to my farm animals. One of my mares was Stoyanka, the other was Mitsa. And my dog was named Lichko. Even my fields had names – Grandma Rada, Vitanov's Meadow, the Cherry Fields. And now my grandkids are Solveig and Kate. When they wrote to say they were coming to visit, me and the wife practiced their names over and over for a week to learn them and not mix them up. On top of that they've now taken to calling my wife Grandma Kate.

Losing Koycho was like being left one-handed, I didn't know whether to work the fields or look after the animals. Our state delivery quotas kept rising; little by little I gave ground and finally caved in. In '52, I joined the co-op. I signed the membership form and brought it to Dragan Peshev. He was the chairman. Stoyan Kralev happened to be there with him. I dropped off the form and left, Stoyan Kralev came out after me. We walked together a ways, me toward home, him toward his place. Kinsman, he said, this whole business should have been over and done with long ago, all those brawls of ours were for nothing. No, I told him, they weren't for nothing. You fought for what was yours, and I fought for what was mine. I'm not joining the co-op of my own free will, but at least I know I fought for my land, and when I die, I'll die on my feet. But once I join the co-op, I mean to work hard. I'm not one for fiddling around, I'm not used to being deadwood.

From that day on my squabbles with Stoyan Kralev came to an end. His reign ended that year too, they removed him from the post of party secretary and made him chairman of the co-op. The following year he in turn made me a crew leader. Everyone said: Ha, now we'll see these two bulls lock horns. We worked together for ten years without any quarreling. Whatever he ordered, I carried it out to the letter. If I said something or other wouldn't work, he agreed. You know more about agriculture, he'd say, if you see something out of line, don't keep quiet about it. About that old business – not a word. And so on till this very day. Not that I've forgotten, you don't forget that sort of thing, but I don't hate him. Later, when they removed him from his post, he went soft, but back in the day he was a man's man. He walked straight ahead, without glancing around, like a real man, and I can't hate a real man. I might argue with him, I might come to blows, but hate him? Never.

Before joining the co-op, I thought the worst thing in the world would be being left without land of my own, but now I see there's something worse. You can live with shared land. You squint your eyes and tell yourself: "I'm working my own land," and you get used to it over the years, just like the workers get used to the factory. Besides, the co-op got off the ground little by little, we weren't left naked or hungry. We earn enough to make ends meet, we've also tucked a little aside. We've got pigs and chickens here at home, they gave us a half acre of vineyards, so we've got wine and brandy, plus our vegetable garden. It's more than enough for this lifetime, right? I'm already past sixty, but I still pull upward of three hundred, if not four hundred, shifts a year. Your grandma Kate puts in two hundred as well. We keep on keeping on, we're healthy, we haven't stopped. What's worse is something else entirely, and there's no cure for that. Every year there are fewer and fewer of us left. Out of two hundred houses, there's barely fifty chimneys smoking, and beneath them at most a pair of old folks knocking about. Out of eight hundred, only a hundred or so of us are left, and they're dying off one by one. We don't go to weddings or baptisms, we go to the graveyard. We've forgotten what the young men's Christmas caroling sounded like, what the children's New Year's ritual was. There are no kids twittering about like back in the day, there are no youngins to sing and strike up a round dance on the village square, it's like we never raised children, never brought up grandchildren.

But anyway, let's raise another toast, everything else can go to hell. Sometimes my soul feels so trapped that I feel like doing I don't know what. Dropping everything just like that and heading off somewhere, changing my skin. It's not easy getting old, my boy, take it from me…

PART THREE:

NIKOLIN "LITTLE HORN" MIYALKOV
AND IVAN "PAINKILLER" SHIBILEV

WHEN THE SIX MEN set out for the woods, Nikolin Miyalkov took up the rear, yet he was the most impatient for them to leave the village behind as soon as possible. Like the others, he, too, pretended he was going to hunt wolves, but his true goal was to get Ivan Shibilev alone and speak to him man-to-man. He had been wanting and anticipating this encounter with aching impatience, yet had not made up his mind to go over to Ivan Shibilev's place. Many complicated and contradictory feelings had prevented him from asking a single, solitary question – bashfulness and pride and fear and hatred – and so this long-desired meeting had become an ominous inevitability. Ivan Shibilev might just pass him by with scorn, laugh at him, or tell him the truth, and the more vehemently he strove to uncover this fateful truth, the more he was afraid of it.

Ivan Shibilev, in turn, breathed a sigh of relief when the lot he drew took him far from Nikolin Miyalkov, because something had happened between them which made him keen to avoid the other man. For this reason he hadn't left his house for a whole week, but on the eighth day he couldn't stand it any longer, got dressed, and dashed down to the tavern. There the traditional "Eucharist" of new homemade wines was beginning, they made room for him at the big table, where, among the other men, the hunters from the local hunting club had also taken seats. They invited him to taste the wine, and so he stayed there with them. He could have made up some excuse to go home, especially since one of those at the table was Nikolin Miyalkov, the reason he had not stuck his nose out of doors for a whole week, yet he stayed, perhaps precisely because of him. The cheerful atmosphere in the tavern took the edge off his uneasiness, which gave way to some vainglorious pride which refused to allow him to appear guilty or frightened in front of Nikolin Miyalkov. From what he could tell, no one in the village had found out what had happened between them, and this allowed him to deftly hide his feelings from the others. As always in such situations, he cracked the others up with his stories and jokes, yet at the same time he was unwittingly watching Nikolin, who was sitting across from him. He noticed that a whitish-blue ring had formed around his mouth, his cheeks were sunken, while his eyes burned with that dry, sharp glitter that revealed deep inner pain. And he wasn't mistaken, because Nikolin ever more often and more probingly fixed him with his fiery gaze, in which pain, fury, and hatred could so clearly be read that Ivan Shibilev began thinking up ways to slip out of the tavern. At one point it seemed that Nikolin was looking at him with such unbridled hatred and had started to get up, as if to reach across the table to punch him in the face, but at that moment Salty Kalcho pushed away the soda bottle which they had poured the wine into, covered his face with his hands, and burst into tears. Many of those around the table had been at his late daughter's ill-fated wedding and remembered the incident with the punctured soda bottle.

This sinister memory made the men shudder, sensing that something very bad could happen between Salty Kalcho and Zhendo the Bandit, and it was right then, Lord knows why, that the idea of the wolves being spotted in the vicinity of the village popped into Ivan Shibilev's head. He, of course, was joking so as to dispel the gloomy spirit of revenge reigning over the tavern, which could spark and detonate Nikolin Miyalkov's hatred as well. But imagine his surprise when Nikolin of all people, who was the head shepherd and who should know better than everyone whether wolves had been spotted and whether they had stolen sheep, instead of catching him in this lie, was the first of the hunters to get up from the table and announce that he was going to get ready for the hunt. To Ivan Shibilev's even greater astonishment, the other hunters followed him without a moment's hesitation, so he had no choice but to leave with them.

As we already know, Ivan Shibilev dawdled for more than half an hour at home, in the hope that the others had taken everything as a joke, but they wouldn't hear of turning back and even made him lead them toward the woods. According to the lots they had drawn, he, Zhendo, and Stoyan Kralev would head for the southern edge of the woods, since from there it would be easier to get down to the Inferno where the chase would start, while Nikolin took up his post in the blind, and as always, when he thought about Ivan Shibilev, he started from the very beginning, from the day they had met.

It was the fall of 1942. Back then he had been living and working on Mihail Devetakov's estate in the neighboring village of Orlovo. That same year, Devetakov, for reasons unknown, had decided to sell half his land and had sent Nikolin to our village to ask Stoyu Barakov whether he would also like to buy part of his land. When he came to the first gate in the village, Nikolin stopped the buggy and looked into the yard. He wanted to ask where Barakov's house was, so he wouldn't have to wander every which way through the village searching for it. Judging from the single chimney on its roof, the little house he had stopped in front of had one or two rooms, while its face had only two windows and a door without an entryway. The yard was fenced in by a thorny hedge overgrown with elderberry, the wooden gate was rotting and held together by tin rings, while a gourd with a long winding neck had been hung on the door. A donkey was rolling around in the mud, kicking up dust. The grass in the yard had been grazed in circles according to where the picketed donkey could reach – the circles overlapped and created strange geometrical shapes in all possible hues of green.

Nikolin had just decided to continue on his way when the horse shied, snorted, and jumped aside. A flat-bottomed *kalpak* rose out of the elderberry thicket, and from beneath the *kalpak* – an old man's sheepishly grinning face.

"Hold yer horse so it don't bolt!" the old man said, coming out into the open and clutching at the strings of his breeches. "Today is my brother-in-law Dimitar's name day, so we drank a few rounds to his health. But on my way back home I got struck with such a wicked case of the trots that I couldn't even reach the privy. Just so you don't think I'm hatchin' a nest of eggs, squattin' in this here hedge."

The old man was dressed in a new violet quilted jacket and fawn-colored breeches and was shod in new shoes, he looked neat and clean, yet somehow sluggish and at loose ends. While tying up his breeches, he looked the stranger up and down more with anxiety and even fear, rather than curiosity.

"Well, come on in, then, come into the yard, no reason to stand out here on the road!"

He turned to open the gate, but spotted his sash in the bushes, fished it out, and started winding it around his waist.

"I won't be coming in," Nikolin said. "I wanted to ask you where Stoyu Barakov's house is."

"Just a second now and I'll tell ya, just wait a cotton-pickin' second!"

The sash was five or six yards long and such a bright red that it stood out against the green grass like an ember, and that ember seemed to be burning the old man's hands. He had grabbed one end and was trying to stuff it under the ties of his breeches, but kept dropping it, getting it tangled up in his legs or winding it in the wrong direction. Nikolin jumped out of the buggy, grabbed the free end of the sash, and held it taut.

"Come on now!"

The old man started spinning around, while Nikolin slowly came toward him, letting out the sash little by little. The old man couldn't keep his balance and staggered; when he finally managed to wind the sash around his waist, he flopped against Nikolin's shoulder and belched so profoundly that the sour scent of brandy mash surrounded them.

"I'll be damned if that sash ain't as long as from here to Vladimirovo! I got dizzy before I reached the end of it!"

Nikolin climbed into the carriage and started off, and the old man trotted along beside him.

"Hey, weren't you coming to see me, sonny!?"

"I stopped to ask you where Stoyu Barakov's house is," Nikolin said. "That's where I'm headed."

"Well, why didn't you say so, my man? And here I thought you were coming to see me. So Barakov's house, you say? When you reach the fountain, hang a right. As soon as you pass the school, keep left and you'll see it. A big house, two stories. But wait, wait! I can take you there myself, why the heck not?"

Nikolin stopped the horse, the old man climbed in, and no sooner had he sat down than he had managed to find out more or less all there was to know about Nikolin and also to bare his soul in return: "Well, as for me, I'm Grandpa Koyno, but they all call me Grandpa Kitty Cat. So while I was squattin' there in that thicket, what do I see but some fancy carriage coming up the road and stoppin' right in front of my gate. In that carriage there's a fellow dolled up all city-like, so I say to myself, he's gotta be from the tax office, either a taxman or a repo man. Around Saint Dimitar's Day the villages are crawling with 'em, 'cause by then all the crops and the livestock have been brought in. Can folks of our station get away without payin' taxes, I ask you? No, sirree. Two years ago one of 'em grabbed hold of me again on Saint Dimitar's Day, just as I was lying there in the shade of the shed. I'll take the last bite out of your mouth, he says, I'll rip the shirt off your back, he says, but this time, by Jove, I'm not going away empty-handed. He'd come with a policeman, so thrashing him or running away was no use. He went into the barn, grabbed a dozen bushels of wheat, swiped two lambs from the pen, at long last picked out exactly what he needed, and took to his heels. And nowadays they're sayin' that Russia's going to war, they're sayin' that our dear old Bulgaria's gonna get dragged into it, they're talking about mass mobilization, about requisitionin' food and livestock. This fellow, I said to myself, ain't here to spread good cheer, since he's watchin' me, waitin' for me to finish my business. I can squat here till the cows come home, I says to myself, and I still won't be rid of him, so I may as well hitch up my drawers and charge on ahead, so help me God. And here you're one of Devetakov's people."

Grandpa Kitty Cat didn't look like a cat, he had a longish face with sunken cheeks, squinting eyes hidden like mice beneath his brows, a gray moustache trimmed to his upper lip, so Nikolin thought they must have stuck him with this nickname completely randomly, provided, of course, there was nothing feline in his nature. But Nikolin didn't notice anything of the sort, because he spent only an hour or an hour and a half with him. Barakov wasn't at home, so they turned back and along the way Grandpa Kitty Cat started inveigling Nikolin to come visit him. After the misunderstanding between them had been cleared up, the old man, freed of any inhibitions whatsoever, once again gave himself over to the exalted mood he had left his brother-in-law's house in. When they reached his house, he fell into such maudlin gushing that you'd think he'd fallen in love with the unfamiliar young man, and outright begged him: "Come on now, my boy, humor an old man! You seem like a nice fellow to me, come sit for a bit and let's shoot the breeze! Your estate's just a hop, skip, and a jump away, you'll fly in that buggy of yours and be home inside of an hour. We're not mighty landowners, but since we don't have nothing else, we pay back a good turn with fine conversation. It just ain't right for you to pass up my gate like that!"

Along the way, Nikolin had firmly refused to stop by the house, because he could see that the old man was three sheets to the wind and was inviting him in without his family's knowledge, and under such circumstances, he didn't dare set foot in a strange home. But Grandpa Kitty Cat was wheedling at him so insistently, so kindly, and with such childlike naïveté, that Nikolin decided to stop by his place for a short while, just long enough to humor the old man. Besides, he was thinking that when he left there, he would go looking for Barakov again and perhaps this time would find him at home. He tied the horse to a tree without unhitching it, and Grandpa Kitty Cat led him into the yard, where there was a little flower garden in front of the house, and graciously installed him on a three-legged stool. Then he pulled down a low table that had been hanging on the garden fence, set it in front of Nikolin, and darted into the house.

The garden was awash in autumn flowers – kaleidoscopic Michaelmas daisies and dahlias, scarlet geraniums and yellow marigolds, asters and carnations. The air was steeped in fragrance, heavy and still, like years-long solitude, gentle and sad, sweetly unbearable and achingly enticing. Nikolin took it in not only through his nostrils, but also through his skin, he felt it on his face and hands like the touch of someone's palm, and thought to himself that this scent resembled the life of this old man who, it seemed, lived all alone in the little house with its flowers and hedge, with the donkey and a few sheep, and that was why he was so eager for company. He looked around, trying to discover traces of other people, but saw neither clothes nor shoes nor any other thing. Ten minutes or so had gone by and Nikolin was feeling anxious about sitting alone in a stranger's yard, yet leaving without saying goodbye to the old man would be even more awkward. As much time again passed and Grandpa Kitty Cat finally came out of the house. In one hand he was holding a green bottle, and in the other, two glasses as big as thimbles, slipped over his finger tips as if they truly were such.

"Tarnation, if this bottle had been a snake, it would've bitten me – right under my nose and still couldn't find it! I looked high and low for it, rummaged around in the pantry, turned everything topsy-turvy, and there it was, right in the cupboard," he said as he pulled the paper stopper out of the bottle and filled the glasses. "Well, cheers and welcome to my humble abode!"

The brandy was greenish-yellow and murky, smelling of sour mash gone bad and leaving a burning, unpleasant aftertaste. Nikolin took a sip and its acrid whiff went down the wrong pipe, he started coughing and tears sprang up in his eyes.

"Darn if I didn't forget the appetizers!" Grandpa Kitty Cat fretted. "Let me see if I can rustle up some tomato or other."

He drained his glass in a single gulp and went to get up, but right at that moment a young woman passed by the rosebush, coming toward them. Nikolin had spotted her as she was crossing the yard, but somehow couldn't believe his eyes, so unreal did the girl's appearance seem to him. It crossed his mind that she, too, was a stranger like he was and like him had stopped to ask for directions at the first house she had come across, but at the same time he noticed that the girl hadn't called out from the garden gate, as a stranger would. She walked like city women, as if on tiptoe, while her arms were folded beneath her chest. Grandpa Kitty Cat only saw her when she welcomed the guest and gave him her hand. Nikolin got up off the stool, took off his hat, and stayed standing.

"Hey, now there's my girl! There's my little girl, my little sweetheart!" Grandpa Kitty Cat exclaimed, and laughed out loud. "We live here together just the two of us, spoilin' each other rotten. We're just a couple of orphans, we are, me with no wifey, she with no mommy. Just like…"

"Dad!" His daughter cut him off, as if scolding a small child. "You've had too much to drink and now you're talking nonsense."

"For shame, Mony, what do you mean, I've had too much to drink? Your uncle Mitya and I raised a few glasses, so his name may live on, and that was that. Mony, this boy here's from Devetakov's estate. He's a fine lad, a good lad, I've taken a shine to him, but he doesn't drink, nary a drop! Here's to you, Nikolin, my boy!"

He tossed back another shot of brandy and it finished him off completely, he was thick tongued, reeling back and forth on his stool. He ran the risk of falling right off it when Mona grabbed his arm.

"Dad, get up and go to bed!"

Without a word or sign of objection, Grandpa Kitty Cat got up and his daughter led him into the house. Nikolin was left alone again and was again anxious, especially since finding out the girl was the lady of the house. She had left him without a word, so that meant he should go. He had untied the horse's reins and had one foot on the mounting step of the buggy when he heard her voice behind him. In just a few minutes she had managed to change into a different blouse with light-purple flowers, a tight, dark skirt, high-heeled shoes, and now here she was stepping lightly and gracefully toward the carriage. The twilight had imperceptibly plunged everything around them into dark shadows, only her hair, reflecting the final gleams of the sunset, shone like a spray of coppery-golden wheat.

"Are you going, Mr. Miyalkov? Why so suddenly? Daddy said you'd only just arrived," she said as she came toward him. Her voice was muted and soft, her bluish-green eyes looked even lighter in the dusk. "Don't pay him any mind, he got drunk and had no idea what he was doing and saying. He only drinks once or twice a year, it hits him hard and he can hardly stay on his feet."

"He's an old man, who can blame him?" Nikolin said, still grasping the seat of the carriage with one hand. "He had a few drinks and was in high spirits. He showed me Barakov's place, we chatted a bit, and he invited me to sit awhile."

"Haven't you come to our village before?"

"I've never had reason to pass through this way. We're only half an hour away, but I've never been here."

"And I haven't seen you before," Mona said. "I've been to Orlovo plenty of times, but I haven't seen you. But why are you rushing, why don't you stay for a bit?" She was standing a foot away from him and Nikolin could catch the scent of her perfume. *She must be a teacher*, he thought, *since she's dressed like those city ladies who come to visit the estate, her manners are like theirs, and she smells nice, like they do.* "I'll take you to a wedding."

"To a wedding? What wedding?"

"A girlfriend of mine from the neighborhood is getting married, just right down there, a few houses away. You can meet the local young people, have yourself some fun." Mona was looking at him calmly and probingly, her head slightly tilted toward her shoulder, but he kept silent. "Why are you so hesitant, you'd think I was asking you to walk on hot coals! Come on, at least walk me there, since it's already dark and I can't go on my own. If you don't like it, you can turn around and head back to your estate."

Going to a wedding, in a strange village no less, and with a girl on top of everything – that really was the equivalent of walking on hot coals for him. For eight years, he'd been living on the estate, which was only a mile away from Orlovo, but never once had he gone to mingle with the other young people at working bees, parties, or celebrations. Talking to unfamiliar people stirred up some anxiety and tension within him that he couldn't overcome. Incidentally, we'll get to that side of his character a bit later, let us just add now that he had only rarely had occasion to talk to women, and only then with those who had come to visit the estate. In their presence, he felt bashful and awed, as servants feel in front of ladies of the highest standing. As far as he was concerned, Mona, too, belonged to this category of ladies, whom he was used to obeying and serving, thus he had no choice but to escort her to the wedding.

This wedding turned out to be one of the most important and most harrowing events of his life. Two lanterns had been hung in the yard, and beneath them stood barrels of wine. Men were crowded around the barrels, pouring wine from the spigots and drinking, the young people were dancing to the sounds of an accordion. Mona led him through the crowd to a veranda, where a large table had been laid out, there they were met by the bride, who settled them into the room with the "hostage." Ivan Shibilev, that was the name of the hostage at the wedding, politely introduced himself to Nikolin and made room for him between Mona and himself. He found himself for the first time in the company of so many and such unfamiliar people, and when amidst the general hubbub he traded a few words with Mona and Ivan Shibilev, he was surprised that he didn't feel the same anxiousness that had almost stopped him from coming to the wedding. All that lavish eating and drinking, the music, the songs, the dances, and the jokes were for him a discovery which he had never even suspected existed. And no one paid him any particular attention, just those who were closest to him at the table raised their glasses to toast with him from time to time, all of them were gripped by some unbridled, spontaneous merriment, they were talking loudly without listening to one another, shouting, singing, trying to outdance each other, and now look, the charming young man who had made room for Nikolin next to him suddenly stood on the threshold between the two tables, dressed in colorful clothes, with a red rag around his neck in lieu of a tie, with a child's hat on his head and a violin in his hands.

The table fell silent and they all got ready to watch and listen to Ivan Shibilev's "artistry," while the young people crowded around the veranda. In front of everyone's eyes, Ivan Shibilev made a funnel out of a newspaper, pulled an egg out of it, put it into his pocket, then pulled out another and yet another. The audience was struck dumb with wonder, only one young man stepped forward and said that he'd seen tricks like that with eggs when he was in the army, only they weren't real eggs, but wooden ones. Ivan Shibilev fell silent as if caught in an act of chicanery, then suggested somehow uncertainly to the young man that they bet a box of candy if he would test the eggs with his teeth to see if they were real or not. The young man was sure he would win the bet and bit the egg clear in half, and yolk dripped from his mouth.

The crowd burst into thunderous laughter, Nikolin laughed right along with them as he watched the young man spitting out shards of eggshell as stringy yolk trickled off his chin. For a whole hour laughter welled up in his chest, his heart was cheerful, free, and light, as if he had found himself in a world of carefree joy. After the trick with the egg, Ivan Shibilev played the melody of a sad love song. His violin was peeling and cracked in places, like the violins played by the old Gypsy fiddlers he had bought it from, and it's no surprise that he played like them too, with lots of variations and flourishes, husky, yet sweet, and to Nikolin the violin seemed to be singing the words of the song: "Oh, mother, may he be damned, thrice damned, he who loves a girl but doesn't take her to wife!"

"Play another one, play another one!" the crowd shouted.

Ivan Shibilev put the violin back under his chin and started imitating various animals and birds. This was his latest musical number. The audience thought he was scraping away at the strings as a joke, but when the braying of a donkey burst out amidst those scraping sounds, they again erupted in laughter. This was followed by the barking of a dog, a decrepit lop-eared dog lying somewhere in the shade resting his old bones, and as soon as it sensed a stranger in the yard, it just barely raised its head from its paws and let out a few yaps, just enough so as not to shame itself before its master. After the dog, a cat meowed, then a rooster crowed, lively and vociferously, with those quiet throaty sounds at the end that wrench themselves out of its lungs when it takes a breath. After the rooster, a hen cackled "cluck-cluck-cluck" and Nikolin could see in his mind's eye the hen strutting dazedly around the yard on a hot summer day and pecking here and there, not because she's hungry, but out of boredom, jabbering her chickenish nonsense to herself. Finally it was the songbirds' turn. Ivan Shibilev put his hands on the upper end of the violin's neck and out from under his bow flew the sonorous trills of the nightingale on May nights when it is giddy with amorous passion and improvises with reckless inspiration. Amidst these coloraturas from time to time either the fragile monotonous refrains of the finch would call, as if someone were tapping with a fork on a plate, or the soft recitative of the oriole was heard, curled at its end like a comma, or the alto aria of the blackbird hidden somewhere among the cold and thick branches of the tall trees rang out, its song bursting forth from deep in its lungs. Ivan Shibilev wrested an avian choir from the strings of his violin and directed it at the same time, turning the chilly autumn evening into a cloudless spring morning, when the world of birds is overpowered by the gentle urge to create.

Then a shot rang out, the women screamed and covered their mouths with their hands, the room filled with smoke and fumes, a sinister silence fell, and all eyes turned to the father of the bride. He lifted up a soda bottle tied with a red ribbon, then a white cloth was shoved under his nose, his wife shouted something and started beating her head with her fists. The wedding guests froze to the spot, some smiling spitefully, others stunned and flustered, the white cloth was being passed from hand to hand, they started wrangling over some land, they were crammed cheek by jowl in the room, it grew as stuffy and tight as in a hole. After some time, Nikolin learned what had happened at the wedding, since the rumor soon reached the estate, but at the time he had sat there bewildered and crestfallen, unable to fathom how after so much singing, dancing, and laughing such confusion could suddenly take hold and cast a pall over the wedding's good cheer, just like a hailstorm suddenly whipping up out of a clear blue sky, pummeling the crops with icy pebbles and flattening them to the ground in one short minute. The stuffy air suffocated him, his head began to spin, he wanted to ask Ivan Shibilev what was going on, but the hostage was gone, and Mona had disappeared too. He tried to get up and go outside, but behind him was a wall of people standing so tightly packed together as if they had fused. He finally made his way out around midnight with all the others, drove his carriage out of Grandpa Kitty Cat's yard, and headed for the estate.

The image of his daughter would constantly slip into his memory of that wedding and his first meeting with Ivan Shibilev, as sometimes happens in a phone conversation. You're talking to someone on the phone and from time to time you start hearing an unfamiliar voice, then it disappears, only to entwine itself in the conversation again – at first soft and unclear, then growing stronger and clearer until it takes over the line and you can no longer hear the person on the other end. In the same way, the memory of his daughter now also displaced in his mind that distant memory, because the memory of her was stronger. A week or so ago he had run into her on the street in the upper end of the village on his way home from the sheep pen. She was dressed in a gray topcoat with a leather collar with some sort of fluffy hat on her head, with bright-yellow, almost white, boots on her feet. He recognized her by the boots, otherwise they might have passed by each other. It was growing dark already, and she was slinking along the fence in the dark quickly and stealthily, which made her boots shine like two flames.

"Mela, my girl, is that you?" Nikolin called when she had already passed him.

"It's me," she said, and stopped reluctantly.

Instead of the girl stepping toward her father, he went over to her to greet her.

"Well, you're a sight for sore eyes! So you finally came home! So I see this girl coming along toward me and I says to myself, that sure does look like Mela. But why didn't you write me to come meet you? How'd you get here?"

"I took a bus to Vladimirovo, then a truck from there."

"Have you forgotten where we live, honey? Our house is down on the lower end. Let's go get you warmed up, you must be freezing."

He reached out to take her valise from her hand, but she hid it behind her back, was silent for a moment, then said: "I've got to go somewhere else first."

"Come on, now, where are you going to go in this darkness? Come on home first, get warmed up, then go out. Let's go, my girl!"

The two of them set off together, Nikolin could not hide his surprise and delight and started telling her that lately he had dreamed of her often, and what do you know, his dreams had come true. He asked her whether she would stay for the holidays, where she worked and what she did, but she answered evasively, hurrying on ahead. When they came to the cross street, she took her valise in both hands and turned her head aside.

"I'm going up this way."

"But why, honey?! Aren't you going to come home first..."

"Oof, you and your questions, questions, questions!" She interrupted him as if wanting to get away from some pest blocking her path. "I told you, I've got something to take care of."

She took a few steps and stopped with her back toward him, then slowly started coming back. Her face, veiled by the dark cobwebs of the twilight, looked perfectly white, and her eyes were two dark caverns.

"Since you want to know where I'm going, I'll tell you. I'm going to Ivan Shibilev's."

Her words slapped him in the face like fire, he closed his eyes, and when he finally got ahold of himself and wanted to ask her if she would be at Ivan Shibilev's for long, she was no longer standing in front of him. She had disappeared so quickly and quietly, as if she had turned invisible or flown off like a bird.

At home he grabbed a chicken and slaughtered it on the chopping block. While waiting for its death throes to end, Nikolin watched as a pig ran across the yard with a mouthful of hay and hid inside the pigpen. *A nasty cold front is coming,* Nikolin thought to himself, and only now heard a distant blustering from the north. A flock of crows flew like black clouds over the yards, swooping low over the houses then suddenly soaring high into the sky, filling the expanse with their anxious screeching. He set water to boil and went into Mela's room to light the stove. He had built it onto the house before Mela was born and the three of them, Mela, her mother, and he, had slept there. The two older rooms had been woven from sticks and dug into the ground, while the new room – made of bricks, spacious, light, and raised up a step – looked like a patch of new cloth on an old shirt. As a schoolgirl, Mela had taken over the room, she slept there, did her homework there, and wouldn't even let him set foot there, and when she left she locked up the room with a padlock. Later, too, when she lived in the city and didn't come home for a whole year at a time, he went into the room only rarely to see whether the roof was leaking or to clean the cobwebs from the ceiling. Every time he went in on tiptoe, because it seemed like Mela would jump out of some corner and scold him: "This is my world, and my world alone!" she would tell him. "And no one is allowed to sully it with their presence!" The four walls of the room were covered from floor to ceiling in colorful theater posters, photographs of actors both large and small, in color and black and white, in various poses, smiling and teary-eyed, furious and licentiously cheerful, wearing village clothing, royal robes, or even half naked, all of them somehow unreal, mysterious, and inspiring an inexplicable uneasiness. And Mela's clothes, belongings, and jewelry had always been scattered about the floor, on the table, over the chairs, and in the wardrobe, the bed would be left unmade for weeks, while her comforter looked like a den – however she had crawled out of it in the morning was how she would slip under it in the evening. But Mela felt at home in that flea market of a room, she would stay in there for whole days, and Nikolin could hear her pacing from one wall to the other muttering something, shouting, laughing, crying, getting angry, or ordering someone, "O my dear husband, regain my honor with your sword!" or, "My soul yearns for you as the morning yearns for a ray of light!" Nikolin had remembered these words and many more, without understanding what they meant, and he grew ever more used to the thought that his daughter did indeed live in some world of her own, which he did not and could never understand. Deep inside, he did not approve of this world and her way of life, yet at the same time he told himself that he was a simple, uneducated man and had no right to meddle in her business. What bothered him most was how during vacations she would not lift a finger to help around the house or in the fields, as the other girls did. She spent the days in her room and the evenings at the youth club, coming back at midnight or sometimes even at dawn. She could go for days without eating, and never touched the pots and pans to make lunch or dinner, instead waiting for him to come home from work to make her something to eat. Ever since she was a child she had been headstrong, careless, and neglectful of everything around her in the house. No matter how hard they had tried to teach her to put everything back in its proper place, her toys, notebooks, and textbooks were constantly rolling around on the floor. Her only true concern was dressing herself up like a big girl, she wouldn't wear just any old dresses or blouses, but had to touch them up herself. But otherwise she was a smart, curious, loving, and charming child, and with this she made up for all her carelessness and neglectfulness around the house. She was first in her class at school, she played the lead part in all the school plays, her teachers said she had a bright future, and Nikolin was very proud of her.

Now it was cold in her room, it smelled musty, like mothballs and faded paper, Mela's world of theater posters and actors' photos on the walls had been ravaged by flies, it was yellowed and dead. No other traces of her besides that dead world remained in the room, there was not even a button left of her, Nikolin only now noticed this. He opened the window for a bit to let in fresh air and as soon as he got the stove lighted he went into the other room. He dipped the chicken in the boiling water and started plucking it. There wasn't time for stew or some other dish, but he would at least boil the chicken and make soup from the giblets. Mela must be freezing from her travels, a bit of soup would do her good. He put the giblets in one pot to boil and put the chicken in the other, and the whole time he was thinking how nice it was that she'd come home for the new year's holidays. Tomorrow or the next day I'll put the pig under the knife, we'll make some sausages and black pudding and then Mela will go on her way. Who knows how long it's been since she's had that kind of thing, in any case I wonder how often she eats and what she eats? Last year I gave her money when she left. Is that enough? It's enough. When you need more, just write, I'll send some. Okay, I'll write. But she didn't write. But now look, she came home!

He thought he heard the front gate creak and dashed outside. He had left the light on in the yard, he could see the gate, but it was closed. The branches of the acacia tree were creaking in the gusts of wind. In the darkness of the gardens it was as if there was a huge blacksmith's bellows, someone was pumping the handle of the bellows ever harder and more often, the stream of air bent the branches of the acacia, rubbing them together, it swept up the dry leaves and whirled them in a funnel, a tin lid fell from the mouth of the funnel with a clatter, and the rooster's crowing rang out like an echo. There's a nasty cold front coming, he thought to himself, and went back inside. The two pots were bubbling, the room was warm, the alarm clock showed nine o' clock. He took the boiled chicken out of the pot and left it to cool, he took the soup off the burner as well and went about setting the table. He put on a new tablecloth, plates, forks, spoons, he also brought out a little flask of new wine, murmuring to himself the whole time: "I'll put this here, and that there. No, wait, that's not right, now there it is. Now I'll wipe down the glasses real nice with a towel. That one's for Mela, this one's for me. Mela's glass should be closer to the stove. She'll come back freezing cold, she'll sit by the stove to warm up. I'll pull the table a little closer to the stove. Just like that, there we go. I'll pour the wine later, it should only be poured once we start eating…"

He did all of this deliberately slowly, several times over, and was talking to himself so as to scatter his painful thoughts and not to allow them inside himself. He could sense them hovering about him, stalking him from all sides, jostling to burst into his head. And then it was eleven o'clock, midnight passed, and Mela still hadn't come home. There was nothing more he could do, he sat down on the bed to wait and even as he was sitting down the thoughts that had been crouching around him the whole evening like a pack of predators with bristling fur and bared teeth bloodthirstily pounced on him and started tearing away at him. He had no more strength to drive them away, he lay down on his back and with a sweet sort of agony let them rip the living flesh from his body. Mela won't come back tonight, they shouted in unison, she'll stay with Ivan Shibilev, because he…

From his left side a short rifle shot blew in on the blizzard – bang – like those short dry sounds made by a flyswatter. About one hundred feet away from him, Salty Kalcho was standing in the blind; what on earth could he be shooting at in this blizzard? In any other case, he would have been on his guard, waiting for some game to come his way as well, but now the shot only reawakened his memories of another short, dry shot he had heard in 1945 in the backyard of the estate. There had been a little corn left in the fields, they had harvested it and were hauling it back in the cart, they ate lunch in the kitchen, and Devetakov went upstairs to rest while Nikolin went to shuck the corn. He sat in the cart and to save time, he tossed the shucked cobs right into the mouth of the crib. After about an hour he got thirsty, and before going into the kitchen, he saw Devetakov standing on the veranda, washed, combed, and changed, as always after coming back from the fields. Since early spring he had put a little varnished table and chair on the veranda and in his free time he would sit there. There was always an open book on the table, but Nikolin had noticed that Devetakov was never looking at it, instead he stared straight ahead at the fields, as if trying to discover something there, or perhaps he had discovered it and just couldn't get enough of the sight. Nikolin had stopped many times behind him, trying to figure out what he was looking at in the fields, but he didn't see anything in particular, in early spring, the fields were like carelessly spread aprons, both small and large in the cheerful reseda hue of sprouting wheat, dark brown with stripes of sunflowers or corn, in the summer bright yellow, dark green, and golden, and now black like a tarry sea, deserted, calm, and sad; a person or cart was rarely spotted on the highway that stretched like a white bridge over that sea, and where the highway ended, village houses, white and small as cubes of sugar, could be seen. But Devetakov, with his elbows propped on the table and his head resting in his palms, was always looking out over it, his eyes squinting against the light. Nikolin drank some water, set out toward the backyard again, and on his way heard a pop like the distant shot of a rifle – bang. He climbed into the cart and before sitting down, he looked out over the field. There were two hunters in the village and at that time they were often wandering about the estate. Later, as he shucked the corn, he realized that the shot had come from the direction of the house, so he climbed out of the cart and went to look in the front yard – sometimes the hunters stopped by to ask for water. There was no one there, Devetakov wasn't on the veranda either. Nikolin worked up a sweat pulling the empty cart under the awning by hand, so he went to go upstairs to change into a dry shirt.

The varnished table had toppled over with its legs in the air at the far end of the veranda, and Devetakov was sprawled next to it. He was lying on his right side with his head thrown back. With one hand he was grasping the leg of the table, with the other the collar of his shirt, as if trying to rip it open. Later, when he re-created that tragic event in his memory over and over again, with ever new details, Nikolin recalled that the first thing he saw on the veranda was the book, fallen open with the cover up, after that his gaze fell on the fresh scratches on the floor, and following these scratches as if following tracks, he caught sight of the toppled table, and next to it two sock-shod feet, and only then did he see Devetakov himself with his head thrown back and crammed in the corner. Nikolin froze, not from fear, rather from surprise to see him in such a state. He kept staring at him and wondering why he was sprawled out on the floor: Had he tripped or fainted or what? The fingers of his left hand, which had been clutching his collar, relaxed and his hand slid to the floor. Nikolin grabbed him under the arms to lift him up and carry him to his room, but Devetakov's right hand was clutching the table, dragging it along the floor. "Come on, let go of it!" Nikolin told him, and then he saw the revolver gleaming on the floor, bluish-black and so small that you could hide it in your palm. Only now did he recall the short, dry shot he had heard coming from the house an hour earlier and cried: "Uncle Mihail, what have you done?!" Then he dashed out into the yard. He ran back and forth, shouting in a hoarse voice: "Heeeey, heeey, people, is there anybody here?" But there was no one in the house or yard besides him. And as he was running back and forth and shouting, across the garden he happened to catch sight of Malayi, the threshing machine operator, who was carrying his wife. Nikolin ran over to them and said that Devetakov was lying on the veranda looking more dead than alive, "and plus next to him there's a little volver." Malayi set his wife on a bench and headed toward the house, saying: "I just see Devetakov on ze balcony... I just see him." He felt for his pulse, unbuttoned his shirt, and asked: "Vere ve put?"

Still pale and shaking, Nikolin opened the bedroom door and the two of them laid Devetakov on his bed.

"He dead," Malayi said, taking off his cap and standing for a moment next to the dead man with a gloomy, inscrutable expression. "You go veel-lage, tell priest."

He went back to his wife, while Nikolin went out to the highway and headed toward the village. He didn't think to hitch up the carriage or to ride a horse, but set out on foot. The sun was already setting when he entered the yard of the late cook, Auntie Raina. Only her husband, Grandpa Stavri, was home, they talked a bit, then went to tell the priest. He got back to the estate when it was dark, but didn't dare go into the house where the dead man lay, instead he stayed standing in the yard. Shadows were crawling in from all sides like incorporeal creatures, circling around him and giving off muted, sinister sounds. *It's nothing, I must be seeing things*, he told himself to keep up his courage, but he spun around with the shadows so that nothing could jump at him from behind. But now something was pulling at his clothes from behind, it crawled up and stopped on his shoulders. It had no weight, no soul, but he could sense it on the back of his neck, yet he didn't dare lift his hand to brush it off. He hunched his shoulder up to his ears, hugged himself, and stood there unmoving, but the thing grabbed his throat and started strangling him. He strained to yell for help, but instead of a scream, a muted groan tore from his lungs. *The shadows are strangling me*, he thought, and tried to free his throat. He couldn't feel anything, yet his fingers met resistance and he couldn't tear off whatever was squeezing his throat like pliers. And then he spotted some dim light coming through the dark branches of the trees in the garden. He ran toward the light and saw that it was coming from Malayi's window. He stopped in front of the window and as soon as he stopped, whatever had been strangling him let go of his throat and a weight lifted from his back. He thought about going inside where Malayi and his wife were, but he had never stepped over the threshold of their house and didn't dare do it now.

Malayi was Hungarian and no one knew what long and winding roads had led him to this godforsaken region. He was a husky man in his midfifties, with a hooked, beak-like nose and round, platinum eyes. Eyes seemingly devoid of pupils and closed to the warmth of the soul could only belong to someone completely indifferent, or to a despairing loner. If these eyes were windows onto his soul and if one could peek into their pupils, one would surely see an enormous emptiness. But they never stopped on anyone else's eyes for more than a second and were always looking somewhere aside, as if concentrated on their own emptiness. His eyes, in combination with his beak-like nose and grease-stained work clothes, which resembled bristling plumage, gave him the look of a bird of prey, but an aging one, already resigned and indifferent to everything. His voice, too, was full and hard, but without those modulations that give the sonic impression of feelings. He uttered few words, and even then with an accent that jumped from the first to the last syllable as if going up and down stairs, with hard, closed vowels, but always using the politest of forms: "Boy, COME here if YOU pleases!"

That is what he had said to Nikolin eleven years ago when the latter had just come to the estate and was passing by the garage housing the threshing machine.

"Please be SO kind, geev me HAND here!"

Nikolin understood his gestures more than his words and grabbed the screw that had been pointed out to him. Malayi dug into the tractor's womb up to his elbow, moved some part, and said: "Thank YOU, boy, free TO go!" Nikolin was seeing a tractor for the first time and his astonishment knew no bounds when the huge machine began to rumble and shake at the mere turn of a key, its parts moved and spun as if alive, the garage filled with a deafening racket and a warmth smelling of burning oil. At one point the machinist took a big silver watch out of the breast pocket of his grease-stained work shirt, glanced at it, and put it back in his pocket. He didn't look at the boy even once while he worked and left the garage without saying a word to him. Nikolin stared at the tractor a bit longer and then also went out, and at that time the Hungarian was already entering the yard of the lean-to where he lived with his wife. Actually, it wasn't a lean-to, but a freestanding house with two rooms, a kitchen and a glassed-in veranda on the front of it. Back in the day, Devetakov had left his new threshing machine in the garage year-round, since there was no one in the area to take care of it. And when he had met Malayi by chance on a train, he made him such an offer that the Hungarian immediately took him up on it and came to work at the estate. He had a wife and two children, a little boy, Ferenc, and a little girl, Zsuzsa. After they had finished primary school in the village, they had sent them to study in the city.

When he walked past the fence of the house, Nikolin saw the Hungarian carrying his wife in his arms like a small child. He already knew from Auntie Raina the cook that Ms. Clara was paralyzed, but he was amazed that she was as fragile and delicate as a girl, and that her eyes were so wide and such a clear blue. From then on, whenever he passed by their house, he would always see Malayi carrying her out three times a day, and depending on the time of day, setting her in the gazebo or on the grass in the yard. And every time he would be struck by the gentleness with which the Hungarian, who had managed to change into clean clothes in the span of a minute, carried his wife in his arms, as if carrying a little girl, and how that little girl, like those delicate flowers that draw their living juices from the air, wrapped both her arms around his neck and spoke to him in their language with a gentle and ringing childlike voice. Once or twice a month, Malayi would bring her to the big house to play the piano, and if Devetakov was at home, he and Ms. Clara would speak French together. Malayi would set the sheet music above the keys, sit down at the end of the table with his arms crossed, and gaze at his wife with a smile, and while she turned the round, spinning stool toward the piano and started to play, his harsh and inscrutable face with its nose like a bird of prey's beak would suddenly light up with some inner light and take on a strange expression, at once cheerful and sad, deeply pensive and smiling, while a soft, luminous radiance would stream from his cold eyes and large clear tears would glitter along his dark eyelids. The sounds flew up from beneath Ms. Clara's thin white fingers like invisible birds, circling through the air, touching the ceiling with their fluffy wings, diving down to brush against the stove, the walls, everything, they raced, played like a spring flock of birds, filling the room to bursting. Little by little, Nikolin began to see them as living, multicolored spots that flew smoothly and sonorously through the air, chasing one another, singing or crying with sad, moaning voices, whirling like a vortex and seeming to disappear into the distance, but really entering into Nikolin himself, filling his soul, and causing him to shudder with some impatience, to rejoice, or to feel an inexplicable sweet sorrow.

Nikolin could not go into Malayi and Ms. Clara's house, because he knew that now Ms. Clara was lying on her back in bed or sitting in a chair, talking to her husband in her chirping voice and smiling. She always smiled charmingly and happily like a young girl when she was speaking with Devetakov, when her husband carried her in his arms, and when she sat out in the yard in fine weather or in the garden on the soft grass, and her eyes were such a clear blue and so radiant that to Nikolin it seemed that instead of a face she had a luminous smile. The dim light behind the curtain went out, the darkness around him faded, the sinister shadows once again crept up around him, and he again started bucking, running, and whirling around with them. And while he was spinning and running around the garden, he caught a whiff of a warm scent, steeped in the sour breath of a horse, that enveloped him like a caress. It crossed his mind that he hadn't fed the horses that evening, so he went into the barn. He filled the manger with hay, lay down between the two horses, and spent the whole night calmed and warmed by the presence of those two creatures. And the whole night Devetakov was right there before his eyes, sometimes as he had been on the veranda, with a yellowed face, his blue eyelids screwed tightly shut, other times as he had been eleven years ago, bareheaded in a plaid shirt with rolled-up sleeves. The two of them stood before his eyes side by side, and with great effort he tried to rid his imagination of the dead one, and only to see the living one, and when he managed to do this, he felt a hand on his shoulder, a soft, white, warm hand.

Back then he had been a sixteen-year-old boy. His uncle had brought him to the estate while on his way to the city one day to sell firewood. In the middle of the village of Orlovo, a Turk had stopped them and paid for the wood without even bargaining for it, and led them to the estate. They unloaded the wood, and before they left, a young man around thirty passed by them, bareheaded and in his shirtsleeves, and asked Nikolin's uncle whether he could bring him two or three more cartloads of wood. His uncle promised to do so, and as the young man walked away, he realized that this must be the landowner, Mihail Devetakov, so he ran and caught up with him. He took off his hat and while talking to him, he held his hat over his heart so pleadingly and bent double so slavishly that the young man looked back toward the cart. The two men soon came over to Nikolin.

"Nikolin, my boy, the young master here is looking for a boy to work for him," his uncle said. "Will you stay?"

"Sure I'll stay, why not," Nikolin said, staring at his uncle's feet.

For a year his uncle had been looking to find him work, so Nikolin was not surprised by his decision to leave him at the estate that very minute; besides, he, too, was already eager to leave home. Devetakov could see that the boy was shy, so he tried to win him over. He put his hand on his shoulder, led him toward the house, and told him that he needn't worry about anything, as he was already a big boy. He also asked him what kind of work he would like to do.

"Well, until now I've herded sheep," Nikolin said.

"That's all well and good, but I've already got two shepherds," Devetakov said. "Wander around the yard for a day or two and take a look here and there, then we'll see."

While they were talking, Devetakov had led the boy into the house. It had two stories and was shaped like a horseshoe, there were five rooms on the upper floor, with the two end rooms jutting forward and all connected by a wooden veranda. The middle room, called the "parlor," was the largest and best furnished. It had three windows and a carved wood ceiling, while the furnishings were antiques: a large oval-shaped table with twelve chairs made of black wood, a breakfront with thick, protruding glass panes, two leather sofas, a stove made of glazed tiles, and a piano. Two of the lower rooms were taken up by Auntie Raina and the estate steward, while the others were used for the kitchen, bathroom, and pantry. From the outside, the house appeared unsightly, hulking, and even angry, but on the inside, it was cozy and comfortable, cool in the summer, warm in the winter, and impervious to the harsh winds of the steppe. There was a tiled stove that reached to the ceiling in every room, and this was, in fact, what set it apart from village houses. Way back when, Devetakov's father had built it for a large family, but he ended up having only a daughter and a son. His wife died early of appendicitis, while his daughter ran off with a man when still a schoolgirl and was never seen or heard from again.

They walked along the wooden veranda and went into the western-most upper room. When he saw the colorful carpet on the floor, Nikolin stopped on the doorstep and instinctively glanced at his feet, shod in crude leather sandals over thick woolen socks.

"Come in, come in!" Devetakov said, again putting his hand on the boy's shoulder.

His voice was gentle, affectionate, and inviting, yet Nikolin stepped into the center of the room as if on hot coals and stopped there. In the corner by the southern window there was an iron bed with a head- and footboard covered with a colorful blanket, a little table with two chairs, a brown-tiled stove, tall and shiny as a glazed pitcher, and that was the extent of the furnishing.

"You'll sleep here, Nikolin," Devetakov said, and turned toward the woman who was passing by on the veranda. "Auntie Raina, we've got a new worker, his name is Nikolin. Prepare his bed for tonight, and draw him a bath now. Once he's bathed, give him a shirt and shoes and don't forget to call him for supper. Run along then, Nikolin, go help Auntie Raina heat the water for your bath."

Nikolin turned to leave the room and burst into tears. The sobs rose up suddenly from the depths of his soul like a storm, shaking him all over and overcoming him entirely.

"Are you missing your village?" Devetakov said. "If you don't want to stay here, I'll take you back to your village first thing tomorrow."

"Oh, no!" Nikolin bawled in a hoarse, breaking voice, hiding his face in his shaking hands. "Nooo!"

"He's missing his mom and dad," Auntie Raina said. "Don't cry, my boy, you're a big boy already!"

Devetakov signaled to her to step out onto the veranda and whispered to her that the boy was an orphan so they shouldn't mention anything about his parents or ask him anything about his past. Poor thing, it's all too much for him, she said, her eyes filling with tears. With the instinct of a kind woman, she realized why the boy was shaking with such violent sobs bursting from the bottom of his heart, so she took his hand like a small child and led him to the kitchen. Later Nikolin often thought to himself that if it hadn't been for that woman, he would have run away from the estate that very day and gone back to his own village. She took him in as her own son from the very first minute, comforted him and gave him new clothes, showed him where everything was, and within a few days introduced him to life on the estate. In the morning she knocked on his door to ask him whether he'd slept well and always found him standing near the window, already dressed. It's hard to get used to a strange place, my boy, she would tell him, while leading him to the kitchen for breakfast, because she could see the signs of sleeplessness on his face: His voice was hoarse, his eyes were red, his face pale and anguished.

His life on the estate began so suddenly, it was so new, so fantastically easy and carefree that for months he could not get used to it. He lay awake for whole nights on end, he didn't dare reach out and savor the cleanliness of the sheets that enveloped him with unwonted cool gentleness, he couldn't savor the soft bed, the spacious room, and the calm. The estate wasn't large, consisting of two hundred fifty acres of land, three hundred sheep, six horses, of which two were for riding, again as many oxen, and a few cows. The servants were not too numerous either: Auntie Raina, the two shepherds, the stable man, the oxherd, the threshing machine operator, the steward, and the elderly Grandpa Kunyo, who didn't seem to have any particular occupation. Several days after Nikolin arrived at the estate, the master left to go abroad, as Auntie Raina told him, and didn't come back until after the New Year. During that whole time, no one gave him any specific tasks, but he had been used to working from a very young age and sitting idle pained him. He helped Auntie Raina in the kitchen, bringing her wood, water, and supplies, he also helped the herdsmen. At that time he knew the most about herding sheep and so he spent his free time with the sheep. It just so happened that one of the shepherds got sick and stayed at home in the village all winter, so Nikolin took his place. Every morning if the weather was clear, he would drive the sheep out into the garden to stretch their legs a bit, he tossed hay and corn on the snow for them to eat, watered them at the well, and cleaned the manure from the sheep pen. After the New Year, in the worst cold snap, lambing time began. He could tell which ewe would give birth on a given day, during the night, or on the next day, and didn't let her out of his sight. The ewe would start lying a ways away from the herd for an hour or two at a time, not eating much, and the wool of her belly would be slick with sweat. He would isolate her in the most sheltered part of the sheep pen and wait for hours, because every ewe birthed different – some quickly and easily, others taking longer, with more trouble. The lambs were different too. Some jumped to their feet as soon as they were born, wagging their tails and looking to nurse, while others were born weak as preemies and couldn't get to their feet. There were also cases when a first-time mother's milk dried up, or she crushed her little one or couldn't get it settled at her udder.

When five or even ten lambs were being born a day, Nikolin didn't sleep whole nights, but rather lay fully clothed on the couch in the kitchen, getting up every hour to go to the sheep pen to see if there was a new lamb. He would take it over to the stove to dry it off, and if it had been smothered during the birthing, he would blow into its mouth and rub it as the old shepherds in the village had taught him, thus bringing it back to life. Every morning Auntie Raina found him fast asleep on the couch after a sleepless night, with a lamb next to him on the floor. "Good Lord, this child's going to catch his death with these lambs," she would tell Devetakov. "Tell him to sleep up in his room, he hasn't had a square meal or a good night's sleep since I don't know when!" But instead of telling the boy to sleep in his room at night, Devetakov would often come down to the kitchen in the evening to see the newborn lambs. He had just come back from France and as was his wont after just returning from abroad, he still wore the clothes he had worn there – a homemade wool sweater with a high collar, a knitted cap, and gray, checkered pants. Outside, everything was frozen in ice and snow, beyond the window a blizzard was blustering or a fairy-tale-like white wasteland stretched, while in the kitchen hovered the mystery of birth, of something warm and life-giving, incarnate in the deep, moist eyes of the lambs, in their effort to stand on their fragile legs, too spindly for their bodies, to take their first gulp of milk, and that filled him with childlike joy and excitement. Auntie Raina slept in the room next door and could hear them going to the sheep pen and returning, and would come into the kitchen. "Misho, Misho, you're nothing but an overgrown child!" she would affectionately scold her master. "Run along, get to bed now, it must be the middle of the night! Those lambs will be born with or without your help, God's watching over them from above…"

The sheep stayed at the estate only during the winter months. In the first days of spring, they were driven to the summer pastures, nobody gave Nikolin any specific jobs to do, so he once again hovered around Auntie Raina. She was the cook, but she also took care of the house. During the most intense days of the harvest, her husband and two daughters came to help her, the rest of the time she managed on her own. She had a room on the lower floor, but only stayed there to sleep on the coldest winter days or when she had to stay late at the estate. Since there was no housekeeper to track expenses and maintain the house, in time she had taken over that duty as well. She kept track of everything, she knew how much of everything there was and what the house needed, she kept even the empty desk drawers locked, spent the household budget as she saw fit, and answered to Devetakov down to the last cent. She also gave Nikolin his first salary.

"This here is half a salary, since you came in the middle of the month. From now on you'll get a full salary of eight hundred leva."

Nikolin had never seen, much less possessed, so much money, which for that time was no small sum. For his shepherding work, he'd been paid in kind – with grain, flour, and cheese, which he would bring home.

The sheep owners had fed him three times a day, his aunt had mended or replaced his clothes, and he had had no need of anything more. Now he was fed and clothed better than ever, without really having worked, and on top of everything, they were giving him so much money. Auntie Raina held out the money to him, but he turned aside, as if she were forcing him to do something shameful.

"The poor little darling!" she said. "People will kill for a single lev, and he doesn't dare reach out and take four hundred leva!" She wasn't making fun of him, but wondering aloud how a child who had lived until now in such poverty and isolation could be so repressed that he had lost his sense of self-worth. "You'll go put it up in the desk drawer and lock it. That way month by month, year by year, the money will pile up and someday you, too, will have a house and land like everybody else. You're a bachelor, right? Just wait a year or two and you'll have found yourself a bride. And you'll give half of it to your sisters. The elder one's fourteen, you say, she may be making a home of her own before long, and the younger one'll be soon to follow. Your uncle's as poor as a church mouse, but a girl can't go to a strange home empty-handed." While speaking to him gently and admonishingly, Auntie Raina led him up to his room, split the money in half, and set it in the desk drawer. "This pile here is for you, that one there's for your sisters. Now here's the key, you hide it well somewhere, paying mind not to lose it. When you need money, you'll unlock the drawer and take some..."

That same year and at that same time Ivan Shibilev was living in Varna, hesitating as to whether to start his third year of high school or not. He had passed the first two with flying colors, and without much effort at that, but still, he likely would not have continued his studies if his mother hadn't arrived from the village on business. She was widowed and had taken a second husband in Orlovo, but Ivan Shibilev had refused to move there with her. He spent one day in the house, then told his mother that he couldn't spend another minute there and went back home. All his mother's efforts to integrate him into her new family were in vain. Later she gave birth to a girl from her second marriage, but at that time Ivan was her only child and she had decided to remarry for his sake alone. Her late husband had left more than twenty-five acres of land, a nice two-story house, livestock, and money, but during her four years of widowhood, the estate had started going to pieces. She was young and had no head for business, everyone cheated her and before she knew it, the money had dried up, the land had gone to seed, and of the livestock all that remained were two oxen and a cow. To secure a future for her son, she got married a second time, and as luck would have it, her second husband turned out to be kindly and, like herself, moderately wealthy. He wasn't offended by the boy's hardheadedness, even though he saw how his mother was suffering and was ready to go back to her own village with him. They decided to leave the boy alone and to write to him every day or two in the hope that when the cold settled in and he got lonely, he would want to come back to them. But the boy wasn't lonely in the least, on the contrary, this arrangement suited him very well and he begged his mother not to worry about him. He welcomed her gladly and she saw that he was healthy and happy and that was the most important thing for her. Even the winter did not scare him off. They delivered chopped dry wood to him, put stoves in both rooms, his mother cleaned and cooked for him at least two times a week. And so at the age of twelve Ivan Shibilev started living alone as the master of the house. He was very handy at many things, and even at that early age he started showing the penchants and talents that would later cause his fellow villagers to call him the "Painkiller." Alongside his homework and housework, he played every musical instrument in the village, he wrote poetry and painted in watercolor, and he often stopped by his neighbor's woodworking shop to watch him and to try his hand at the lighter tools.

Ivan Shibilev started his life in the city under the best conditions imaginable. His mother rented him a nice room in the city center with full room and board; that is, he ate with the landlords and had everything he needed to keep himself full, well dressed, and able to concentrate on his studies. His lessons posed no trouble to him at all, he remembered them as soon as he heard them in class, and he finished his homework in less than an hour, so for him the problem wasn't the time spent in class, but outside of it. His curiosity drew him irresistibly toward the life of the city and by the end of his first term he had more or less tasted of all its delights. Every day after school he would rent a bike and pedal furiously down the asphalt path along the Sea Garden, he would drop in at the shooting range, go to the harbor to watch the foreign ships, he would pass by the market or head down the main street, where in the early evening the whole city would come out for a stroll and could be seen in its full kaleidoscopic glory. He was most drawn to the cinema.

There were three cinemas in the city center with the imposing names of Splendid, Gloria, and Olympus, and each of them showed films according to the means and mentalities of the various urban classes. At Splendid, the most comfortable and expensive cinema hall, they showed "serious films," which were watched mostly by the local highlife; respectable housewives, clerks, and tradesmen went to Gloria, while Olympus was overflowing with hoi polloi – gangs of kids, cart drivers, bootblacks, servants, and all manner of folks looking for longer-lasting and less-pricey spectacles. Ivan Shibilev went to all three cinemas, most of all to Olympus, since the films shown there were multiepisode series and were entertaining. You could stay in Olympus from nine in the morning until midnight, you could eat, munch sunflower seeds, and even smoke, thus you could hardly breathe from the dust and tobacco smoke. It was not the Olympic gods parading across the screen, but rather the movie stars of the Wild West. The audience loved best of all Buffalo Bill and his mystical horse, the eternally tobacco-chawing Wallace Beery, Rin Tin Tin the dog and Rex the horse, and many others. Brave and bighearted, they attacked fearlessly and found their way out of the stickiest of situations, were sharpshooters even at a gallop, riding backward and firing two pistols apiece, escaping unscathed from a shower of Indian arrows. Laurel and Hardy, Chaplin, and Krachun and Malcho squandered at least a ton of pies in every film, smashing them in each other's faces, tripping and falling at every step, breaking dishes, causing fires and floods, getting caught up in all sorts of shenanigans, and always outwitting the police. The smoky theater shook with the audience's ecstatic exclamations and uncontrollable laughter.

At Splendid they also showed "forbidden" – in most cases amorous – films, which inflamed the schoolchildren's imaginations to such an extent that they were constantly talking about them and hatching plans to sneak into the theater to watch them. While these films were being shown, two teachers, one from the boys' school and one from the girls', stood at the door like Cerberus and caught the students they recognized; they also took trustworthy students from the upper grades with them to help. Nevertheless, the most creative and daring students managed to get into the theater, and their fame as lucky dogs spread throughout the whole high school. One got in wearing his brother's officer's uniform, another bribed the projectionist and watched the film from the projection booth, yet another strolled into the theater as cool as a cucumber dressed in women's clothing. Feverish teenaged imaginations spun legends about the daredevils who managed to sneak by under the noses of those Cerberuses. No one actually knew who these lucky dogs were, but everyone knew what they had seen in those forbidden films down to the last detail.

Ivan Shibilev went to the cinema almost every night, without paying any mind to the "students' curfew" and without any pangs of conscience for breaking school rules. During the middle of his second term, however, his luck betrayed him and he was caught coming out of Splendid after curfew and his grade for behavior was lowered. His class teacher called him in to remind him that just as in any institution, at the high school, too, there were rules and a code of conduct which had been established over the years and which had to be followed down to the letter. The class teacher was especially fond of Ivan Shibilev, just as, incidentally, all the other teachers were, and made it known to him that if he promised to follow the school rules strictly from now on, he could ask the principal to rescind his order lowering his behavior grade. Ivan Shibilev replied that he couldn't fathom why they were accusing him of violating the school rules when he was merely satisfying an intellectual need after he had prepared his lessons for the following day. To the class teacher it became clear that he would have to punish one of his best students, to "shake him up" a bit, so as not to have to repeat this unpleasant exercise in the future.

Ivan Shibilev was not "shaken up" by the punishment. For him it was perfectly natural, for example, to rework the school monogram engraved on his belt buckle to suit his own taste. He came up with his own design of the monogram and gave it to a smelter in the neighborhood to cast it, not in gold, but rather silver bronze, since he felt this color better matched his suit jacket. For the same reasons, he refashioned both his hat and his jacket. He removed the spring from the hat, roughed up the edges a bit, and bent down the right side of the brim so it looked "more chic," while he added light-blue velvet to the collar of his jacket. His hands instinctively itched to take hold of not just his clothes and other objects at his disposal, but of many other things as well, to change them so as to be better or more comfortable to his mind. He also couldn't stand the large student number on his left sleeve. He hated it not out of vanity or because it made it riskier for him to break the school rules (as we have seen, he did not pay mind to them anyway, as he couldn't see their point), but as a mockery of his individuality. He thought of himself as Ivan Shibilev, student in group 4a, and not as the number two nineteen written on a round piece of cardboard, covered with cloth, and sewn to his sleeve. "Hey you, number two nineteen, get in step, you're throwing off the whole company!" the gymnastics teacher hollered at him while marching the classes around during some celebration. "Number two nineteen, I'm talking to you!" The teacher ran over, out of breath, and shook him by the shoulder, and only then did Ivan Shibilev realize that the order had been meant for him. This happened during his very first term of study and since then he had taken the number off his sleeve. He carried it in his pocket and only in the morning, before going into class, would he fasten it to his sleeve with a safety pin.

His infatuation with cinema continued the whole year with such an intensity that he didn't even want to go home to the village during vacations, so as not to miss a film. As soon as the first shots appeared on the screen, he would fall into a trance and be transported to a magical world which he had never seen before, not even in his dreams. He would leave the cinema hall enchanted and would carry that world around with him for a long time, seeing the characters from the film, sensing them around him, hearing them speak and breathe. Thus he himself started living another, unfamiliar life, taken aback and touched by his own actions: He was a shipwrecked sailor, a roulette player who lost his fortune, a judge, a criminal, a soldier...

At the beginning of his second year, he met the artist Asen Momov. He had gone into the Astra Photo Studio on the main street to have his picture taken, and there amidst the advertising photos hanging on the wall of the reception room, he also spotted seascapes. Apparently no other client had ever studied his pictures with such interest, so the artist noticed this immediately. He also noticed the awe with which the schoolboy listened to him when he started telling him about his pictures and that's how he found out that the boy also "painted a few pictures now and then." He invited the boy to his home to see his other paintings and Ivan Shibilev turned up at his place at the appointed day and hour. Momov ran the photo studio with his father, and in his free time painted the seaside cliffs with wild foaming waves crashing against them, or sometimes the calm sea with fishing boats as well. Very rarely, and only on commission, would he paint still lifes of woven baskets full of fruit or bouquets of autumnal flowers against a colorful tablecloth. He painted in oils, but most often in gouache on small squares of cardboard, and he would go around to all the larger institutions and stores, selling his art. Very rarely, perhaps two or three times a year, he managed to sell a picture to some merchant, and in exchange for goods, no less – cloth for a suit, shoes, or a shirt.

There were several other artists in the city, and they expressed their rivalry through complete scorn for one another. Since Momov had discovered in the boy his own ecstatic disciple, he looked over his pictures, approved of them, and declared himself the boy's patron. Ivan Shibilev was overcome with the same passion for painting as he felt for cinema and poetry, and in the fall he returned from the village with an entire stack of drawings and paintings. The whole summer he had been painting with fierce abandon anything that fell before his eyes: people, houses, animals, scenes of harvesting and threshing. A new drawing teacher had arrived at the school, a young man with new outlooks on art and a talented artist himself. He was delighted by the boy's landscapes and especially his portraits, saying that he had seen his subjects "not with his physical eyes, but with his spiritual eyes." Near the end of the year the class teacher, who taught literature, and the drawing teacher declared Ivan Shibilev a wonder child with multifaceted talents. Besides the straight As he had received in all subjects, Ivan Shibilev had drawn portraits of his classmates and teachers. The portraits were done in oil, gouache, or in pencil, depending on the time and place he had observed his models. At the same time, a cycle of his poems came out in the magazine *Bulgarian Speech*. The two teachers arranged for him to have an art show in the foyer of the high school, which was visited by many students and citizens of the town.

Very soon after these days of universal rapture over his talents as a poet and artist, Ivan Shibilev was fated to be swept away by the irresistible force of theater as well. His landlord's younger brother was a stagehand at the theater. Like most stagehands, he suffered obsessively from being a failed actor and had "dedicated his life" to the stage with a devotion that perhaps even the actors themselves were not capable of. His brothers, one a retired teacher of history (and Ivan Shibilev's landlord), and the other a clerk for the tax authorities, were ashamed of his theater mania, which had caused him to miss out on a normal career, and considered him mentally ill. Everyone from both families and especially the children loved him and gladly welcomed him. He created a jubilant mood wherever he went, he could make faces and do magic tricks, he could imitate people and animals so well that everyone would be shouting with laughter. His name was Georgi, but everyone called him Uncle Zhorko, and in his absence they called him Uncle Bunny as well, as he had a harelip. The very first time they met, Ivan Shibilev recognized in him a kindred spirit; for his part, Uncle Zhorko also appreciated the boy's talents and started taking him to the theater for free. He introduced him to the ushers, they set up a chair for him on the edge of the first balcony, and from there, undisturbed and all eyes and ears, he watched the theater's entire repertoire.

Once Uncle Zhorko asked him to help for a few hours, since one of his co-workers hadn't shown up to work. Ivan Shibilev stayed with him the whole afternoon and from that point on was his unpaid assistant, first only on weekends, then during weekdays after he got out of school. Actually, there was nothing really for him to help with, since Uncle Zhorko and his fellow stagehands did all the work, but he would nevertheless stay on until the end of the performance. He would explore every corner of the stage, watch them installing the sets, sometimes he even managed to peek into the dressing rooms where the actors were getting ready for the performance. Rehearsals were most interesting for him. Outsiders were strictly forbidden from attending them, but Uncle Zhorko managed to hide him in some dark corner behind the set, or if need be introduced him as his nephew. And so Ivan Shibilev got the chance to see and hear what was happening on stage. At first the actors read through their parts and Uncle Zhorko explained that this was table work. During the following rehearsals, the actors recited their lines by heart and started working on the mise-en-scène (as Uncle Zhorko explained), they interrupted the action many times, the stagehands brought more and more set pieces to the stage, the actors put on the necessary costumes, the director followed the play from down in the auditorium, speaking to the actors from there and sometimes running over to them and showing them something before going back to his place. From one rehearsal to the next, from individual words and gestures, the play transformed into a living human story, happy or sad, but always moving to the point of oblivion. Opening night would come as the icing on the cake. A few days before the opening, everyone at the theater, from the doormen to the stagehands to the director, would be overcome by panic and anxiety, they would rehearse twice a day, going over some parts of the play even a third time, the director would dash from the auditorium to the stage and back, shifting set pieces, changing costumes, commanding everyone to keep quiet. Ivan Shibilev, like everyone else, experienced preopening jitters, because he knew all the roles by heart and felt himself a part of the production.

Finally, opening night. The ground floor and the balconies would gradually fill up with people, and Ivan Shibilev would watch through a crack in the curtain and see that there, in the theater, the audience looked completely different, as if they had left their everyday concerns outside;

not only in their Sunday-best suits and dresses, but also in the expressions on their faces, there was a solemnity and a nobility, a softness and a civility, which outside was not noticeable in them. Transformed by the gilded Baroque atmosphere of the hall and the lights, they sat respectfully in the soft velvet seats, whispering among themselves and impatiently waiting for the curtain to rise. Ivan Shibilev knew firsthand that for them, everything behind the curtain was a mystery which they could never catch a glimpse of, and that they would always have to strain their imaginations, just as he had strained his own imagination until recently. None of the hundreds of spectators could guess, for example, that behind the mysterious curtain reigned not complete calm, as it seemed from the auditorium, but on the contrary, backstage was seething with the utmost tension, carelessly done details were being fixed, the stagehands were scurrying about on tiptoe, the director was giving his last bits of advice, the actors were waiting for the curtain to rise, inwardly steeled and concentrated, as if about to face a life-threatening ordeal.

And now the lights go out one by one, the noise gradually dies down, the upper part of the curtain tears into two halves and they sail toward the two sides of the stage. Beyond the footlights a bluish darkness descends and into it, reflecting the glimmer of the stage, peer the luminous stains that are hundreds of human faces. Soon these faces hold their breath, while shortly they start to laugh or to sob, as if what is happening onstage is happening within their very selves. Act after act, and the end of the play comes imperceptibly. The hall quakes with applause and admiring shouts, the actors come out onstage hand in hand, smiling and still worked up from the play, they bow to the audience, hide behind the curtains, and called by the crowd again and again, they come out to take bows. After these minutes of ecstatic applause for the actors and the minutes of glory, which the audience bestowed upon them, Ivan Shibilev thought to himself that cinema, drawing, poetry, and studying were fleeting passions on his path toward the stage, and he made a vow to devote his life to theater. And while his teachers, fellow students, and acquaintances kept telling him that nature had been recklessly generous with him and while they praised him as a famous future poet or artist, he was already striving in his thoughts and feelings toward the theater. The openings of *The Misanthrope*, Stoyanov's *The Master Craftsmen*, and Nušić's *The Minister's Wife* were all coming up one after the other, which would star Krustyo Sarafov, Elena Snezhina, Vladimir Trandafilov, and other touring "luminaries of the stage." In the city's artistic circles, there hardly could have been two people awaiting these premieres more impatiently than Uncle Zhorko and Ivan Shibilev. Uncle Zhorko refused to leave the theater for days on end, sleeping a few hours a night on a dilapidated couch, working furiously the rest of the time so that the performances would want for nothing. Ivan Shibilev went to the theater every night and very often during the day as well to watch rehearsals along with his brother-in-arms. Uncle Zhorko had already managed to show off the boy's poetry printed in *Bulgarian Speech* and the local paper *Literary News*, a few people had even seen his exhibit at the high school, thus almost all the actors knew him and were kindly toward him.

And so the end of his third year of high school came about. He could have finished with straight As, since all his subjects came easily to him, if these subjects had not ceased to interest him. Everything his teachers said filled him with boredom, while exams were especially unpleasant. They turned into a cross-examination, terrorizing his soul and making him feel like a marionette. More and more often he began getting bad grades and his teachers did not hide their regret that day by day his standing at the school was plummeting and he was not making the effort to repeat his initial successes. He thought to himself, *so many people have no idea how high Kom Peak is, or what the chemical makeup of water is, or they don't know how to use a logarithmic table, but still, they're not fools or degenerates, useless to themselves and to society, as they preach to us in class? I wonder whether Sarafov or Snezhina can calculate the volume of a cylinder, and if they can't, how did they become such wizards on the stage?*

Thus he tried to use such sophistic reasoning as a shield against his academic capitulation and as an excuse for his latest obsession. One day perhaps the muses would turn into Furies to take revenge on him for his artistic polygamy and to change his talent into a terrible curse, but for the time being he was filled with such pure aspirations that the thought of such a danger didn't even cross his mind and he believed that he could serve his muses to the end of his life with the same devotion and love. He felt pangs of conscience only where his mother was concerned, the poor illiterate woman who had married a second time just so she could save their property and give him an education. Just as every summer, she moved back to the old house to spend a few months with him, but he stayed with her only two days and went back to the city on the third. He told her that the school required him to stay in the city for a while longer, so she gave him money and her blessings and sent him on his way.

In early July one of the directors, Yanakiev, gathered together a dozen actors and undertook a tour in the region with the Bulgarian classics *Under the Yoke* and *Boryana*. Here and there they were still harvesting barley, but people in the villages had never been to the theater and in the evenings they filled the "hall." In most villages they fed them gratis, and the eternally hungry actors' guild ate and drank their fill and earned a lev or two for summer vacation. Yanakiev had a friend, a colonel from the local garrison and a passionate lover of theater, who lent him a four-ton, canvas-covered truck; hence transporting people and props was quick and easy. Ivan Shibilev and Uncle Zhorko, who also took on the duty of quartermaster, would go to the next village a day or two in advance to secure lodging for the troupe and to prepare the stage in some cultural club, school, or even in a barn.

In one such abandoned communal barn, Ivan Shibilev made his

first theatrical appearance onstage. The actor who had been playing the role of Pavel in *Boryana* broke his leg on just the second day of the tour after an unedifying bender and had to be taken back to the city. Yanakiev assigned the role to Ivan Shibilev without any hesitation, because he knew he would do well in it. He already knew of the boy's passion for theater, thanks to which he had come along with the troupe to work for free, but now he discovered that the young man had other talents as well. He had an exceptional memory and knew almost the whole of the theater's repertoire by heart, he was a skillful imitator, he wrote poetry and recited it well, he drew portraits of people from the troupe, played violin and all the folk instruments, and besides that, he possessed that which is most invaluable for an actor – charm and a strong stage presence. He was slightly taller than average, with brown eyes, a warm voice, and a very pleasant, expressive face, which reflected a cheerful, restless character and emotional purity. After the performance of *Boryana*, the actors congratulated him on a successful debut and wished him further successes. Everyone was delighted by the freshness and earnestness with which he embodied the young village lad Pavel, especially in the moment when he took a stand before the all-powerful king of Alfatar to defend his love to the death: "I won't let Boryana go, she leaves this place only over my dead body!" After a monthlong tour, the troupe returned to the city. Before they went their separate ways, the director asked him to come to the theater around September 1 to play the same role, in case the other actor was not recovered by then, and even if he was, to try him in some other role fit for a young man.

Ivan Shibilev barely waited until mid-August, then left for the city and that very same evening he stopped by the theater. At that time the only people hanging around were Uncle Zhorko and a few workmen finishing up renovations on the dressing rooms. There was a bench in front of the doorman's booth and on the bench was sitting a young woman with dark hair tumbling down around her shoulders. She was sitting with her back to the street, talking to Uncle Zhorko. As soon as he saw Ivan Shibilev, Uncle Zhorko left the woman and came to meet him, his face one big rabbit-like grin.

"Now there's our little actor!" he said, giving his shoulders a friendly shake. "And you've grown a moustache! It looks good on you, it really looks good!"

After they chatted for a minute or two, Uncle Zhorko invited him to sit down on the bench. As he sat down, Ivan Shibilev unwittingly glanced at the girl and through his heart ran that shiver of ecstasy and despair he felt in the presence of a beautiful and unknown woman. *How can such beauty possibly exist in the world and how can I live in that same world without seeing it for more than a moment?* he thought to himself, dazzled by that beauty, and not hearing what Uncle Zhorko was telling him. *That is a flagrant injustice and inconsolable grief for the human heart. Isn't it pointless to live, since this beauty will part from me? Merciful God, please make it such that...* But even before he said it, God had fulfilled his prayer. The workers called Uncle Zhorko into the building and the girl turned to Ivan Shibilev and asked him how long he had been an actor.

"I'm not an actor," he said. He felt as if he were dreaming, and just as it is in dreams, he wanted to look her in the face once more, but some force would not allow him to turn his head toward her and this force was secretly persuading him that if he looked her in the face once more, he would see a gorgon and would immediately be turned to stone. Why, why am I afraid to look at her, he kept asking himself as he went on telling her how he'd by chance filled a role for a whole month and how the director had promised him yet another role in the new season.

"You're so lucky!" the girl said with ingenuous frankness.

"Lucky? On the contrary!" Ivan Shibilev said, shaking his head sadly.

He was speaking honestly, because his happy days, of which there had been many until now, disappeared into a dark abyss the moment he had seen the girl, he felt hopelessly forlorn and filled with inexplicable grief only at the fleeting thought that she would leave and the world would be desolate without her. That very evening, racked by insomnia and loneliness, he would write:

> *The world will be a white desert without you*
> *and in this desert, my days will wither away...*

"The director Malovski promised me a role this season," she said. "Maybe we'll be partners in some play. I'm Genevieve, but they call me Veva. And your name?"

"Ivan."

"Well, I've got to go now!" Veva shook her magnificent hair, ran her fingers through it, and got up. Ivan Shibilev jumped up as if shot off a spring and started walking along with her. "Are you leaving too?"

"Yes!" Ivan Shibilev got up the courage to glance at her in profile and saw that her lips were curled into a slight smile. *That divine smile is for me, because I got up to see her off,* he thought, and sensed how the Weltschmerz disappeared from his soul as instantaneously as it had appeared, making room for wild and daring hope. "Will you allow me to walk you home?"

"Oh, that won't be necessary!" Veva said. "I'm going to meet a girl-friend."

"What a pity! If you were alone, I would have offered to keep you company this evening."

"How very kind of you, but you can accompany me just to the church on the main street. My girlfriend will be waiting for me there."

"I shall be happy to spend a few more minutes with you!"

Ivan Shibilev could not shake off his excitement, he had trouble catching his breath, and since he believed that Veva was a professional actress, he kept speaking to her in that grandiloquent tone he had heard at the theater. The "divine" smiles that lit up her face were indeed for him, but more as ironic smirks at his efforts to prove himself a worthy gentleman for her. She was only two years older than he was and from the outside this difference didn't show. Dressed as he was in fashionable trousers of white shantung and a light-blue shirt, with his moustache and his hair slicked back, a head taller than she was, with broad shoulders and a fine figure, Ivan Shibilev even looked a few years older than she was. However, in terms of life experience he was still a child compared to her, since she could long since faultlessly read men's glances, facial expressions, and desires as easily as reading a simple book. She had needed not minutes but only a few seconds to realize that the young man was still a virgin and had fallen in love with her "at first sight" and was ready to declare his eternal love for her. She also knew from experience that youngsters like him needed to be sent packing in the very first minute and she always did so for completely understandable reasons, but her girlfriend was not waiting for her at the appointed place by the church, the young man invited her to dinner at a restaurant, and she accepted. He radiated a certain charm which caused her to reward him for his clumsy efforts to court her, plus she was not used to spending her evenings alone. She had already noticed that he was not brave enough to look her in the eye and that he spoke in a style unusual for his age, so as to make himself seem like a man who'd been around the block, and that made her feel kindly toward him.

At the restaurant, Ivan Shibilev calmed down and got back into his own role. He had a whole evening ahead of him with Veva, who filled him with high hopes, plus the waiter treated him like a true gentleman ("What would the gentleman like? As the gentleman wishes…") and that only further inflated his self-confidence. Just a few tables at the restaurant were occupied, the two of them were sitting secluded in a small niche, where it was quiet and cozy. Captivated to the point of ecstasy by the girl's beauty, he fell into deep, delicious self-revelation and told her everything, or almost everything, about himself, as only a young man who has just left his boyhood behind him can: with the purest and gentlest excitement, with the most beautiful words in the world and the strongest feelings, because, in telling her about himself, he was declaring his love for her. To restrain his hot gushing effusions, which were beginning to grate on her, as well as to satisfy his curiosity to a certain extent, Veva briefly told him about herself. She had been an actress at the Pleven Theater for two years, but due to jealousy, rumors, and discontent among the troupe, she had been forced to quit. Other theaters had made her offers, but she had decided to stay with the one here, since she had a spinster aunt with a large house where she could live in true luxury. At the end of the last season she had gone to Malovski and he had promised her a role in *Wife for Rent* by some Burali or other, in which she had played the lead role at the Pleven Theater.

That was hardly entirely believable, but the truth was that Veva knew the value of her beauty and had long transformed it into a means of making a living. Not at the end of the last season, but almost a year earlier she had started hanging around the theater and fell first, of course, into the director Malovski's hands. He didn't try to hang on to her for more than a month before passing her off to some of the actors, while they for their part, since they couldn't afford the luxury of long-term romances with such a beauty, passed her on to their friends and fans. Ivan Shibilev found this out from several of the actors, who had seen him with her in the restaurant or on the street, he also heard this from Uncle Zhorko. The latter told him that such girls were always circling around the theater like moths around a lamp in hopes of making it onstage not thanks to their talent and skills, but at the price of their womanly charms. The director Yanakiev, who had decided to take Ivan Shibilev on in his next play, troubled by his lack of experience with women and especially women like Veva, also advised him not to see her and even called her a "spittoon."

After their first dinner in the restaurant, Ivan Shibilev solemnly vowed that he would follow Veva anywhere, at any time, and under any circumstances. She didn't ask this sacrifice of him, on the contrary, over the course of two months she went out with him only five times, while the rest of the time he was stalking her on the streets. When she found this out, she got angry and threatened that if he kept following at her heels, she would never speak to him again. Ivan Shibilev made sure she did not catch sight of him unwanted again, but when he could he kept track of where she went and whom she saw. In the evenings most often she would go to a two-story house near the covered market and after about an hour would come out with another young woman. The two of them would set off down the main street to the Eye of the Sea Restaurant, then they would turn right and go down to the Sea Garden. There the crowds split into various directions, thinning out, and it was easier to follow the two women. As soon as they turned into one of the alleys, two men would be standing before them ostensibly "by chance," they would start chatting with them and walking along with them, at first all together, but soon splitting into couples. As could be seen from their clothes and manners, these were men of solid means, naval officers in white uniforms with dirks on gleaming chains or infantry officers, who when meeting the ladies would press their long swords to their thighs, bow gallantly, and noisily click their spurs together. After a few turns around the garden, the two couples would head for the casino. There an orchestra was already playing and the choppy beats of a rumba or foxtrot carried through the cool evening air, under the generous light of the electric lamps, the dance floor roiled like a living, colorful avalanche. Hidden in the shadow of nearby trees, Ivan Shibilev waited there until Veva and her girlfriend with their two beaus came out of the casino and headed down the street. They walked in pairs a dozen yards apart, holding hands, and when passing through darker spots the gentlemen would embrace their ladies and kiss them. Soon they would arrive at the house by the covered market and go inside. Some nights

Ivan Shibilev would take up his post on the nearby corner and stand there pointlessly until dawn, when the two men left the house.

There were days and nights of even crueler suffering, and those were the days and nights when Veva didn't have anyone to go out with and deigned to take pity on him. He was lurking near her apartment at all hours, Veva could see him through the window, and when she had no other date, she would go out through the main entrance, as she was sure that he would glom on to her. They would take a few turns along the main street then go into one of the restaurants. Veva preferred the Eye of the Sea or Bulgaria, because these restaurants were patronized by the choicest society. Amidst that choice society, just as everywhere else, incidentally, she gave him to understand in every possible way that he should not nurse any hopes of greater intimacy and if she went out with him from time to time, it was only because she could not withstand his stubborn insistence. She behaved such that men unambiguously expressed their admiration for her exquisite beauty, and she not only did not hide her satisfaction as every respectable young lady should, but even provoked such attention with glances and smiles. Men frequently stopped her on the street, and to speak with them, she would turn her back on her escort or would order him to wait for her at a distance; in restaurants men sat down uninvited at their table, there were those who chided her in lieu of a greeting: "Oh, Vevie, looks like the bill's on you tonight!" They were implying that her companion was a mere child and she would have to pay for his dinner. This caused Ivan Shibilev to try to hide his youthfulness. He had gotten two suits made by the most fashionable tailor in town, he wore white pants and white shoes, in the evening he would put on a tie, since his moustache made him look like a young man from a wealthy family. In the village eighteen-year-old boys were seen as marriageable men, and his mother as well as his stepfather saw him as an eligible bachelor and sent him money over and above his monthly allowance. Since he had saved money from the tour as well, he had the means to allow himself to eat and dress well and take his lady friend to the most expensive restaurants. Despite this, she preferred the company of other men, who not only were not in awe of her beauty, but who treated her indecently and even cynically: They looked at her with lustful eyes, invited her on dates in his presence, and smiled knowingly behind her back.

Ivan Shibilev suffered from the fact that he could not see her every day and every hour, but never for a moment did he doubt her moral purity, nor did he ever judge her behavior. She was a true angel, who stood so high above them in the aureole of her beauty that no one was capable of sullying her in any way, just as no one could appreciate her beauty and talent as an actress. He felt an insatiable yearning for her, and to that feeling, so agonizing and sweet, he subordinated and dedicated everything: his poems, which he had written in moments of loneliness in an ecstatic outburst of love, and his hopes, and his dreams, and his work in the theater. The actor he had replaced on the tour was still recuperating, so the director gave him the same role. After a few rehearsals, just enough to get him used to the roominess of the large stage, the play was performed at the end of September, immediately following the season opening. Ivan Shibilev played the role of the young village lad far better than had been expected of him, he was so wildly naïve and so ecstatically gentle toward his beloved Boryana that the audience rewarded him with applause and cries of "Bravo!" The director had entrusted him with the role despite the protests of a few of the actors and now he was glad that this experiment had turned out successfully and promisingly. He was flattered by the hope that he had discovered and paved the way to the stage for a new, fresh talent, and after the performance he sought out Ivan Shibilev to congratulate him and talk about the next role he planned to give him. Ivan Shibilev had dashed out of the dressing room and was feverishly circling around the theater. Veva had promised to come watch him and wait for him after the performance by the entrance to the theater, but it looked as if something unforeseen had come up for her. Two days later he ran into her "by chance" as always near her apartment and she told him that the next day she would be going back to her hometown. Her mother wasn't well and had asked her to come stay with her for a week or two, after which she would return to take up the role Malovski had offered her. Seeing his face go pale and twist from inner anguish, Veva gently kissed him on the cheek, pressed her face to his, and stayed like that for a whole minute. Then she took his hand and led him toward the local park. The city was already quiet, its even breathing could be heard coming from the sea.

"Don't try to comfort me, I'm not a child!" Ivan Shibilev said. "I know that when you leave, I won't ever see you again. Ever! But I won't ever forget you! As long as I live, I will live only with the thought of you!"

"Don't talk that way, Vanyo! You're so young and you're already an actor, your future is ahead of you. I don't deserve you, I'm a frivolous nobody... You'll find another woman who suits you."

"No, no, no!" he cried, taking both her hands and kissing them in tears. "You're an angel, you're the purest, most beautiful woman in the world! You are a saint! You have a good heart and a kind soul..."

He spoke as if in a trance, intoxicated by the agonizing sweetness of confessing his innermost feelings and vowing that she was the first and last and only love of his life. She was looking somewhere at his forehead with mocking attention, as if waiting to see how far he would go in his gushing effusions. Finally, to spare him the banal confession that after they parted he could not live without her and would kill himself, she took him gently by the hand and led him back to his apartment. She had done all she could to put him off her, but instead of being driven to bitterness and despair, he had grown all the more hopelessly attached to her. Now she realized that she had been flattered by the purity of his feelings and due to her own vanity she had given him certain hopes by nevertheless going out with him from time to time. She had let this game go on and now she had to break it off without tiresome consequences for herself – he might spend the night in front of her apartment, waiting to see when she would go to the station.

They parted in front of his apartment, having agreed that she would put off her departure for a few days and that the next night they would meet in front of the Eye of the Sea. Ivan Shibilev fell asleep in his clothes long after midnight and awoke before dawn. *She's leaving today*, he thought, and realized that this painful and bitter thought had pierced his entire being, during the night he had felt it as a foreign body within himself. He folded up his two suits and put them in the suitcase, placed a scroll of poems on top of them, and went out. His landlords were at the vineyard, as always during the grape-harvesting season, and he left them a note saying he would be back in about a week. He locked the front door and ran to the square by the men's high school, where he caught a phaeton to the train station. When he arrived there, Veva and her girlfriend were standing in front of the second wagon after the locomotive. Veva got into the train and stuck her head out the window. At the ticket window they told him the train was leaving in five minutes for Sofia via Pleven, he bought a ticket and through the eastern entrance went out onto the platform and climbed into the last wagon. By the time he reached her wagon, the train had already left the station, and Veva was preparing to enter her compartment. When she saw him, she looked scared, she stared at him and didn't know what to say.

"Good God! So you're… traveling too?"

"I'll go with you a ways," Ivan Shibilev said, as if it were a matter of walking her to the next street over. "I wanted to wish you a safe trip!"

Veva immediately changed her expression, smiling sadly and saying that she was touched by his attention. She had been at her girlfriend's until late the previous night, and when she had returned to her apartment, she had found a telegram from her sister. It said that their mother was on her deathbed. She hadn't slept a wink the whole night, at dawn she had packed her bags and gone to her girlfriend's to tell her of her sudden departure.

"How nice that you came!" she said again, stroking his arm. "Now I really do believe in telepathy. I was thinking to myself what would happen if Vanyo were to find out that I was leaving so suddenly and came to say goodbye! And now look, you're here! Except that I'm very tired. I need to rest for a bit, and then we'll talk."

She went into the compartment and sat down by the window, where there was a free seat. She leaned back against the headrest and closed her eyes, while Ivan Shibilev remained standing in the corridor just like that, so he could watch her through the glass window of the door...

In Nikolin's first years there, time seemed to stand still, since no changes came to the estate. The seasons came and went, and with them the sowing and threshing, Devetakov would go abroad for a month or two, the Hungarian would bring Ms. Clara to the parlor from time to time to play the piano, on the major holidays or in summer, guests would come to visit. Even the declaration of the Second World War was a nonevent for him and the other workers, since its echo reached the estate quite faintly and dimly. In '42 they called up a few of the village men from the reserves and sent them to the newly acquired territories, planes started flying overhead toward Romania quite often, from where, when it was still, one could hear a distant rumble, but even these events did not bring any change to life on the estate. The only significant event was the sudden death of the cook, Auntie Raina. She had gone home hale and hearty one evening, and the next morning her husband came to tell them that she had passed away. Nikolin was very attached to her and later thought to himself that with her death things at the estate started going downhill. In the autumn of that same year Devetakov announced he was selling half his land. This sale came like a bolt from the blue and no one knew the reason. Some of the workers said he had accumulated lots of debts that couldn't be put off, while others claimed he was getting ready to go abroad and stay there for a good long while. Devetakov asked a fair price and the wealthier folks in the nearby villages bought up the land. After the sale he spent almost two weeks at his city house and came back with the blueprint for a new school in the village. Back when Devetakov was studying abroad, his father had already laid the foundations, but his death had prevented him from finishing it. When he was done with his studies, the younger Devetakov decided to finish building the school, but years passed before he hit his stride as the new master of the estate, and in the meantime the villagers had hauled away the construction materials little by little for their own uses. The old four-room schoolhouse was rickety, which was the only reason the school inspectorate refused to allow a junior high school to be opened in the village. The villagers volunteered to work on the building the whole winter and summer, and by the fall the new school with its seven classrooms and two offices was ready and outfitted with the necessary supplies.

Nikolin noticed that during the sale of the land and the building of the school, his master had started to drink a bit with the buyers and builders. He had never seen him drink before, even though he loved treating his guests to all manner of drinks imaginable. These beverages had been gathered from all corners of the country and abroad and stood lined up in a cellar beneath one of the barns. The elder Devetakov had had a passion for collecting alcohol of all kinds and to this end had made a special underground storage cellar lined in oak paneling with built-in shelves and ventilation. He himself couldn't stand alcohol and had hardly drunk a bottle of wine over his lifetime, but he loved having guests and was truly gratified when he could surprise them with drinks heretofore unknown to them. He kept his hobby a secret, as was the underground cellar, in order to play the role of the magician in such cases ("Name a drink and in a minute, it will be in your hand!"). He entrusted this secret hobby to his son, who took it as a paternal bequest and began collecting Bulgarian and foreign liquors and treating his guests. For some time now, however, he had begun treating himself as well. When bringing Devetakov his supper, Nikolin always saw a bottle and a half-drained glass on the table. He would go eat his own supper, finish some work in the kitchen, and when he went back to clear the dishes, he would find his master's food sitting untouched or barely picked at. Devetakov would take sips from the glass and stare into his book, while Nikolin would scold him: "You haven't eaten a thing, what's this nonsense?"

"I've eaten my fill. Clear the dishes!"

"Eaten your fill, my eye! You've pecked at it once or twice – you call that eating your fill? You better worry about eating first, then you can drink yourself silly with that rotgut! A single whiff of it is enough to make your nose fall off."

During their long years of living under one roof together, Nikolin had managed to somewhat overcome his shyness and sometimes permitted himself to indulge in that rough-edged protectiveness which simple folks use to express their fond devotion to the ones they love. Even though he was almost half his master's age, he unwittingly acted the role of an elder man when he felt that Devetakov was doing childish things such as, for example, selling his land and building a school, which cost him many head-aches and expenses. He was also worried about the change that had come over his master. After drinking a glass or two, Devetakov would withdraw into himself, and some warm shadow of grief and resignation would settle into his eyes. Already years earlier he had noticed how that shadow would suddenly darken his eyes like a storm cloud even when he was cheerful and chatting with guests and friends, when he was reading a book or working on something in the yard. He had also noticed that in such cases he radiated a sort of silence that muted all noises nearby and at the same time gave off a sense of somber alarm and unease. He caught this with his senses, just as animals sense uneasiness in nature's silence before a sudden atmospheric change, and since he couldn't make sense of it or find a word for it, he simply called it "that quiet thing." There had been times when the two of them had been galloping on the horses from the woods back to the estate, or traveling to the city or having dinner, when suddenly he would sense in some inexplicable way that "that quiet thing" had started emanating from his master, transforming him. Nikolin would wait for him to leave off his usual routine and he was never mistaken – Devetakov would shut himself away for a few days or weeks in the room with books, or he would go to the city or would undertake something unusual. Now, after he'd sold his land and built the school, one morning when it was still dark, without preparing for a long journey as he usually did, he asked to be driven to the train station and left to go abroad with only the coat he was wearing and a single small suitcase.

After Auntie Raina's death, Devetakov entrusted to Nikolin the house and all the rights and responsibilities the deceased woman had had. He kept everything under lock and key as she had, he knew how much and which things were in every room and the whole house, he met guests and settled them into their rooms, he delivered and distributed the goods for the kitchen. A new cook was hired, Dobrinka, who had just come back from many years of domestic service in the city, a jaded, lonely, and bitter woman. Like every peasant who has "gone out and seen the world" and learned a bit of her rights, Dobrinka, as soon as she set foot on the estate, imported and kindled amidst the workers that antagonism that, albeit in naïve form, exists in even the smallest social groups. After the death of the former cook, her room remained locked for a long time with all her things inside; the new cook was given a room in one of the annexes and this was grounds to loathe the master, and Nikolin along with him. The young man irritated her with his monk-like meekness, she saw him as the master's stool pigeon hidden behind a mask of hypocritical kindheart-edness. When the old cook's family came to collect her belongings, the room on the ground floor was once again free, but Nikolin did not dare settle the new cook there without the master's permission and she hated him for it. Grandpa Kunyo also suspected Nikolin of spying on him and telling the master about his thefts. Back in the day the elder Devetakov had taken him in out of pity to oversee the workers, but he turned out to be a good-for-nothing brawler and drunkard who stole from and made free with the estate more than any of the others. Despite this, Devetakov didn't drive him off, but entrusted him to his steward, Halil Efendi. Halil Efendi was fair and strict, but still he couldn't get the old man to walk the straight and narrow. Grandpa Kunyo, once he saw that the Turk wasn't going to put up with him, would stand before him like a dog with its tail between its legs, but the minute he was out of his sight, he'd be back up to his old tricks. He swiped everything he could from the estate, sold it to the villagers, and would carouse at the pub for days on end. He soon was in thick with the cook and once he goaded her to bring Nikolin's dinner up to him in the parlor. That day Nikolin had the flu and was lying on the sofa, he ate a bit and then went to lie down again. The next day the scene repeated itself, and on the third day, when he was recovered and went down to the common dining room, the cantankerous old man leapt to his feet, bowed, and called him "Mr. Miyalkov." Grandpa Kunyo always came to lunch and dinner tipsy, played the clown, and entertained the others with various stories he'd heard at the pub. For some time now they'd only been talking about war and politics at the pub and he conveyed those conversations to the estate. "The Russians have got those Germans stuffed in a sack at Stalingrad," he spoke excitedly, taking a swig from the flat flask which had once held soybean butter and which he always kept in the inside pocket of his jacket. "Just like that, like you stuff a dog in a sack. It growls and kicks and whimpers, but it just can't bite. That's how

Germany is now. Big Brother Russia's laying into 'im, and he's just whimpering and baring his teeth till he kicks the bucket. Let that be a lesson to our fascists here" – he pounded on the table, looking at Nikolin and shaking his head menacingly – "Now they're explooting us and drinkin' our blood, but soon we're gonna stuff 'em all in the sack and grab our cudgels! Once we give 'em a nice hard pounding, there won't be any mine and yours, we'll all be equals. What god said that one fellow'll have estates, pile up money, and go trotting off to foreign parts, while others'll be slogging like slaves for a crust of bread?" "You only seem to slog away at the pub," the others said and laughed. "Go ahead and laugh, yous," Grandpa Kunyo said, "'cause you're blind and can't see what a sorry state you're in. They strip the skin off your back and you stay silent as oxen. They say I've taken to drink. What, you think I drink out of happiness? No, I drink out of misery! This's gone missing, that's gone missing, I'm always the one left holding the bag, I'm always the one to blame. They say I've stolen from the estate! I haven't stolen and I'm right furious I haven't. As if it'd be more than a fleabite to the master if you took a half bushel of grain or a basket of chaff? They oughta take his everything, down to the last crumb, 'cause it's been plundered from the people, it oughta go back to the people..."

And so, Grandpa Kunyo, exalted by alcohol, was the first at the estate to talk about war and politics and to proclaim the principles of the future socialist revolution. No one besides the cook Dobrinka, however, took his prophecies seriously. The shepherds and the ox herders were all elderly and practically illiterate men, they took no interest in international events. The pub was the place for talking politics, while they lived cut off from the village for months at a time and took the old man's haranguing for drunken blather. Even though he was young, Nikolin like them only understood those events that took place right before his eyes. The old man's constant barbs made him uneasy and he stopped eating lunch and

dinner with the other workers – he either waited for them to leave the
dining room or took his food up to his room.

The autumn rains came, making the trees bare and the ground muddy.
Fog lay over the empty fields like deep sorrow, and amidst that sorrow
the estate stood like a forlorn orphan. The days were short and dreary;
instead of sun, for an hour or two some cold pale glow would appear in
the dark-blue sky, and then darkness would again settle over the estate,
muddy-white and bloated from moisture like a wet hemp rug. The master
had told him to turn on the radio or the gramophone whenever he wished,
but Nikolin couldn't make heads or tails of them and was afraid he might
break them. During the day he was busy with housework, but he spent
his evenings alone. He ate supper at the big table in the parlor and after
that would go to light the stove in his master's room. He lit it every night
after Devetakov's departure, even though he knew that he would return
in a month at the earliest; in this way he fed his illusion that his master
was there and might walk into the room at any moment. He would sit
on the upholstered stool by the stove, sensing with satisfaction how the
amber-colored tiles gave off an ever-stronger heat, filling the room with
coziness and a sorrowful calm, while outside the wind was whistling and
rain spattered against the windowpanes. The big gas lamp threw soft yellow light on the family photo, from which peered the elder Devetakov, his
wife, and their two children. The father and mother were sitting in high-
backed chairs, he in a soft hat with a starched collar, a tie, and a small chain
running from one pocket of his waistcoat to the other, with retouched
eyes and a moustache, she with an oblong, gentle face and a thin neck,
with puffy sleeves and a thin, weak hand resting on her son's shoulder,
with an aureole of the mysterious and romantic beauty that women from
a past and unknown world always emanate. Her son, Mihail, was sitting
on a little stool in front of her with close-cropped hair and in a sailor suit,
looking slightly aside with his mother's timid, wide-open eyes; his sister

was sitting next to him, a vaguely smiling girl in a schoolgirl's beret and two long braids hanging over her shoulders. Directly beneath the photo, the brass balls of the bedstead gleamed like two little suns, and beneath them lay the bedspread, its soft flowers spilling out across the bed. In his solitary concentration, Nikolin could see his master lying on that bed with feverish eyes and his gentle, oblong face like his mother's, as he had seen him in bed sick with a cold. He would bring him warm milk or tea several times a day, and Devetakov would always say: "Thank you, Nikolin! Don't come any closer so you don't catch my cold!"

Then he would go into the other room, where the books were, lined up in bookcases of dark wood. They took up the two opposite walls from floor to ceiling and were so tightly packed next to one another that Nikolin could not fit even a finger between them. He had never opened any of those books, but he could stand amongst them for hours filled with awe and reverence, since it seemed to him that between their covers a different, exalted, and mysterious world lay locked away, which only his master could peer into and grasp. He had seen him sitting in the small leather armchair with an open book, absorbed for hours, he had seen how his face had changed, now cheerful, now sad, he had heard him laughing or breathing a deep sigh.

In early March Devetakov came back from abroad. Even though he was tired and had grown thin from the long journey, he looked cheerful and inspired, he radiated a sort of softness and calm and Nikolin thought with joy that it wasn't "that quiet thing," which made him sad and indifferent, but some other thing, kind and invigorating. As always, he had brought back presents for the servants and the Malayi family. The Hungarian seemed to be waiting for him, he took the present with a letter and in turn gave Devetakov a letter addressed to him. As long as Malayi had been living on the estate, he had passed hundreds of letters from Ms. Clara to Devetakov and from Devetakov to her. Nikolin had seen her letters on Devetakov's desk, short notes written in French on powder-blue paper and placed in the same, oblong envelops. Every exchange of letters was followed by an exchange of books, or Clara and Malayi came to visit. They came now, too. Nikolin noticed that they were far more excited and cheerful than other times, especially Malayi, who, despite all his efforts to appear sociable, always remained silent and impenetrable; this evening he was not himself at all. His dark face with its hooked nose, which gave him the look of a bird of prey, was lit up by some inner light and joyful impatience, and he started speaking as soon as he stepped through the door, holding his wife in his arms. After dinner, Ms. Clara sat down at the piano and while her exquisite white fingers wrested soft, gentle sounds from the keys, smiling, she broke into some cheerful song. Then they listened to the news on Radio Sofia, from Moscow and London. The main news reported on the radio stations was the end of the winter campaign on the Eastern Front. The German army had been forced to retreat almost four hundred miles, and the Northern Caucuses, Stalingrad, the Rostov Region, and the Kursk Region, along with many others, had been liberated. The German Army had lost almost half its military might.

"Germany has lost the war," Devetakov said after switching off the radio. "It had lost even before it began."

"Are you so sure, Monsieur Devetakov?" Ms. Clara asked. "The end of the war is still unclear."

"It's more than clear, madam, above all to the Germans themselves. They are no longer fighting a war but a desperate skirmish to save their own prestige. Shortsighted, narrow-minded, and empty-headed politics finds its satisfaction in prestige alone, it is ready to die, just so as to come out of the defeat with some honor, even if that honor is death itself."

Devetakov told them about his stay in France, about the moral and material destitution crushing Europe, about everyone's despair and hatred of fascism and war, about the death camps where millions of innocent men, women, and children were being murdered. Ms. Clara started to cry. Malayi sat next to her, and no less moved himself, he began stroking her hands and speaking to her in Hungarian.

"Forgive me!" Ms. Clara said after getting ahold of herself. Unlike her husband, she spoke Bulgarian like a Bulgarian. She had learned the language alongside her children and in her solitude she had read almost all the books in Devetakov's library. "We've been living like one big family for twenty years now, but we have never spoken about politics, not even about this war. The defeat of the Germans at Stalingrad was a true holiday for us, the greatest cause for celebration we have had since coming to Bulgaria."

"Perhaps your exile will come to an end very soon and you will return to Hungary."

The two of them exchanged surprised glances, murmured something to each other in Hungarian, then Ms. Clara asked: "How did you know we were exiled?"

"From my deceased father."

"And how did he know?"

"From the police, madam. A few days after you arrived at the estate, the police came looking for you. My father took care of the whole business with the district constable, whom he knew, and he struck you from the list of 'undesirables.' My father was not interested in politics, but he was a democrat by conviction and had no love for the monarchy."

That evening Nikolin learned the secret the family had been hiding for many long years. Janos Malayi had just graduated in machine engineering and had started work at a factory in Budapest when he met the famous revolutionary Bela Kun. This happened in 1918. Bela Kun had secretly come back from Russia to take part in the founding of the Hungarian Communist Party. In the following year, a Soviet-style republic was established in the country. Bela Kun was appointed People's Commissar for Foreign Affairs and took on the young engineer as his assistant. The republic lasted only four months. After its defeat, Bela Kun emigrated to Austria, while Malayi was arrested and sentenced to death. His comrades, including a Bulgarian student by the name of Karov, helped him escape from prison. He hid in underground safe houses and communicated only with Karov, whom the authorities did not suspect of being involved in revolutionary activities. He had married Clara a month before the revolution, without her parents' knowledge. Her father was a high-ranking official in the Ministry of Education and flatly refused to allow his daughter to marry the young engineer, whom he knew to be an active communist. Clara had graduated from a French college and her father had plans to marry her off to someone from the highest society. After Malayi's escape from prison, Clara kept in touch with him through Karov and went to see him at the safe houses. Karov managed to arrange for Malayi to flee to Bulgaria with the help of a railroad worker. Clara decided to follow him and started living with him in his underground apartment. Karov found a fake passport for her as well and the three of them left for Bulgaria in a freight car...

Karov was from the Pleven region and took them to his home village. They spent a few months at his house, then they found work for Malayi at a steam-powered mill in another village near Pleven. There, in a shanty by the mill, they lived for almost three years; their son and daughter were born there. The September Uprising broke out in Bulgaria and after it was crushed, the authorities came after Karov. Now they hid him, as he had hidden them in Budapest. He often spent the night with them, and sometimes would stay for several days at a time. One night he told them that he was leaving for the Soviet Union, they said their farewells and never saw or heard from him again. It seems that the police had been keeping him under surveillance and several days after he disappeared, a pair of policemen came asking about him and searched their home. They found no trace of Karov, but their visits grew more and more frequent, the police interrogated them and claimed that very soon they would bring

Karov back to visit them. Thus several months passed, there was no sign of Karov, and the police never brought him back – had he managed to cross the border or had he been killed? Being kept in the dark was agonizing and made them extremely edgy until they finally decided to take a most desperate and foolhardy step, which would give them away to the authorities – they decided to set out and go wherever their path might lead them. One day off they took a stroll with the children down to the railway station which lay half a mile from the village and got on the first train that came through. A man was sitting alone in a compartment, they asked whether they could sit with him and he politely invited them in. The man was the elder Devetakov.

The blizzard was still raging. It was no longer snowing, only a strong wind was blowing, scooping up the snowbanks and turning them into white dust clouds. During the lulls, the air grew clear and only for an instant Nikolin could see how down in the Inferno the white dust cloud would settle and at the next gust of wind would swirl up again like boiling milk, veiling everything before his eyes. His feet were not yet numb with cold, because he was stamping them on a thick layer of fallen leaves, but his fur coat was short and the cold was piercing his thighs. *Mela's got the house all warmed up, when I get back tonight I'll soak my feet in salt water, I'll go to bed and get up tomorrow morning as good as new*, he thought to himself and a sharp pain jabbed through his chest like a knife. *I mustn't think of her, I mustn't think of what happened a few days ago. If I keep going over it in my mind, my heart will give out and I'll collapse here and die under the snow.* With tremendous effort he redirected his imagination back toward his memories of the past, which, thanks to the years, had lost their sharpness and did not cause him any anguish. He had never made sense of these memories as clearly as he did now, while standing blind in that white blizzard, or perhaps it was precisely because of this that he grasped them, because he was blinded and was seeing his past with his spiritual sight. He realized that something unusual had happened to him, as if he was having some intellectual revelation, just as fervent believers at a given moment or hour receive divine enlightenment. Only now, amidst this raging winter storm in some inexplicable way, he suddenly understood and made sense of all the events, words, and conversations between Devetakov and his numerous guests on all sorts of questions, which he had heard, seen, and experienced, but due to his youth and near-illiteracy he could not then understand. Those memories had slumbered in his mind like a seed in the ground throughout the long winter and now they came to life and sprouted from the warmth of his anguish, fresh and clear down to the smallest detail. And thus, thanks to the revelation that had overcome him like a divine blessing on that difficult day, he was able to transport himself back into the past and to alleviate his pain. There was only one event from the past that he didn't understand – why did Devetakov take his own life?

"That man speaks with the sky," Halil Efendi had said when leaving the estate for good.

He was around forty-five years old, broad-shouldered and strapping as a wrestler; he was as wise and fair as he was strict and merciless to lazy and careless workers. He attached lead ballast to the plowshares and if a tractor driver plowed too shallowly or tried to rush through the plowing too quickly, he took him down from the tractor, gave him a good couple of slaps, and threw him off the estate immediately. He dressed like a European, spoke Bulgarian like a Bulgarian, read books, and wrote with his left hand. He kept the estate's ledger using that simplest of folk accounting systems – "give and take" – which consisted of a notebook with hard covers. On the left page he wrote the worker's name and on the right, who had done what and what he was owed, what had been sown and what was produced from the land, what was sold and what was left over, expenses and income from the threshing machine, the livestock, and the fowl. On Saint Dimitar's Day he opened up the notebook and gave every man what he was owed down to the last penny, and after that "a little something extra, from the master," according to the worker's merits – a few pounds of wool, a change of clothes, a bushel or two of grain. This payout was done in front of all the workers, so that no one could complain he had been wronged.

Halil Efendi left the estate because there was no longer any estate. A month after he had come back from abroad, Devetakov donated seventy-five acres of land to the village municipality, leaving only twenty-five for himself. He paid off the servants more than handsomely and let them go. Halil Efendi was the last to leave, because he had to hand over the ledger of accounts to Devetakov. The two men said their goodbyes without shaking hands, Halil Efendi bowed to Devetakov and quickly left the room. Nikolin went to see him out to the front gate and it was then that the Turk said that Devetakov spoke with the sky. Nikolin didn't understand what he meant by these words, and he didn't dare ask, but from his face he could see that he did not pity or reproach Devetakov for giving away his land, and that showed that he didn't consider him mentally deranged, as word in the village had it.

Nikolin didn't think he was deranged either, because his master seemed livelier, more cheerful, and more spiritually sound than ever. Before, Devetakov had worked in the fields with the hired hands, but only for a week or two, and somehow in a lordly way, as if for amusement or, as Nikolin thought, so people wouldn't say he was lazing around in the shade while the common people baked in the heat. Now, however, it seemed he had decided to become a true villager, and the two of them were in the fields from early spring until late autumn. Even though they plowed with a tractor and threshed with a threshing machine, farming twenty-five acres was no small feat for two men, they had a lot of manual work to do, they had two horses, two dozen sheep, and fowl that they had to take care of. Devetakov was baked like a brick from the sun and wind, husky and sprightly as a young man, sociable and affectionate, he had a hearty appetite, and at night he slept soundly and deeply. And so it was until the spring of 1945.

The biggest event during that time was the arrival of the Red Army. They didn't pass through Orlovo, so people from the surrounding villages went to see them in Dobrich. Nikolin went to see them as well, along with Clara and Malayi, Devetakov went too. The previous evening Malayi had come to the house and announced that the Soviets had crossed the Bulgarian border, then he brought Ms. Clara over as well. They were dressed in their holiday best and so excited that they spoke over each other and laughed loudly. Nikolin served dinner and brought out a bottle of wine, they toasted the Red Army, Ms. Clara played the piano, they listened to the news, and in the morning Nikolin drove them to the city. Devetakov's house was on the main street, Ms. Clara and Malayi stayed on the balcony, while Nikolin went down into the street. The troops came on tanks, in trucks and horse-drawn carts, the people blocked their path, everyone was shouting *"Zdravstvuyte, bratushki!"** and giving the soldiers flowers, bread, and wine...

No guests from the city or from Sofia had come to the estate in a year or two, and after the Soviet Army's arrival on September 9, no one came from the village, either. Only Ilko Kralev from Ravna would drop by from time to time to bring back or borrow some books from Devetakov. Two years earlier another young man from the village of Zhitnitsa would come as well – Alexander Pashov, and he and Ilko Kralev often dropped in at the same time. Both were students in Sofia, Pashov was studying medicine, while Kralev was studying law. Pashov would arrive by train, but Ilko Kralev came and went by foot along the highway. During vacations and especially over the holidays their visits would last several days, as Devetakov would not let them leave. The three of them would sit in the room with the books, or if the weather was nice, they would stroll through the fields or sit on a bench in the garden, and they were always talking, always reading some book. Since Pashov had left to go abroad, Ilko had come to the estate on his own. Devetakov was extremely fond of him and had told Nikolin to give Ilko the key to the library in his absence so he could take whatever books he needed. The last time he had come, around the New Year, Ilko had been spitting into a flat tin box which he kept in the pocket of his coat. He and Nikolin were the same age, and upon leaving he said: "Don't be fooled by my well-fed look, mate, I'm rotten on the inside, this consumption is eating away at me like a worm."

But lo and behold, in the spring a guest came to visit them. They had been sowing corn and came back home late in the afternoon. As soon as they entered the yard, a woman came down the steps from the veranda and walked toward them, stepping lightly and somehow stealthily through the wide yard, she greeted and gave her hand to Devetakov. Nikolin recognized her immediately – the wife of Alexander Chilev, a merchant from Sofia. She was every bit as pretty and slender as he had remembered her from several years ago, yet her beauty seemed somehow worn out and sad, while her clothes were simple and dark, as if mourning a loved one.

"Oh, Michel! We shouldn't have to meet this way!" she said, her eyes filling with tears.

Devetakov said nothing, just kissed her hand and led her toward the house, but she continued: "Alexander is in prison. And Lily is not doing well…"

That must be her little daughter, Nikolin thought, and remembered a little girl, dark-eyed and pretty like her mother, who had come to the estate with her parents. She was a curly-haired, rambunctious, and mischievous child, she roamed around the yard and the garden all day, climbing the fences and the trees, and not giving the birds a moment's peace, so her mother had made Nikolin keep an eye on her. He washed up, changed clothes, and went into the parlor. Devetakov and his guest were sitting at the table across from each other, talking. He passed behind them and set about lighting the stove, their visitor didn't seem to notice him. She had propped her chin in one hand and was holding a cigarette in the other. She spoke softly and her voice carried through the room, gentle and sad like the rustling of fall leaves.

"Pork lard is a thousand leva for half a pound and still there's none to be found. Which would be fine if there was cooking oil, but there's none of that, either. If only I were in Sofia, I'd manage somehow, I've got friends and relatives there. Here it's like I'm in hell. Everyone flees from me as if I've got some disease. They're far better off, those women whose husbands are working and earning a little something. Did you know that Elena's here too?"

"Elena who?"

"Sarmashikova. She's been here for ten days, but I only found out yesterday. Looks like she hasn't so much as poked her nose out of doors. That lawyer Malinov's wife told me. I thought he'd come to visit you. He was working on some construction site. Lots of our people have been sent to this region."

The woman fell silent, lost in thought, her pretty face darkened, tears glistened in her eyes. Devetakov was silent as well, and when Nikolin finished with the stove, he told him to prepare dinner.

"We do our own cooking here," he added. "Nikolin is the head chef."

"I'll cook," the woman said, getting up. "Just give me an apron or a towel to put on."

Nikolin led her to the kitchen, gave her a leg of pork and everything else she needed, and asked her if she wanted help, but she told him she would prepare everything herself. He left the kitchen as if banished and went out under the awning to chop wood. *Well, look how far she's fallen, the poor thing*, he thought to himself while chopping wood. *There's no lard, she says, there's no oil, there's no meat, prices are sky-high. But we've got everything here, as much lard and flour and oil and meat as you could want.* He pitied her and felt some kind of superiority over her. This feeling seemed indecent to him and he told himself that he shouldn't be acting "bigheaded" with her, yet at the same time he was pleased to see her cooking for him with her "dainty little white hands." Then he reproached himself again for thinking such a thing about a helpless woman, and again he remembered that of all the women who had come to the estate back then, she was the most pretentious and snobbish, she hadn't known his name and had merely told him: "Hey, boy, go see where my daughter is!"

Guests had come to the estate, most often around the major holidays, all people of means – merchants, neighboring landowners, industry bosses, and scholars. They would take the train to the city or to the station in the village and Nikolin would drive them to the estate in the carriage. When the weather was warm they spent their time outside, eating lunch and dinner on the veranda or in the gazebo in the garden, while in the late afternoon they would go out for a stroll in the fields. In late fall or winter, they stayed in the parlor, where the table was piled high with food and drinks at all hours of the day and night, they would play the radio or the gramophone, bang away on the piano, dance, play games, laugh, and horse around until the wee hours of the morning. Auntie Raina waited on them, but when there were lots of guests, Nikolin would help her. Auntie Raina would set the table and bring food and drinks, while he would bring the full pots from the kitchen, plus pans of *banitsa* or roasted meat. He was always anxious when amidst the guests, especially during those first years, because he instinctively sensed that they felt distrust or contempt for him, he also caught those discreet glances that were exchanged in his presence as a sign that they needed to change or break off their conversation in front of the estate's coachman. Over time, the regular guests and even those like General Sarmashikov and his wife, the Sofia grain trader Chilev and his family, and other high-ranking people got used to him, just as they had gotten used to the rustic simplicity of Devetakov's home, with the iron twin beds, with Auntie Raina's rich dishes, with the homemade pickles and "desserts" of pumpkin with molasses, fried bread, pancakes, rice pudding, and donuts. They jokingly called him "the valet," permitted themselves a certain looseness of tongue, and acted more spontaneously in front of him – as if in front of a person whose job from then on was to be the sole witness to their encounters and conversations, as all servants are; they had fun with his excessive bashfulness, under the pretext that it gave him a certain "charm" of an immaculate village lad. He, of course, found nothing degrading or insulting in the fact that these ladies and gentlemen and even their children looked down on him. Like every man of the people he was exactly proud enough to realize his place with respect to these people, and that was the place of a servant.

The lady did not look at him even now, nor did she say anything to him as he lit the stove, she was working at the kitchen table with her back to him in silence. He went out to do some work in the yard and stayed there until late. When it was dinnertime, he passed by the kitchen and saw that the woman was no longer there and went out to wash his hands. She had left a plateful of food, bread, and a fork on the table, and this showed that Ms. Fanny did not want him upstairs in the dining room. He ate alone and when he went upstairs to his room, he saw the lady and Devetakov having dinner in the parlor, he with his back to and she facing the windows. Her face, illuminated by the lamp, was flushed and smiling, her dark, glittering eyes flashed with sparks of happy excitement, she had changed her clothes and her hairstyle and now looked as young and fresh as a girl. He went to bed, but was restless, some vague alarm was gnawing at him and making him listen closely to the muted music and voices coming from the parlor. When these sounds died down an hour or two later, the door to the parlor clicked shut, and footsteps could be heard along the veranda, he leapt out of bed and pressed his eye to the keyhole. Ms. Fanny and

Devetakov went into his bedroom. Without realizing what he was doing, Nikolin got dressed and tiptoed into the parlor. Amidst the mixed scent of wine, cigarettes, and food, his virginal senses caught that delicate fragrance of perfume, which female guests to the estate left in their wake. He stepped over to the wall separating Devetakov's room from the parlor and listened. He couldn't hear anything but the fast heavy beating of his heart, yet he stood with his ear to the wall as if mesmerized. At one point he thought he heard whispering and stifled laughter, he strained his ears to their utmost and froze. Only the distant sounds of the spring night reached his ears and it was then that he realized that behind the wall was not the bedroom, but Devetakov's library. He went back to his room and lay in bed. Some wild curiosity was tormenting him, he strained his imagination to such an extent trying to guess what that unusual and shameful and mysterious thing was that was happening between the two of them in the bedroom that his head felt heavy and he finally fell asleep at dawn. Around nine o'clock Devetakov woke him and ordered him to take the lady to the station. Ms. Fanny did not say a word the whole way, she sat huddled down in the collar of her coat, looking aside. The train station was only a mile from the estate, but Nikolin drove it at a gallop so as to shorten the awkward ride. The buggy bounced along the uneven highway, the lady's suitcase, stuffed full of food, bounced on her lap, but she kept silent, still looking aside.

Nikolin was not only surprised and disconcerted but also horrified by what had transpired between Ms. Fanny and his master. He had never seen him retire with any of the ladies who had come visiting, nor had he ever heard of him having affairs with women. Devetakov's sleeping with Ms. Fanny awakened in Nikolin not only subconscious feelings he had never before experienced, but also an aching jealousy, as he had gotten so used to the thought of his master as a pure and uncorrupted person who belonged only to him and who would never share his life with another.

He was afraid that the lady would come back again and was very alarmed a dozen days later when he heard Devetakov speaking to a woman on the veranda. He took her for Ms. Fanny and was about to turn around, but the woman looked at him and said, her face a mask of wonder and fright: "Michel, who is this character?"

"It's Nikolin, Mishona darling! Have you forgotten him?"

"Oh, Nicky, my dearest Nicky, is that you?" She laughed with her wide, bright-red mouth that stretched nearly to her ears, rushed toward him, and pinched his cheek with her sharp nails. Nikolin drew back, flustered, but she flung herself at him, threw her arms around his neck, and pressed his face to hers. "How hulking and frightening you've become, Nicky!"

"Mishona, leave the boy alone!" Devetakov said, taking her suitcase to the guest room. "Come on in!"

"Nicky, you've forgotten me, sweetie! Don't you remember Mishona?"

"I remember you, how could I not?" Nikolin said.

Up until a few years ago, she, too, had come visiting, but not alone, always with the Chilevs or the Sarmashikovs. Back then she looked younger and fresher, but she was still every bit as lean and thin-waisted. Once General Sarmashikov had brought a colonel to the estate who got very drunk and wanted to strip Mishona naked in front of everyone. She slapped him across the face, the colonel got angry and began cussing her out. Mishona, not to be outdone, let fly at him such a foul curse that everyone burst out laughing, the colonel burst out laughing too, and the whole row died down. Still not rested from her journey, she, like Ms. Fanny, immediately set about cooking. She herself came looking for him in the yard, asked for wood and went into the kitchen. *These women, they're hungry as bitches*, Nikolin thought to himself as he brought the wood, *before they didn't even know where the kitchen was, but now you can't get them out of there.* He gave her the ingredients and was about to leave when she stopped him.

"You'll stay here with me while I'm cooking! Sit down right over there, in that chair!"

Nikolin sat down at the table, took a knife, and started chopping an onion, while she sliced the meat. She worked quickly and skillfully like a seasoned cook.

"Why so silent, why don't you talk to me?"

"What have I got to talk to you about, ma'am!" Nikolin said.

"Everything. I don't like quiet people. But you're so sweet, I could just eat you alive."

Nikolin blushed and got up to leave, but she grabbed his hand and pulled him back to his chair.

"Stay here with me, dearie, otherwise I'll be mad at you!" And then, suddenly seeming sad, she fell silent, lost in thought, and then asked him: "Do you smoke?"

"No."

"Then I'll light up."

She pulled a small metal cigarette case out of the pocket of her skirt, took a cigarette, and handed a match to Nikolin.

"Give me a light, you are a gentleman, right? Come on!"

Nikolin hesitated, as if it were shameful to give a light to a woman who smoked, then he struck the match and brought it to her mouth. Mishona pulled her chair next to his and crossed her legs.

"Okay, now tell me all about it!" she said, taking a drag on the cigarette, making a little ring of smoke and watching it rise upward and disperse, then she broke into a grin.

"Tell you all about what?"

"About Ms. Fanny."

Nikolin turned away.

"Did she sleep with Devetakov? Come on, tell me!"

"How should I know?"

"Come on now, Nicky, look me in the eye, look at me!"

She grabbed his face in both her hands and turned it toward her. Niko-lin pulled away, but she locked her hands behind his head and wouldn't let go. Sweat rolled down his back from shame and fear that Devetakov might come in and find them like this, her hanging on his neck, breathing in his face with her big smiling mouth and fawning all over him.

"Tell me now, did Devetakov and Fanny sleep together?"

"They did…"

"And did you sleep that night? Not with her, but in general, did you sleep at all that night?"

"I slept, what else would I be doing?"

Mishona laughed loudly and bent over double.

"You're lying, you're lying, you didn't sleep a wink!" she was saying through her laughter, hardly able to catch her breath. "You must've been listening through the wall, huh? Tell me, did you listen in on them?"

Nikolin blushed and again tried to pull away, but she locked her hands even more tightly around his neck.

"Well, why didn't you ask to sleep with her too, Nicky? She would've said yes. That's how she is, that's why she came to see Devetakov. Only yesterday Mrs. Chileva had her nose in the air, and now she's going around like a whore sleeping with men for a loaf of bread and a pound of lard. No more money for her, no more spas abroad, no more car, no more big business deals with the Germans. It's all over, and to top it all off, they tossed Mr. Chilev in the clink. But they better be happy with that, because they could've sent him into the hereafter. So ask her, Nicky, just ask her! Aren't you a man, what are you blushing for! Listen, Nicky, listen, sweet-heart! One of these days a general's wife will show up here. You know her – Sarmashikova. You've got to get your hands on her no matter what. She'll do it for a pound of flour. You'll be doing my heart a whole heap of good, I tell you. She's been in the city, too, 'on vacation' for a week now, because they sent the general to keep Chilev company. She's pretty, too, that general's wife – I'd be willing to bet you'll like her more than Fanny. If you have her once, it's enough to last you a lifetime. She'll be happy, too, and she'll come running to you every day. Don't pity her, because she's never pitied anyone. She's spent her whole life trampling weaker folks."

While saying this, Mishona was gently stroking his bristly chin, while he sat there as if paralyzed, wondering why on earth he was letting this woman touch his face and at the same time experiencing a dual feeling of shame and pleasure at her closeness. She pulled her hand away, lit up another cigarette, and fell silent. The pot started boiling, steam was rising, the smell of food filled the room, in the stove the fire was crackling. The setting sun hid behind a cloud, the kitchen grew dim, and darkness lurked in the corners. Smoke from Mishona's cigarette rose straight up, then curled and crept along the ceiling like thin white fog. Mishona's face grew long and pale, her lips trembled like a child's, and she seemed to be trying not to cry, but the tears gushed from her eyes and ran down her cheeks. Nikolin felt uncomfortable, he turned his head aside and started to get up, but she again grasped his hand.

"Why do you want to get up? Because I'm crying? No, I'm not crying," she said, smiling through her tears. "The poor little thing, he feels ashamed to see me crying. You're so good and pure-hearted! You won't have an easy time of it in this life. But who knows, maybe you'll get lucky… I just remembered something and it made me sad. I remembered sitting with my grandmother in the kitchen one spring evening. I was holding yarn in both my hands and my grandma was winding it into a ball. Just like now, the kitchen was growing dark, the windowpanes turned bluish, the fire blazed brighter in the mouth of the stove… What I wouldn't give to go back to the village, to sit with Grandma by her stove!"

Mishona told him all about her childhood, and then her whole life story. She seemed lost in some sort of reverie, and Nikolin could see that she was not telling it to him, but to herself – in that way a person confesses with a pure heart and a pure soul. Her story was rambling and confused like a dream, and later, when Nikolin thought about her, he could only remember a few separate incidents from her life. She had graduated from high school in her small hometown, and since she didn't have the money to study at the university, she started working at a trading firm in the regional capital. The owner of the firm had a son, they fell in love, and she got pregnant. When the elder Goranov (that was the father's name) found out, he gave her two months to get rid of the child and she did, but she told him she wanted to keep the child and raise it on her own. The old man was frantic and one evening he came to her apartment. While the landlady was opening the door, Mishona managed to wind a sheet around her middle and showed him into her room, pretending to be pregnant. She knew he would never accept her as a daughter-in-law, so she decided to torment him to the extreme. The old man all but fell on his knees in front of her, begging her to go to some other city and have the baby there, he promised to give her money that would allow her to live in the lap of luxury, he promised to will the child money or some property. She refused. Then the old man set a whole pile of money on the table and advised her to think it over one more time. If she did what he asked of her, she could keep the money for herself; if not, she should return it to him. At first, she was tempted by the money and decided to keep it, go to Sofia, and enroll in the university. The next moment, however, fury seized her, such intense fury that she didn't even know what she was doing. She put the money in a shopping bag and decided to take it to the trader's home that very minute. Not only to return it, but to throw it in his face on the doorstep and then leave. She put on an old dress, covered her face with a scarf up to her eyes, and went out. She had only gone a block when she saw the elder Goranov turning down the main street. The main street was the city "promenade" and at that time of day it was always teeming with people.

Right in front of a restaurant two men stopped Goranov and started chatting with him. Mishona stood in front of a shopwindow and recognized the two men, they were traders like Goranov. And then she got the idea of throwing the money in his face right there and then, on the street, in front of his colleagues and the whole city. She ripped the paper bands holding the wads of bills together, stirred them up in the bag and walked over to the three men. Disguising her voice, she said she had something to give to Mr. Goranov, but he didn't hear her over the noise of the crowd, while the other took her for a beggar and pushed her away. She stepped even closer, pulled a wad of bills out of the bag and threw them in Goranov's face, but he turned aside. The other two men looked at her, stunned. Then she threw another handful of bills in his face, then another and another, until her fingers reached the bottom of the bag. She slipped into the crowd and hid in an entryway, pulled the scarf from her face, and stood on the opposite sidewalk watching the scene that unfolded. The crowd had formed a ring around the three men and was gathering up the money scattered at their feet. They were trying to get out of the ring, yelling, frightening, but the whole of the promenade came swooping down on them like an avalanche, squeezing between their legs, pushing them, crushing them. Men and women were rolling around, screaming, suffocating, fighting, and if someone managed to grab some bill, the others threw themselves on him to take it or shoved him out of the crowd. A squadron of policemen arrived, but when they saw the scattered money, they, too, hurled themselves into the fray to collect it, making the chaos even more complete. The crowd finally scattered around midnight and then Mishona saw the elder Goranov lying on the sidewalk as if dead. The police picked him up and took him to the hospital.

When she got home to her apartment, Mishona saw that some money was left in the bag. She counted it – around fifty thousand – and she was amazed that Goranov, who really was filthy rich, would have paid such a high price to hide a bastard grandchild from society. She thought she had thrown all the money, but since there was still fifty thousand left, that meant Goranov must have given her no less than two hundred thousand. She left for Sofia the next day, checked into a hotel, and went to Chilev's trading bureau. She knew the address of many trading firms with which she had corresponded, but she went to Chilev, since his office was closest to her hotel. Chilev was a wholesale trader, an exporter of grain, leather, and wood, he had business ties to Goranov and had frequently come to his office. She told him she had quit her job a month earlier and come to Sofia to study at the university, but since she didn't have enough funds, she was looking for a job to help support her studies. Chilev recommended her to a relative of his who hired her, she found an apartment and so started living in Sofia.

The provincial newspapers, and later those in the capital city as well, wrote for a long time about the bloody brawl on the main street of that regional city with ever greater details, but the name of the woman who had thrown three hundred thousand leva (later it became half a million) in Goranov's face was never mentioned, since no one had recognized her. Goranov was in the hospital with multiple fractures, fighting for his life, but he remained silent, afraid of bringing scandal upon his family and his firm. Just as earlier, Chilev went on business trips to visit the younger Goranov, who now was heading his father's firm, and from the local business circles there he learned that Mishona had had intimate relations with the younger Goranov which were cut off suddenly and she had left the firm. Chilev frequently stopped by to see her, treated her very kindly, and one evening invited her to his home for dinner. She accepted his invitation and there at his place she met the Sarmashikovs. From the conversations about the Goranov incident, she guessed that the attention being lavished on a poor secretary like herself was due to their curiosity not so much to find out more details about the scandal, but to understand how that woman could have thrown so much money onto the street and where she had gotten it. They weren't particularly interested in the woman herself, since they were almost certain it was Mishona. Their suspicions were wholly confirmed when she invited them over in turn and they saw that she lived in a luxurious apartment in the center of town, something a simple secretary could never afford in any case, unless she was rich, and not simply rich, but a millionaire, since, in a fit of rage, bitterness, or vengeance, she had thrown half a million leva into the street. Thus, she started playing the role of the millionaire heiress, and when they asked her how she knew French (she had conducted Goranov's correspondence with foreign firms in French), she replied that her aunt had graduated from some college in France and had adopted her, and she had started studying the language with her. After her aunt's death, she had taken private lessons, or so she said. She also said that she was descended from an old but poor family, but had recently received a humble inheritance from her grandfather, which allowed her to rent a slightly more spacious and comfortable apartment.

The next year, Ms. Fanny and the general's wife Sarmashikova went to Paris without their husbands and invited her to serve as their translator. By chance they met Mihail Devetakov, who was in his last year of studies there. He showed them the sights of Paris, stopped by the hotel almost every day to see them, and so they grew close. They invited him to visit them in Sofia and he did. Every time he left for or returned from abroad, he would stay for a few days either with one family or the other, he even stayed at Mishona's place. Later, they, too, started going to visit him once or twice a year, and always together. For Chilev, this friendship with Devetakov was profitable, because he bought grain from him and, through him, from other landowners, while the general took care of one of his army duties with these visits – he was an inspector for the military units in the region.

The two families' benevolence toward Mishona was not selfless. For one, they considered her very rich, and what's more, Chilev and the general began visiting her on their own, unofficially. At first she was flattered by this attention, but when they started bringing her little gifts and courting her, she realized they had made a friendly pact to share her. She acted as if she had not guessed their intentions, and this just seemed to inflame them all the more. She nevertheless managed to deflect their lustful exertions, yet her provincial naïveté made her feel indebted to them for their generous adulation. They took advantage of this and as a sort of consolation for their wasted efforts to seduce her, they asked her – first Chilev, then General Sarmashikov – to let them use one of her rooms when needed and she agreed. But their wives had also asked her for the same favor. Ms. Fanny, after swearing to Mishona her truest friendship to the grave, asked her to let her use one of her rooms for a very important confidential conversation with a girlfriend, with whom, for a number of particular reasons, she could not meet elsewhere. Later, the general's wife, too, had a similar conversation with a girlfriend in the same room. Her apartment had a separate entrance onto the street and turned out to be very well suited for confidential conversations. And so she became a procuress for both families. They introduced her into so-called high society and she was forced to conform to the manners of this society. She lived in grand style, organizing lavish dinners at her home, dressed in the most elegant fashions, went abroad every year, and did not deprive herself of any luxuries. She had lovers, too, as was fitting for a woman in high society, even though she could have married well. Her longest affair was with a young and very talented lawyer. She acted as his patron, as he was still at the very start of a brilliant career. She was ready to marry him, but he, precisely because he was a very talented lawyer, managed to make very good use of her patronage and to dump her after he found out via channels known only to very talented lawyers that she was no millionaire at all, but simply a not particularly chaste provincial girl ("Alas, he was right about that," Mishona admitted) obsessed by some plebian mania for living like an aristocrat, and thus had lost her moral bearings due to her lack of an intuitive sense for a world from which she had taken only what was superficial and tawdry ("That was true, too!" Mishona confirmed). The young and talented lawyer told her this with cynical frankness not out of moral considerations, but because he knew that she, after refusing to invest her money in any profitable enterprise whatsoever, always hampered by her plebian fear of entering the lupine world of business deals, had only enough funds on hand so as not to fall into abject poverty. The two families found this out and did not hide their contempt for her, yet they could not possibly ostracize her from their circles, as she was their procuress and rival. She was every bit as contemptuous toward them, yet she stuck to them like glue so as to savor their fall and to justify and make her own fall somewhat easier to stomach. Only one person from their numerous acquaintances was worthy of respect – Mihail Devetakov. He was so intelligent, noble, and morally superior that even they, depraved women that they were, fell under the spell of his charm and fought between themselves a secret rivalry to earn his esteem, even though they did not feel worthy of such esteem...

The lid of the pot was jumping from the pressure of the steam, droplets were running down it, falling on the firebrands and hissing. Mishona fell silent, listening. She had had her eyes shut the whole time and when she saw Nikolin next to her, she seemed startled and jumped up off the chair. Then she laughed and lifted the lid of the pot.

"The food is ready! Let's have dinner!"

"You two go ahead and eat, I've got some work to do," Nikolin said.

"You don't have any work to do at this hour, darling! We'll have dinner together. Help me take everything upstairs and set the table. You are the head chef, aren't you?"

After dinner, they stayed at the table, listened to the radio and talked about many things. The whole time Nikolin could not shake off the nagging thought of where Mishona would sleep – in a separate room or with Devetakov, and whether he would accept her, after he had slept with Ms. Fanny. When the last news bulletin on the radio finished, Devetakov said "good night" and went to his bedroom. Nikolin wanted to help Mishona clear the table, but she told him to go to bed and so he did. The moon dangled right in front of the window as if hung there and filled his room with a white, ghostly light. From the parlor he could hear the clinking of plates, he also heard Mishona's footsteps on the wooden floor and he followed her movements anxiously. She went into the neighboring room, which was connected to the parlor, put wood in the stove, then he could hear her footsteps by the wall where the bed was, and then there was silence in the house. Nikolin calmed down, but not ten minutes had passed when the door to his room opened slowly, and cautiously, Mishona came in and silently made her way toward his bed. She was in her nightgown, her hair was swept up in a bun, which made her neck look as thin and delicate as a doe's. Her nightgown was low-cut and her breasts, bluish white like milk, were partially exposed. She walked like a ghost, smiling and bending slightly forward, she sat down on the bed and touched his face. Nikolin lay there as if paralyzed, not daring to breathe, while she slipped her hand down his shirt and dug her fingers into the bristly hair on his chest. Her hand was hot as tongs, her face radiated the dizzying scent of cigarettes and perfume. Nikolin got ahold of himself and retreated to the other end of the bed.

"Where are you running to, dummy?" she whispered, moving next to him. "You can't think I'm going to sleep with you! I just came to show myself to you, to let you touch a woman, so you don't die wondering." She took his hand, placed it on her breasts, and Nikolin felt something warm and soft as jelly in his palm. "Touch me, darling! Come on, Nicky, touch me!" she said, leaning ever closer to his face, warming it with her breath, but he had clenched his hands into such tight fists that no power on earth could have opened them. Then she whispered something dirty in his ear, took off her nightgown and was naked. Nikolin closed his eyes, but she dived under the covers and pressed herself to his body like a leech. She stayed next to him for only a minute or two, but touched him everywhere most shamelessly, then put on her nightgown and left.

Nikolin was afraid she would come back, so he leapt out of bed and locked the door. He didn't hear any noise out on the veranda, but he stood by the door, ready to hold it shut with his shoulder if Mishona tried to come back in. Only when he heard her go to bed behind the wall did he lie back down too, pulling the covers up over his head.

"Nicky, I'm begging you, don't think badly of me!" she said the next day as he was driving her to the station. "I'm sorry I joked around with you like that. You won't think badly of me, will you? Promise me!"

"I won't," Nikolin said, but was on his guard in case she tried to play some other joke on him.

On his way back home, and over the following days, he thought only of her, wondering what kind of person she was and not being able to come up with an answer. He remembered how even years ago she had teased him: "What a wild sort of handsomeness that boy has!" she would say, and invite him to dance, while he, wishing the earth would swallow him up from shame, would run outside, hounded by the guests' laughter. He didn't know where she was from, why she was called Mishona, whether she was married or not, just as he didn't understand whether she was just making sport of him or really wanted to draw him closer. Now that he knew how much she had been through in her life, he thought that she had a good and compassionate heart and wasn't haughty like the other women, but he felt some instinctive fear of her, the same fear village men feel toward loose city women.

Soon after Mishona left, Mrs. Sarmashikova – or Madame General, as they once had called her – arrived in a cart from the village. That morning Devetakov had left for Varna and hadn't said how many days he would stay there. Madame General stopped in the yard hesitantly, then went into the house and set her oilcloth shopping bag on the chair. After that, everything unfolded as it had with the other visitors. She also asked for ingredients to make dinner, he gave her what she needed, showed her which utensils and pots and pans were in which cupboards, and went about his work in the yard. Of all the women who had come to visit the estate, Madame General was the least talkative and somehow indifferent toward the others. Her thoughts seemed to be far away and only from her faint, almost imperceptible smile could you see that she was listening to and following what was being said around her. Nikolin had never exchanged a word with her, but she struck him as the most pleasant of them, he loved looking at her and hearing her deep, sonorous voice. She was at that ripe age when women tend to plumpness and become rounded, but not only does this not detract from their beauty, it gives them a particular appeal. The previous guests had said that she would come to the estate without fail, and Nikolin had secretly been waiting for her with an excitement that he could not explain. Mishona had turned his chasteness upside down and awakened in him an attraction to a woman, and that woman was Madame General. When he remembered how Mishona had come to his bed that night, her image in some inexplicable way turned into Madame General and she would tell him: "Come on, touch me!" He dreamed shameful, agonizingly delicious dreams of closeness with many of the women he knew, he even dreamed of the deceased cook, Auntie Raina, who was sitting on a chair in the kitchen, lifting the skirt of her dress to her thighs and telling him: "Look here, my boy, look what I've got up under here!" She and all the other women with whom he committed such unbridled and shameful fornication had the face, voice, and body of Madame

General, he sank into her incorporeal flesh as if into an abyss, only to awaken exhausted and swimming in the sticky wetness of pollution.

He assumed that Madame General, like Ms. Fanny, would not invite him to dinner but would leave his food in the kitchen, so his heart skipped a beat when she called him by name from the veranda. He quickly washed up and went upstairs, his knees shaking and slightly out of breath. Madame General had set the table and was waiting for him. She pointed at the chair across from her and said: *"Bon appétit!"*

"Thanks, same to you!" Nikolin replied.

Madame General handled her silverware daintily and quietly, she lifted the fork slowly toward her mouth and chewed just as slowly with her mouth closed. Nikolin was nervous, he ate as slowly as she did and did not even taste the food. As he had noticed earlier, her thoughts were far away and she was staring at some point in space in front of her. From time to time he dared to glance at her generous, rounded breasts, which welled up beneath the light-blue fabric of her dress, at her face with its slightly prominent, dark cheekbones, and the dark circles beneath her eyes, which made them even larger and deeper, her dark hair gathered at the nape of her neck in a clasp with a silver pin. At every noise outside, she stopped eating and pricked up her ears, and for the first time since he had been living with Devetakov, Nikolin hoped that he wouldn't come home that night. Madame General glanced at the little watch on her wrist and said: "Michel won't be coming back tonight. The evening train has come and gone." She wiped her lips with her napkin and sat back in her chair.

"Wait, I forgot to get wine," Nikolin said, to keep her longer at the table, but she said she didn't drink. "I don't drink either, but I just thought because of the guest…"

Nevertheless, when Madame General began clearing the table, he went down to the storeroom beneath the barn and drank half a bottle of wine in a single gulp. His face blazed up immediately, and his head felt pleasantly dazed. He went back to the house but didn't find Madame General in the parlor. He thought she'd gone outside, so he sat down to wait for her. Not imagining that she would have gone to bed without telling him, he went to the door of the room where she had once slept with her husband during their visits, grabbed the knob and turned it, but the door was locked from the inside.

"What is it?" Madame General called.

"Uh, nothing... I was just wondering where you were..."

"I've already gone to bed."

He stood in front of the door, tempted to say something more to her, but then he felt ashamed and went to his room as if duped. His only hope was that Madame General would come looking for him the next day, asking for food to take back to the city. Mishona had told him that she, like Chileva, had been forcibly resettled from Sofia and was hungry and wouldn't leave empty-handed. But in the morning Devetakov came back, filled her bag with food, and Nikolin drove her to the train station.

And so it was the whole summer. The three women would come, spend a day and night there, and go home with their suitcases full, without ever running into each other as if by mutual agreement. But "that quiet thing" had again settled in Devetakov's soul. The three women, it seemed, were familiar with this state of his from before or simply pretended that they didn't notice it, and were not offended that he wasn't as attentive and polite with them as before and didn't even greet them or see them off, spending all day in his room or walking around the garden, withdrawn and indifferent to everything and everyone.

One day, who knows how or why, the three of them all arrived, first Mishona on the morning train, then Ms. Fanny and Madame General on the afternoon one. That day Nikolin was out working in the fields and came back in the late afternoon. The visitors were sitting in the gazebo in front of the house. Mishona met him in the yard and made him come sit with them. As soon as he sat down he realized that the visitors were not in a good mood, not only because they had crossed paths and they couldn't stand each other, but also because they'd had an argument. Their faces were drained by that paleness which drains ladies' faces when they are furious and have to keep their temper. All around it was quiet and cool as befitted the sunset after a sweltering day, a light, translucent darkness crept up from the fields. At one point, Ms. Fanny said out of nowhere: "Nikolin, please bring me a glass of water!"

"No," Mishona cried, grabbing him by the arm. "Don't you dare move! Her throat is dry from spewing spite, let her go drink water in the kitchen."

"Don't make a fool of yourself in front of the man, you shameless hussy!" Ms. Fanny said quietly, getting up from the bench.

Mishona broke into ringing, malicious laughter.

"What, is anyone a more shameless hussy than you? Don't you make a living by…" Here she said something vulgar, which made Nikolin bow his head. "Back in the day, you cuckolded Chilev for fun, now you do it out of necessity."

"Scum! You spend your whole life eating our scraps, and now…"

"'Cause you priced me out of the market." Mishona clicked a crude military cigarette lighter made of a cartridge case and lit up a cigarette. "I'll tear you to pieces if I have to, but I'm never letting you set foot here again. Earn your keep somewhere else! You're still healthy, you'll still last through plenty of men…"

"Shut up!" Madame General couldn't take any more. "Why are you fighting, why are you talking such nonsense!"

"My utmost respects to you, Madame General!" Mishona turned to her. "I beg your pardon. Stay calm, my dear! If you're in a bad mood, you won't truly be pleasing to Nicky. Isn't that right, Nicky? You don't like sulky women in your bed."

"You worthless trash! I spit in your ugly face!" Ms. Fanny said, and spit in Mishona's face.

Mishona jumped forward and gave her such a slap in the face that

Ms. Fanny shrieked and staggered backward. Madame General grasped her by the hand and the two of them went inside the house. Nikolin stood as if paralyzed, not knowing what to do.

"Don't you give them even an ounce of food!" Mishona told him. "They stuffed themselves on other people's pain back in the day, now let them earn their own daily bread. Don't you even drive them to the station, if they go to leave. Let them go on foot!"

But that very evening Nikolin drove them to the station and gave them a trunk of food "for the trip" to share between them. Very early the next morning he drove Mishona to the station, too, and gave her a suitcase full of food.

"Forget last night's brawl, Nicky!" she said as they parted, bursting into tears. "That's what we are, bitches. Three hungry, low-down bitches."

Those were her final words, he never saw or heard from her again. Devetakov killed himself only a few days after their departure. No one from the village came to his funeral besides the ancient Grandpa Stavri, the late cook Auntie Raina's husband. The four of them buried him under the old walnut tree at the far end of the garden – Nikolin, Grandpa Stavri, Malayi, and Ms. Clara. A few days later he and Malayi were called into town, to the notary public. The dead man had left a will, the notary opened it and read it. Devetakov had willed the twenty-five acres and the house to Nikolin, the threshing machine and the tractor to Malayi, and his library to Ilko Kralev from Ravna. That very same minute Malayi signed over the threshing machine and the tractor to the village. A week later he and Ms. Clara left for Sofia, where their son and daughter were, and from there – for Hungary. A car came from the city to pick them up. Malayi hugged Nikolin, and Ms. Clara kissed his forehead and started to cry. That's how he remembered her – with tears in her merry, blue, girlish eyes. They organized a demonstration, gave speeches, and the whole village saw them off triumphantly, since they were communist emigrants

and the Hungarian government had requested their return from the Bulgarian government.

Nikolin was left completely alone. No one came looking for him for
any reason, while he had no one to visit. During the day he worked in the
yard or in the fields and didn't feel so lonely because he could see people
in the fields and on the roads, but the nights were unbearable. The dead
man's ghost hovered around him, Nikolin dreamed of him every night,
while during the days Devetakov himself seemed to be in the room and
he kept waiting for him to step out onto the veranda. Before he realized it,
Madame General also began appearing in his dreams. She would be sitting
across the table from him, she would reach over the plates, take his hand
in hers, and tickle his palm with her fingers with an expectant, seductive
smile, the table would split in two, she would come closer and closer to
him, pressing him to her breasts. Other times he would be carrying her in
his arms just as the Hungarian had carried his wife, or else she would slip
naked into his bed and scorch his ear with her breath: "Come on, touch
me, aren't you a man?" while Devetakov would be sitting by the stove,
he would raise his eyes from his book with a sad smile, shaking his head:
"Oh, Nikolin, Nikolin, so this is who you really are?" After such deliciously
agonizing dreams Nikolin would think of Devetakov as if alive and would
suffer pangs of conscience that he had profaned his master's memory. He
would go to his grave and pray for forgiveness with his whole heart and
soul: "This grass still hasn't grown over your grave, Uncle Mihail, and this
is how I, miserable ingrate that I am, repay you for putting your hand on
my shoulder and becoming my mother and father. You didn't sleep with
Ms. Fanny that night, Mishona herself told me how pure your soul is, and
I know it, too, since you never sullied yourself with a woman before my
eyes, and now I'm defiling your precious memory by dreaming of you
with a woman. My whole mind and soul rails against these dreams, but
they keep coming to me when I'm fast asleep, they stalk me and swoop

down on me like a band of thieves. I won't sleep at night, I'll sleep only during the day so I won't dream!"

After making this vow, he didn't sleep for several nights. He pounded sunflower seeds from the heads, chopped wood, and did all sorts of tasks that could be done on moonlit nights, then in the morning he would go out to the fields. On the fourth night, when he could no longer fight off sleep, he lay down in the bare wooden bed of the cart so as not to sleep soundly, he also tied the dog to the wheel to awaken him with its barking. But Madame General appeared again. The dog sensed her and began barking fiercely at her, but she wasn't afraid, she was smiling as she stepped toward the cart. The dog jumped at her, biting her dress and tearing it to pieces, but she just stood there smiling until all her clothes had been torn off and she was left in her nightgown. She got into the cart and lay down next to him, while the frenzied dog kept trying to bite her. Nikolin kicked it in its bared teeth and then saw that it wasn't the dog, but Devetakov, who was holding his injured head and sobbing. No matter how vigilantly he stayed awake, no matter how much he tormented himself for nights at a time, as soon as exhaustion got the better of him and he closed his eyes, Madame General would come to him out of the blue and take him in her affectionate arms. And so it was until one day she appeared to him when he was wide awake. She had heard of Devetakov's death only the day before and had hurried there to see what Nikolin was doing, how he was managing all alone in that big house.

"Good Lord, how thin you are, as if you haven't eaten in a month!" she said. "The dead are the dead, the living must go on living. You're young, you've got your life ahead of you, don't think about the dead."

She spoke and looked at him as if Devetakov's death hadn't made a particularly strong impression on her and she had come to the estate only out of concern for him, to help him if he needed a woman to lend a hand, and to dispel his loneliness. She was not wearing any signs of mourning, while in the expression on her face, in her eyes, in the softness of her sonorous voice, Nikolin sensed a cheerfulness in which he caught a hint of sympathy and a desire to comfort him, as one would comfort a loved one going through hard times. And that wild and shameful passion that pushed him so recklessly toward this woman again overcame him in full force and he forgot the spiritual torments they had caused him in his dreams. He had always assumed and believed that his attraction toward her was as indecent as it was pointless, since a general's wife would never permit herself intimacy with a person like himself, but now he had a certain premonition that she would allow just such intimacy. From experience he knew that first she would set to cooking, so he suggested that they both go down to the storeroom together for supplies. They went into the barn, he lifted a trapdoor with a metal ring, revealing wooden stairs beneath it. He lit a lantern, climbed down the stairs, then shouted up: "Come on, climb down!"

"Give me your hand, I can't see anything!" she said. He gave her his free hand, she stepped on the ground and tottered, clutching at him to steady herself and in so doing embraced him such that her chest pushed him back. The embrace lasted only a moment, she gave an affected shriek and let him go. "Oof, I almost lost my footing! But what if someone closes the trapdoor from above and leaves, what will we do down here in this cellar?"

She was talking and giggling flirtatiously like a young girl, just as in his dreams, and Nikolin expected her to reach out and stroke his face, but she was looking at the tins lining the walls and reflecting the light of the lantern.

"What are those?"

"Those two are full of lard, the other two are full of cooking oil." Nikolin took a step forward and the lantern light revealed what other foodstuffs were there: braids of onions and garlic, potatoes, an earthenware jar of rice, smoked pork legs, a chest full of flour, crates full of all sorts of beverages, while from the ceiling two rows of flat sausages hung from poles. Madame General's hand shot toward them like an arrow, took down a sausage, and the next moment her cheeks puffed out like fists. Nikolin was aghast by the ravenous glint in her eyes, which also lights up the eyes of starving dogs when they find a scrap of meat and swallow it without chewing, growling with satisfaction. Madame General was also swallowing the sausage without bothering to chew, a voluptuous growl was coming from her throat. Once she had devoured half the sausage, she choked, coughed, and only then seemed to notice that she was not alone.

"Have a bite, Nikolin!" She tried to put the half-eaten sausage in his mouth, convulsed with affected, forced laughter. "It's really delicious, but so spicy that I choked."

Nikolin took an empty crate and started putting food into it. He could see that Madame General was ashamed and was trying to cover up her faux pas, but at the same time he could tell that she hated him. He, too, felt ashamed for allowing himself to tempt a starving woman, just as hunters lure hungry game into their traps with bait. As soon as he had invited her down to the storeroom with him, where outsiders had never set foot, his conscience jumped as if stung: "You want to show her how much food you have, to lure her into coming again!" But this inner voice calling from the depths of his conscience was so weak and uncertain that his passion had drowned it out. During lunch Madame General was cheerful and chatty as never before. She was sipping the French wine she had taken from the storeroom and was smiling at him, her face flushed like a peach, asking him what she should do – go home that afternoon or stay till the next morning?

"Do what you like," Nikolin said. "I'll leave you the key to lock up the house, because I've got to go to the village and I don't know if I'll be back by tomorrow. My sister is sick and my brother-in-law came here yesterday to call me to her."

"You don't like my company, I can see it," Madame General said. "Give me your hand and admit it!" She reached across the table and, just as in his dreams, took his hand in hers. "If you're enjoying my company, you'll put off going until tomorrow and I'll stay here tonight. Look what a fine time the two of us are having, because we are both lonely." Her hand was cold as ice, her face had gone from pink to white, and her smile had turned to a grimace, as if she was desperately trying to suppress some sharp pain. Nikolin could see she wasn't herself and, not knowing what to do, pulled his hand away from hers and got up, while she put her head down on the table and whispered: "Good God, how far do I have to... No, you don't like my company, admit it!"

"Of course I like your company!" Nikolin said. "But I've got to go. Since they've come to call me, that means my sister is really sick. The next time you come, you'll stay the night and we'll have a nice chat."

Madame General lifted her head and looked at him, smiling. "God almighty, the wine has gone to my head. Forgive me, Nikolin!"

"There's nothing to forgive you for," Nikolin replied. "The wine went straight to your head, that's exactly the reason I don't drink it. Now I'll go get a little something for you for the road, as we need to get going."

It pained him to lie about his sister, but it pained him even more to watch her trying with all her might to suppress her dignity and pride so as to steel herself for this most desperate act. *And all of that just for a loaf of bread*, he thought to himself on the way back home, after he had driven her to the station with a bag full of food, as always. *Just a year ago she was a general's wife, now she's homeless and penniless, what must she be going through to come here to beg from a servant like me! How much agony must it have cost her to play up to me just for a pound of potatoes or a sack of beans! She hates me and is disgusted with me, and with good reason.* This is what Nikolin was thinking, repulsed by his own lustful desire for this wretched woman, who had fallen from life's highest rung to its lowest, but during the night he once again dreamed of her legs, as he had seen them on the ladder in the storeroom. They had come down rung by rung, rounded and pink in the lantern light, he could not resist the temptation, with a finger he stroked the smooth, warm skin and then he heard her laughter above his head. She was laughing loudly in two voices, one deep and sonorous, the other thin and faltering, and these voices turned into an anxious dog's barking. Frightened, he woke up. The two dogs were barking at someone over near Malayi's house. He jumped down from the cart where he had been sleeping and headed in that direction. The night was as light as day, he could see the dogs lunging at the fence of the deserted house. Someone yelled at him to stop and Nikolin could see the intruder in the shadow of the house. He stopped by the fence and asked who was setting the dogs off at that hour of the night and what they were doing there.

"I'll tell you what I'm doing, you kulak's bootlicker!" the man shouted. "If you take one step closer, I'll blow you away! Get the hell out of here!"

Nikolin was not frightened and stepped toward the dark side of the house to see the intruder up close and then a shot rang out and the bullet whizzed right over his head. He stepped back, calmed the dogs, went back into the yard, and from there watched two men empty out Malayi's house and load everything into a cart. They worked calmly and nonchalantly, he could hear them discussing what to fit where, the room inside was lit up by a lamp or lantern. They loaded the cart, turned out the light, and headed off toward the village. They came back the following nights and when there was nothing more to steal from the house, they tore out the windows and doors and carted them away. They soon fell to attacking the outbuildings as well. They carried off the roof tiles, the doors, the wood beneath the awnings, in the end they even carried off the plows. Nikolin watched them from his room and could do nothing to stop them. He didn't know where they were from and who they were, whether it was one and the same or different people, but he could hear them threatening that if he tried to resist or went to the authorities for help, they would send him to serve Devetakov in the afterworld as well.

At that time his two brothers-in-law turned up like vultures, having caught the whiff of carrion all the way from the village. They said they had heard Devetakov had willed the property to him and that it was being plundered by the villagers, so they'd come to help defend him from thieves. As the late cook Auntie Raina had advised him, starting with his very first salary he had set aside half for his two sisters so that each of them eventually had twenty-four hundred leva. That was a lot of money for that time, when the villagers still bought and sold by barter, and cash money was like solid gold. When they were still young, he gave them each a hundred leva for their dowries and other necessities, then later began buying them land for their dowries as well. Again following Auntie Raina's advice, this was done for him by the estate overseer Halil Efendi. He was an experienced and honest man, he bought only the best land and when his sisters were of marrying age, they both had nearly fifteen acres. Both of them married the sons of moderately wealthy families, had children, and lived very comfortably. But Nikolin's in-laws and brothers-in-law, and alongside them his sisters as well, turned out to be greedy, insatiable people. His generosity led them to believe that he had somehow gotten under the skin of his master, whom they knew to be a crackpot who had accumulated much money and land. They visited him a few times a year, he also would go to visit them, and every time they saw each other, they tried to wheedle more money from him – one had started building a house, the other wanted to buy a horse or a cow. The more he gave them, they more they asked him for, because they thought that he, too, like his master, was a bit of a crackpot and didn't understand the value of money.

It just so happened that the night his brothers-in-law arrived that the thieves tried to steal the sheep from the barn. Nikolin had been expecting them to go after the livestock as well and that night had tied one of the dogs to the sheep pen and the other to the barn by the cows. Since they couldn't drive away the dog, they killed it with a chain and went about their work as usual without a whit of discretion. One waited with the cart by the door of the sheep pen, while the other two caught the sheep and tied their legs. His brothers-in-law grabbed an axe apiece, cornered them in the pen, and went at it hand to hand. The fellow in the cart managed to get away, but the other two took such a beating that they hardly made it out of the yard of the estate. His brothers-in-law had come to guard the estate, but they turned out to be the worst bandits of all. They stayed at the estate for two days and didn't leave him in peace until they had made off with one of the horses, the cow, and half the sheep. Since the villagers had turned a greedy eye to the estate, they said, they would rob it blind down to the last brick, because it was a kulak's estate, and since that's the way things were, why leave it to be plundered by strangers? He gave them what they wanted and sent them on their way.

This was the miserable state we found Nikolin in when Ilko Kralev and I went to the estate to pick up the books Devetakov had willed him before his death. Nikolin was very glad to see Ilko and even wanted to shake his hand, but Ilko told him to keep his distance.

"Don't you know I'm sick with tuberculosis?"

"You'll get better," Nikolin said, looking at him long and hard. "There's no sickness in your face."

He was a handsome young man with expressive, tired, and sad eyes, there was sorrow in the dark hollows beneath his cheekbones, and in the corners of his mouth when he smiled, and in his voice, soft, lilting, and slightly hoarse when he was saying how good it was of us to think to visit him. Ilko first wanted to see Devetakov's grave, and then we would get down to work. The leaves of the walnut tree with the color of hammered gold had covered the oblong pile of dirt, asters lay at the base of the wooden cross. Their fresh fragrance mixed with the underlying scent of the walnut leaves, filling the warm, still air with that gentle grief that lends a sorrowful charm to the first autumn days. "Why?" Nikolin said, tears springing from his tired eyes. "Why did he take his own life?"

Ilko Kralev and I had asked ourselves the same question many times after we had learned of Devetakov's death. Rumors abounded about the reasons for his suicide and since at that time the only thing people were writing or talking about were the People's Courts* and the sentences handed down to political criminals, most people claimed, under the influence of these events, that the reason for his death was political. Like every wealthy landowner, Devetakov had quite naturally been against the new government, he had been mixed up in political schemes and had killed himself out of fear of being discovered and brought to account for these deeds. His building of the school and donation of seventy-five acres of land to the village was explained as an attempt to atone for his guilt in the eyes of the new government, since he had foreseen these events a year in advance – just as everyone had, incidentally.

The only person who could know or even guess the reason for his suicide was Nikolin, but he, too, had not noticed anything strange in his master's behavior besides "that quiet thing" that came over his soul from time to time. Ilko recalled that over the past few years when he had met and talked with Devetakov, he had noticed "that quiet thing" in him; Alexander Pashov, with whom he often visited the estate, had noticed it too, but the two of them had explained it away as a state of deep internal concentration. Devetakov was "quiet" and calm by nature, but not indifferent. He spoke and argued with great passion, but without any external indications of that passion. They would talk about history, literature, philosophy, politics, and so on, as well as the so-called "accursed questions." Devetakov did not preach pessimism, yet he also was not an "ecstatic admirer" of the current world order, in the sense that he looked upon this order with condescending irony, and upon life as something foist upon one, which a man in any case had to resign himself to, while this resignation was wisdom itself. Death was not his "pet topic," unless of course he had purposely avoided it, not wanting to impose it on the others, and Ilko could not reconcile his suicide as an act of superhuman will with a person with such a contemplative, gentle, and inwardly focused nature.

For several days we packed up books, brought them to the village, and piled them on the dirt floor of Ilko's rented room. Morose from his lonely nightmares and deprived of human contact, Nikolin was desperate to cater to us and to keep us there with him as long as possible. He cooked us wonderful lunches and dinners, and in the afternoons he came to help us, and with artless candor he told us all about Devetakov, himself, and everything the reader already knows. He was confused and tormented, he couldn't see how he would live from then on and asked us for advice. Ilko asked his landlord Anani to rent out the other room, and once he agreed, he suggested that Nikolin rent the room. Nikolin was glad, but now he didn't know what to do with everything in the house – should he move it somewhere or just leave it? Ilko made a call to the city and a truck arrived with a few workers. And so the rug from the parlor, the piano, the elliptical table, a few leather sofas, and other larger pieces of furniture were taken away to various public institutions.

All we had left to do was to pack up and transport the books from the lowest shelves of the bookcases when Ilko found a roll of papers tucked between the pages of a French novel. The first sentence, which had been continued from a previous, missing page, caught his interest and he read all the remaining pages. They were numbered, but not in order and there was no connection between them. They were written clearly in black ink, but with many things crossed out and added in, which led us to believe that they were excerpts from the draft of a diary or notes for some essay. Ilko looked through all the volumes at his home in hopes of finding the whole manuscript, but alas, he did not discover a single line more. Years later I copied down this roll of papers from Ilko's notes, and now I am tempted to insert them into my story, even though I realize they do not hold any original thoughts. Besides that, Devetakov is one of the most episodic characters in this story, the reasons for his suicide will hardly pique the reader's interest, and yet I cannot pass over in silence these pages, from which gush an inhuman thirst for life and an apocalyptic horror of death. So here is the sentence, with which the roll of papers, whose first half is missing, begins:

> ...*from which it follows that the instinct for life is stronger than its meaning.*
>
> *How I hate Nature! If only because I came into this world not of my own free will, but of her will. She thrust me upon the world. She is a blind force which creates indiscriminately, with no plan, no goal, nor any emotion.*
>
> *Before man invented something as simple as the wheel, and many other things of that sort as well, thousands of years had to pass. To create the most complicated thing in the world – man himself – all that is needed is a blind instinct. No one thinks when creating a person, because he has given himself over to carnal passion. What's more, a person is often born from unregenerate drunkenness, from violence or from flirtation, from accidental encounters, by accidental people. Despite this, Nature endows him with a mind, feelings, imagination, he can feel pain and spiritual excitement. Therein, too, lies her baseness, if we can charge her with this vice.*
>
> *My father died of a stroke at the age of fifty-five. He was exceptionally vigorous and strong. They say that in his youth he wrestled at village fairs and often beat the strongest contenders. He had a gentle nature, a subtle sense of humor, as well as musical talent. I remember how he would "play around" on the flute or violin during his free time. He played by ear. He would perform Russian romances and other melodies he had heard from other musicians and most often from gramophone records.*

Studying music was unthinkable in his day and age. My grandfather, a half-literate peasant, didn't want to hear about any studies whatsoever. My father left school after seventh grade, but he was naturally intelligent and, unlike the other large landowners in these parts, read books by Bulgarian and foreign authors. He bought my sister a piano, hired a teacher for her from town, but she didn't show any aptitude for music. Much to his chagrin, I showed no interest in music either. But as a consolation, he was very proud that I graduated from university abroad.

My father was generous and loved guests. He loved to wine and dine them, to treat them to various drinks and to listen to their conversations. The guests – who were always different – created a holiday atmosphere for him. He was very social and in their presence felt inspired, joyful, and happy. But as luck would have it, it was in the presence of guests that he fell ill. He went to the other room to get something, was gone a long time, and when we went to look for him, he was lying on his back on the bed. He couldn't speak or move. We called a doctor in the morning, and he found that my father had had a stroke on his right side. From that day on, my father was mute and paralyzed. I was horrified. I kept asking myself why such a kindhearted man with such a lust for life would be punished so cruelly by fate, why wasn't he at least sent some more tolerable illness. He who had done Ms. Clara such a good turn was now suffering even more terribly than she was. He would sit in the house all day, or, if the weather was good, out on the veranda. But the worst and most unbearable part was that he was aware of his own suffering. His mind was completely intact, but instead of words, bellowing came out of his mouth. He suffered most when the man we had hired from the village undressed him, wiped, and dried him. Then he would bawl like a child, staring at the icon of the Virgin Mary – perhaps he was praying to her to end his misery as soon as possible. I had never seen and will never see such terrible suffering in anyone's eyes.

Yes, nature not only causes man undeserved suffering, she downright mocks him.

An ancient king said to a poet who had praised him in an ode and compared him to the sun: "Before you compare me to the sun, you need to see my chamber pot!" The king was sincere and spoke the truth.

Before we fall in love with a woman, we, too, must first of all see her "chamber pot." Even the most tender love between a man and a woman is nothing but a sexual urge. Trite, but true. Otherwise lovers would still delight in and enchant each other from afar. They wouldn't feel attraction to each other the very moment they met or even before meeting. And perhaps this is precisely the reason that man since time immemorial has glorified the object of his attraction as an unearthly creature and has called this attraction "love." He sings the praises of his love precisely because he doesn't dare call it by its true name, so as not to lower himself to the level of animals. In this way he rises in his own esteem. Animals mate only at certain times of year so as to further their kind, while man does it constantly for pleasure alone, which degenerates into fornication. And fornication leads to tragic consequences. Man's love is corrupt. It serves as a medium of exchange for espionage and all sorts of shady undertakings.

In this way, man shows that his love is an instinct from whose power he cannot free himself, not even when he sees that it could cost him his honor, his freedom, and his life.

I have to kill this instinct within myself. It suppresses my will and my freedom. I must also kill the feeling of ownership. It is one of the worst vices. A crime against those who live in squalor and want. What do I need all this land for? I have a little money in the bank, deposited there years ago by my father, it is enough for me. From now on I have nowhere to travel to, I have nothing to buy. I want for nothing.

If I give my land to the poor villagers, I will make them happy their whole lives. Not only them, but their children as well. I sense that I will be happy too. Or at least I'll be trying to make sense of my life to some extent. Going on living as I have until now is unbearable. I'll go to the villagers and, for you – this much, for you – that much! How simple it all is, yet for years I have not been able to do it. My will is not strong enough, I have the feeling that I will be left helpless and insignificant, without support and solid ground beneath my feet. But it won't be like that. Since I know that I myself have deprived myself of something, I won't miss it at all. If only I could at least sell my land at half price, but I can't even do that. Because I am greedy and depraved. Because I am a true evildoer. And I haven't even lifted a finger for thvis land. I inherited it.

On March first I will go to the town hall and will look at the property tax records. I will see how much land the villagers have and give mine away to the poorest of them.

On March first, and not a day later!

They say that a supreme harmony exists in nature. In fact, chaos reigns there. Even the ancients, and after them the Christian thinkers, too, have said that nature is imperfect. However, there are some "great minds" who find harmony even in the existence of the millions of kinds of insects, all manner of reptiles and lower organisms. The mosquito, they say, feeds on the blood of man and the other animals and that is in accordance with natural harmony. The subterranean creatures, too, which never see daylight and destroy the poor villagers' crops, are also part of this harmony. Wars, violence, the devouring or killing of those weaker by the stronger maintains the supreme balance in the world. This balance is immoral and bloodstained, but scholars and philosophers accept it and justify it in elegant systems. They can't understand nature, so they create systems to show off their intellectual prowess to the world. They even go so far as to consider death necessary for this natural harmony. While death is nature's most criminal act. It robs life of meaning.

Since the most ancient times people have been tormented by the transience and pointlessness of life. Gilgamesh, the hero of the Ancient Babylonian epic, was horrified by death. He met with all the wise men of his time, seeking consolation from them, but they all told him that the gods had doomed men to death and kept immortality for themselves. It would have been better if we had never been born than to have to live in a world of sin and suffering without understanding why things happen as they do – so says the Book of 4 Esdras.

In Ancient Greece, which distinguishes itself with its life-affirming philosophy, we find no less grief and sorrow. "For of all creatures that breathe and walk upon the earth, there is none more miserable than man," says Homer in the Iliad. And in the works of many of the early poets such as Simonides, Theognis, and others, written in the sixth century before the Common Era, there is much hopelessness: "Best of all for mortal beings is never to have been born at all, nor ever to have set eyes on the bright light of the sun."

Later, Sophocles, too, would say: "To never have been born may be the greatest boon of all."

Centuries later we also hear Pascal's sad howl: "You have no foundation beneath your feet, beneath us is the abyss. It is terrifying to feel how everything you have disappears."

There are philosophers who claim that the suffering and death of the individual atones for the happiness of humankind. Death is evil, of course, but in this case it is transformed into a virtue. From it is born new life that eternally renews itself. From here stems the theory of immortality through the generations or even through some action. A pitiful consolation. Or more precisely a posthumous indulgence of our vanity. I'm not there, but my children, grandchildren, and everyone from my "line" will live one after the other and I will live on through them. Do my father, my grandfather, and my great-grandfathers live on through me? No, of course not. I am alive, and they are dust, or not even dust, rather nothing. Just some names, some ideas, long-forgotten ones at that.

I am gone, but I will live on through my deeds in the minds of future generations. An even more pitiful consolation. So what of it that someone at some point will open a book and perhaps read that so-and-so did such-and-such for the good of humanity? He invented a machine, painted a picture, uttered a wise, immortal thought. What good have Archimedes or Socrates, for example, done for humanity? Or Shakespeare, or Michelangelo? None whatsoever. Literally, none. They've distracted themselves with various endeavors and ruminations so as to divert their thoughts from their inevitable death. They have distracted themselves and others and this is the only good they have done. At any rate, humankind keeps on dying as before and all those Aristotles and company are nothing but names written in books.

I don't want to be any one of those grand names, I want to be immortal. To live even after the end of the world. Let them live on "in the minds of grateful humankind."

The Ancient Greeks, as we know, bowed down before implacable fate, which renders the separate individual helpless in the name of shared universal harmony. Heraclitus was awed by the constant stream of life that flowed thanks to the death of the individual man. Thus the immortality of the human race is assured.

After a man dies, what good to him is the life of nature, of the universe! What meaning does my sacrifice have for maintaining the life of the universe, since it is not a living creature and cannot be aware of it? Since it exists, both with and without me? Nature constantly creates through the power of its blind instinct and constantly kills, thus the world, in fact, is an endless graveyard. This alternation of life and death, of birth and disappearance into nonbeing, scared Heraclitus himself, too, and in the end he compared universal harmony, the life of nature, to a heap of trash or some such thing.

Today Malayi brought Ms. Clara to play the piano. While she was playing (at this point very poorly and painful to listen to), I was thinking of what a tragic thirst for life this woman has. When she and her husband arrived here, she was such a pretty young woman that people from the surrounding villages, as well as our acquaintances from town, came just to see her. We already knew that she and her husband were political emigrants. In our eyes her selfless love and self-sacrifice gave her the halo of a saint. After a year or two she became paralyzed and we were all stunned. Whenever death is mentioned, she pales in horror.

Her suffering, one might say, is nothing in comparison to

that of one of my cousins. He is forty years old, but he cannot walk or even sit. He crawls around on his hands and knees, and outside in the yard, they take him out in a handcart. He looks like a four-legged insect. Outsiders, if they happen to catch sight of him crawling around on the floor, are horrified. Two or three times a month, I get a note from him asking for some books. He reads all sorts of books, but prefers those that describe journeys to far-off lands. You can talk about anything with him, as he is a true encyclopedia. He remembers not only what he has read in magazines and newspapers, but also what he has heard on the radio. He knows all the political happenings around the world, all the politicians' names, as well as the movements of the military units along the German-Russian front. He knows French and speaks only French with me. He learned it with a private tutor.

His memory is well trained, but not mechanical. As a child he had two teachers and since he could not write, he had to learn his lessons by heart. They don't hide him from me, because we are relatives, and I bring him books and newspapers that his brother, whom he lives with, cannot always find for him. When Licho (his name is Iliya) and I talk, he lies on his stomach on the bed, and I sit in a chair across from him. Our conversations are encyclopedic. From everyday problems to philosophy.

Sometimes we talk about life and he says that he is a heap of suffering. I have been punished by God more than all the people on the earth, he says, why am I alive? I am a freak. Why don't I die or put an end to my torments?

That's what he says, but as soon as he gets a little cold or sneezes, he wants them to call a doctor right away. Yes, the instinct for life is insurmountable. It is stronger than the worst suffering, than the most hopeless despair, than the meaning of life.

How can I overcome that blind, incomprehensible force? Was it Euripides who said that perhaps life is death, and death life? If this is the case, then crossing over from one state to the other should not be so frightening.

These notes are by Alexander Pashov. This is his handwriting. I remember how his notes looked when he was talking about Lenin's The State and Revolution, *a Russian edition printed abroad, which I brought him from Paris. Ilko Kralev also managed to read it.*

How pure the two of them are, in love with humankind. Platonically in love. They are ready to sacrifice themselves on the "altar" of their ideals. How they thirst for knowledge and action for the good of the poor and downtrodden classes! I do not share their ideology. It is the most humane of all ideologies, but it is impossible to put into practice. Man is built far more complexly than young idealists and other theoreticians think. Yet still I admire them, because their ideals are noble, selfless, and lofty.

In them, I see myself at their age. Didn't I, too, "embrace" suffering humankind? I wanted to become a village teacher to teach the peasants to read and write. A doctor, so I could heal them free of charge. A lawyer, to fight their cases for them and to defend them in court. My father didn't laugh at me and didn't oppose me. As I found out later, he had gone through his own phase of romantic populism and patiently waited until life showed me its other faces as well.

I envy the two young men their pure, sincere faith in the fulfillment of their ideals. What happiness it is to believe. If I felt any happiness in my youth, it was because of my faith that if I sacrificed myself for the people, I would make them happy. Now I cannot believe. I want to but I cannot. Now I know that no ideals and no revolutions have changed or will ever change man. The theoreticians, and especially the materialists, do not know human nature. For them, man is a material with which they try to realize their theories in practice. They don't want to know that man is an abyss, whose bottom no one has yet managed to glimpse.

The communists, like all revolutionaries, also believe that their idea is the most just and the most applicable to social life, hence everything before them was imperfect. But who would make a revolution if he didn't believe that his cause was the final word in human justice?

Revolutions are carried out with violence and I've always wondered how you can reach a humane end with inhumane means. Some time ago, when I was talking with Alexander Pashov and Ilko Kralev, this question arose and they tried to prove to me that the revolution (they meant the socialist one) is not and could not be unethical and immoral. Revolution is a fundamental change to the economic – and as a result also to the spiritual – life of society. Every day we make revolutions in various spheres of life, albeit on a smaller scale. Watering crops, spreading manure, interbreeding animals with the goal of getting a better breed, medicines, surgical operations, science as a whole, and civilization – are these all not "violence" against evolutionary development? Revolution is necessary to man.

Thus laid out with simple and clear examples, the motives for revolution look logical and convincing. In other conversations on similar topics Alexander Pashov and Ilko Kralev freely cited economists, scholars, and philosophers, and I have the feel-

ing that, theoretically, they are very well prepared. Especially Alexander Pashov, who thoroughly knows the works of Marx, Lenin, Plekhanov, Stalin, and others. On the whole he is exceedingly well read for his age. He is able to improvise and to convince his interlocutor calmly and logically, without pushing his knowledge on him. Conversations with him are democratic, if I may put it that way. On top of this he is reserved and resourceful and it seems that he lives a Spartan lifestyle, despite the comfortable conditions his father has secured for him. Overall, I feel he has all the qualities necessary for a public figure, for a functionary of the highest rank or even a party leader.

But he is also a theoretician, and a young one, at that. Panta rhei and the fact that you can never step into the same river twice means that it is changing every moment. But this is a mechanical change. The materialists attribute this characteristic to man as well, but the analogy is faulty. Man changes, but also mechanically. He improves his material and technical culture, but in the moral sense he does not change. And the goal of every revolution is precisely moral change.

I envy the dead. They have overcome the horror of death and have crossed over into the void. Why do I feel horrified by that void? Billions and billions of people have sunk into its bosom, I, too, will sink into it. The years I have left to live out will be filled with an anticipation of death and a horror of it and that agonizing anticipation cannot be justified by anything. The man who has reached the truth that life is meaningless should not fear death. Free and happy is he who can arrange his life as he sees fit. Finally, if I'm deprived of this earthly life, I have nothing to lose, but if there is life "up above," then I have everything to gain.

Yes, here is the only meaning of life – immortality.

If there is no second life, nature is a criminal. A recidivist. But where would that second life take place? Here on earth? No. "Up there," in the other world? It does not exist, it was made up by religions. And religions are the most indisputable proof of man's striving to overcome death. All of man's activities ever since he has existed have been a struggle against this so-called natural necessity. Belief in the afterworld is a negation of death. Religion is a hope for immortality. There are real hopes, for example, the hope that next spring what was sown will sprout, grow, and in the summer bear fruit. The likelihood of natural disasters destroying what was sown is only one percent, and not even every year. But there are also fantastical hopes. One of them is the hope for the afterlife, resurrection.

Man's thirst for the immortality of the soul is so great that he goes to absurd extremes to believe in that immortality. Religions say that God created man, when it is precisely the opposite. Man created God as a belief and a hope.

Where is God to help and console us?

Everything is possible for God, religious thinkers claim. But some add that there is no absolute guarantee of his existence. Man can always doubt and deny him. We ought not seek to discover him through the path of reason, he is not in ordinary being but in spirit. And since everything is possible for God, then faith in him is a struggle for possibility. It opens up the path to immortality.

Yes, God is our only hope, our one salvation. If we manage to raise ourselves up to his level, we will conquer the void. Only we mustn't forget — God cannot be reached by the path of reason. Our reason is mistrustful and limited. It seeks truth, justice, and goodness here on earth via a logical path and thus creates law,

and through the law creates sin. Reason has created man's greatest suffering, but who created man himself? God, of course, who
else could it be?

But why?

Some philosophers answer this question by saying that God
created everything, but reason and morality have not been created. They are primordial. A fine answer, what more could one
say? An escape hatch from the labyrinth of that clear contra-
diction. That way an answer is also assured for the question of
why God is so indifferent to man's fate. Since he did not create
morality, goodness, too, is not his creation. He exists incognito
in this world and has nothing to do with wisdom, morality, and
truth. They have been thought up by reason.

To the ancients' reasoning that regardless of whether the
soul is immortal or not, we must be virtuous, Saint Augustine
replied with an aphorism: Namely, that pagan virtues are merely
splendid vices.

Splendid indeed, but an aphorism nonetheless.

What's more: "God is everywhere from whence ignorant
people come and worship the sky."

And why did Jesus teach us virtues here on earth? He really
did say that blessed are they who are not tempted by virtue, but
at the same time he counseled us to give one of our shirts to the
poor. Is that not a virtue?

The other day Ilko Kralev told me Alexander Pashov had left
half a year ago for Switzerland to study medicine there. I had
been asking Ilko about him for a long time, but Ilko had claimed
not to know where he was. He only told me a few days ago. I
have the feeling that despite being such good friends, or perhaps

precisely because of this, Alexander Pashov's making such a move during the height of the war was a mystery to him. This is why I did not consider it necessary to tell him that about two months ago I had seen Pashov in Zurich, on my way back from Munich. I was trying to slip into Paris with a heap of recommendations from Sofia acquaintances, but only made it as far as Munich. At first I wasn't completely sure that the young man I saw at the Zurich hotel was Pashov. Since I didn't expect to see him abroad, in the first instant I thought I'd mistaken someone else for him. Later, as I all the more often and in ever greater detail re-created my memory of his gait, his height, the expression on his face and in his eyes, the more I became convinced that it had been him. We passed within a few feet of each other by the reception desk. I was going into the hotel, he was coming out. His gaze fell on me for a bit longer than usual and when I opened my mouth to greet him, he turned away and hurried toward the exit. He was dressed elegantly in a light overcoat of gray cloth, a wide-brimmed gray hat, and gray gloves.

Now I was absolutely sure that it was him, so sure that I wanted to catch up with him. But then I thought that since after having visited my home regularly for three years, he pretended not to know me, with that he was trying to tell me that he had serious reasons to pass me by. What could these reasons be? He didn't come to see me that evening, nor on the following morning. The hotel administration told me there was no one by that name registered at the hotel. The gentleman I had seen here had likely come to meet someone. Throughout my whole return journey and even until recently I had been trying to explain to myself why he had passed me by in that Swiss hotel and finally came to the conclusion that perhaps he was working in international espionage.

*What a dreadful world! What a complicated creature man
is. If Pashov was working as a spy, which side was he on? The
fact that he spoke so passionately about communism did not at all
mean that he was serving Soviet Russia, on the contrary. Perhaps
he preached communist ideas so openly in order to hide his work
for the fascists.*

*I have gotten quite a lot of information about Soviet Russia
from the French press. It is extremely contradictory. Some are
horrified by the harsh dictatorship there, others are ecstatic about
the Soviet government. A government that is waging a difficult
war against the economic backwardness of Tsarist Russia, in the
name of the masses. Some Frenchmen, as well as other foreigners
who have visited Soviet Russia, say that a great renaissance of
humankind is underway there.*

*But I am familiar with fascism. Both here in Bulgaria and
abroad. It is a political paroxysm. I saw it in occupied France,
I saw a democracy crushed under a heavy boot. I also saw it in
Germany. Nowhere else has such a herd-psychosis been forced on
a people. Nowhere else has individuality been so suppressed and
unified on account of a mediocre, bloodthirsty Führer. And on
account of a suite of windbags. How can a people be ruled by a
band of bums with the impudent self-confidence that they will
transform the world? How we praise "the people," when they are
nothing more than a mob whom anyone can oppress if he has
the ambition and the talent for it. Death has a hand in this, too.
Fear of it turns people into a herd. The oppressor, the called-upon
oppressor, knows this.*

*Fascism is madness. How could Alexander Pashov serve
such madness? Is it possible for a monster to be at work in a
person like him? I don't want to believe it, but who knows? You
can expect anything from a man.*

And so, to secure immortality for ourselves, we must reject rational thinking. Faith begins where thinking ends. Could there be a more impossible condition for immortality? And how was this truth reached if not through reason? Isn't it the case that as soon as a person opens his eyes to the world, he wants to see, touch, and find out everything? He asks a hundred questions a day and this is reason.

Your God, who does not want the impossible, is not God, but a repulsive idol. This was said by one of Dostoyevsky's characters. The one from underground. An old, ancient biblical chimera transformed later by religious writers into an irrevocable condition for true faith. Isn't it true that even ancient Abraham, at God's first call to sacrifice his son Isaac, raised his knife, ready to slaughter him like a lamb? And if God hadn't stopped his hand, he would have killed the boy without batting an eye. But God, of course, stopped his hand, thus we can't really find out how strong Abraham's faith actually was. And whether he was truly prepared to kill his son.

What a shallowly constructed legend. Its whole point, if it has one, lies in the fact that faith is an unbelievable paradox and it is precisely this paradox that can transform a murder into a sacred act. And return Abraham's son to him.

But to believe like Abraham, I must lose my individuality, suppress my will, lose my I. Give up my soul. "Any one of you who does not renounce all that he has cannot be my disciple." Or: "If anyone would come after me, let him deny himself and take up his cross daily and follow me. For whoever would save his life will lose it, but whoever loses his life for my sake will save it."

Some Ignatius or other, brought to Rome to be ripped apart by wild beasts, begged the Christians there not to try to save him. "Nothing can stop me from going to join Christ. I would rather

die for Jesus Christ than rule to the utmost ends of the earth. I
am burning with desire to die as he did." Indeed, whole gener-
ations of martyrs joyfully accepted death out of love for Christ.
And they even hungered to give themselves over to the greatest
suffering and death so as to experience his agonies and death.

Mystics. Or people with troubled minds, freaks, madmen,
prone to fainting fits, mentally ill. They dream of God or see
God while wide awake and imagine that they are one with him.
Pascal, too, was given to raving in moments of spiritual crisis.
He was mentally ill, too.

Today I listened to a speech of Hitler's on the radio and
now I think that rulers and especially dictators actually use the
tried-and-true practices of religion. They, like God, demand total
submission and devotion to the death from their subjects. They
don't acknowledge anyone's personal freedom and individuality
at all. Or they acknowledge it on paper, but in actuality suppress
it with every means at their disposal.

The truth is that there should be a God, but there isn't. Oh,
if God did exist, he would not live "incognito" in this world.
He would not be so indifferent to people, he would not put them
in such difficult, impossible conditions in order to unite them
with himself.

But I am getting confused. I am confused. Isn't God spirit?
If he exists, he really must be spirit. The world we live in is so
absurd, so pointless, that perhaps only uniting with the spirit
will save us. Now therein lies the mystery of religion. In reality,
it is a struggle for a good life here, on earth. It tempts us with
resurrection in the afterworld, because here we are doomed to
meaningless death. Hence it follows that our salvation is in the
spiritual world. As soon as we accept this, that insurmountable
natural necessity will no longer exist for us. In this way we will

already be made perfect and we will have lived out our lives happily here on earth, and that is the meaning of our existence.

As far as the afterworld, resurrection, and eternal life are concerned, that is now eschatology. A dream – and none of the living can ever find out whether this dream is attainable or not. But after we've lived out our lives so happily, we won't even have any need for it. Religion is beautiful, perhaps the most beautiful poetry ever created by man.

Just poetry.

While death, absurd, senseless death, still hangs over man's head like a terrible judgment. The thought of it strips the rest of my life of meaning. To overcome it, I must accept it. Yet I have not the strength for this. The eternal darkness into which I must sink plunges me into horror and paralyzes my will. I cannot, I cannot overcome my instinct for life. This blind force holds me in its clutches.

How happy are those madmen, those poor in spirit, those freaks, the mentally afflicted, who burn with impatience to die so as to go join their God.

Ilko Kralev is ill with tuberculosis. He is sentenced to death. Does he know it? He shows no sign, literally no sign, that he is suffering. He spits into his tin box so conscientiously, as if carrying out some ritual. From whence that self-control? Or is his hope stronger than despair?

Why does he not rail against this absurdity?

In the first days of October, Nikolin hitched up the carriage and set off for Ravna so as to move in with Ilko Kralev. He had loaded up the most necessary of his possessions – two suitcases of clothes and bedding, a trunk full of kitchenware, food, and a cage full of a dozen chickens on top of everything. He was bringing them for Ilko, who lived a solitary life, without any possessions whatsoever, plus his illness demanded nourishing food. He had known him for a long time and believed that he was the only person after Devetakov that he could live with. To him, Ilko seemed to resemble Devetakov in nature and even in his outward appearance, thus his life with Ilko would be a continuation of his previous life. He, just like Devetakov, could not live without books, let him read, I'll take care of the housework, I'll cook for him and take care of him until he gets better. Tomorrow I'll go back to the estate to get the rest of the birds, the pig, and whatever's left of the food, plus the money I have will last us a long time.

While hatching such plans about his future life, he had reached the first house in the village without realizing it, and he would have passed it by if someone hadn't called him by name: "Nikolin, why are you just passing us by like that?"

By the gate stood the blond girl with whom he had gone to that ill-fated wedding with the disgraced bride two years earlier. He had long remembered that wedding, and the blond girl along with it. Over time the memory had faded, but when he saw her by the gate, he immediately remembered her name, he remembered his unusual meeting with her father, Grandpa Kitty Cat. And everything was exactly the same as he had seen it a few years ago – the rotting gate with the gourd slipped over the side post, and the dunghill at the far end of the yard where the donkey was rolling around, and the grass grazed in circles, and the house nestled amidst the bushes and trees. Even the time of day was the same, late afternoon, the sun was shining just as brightly and the thorny hedge was already casting a bluish shadow. And Mona was the same. She was looking at him as she had then, with her head cocked slightly toward her shoulder, and was smiling, her hair gleamed in the sun like a stalk of ripe wheat. She came over to the carriage and gave him her hand.

"So you've forgotten me, have you?"

"I haven't forgotten you," Nikolin said. "I just didn't see you."

"How could you pass us up without stopping by! Your buggy's loaded up like a Gypsy's cart, where are you headed to?"

"I'm going to Ilko Kralev's…"

He wanted to add that he was going to live at Ilko Kralev's, but she, just as her father had done back then, opened the gate and invited him to stop by their place for a short while so politely that he couldn't refuse. He tied up the horse without unhitching it to the same tree and Mona invited him to sit on the three-legged stool next to the same rosebush in the garden in front of the house. She chatted with him and behaved so familiarly with him that he got the feeling that they had met here in the flower garden not two years ago but two days ago. The crooked gate squeaked and Grandpa Kitty Cat came into the yard. He looked at the buggy from all sides and cried: "Well now, if this buggy ain't one of Devetakov's! And lookee here, Nikolin's come to visit! Where have you been, my boy? So much time has passed and you haven't thought to look us up! We heard Devetakov passed away, may he rest in peace, and me and Mony here were wondering whatever happened to Nikolin. And now here he is – alive and kicking." Grandpa Kitty Cat was the picture of affability and was beside himself with joy, as if seeing his dearest friend. "But why are you sitting out here? Why don't you go into the house? Mony, invite our guest in."

"I invited him in, but he turned me down. He's in a hurry."

"Where do you have to hurry to at this time o' day? It's already getting dark." Nikolin got up, but Grandpa Kitty Cat put a hand on his chest. "You go ahead and hurry, my boy, but it's not a matter of life and death. Cool your heels for a bit, let's chew the fat, then you hurry on your way! Yessiree!"

Nikolin was used to living in the large house and the room looked like a matchbox to him, the ceiling beams hung right above his head like the ribs of a skeleton, the light of the sunset was filtering through the little window as through a knothole in a barn. It was spick-and-span, but meagerly furnished and impoverished. The square table, covered with a hard and shabby oilcloth with red flowers, three wooden chairs, a small stove with a crooked pipe, in the corner stood a wooden bed, above the wooden bed a square piece of needlepoint with square pieces of home-made cloth, embroidered with red and green crosses and flowers, just like the ones his mother had once embroidered. The little rugs on the floor woven from colorful rags, and the copper basin with the dented-up aluminum pitcher, and the gas lamp with its round, fly-encrusted mirror reminded him of the poor, old, and shabby furnishings in the house where he had been born.

"You're coming from a lordly life, you're used to nice things, but don't find fault with us or be disgusted by us," Grandpa Kitty Cat said, as if guessing his thoughts. "As long as you've got a big heart, the rest'll figure itself out, that's what I say!"

"That's the truth," Nikolin said. "As long as we're healthy and happy, what more could a person want!"

Mona was coming in and out of the room through a small door to the pantry, bringing bread, cheese, a potato stew, finally she also brought out a wicker-covered jug of wine.

"It's still young," Grandpa Kitty Cat said, pouring it into chipped little glasses left over from Lord knows when. "My brother-in-law gave it to me the other day to try it."

The wine had the scent of ripe grapes and its taste was sweet and sourish. As soon as they'd taken their first sips Grandpa Kitty Cat couldn't contain his curiosity any longer and started grilling him, as was fitting, from A to Z, about how he'd been living since they'd last seen him and how he figured to go on living in the future. Nikolin wasn't bothered that he was quizzing him in such detail, because he could sense in his curios-ity the sympathy that his soul had been longing for. He told them about Devetakov's death, about the thefts from the estate, and about Ilko Kralev, whom he was going to live with.

"Don't you even think of it, my boy!" Grandpa Kitty Cat said. "How're you gonna live with those two sickos under one roof? One of 'em consumptive, the other's face rotted away, if you don't catch TB you'll get sick just from looking at them. Mony, you tell him too!"

"As if he would listen to me!" Mona said. "He's a man, let him decide for himself. Ilko ran away from home to not infect his family, while others are going to him of their own free will to catch consumption."

Nikolin didn't know what to say. The old man's advice was sincere and well intentioned, but, on the other hand, Ilko was the only person he could take shelter with. Otherwise he would have to go back to the estate this very minute, to condemn himself to loneliness again, and to spend his nights fighting ghosts and thieves. It was better to die with the sick man than to live exiled like that from the world.

"You're a fine lad, Nikolin, my boy! From the first moment I laid eyes on you, I knew what kind of person you are," Grandpa Kitty Cat said, a vague smile veiling his face. "I just can't figure out why you've got it in your head to waste your life on Ilko. That damned TB cut down plenty of folks here in the village, it doesn't show any mercy. If you don't have anywhere to go, stay here with us. I mean it! Stay here a day or two, think it over, and then decide, don't just go running blindly off any which way. Are you gonna spend your whole life worrying about the sick and the dead? If you like it here with us, stay as long as you like. We won't throw you out, we won't let you go hungry. And besides…"

"Dad, you'd better get to bed," Mona said, taking the glass out of his hand.

And again it was like the first time he had visited. The old man walked over to the bed as if enchanted by his daughter's words and started getting undressed. He left his hat, quilted jacket, and shoes on the floor and slipped under the blanket in his breeches. Soon a steady purring could be heard from under the blanket. Mona seemed angry or ashamed at her father's words, and Nikolin once again got up to leave.

"Stay a little while longer to chat," she said, glancing over at the bed. "He's asleep as soon as his head hits the pillow. Where are you going to go at this time of night, it's already dark outside. I can see your heart is heavy, the loneliness is torturing you, you don't have anyone or anywhere to turn to. Why do we make you uneasy?"

"I do feel uneasy," Nikolin admitted. "I'm not used to letting night catch me in strangers' houses."

"What, are your other troubles not enough already that you need to add that worry to the pile? Good God, so there are people who can be made to feel uneasy even by us!"

A thin, gentle smile lit up Mona's face and it was as if this smile caressed his soul. There was none of Mishona's depraved teasing in it, nor any of Madame General's suppressed scorn. The one, after wasting her life in careless frivolity, made sport of him and turned him into a wastebasket into which she threw the trash of her soul, while the other, having lived until recently in luxury, bit her lips to overcome her pride and hatred of him, so as to beg a bag of food off him. From the start he had felt awkwardness and an inward fear of these women, because he knew that between them stood a high and hard wall, which separates a servant from ladies of high standing, and perhaps because of this they were a mystery to him, which gave rise to a vague urge to peer into that mystery. His attraction to Madame General was blind and reckless and it turned into a painful humiliation, and when he started to feel sorry for her, he felt guilty in her eyes and felt a sense of disgust toward himself. At his first meeting with Mona, he had also felt her to be far superior, since he had assumed that she was a teacher or a secretary, and most of all because she was a pretty girl whom he'd never met. Now he felt calm with her, as we all feel calm and trusting with our equals.

"From now on, you'll have to get used to living with strangers, since you're lonely on the estate," Mona went on. "Living alone is no life at all."

"It's tough," Nikolin said. "Even if you've got a house like a palace, and even if you've got land, since you're alone, it's like you've got nothing. A man can't enjoy anything by his lonesome."

"I'll make up a bed for you in the other room, get a good night's sleep, then do what you have to do tomorrow."

Nikolin put his hat on his head, stopped by the door, and asked: "Where should I put up the horse?"

Mona led him to the barn, where there was only one cow, tied the horse to the end of the manger, and the two of them went back to the house. Grandpa Kitty Cat was sleeping with the covers pulled up to his chin like a child, with his eyes half open and his hands on his chest. Mona called Nikolin into the other room, showed him the bed in the semidarkness, and went out. He stood in the middle of the room until his eyes got used to the darkness, undressed, and tiptoed over to the bed. It was wide like all village beds, filled with straw and covered with a striped blanket. The straw rustled at his every move and gave off the scent of dried grass, in the middle there was a dip formed by Mona's body. The strip of light coming from under the door went out and the house sank into silence. He didn't dare move, as he felt that the rustling of the mattress would be heard in the other room, he lay on his back with his hands behind his head and stared at the blue square of the window. He was thinking about the twists and turns of fate that had brought him to a girl's bed completely by chance, and was wondering whether some happy omen was not hiding in this happenstance. He was also wondering what the old man would say if tomorrow and the next day and the day after that he were to stay at his house, would he really take him in, as he had promised that night, or was his invitation merely drunken blather? If his invitation was sincere, that meant he wanted him for a son-in-law, otherwise how would he let some young bachelor live in his home? And would Mona have him, or would she send him on his way with a wave and a smile, as all guests are sent off? He had never thought of marriage and now it seemed to him as absurd as it did pleasant, because he could not get the image of Mona out of his mind.

I won't fall asleep, I'll get up early and leave, he kept telling himself, sensing that the silence was rocking him into some sweet daze, his thoughts were scattering and his eyelids were growing heavy.

He woke up late, feeling as light and chipper as a person who has slept soundly after many sleepless nights. Grandpa Kitty Cat had gone to the fields in the donkey cart to bring back a little corn, but Mona was waiting for him in the other room. She had put breakfast on the table and was sewing on some cloth such that when he opened the door, the first thing he saw was her, with her hair neatly combed back and tied in a bow, as pretty and tidy as a doll.

"I really overslept!" Nikolin said, when he saw the sun was almost at high noon. "Why didn't you wake me up?"

"Since you feel like sleeping, sleep. There's no work waiting for you. Why don't you shave?"

Nikolin was overcome by a pleasant sense of carefreeness that he had never felt before. The sorrows, worries, and loneliness that had suppressed his heart's youthful impulses disappeared as if miraculously and he gave himself over to the hope for a new life, easier and more cheerful than his life thus far had been. Wherever he turned, his eyes saw only beauty and tranquil joy, as if the world around him had transformed itself in only a single night. The warm autumn day was quiet, calm, and lovely, the little house was lovely and cozy like his parents' home, and from the flowers in the garden wafted a sweetly sad scent, and Mona was the loveliest girl he had ever seen in his life. He was so dazed by this joyful premonition of his future life that he didn't even stop to think whether he was annoying her, whether she was not being so polite to him merely out of decorum, waiting for him to realize on his own that every visit must come to an end. He took the cage of birds out of the buggy to let them roam around the yard with the others and caught one. He asked for a knife, slaughtered it, and handed it to Mona. She went to the summer kitchen to light a fire, while he took one of his two suitcases and carried it into the room. The suitcase was made of yellowish-brown leather, while its inside was covered in blue silk. It was full of all the shaving implements he had found in the house – two razor strops, brushes, two straight razors, a whole dozen bars of soap, a little bottle of cologne, and face towels. Mona scooped him up a pitcher of warm water, fixed a little mirror to the chimney of the hearth, and he shaved. Then they plucked the chicken – she held it by the legs and he by the head – they cleaned it, sliced it, and set it in the pot to boil.

That's how Grandpa Kitty Cat found them at noon, sitting together in front of the hearth of the summer kitchen. Nikolin expected him to ask what he had decided – would he be staying with them or going – but the old man seemed to have forgotten that he had been their guest only since last night, and called him to help push the full cart behind the house next to the corncrib. During lunch he also did not ask, and when he got up from the table, he went off into the village on some errand. Mona and Nikolin went behind the house to shuck the corn and by evening, they had finished it. Grandpa Kitty Cat again lay down and fell asleep instantly, while Mona made up Nikolin's bed in the other room. He had just laid down when she came in to him. She stood by the bed for about a minute, then sought out his hand and took it in hers.

"I came to visit you, hey, wake up! Do you want to talk?"

His throat was tight and he said something that even he did not understand. He squeezed her hand tightly and starting drawing her toward him, breathless from excitement and bashfulness.

"Don't pull me like that or I'll get mad and leave!"

He let go of her hand, ashamed that he couldn't say even a word of what he had been thinking of telling her all day. She leaned over him and started stroking his face with one hand, and his shoulders with the other.

"You may think badly of me, but I…" she said, sinking onto his chest and pressing her face, hot and wet with tears, to his. "Don't leave me, I've taken a liking to you."

Nikolin didn't realize how she had stripped down to her blouse and slipped under the covers with him, nor did he know how he ended up on top of her between her naked thighs. Her hands were locked around his waist like a ring and that ring was pulling him toward her, while she was moaning: "Oh, it hurts!" *What hurts, why does it hurt*, he thought to himself and tried to pull away, but the ring of her arms pressed him ever more firmly to her body. As soon as he felt her warmth, she again let out long, muted moans and again pressed him to her, while he kept wondering what was hurting her and why. This went on for a long time, a very long time, to the point of exhaustion, and he finally felt himself sinking into some warmth and his body all at once relaxed into sweet helplessness.

In the morning he hitched up the buggy and headed to the estate. He and Mona had decided to get married the coming Sunday and he wanted to take a few things for their future household. Grandpa Kitty Cat had already quizzed him as to what was left in the estate house, and having gotten wind of big game, he set off in his donkey cart after Nikolin and he wasn't disappointed – the housewares had not yet been plundered. He ran from room to room, shouting: "This ain't a house, but a royal palace!"

Nikolin took a few tablecloths, a crystal pitcher with glasses, a pair of boots, forks, spoons, plus a few more housewares and wanted to leave, but Grandpa Kitty Cat grabbed on to the door handle and refused to let him lock it.

"Are you plumb out of your mind? You're gonna leave all this loot to be plundered by strangers?!"

"I don't need that junk, nor do I have anywhere to put it."

"You call this junk?" Grandpa Kitty Cat was walking around the parlor, touching the furniture. Give me the keys, you go on back if that's what you want. I'm not budging from here till I've taken what needs to be taken."

Nikolin didn't feel like arguing, so he gave him the keys and left him to run wild in the house. He'd only been away from Mona for an hour, and already it seemed that he hadn't seen her for a whole eternity, he hurried to get back as soon as possible to see her, to hear her voice, to delight in her presence, to make sure it wasn't all just some happy dream, but that he was happy wide awake.

Grandpa Kitty Cat returned late that afternoon with an overloaded cart. And the next day he went back to the estate with a horse cart he'd borrowed from his friend Petko Bulgaria. For several days the two of them set out and came back with the cart crammed full, until they had carried off everything that wasn't nailed to the floor. And so, if Nikolin was in seventh heaven, then Grandpa Kitty Cat was even a little bit higher than him, in eighth heaven. He, too, was living in another world, in the world of that old fairy tale in which the daughter of a poor peasant marries the king's son. The house, the barn, and the yard were filled with leather sofas and armchairs, with Persian rugs and tables, beds with bedsprings and chests of drawers, tins full of lard and cooking oil. He'd also brought the radio, the gramophone, the paraffin lamps, the chickens, the geese, the turkeys and a pig, the shovels, the picks and axes; there, too, were all of Devetakov's clothes, underclothes, and shoes, as well as the little varnished table he had been sitting at the day of his suicide.

Mona wanted to have a civil wedding, because they weren't prepared to throw a big reception, and in any case the house was so crammed full of things that they could barely make their way through the cramped space. They signed their names on the dotted line at the village soviet, came back home and had lunch, and that was the extent of their wedding celebration. Nikolin had decided to build a new house the next year, but the close quarters forced him to move up his plans and only a few days after the wedding he started looking for builders and materials. The village was uneasy, there were rumors that a cooperative farm would be founded, rumors of a new war, of nationalization, of state delivery quotas, people had split into parties, they went to meetings every night, arguing, fighting, settling old political scores. Nikolin knew about the happenings in the village from Mona, who went to the youth meetings and informed him of everything, but these events didn't interest him, much less move him. Up until then he had lived far from social life and he knew neither the passions nor the problems of that life. He had given his entire being over to the magic of female flesh, which made him deaf and blind to the world around him, and only in his fleeting moments of sobriety did he wonder and try to figure out with no success why people split into parties, why they argued and fought, when there was so much love and so many caresses in life, so much happiness and beauty.

The local folks from the village in turn wondered what kind of person this newcomer was. They knew he had twenty-five acres of good land and a big estate house, they figured he had money, too, and the word was that he was either very foolish or very presumptuous to be setting out to build a new house at a time when no one was sure of his property, and most were getting ready to flee to the cities if they founded a co-op. Because they didn't know his nature and since he kept his distance from everyone, the locals felt a mix of jealousy, scorn, and curiosity toward the newcomer and no one tried to get to know him. The only one in the village to stop by his house was Ilko Kralev, and he did so only very rarely, since he was sick.

Nikolin didn't manage to find materials, so he built only another room onto the old house. By the New Year, the room's plaster was dry, they outfitted it with Devetakov's furniture and moved in. In January Mona found she was pregnant and gave birth to a little girl at the end of May. After she got up from childbed, she went down to the village soviet on her own and officially named her Melpomena.

The first order of business for the village wiseacres was, of course, to stick the newborn with a nickname, so in case, God forbid, she were to die before she was registered down at the soviet, they would have some way of putting her down in the books in the afterworld. They nicknamed her without any particular creative exertion, instead making use of traditional familial succession – they added an adjective to the mother's nickname and the newborn became the Little Grand Dame. Then the child's name caught their attention. No one had heard that name in these parts and the local wiseacres gave their all trying to get to the root of it. They dug around in Grandpa Kitty Cat's family tree back nine generations, they dug through Nikolin's and even Devetakov's, but their etymological investigations led nowhere. Finally Mona, after savoring the satisfaction of keeping them in the dark for a long time, explained that she had named her daughter after some goddess of the theater. On its own, this explanation didn't mean anything to them, but since it was a question of theater, it was clear to everyone that only Ivan Shibilev was capable of coming up with such a name. For the time being the wiseacres were silent regarding the mystery surrounding the child's paternity. It had been born in the seventh month of the marriage and perhaps it was premature, but it just might turn out to be the offspring of one of Ivan Shibilev's countless "tricks."

However, the village did not accept the name in its original form and ruminated on it for a long time until it fit every mouth. To give it a local flavor, the name had to be stripped of its exoticism and strangeness and be ironed out till it was smooth as a white bean, so as not to prick the palate when pronounced. After this prolonged articulation, in which the young and old alike took part, from Melpomena, through Mena, Melpa, Melmena, etc., the name arrived at its most perfect form – Mela.

Only Grandpa Kitty Cat had no inkling that his granddaughter bore the name of the ancient muse of tragedy, and from the looks of it he had no inkling at all that his granddaughter even existed. He rarely picked her up and never boasted to anybody that he had the most beautiful and cleverest grandchild in the village. While his granddaughter made her first attempts to charm those around her with toothless smiles and to enrapture them with her cooing, Grandpa Kitty Cat was living out his material ascendency and all his attention was fixed on how to savor it to the hilt and, more importantly, how to show it off. As always, he got up in the morning after the sun had risen, went out into the yard, and yawned three times, and his yawns sounded like a cat's meowing – meeeooow – hence the source of his nickname. Depending on the weather, his meowing could be heard throughout the whole village or just in the neighborhood, but in any case it always carried past two houses to the third, from where at the same time came the tobacco-fueled coughing and hacking of his friend Petko Bulgaria. "Mornin', Koyno, mornin', Petko!" After this exchange of morning greetings complete with meowing and coughing, Grandpa Kitty Cat would wet two fingers from the spigot in the sink, touch them to his eyelids and thus quickly and economically wash up. If it was a holiday and sunny, Grandpa Kitty Cat would stretch out somewhere in the yard or garden. There were little niches everywhere strewn with hay or some little rug where he loved to lie down and nap like a tomcat. About an hour later, Petko Bulgaria would show up and say: "Long live Bulgaria! What'll it be today?" The order of the day was whatever Grandpa Kitty Cat wanted – backgammon or sixty-six with cards made out of cigarette boxes decorated with little crosses, squares, radishes, a priest, a boy, and a girl. They would settle into some feline lair and play without a whit of gamblers' zeal, lazily and silently, for lack of anything better to do. Just as in the morning when they exchanged greetings with meowing and coughing, when they were playing they would have one and the same inarticulate dialogue: "Mmm?" "Uh- huh!" "Mmm?" "Uh-huh!" This dialogue could be an expression of classical sloth, but it might also conceal some deeper meaning, known only to the two of them, for example: "I really stuck it to you that time, didn't I?" "Not so fast, don't you know in the end you'll be the one getting walloped!"

Every weekday Grandpa Kitty Cat faced the same dilemma – to go out to the fields or not. It always seemed to him that he could put off the job until the next day, but when he saw his neighbors filing out toward the field, he would decide that he and Mona should go too. Immediately, however, some clairvoyant premonition would overtake him that it might rain or that a strong wind might come up. He would strain his mind to remember how the sunset had been the previous day, had it been wrapped in bloodred clouds or not, had the roosters been crowing at any old time, had there been a halo around the moon, and if he remembered any of these omens, he would put off the work until the following day. Thanks to his meteorological acumen, acquired over the years through close observation of natural phenomena and the behavior of animals, Grandpa Kitty Cat could guess the weather forecast a day in advance and never once had he allowed the elements to surprise him far from home. Even when his forecasts were inaccurate, he still managed to outrun the elements, because the whole day while he was hoeing, reaping, or mowing, he never took his eyes off the sky. If a cloud appeared, even if only as large as his hat, he was ready to ditch his work and hightail it back to the village. Such clouds often appeared in the worst heat waves of summer, floating like balloons through the azure sky, their shadows passing over the heat-scorched field like ghosts. Sometimes they swelled, turning from golden to ashen blue and showering a few droplets down. One of these droplets would inevitably strike Grandpa Kitty Cat's straw hat and he would immediately grab his bag from the pear tree: "Mona, let's go!" And they would leave right in the middle of the day so as to escape the rain that never fell. Only then would people from the neighboring fields look up and say: "Koyno must've felt a raindrop!" Koyno Raindrop, that was Grandpa Kitty Cat's second nickname, which was used only when he was working in the field, hence very rarely. All in all he had about five acres and no matter how symbolically he and Mona worked the land, they somehow managed to sow, hoe over, and reap it – sometimes on their own, sometimes with the help of his brother-in-law, relatives, and neighbors.

Nikolin transformed their lives like a magic wand. Their house expanded by one room and was filled with luxurious furnishings, their land grew from five acres to thirty, and they had cold hard cash on hand. Mona no longer had to stalk the chickens in their nests for eggs to trade for a piece of cloth from the village shop; now Kichka Kraleva made her blouses and skirts of the finest cloth, which she bought from the city. Now she really had become a grand dame, curvier after giving birth and somehow wantonly beautiful, self-assured, and fully aware of her feminine charms. Grandpa Kitty Cat also changed his attire, by refashioning and altering the clothes he had swiped from the late Devetakov's wardrobe. Nothing quite fit him because he was short, so he looked like a boy wearing his older brother's hand-me-downs. The only thing he couldn't replace was his red quilted jacket, since Devetakov's suit coats were too big for him, but to make up for it he wore a pocket watch on a silver chain that he had found on one of his marauder's raids on the estate house.

"Long live Bulgaria, I tell you, Koyno, you sure did strike gold!" Petko Bulgaria would tell him every time they played backgammon or sixty-six.

"Better to be born lucky than born rich!" Grandpa Kitty Cat would reply with the satisfaction of a man convinced that lady luck was obliged to favor him at any cost. "I may not be much of one for digging in the fields, but this time I struck gold and then some!"

They would be playing as always in their silent, lazy way, out of a lack of anything better to do and conversing inarticulately: "Mmm?" "Uh-huh!" Now, however, they did not hole up in some feline lair in the yard or garden, but sat in the house or, if the weather was nice, under the awning of the barn. Grandpa Kitty Cat would sit in the dark-brown leather armchair, while Bulgaria would take the chair upholstered in red velvet, and they would play on the little varnished table that Devetakov had been sitting at on the day of his suicide. Grandpa Kitty Cat loved nestling in that deep armchair that swallowed him up to his ears in its maw, he couldn't get enough of its softness and the distinctive scent of the leather. Even though his straw mattress had been tossed out long ago and replaced by a bed with springs, by day he purred away in the armchair and sometimes even spent the night there. His other favorite item was the gramophone. The young couple had moved into the new room and taken the radio, leaving the gramophone to him. He would put it on when he was napping in the house or outside, he'd also put it on when he and Petko Bulgaria played backgammon. There were lots of records with all kinds of music, their melodies were strange and unfamiliar, but Grandpa Kitty Cat played them so people would know he had a gramophone at home, the likes of which could only be found at the community center. In nice weather, he would take the gramophone outside, its snoring, shrieking, and gasping melodies would waft over the village and everyone nearby would stop to listen to them.

But out of everything, Grandpa Kitty Cat was most addicted to the buggy. He would hitch up the horse, sit in the shiny two-wheeler, and set off to make the rounds of the village at any old time of day. The handsome gray horse stepped slowly and solemnly, while Grandpa Kitty Cat sat even more solemnly in the seat, all ears and eyes to see whether people were looking at him and whispering. He especially liked going down to the village store in the buggy at dusk, where the men gathered to shoot the breeze, or to the *horemag* – a combined hotel, restaurant, and store. Earlier he had never set foot there, because he didn't have a cent to order a glass of wine, but now he would sit there for hours on end. He couldn't stand alcohol and cigarettes, but he ordered both one and the other, so that everyone could see that he had a purse and that his purse was chock full. Indivisibly by his side, of course, sat his loyal friend Petko Bulgaria. They were like two peas in a pod and the sudden difference in their material standing did not undermine but only strengthened their years-long friendship. Bulgaria did not feel that envy arising from differences in material standing which divides the rich from the poor like a chasm; on the contrary, he became all the more attached to his friend and became his orderly of sorts. He had a little land and a son to work it, he went around as ragged as a tattered flag and was so scrawny that, as the locals put it, you could hear his bones creaking a mile away when he moved. He was the very personification of destitution, which only underscored Grandpa Kitty Cat's superiority in every respect. Bulgaria reinforced that superiority with his toadyism and verbal praise for his friend, and as a reward for his efforts Grandpa Kitty Cat magnanimously allowed him to taste of the earthly blessings fate had so generously bestowed upon him. The two of them did everything together, they rode in the buggy wherever and whenever the spirit moved them, they went to visit the neighboring villages, listened to the gramophone, and at the *horemag* Bulgaria drank the wine and smoked the cigarettes that Grandpa Kitty Cat ordered for prestige alone.

At first the locals looked upon Grandpa Kitty Cat as a lucky devil who had won the state lottery, with surprise and a bit of envy, but without hard feelings, since he had attained his prosperity through blind chance, which is blind precisely so it can show its favor to one in a million. He, however, was not capable of enjoying this blessing of fate humbly and decently and was constantly irritating people with his nouveau riche antics. At that time everyone was worried about impending events and didn't know what tomorrow would bring (the agitprop brigades for the cooperative farm were after them day and night, committees were going door to door to collect state quotas of grain, wool from slaughtered sheep, and milk from dry cows), but Grandpa Kitty Cat looked down on all that from the heights of his newfound abundance and said: "I delivered my quotas, yessiree! The grain and the wool and the milk to boot. Whatever we didn't have enough of, my son-in-law bought on the black market, and we rounded out our deliveries right as rain. I can sleep soundly at night."

His insolent smugness, his round pink face, and the satisfied glint in his beady little eyes soon turned him into a living caricature, and the local folks' good-natured mockery mutated into scorn and hatred. Few sat down at his table besides Bulgaria, and when they did it was only to toy with him and laugh at him later. As subsequently became clear, the family's brief economic ascendancy was due to a mix-up on the part of the authorities in the two neighboring villages. Nikolin had abandoned the land he'd inherited from Devetakov as soon as he left the estate, but the authorities in Orlovtsi had absentmindedly thought he was delivering his quotas here in our village, while our folks here thought he was giving them to Orlovtsi. Only when it came time to found cooperative farms in both villages did the Orlovtsi people discover that Nikolin owed them deliveries for twenty-five acres of land, a cow, a pig, thirty sheep, and they forced him to hand them over. Nikolin bought the grain, the milk, and the meat on the black market, his savings melted away completely, and he became a founding member of the co-op with five acres of land. Alongside his wife, who often brought him to the youth club parties, theater performances, and on visits to fellow villagers' homes, he little by little joined society, and again under his wife's influence he started to participate in some community endeavors. We lived in the same neighborhood and he was among the group of landowners Stoyan Kralev had charged me with recruiting for the future co-op. Knowing the story of his life up until now, which had been spent in lonely and sad isolation, and also knowing that interacting with other people perturbed and upset him, I never supposed he would agree to join the co-op as soon as I opened my mouth. He didn't even give me the chance to "propagandize" him when we met in the street one evening and he invited me to his place to see his little daughter. Mona showed no interest in our conversation, which revolved around the future co-op, while the head of the household and the owner of the land didn't put up the resistance I had expected. He made some exclamations that gave me to understand that since the land would become the property of everyone and since "everyone would work it," that "everyone" clearly excluded himself. He agreed with only a single condition – that we not touch his horse and buggy, "as for the rest, they can do what they like with it."

Anyone else in my place likely would have been surprised by how lightly these people took joining the co-op, especially knowing that almost all landowners came to that decision after dramatic equivocations and teeth-gnashing. Since we were neighbors and I had the chance to observe them up close, it wasn't difficult for me to explain why they "stepped from one era into another" with such indifference – they were possessed by feelings and passions so strong and insurmountable that they were blind to everything happening around them in that difficult time. Grandpa Kitty Cat was living out his second youth, he had gotten it into his head to find himself a "granny" and tirelessly disconcerted the elderly widows in our village and the surrounding ones with his belated Don Juan shtick. He and Bulgaria went around on "matchmaking visits" but could never quite find a lady to their liking. They were capricious and hard to please, because the candidates offered themselves up willingly as soon as they saw the groom step out of his buggy all rounded and rosy-cheeked and self-assured, such that his looks alone said: "Whoever makes a match with me will come into my house wearing only her slippers, leave the rest to me!"

Nikolin was completely devoted to his wife and child, for him everything in the world was just and beautiful. He didn't even worry about the state of his home, where the Baroque exquisiteness of Devetakov's furnishings was so grotesquely combined with things suited to an impoverished hovel; he didn't notice the plebian boasting and clownish antics of his father-in-law, which made them the laughingstock of the village. Mona was preoccupied by her love for Ivan Shibilev and by uneasy thoughts about the future of this love. At first they had been "paired up," as the village did with young men and girls who showed a liking for each other or simply because they lived in the same neighborhood and were frequently seen together. This "pairing up" didn't mean there was any romantic connection between the young people, it was a playful vow between the boy and the girl and only rarely ended in marriage. They had paired up Ivan Shibilev and Mona this way when she had become a young woman, because they always saw them together in the community center rehearsing plays or creating some cultural-education program for the youth club parties. Ivan Shibilev gave her the romantic leads, put her name first on the playbills, and was ecstatically enthusiastic about her acting, while she for her part repaid him with selfless devotion even in the theater troupe's difficult early years when girls were not allowed onstage. She joined the troupe while still in middle school, along with Kichka Kraleva, and hadn't left the stage since. Due to a dearth of women, Ivan Shibilev often gave her two roles in one and the same play and she managed to transform herself into an elderly woman and a young girl equally convincingly. She was the village's unequivocal beauty, and Ivan Shibilev dressed her and made her up such that onstage she looked even more charming and brilliant.

The village realized that her love for Ivan Shibilev was fateful when she became a young woman and the bachelors started circling around her. Candidates turned up not only from our village and the neighboring ones, but from the city as well, they were everything from simple to educated, rich to poor, and all were sent packing with their tails between their legs. Finally the son of Rich Kosta from Vladimirovo tried his luck, too. Rich Kosta really was the richest villager in the region, he had one hundred and fifty acres of land, a steam mill, and two stores. He was so sure of his success that he sent his matchmakers to see Grandpa Kitty Cat in broad daylight in all their old-fashioned splendor, in a painted sleigh pulled by four horses, with gifts, bagpipes squealing, and guns blazing. The matchmakers didn't even haggle, but asked what day the engagement would take place. The engagement never did take place, because they never so much as caught sight of the would-be bride. When she found out about their arrival, Mona hid at a cousin's house and only came home the next day. Before running away from the house, she had told her father not to negotiate with the matchmakers, but to send them away. But how can you send away Rich Kosta's envoys? In the morning, Mona found her father as crestfallen as a newly bankrupted millionaire, a bankruptcy that was entirely his daughter's fault. His despair had transformed him from a sleepy Kitty Cat into an enraged lynx, and as soon as he saw her, he leapt in front of her in a single bound, ready to sink his claws into her face. This transformation came over him for the first and final time and lasted only a second, because the next moment he once again had become a peaceful house cat. His daughter's blue eyes, which so bewitched the young men, hypnotized him like the eyes of a snake, robbing him of his will. Nevertheless, he managed to pour out his rage at the top of his lungs.

"Your mother! You're just like your mother!" By affronting the memory of his deceased wife, who when alive, it seems, had hypnotized him with her gaze in exactly the same way, Grandpa Kitty Cat indirectly wanted to affront his daughter, except that she was not insulted in the least, so he couldn't contain himself and shouted: "I know why you're acting so high and mighty. Because of that jester Ivan Shibilev, whose hammer never falls in the same place twice. He'll put such a banana peel under your feet that when you fall there'll be no getting up!" After uttering that sad prophecy, Grandpa Kitty Cat lay down on his bed, pulled the covers up to his chin, and fell silent before adding: "Turning away Rich Kosta's matchmakers! I can't even get my mind around it!"

The other villagers were also astonished by Mona's recklessness. They had gotten used to making sport of her suitors, and as soon as a new one turned up, they would wait to see how she would "send him packing." But to turn away Rich Kosta's envoys, and to do so as if turning away a beggar from your door no less, this was more than recklessness. But what the cause of this recklessness might be – whether foolishness, capriciousness, or madness – no one could say. However, this mystery was soon solved. After the incident with Rich Kosta, Ivan Shibilev came back to the village – as always, no one knew where he was coming from and how long he would stay – and it was then that our locals noticed that he and Mona met on the street every day or in the evenings at the community center, from where Ivan Shibilev would see her home. Now it became clear that they were bound by love, a love as great as the sacrifice Mona was making for Ivan Shibilev. Some, of course, felt sorry for her and even gloated over her misfortune, depending on to what extent they had been aggrieved by this rivalry or her disregard, but everyone was bewildered as to how she could be so blinded by her love for Ivan Shibilev, since no one in the village could say what kind of man he was. When Ivan Shibilev did something good, and he could do lots of good things, everyone was struck with admiration for him and even declared him the village's pride and joy. On the other hand, when he got up to his crazy tricks and mischief, and he could certainly get up to such things as well, they unanimously declared that despite everything, he was nothing but a ne'er-do-well, a scapegrace, a buffoon, a ladies' man, and even a charlatan. Every day they found him in a different mood, sometimes completely absorbed in some undertaking, polite and courteous, other times neglectful of everything, hardheaded and spiteful, and this hindered them from seeing his true self. Mona knew him better than everyone, his inconstant character caused her the greatest suffering, yet she nevertheless loved him just as he was – restless and exulted, confiding and withdrawn, sad and serious, carefree and cheerful. When he gave her her first role in the community center troupe, she had been ten years old, and he twenty, as patient and affectionate with her as an older brother with a younger sister. Even back then she had become attached to him, just as little girls grow attached to good teachers. Over the years this attachment transformed into awe, and from awe into love, a love that can only spring up in the uncorrupted heart of a village girl, bashful, pure, and utterly devoted. She burned with shame merely at the thought of going up to him and telling him how much she loved him and that he was the only meaning in her life, and that the world began and ended with him and him alone.

She declared her love to him by catching his meaning from a glance or a single word, by listening to him enraptured for hours on end, she was ready to follow him anywhere at any time, she declared her love for him most fervently onstage, when the two of them were playing a pair of lovers, as always. These roles always involved declarations of love, there were also scenes in which the man abandoned his beloved for various reasons, and Mona would act them out with such feeling that she was bathed in tears, moving the audience to tears as well. Her love for Ivan Shibilev had become legendary and everyone tried to guess how it would end – in marriage or in heartbreak. Mona was already twenty-one years old, making her an old maid by implacable village statistics; she kept turning away her numerous suitors, while Ivan Shibilev neither married her nor cut her loose to try her luck elsewhere. "He's like a dog on a haystack – he won't eat it, but he won't give it up, either" – that's what the villagers would say, taking Mona's side. When she spoke to him onstage with tears in her eyes: "Don't leave me, I shall wither and die for the love of you, I shall take my own life!" the public would jump to its feet, yelling at Ivan Shibilev: "Marry her already, you scoundrel! Why are you toying with the girl, why are you torturing her, may God strike you dead!" While to Mona, they would yell: "You've wasted enough tears on him, send that charlatan packing and find yourself a real man!"

No one suspected that their love was pure and uncorrupted by carnal passions. Ivan Shibilev, despite his unbridled nature, had not laid a finger on Mona, besides in their theatrical performances, and even then only before the audience's eyes. Even when they were alone in the community center or on the street in the evening, he had not permitted himself anything more than a handshake.

There could be several possible reasons for his platonic relations with Mona; however, one appeared the most likely – his desire to relish their purity. We shall return to these reasons, but for now we must briefly recall the circumstances that gave rise to them. Where had we left off the story of Ivan Shibilev? Oh, yes, on that late afternoon when he could not find Veva among those getting off the train. From his conversations with her he had gotten the impression that she had grown up and lived in that city, hence it was only natural to look for her there. He asked about her at the theater first of all, and he didn't ask just anyone, but the two stagehands, because he felt they would know the theater's artistic troupe better than anyone. They told him they didn't know any such actress, nor had they ever heard of her. To him, it seemed like his life had suddenly been split into two halves, and if in the first half there were still some memories, both joyful and sad, in the second, the future half, there would be nothing but anguish, meaninglessness, and hopelessness. And this hopelessness was making his heart bleed when someone tapped him lightly, yet insistently, on the shoulder. He raised his head and through his tears saw a woman standing in front of him, with her hand on his shoulder. It was Darina Mileva, or Darya, as they called her, whom he had known from the Varna Theater for a year and with whom he had spent a whole month on tour.

Darya was twenty-eight or twenty-nine years old, but was already an established actress. Without being brilliant, she was one of those actresses they call a mainstay of the theatrical collective, and whom directors entrust with roles with complete confidence. She was hardworking, calm, and so natural onstage that everywhere she had performed around the country she had become the audience's favorite. Like most provincial actors at that time, she didn't stay in any one place for long, but this was not due to external, but rather to personal, reasons. Her husband, whom she had married at the age of nineteen, was also an actor, a typical provincial crank, a drunkard and brawler, whom they took into theater troupes only because of her. Soon after their marriage he slid into complete alcoholism, Darya ran away from him several times, but he refused to grant her a divorce; instead, he staunchly followed her all around the country to disgrace both Darya and himself with his rows in front of their new co-workers. Sometimes he would disappear for months or even a whole year, writing her all the while (without ever telling her his address) that he could live without her, that he would grant her a divorce, and that he would never come looking for her, but then he would do the exact opposite, arriving unexpectedly, barging into her apartment most brutally and sponging off her. Darya pitied him, as one pities a sick and helpless person, but in the end she would not be able to stand his drunken benders and would look for work in a different theater. Despite these forced resettlements and her unhappy married life, she was still fresh faced. She was petite, but hardy like fresh fruit, with dark hair and smooth skin, such that she could play women of all ages equally convincingly.

"Can I believe my eyes?" she said, seeing him standing there helplessly, leaning against the wall by the entrance to the theater. His face, where traces of dried tears could be seen, and his moist, darkened gaze radiated inconsolable grief, which he could not hide in any way, nor did he try to hide it. His first question for Darya was whether she knew an actress by the name of Genevieve (Veva), and she immediately understood the reason for his grief, which, incidentally, made him so sweet and endearing that she didn't have the heart to leave him on his own and invited him to her home. After many years of wandering, she had finally come back to the house where she was born. It was old and cozy, with a broad yard sunk in flowers and fruit trees, with three rooms on each of its two floors. After dinner,

Darya took her guest on a walk around the city, they strolled down the main street, sat for a while in a pastry shop, and went back home. During their walk, he told her everything, she heard him out with sympathy and settled him in to one of the rooms to get a good night's sleep, so in the morning, well rested and calm, he could decide what to do from then on. The next morning her guest asked her where there was a hotel, so he could rent a room for several days, and she told him that under no circumstances would she allow him to go to a hotel, and that as long as he was in the city, he would be staying with her. She assumed that when he looked for and couldn't find his Veva, he would leave, but he, it seemed, had no intention of leaving so soon. During the day he would go out and about several times, writing poetry, reading books or newspapers, or drawing, while in the evening, if there was a play, he would go to the theater, where Darya had arranged for him to get in free.

After the performances, he would wait for Darya to remove her makeup, she would take his arm, and the two of them would go home. They always ate dinner alone, because Darya's parents were asleep by that time. Her father was paralyzed and half blind, but her mother was still healthy, yet constantly busy with her sick husband and the housework, so she could not wait up for them. After dinner the two of them would go up to Darya's room and stay there until midnight. If she wasn't learning a new role, for which Ivan Shibilev acted as her partner, they would read poetry, play various games, and their games became more and more erotic until one night Darya ravished him. It really was ravishment, because Ivan Shibilev seemed attached to her, her closeness excited him, yet every time they accidentally touched he would bashfully and timidly pull away, and this indecisiveness was due to a trauma of an erotic nature. His will had been tormented so terribly by the obsessive thought of a single woman that he was in no state to do anything to free himself from that thought. Darya knew from experience and observation that chaste nineteen-year-old young men fell in love platonically "for their whole lives," yet at the same time were tortured by the mysteries of female flesh, they were ashamed of this feeling, which debased their hearts' purest impulses, but as soon as they experienced female flesh, they somehow matured all at once and became more reasonable. She freed her young friend from this primordial and agonizing mystery not, of course, out of pedagogical inducements, but under the impetus of a long-suppressed passion, at the same time freeing her own will as well, since she, too, bashful and "wild" to the men who had tried to court her, had been traumatized by the unusual state of her marriage.

At a more mature age, Ivan Shibilev would realize that when we praise our fiery, pure, and one-and-only love as the supreme gift from the heavens, we are actually praising and deifying our carnal attraction to the opposite sex. At that time, of course, he had no way of knowing this and lived according to the laws of that other, equally ancient and indisputable truth, that youth is the time of the flesh, and he didn't realize how his love for Veva, extolled in his poems and proclaimed with so much anguish, had turned into some vague dream-like vision and disappeared, only to be reborn in his love for Darya. Becoming a man is a complicated and painful process, as is every passage from one state to another, accompanied not only by the urge to discover the mystery of female flesh, but also by shyness, fear, and doubts, by powerful explosions of boldness as well as slumps, low spirits, and deathly despair. Several months of Ivan Shibilev's life tumbled into the abyss of an exhausting bacchanalia, and when he finally got ahold of himself and came to his senses, he truly had gained a certain self-confidence in his manhood and became more reasonable, insofar as a person like him could be reasonable at all. In the meantime Darya had introduced him into theatrical circles, and just as everywhere, here, too, Ivan Shibilev quickly won everyone over, including the director of the touring troupe. This director and the director of the

Pleven Regional Theater put on five plays in one season with a cast of fourteen members, most of whom were local amateur actors. As can be seen from the memoirs of actors from that time, quickly cobbled-together productions (there were even cases of plays being put together in two or three days) were a common occurrence at some of the provincial theaters, which clearly showed their amateur, and at times unscrupulous, nature. The reasons for this were above all material, since the provincial theaters at that time did not receive or received only very little financial support from state and public institutions. To guarantee a decent income, theatrical troupes staged two hundred or more performances in dozens of towns and villages in a single season. Given these conditions, it was not difficult for the most enthusiastic citizens to join a theatrical troupe, much less for Ivan Shibilev, who could memorize his role on the first read-through, and who had some experience onstage to boot. He performed three roles in three of the plays quite successfully and perhaps would have stayed at that theater for a longer time if Darya's husband had not returned.

He was around forty, quite tall and broad shouldered, with the weary face of an alcoholic, and most importantly of all, he was at the height of yet another bender. As soon as he had arrived in town he had had a few rounds with friends and had learned from them that his wife was living with a young actor, and as soon as he set foot in the house he barged into Ivan Shibilev's room and hurled himself at him. Ivan Shibilev was surprised by his unceremonious entrance, but recognized him immediately (Darya had described him to a tee), and although he was good and scared, he nevertheless was not cautious, since he couldn't believe the man would dare to rough him up. Her husband was not speaking, but roaring, he asked Ivan Shibilev what he was doing in his house, called him a dirty bastard, knocked him to the floor, and started choking him. Even though he was half his age and in far better shape, Ivan Shibilev barely managed to wrench the man's hands from his neck and to catch his breath; he wriggled out from beneath him, but the man stuck out his leg and tripped him. Ivan Shibilev fell and while falling, cut his forehead right between his eyebrows on the edge of the stove, blood poured into his eyes and down his face. He jumped to his feet again, and, blinded, felt his way to the door, but then the drunkard pushed him from behind. So as not to fall down the stairs, he clung to the railing, but the other man grasped him by the ankles and started dragging him down. This is how Darya found them. Frightened by this scene, she screamed and darted forward to break them apart, her mother appeared as well and shoved the drunken man into one room, while they bandaged Ivan Shibilev's wound in another. In the evening of the same day he moved into a hotel and spent around a week there before leaving the city.

The conclusion of their affair was as sudden and quick as it was invidious and dangerous – if they had been caught red-handed "at the scene of the crime," it might have cost him his life. But the worst part was that Darya, after taking him to the hotel, did not come to see him again, nor did she try to contact him. Ivan Shibilev didn't dare go looking for her at the theater, so as not to bring the scandal there as well; he waited five days and on the sixth left the city. And thus began his many odysseys, which differed only in the cities where he would spend some time, and in the professions he practiced there (as an actor in some amateur or professional troupe, as an artist, as a ballad-monger in the circus, as a soldier for two years, a housepainter, a musician in pubs and restaurants), but in their essence they were all the same, because everywhere they accepted him gladly because of his charm, talents, and his "golden hands," the men were fond of him, the women fell in love with him, and in the end, due to some subconscious recklessness or excessive sensitivity, he would get himself caught up in a situation in which these very same people, especially the women, seemed to unwittingly, yet inevitably, aggrieve him and leave in his soul some impurity, disappointment, or even despair, and then absolutely spontaneously, he would rush back to his Ithaca, his native village. But what would he find there? Ignorance, slovenliness, coarseness, but also spontaneity and calm, and something that seemed like signs of life. Everything would be sunk in a deep layer of dust, mud, or snow, grayish, shabby, and muted, such that it weighed on his soul with a soft, caressing quiet, in which he could hear the beating of his heart.

As always after his return, not a week would pass and he would start sensing, hearing, and seeing how in the bosom of this desolation life was sprouting, growing, and finally bursting forth in the woodworking shop, at the tavern, in the little mud-brick community center, in the school, and even in the church with Father Encho. In the woodworking shop he would make frames, or a table or chair, in the tavern he would entertain the locals by playing various instruments, in the little church, sitting with Father Encho in the narthex by the stove, he would paint a Virgin Mary, a Jesus ascending to heaven, or whichever icon the old priest happened to need, at the community center he organized parties or plays, at the blacksmith's he would build a reaping machine out of scraps of iron, like the ones he had seen wealthier folks in the neighboring villages using, to help lighten the harvest's heavy workload. The reaping machine would work for a day, a week, or a summer before disintegrating into its constituent parts, because there was no one to fix it.

Ivan Shibilev would already be flying off to or would have flown off to his next odyssey, toward life in the cities and towns, a life delusive with the magic of the unknown, filled with delights, ostentation, and bitterness, with an insuppressible thirst for fulfillment, enticing and severe, beautiful and freakishly ugly, only to return once again to the village exhausted and disappointed, with oversaturated senses and a tormented mind. Besides his mother, Mona was also waiting for him, and over the years she had grown from a little girl into a young woman. In his constant association with her there was a dose of egoism, albeit subconscious, because he would come running, dogged by the malevolent storms of his worldly exploits, to take shelter beneath the eaves of her moral purity, to drink from her the strength, consolation, and reassurance that would cleanse him. Perhaps this is how we should explain his complex and platonic relations with her, so uncharacteristic of his nature, and perhaps also with his fear of desecrating her honor and life so fatefully: One misstep and his quiet harbor could change into a prison.

And so it was until the night of Radka's wedding. That same night, along with wretchedness over what had happened, for the first time Ivan Shibilev had felt another emotion as well the moment he saw the young man from the other village, whom Mona had brought to the wedding, and that emotion was – let us not beat around the bush – jealousy. To be jealous on Mona's account, that seemed to him, no matter which way he looked at it, strange and almost absurd. She had grown up and become a woman in front of his eyes, thus he had gotten used to thinking of her as some kind of half child half woman, he had also convinced himself that he had some sort of right to her, just as she owed him some sort of filial piety, as it were, so it seemed unbelievable that one day she would have a relationship with a man. That evening, however, when he saw Nikolin, he also saw Mona in a different light and realized that she was already of a marriageable age (how beautifully that was written on her face!) and that she had long been waiting for the moment when he would ask for her hand, or if he did not want her, when he would "set her free," so she could marry someone else before she got too old, regardless of whether she loved him or not. She had brought Nikolin, with whom she seemed to have relations, to the wedding to remind him of her innermost longings, of his negligence of her fate as a woman, and perhaps also as proof that, in any case, she had a man waiting in the wings whom she could marry whenever she liked. He also thought to himself that she, alas, had every right to do so, since she couldn't spend her whole life serving as the safe shore after his shipwrecks, without him having clarified his relationship with her. He told himself that it was humiliating to feel jealous of this simple young man, but every time he caught sight of Nikolin, jealousy pierced his heart, and with great effort he managed to hide it by entertaining the others with magic tricks and musical antics. Nikolin's presence made an impression on everyone, he attracted their gazes and they openly admired both his clothing, which was slightly different from ours, as well as his face, that of a handsome, righteous young man who emanated charm, bashfulness, and virtuousness. Ivan Shibilev found it unpleasant when some of the women most unceremoniously looked from one young man to the other, comparing them as rivals, while others, likely tipsy and in heightened spirits, spoke openly in the newcomer's favor. But the most unpleasant and insulting part was that Mona, too, saw and heard them praising the stranger and, instead of showing them in some way that she had nothing to do with him, kept whispering in his ear confidentially and smiling at him. *She's a woman, what can you expect,* Ivan Shibilev thought to himself. *She didn't dare admit to me that she had a boyfriend, and now she's showing him to me in front of the whole village, perhaps without realizing how cruel she is being to me.*

At that moment, with his pride wounded and in a fit of jealousy, Ivan Shibilev went out into the yard and stood in the shadow of the barn. A minute later Mona threaded her way through the crowd and went over to him. From the look he had given her, she had understood that he would be waiting for her outside and she had followed him. Ivan Shibilev took her by the hand and led her toward the garden, and from there through the fields. They walked in silence, from time to time she felt his fingers gently squeezing her wrist, as if trying to tell her something he could not or did not want to put into words. After a half an hour, the winding strip of the path, lit up by the silvery glimmer of the stars, led them to the vineyard. They slipped into the narrow rows between the vine stumps, he walking ahead, and she coming after him, they wound to the left and right until they ended up in front of the watchman Salty Kalcho's hut. Ivan Shibilev lowered the latch on the door and went inside, she went in after him. Inside the hut there was a straw bed covered with a rug, and a few dishes in the niche of the hearth: a small pot, two earthenware bowls, a gas lamp, a pitcher, and matches. Ivan Shibilev lit the wood in the hearth and the hut filled with the scent of savory, mint, and ripe grapes, which were hanging in bunches from the ceiling. They stood for a while staring at the fire's living flames, then Ivan Shibilev turned to her, embraced her, and set her on his knees like a little child…

Years later, Mona superstitiously thought that the night in Radka's father's hut was a bad omen for her, because that same night Radka and her father had been the unhappiest people in the world, while she had been the happiest. Fate had been trying to give her a sign that it was unfair and unnatural for her to be so insanely happy when her friend was standing on the edge of the abyss that was death. But she didn't notice this sign… That is also what she thought when she saw Nikolin coming up the road from Orlovo and she decided to take the most desperate of steps. She told herself that she shouldn't deceive such a good and innocent person, but she nevertheless put all her effort into making him feel at home and keeping him by her side. She had already realized two years ago, after speaking to him for only half an hour, that he was a good man, inexperienced with women and a virgin, she realized it even more clearly that night when she seduced him in her bed. She knew she shouldn't make him a sacrificial lamb, but her desperation, stronger and more ruthless than any moral inhibitions, was leading her toward deceit and treachery just as surely as one leads a blind man to the other side of the street. Her desperation also contained a measure of vengeance toward Ivan Shibilev, the pathetic and pointless vengeance of a woman in love, who has no other means to fight her beloved's indifference.

After that night in the hut, Ivan Shibilev had disappeared for months, but he would let her know where he was, what he was doing, and when he was thinking of returning. The village councilmen had opened his first letter and the whole village knew its contents, so from then on Ivan Shibilev came up with a code that no one could break. He sent her books of plays, magazines, old newspapers, and all sorts of printed materials, in which certain letters were underlined very lightly in pencil. Mona copied down the individual letters, arranged them into words and sentences, and thus pieced together his letters. In every letter Ivan Shibilev promised her that he would be back soon and then they would talk, and to her that meant that he would finally propose marriage to her. When he did return, he would indeed talk to her, but about completely different things: how he had acted in some theater group, how he had helped some artist or played at some restaurant. Every evening he came to pick her up from home, or, if the weather was bad, he would sneak into her room through the window. All their meetings ended with the slaking of his unquenchable passion and that was all they had to "talk about."

Over time, Mona began to gain some confidence where he was concerned and reminded him that the years were passing by for her and that it was time they settled down. Tormented by anticipation, doubts, and fear that someone would see them sneaking through the gardens and fields at night, she would sometimes become hysterical, kicking up a fuss and giving him an ultimatum – either they get married or they split up. After such scenes, Ivan Shibilev would not come to her and she would set out looking for him in the village. She doubted his devotion, she suffered heretofore unknown fits of jealousy, which, together with the anguish of loneliness and uncertainty, ate away at her soul. She knew that marriage would be a heavy burden for a scapegrace like him, yet she nevertheless believed him when he, flustered and frank as a child, would tell her that no matter what happened, he would never leave her, ever. She believed him and even felt guilty for offending him with her mistrust, she sought and found reasons to justify his wandering and thus created a vicious circle of illusions from which she could not escape.

In the two months since she had realized she was pregnant, she had had no word from Ivan Shibilev, she didn't know where he was and when he would return. It was a difficult pregnancy – her breasts swelled and hardened, certain smells made her nauseous, she slept only a few hours until midnight and then would get up every hour to throw up. She felt better in the afternoons, but even then she didn't dare go out into the village, because every woman would see that she was pregnant as soon as she looked her in the eye. The season protected her from curiosity as well, the villagers were harvesting their melon fields, followed by corn and grapes in the vineyard, such that none of her girlfriends stopped by to see her, but this also meant she had no way of finding out whether Ivan Shibilev had come back. At other times only one person from the village need spot him and within a minute everyone knew of his arrival, she would know it too from the face of the first person she met. No matter who that person might be, man or woman, on their face would be a strange expression of treacherous sympathy, scorn, and malice: "Your little boyfriend is back, go run to meet him!" Happy news, but also a sign that everyone made sport of her feelings, that the glorious time was long over when she had sent away her most brilliant suitors with a capricious grimace like a king's daughter, and when those same people had looked at her with bewilderment and reproach, but also with respect.

Sometimes deceptive premonitions or noises similar to the multiple signals that Ivan Shibilev had thought up for their secret meetings made her get up and go out late at night, tingling with impatience to peer into the shadow of the trees and to prick up her ears. The deluded beats of her heart echoed in the silence and she would head down the street to see if Ivan Shibilev's window was lighted up. In those warm, mystically white, quiet nights, her hope of settling down once and for all with Ivan Shibilev grew old with every hour, turning into a dark and ugly desperation. Ivan Shibilev might not return for a whole year or he might return earlier, but she didn't know how he would take the news of her pregnancy – would he want to get married or would he wander off somewhere again? Deep in her heart she suspected that he was capable of leaving her alone again, even pregnant, because she knew his soul, and it was an incomprehensible soul, angelically loving and demonically cruel.

The news that Devetakov had willed his books to Ilko Kralev and his twenty-five acres of land, house, livestock, and everything else to Nikolin had made the rounds of the village a couple of days after Ivan Shibilev had left for the city. Anguished over yet another impending separation, Mona had not tried to stop him because she was convinced that this time he would neglect all his other business and stay with her. Only half a year earlier she had sent away Rich Kosta's matchmakers in the most scandalous way, and she believed that Ivan Shibilev more than anyone would appreciate her gesture, which she had made only because of him. But it seemed that Ivan Shibilev had appreciated it in the opposite sense – since Mona, already compromised and labeled an old maid, had rejected her most advantageous match for marriage, that meant she was so firmly and fatally bound to him that she would never under any circumstances find another man. Wittingly or unwittingly, Ivan Shibilev had taken advantage of her slavish devotion, and wounded by his carelessness, she, for the first time, felt that her heart could not bear this love for him and that she would have to free herself somehow from its torments. And when she heard them talking about Nikolin in the village, she recalled how she had met him at her home and how even then she had sized him up with the insight of an experienced woman – simple-hearted, lonely, and uncorrupted, despite his twenty-seven years. He was more handsome than Ivan Shibilev, and charming in his unawareness of his own handsomeness, while his soft

Russian leather boots, wide-brimmed hat, black northern-style jacket, and white shirt, the likes of which no one in these parts wore, gave him the look of a tidy and staid young man. She mentally pictured herself next to him, resting heavily on the unshakable stronghold that he was, and realized that she was calling upon his image for help because it could comfort her in hours of spiritual anguish. But this mental comparison of him with Ivan Shibilev was a fleeting and painful game of the imagination, born of an impulse of subconscious vengeance and hatred toward her beloved, who had caused her such suffering precisely because of her love for him.

The evening of that same day her father mentioned Nikolin like an old friend or relative. "Well, what do you know, our boy Nikolin has become a real fat and flush landowner!"

"What's this 'our boy Nikolin,'" Mona snapped at him. "You had a drunken chat with him and now it's 'our boy Nikolin.'"

"That's how it is!" Grandpa Kitty Cat said. "Sometimes you spend your whole life talkin' with someone and you still don't understand him, but other times you can understand a man's soul from a single word. May the good Lord give you such a man to live with, then…"

He wanted to say something more, but he prudently fell silent out of fear of making her angry. After the numerous matchmaking fiascos and especially after the incident with Rich Kosta, even the accidental mention of some bachelor's name drove her into a fit of fury, and his feline nature could not stand such agonizing scenes. Now, however, Mona was not angry with him, even though she had understood his obvious hint, as she was strongly taken aback that her father, too, due to some strange insight, only that very day had suspected as she had – as contrary to common sense as it might seem – that Nikolin sooner or later would somehow become involved in their lives in one way or other. He never spoke of it again, not even on the day when Nikolin became a part of their family, as if he had long since foreseen it as something perfectly natural and inevitable.

Ivan Shibilev turned up in town after their wedding, disappeared, and showed up again after the birth of their child. *He deceived me and humiliated me, I hate him,* she would tell herself, feeling such hatred for Ivan Shibilev that she burned and destroyed everything that reminded her of him: his decoded letters, the portrait he had drawn for her and given to her, the shoes, blouses, and cheap trinkets he had brought to her on his every return. She strolled around the village with her "proudly" swelling belly, to show everyone that she was not hiding her pregnancy, but rather was proud of it. To her girlfriends who said that her pregnancy was progressing more quickly than usual, she unambiguously hinted that even if it were born in the seventh month, her baby would be a *devetache* or nine-monther, alluding to Nikolin, whom everyone at that time called Devetaka. Radka's wedding, where she had introduced him to many people, was her surest alibi for her relations with him. No one dared accuse her that this hidden affair was unfair to Ivan Shibilev, since it had ended in marriage, all the more so since Ivan Shibilev (here Mona smiled with that cynical and deadly irony which only a vengeful woman is capable of), due to his own, albeit belated, admission, was not capable of doing a man's duty. This explained the reason for her unexpected marriage to Nikolin and gave the locals the great satisfaction of mocking Ivan Shibilev's manly feebleness and at the same time censuring him for having given the girl false hopes for so many years. Only the most insightful of the local wiseacres, who had a subtle sense for such things, were skeptical of the Grand Dame's declarations. They, of course, could not establish whether or not Ivan Shibilev was lacking in manly merits, but from experience they knew that in such cases they needed to reserve the right to the last word on the matter. But there were only a few such doubters, while all the others believed Mona and told her "Atta girl!" for finally giving Ivan Shibilev the boot and becoming a proper wife and mother.

Intoxicated by her passion to dethrone her one-time idol completely, Mona also gave up her theatrical activities at a time when the stage was most needed to convince the villagers to join the co-op. Despite the promises and cajoling of Stoyan Kralev and his wife, Kichka, Mona's best friend, she declared that because of Ivan Shibilev she hated the theater and everything that reminded her of it. And so two years passed. One day, at the end of May, as she was coming back from the store, Mona saw Ivan Shibilev go into the community center and she followed him. She didn't ask herself whether he was alone or not and how he would behave toward her, she simply pushed the door open and went in. A wooden frame stretched with canvas, upon which the dark contours of a portrait of Georgi Dimitrov had been sketched, was leaning against the wall by the stage. In front of the painting was a box of paints, brushes, and scrolls of paper, but Ivan Shibilev was not there. The dark-green curtains were pulled back on either side of the stage and tied with rope, while the stage itself was semidark and disconcertingly quiet with its bare, dirty walls and uneven wooden floorboards.

Mona climbed up onstage and walked toward the door of the little room that served as a dressing room and prop storage. There was no other exit from the room and Ivan Shibilev could only be there. An icy chill crept over her body, while her hands started shaking so badly that she could not grasp the door handle. She stood like that for almost a minute, her shaking growing ever more uncontrollable, an inexplicable horror gripped her, as if she was about to hurl herself into an abyss that she could never climb out of. At the same time, some sinister force kept driving her forward and she turned the door handle. Ivan Shibilev was standing up against the wall with his hands hanging down along his sides, so motionless that in the first instant Mona thought he was a prop. She took a step forward and his figure stood out in the dim duskiness. He looked at her with a furtive, concentrated gaze and kept silent. She put her arms around his neck and felt him coming to life, bending his face toward hers, while his hands warmed her body...

Nikolin found out about his wife's extramarital affairs about a year after her first infidelity. This affair was so obvious that even his most spiteful detractors didn't bother whispering it in his ear, so sure they were that he knew about his wife's dalliances. Judging, however, from their peaceful family life and especially the joyful expression on his face on those occasions when he was seen around the village with his wife and daughter, it seemed that he wasn't perturbed by these dalliances at all. Such indifference, worse than any imaginable vice, was unnatural and unheard of in the history of the village, so locals began rubbing his nose in his wife's unfaithfulness, in order to find out why he didn't want to hear about it – was he mentally unsound, a freak of a man, or did he simply lack the strength to bear the bitter truth? Witnesses to Mona's infidelity showered him with indisputable proof, but he kept silent or smiled and continued on his way. This confused his "well-wishers," faced as they were with such a chump of a cuckold, the likes of which had never been seen in these parts.

While for him, it was too absurd to be true, that which people so diligently took upon themselves to show him. Neither his mind nor his heart could accept the idea of his wife "running around" on the sly with some other man, because he didn't see the point in that. Mona gave him her wifely caresses with true passion, and before accusing her of being unfaithful, they needed to experience the magic of her smile, to take the child from her arms and hear her say: "Come on now, snuggle up to Daddy!" For Ivan Shibilev, whom everyone named as his wife's lover, Nikolin felt such respect and admiration that for nothing in the world would he have believed that Ivan Shibilev was giving him cuckold's horns. It was impossible for a person like Ivan Shibilev – intelligent, with the Midas touch and so many talents – to be sneaking into his marriage bed and stealing his happiness, just as one would steal livestock or property. Not only was he not jealous of Ivan Shibilev on his wife's account, he was even happy that she, too, was a good actor in the community center plays. The two of them moved the audience to such laughter and tears that when the curtain call came at the end of the play and everyone was yelling "Bravo!" he would flush with pleasure, filled with pride in his wife. He equated skills, talent, and erudition with goodness and honesty, but his "well-wishers," frustrated by his obstinacy, stupidity, or blindness, grew even crueler, and to bring to light the truth that was owed to the world, they started proving to him that even the child wasn't his, but Ivan Shibilev's.

However, at that time, there was hardly a happier person than Nikolin. He was already a shepherd in the cooperative farm and grazed the flock entrusted to him in the stubble fields where there was plenty of grass; until it became trampled down, the whole village would let their livestock out there to graze. The days were hot and the stubble fields unfolded beneath the bright sun like a golden, white-hot infinity. Around ten o'clock the sheep began to gather in groups and started lying down, and then Nikolin would drive them back to the village. As a child he had herded a few dozen of the neighbors' lambs and since then he had dreamed of having a large herd, with a donkey and dogs, and now his dream had come true – he had a herd of two hundred sheep, a donkey (Grandpa Kitty Cat's Drencho), and two dogs. Drencho, who led the herd, carried in his packsaddle a water keg, a sack of food, and a hooded cloak. For Nikolin it was truly a pleasure to see him plodding calmly and steadily with the stateliness of an ancient leader, and to watch the sheep trailing after him single file in a long line, while the two dogs walked on either side like guards, ostensibly indifferent but ready to hurl themselves at anyone who came near the herd. Nikolin himself walked somewhere in the middle of the herd with his crook slung over his shoulders and his arms hanging on it, listening to the melody of the full-throated sheep bells and the delicate tinkling of the copper cow bells. The long, dark-brown line of the herd would creep like a snake with barely perceptible tremors, raising a white stream of dust and entering the village to the even rhythm of the bells. Drencho would reach the old mulberry tree with its hard, dusty leaves first, then the sheep would enter the dairy, a round space fenced off by a low stone wall with two narrow openings across from each other. While unloading the donkey's pack, Nikolin would yell at the top of his lungs a few times: "Come on, come ooooonnn!" and old women with their copper pails and their grandchildren in tow would come from the families who were part of the co-op. The women would sit on flat stones in two lines, one across from the other in front of the openings to the dairy, while the children would chase the sheep out one by one. Soon the humid air would be filled with the sweetish scent of musty wool, manure, and fresh milk, and amidst the clamor of the women one could hear the gentle, muted ring of streams of milk hitting in the empty pails. Drencho would saunter away from the dairy like a soldier freed from sentry duty and would roll around to his heart's content in the dunghill next door, stretching out in the sun, the dogs would also lie down nearby, while the sheep that had already been milked would dart with bowed heads to the mulberry tree and huddle up next to one another in the shade. Nikolin would go home to eat lunch, nap for a few hours, and finish some man's work around the house. The house had been left without a man since Grandpa Kitty Cat had passed away after the founding of the co-op. His only condition upon joining the co-op, as we already know, was that they leave his favorite means of transport at his disposal, and Stoyan Kralev had honored this request. They rounded up the co-op members' land and livestock, but just as before, Grandpa Kitty Cat continued to parade around the village in the two-wheeled buggy, shoulder to shoulder with Petko Bulgaria, inciting the villagers' hatred. One night the wheels of the buggy were taken off and stolen away, while the horse was driven to the common barn. Grandpa Kitty Cat spent a whole day and night curled up like a cat in Devetakov's leather armchair, and in the morning Petko Bulgaria found him dead.

Late in the afternoon when it cooled down, Nikolin would again drive the herd out to the pasture. He loved standing propped on his crook like the shepherds of yore, watching the sheep fiercely tearing away at the soft grass and the sun, ever larger and flaming, descending toward the blue line of the horizon and slowly sinking into it; its glow would grow pale and everything around would be awash in a soft, translucent light, and in this light the night would come as if on tiptoe into the stubble fields, its footsteps crackling softly and sonorously. On such evenings he often heard one of the shepherds or horse herders nearby saying that his little daughter, Mela, was not his but Ivan Shibilev's, they pretended not to notice him in the dusk, yet they yelled so loudly that their voices carried through the whole vicinity. Nikolin would smile and pass by with his herd. The cruder and more insulting the rumors about his wife were, the more unbelievable they seemed to him, hence the less they hurt him. Instead of falling into fits of jealousy and despair, as his "well-wishers" assumed he would, their efforts to open his eyes gave him a strange feeling of satisfaction. More or less the entire village had taken it upon itself to destroy his happiness, so that meant his happiness was huge and invincible. He stood alone against the village and won the battle with a single, solitary weapon – his faith in his wife. But people didn't want to settle for his foolish faith, especially since it undermined the village's moral principles and encouraged debauchery.

Ivan Shibilev and Mona had become so brazen that they could not hide their affair in any way. They were being followed day and night, thus no matter how imaginative Ivan Shibilev might have been, his trysts with Mona could not be kept secret. His every new move was followed and exposed, every signal was decoded. Finally it was the authorities' turn to become involved and to put an end to this "moral corruption" as the party secretary Stoyan Kralev put it. This job turned out to be very difficult, if not downright pointless. On the one hand, Mona was a friend of his family, thus he and his wife, Kichka, found themselves in a delicate situation when the public conscience rose up against Mona's amorous adventures and demanded that she be censured and reined in somehow by the leaders of the village. On the other hand, Mona had taken part in the theater troupe since she was a child, when no other woman in the village besides Kichka Kraleva had wanted to set foot onstage, she had been the first of the young people to wear the clothes and hairstyles that Kichka had presented to the youth as a weapon in the fight against the old fashions; in short, of all the young women, Mona best and most prominently fulfilled the duties assigned to her by the party in the past and even now. Stoyan Kralev and his wife had tried to hint to her many times that she must put an end to her affair with Ivan Shibilev, but she would just keep silent and such a gentle and innocent smile would appear on her face that they didn't dare bother her further. The couple's love affair, however, was constantly on the tip of the village tongues, while the opposition, who used any and all means to denounce the communists, had even made a popular song about it, since Ivan Shibilev and Mona were both party members. More than anyone, Stoyan Kralev felt an organic hatred of and disgust at their dissipation, but due to various reasons, especially those of a public nature, he still had not gotten around to denouncing and punishing them. The two of them had shouldered almost the entire burden of propagandizing both in the past and now, and had done such a good job of it that they had won over at least half the village to the side of the Fatherland Front, to say nothing of the joy and excitement they had brought people with their performances. However, he could no longer remain indifferent to their licentious affair, so he sent his people to call Mona down to the party club and she came with her little girl. The latter was not yet three years old and she knew Stoyan Kralev, since he had come to see her mother many times, and as soon as she saw him she began showing off for him, diving under the table and touching everything in the room.

"You should've come by yourself," Stoyan Kralev said.

"Why?"

"Because this isn't a conversation for little ears. Come back this afternoon at five, but by yourself!"

Mona gave her daughter a little rubber ball, led her outside to play by herself, and came back in.

"Me, you, and Kichka have talked about this business of yours before," Stoyan Kralev went on, "but now we've got to talk about it again."

"What business of mine?"

"That business with... Ivan."

"What is there to say about it?"

"What do you mean, 'what'? The whole village is outraged..."

Stoyan Kralev had expected that when he started talking about her extramarital affair, she would become flustered and ashamed, or would try to justify herself in some way, but Mona was sitting quietly with her hands on her knees like a little girl, looking him in the eye with a barely perceptible smile. That smile, whether sarcastic or judgmental, startled him and caused him to fall silent for a minute. In that smile there was beauty and shamelessness and the licentiousness of a woman who has given and received everything from such a long-awaited and secret love, as well as scorn for everything and everyone who might try to take that love away from her. The longer he looked at that smile, the more Stoyan Kralev understood her and the more exasperated he felt. He nevertheless got ahold of himself and calmly advised her "as a friend" to get her personal life in order such that it "wouldn't be grist for the rumor mill." Mona heard him out silently and said only "goodbye" as she went to leave.

"It's not clear to me whether you agree with what was said here or not?" Stoyan Kralev asked while walking her to the door.

"I'm outraged by the whole village!" Mona said, a deep flush coming over her face.

"What? *You* are outraged by the whole village? Come on back here for a second and sit yourself down!"

"Why should I come back? To listen to your sermon again? I already heard you out."

"I'm speaking to you as your comrade, who wants what's best for you, while for you it's in one ear and out the other. Is that how it is?"

Mona was looking him straight in the eye and again a mocking expression came over her face. *She is depraved and insolent*, Stoyan Kralev thought to himself, turning away from her.

"Hasn't it ever crossed your mind that your affair with your lover is immoral, comrade? Hasn't that at least once crossed your mind?"

"Why is it immoral? Is there such a thing as immoral love?"

"There is! And it's your love affair with Ivan Shibilev. If a married woman's perverse relations with her lover can even be called love."

"I know what love is, not you!"

"All you know how to do is hump like dogs in other people's yards! It's moral degeneracy, not love!" Stoyan Kralev was standing with his back to the door, as if afraid that Mona would run out, and as always in such situations, gave free reign to his temper. "The village is up in arms over you two, but you don't have a whit of conscience or shame. You're communists, come to your senses before it's too late, get ahold of yourselves!"

"I live in this world because I love one man. No one has the right to judge me," Mona said, and went to leave, but Stoyan Kralev blocked her way.

"Every decent person has that right."

"Even the opposition?"

"In this case, even the opposition. No matter what kind of people the opposition might be, we can't reproach them for depravity. Which is why they're rubbing their hands with glee and saying: Look what kind of people are holding power and controlling the people's property! They made the land common property, now they'll make the women common property too. Don't you understand that right now everyone is watching us, following our every move? We are obligated to set a good example in every respect. And why do you bring such shame on your husband, why do you make such a good man unhappy? Doesn't it weigh on your conscience that as his reward for saving you from Ivan Shibilev's clutches and giving you a home and family, you repay him with torment?"

"Let me go!" Mona screamed, stifling her sobs, her face contorted by spasms. "You are cruel and merciless; when it comes to people's souls, you only know how to give orders. You have no heart or soul!"

"Because I'm trying to advise you to do what's right? Does your beloved have a heart and soul? If he did, would he roam the whole world over and only come back to you when the spirit moves him? You abandoned your family for him, had his child, and he…"

Mona screamed something, yanked on the door handle with all her might, and jumped outside.

Shortly thereafter, Stoyan Kralev sent for Ivan Shibilev to come to the party club on urgent and important business. While waiting for him, he paced around the room from wall to wall, telling himself to keep completely calm, since he knew Ivan Shibilev better than anyone and suspected that the conversation with him would be tense and difficult. The reader will find out later in our story what great political and educational work the two men had carried out before the communist coup of September 9, when besides their ideological unanimity, they were also bound by friendship. In the "new life," however, both their work and their paths had turned out to be very different. Stoyan Kralev became party secretary and took over the leadership of the village, while Ivan Shibilev shuttled between the village and the city as always. He had been with the Shumen Theater for barely a year, where he had been appointed under Article 9, and this was exactly what Stoyan Kralev wanted to find out — was he settled down in Shumen for the long haul, and if so, that gave him the chance to have a more specific conversation about his relations with Mona. It was a delicate question, no two ways about it, but Stoyan Kralev was most worried about Ivan Shibilev's character, a person with a change-able mood, with his own ideas and principles about life, cheerful, gentle, devoted, and accommodating, ready to give up everything he had for others, but sometimes willful, dejected, and headstrong, which, of course (to be perfectly frank), did not prevent him from doing a great deal of party and educational work and thus becoming the darling of the village.

And so, Stoyan Kralev did not expect anything good from the impend-ing conversation, but he also did not expect that it would turn into a row and bring about a complete rupture between the two of them. As he suspected, Ivan Shibilev acted as if there was nothing blameworthy about his relationship with Mona and that this affair did not make her look bad in the eyes of the village, nor did it destroy her family. Love is freedom of the spirit, the holiest of holies for man, free is he who loves, while he is a slave who is not free to experience love, he said, as if reciting some monologue onstage. His monologue continued for several minutes in that same spirit, abstract and vague, and Stoyan Kralev began to lose patience. No matter how he told himself to remain calm, his nerves became more and more strained and he again began pacing around the room, the right corner of his mouth twitching unwittingly in a nervous tic. He, of course, immediately realized that Ivan Shibilev was trying to bamboozle him with learned palaver in order to gain some time and to turn the conversation in another direction. And he was not mistaken, since Ivan Shibilev really was reciting from memory a monologue about love from some classic play. He, in his turn, knew Stoyan Kralev as well as he knew himself, and as soon as he realized that he had called him down not only in his capacity as confessor, but also in his capacity as aggressor, he wanted to deprive him of the pleasure of ordering him around and at the same time to show him that he had no intention whatsoever of listening to his dogmatic judgments about morality and so forth. Without feeling hatred or any other negative feeling toward Stoyan Kralev, he had long not been able to stand his semiliterateness, which, combined with his self-confidence as the ruler of the village and as a party activist of the broadest scope, was cause for mockery and pity.

"Let's leave aside this highfalutin talk," Stoyan Kralev said. "I know you're an actor and all that. Let's speak in simple and clear human terms. So why don't you tell me, without twisting and turning it all fancy-like, what are your true intentions toward that woman? Are you going to leave her in peace to tend to her family or will you take her with you?"

"I'll tell you in simple and clear terms. These things cannot be said either in simple or in complex terms. I cannot explain it, and even if I could, why should I have to confess to you?"

"Not to me, but to the party!" Stoyan Kralev said.

"So that means you don't have your own opinion."

"I do, and it coincides completely with that of the party. I'm talking to you as one communist to another. I'm raising the question from the party's point of view, not from a personal one."

"So you're trying to say that you identify with the party." Stoyan Kralev didn't understand this and fixed him with an angry, questioning glance. "You've called me down here to judge me in the name of the Bulgarian Communist Party, that means you identify with the party. Just like the priests – they condemn or approve not in their own name, but in God's name. In that case, I'd better be careful. If I don't give you the answer you want, that means I'm not giving the party the answer it wants. If I insult you, I'm insulting the party. But I already told you that love is sacred and inviolable. How can you expect and demand of me that I confess my innermost feelings and intentions to you? This is blasphemy not only against my feelings, but also against me as a individual."

"Listen, Ivan, listen, my brother! We're not in the theater and we're not playing parts. You know very well that the party stands above all, above any personal feelings and so on. Love has a party and class character and since that's the case, the party has the right to meddle in the communist's intimate life when that life is dissolute and sullies communist morality. Let me ask you again: Will you quit running around with that woman or not? If you keep carrying on, then there's no place for either of you in the party, I'll have you know. Rumors about your love affair have reached the party's regional committee and from there several times they've most strictly ordered me to take a stand with respect to this business. The party will not allow two communists to run wild in front of the whole village. How can two communists allow themselves an adulterous affair? This is a crime against our sacred communist morality. As you know, the nationalization of property is just around the corner, and we communists need to lead the charge on both the political as well as the moral front. Otherwise people won't follow us. As soon as the question of collectivization is raised, everyone, especially the opposition, points out a list of reasons not to join the cooperative farm, and one of those reasons is your love affair with Mona. Ivan Shibilev, they say, back in the day was always telling us about communism and the kolkhoz, but now look what his communism really is. He whores around with other men's wives, footloose and fancy free. Is that true? It's true. I've heard that you go around with other women at the theaters or wherever it is you wander off to. Since you've got other women there, why run around with this one? Or if you really just can't do without her, take her and make her your lawful wife. Your love is sacred, isn't it? Sacred, but only in word and not in deed, it seems, since otherwise you go about your usual philandering. Things can't go on this way. Either you leave that woman in peace or you take her with you to Shumen. With the child, of course, because she won't part with the girl. You'll have to adopt her."

Stoyan Kralev proceeded to explain the law on divorce, mentioning several times that Mona, if she got divorced, would take the child with her, in order to goad Ivan Shibilev into admitting that the child was his in any case. If he admitted it or even hinted at this in any way, Stoyan Kralev would have pressed his back to the wall all the harder and disarmed him completely. Ivan Shibilev listened to him with his charming smile on his face and at a certain point chimed in, as if completely casually:

"Who died and made you God?"

"What?" Stoyan Kralev pretended not to have understood this, but the deep flush that instantly sprang up on his face made it clear that he had understood very well and was deeply offended.

"I said, who made you the village dictator?"

"Listen," Stoyan Kralev shouted. "You better watch what you say!"

"I'm all eyes and ears and I'm watching and wondering how a semi-literate peasant, who up until yesterday was stitching away at his thick homespun cloth, is now standing in front of me with the self-confidence to act as the master of my thoughts and feelings, of my heart and soul. And the most tragic part is that you yourself believe that you have the right to stick your dirty hands into people's souls with impunity. Love, you say, has a class- and party-based character. Who taught you that supreme idiocy? If it was me, then just shoot me now and know that you've done a good deed. Such a cynic deserves no less. Oh, Stoyan, my boy, who would've thought that you'd turn into such a homespun tyrant? Our sacred ideals, for which we were ready to give even our mother's milk, what craftsman's hands have they fallen into, hm? And just look how you've transformed yourself! A jacket à la Stalin, a cap à la Stalin, a moustache à la Stalin, and your left hand tucked into the buttons of your jacket à la Stalin. You're Jughashvili to a tee! No, Kraleshvili! Not only you, Comrade Kraleshvili, but also the comrades from the regional committee have no right to meddle in people's personal lives!"

While he was saying this, Ivan Shibilev was smiling mildly and condescendingly, as if telling a stranger a funny story. Stoyan Kralev was so stunned by his insolence that he was literally choking with rage. No one had ever dared insult and humiliate him to such an extent, and with such calm and unabashed arrogance, no less. The worst part was that Ivan Shibilev spoke as if he could see into his soul like looking into the palm of his hand, and there is nothing more terrible than being judged by someone who knows even the most inscrutable corners of your soul. In the face of such a person you either have to throw up your hands or hate him down to the marrow of your bones. Stoyan Kralev wanted to make him understand once and for all whom he was dealing with, but he couldn't think of anything, he kept staring straight ahead, keeping silent with his lips pressed tightly together, he was so shocked at Ivan Shibilev's impudence. Ivan Shibilev said he had some urgent business and left, as if the two of them had merely exchanged the most common of comradely pleasantries.

About a week later Stoyan Kralev called a party meeting, which was also attended by a representative of the party's regional committee. The meeting's agenda consisted of a single item – reconsideration of Comrade Ivan Shibilev's party membership for several reasons: having expressed mistrust in the regional committee of the BCP, spiritual and moral depravity, and nonobservance of party discipline. The only serious accusation was the last one, due to his frequent absences from party meetings, but Stoyan Kralev himself had declared with respect to these absences that for a true communist, the party was everywhere, as God is for believers.

Now, however, he began his accusations precisely with the fact that Ivan Shibilev attended party meetings once in a blue moon, sometimes due to his absences from the village, sometimes due to negligence, while according to the regulations this was punishable by expulsion from the party organization. His surest argument for expelling Ivan Shibilev from the party were his amorous affairs, which would surely provoke the greatest outrage from party members, but that, to his greatest astonishment, did not happen. Those very same men and women who had turned his romantic liaison with Mona into a song (Stoyan Kralev had suggested they expel her as well, but the committee had refused, so as not to create even more upheaval in her family), when they found out he was to be expelled from the party, were taken aback, and when it came time to express their opinion, no one wanted to speak. Stoyan Kralev had worked over a dozen people in advance who had promised to support him, but now they, too, sat silently with their eyes fixed on the floor. He was forced to call on them by name and give them the floor, but they hardly got up from their seats, crumpling their hats anxiously in their hands, sighing or muttering that they didn't know what to say, or that just as there is sin, there is also forgiveness, that a dog goes to a bitch that flips up her tail, and so on. Finally a tall, one-eared villager, without having been given the floor, stood up and called out as loudly as his voice would allow him: "Ivan Shibilev might be able to live without the village, but the village can't live without Ivan Shibilev!"

At this, the party meeting livened up. People whispered amongst themselves, female laughter rang out, while someone suggested the meeting be brought to a close. The buzz that swept the room supported the one-eared man's statement, more voices were heard calling for the end of the meeting, because it was wrong to expel a person like Ivan Shibilev from the party. These fragmentary protests, uttered softly and meekly, also expressed the people's love for Ivan Shibilev, ne'er-do-well and charmer, wild man and sweet-talker, actor, artist, and the man with the golden hands, Ivan Shibilev, who over the years had become something like the village's spiritual sustenance. Stoyan Kralev said something to the representative of the regional committee, then gave the floor to Ivan Shibilev.

"I have nothing to say!" he called from his seat.

He was sitting at the end of the front row, right near the podium itself, listening and watching at almost point-blank range the deliberately serious, practically gloomy faces of Stoyan Kralev and the regional committee representative and was thinking that this whole business about expelling him was a clumsily orchestrated frame-up which even the simple village people were mocking. When Stoyan Kralev asked him whether his silence meant he was in agreement with the party bureau's decision, he replied that it did not indicate agreement, adding that the decision by the regional committee was also unfair, since it was slander against him.

"Slander, you say?" the representative of the regional committee piped up. "So that means that the regional committee of the Bulgarian Communist Party is a slanderer?"

"You don't need to twist my words around. Stoyan Kralev slandered me in front of the committee."

"A party secretary is incapable of slander!" the representative cried, getting up from his chair. "The party does not pick slanderers as party secretaries. That should be as plain as day."

"I have no intention of arguing with you. I've never seen or heard of you before. You've been ordered to make a decision to expel me, so expel me!" Ivan Shibilev said with a smile. "Everything has been decided in advance, why should we waste our time with empty words?"

Sweat broke out on most people's faces, everyone had fixed their heavy, unmoving gazes straight ahead, the musty air was weighted with the scent of onion and sour sweat, although the most sensitive noses could also catch a whiff of ripe wheat, which was wafting in through the window facing the fields. Midnight had long since passed, roosters were crowing in the distance, the room was getting warmer and stuffier, the people, exhausted from working in the fields, were dozing off in their seats, their dark faces scorched like charred logs. Stoyan Kralev once again began calling people by name to vote, first the dozen or so he had worked over, then the rest of them. They stood up one by one, anxious and flustered, and raised their palms to their noses agonizingly slowly.

After he was expelled from the party, another misfortune befell Ivan Shibilev right as he had learned his two roles for the season and was preparing to go to Shumen. Only a week was left before his departure when Father Encho stopped by and asked him to repair the icon of Saint George the Dragon Slayer. Ivan Shibilev was an atheist, but he painted icons for the church with pleasure because the work was interesting to him. Stoyan Kralev many times had meant to turn the church into a youth club or a storehouse for grain, but the regional committee would not let him. The church, of course, stood practically empty. Church weddings and baptisms were not legally recognized, the young people were antireligious, while the older people were afraid to enter the church, thus Father Encho's flock consisted of a few dozen elderly folks like himself, who tottered down to the church once a week to light candles in memory of the dead. In 1949 the roof of the church began leaking in many places from the spring rains and the icon of Saint George got wet. The workman who repaired the church's roof damaged the icon even further, so Ivan Shibilev painted a new one. A few days after he put it in the place of the old one, two policemen came to get him in an old jeep and took him to the regional committee of the party. Ivan Shibilev was convinced that they had decided to return him to the party's ranks and went into the committee in the best of moods. Stoyan Kralev, Kozarev (the regional committee representative), and two other party secretaries were waiting for him. All four of them were so somber that they didn't even return his greeting, and without any word of introduction shoved the icon of Saint George in his face.

"Did you paint this?"

"I did," Ivan Shibilev said.

"Explain to us what you've drawn here."

"Saint George battling the dragon..."

They set the icon on a chair and forced him to sit across from it, while they stood on either side of him. Saint George, a young man in a scarlet cloak with a silver helmet, sat astride a white, enchantingly beautiful horse and with a forceful blow had driven his spear into the mouth of one of the dragon's two heads. But this head was the head of the party representative Kozarev, somehow freakishly frightening, biting down on the spear's head with bloody teeth. The dragon's body resembled a frog covered in poisonous green scales, with a pinkish-white belly, spiky legs, and a mousy tail curled into a circle. The second head was that of Stoyan Kralev, already dead, with eyelids half closed over the whites of his eyes and a black moustache over the mouth, from which dark-red blood was flowing. This bloody battle was being fought against the background of a cheerful meadow of blossoming trees, the silvery glimmer of ripe wheat, and a cloudless blue sky.

"We've all seen dragons drawn in children's books, we've also heard about them in folktales, but we've never seen the likes of this dragon here, with human heads, and the heads of party functionaries at that," said one of the secretaries. "Why have you insulted our comrade leaders, why did you turn them into monsters? And is that just a coincidence?"

"I don't know how it happened," Ivan Shibilev said, and he wasn't lying, nor was he afraid to take responsibility for this "insult." He had worked on the icon so feverishly that he truly wasn't in any condition to explain how all this had happened. He only remembered that while he was drawing, the two of them had been before his eyes, they had made such a strong impression on him when they expelled him from the party. During the whole party meeting, he had felt that they were attacking him like a pair of predators, and since they were raising one and the same accusations against him in one and the same way, it had seemed to him that they were really a single beast with two heads. Thus, while he was drawing the saint battling the traditionally two-headed dragon, he had unwittingly painted both their images. He had done it unintentionally, under the influence of the intense internal agitation they had caused him, and he was in no condition to explain how it had happened. So many and such serious accusations were showered on him that he was unable to exculpate himself. The most serious accusation was that of criminal abandonment of communist ideals and of having fallen under religious influence. It was true that before September 9 he had fought most doggedly against religion; thanks to this, most of the young people had become atheists, but this service of his, rather than alleviating his situation, made it worse. It was one thing for an ignorant peasant or a person without class consciousness to fall under the priests' influence, but it was quite another when that person was a former self-declared atheist and communist who had betrayed his convictions precisely at the moment when the party was waging such an intense and uncompromising battle against religious fallacies. The bourgeois elements of society would certainly take advantage of this situation and point to him as an example of how a once-convinced communist renounced his ideology and accepted the idea of God and religion. However, was this communist in the past even a real communist, and not a subversive and a traitor who now, supported by the reactionary forces, was showing his true colors?

Ivan Shibilev tried in vain to show them that their accusations were absolutely unfounded and even insulting to him, that whether right or wrong, he looked upon icons as art, and not as a means of religious propaganda. As far as his personal business and intimate life was concerned, no one had the right to meddle in them, because no one could command people's feelings and tastes. With this conclusion, Ivan Shibilev rejected all their charges that he was guilty, and as for the self-criticism that was expected from him as an (albeit former) communist, it didn't even cross his mind to engage in it. They sent him away even more coldly than they had greeted him. That same night he learned from Father Encho that the chairman of the village soviet, Stoyu Barakov, had given the icon to Stoyan Kralev the previous day. Barakov had stopped by, ostensibly to see how repairs to the church were going, seen the icon, taken it down, and carried it away that very minute.

Late in the afternoon on the following day, Ivan Shibilev's neighbor told him they were going to burn the "icons." Ivan Shibilev was reading a book on the veranda; he threw it down and headed toward the church. I happened to be in the village that day and learned about this impending event from him when we met by chance in the street. He was very agitated, he grabbed my arm and led me to the church. Quite a few people were already gathered in the churchyard, mostly young men and women, whom – as we learned later – Stoyan Kralev had called up to be present at the icon burning. Stoyan Kralev himself was nowhere to be seen in the crowd, he was also not in the church, as Ivan Shibilev and I saw when we went in. The door was open, but there was no one inside. I hadn't gone inside there since I was a child and our teachers had led us to the church on the major holidays, and now I experienced a peculiar feeling of awkwardness and curiosity. I was surprised that inside the church, which seemed as small as a matchbox to me, it was not as oppressive and gloomy as I had imagined, but rather solemnly bright and peaceful. The icons, too, were not as uniform or darkened from candle soot as I had remembered them from my childhood, they emanated a varied, warm light that caressed the eyes, life welled forth from the saints' faces. I got the feeling that these faces were familiar to me and that through their eyes, those near and dear to me were looking at me from a familiar background. And indeed, the longer I looked at them, the more clearly I recognized them. God the Father, for example, placed in the center of the iconostasis, was old Father

Encho himself, with his fine white beard, with his desiccated hand raised to make the sign of the cross and a golden nimbus around his head, staring straight forward with a stern and even cold, piercing gaze, against a background of silvery-green wheat fields, crisscrossed by the brown strips of the roads. To the left of God the Father, in the image of Saint Petka, the patron saint of the little church, Ivan Shibilev had painted his mother, with their house and yard in the background, while in the yard stood two horses hitched to a cart. To the right was Jesus with a small, barely sprouted beard and a thin moustache, with wide-open eyes and the oblong face of one who has suffered, and that was the face of Ilko Kralev, from the time when he had cavities in his lungs and was fighting for his life. Many more men, women, and young people had been painted as saints, every one of them bright and joyful against the backdrop of the local landscape. Mona, of course, was among them as well, a young, gentle, and smiling Madonna with slightly squinting blue eyes, in a red heavily draped robe; in her lap was the young Jesus, who was a copy of Mona's daughter, who in turn was a copy of the artist himself.

I was even more stunned by the fact that Ivan Shibilev had not told either me or Ilko Kralev about his work in the church, even though the three of us were good friends. There had been a time when he had read his poetry to us, showed us his paintings, and even shared his most personal problems with us. Once, for example, we had gotten together at his house and he had showed us a portrait of Mona, jokingly telling us that he was our local Leonardo, since he, too, was interested in many things and since he also had his own Mona (Lisa) to boot. I asked him whether he had had any particular reasons for painting these icons, and doing it in secret at that, and he explained to me that he hadn't done it in secret and hadn't had any particular reasons for doing so, but the circumstances under which he had painted them were such that he hadn't had anyone to show his icons to. He had painted them over many years at Father

Encho's request. The old man would realize from time to time that he was missing some saint or some biblical story that he had seen in the churches in the neighboring villages, and would ask him to paint it. He had taken on this work with pleasure, because he found it interesting and pleasant, and plus, the church was the only place he could hang up his works and make them "community property." This community consisted of a few dozen elderly men and women who stopped by the church on holidays to listen to Father Encho's snuffling sermons. All of them, aged to the point of blessed ignorance, didn't even look at the icons, except when crossing themselves in front of the Virgin Mary, and even then without really seeing her, because it was placed too high up in the iconostasis for their shortsighted eyes. Incidentally, over the years Ivan Shibilev had replaced the old icons with his own. Most of the old icons had been painted by some Petko or other, a newcomer to the village and master cart maker. They were messily painted, gloomy, and even sinister, and did not possess any artistic merit. Ivan Shibilev saved only five old icons that had ended up here, Lord knows how. They were the work of a talented, unknown master from more than a century ago and stood out from the rest as true masterpieces. Thus, Ivan Shibilev was perhaps the only artist in Bulgaria who had at hand a permanent exhibition hall in which to display his works, without anyone but him having actually seen them. Even Father Encho, due to his shortsightedness and ignorance, didn't bother looking at them, but was satisfied since the empty places on the church walls were filled with the necessary inventory. The only competent visitor turned out to be the chairman of the village soviet, Stoyu Barakov, who managed to recognize the images of Stoyan Kralev and the secretary of the regional committee Kozarev in the two heads of the dragon, which had become the grounds for the icons to be burned.

An unfamiliar policeman came inside and asked us to leave, and when we went outside, we saw Stoyan Kralev and the younger Barakov in his police captain's uniform talking to a group of young people. After getting out of prison, Miho Barakov had started working for the police for several years as an assistant, and now, at the tender age of twenty-four, he was the chief of police in the regional capital. He was handsome with his black moustache and white face, in brand-new full military attire, shining from head to toe; he commanded respect and even awe not only because of the fact that he occupied that important post at such a young age, but precisely because at that young age he was able to comport himself like an established man of twice his age, to carefully measure his every word and gesture and to keep his composure in all cases. Deep inside, Ivan Shibilev did not really believe that Stoyan Kralev would burn his icons, as he had announced he would. He had read somewhere that in the Soviet Union they punished destroyers of icons most severely, but the party's regional committee here had no way of knowing that. Stoyan Kralev could not possibly attempt to destroy the icons single-handedly, and surely he had gathered the people in the churchyard to show those which had been painted by Ivan Shibilev, to expose him as a renegade and thus to justify his expulsion from the party. Ivan Shibilev was still nursing a certain hope that the icons would be spared, but as soon as he saw Miho Barakov and the policeman he had brought with him, all at once he became extremely nervous and whispered to me: "That guy here is a bad sign."

In the meantime people kept arriving from all corners of the village, Father Encho eventually turned up as well. Bent over from old age, he could hardly shuffle his slippers along; he would stop, leaning on his cane, to catch his breath before again continuing onward. His kamelaukion, faded by the sun, had tipped to the back of his head, from which a lock of hair hung; behind his thick glasses his eyes looked freakishly large and turbid. As soon as he arrived he asked after Stoyan Kralev and went straight over to him, while the crowd fell silent to hear what the priest would say to him.

"Stoyan, my boy," Father Encho cried, "I baptized you and married you in this here church; when you were a child, I gave you the holy communion here, and now you want to burn God's holy icons."

Stoyan Kralev looked at him with a smile, as one looks at a child who asks irrelevant questions.

"That's true, Father, that's true. Except that these are not God's holy icons but a bunch of dabblings by your friend Ivan Shibilev. You've been pictured here too, along with a lot of other folks from the village…"

Ah, so he came to look at them! Ivan Shibilev noted anxiously, while Stoyan Kralev went on loudly so that everyone would hear him: "Since they are not saints, but our local sinners, they have no place in the church…"

"God is looking on from above, my child!"

"Perhaps he is looking on, but when we look up, all we see is air. You don't see anything either, but still you bow and cross yourself before him."

"God lives, my child, he lives! If he didn't live, we wouldn't live either."

"You talk about God as if you'd just gone to visit him this morning to drink coffee."

"God doesn't show himself to anyone. He is the mystery of mysteries…"

"You believers use cheap tricks, Father. God is a mystery to people, you say. He doesn't want to show himself to them, he hides from them, how can they believe in him then?"

"Since you haven't seen communism, why do you believe in it?"

Laughter rang out and a buzz swept through the crowd.

"Look what our good father here is hinting at! Communism, Father, is scientifically proven, and its first phase, socialism, has already been established in the Soviet Union. Many people have gone there, they've seen it, they've touched it with their own two hands, as it were. But what is your belief based on? They tell you: God exists, and you believe. Could there be anything more foolish than closing your eyes and believing in something that you can't see, hear, or smell? We all know that old folk saying: 'Pray to God, but keep rowing to shore.' What are the people trying to say with this proverb? That you shouldn't wait for God to help, because he's not there at all, instead you have to help yourself. Simple folks figured this truth out for themselves from experience, while you priests keep confusing their minds and deluding them. There's so much injustice, so much hunger and sickness, so much human tragedy in this world, while your almighty God just sits up there with his hands crossed over his chest, watching the show. How can you believe in him after that!"

"Faithlessness is death, my child! One day up there..."

"Ah, are you hinting at the afterworld?" Stoyan Kralev interrupted him. "When someone comes back from there and tells us what he's seen, we'll think about it then. If there is another life up there, then we'll repent before that old God of yours, he'll forgive us and let us into heaven..."

Father Encho wanted to say something more, but someone grabbed him under the arms and carried him out of the crowd. It was his son, a man around fifty, pale with worry over his father's words.

"Don't mind his prattle, he's an old man, he's lost track of the years and his tongue!" he said to Stoyan Kralev, and led the old man away toward his home.

This short verbal wrangle with the priest served as a good prelude for Stoyan Kralev to launch into the antireligious speech the situation demanded he give. He had many years of experience in giving speeches before the villagers, he knew very well the rules of this art, as well as his listeners' mentality. He spoke loudly, clearly, and inspiringly, he skillfully made use of intonation, pauses, and gestures, and used folksy terms and examples which were easy to grasp and remember. He renounced religion, comparing it as all atheists do to opium, which the bourgeois ideology uses to lull the people's consciousness to sleep. To convince his listeners, he had to prove the nonexistence of God using the arguments of the semiliterate priest, who, in all likelihood, had stated them without understanding them. It was not difficult to refute and mock these arguments, since Stoyan Kralev relied on village realism. He did not have even the slightest inkling that he had taken up a topic as old and complex as the world itself, over which hundreds of philosophers had racked their brains.

"It's as if they're telling you: Put the pot on the stove and wait for the stew to boil, without having put either meat or vegetables in it. That's how it is with religion: Believe in God, even though you don't see or hear him!"

It turned out that as Stoyan Kralev was speaking, the icons were being brought out of the window on the other side of the church and lined up along the fence, while before them lay piles of dry wood. The people examined them with the greatest curiosity, recognizing the faces of many locals, and soon they began asking Stoyan Kralev why they had to burn such beautiful pictures. He took out a match and lit one of the piles of wood, but Ivan Shibilev darted forward, pushed his way through the crowd, grabbed two icons, and shouted: "Barbarians! Medieval inquisitors! You're the ones who should be burned at the stake!"

Some time later, when we met again and recalled this incident, Ivan Shibilev told me that he had never before fallen into such a frenzy.

"I now realize," he said, "that their goal was to drive me to the point of exasperation, and I really was gripped by such a fury that I would have been capable of doing Lord knows what if they'd goaded me. I knew that they'd decided to sacrifice me to prove to the opposition that they were merciless toward their own as well, when necessary. I knew what was waiting for me after all that and still I couldn't control myself, I hollered at Stoyan Kralev and Miho Barakov and showered them with the most insulting epithets."

The two icons that Ivan Shibilev took were the images of his mother and Mona. The policeman caught up with him, blocked his way, and tried to take them back, but Ivan Shibilev shoved him hard in the chest and quickly headed for home. The crowd watched him in total silence until he disappeared around the corner of the nearest house, while Stoyan Kralev, pale and trembling, shouted: "Comrades, do you know why Ivan Shibilev went berserk when we threatened the icons? Because he painted them. We, comrades, are laying the foundations of socialism, of our bright future, we are toiling, depriving ourselves of many things, not getting enough sleep, not getting enough to eat, while he's chumming around with that doddering old geezer of a priest Father Encho and painting icons for his church. Has he really fallen into the religious fallacy, or have we been nurturing a snake in our bosom? We heard how he defamed both myself and the head of the police, how he even shoved a policeman. How can he permit himself such brazenness before the eyes of the whole village unless he is a person, whether consciously or not, who is pouring fuel into the fire of our class enemy? And all of that because of these splotches of paint here."

Stoyan Kralev grabbed several icons and threw them into the flames. The scent of turpentine and paint filled the air, the dry wood crackled and flared up. On one of the icons Jesus was painted in the image of Stoyan Kralev's brother Ilko. His face, already tormented with suffering, went dark, covered with boiling drops of oil, then wrinkled up and disappeared. An image of Stoyu Barakov as Judas, with his close-cut, bristling hair, sitting at the end of the table guiltily listening to Jesus's words, also disappeared in the same way, as did Nikolin Miyalkov as John the Baptist, Auntie Tanka Dzhelebova as Saint Mina, along with another dozen locals, old and young, painted in bright biblical cloaks with golden haloes around their heads.

Early in the morning Ivan Shibilev was arrested and taken to the city; several days after that he was sent to a labor-reeducation camp. The precise reasons for this punishment became known from Ivan Shibilev himself after he was released. They accused him of spiritual and moral depravity, of spreading religious propaganda, of insubordination and physical assault of a member of the police force, and so many more things that, as Ivan Shibilev himself put it, he was amazed they didn't string him up in public or throw him in prison for life. In time it came out that despite the numerous accusations against him, the regional committee thought that after his expulsion from the party, it would be over the top to impose yet another punishment on him, and they decided to release him after a good dressing-down, but the head of the police insisted that he be sent to work for some time, so as to learn to weigh his words and deeds more carefully.

The camp was located in the village of Obrochishte, where there was a state-run cooperative farm. Ivan Shibilev later told us that his stay there was neither as long nor as grueling as he had expected. The head turned out to be one of the twelve Communist Youth League members tried after the organization had been crushed, and he had spent time in prison with Miho Barakov; he had then been a young laborer but was now a thirty-year-old lieutenant in the police. After reading Ivan Shibilev's dossier, he questioned him a bit and then appointed him head buyer of the vegetable brigade. This brigade worked the vegetable garden in the neighboring village of Kranevo, located on the seashore in the picturesque valley of the Batova River. On holidays and weekends, when he was given leave, he would stop by the pub and play clarinet, he would also play at parties, recite poetry, do magic tricks, and tell jokes – in short, here, as everywhere he had worked before then, he won over both the camp leadership and his fellow brigadiers, as well as the local villagers.

Of course, he was deeply insulted at having been sent to do forced labor, yet still his character did not permit him to fall into any deep and hopeless funk. He didn't hold grudges, plus his tendency to get swept away by various pursuits distracted and calmed him. And thus his eight-month stay there might not have left any lasting traces in his life if it hadn't been for the accident with Mona. For a whole month after his internment, she didn't know anything about what had happened to him, and there was no one who could tell her. Stoyan Kralev assured her that he, too, didn't know anything about his whereabouts, while Miho Barakov, whom she managed to go see, told her that he had been sent for several months to some farm in southern Bulgaria, but even he didn't know where. Ivan Shibilev could have written her as soon as he had arrived, but he knew his letter wouldn't reach her with the postmark of the labor-reeducation camp. A month went by before he managed to send her a play and a letter in the name of a girlfriend of hers from Tolbuhin, written by the co-op's accountant. The elder Barakov called Mona down to the village soviet to give her the booklet, which he had leafed through page by page, but kept the letter to himself in any case. At home, Mona put together the marked letters and pieced together the message. Ivan Shibilev wrote her that he was alive and well and feeling fine, but she was sure he was writing that only to reassure her. Like everyone, she, too, thought that the camp was hell on earth, where they tormented people and kept them on the brink of starvation. Since the local authorities had been hiding his whereabouts for so long, she thought that meant he really had been sent to hell and that she had to go see him at any cost, even if only for a minute through the fence. She couldn't shake the thought that he was imprisoned only twenty-five or thirty miles from the village and she was constantly hatching plans of how she could go to see him. His letter arrived at the height of threshing season, so to be absent from the village for personal reasons even for half a day not only was inconvenient but was downright blameworthy. So she waited until the first few days of fall, when the co-op freed the draft animals from fieldwork. During that time she was constantly doubled over from stomach pains, and she even fainted in front of Nikolin. He asked for a horse cart from the co-op chairman and even before dawn sent his wife to the city to see a doctor, while he stayed at home with

their daughter. It was about a dozen miles to the city, and as much again
to Obrochishte, and so as to make it back to the village by nightfall, Mona
whipped the horses into a gallop as soon as she left the village. The road
curved around a small glade of acacias, right in the bend a motorcycle with
a sidecar popped up, coming straight at the horses. They stopped short,
while Mona pitched forward over the cart rails onto the shaft. The next
instant the horses bolted forward, bore off into the stubble field, turned
around, and galloped back toward the village. The motorcyclist, who was
a courier from the city, reported the incident at the village soviet, only he
hadn't seen which street the runaway horses had turned down. He and the
policeman set out to look for them, but then men arrived, carrying Mona
in a blanket. They left her in the village soviet and sent the motorcyclist
to the neighboring village for a doctor. He arrived half an hour later, but
not in time to find Mona alive. He said she had already died when being
dragged under the cart.

Ivan Shibilev's life underwent a change, the likes of which no one
expected for a person of his character. His insatiable passion for roaming,
for theater, where he now could become a full-time actor, for books and
for drawing and for many other things suddenly turned into another, even
greater passion – for his child. Up until Mona's death, he somehow could
not feel that the child was his own. From the very first, when she claimed
it was his, he suspected she was doing it to hold on to him as long as possible. For a woman like her, whose love had not been fully reciprocated
and who had been compromised, it was absolutely within the realm of
possibility that she would use a lie to get revenge or at least to torment
his conscience for some time. Even after Mona's marriage, just as before
he did not clarify his feelings for her, he got swept away by other women,
but with his every return to the village, he would somehow completely
naturally return to her, without considering the consequences of this
affair. When he found out that she had gotten married and had a child,

he didn't feel pain or jealousy, but rather a certain dissatisfaction, as if he had been deprived of some convenience that he had grown accustomed to over the years. There was also a time when he avoided seeing her, because he felt disgusted by the thought that she was coming from her husband's bed or from his child's arms. The very first time they met after her marriage, Mona, who was extremely worked up and sobbing, had told him that the girl was his and that she had named her Melpomena, because he had told her more than once that if he someday had a daughter, he would name her after the patroness of the theater. He did not believe her, yet unwittingly he began peering at the child and gradually discovered that she resembled him. Nevertheless, if Mona hadn't died, he likely would have worked in some theater or somewhere else, he might even have gotten married and had children and lived far from the village. Mela would never have found out that he was her real father, and it just might have happened that he never would have seen her again as long as he lived. But as it was, after Mona's death everything within him was subordinated to the single goal of remaining close to the child and not letting her out of his sight.

Nikolin could not look after the child himself and shortly after her mother's death, he hired an elderly woman, Mona's aunt, to take care of her. To Ivan Shibilev it seemed that this aunt did not take care of the girl as she should, that she didn't feed her enough and keep her clean and tidy. When the weather was nice the girl would go out into the street to play with the other children in the neighborhood, and Ivan Shibilev always found time and excuses to pass by that way to see her. For a long time after her mother's death, in the little girl's eyes, which were a warm brown and slightly slanted up toward her temples just like Ivan Shibilev's eyes, there was some hidden sorrow, which gave her the look of a lonely, abandoned child. She had long known Ivan Shibilev, because she had often seen him in the street, the community center, or in other places where her mother had spoken to him. At these meetings, he always gave her some treat, and when she was little, Mela had grown so accustomed to these treats that she herself would reach toward his pockets. Several days before they sent him to the labor camp, Ivan Shibilev had run into Mona and the girl by chance on a side street and in a rush of feelings for the girl he had taken her into his arms and showered her with kisses. At the camp he had often recalled that sweet, heady scent of a child's flesh, which the little girl still gave off, and his heart would be filled with tenderness. Now that she had been left without a mother, he wanted more than ever to hug and kiss the girl, but she had changed, she no longer took sweets from him and even avoided talking to him. Auntie doesn't let me take anything from you, she would say, turning her back on him, when he would meet her and try to talk to her. The old woman likely knew, as did everyone in the village, that he was her real father, and didn't want to let him near her.

With a heavy heart Ivan Shibilev waited for her to grow up and start school. So he could be with her more often and more closely, he founded a children's theater, selecting children from all grades, and by May 1 they had put together two plays. They were so popular that people even came from the neighboring villages to watch them. The little stage in the old mud-brick community center was transformed into a fairy-tale nook where the children, dressed in brightly colored, beautiful costumes, danced, sang, and recited to the accompaniment of a choir. During rehearsals, Ivan Shibilev had the chance to see Mela, to talk to her and to stroke her hair several times a week, and those were his happiest days and evenings. He had decided to stay where she was, but he had no job, the village leaders didn't know how to act toward him and what job to give him. They hoped that after a week or two, as had always been the case until now, he would take off for the city, and after everything that had happened to him, perhaps he would never come back to the village again. It was the winter holidays and every night people came to invite him to get-togethers,

Christmas Eve celebrations, and name days. Stoyan Kralev and Barakov sent people to these gatherings to watch and listen to him at the homes he visited, but all their spies reported one and the same thing – Ivan Shibilev didn't talk about politics or even about village business, when they asked him how the labor camp had been, he would say that he'd had a nice rest there, he'd picked more peppers and tomatoes than you could shake a stick at, and had played clarinet in the evenings. Stoyan Kralev and Barakov didn't know how to interpret his behavior, as resignation or as spite hidden behind a calm veneer. In any case, the two of them were on their guard where he was concerned, because you never knew what to expect from a person like Ivan Shibilev.

One day in the early spring he himself came to see them at the party club, where the two of them were discussing plans for the impending sowing time. As soon as they saw him on the doorstep, they both stood up as if on command and stared at him, trying to guess his intentions. These intentions, of course, could not be peaceable in any case and Stoyan Kralev, expecting some show of vengeance, put his hand on the handle of the drawer where he kept his pistol. Barakov was clearly very unnerved and even frightened. He had no means of defense if the need arose and when he saw Stoyan Kralev trying to open the drawer, he stepped to the side and stood next to him. But Ivan Shibilev closed the door behind him, greeted them, and just stood there. They did not return his greeting and kept looking at him with undisguised suspicion.

"I've been waiting for more than two months for you to call me in, so here I am finally coming to you," Ivan Shibilev said, smiling somehow guiltily. "Aren't you going to find some job for me here in this village? Or should I start going around begging?"

The two village leaders exchanged glances, then Stoyan Kralev pointed at a chair by the wall.

"Sit down! Aren't you going back to the theater?"

"I have no intention of going back."

"For how long?"

"Forever."

"Should I believe you?"

"Do what you like, but I'm staying here."

"Fine," Stoyan Kralev said after thinking it over. "You'll have your answer tomorrow. Stop by around noon."

Ivan Shibilev left, and the two men stood there staring at the door in silence – they felt shamefaced and guilty in his presence, whereas he had acted as if nothing bad had happened between them.

"You know what a playactor he is, he makes himself into whatever he wants to be," Barakov said. "When he feels like laughing, he laughs, when he feels like crying, he'll shed the biggest crocodile tears you've ever seen. He acts like butter won't melt in his mouth, but who knows what he's got up his sleeve. His type are fair-weather friends. I don't trust him as far as I can throw him."

Stoyan Kralev also didn't believe he would stay around and thus was generous with him. They appointed him as accountant in the co-op in the hopes that after a few months he would dash off somewhere and leave the position free, since it had been intended for a girl from the village who would finish with her accounting courses in July. But July rolled around, the girl came back from her studies to take up the accounting duties, but Ivan Shibilev stayed in the village and had no intention of leaving it. They were forced to assign him to the woodworking shop, since he had a knack for woodworking, but since there wasn't enough work for three men there, the following year they sent him to the machine-tractor station. They shoved him off from job to job, from place to place, always in the hopes of finally being rid of him, but never once did he raise his voice in protest or accuse them of unfairly having expelled him from the party and having sent him to a labor camp. He only rarely recalled these unpleasant things, and even then without malice or hard feelings. They were like nightmares, which he would forget a minute after having been reminded of them for some reason. His desire to live with and for Mela was becoming more and more overpowering, and his heart had no room for other feelings or thrills besides her. Almost every day or every other day he looked for convenient excuses to catch a glimpse of her at least for a minute, when she was playing with the other children or on her way to or from school. He didn't dare stop her on the street or caress her, for fear of awakening Nikolin's jealousy and suspicion. In bad weather, when it was snowy or muddy, Nikolin would take Mela to and from school. Ivan Shibilev watched how he would pick her up and press her face to his and his heart would sink in anguish.

In the meantime the elderly woman looking after Mela got sick and passed away, and now Nikolin was looking after his daughter on his own. How long would things go on this way and would Mela ever learn who her real father was? How could he hint at it to her at this young age? If he tried to tell her in some way, she surely wouldn't understand him, and even if she did understand – she would be torn psychologically, traumatized, and Nikolin wouldn't let her see him anymore. On the other hand, if he left her to find out later, she would grow so attached to Nikolin that she would never part from him for anything in the world. There was only one possible way to make her attached to him: theater. Only there could he be close to her, envelop her in attention and tenderness, satisfy her childish caprices. And everything turned out as it once had with her mother. Mela was quickly and permanently drawn to the stage. She liked getting up in front of people, with them clapping and admiring her. She learned her parts at the first rehearsal, she was agile and inventive, she could embody different states so naturally that after only a few performances she stood out as the most talented child in the village. Ivan Shibilev was happy when leading rehearsals for a play or student performance, which allowed him to spend many hours and whole days with Mela, to make her up and costume her such that she truly became a little angel. In irrepressible outbursts of affection, he took every opportunity to hold her little hands, to stroke her and kiss her and happily noticed that she accepted his caresses ever more calmly, asked him to explain some lessons to her or told her what her father had said or done at home. In this way Ivan Shibilev found out that Nikolin was having a hard time looking after her himself, and he was afraid he might get remarried. A rumor was going around that Nikolin was going to marry a widow with two children, and that possibility cast a dark cloud over Ivan Shibilev's happiness, because the stepmother, like every stepmother, would shut Mela up at home and load her with housework right when she was growing attached to him.

Folks from the neighboring village really were trying to make a match with Nikolin, but he could not even think about a second marriage. After Mona's death he had fallen into such despair that many people thought he would go out of his mind from grief. When he saw her body, he fainted, and at her funeral he again lost his self-control, sobbing heart-wrenchingly and asking her like a child: "What did we ever do to you, our dear sweet mother, to make you leave us alone? You'll never come back to us, it's better for us to come to you! Why are you leaving us here to suffer, dearest mother, take us with you!"

His grieving moved people to tears, but also unsettled them. Mona's aunt, the same woman who would later look after the child, led Nikolin home by the hand and kept watch over him the whole night, afraid that he might make an attempt on his own life. Nikolin was lying on his back, raving deliriously with open eyes. In front of his eyes appeared – sometimes separately, sometimes together – all his departed loved ones: his parents, his uncle, Auntie Raina, the cook from the estate, Mihail Devetakov, and Mona. They all smiled and called him to come join them, only Mona begged him to stay at home, to look after their child and to come to her grave to tell her whether the girl was alive and well. The cook Auntie Raina led him around the vegetable garden while handing him hot dishes of food, and at the same time gently advised him to tuck some money away for rainy days; his uncle was sitting near a tree, big tears rolling down his cheeks, and saying in a thin, womanish voice that all the lambs this spring had been born naked as jaybirds; Mihail Devetakov was sitting on a pile of books, drinking tea from a colorful porcelain cup, and saying: "She is dead. Up until yesterday, she was a person, now she is nothing. How is it possible to change from something into nothing?" "What do you mean, 'nothing,'" Nikolin would say: "I can see her, I can hear her, she ordered me to tell her about our child, how can that be nothing?"

For a long time, when he had the chance, Nikolin would go to Mona's grave every day. The cemetery was close to his house, so he could go there at any time. Nikolin did not light a grave lamp or a candle as the old women did, but he always kept the grave clean. He had hidden a hoe in the bushes and every time he went he would hoe around the flowers and clear away the weeds. While doing this or while sitting by the cross, deeply lost in thought, he would hear Mona's voice coming from the ground every time, muted and distant, yet so clear that he understood her every word. Mona would ask first of all about the girl, and he would tell her in the greatest detail how she had gotten up, what she had eaten, what she had said, whom she had played with, and what she had played during the day.

"Did you comb her hair?" Mona would sometimes ask. "Don't let her go around dirty and unkempt! Tie the blue ribbons on her braids. They are in the wardrobe, on the upper-left-hand shelf."

"Your aunt ties on her ribbons... She cleans her plate and plays either by herself or with the other kids in the neighborhood."

"Does she ask about me?"

"She does. Why doesn't Mommy come home? We tell her that you've gone to the city to a doctor to get well, and she keeps asking when you're coming back."

"She'll be starting school this fall, make sure to get her shoes and warm clothes."

"I've already gotten everything ready. Today she learned the letter M. The mousie makes music, she was saying, the mousie moves. She was saying that over and over all day..."

While talking to Mona, Nikolin felt heavy spasms welling up in his heart and tightening his throat, round, hot tears ran from his eyes, and he was overtaken by a deep, sweet grief that filled his soul with the purifying blessing of human weeping. This was the howl of his very being, which in some inexplicable way lightened his soul, his grief for Mona little by little transformed into a resignation to fate and the hope for a new life devoted to his child. Even before, he had been strongly attached to her, but now that she was left motherless, he felt called to be her only support and mainstay. But the child, too, turned out to be the only mainstay and meaning in his life from then on. He wanted to quit shepherding, so as to be closer to his child, and Stoyan Kralev honored his request and appointed him as a brigadier in the animal husbandry brigade. He worked in the village and could stop by the house several times a day.

The old woman he had hired to look after the girl had gotten sick already in the second year and passed away, and since then Nikolin had been taking care of Mela on his own. All the usual childhood illnesses came one after another: measles and chickenpox, mumps, whooping cough, scarlet fever – all of which Mela got before she was ten. Her last serious illness was malaria. Every day at noon she would start shivering with cold, her teeth chattering, her body convulsed by seizures. He would pile several blankets on her, but she kept trembling with cold, yet after an hour she would be burning up and wanted to be out in the cold. Nikolin would strip her down to her undershirt and take her into the cool shade of the walnut tree, he daubed her lips and forehead with water, but the fire inside her burned ever hotter and she lay limp in his arms as if dead. This went on for two whole weeks, and during the worst heat wave of July, at that. No medicines helped at all and she was so exhausted that she couldn't even walk from the house to the street on her own. Finally Nikolin cured her on his own following an elderly woman's advice. He boiled walnut leaves and he bathed Mela every night in the water, which took on the color of iodine. After the seventh such bath, she took a turn for the better, her emaciated little body and limbs, which looked like sticks, grew rounded again and by the fall she was completely healthy.

Nikolin had thought she wouldn't make it many times that year and had fallen into despair, hundreds of nights he hadn't slept a wink and cried as he watched her succumbing to the illness and turning into a tiny bloodless doll. At the worst moments he would go to the graveyard for a minute to talk with Mona, he would ask her whether the child would recover, but he could no longer hear her voice. He would take her silence as a bad omen and would return home, his heart heavy. Mona either didn't dare or didn't want to give him such terrible news, which could only be the child's death. He stayed awake whole nights, cleaning and cooking, sewing and patching clothes, exhausted to the point of complete helplessness, he lost weight and went around as unkempt as a hermit, many times he woke up on the floor, and sometimes even out in the yard, where he had fallen, overwhelmed by the need for sleep. But thank God, the sicknesses passed one after the other, Mela got better, grew stronger, and at fourteen she was already a slender and pretty girl. She had wanted to continue her education since she was young, so Nikolin sent her to high school in the city. Whatever he earned at the co-op, whether in cash or in kind, went to support her. Once a month he went to the city to leave money for her, while he scraped by as best he could. During her third year, Mela didn't come home during Christmas vacation, but sent a letter saying that she had to stay in the city to take part in some New Year's program. She wrote that she would come home during Easter break, but she didn't come then, either. Nikolin waited a week for her and when he didn't get a letter, he went to the city to see why she hadn't come home. Her landlady said that Mela had left school at the beginning of the year, had become an actress, and had moved into another apartment. He looked for her at the theater, but the doorman said that some Mela had been hanging around there at one point, but that was a long time ago.

Mela finally came back in the autumn. She had spent almost a year at the Burgas Theater and now she wanted to rest. She didn't give her father any further explanations, but even this was enough for him. To him, the most important thing was that she had returned alive and well, so where she had been and why didn't matter anymore. His heart filled with joy and hope, even though Mela was neither happy nor calm. She spent her days alone in her room, talking aloud to herself, while in the evenings she would go to the community center and come back late. Nikolin made food for her, but she hardly touched it and quickly went to her room. He wanted to talk to her, to ask her how she had gotten along in those far-off cities, whether something wasn't bothering her, but as soon as he brought it up, she would fall silent or give one-word answers, and even then with great reluctance. Nikolin could see that she didn't want to confide in him, and with sadness he asked himself how she could possibly have changed so much, it was as if only yesterday she had been that cheerful, playful, loving child who had met him with happy shrieks at the door and had thrown herself into his arms crying: "Daddy! Daddy!"; as if she was not that same little girl who only a few years ago had taken medicine from him, her face burning with fever and her eyes wide open and trusting. Sometimes he thought to himself that his daughter was now a young woman and her "troubles" were a woman's troubles, but he didn't dare ask her, he was afraid of making her angry and causing her to go off to the city even earlier. But she didn't stay longer than two weeks. One morning an old beat-up truck with a canvas cover pulled up to the house and honked its horn. An elderly man climbed out of the cab and asked after Mela. She had heard the horn and signaled to the driver to come in. She led him into her room and a minute later he carried out a large bundle, put it in the truck bed and came back again.

"It's the rug Mom was saving for me," she said when she saw her father standing in the yard watching in amazement as the stranger carried off various things. "I'm taking the armchair, too, because my apartment is empty and I don't have anywhere to sit."

She asked the driver to wait for her, got dressed, grabbed her suitcase, and got in the cab next to him.

"Why leave so suddenly, Mela, honey?" Nikolin was saying, flustered and alarmed by her sudden departure. "If you'd told me a day or two in advance, I could've put together something for you for the road."

"I don't need anything," Mela said.

"What do you mean, you don't need anything, my girl! You're going to live among strangers…"

While grumbling away like this, he had managed to put a loaf of bread, a chunk of cheese, a couple of links of flat sausage, and a slab of bacon in a bag for her, he gave her all the money he had on him and sent her on her way.

She would always come and go so suddenly, always carrying off some piece of Devetakov's furniture that her late grandfather had dragged back from the estate so many years earlier, and he always saw her off with a heavy heart, not knowing when or how she'd be back again. Tormented by loneliness and uncertainty, he often wondered whether Mela wasn't lying to him that she was acting at some theater, and if she was acting, why was she always going from city to city? How could he set her straight, how could he tell her that that kind of life would ruin her when she was still young and green? Filled with love and awe for her, he didn't dare scold her or give her advice, since he realized that as a simple, illiterate peasant he was far beneath her and had no right to meddle in her life. Her nose was always buried in a book, she was always sharpening her mind, how can I, who can hardly count the fingers on one hand, sit her down to teach her reason and common sense! That's how he consoled himself, but deep in his heart he knew that his daughter wasn't living as she should. He saw something indecent, affected, and crazy in the fact that she would spend whole days shut up in her room like a prisoner talking to herself, laughing, crying, or yelling at someone, even though he knew that she was learning some part. One time she didn't come back for ten months and he realized that only Ivan Shibilev could know something about her. The two of them put on performances together every vacation at the community center, Ivan Shibilev himself had been an actor in the city in his younger years, he had taught her to act since childhood, so she surely had confided in him. Nikolin met him by chance that very same day in the street and was very surprised to see that Ivan Shibilev was extremely flustered and even went pale, as if Nikolin had insulted him with his question.

"How should I know what theater she's at!" He acted as if he was in a hurry and went on his way.

"Sorry if I somehow…" Nikolin watched him go and added to himself: "Since you don't know, you don't know, but why get so mad when I ask you?"

Ivan Shibilev knew exactly where Mela was and what she was doing, but he wouldn't tell Nikolin for anything in the whole world. This chance encounter with him not only upset him, but it scared him as well. He thought that Nikolin had already found out how far his relationship with Mela had gone and had decided to try to get even with him for stealing away his daughter. He spent several days expecting Nikolin to come looking for him, he locked the doors of his house during the daytime and went around the yard on guard, but Nikolin did not come. After some time they met again by chance and Nikolin greeted him and passed on by. By the look on his face he didn't seem to be harboring any feeling of hatred, but rather something like awkwardness, and once again Ivan Shibilev was faced with the man's mysterious character, wondering whether he was monumentally stupid, naïvely trusting, or completely lacking any personality whatsoever. Thus he reached the conclusion that he did not possess a sense of self-respect and pride, hence there was no reason to fear him. Sometimes, however, who knows why, he was gripped by the suspicion that the man's calmness hid a great internal strength, and if that was the case, he knew about his late wife's extramarital affairs (many of his informers had bragged publicly about how they had told him this and how he had kept silent or just smiled foolishly) and that the child was not his, but he had borne everything, because his love was stronger than jealousy and humiliation. Perhaps he was one of those types who got a thrill out of his own suffering, or else one of those who got satisfaction watching others, after having found out their secrets, playing hide-and-seek and pretending to be honorable, while at the same time, they knew that he knew that they were deceiving him? In that case it turned out that Nikolin had been watching him and Mona the whole time through a peephole, he had heard their every word, he had followed their every move. When he imagined that, Ivan Shibilev experienced some strange feeling of outrage and helplessness, as a person feels when he finds out that he has been watched in his most intimate moments.

Time proved that such thoughts were mere fantasies born of books and theater, or the figments of his guilty imagination, yet still Nikolin's character (if he had any character at all) again and again appeared before him as a mystery. It was unthinkable for a man to know that his wife was having an affair with another and that their child was not his own, or not to suspect the one and the other when he had been told so clearly and so many times that both the one and the other were true, and after all that to act so indifferently toward his rival. There was something monstrous in that and precisely this would turn out to be the most difficult obstacle to surmount in tearing Mela out of his clutches one day, since no one could in any way prove to him that she was not his daughter. On the one hand, Ivan Shibilev's relations with Mela had advanced to the point that in her letters she addressed him as "my dear second father," jokingly explaining that she called him that because he understood her and cared for her no less than her real father. In conversation she didn't call him that, but had already confided in him that she had received anonymous notes from fellow villagers telling her that he was her real father. Ivan Shibilev didn't deny, but also didn't confirm, this, because he was afraid that she would announce it to Nikolin in a way that would wound him so badly that he would keep her at home or turn to the authorities for help. He placed his hope in time, which was on his side. He wrote to Mela using the code he had developed for her mother, but with different names, since no one suspected they were in correspondence. With touching frankness, Mela would tell him about herself, and this, instead of making him happy, flung him into despair. She was following in his footsteps with such stunning precision that in her he could see himself at that age. She, too, had been a good student, but had also left high school in her third year, swept away by theater and music, and she, like him, could not resist the urge to wander. At the age of fifty, Ivan Shibilev had looked back on his life and was forced to admit that he hadn't lived it as he should have. This thought was especially insistent on those days when he felt the whole weight of the mediocrity and poverty of spirit that surrounded him, when he felt his talents fading from year to year as he became more and more of a villager at heart. He was conscious of and suffered from this rustification, yet he couldn't manage to overcome it, he had become so firmly and permanently caught in the trap of this simple life, filled with the most basic needs, stirred up by political intrigues and concerns about private ownership, a life that had turned him from "our Leonardo" into a village painkiller.

In fact, he hadn't had any particular ambitions and had lived solely following the urges of his many talents and passions, thus looked at from the other side, his life hadn't been spent so badly after all, on the contrary, perhaps it had even been a happy one. Yes, it had indeed been happy, because in that complicated time, oppressive in its intense political struggles, social upheaval, and wars, he had lived free as a bird and flown off wherever his desires had led him. Wasn't that real life – to be working constantly, regardless of what, for whom, and where, and at the same time to be following the call of your aspirations? And even now, at this age, wasn't he still playing at weddings and fairs like your average, ordinary tavern musician? At every village celebration and fair in the vicinity he would stand up in one of the seats of the Ferris wheel and play while in motion – clarinet or violin, and would perform joking songs or poems:

> I've got two little neighbor girls
> Two neighbor girls, with silks and curls
> The dark-eyed beauty's name is Ginka
> While the blonde is called Kalinka

Or (to the tune of "Greensleeves"):

> Alas, my nose doth run and run
> I've blown and blown it continuously
> My handkerchief has been wrung, and wrung
> Disintegrating, and that's why you see...

He would wipe his nose on his sleeve, while down below the audience would cheer approvingly and clap. He realized that his jokes were shallow and even trite, but he couldn't resist the temptation to make them laugh, to amuse and entertain them, to see their smiles and the warmth in their eyes. He had long ago noticed that people were at their best when they were laughing or crying from the bottom of their hearts. In the first case they forgot their troubles, while in the second they regretted all the wrongs they had done to others or forgave those who had done them wrong. Every time he would discover that those listeners who were known as malicious, thieving, and two-faced, when they laughed or cried, it was like they were born again and became completely different people. And he himself, while acting onstage, singing, or playing, felt at his best and happy, he was gripped by ecstasy and ready to give away what was most precious to him if they asked for it, or to perform the most heroic feats in the world.

But if he nevertheless found that he hadn't lived his life as he should have in his younger years, it was because of the life Mela was leading. It seemed to him that if he had lived differently, she, too, who was now going down his very same path with some fatal tenacity, would be living better. But whatever his former life had been, good or bad, happy or not, it was the life of a young man. He had found himself in unpleasant and difficult situations, in which a young girl like Mela would be unconditionally ruined. He knew a lot about her even back when she had started high school, because he always found an excuse to meet her or visit her "by chance," while recently, when they had definitely grown close, to stay with her and even spend months living in the city where she was living. He would turn up at the slightest hint that she was facing some difficulty or had to make an important decision, so as not to allow anyone else to come to her aid, since that someone else could only be a man. She was very beautiful and feminine and, as she had already confided in him, men had been after her even when she was still in high school. Now, wherever she went, men flocked around her, she had "tons" of suitors, especially among actors, musicians, and artists. They all tried to flirt with her, while the directors who gave her parts in their plays wouldn't leave her in peace. Women always hated her, were jealous of her, and gossiped about her behind her back, she despised them and gave as good as she got, and thus she would be forced to look for work in some other city...

Ivan Shibilev was painfully familiar with the alluring, glittering, and bittersweet life of a young amateur actor, filled with feverish hopes of success onstage, with tension, failures, and rivalries with professional actors, with intrigues and love affairs, with jealousy and hatred, it was the life of people striving to scale the heights of capital-A Art and fame, people who were noble and treacherous, poor and generous, naïve and merciless in the struggles for parts and success. In any case, he couldn't tear Mela away from this life, which he compared to a sea of passions, so he was at least trying to teach her to swim a bit better so she wouldn't drown in the very beginning. Her talent, if she had any, had not yet blazed forth, at twenty she had achieved a few modest successes in several small roles, and this made her anxious, closed-minded, and quarrelsome. Her situation made her easy prey for men, and Ivan Shibilev invested all his efforts in convincing her that she shouldn't trust the fleeting impulses of her heart, which are most often deceptive, and that she shouldn't abuse her womanly charm – her beauty might win her the goodwill of some directors and theater managers, but such success would be fake, bought at the price of her degradation. True success was achieved only through hard work and patience, and through an honest appraisal of one's own abilities, thus if she didn't succeed in theater, she would remain a decent woman without pangs of conscience and spiritual wounds that would haunt her her whole life long. Finally, to move her and play on her sense of pity, he threw down his final ace – he told her how after her mother's death, he had given up his acting career right when they had appointed him to the Shumen Theater under Article 9, so he could dedicate the remainder of his life to her alone and to her future. She was truly touched by his self-sacrifice, she burst into tears and promised to be more sensible from then on. They had this conversation in her apartment in the regional town of R., where she had moved at the insistence of the director of the local theater, who had promised her parts in two plays.

That same day Ivan Shibilev went back to the village, and three months later, a dozen days before the New Year, Mela arrived and went straight to see him. For the first time she entered his home, for the first time she called him "Daddy" and threw herself into his embrace. He scooped her up in his arms and crying tears of joy, he began kissing her forehead, her eyes, her hair, and her hands, as one kisses a small child.

"My darling, my sweet little daughter, my little girl, my heart's delight!" he said, out of his mind with excitement while carrying her around the room and showering her with kisses, yet at the same time a bad premonition was gnawing at his heart, precisely because she had returned so suddenly and come straight to him, without stopping by her former home. She had lost weight and was pale, her eyes, which seemed large and dry, burned with anguish and anxiety, her whole body was painfully tense.

"Something terrible has happened!" she said, once they were sitting down across from each other.

And she told him how the manager of the theater, who was also a director and actor, had started insistently making advances on her and declaring his love. They had known each other from her previous theater and when he had left for the town of R., he had told her that if she would come there, too, he would give her parts regularly, and most importantly, he would convene a commission from Sofia, headed by Boyan Danovski, who was a friend of his, and if she did well in her role, they would accept her into the National Academy for Theater Arts without a competition. He was forty years old, divorced with two children. He welcomed her very kindly and even helped her find an apartment, and he really did give her a part and they began rehearsals. He often invited her to his place, but she would either decline or go with others from the theater, but for some time now she had begun visiting him on her own, and as luck would have it a week earlier he had died from a heart attack when they were together during the night. Frightened out of her wits, she had started screaming and woke up the landlords. When they realized what was going on, they detained her and called the police. Interrogations and medical examinations followed, then finally everything was over and she had come home to think over what to do next.

Ivan Shibilev was listening, horrified yet moved that during one of the most difficult moments in her life, Mela had come to bare her soul to him, her real father. They stayed up late talking, and right as they were going to bed, there was an insistent knocking on the window. Ivan Shibilev turned out the light, opened the window a crack, and saw Nikolin standing down in the flower garden.

"My apologies," he said, his voice hoarse. "I came to ask about Mela. She told me tonight that she was going to see you, and she hasn't come back the whole night."

"She's not here, what would she be doing here at my place!" Ivan Shibilev fell silent before adding: "She stopped by for a bit at dusk to borrow a book and went on her way. She was here with a colleague who drove her by car. Their theater is visiting the nearby villages, so she stopped by to borrow the book."

Nikolin stood there for a few seconds, staring at the dark window, sighed deeply, and left. Ivan Shibilev lay down, but after a short while he got up out of bed and went into the other room where Mela was. They had decided that she would stay a few days to rest and calm down, but now they would have to come up with another plan. All signs indicated that Nikolin could sense her presence, he would come back looking for her again or would lurk around the house, he might even complain to the village leaders. That would stir up a scandal, the authorities would return

Mela to him as her lawful father, and that was exactly what he couldn't allow to happen. They decided that Mela would go to Plovdiv to stay with his mother, that is, her real grandmother, who had long since moved there with her husband to take care of his half sister's children. Once the children had grown up, the brother-in-law had bought a new apartment and left the old one to the elderly couple, and Mela could live with them for the time being. Ivan Shibilev wrote a letter to his mother telling her to take care of her granddaughter Mela, and the next morning when it was still dark, he took her to the bus in the neighboring village, from where she would go first to Tolbuhin and from there catch a train to Plovdiv. As for the next step, Ivan Shibilev was hatching plans to find work in Plovdiv or some city even farther away, to move there with Mela or even to follow her from city to city, if need be. Even if he somehow found out where she was, Nikolin was hardly likely to follow her. He didn't know any trade besides sheepherding and living in a city was unthinkable for him, so even if Mela was still formally his daughter, in actuality she would be living with her real father.

Nikolin, for his part, went back home and only then saw that in his anguish he had torn up the whole blanket, turning it into a heap of rags and scraps of wool. The pile resembled some shabby creature lying dead on the bed, and while he was looking at it, gripped by horror, his thoughts swooped down on him even more viciously like vipers and called out one after the other: "Mela is Ivan Shibilev's daughter. Even the dogs have known it since way back when, you knew it, too, you just didn't have the courage to admit it!" "No, I didn't know," Nikolin would answer them. "I heard it, they all told me, but it was like I didn't know it because I didn't believe it. People talk all kinds of nonsense, you can't put a padlock on their lips. Mona was my wife, so how could our child have a different father? How, tell me! Mela is my daughter, I brought her into the world, I raised her since she was nothing but a slab of meat…"

Nikolin again recalled how, when he saw her for the first time after she was born, she did look like a dark-red slab of meat, with her yellowish face and little eyes tightly shut. He remembered, as if they were happening right there before his eyes, all the most important events and moments from her life: her first smile with toothless gums, her first coos and bab-bling, the first step she took on her own, the first time she called him "Daddy"; he remembered washing her little bottom, how he had been intoxicated by the sweet scent of her delicate flesh, how she had written her first letter and sung her first song. *Was all of that a dream, or was it real,* Nikolin wondered. It was real, but why would Mela go to Ivan Shibilev after she hadn't come back to the village for nearly a year, why would she go straight to him and stay there all night? The vicious thoughts asked and answered their own question: *So as never to come back to you again! – What do you mean, she won't come back, where would she go? I mean, she may really have stopped by for some book and left right away again. Those two have been close for a long time, didn't he teach her theater as a child, of course she'd turn to him for advice about her business, who else would she ask?*

While he was thinking this, Nikolin remembered that earlier that evening, when Mela had been standing in front of him in the street, her resemblance to Ivan Shibilev had suddenly struck him, such an obvious and strong resemblance that pain had pierced his heart. Only for an instant, but precisely in that instant when she told him she was going to Ivan Shibilev's and her face looked more elongated than usual and her eyes were squinted. He had seen that expression many times on Ivan Shibilev's face, when he was excited or flustered, when out in the fields hunting, in conversation with others, or most of all when he was performing some part: the expression of an anxious or angry person. He couldn't remember having looked for a resemblance between Mela and Ivan Shibilev in the past, even though many had hinted that she was the other man's daughter, nor had he ever doubted his wife's honor. That night, however, as if he had been suddenly cured from amnesia or awakened from deep oblivion, he remembered moments in which, albeit against his will, he had discovered an obvious resemblance between the child and Ivan Shibilev. He had been especially struck by this resemblance when he noticed it for the first time. Mela had been seven then and was going to school. In bad weather, if there was snow or mud, he would carry her in his arms from school to home. One rainy day he was a bit late and she had started out toward home on her own. The little wooden bridge over the gorge had been washed away by a flood and Ivan Shibilev, who just happened to be there, was carrying Mela through the water, her face pressed to his. Then Nikolin saw from up close how much the child resembled him.

Over the following years, until puberty, the girl was changing constantly and quickly, the features of her face would sometimes resemble her mother's or her aunt's, sometimes Nikolin himself, or even one of his sisters. After puberty her resemblance to Ivan Shibilev became all the more obvious, especially to someone determined to find it at any cost. But by that time Mela was studying in the city, he saw her only rarely and forgot about the resemblance, and whenever she came home, he was so overjoyed and excited that he couldn't think of anything besides how to coddle her and keep her with him as long as possible. He recalled that many times he had sensed or noticed some intimacy between Mona and Ivan Shibilev. Several times he had seen them talking in some side street, he would be holding the little girl in his arms, giving her sweets, and stroking her. He had also happened upon them in the community center, where they rehearsed, and from Mona's face he could tell that she was not pleased to see him, and on the way home she always found a reason to get angry with him. He had also seen the two of them returning from the neighboring village. They had gone there to put on a children's play and at sundown they were returning along the road by foot. They were walking about a hundred steps behind the children and they passed him by without noticing him. He had let the herd graze by the road and was sitting in the stubble field when the two of them walked right past him. They were walking into the sunset and their faces were happy, she was saying something and laughing vivaciously, as he had never heard her laugh at home…

When dawn had finally broken and he had to go to the sheep pen, Nikolin happened to notice his leather gloves under a chair in the corner and felt the heavy weight on his heart suddenly being replaced by a sweet lightness, some life-giving stream rushed through his whole being, filling him with calm and hope. He had been looking for those gloves since the weather had turned cold, and the fact that he had found them for him was a joyful omen. The local men wore knitted mittens; of everyone in the village, only he had leather gloves with five separate fingers. He usually wore them on holidays or when he went to the city to bring something to Mela, but since they had gotten worn, he had started wearing them every day. "Here, Daddy, something to keep you warm!" Mela had told him several years earlier, when she had given them to him during one Christmas break. She made him try them on immediately to see whether they fit, then smiled and said that they looked good on him and since they were lined on the inside with cotton wool, they would keep him warm in the winter. Now Nikolin saw her smile, so happy-go-lucky, heartfelt, and daughterly, he heard her voice ("Here, Daddy, something to keep you warm!") and thought to himself that Mela had always been sweet and kind with him, because she was his biological daughter and his alone, she could be no one else's.

A few photos of her and her mother, every object the two of them had touched, a good memory of them was enough to restore his belief that Mona had been a faithful wife, and that Mela was their birth daughter. *Besides, when have you ever heard of a young woman suddenly leaving her father and taking some other man as her true father? And if Ivan Shibilev truly was her real father, why hadn't she gone to him earlier?* he asked himself, answering that he had let himself be swayed by gossip, it had led him into a great delusion, thus all his doubts were ungrounded and futile. That's what he thought during the day when he went to work and was distracted by other people, but at night loneliness weighed on him like a huge stone and those bloodthirsty thoughts again pounced on him, mercilessly tearing up his heart.

He had spent many years in solitude and this had pained him, but the pain wasn't so unbearable, since he had lived in the hope of Mela coming back during vacations. He was also not particularly worried about her future. As a young girl with an education, she would surely get married and live in the city, as most educated young people did. But wherever she might live, she would be his daughter. From time to time he would go to see her, she would come visit him, and he might even live out his old age with her. Why not? Of course she would have children and if there was no other elderly person in the household to look after them, he would take on that task. But if he knew that she would never again set foot in his home, that he would never again hear her voice, never see her eyes...

Tormented from being torn in two directions, he knew the whole time that the truth about Mela was in Ivan Shibilev's hands. What his life would be like from then on depended on this man – would it be calm and happy or filled with bitter, unbearable suffering? Seized by a blind urge for revenge, for seven days he had killed him seven by seven times over for being his wife's lover, and for the fact that Mela was his daughter, he had fallen to his knees before him in gratitude, after hearing from his lips that it was all nothing but gossip and lies, and that he had never had an affair with Mona, and that Mela was his, Nikolin's, daughter.

Now he was no longer afraid of the fateful truth, because he no longer had the strength to bear the uncertainty and was tormented by impatience to find out the truth from Ivan Shibilev as soon as possible. Whatever this truth was, whether good or bad, in both cases it would be like a salve for his tortured soul. However, he didn't know which of the blinds Ivan Shibilev would come toward or if he would come toward them at all. He himself had suggested the wolf hunt as a joke or Lord knows why, but as soon as they set out he had tried to wheedle his way out of it, and if the other hunters hadn't pressed him, he would now be nice and warm at home. Perhaps even now he was already at home. This thought upset Nikolin, so he left his blind and went down into the Inferno.

In the meantime the blizzard had quieted down, the forest, sunk in snow, was awash in a milky light, and the black trunks of the old oak trees started to appear dimly like ghosts. Nikolin walked around the high drifts in the sheltered places, then waded down the slope, knee-deep in snow. It was growing ever quieter and lighter, such that a few minutes later he noticed a person barely crawling toward the south side of the Inferno. *He's going back around the other side of the forest, he feels guilty, he doesn't want to run into me,* Nikolin thought, and hurried to catch up with him. Ivan Shibilev was not running from him, he was running from death itself. When Ivan had gone down into the Inferno with Stoyan Kralev and Zhendo the Bandit, he had let them go ahead, and as Nikolin had suspected, he had decided to go back to the village and then later to lie to the other hunters that he had gotten lost in the blizzard and had been unable to find them. He wasn't forced to lie, however, since he really did get lost. The blizzard was blustering so terribly that he couldn't see even a step ahead of himself, so he trudged on every which way. He had thought to reach the southern end of the valley, where it widened out like a funnel and fused with the plain, and from there to turn toward the village, but instead of coming out on the plain, his path kept getting steeper, and the snow ever deeper. He sank up to his waist in the drifts, he doubled back, wandered to the left and the right, while his strength was being sapped by the minute. He also was not dressed for hunting, he hadn't even taken any bullets, so now he could not even fire off a few shots so the others could come to his aid. But they surely had left and were now drinking wine at the tavern. In good weather the hunts here lasted around twenty minutes, while now it had been more than an hour. Why would those fellows sit freezing in this blizzard for so long since they knew the wolf hunt had been a joke?

The thought that he was left alone and helpless in this hell horrified him. He had no strength left to wade through the deep snow, but he knew that if he stood in one place for more than a minute, he would freeze to death. He dropped his rifle in the snow and started off again. One minute of wading, one minute of rest, without taking his eyes off his watch. He felt the snow piercing the skin of his stomach and chest, how his lips, cheeks, and nose were freezing and he could no longer feel them. After an hour and a half, the blizzard began dying down, the snowflakes thinned, and a grayish-white spot appeared in the sky. That's south, that's the way I need to go. And again, one minute of rest, one minute of walking with his final ounces of strength. There was only one thing he must not let happen – he must not fall. But Nikolin found him fallen, his lips cracked from cold and his face bluish, rolling around in the snow in rubber shoes over thin socks and a thin, short fur jacket. Nikolin grabbed him under the arms and helped him stand up. A minute later Ivan Shibilev tried to talk and blood trickled from his mouth.

"Good thing you showed up. Or I would've stayed here," he said with such a slur that Nikolin could hardly understand him.

He grabbed him under the arms again and led him up to the gnarled pear tree where the path to the village should be. When they stopped to rest Nikolin pounded his back with his open palms to warm him, rubbed his hands in his own, and made him stomp in place. Thanks to these breaks and massages they reached the pear tree, Ivan Shibilev pulled himself together and started telling him how he had gotten lost down there, in the Inferno. Nikolin stood in front of him and asked: "A week ago I came to your place one night to ask you if Mela was there, and you said she wasn't. Did you lie to me then?"

"I lied," Ivan Shibilev admitted. "I didn't dare tell you the truth. I was afraid you'd start yelling and that you'd take her back home."

"Well, what did you have to be afraid of? It's not like she's your daughter or some relative, so she could spend the night at your house?"

"She is my daughter. Everyone knows it, I thought you knew it too."

"You're saying that back then you had something with her late mother?"

"That's how it was. The whole village knows that too, and so do you…"

How simple it is to talk with him, and here this whole week I couldn't make up my mind to do it, Nikolin thought to himself, astonished at his own calmness as he heard that his late wife had been Ivan Shibilev's mistress and that Mela was the other man's daughter. *Now there's the truth that I was racking my brains over all this time! The truth, the truth, the truth!…* He was walking back toward the village, this word on his mind the whole time, filling his entire being, he felt it as a foreign object in both his heart and his soul, and in his thoughts. The word gradually weighted down his heart so much that he could not carry it any longer, he stopped breathlessly, and so as to free himself of it, cried out several times: "Oooh! The pain! The pain! Ooooh!"

His cries, resembling a wolf's howl, were answered by a dog's barking, and only then did he see that he had reached the first houses of the village. He imagined how he would go to his house and find it cold and empty, and not just temporarily, but for all time, until the end of his life, and a heavy feeling of hopelessness once again gripped his heart. *How is it that my whole past has been a lie, and that my future is nothing?* he thought. *It can't be! Let Ivan Shibilev say what he will. The truth is not in another man's words, but in my heart. The truth is in me alone and no one else can prove it with any evidence whatsoever. Ivan Shibilev wasn't in his right mind, his brain was frozen and he didn't know what he was saying. Plus, Mela hasn't told me that she's not my daughter. She's of legal age, what would have stopped her from telling me until now?*

Nikolin set out toward his home, but some force kept pulling him back, and this force was doubt, which had once more seized him and which he could not overcome. He doubled back in his tracks to return to Ivan Shibilev, once more, for the last time, to hear the truth about his daughter. Now more than ever he was afraid that Ivan Shibilev would reconfirm what he had told him, but his hope was also alive and awakened. It screamed in his soul and railed against his faintheartedness so loudly that he grasped it as a drowning man clutches at a straw. "Ivan Shibilev really might not have been in his right mind," he kept telling himself. "He had been snatched from the jaws of death, he could hardly stand on his feet, so he might not have heard what I was asking him or might not have been talking to me, but just babbling. Just tell me that what you told me an hour ago was not true!" Nikolin cried. "Say it with just one word, one glance, one nod, with silence. Don't say anything when I ask you! Even that would be enough. I'm not asking anything more from you."

Ivan Shibilev was nowhere to be seen and Nikolin thought that he had gone home the other way around the village, so that they wouldn't meet again. He was nearing the crooked pear tree when he saw him lying facedown in the snow. He called out to him, then grabbed him by the shoulder and rolled him over onto his back. Ivan Shibilev's face had gone from purple, as he had seen it an hour ago, to bluish-white, and his mouth was full of snow.

PART FOUR:

STOYAN "MAN OF STEEL" KRALEV

(FROM ILKO KRALEV'S NOTES)

AN OLD BEAT-UP BUS belonging to a Varna man went from Varna to Zhitnitsa. In the morning around nine I got off the train from Sofia and caught the bus. It was market day, there were a lot of passengers from the villages, so I barely managed to find a spot in the back seat. As always, the bus stopped halfway on the road to the village Izvor. All the passengers got off to drink water or stretch their legs for fifteen minutes. I was going to get off too, but such a coughing fit came over me that I sat down in one of the front seats near an open window. Something cracked beneath me, I looked down and saw a newspaper. I unfolded it; inside was a gramophone record, shattered into pieces. I got so anxious that my head started aching. There were poplars growing by the water fountain, beyond them began the old woodcutting area grown over with oak brush. Most of the passengers were sitting or strolling through this brush, and among those hanging around the fountain, I didn't see any familiar faces from our village. Finally the passengers began getting back on the bus and taking their seats. I was standing up with the broken record in my hand, waiting for its owner to come looking for it. Then I saw Nusha Pashova from Zhitnitsa. Years ago I had gone to her home to visit her brother, I remembered her as a young girl in her black schoolgirl's smock with white collars, but now she was dressed as a young lady in a suit the color of oranges, against which her dark, sparkling eyes and her hair, which was pulled back into two thick braids, stood out. She radiated such beauty and freshness amidst the sweltering afternoon heat and workaday coarseness of the other passengers that I wanted to hide from her. Precisely because of the dejected state I had been in for several months, I had not noticed her on the bus. I had been sitting in the back seat, staring straight ahead and not daring to move, so as not to start coughing from the heat and spitting up blood in front of everyone. Besides that, I was already sure that the record I had broken was hers and I would have to tell her.

"Hello, Mr. Kralev!" she said, stepping in front of me. "I noticed you back in the city when you got on the bus, but I didn't have the chance to call out to you. I didn't see you among the passengers outside, by the fountain..."

"I didn't get off, as I was busy making trouble for you, Miss Pashova. Is this record yours?"

"Yes."

"I broke it out of carelessness. Please forgive me, I'll pay for it or buy you a new one at my earliest convenience. What was it?"

Nusha took the newspaper with the broken record from me and threw it out the window.

"Some popular song. My landlady gave it to me. You can sit here, the seat has freed up. You may also congratulate me," she added as we sat down next to each other. "I successfully graduated from high school and now am standing with one foot on the threshold of life, as our class teacher informed us."

"Congratulations. As for me, I'm already beyond the threshold of life."

She didn't grasp the double meaning in what I said and turned toward me.

"That means you've finished the university. I accept your congratulations and give you mine in return!"

The bus had started off and we continued talking in this unnatural and affected way, like people who feel some kind of mutual awkwardness or are hiding something important that needs to be said. We had something to say to each other, but this was not the place, the villagers sitting around us were constantly eavesdropping with undisguised curiosity. Besides, I was waiting for Nusha to begin the conversation, only after we had gotten off the bus. But she couldn't contain herself. As soon as we neared their village, she leaned toward me and asked whether I had gotten the letter she had written me about half a year ago. Actually, it wasn't a letter, but a note of a few lines, not addressed to anyone and unsigned. The anonymous author had asked me whether I knew something about L. and to report "where I should," but only in case I had something to tell. I never doubted for an instant that the letter was from Nusha. I had not seen her handwriting before then, but I immediately realized that she was talking about her brother, Alexander. At the university, the other students and everyone called him Sasho, but in the village and in his family, he was Lexy. He liked me to call him that as well, as his fellow villager and friend. In early 1943, Lexy had quit the medical school where he had studied for two years and left for Switzerland. He had left legally, and at first his extreme discretion was puzzling to me, as well as insulting, as we were close friends. Our mutual acquaintances were also surprised by his departure. He hadn't shared his plans with anyone, not even his family, judging from Nusha's note. None of them had found an excuse to stop over at our village and ask me about him. It was only a year after his departure that Nusha contacted me, and anonymously at that. I told her that I had received her letter, but that I hadn't answered due to the conditions laid down in the note itself.

"How did you know that I was the one who had written you?"

"By intuition. And, of course, from the abbreviation of his name. I'm sorry that even now I don't have any information to give you."

Nusha looked at me with shining eyes and gently nudged me with her elbow: "Don't feel sorry, Mr. Kralev! We will arrive in a few minutes and then I will tell you something."

The bus stopped at the edge of the village by the church. We got off and headed straight toward the center of the village. As we walked past the church fence, Nusha stepped off the road and led me into the shade of a mulberry tree. There was a bench under the mulberry, we sat down and she told me that a month ago they had gotten word from Lexy. He was serving as a doctor in the Soviet Army. Doubt must have been written on my face, because she looked me in the eye and asked: "You don't believe it? If you don't believe it, that means you didn't know my brother. Someday perhaps I'll show you his letter, but not now. Not now!" And while she was saying this, she took an envelope addressed in German out of her purse and handed it to me. "Read it, read it, you know German, right, read it!"

The letter was written in German by some "Soldat" by the name of Asclepius, who declared his most fervent love to "Fräulein Pashoff" and recalled with great tenderness the days he had spent with her during his short stay in Bulgaria. The soldier promised to greet her very soon with news of a German victory, after which he would come to take her to Berlin. There they would get married, have two boys and two girls, and so on. It was Lexy's handwriting. I knew it as well as my own, I could also compare it to notes from the time when I had asked him about some phrases in German and he had "scrawled" them in my notebook. He spoke excellent German and Russian and sometimes liked to speak with me in both languages. There was no doubt he was the author of this letter, but for now Nusha didn't even want to imagine under what circumstances it had been written, and how from Switzerland he had ended up on the front in the Soviet Army. She was happy that her brother was alive and was glowing with excitement.

"Oh, Mr. Kralev!" She spoke in a trembling, ringing voice. "We have so many things to be happy about, don't we? My brother is alive, and I fin-ished high school, and you finished the university! Yes, we must celebrate! I won't let you leave for your village right away. First you must stop by our place, you'll rest for a bit and then be on your way. You've spent the whole night on the train, I can see the exhaustion written on your face, you look almost ill. Come on!"

I told her that I was indeed a bit tired and that I would rest, but here on the bench, and that I couldn't go to their place right now. I said goodbye, but promised that I would take advantage of her invitation in the next couple of days.

"I didn't expect you would take news of my brother so indifferently!" Nusha said. "It's because you don't know how much he loves you. What wonderful things he told me about you! But if I tell them to you, it'll make me cry, I'll just burst into tears."

A tear glittered in her eye and she turned away. We sat silently for a minute and I could feel how in that silence something intimate, sweet and yet vague was arising between us. I didn't know what to tell her, I was confused and flustered. After my nightmarish days of loneliness and despair, my heart was seeking closeness and warmth. I was ready to stay with her for a long time and visit her home, but one circumstance held me back, a bitter and terrible thing that I could not share with her. It had to do with her father, and it threatened not only his honor and his life, but his entire family. I could not set foot in their home under any circumstances.

"But you must know," Nusha continued, "that if my brother doesn't come home, if he dies on the front, one of the people he loved and respected the most was you. He often told me that, he told it to my parents, too, and they love and respect you as his good friend and comrade. Farewell! Forgive me!"

Nusha got up from the bench and set off. I watched her stepping into the lush, clean grass along the churchyard fence somehow timidly and gracefully, and suddenly a terrible loneliness gripped me, such as I had never felt before. I caught up with her on the road.

"Nusha, I'm not only tired and look sick, I really am sick. That's why I can't come to your house."

Later I tried to convince myself that I had told her about my illness as an excuse not to go to their place. But it wasn't true. I realized that I shouldn't give in to my cowardliness, yet still I told her that I had tuberculosis. I was looking for sympathy and tenderness from someone and my feelings told me I would find them in her.

"You must have been sitting in a draft on the train and gotten a cold," she said, and smiled. "You men, as soon as you sneeze or cough you immediately imagine the worst. I'll make you oregano tea and you'll be fine by this evening. I also caught a cold on the train on my way back from vacation, and that's how I got better."

My way to the village passed by their house. When we reached the gate, the side door opened and Nusha's mother came out. She greeted me and when she found out that I meant to continue on my way without stopping by, she started wailing and inviting me in in that thin, shrill voice that village women use when they are excited, so that the entire neighborhood already knew who had come to visit. A few minutes later I was sitting under the trellis, while Nusha and her mother were bustling around the kitchen. Nusha's father, Bay Petar Pashov, appeared from behind the outbuildings, dressed in faded denim overalls, bareheaded, with his sleeves rolled up to his elbows. As he passed by the trellis, he caught Nusha's voice coming from the kitchen, stopped, listened, and then went over to the house. Wild rosebushes were growing around the trellis, so he only saw me when he had reached the table.

"Well, it seems we have a guest!" he said, appearing pleasantly surprised. "Whatever made you think of us! You're more than welcome here!"

I went over and reached out my hand to shake his.

"Nusha and I arrived together. We met on the bus."

"Is that so? I just heard her voice, so I said to myself, wait, let's see if she's come home. We've been expecting her for a week now, as soon as the bus arrives, her mother's eyes are on the road. Sit down, sit down."

Nusha came out of the kitchen with a tray and came over to us. In such moments, outsiders are extraneous and I felt like a fifth wheel at their reunion. But her meeting with her father, just as with her mother, passed without unnecessary ceremoniousness, as such meetings do in the village, incidentally. Nusha set the tray on the table, went over to her father and kissed his hand, while he gently touched her shoulder.

"Well, young lady, congratulations on your high school diploma!"

"Thank you, Daddy!"

"Now are you going to take up the hoe, start teaching school, or will we throw a wedding party?"

"I don't know, Daddy, we'll see."

"Is that tea? The Russians haven't even come yet, and you're starting to greet our guests *à la ruski.*"

"Mr. Kralev caught a cold last night on the train and needs to drink tea. You ought to congratulate him as well, Dad! He graduated in law."

"Well, then we need something stronger than tea! A nice grape bran-dy'll fix him right up. Your mother knows which one to serve."

With this short, joking conversation, they exchanged their greetings and Nusha went into the kitchen where her mother was. Bay Petar con-gratulated me on finishing university and said he hoped I would become an important lawyer or judge. Then he asked me whether I knew they had gotten a letter from Lexy.

"Nusha let me read it just now."

"I told her to burn it, but she… You know how girls are!" He took a cigarette out of the pocket of his denim jacket, tapped it on his fingernail, and lit up. "I don't understand this business. He told me he was leaving for Switzerland when he'd already bought his train ticket. Why do you feel the need to traipse around abroad, I told him, it's wartime, anything could happen. Medicine here is nothing, he says, I'll go and finish up there, so I know I've learned a profession as it should be learned. It crossed my mind that maybe they were after him because of that business of yours, maybe he'd been betrayed or something of the sort, but I didn't dare ask him. He wouldn't have told me anyway. He surely told you about his intentions to go abroad. He told me himself that you were the best of friends."

When I told him that Lexy hadn't told me that he was going abroad, he was very surprised and clearly did not believe me.

"If he didn't tell you, who else would he trust about these things?"

"He was acting according to the strict laws of conspiracy."

"Whose conspiracy?"

"What do you mean, 'whose'?"

"Okay, fine, let's say that's how it was. Because of that same conspiracy you won't tell me the truth either. I get it. But what do you think? Was the letter written by him?"

"The handwriting is his."

"But what if he wrote it looking down the barrel of some gun?"

"What gun?"

He didn't manage to answer me, because the women came over to us and started setting the table for lunch. Nusha saw that my tea had been left untouched, so she tossed it into the garden and promised to brew me another one after lunch. Her father lifted his glass to her, but she interrupted him and said that first we needed to toast Lexy.

"Quiet!" her father scolded her. "Now even the stones in the fence have ears! Fine, we'll first raise a toast to him!"

He drained his glass in a single gulp, I took a sip, while the women merely raised their glasses. Nothing more was said about Lexy. His mother, it seemed, was the least informed about the whole business and about his fate and throughout the whole lunch she was looking at me, expecting me to say something about him. From the look on her face I could guess what strong and conflicting emotions were running through her. The father talked about the upcoming harvest and other agricultural matters, but he, too, did not manage to hide the fact that the only thing he cared about was his son's uncertain fate. Only Nusha looked unpremeditatedly happy. Her entire being emanated a lovely radiance, which transformed everything around her with the magic of her girlish beauty and purity, making it gentle, exquisite, and beautiful. I felt that radiance penetrating into my heart and illuminating it with cheerfulness and calm, and felt my despair at my illness, my doubts and fears, giving way to those bright feelings that we are accustomed to calling the hope for happiness.

We were finishing lunch when someone knocked on the gate. It turned out to be someone from my village, he had come looking for something from Bay Petar Pashov. The two of them spoke in the yard, then the man left. I realized that he'd come by cart, so I grabbed my suitcase and said goodbye to my hosts. The three of them saw me out to the street and stayed there until the cart turned past the last house. My visit to them had been accidental. If Nusha and I hadn't met on the bus, perhaps I would never have met her or her parents again due to the tumultuous events that ensued. Now I had a premonition that precisely these events would bring us together again, and that premonition was vague and alarming.

After an hour or so I was home. I found Stoyan and Kichka in the tailor shop, he was cutting cloth on the counter, while she was sewing on the machine. As always, the villagers had their summer pants sewn right before harvesttime and the counter was stacked with rolls of blue denim. None of our reunions after my returns to the village had ever been this emotional. As soon as they saw me on the doorstep, Stoyan and Kichka left off with their work, rushed to hug me, and instead of saying "welcome," they shouted like children: "We won, we won, we won!"

While I had been in Sofia, we had constantly been writing letters back and forth, but of course exchanging news or making political commentaries was out of the question. Only now, undisturbed by anyone, could we share our joy over the events on the Eastern Front. The large map of the Soviet Union, which Stoyan had earlier hid in a corner of the barn, now hung in a visible place in the tailor shop for the whole village to see. With great anguish we had stuck the little red and blue flags ever farther into Soviet territory, from village to village, from town to town, to Moscow, Leningrad, Stalingrad, and the Caucasus. Now the flags were moving in the opposite direction, the red was pursuing the blue, in many places they had them completely surrounded, condemning them to certain death; flags "triumphantly waved" above Vyborg and the territory of the Belarusian Republic. A second front had been opened by Allied troops in Normandy, fascist Germany's death throes had begun, Ivan Bagryanov had been appointed prime minister of the Bulgarian government. The Bulgarian partisan movement had become a political and military force to be reckoned with. Stoyan and I worked until the evening, commenting on the military events on the fronts to the east and west; of course, we also talked about my future work, while Kichka went to get their daughter from Kichka's mother. During these days of intense work she couldn't take care of both the child and the household, she had to help Stoyan in the tailor shop, now I took her place as well. Back in my school days, Stoyan had taught me how to sew summer pants, so during vacation times I helped him.

After dinner I asked to sleep outdoors under the awning of the barn, but Stoyan and Kichka refused. Strange characters wandered the village at night, they said, keeping the house under surveillance, and they might suspect that I was sleeping outside to keep in contact with illegal fighters. I didn't dare tell them I was sick, so as not to spoil their mood on the very first day, and spent a long time convincing them that after exhausting myself studying for exams in a small, stuffy apartment, I needed to sleep out in the open so as to refresh myself and rest up. Stoyan and I carried the wooden bed under the awning of the barn, and Kichka made it up. Early in the morning she heard me coughing and as soon as I came inside the house, she began scolding me for not listening to them. I could no longer hide my illness, particularly since it was dangerous for them and especially for the child. The two of them were stunned but tried to comfort me.

"You're fine," Kichka said, but I noticed how she unwittingly pulled away from me and glanced toward the girl, who was still sleeping. "So that's why you didn't hug Lenka, but only watched her from a distance…"

During vacations, Lenka was constantly in my arms. Even when she was a baby, I had felt some atavistic pleasure in cuddling and coddling her, breathing in the scent of her delicate flesh, watching in her and through her how a person gradually changed from "a hunk of meat" with animal instincts to a conscious being who was aware of the world. Now she was four years old, the age at which a child is innocently tempted by curiosity about everything around it, sweet, illogical, and amusing in its endless questions and answers, when it draws a person as a cross with two support beams below instead of legs and a dot instead of a head, and when the child is exactly such a little stick figure itself. The thought that from now I would no longer be able to hold the girl in my arms, to stroll around the yard and fields with her, to visually transform myself into everything she wanted to see, to joke around with her, to make her laugh and to comfort her, it was this and not the thought of my illness that pierced me with the sinister insight that the remainder of my life would be spent in exile from the lives of others.

"If you really are sick, you need to go get treatment starting tomorrow!" Stoyan said. "You know where and how, and as for the rest, don't worry about it. We'll gladly pay whatever it costs, but we'll cure you."

Stoyan was shaken to the very bottom of his soul, but he talked about my illness as if it was something passing and did all he could to seem calm, which is precisely what the loved ones of the terminally ill do. Several people in the village had died of consumption. Their faces took on a deceptive freshness from the hearty food and rest, but over time they grew as yellow as overripe cantaloupe, and right before death itself – as snow-white and translucent as death masks. In the winter they slept with the windows open, while in the summer they strolled through the gardens and fields, or sat somewhere in the shade, lonely and doomed to waiting for death. Kichka furtively peered at my face when she passed by me, in her thoughts she saw me as one of those living dead and could not hide it.

"Good God, why just now?" she said once, while we were discussing where and when I would take treatment.

Why just now! This was the most fitting exclamation that could come from the lips of a young and happy wife and mother. Did I have to come down with tuberculosis and die just now, when I had graduated from the university with such effort and privation, when our aspirations, nursed for years amidst destitution and dangers, doubts and worries, were now almost a reality, when the doors of the future were opening before us unto a new life, full of joy and happiness? The doctors in Sofia had recommended mountain air, hearty food, and peace and quiet as the only chance for a cure, and I needed to leave for a sanatorium for lung diseases. I was torn and put off that departure for a whole week. "Just now" the great events were unfolding, I wanted to meet them and experience them with my family, and not in a sanatorium for the living dead. I had dedicated my whole conscious life up until that point to these events, as immodest as that declaration might sound to some. Yet I could no longer stay in the village. I couldn't sleep under the awning of the barn any longer, eating separately and keeping the whole family in fear of infection. We decided that I would go to Varna on Saturday to see a famous doctor, and from there I would go to the sanatorium he recommended. Kichka got everything ready for my trip, while Stoyan found a man who would drive me to the bus in Zhitnitsa.

We decided that at noon on Friday, but late in the afternoon Nusha came to our place. Stoyan and Kichka were working, I was sitting by the door, reading a book aloud. Nusha's appearance surprised and disconcerted me so greatly that I froze for several seconds. Then I got up, shook her hand, and led her into the tailor's shop. Stoyan and Kichka seemed to take her as some vision, they looked at her without returning her greeting and without budging from their places, so unearthly and delicate did she seem in that stuffy, messy, wretched room. My heart started beating fast and painfully, I felt pathetic in my overexcitement, yet I could not get ahold of myself and acted completely flustered. First I offered Nusha a chair to sit in, then I introduced her, then I invited her to go outside into the fresh air. In short, I was not in my right mind. When we went out onto the street, Nusha told me that she had gone to the town hall to take care of some business for her father, and after that she had wanted to see whether I had gotten over my cold from the train. The cart she had arrived in was pacing in front of the town hall and the cart driver was waiting for her. Nusha told him to go on ahead, and we started out on foot. We soon reached the edge of the fields and set off across them.

Now here's the strange thing: I don't remember what Nusha and I talked about over the course of an hour as we walked through the fields. No matter how I rack my memory, this hour of my life remains a blank. I don't even recall the expression on her face, nor what she was wearing, nor whether we made plans to meet again. I seem to have fallen into an incorporeal, oblivious state, somewhere beyond myself and the world. As far as the length of time I spent with her, I found that out from my brother and sister-in-law.

"Well, you certainly hurried to get away from the girl! It's hardly been an hour since you left. Who was she?"

At that moment it was as if I had awakened from a dream, I remember how the two of them set aside their work and were all ears. It was more than obvious that until now they had been talking about the girl and not only had they liked her, they were even proud on my behalf. What's more, they were so enchanted by her beauty that they hadn't heard or remembered her last name. Never before had they showed any curiosity about my personal life. My brother lived and breathed the events of the war and often said that now wasn't the time for personal life and that we needed to devote everything we could to the struggle. But now the struggle was nearing its end and how nice it would be for the victory and my personal happiness to arrive at our home hand in hand. I could more or less guess such thoughts from their faces and I had no doubt they were sincere. At another moment perhaps I would have considered the circumstances and tried to prepare them better, but now I was not capable of that, I told them who the girl was. In just an instant my brother's face changed color and expression several times in ascending degrees of intensity, if I can put it like that. It went dark, then pale, and finally beet red. Judging from these changes, he had quickly felt disappointment, alarm, and finally rage, one after the other.

"Petar Pashov's daughter! Are you crazy? How... how... how!" He started choking. "How dare she set foot in our house? Did you invite her, or... No, she wouldn't decide to come here on her own."

"She came on her own," I said. "I didn't invite her."

"That can't be! She didn't come here on her own, just like that, only to say how-do-you-do. Someone sent her or called her here. You were struck dumb as soon as you saw her, that means she must've had a reason for coming. But then again, maybe she did come of her own accord." Now his face radiated a spiteful irony. "Those types come running after men on their own, especially now. She'll slip not only into your house, but right into your bed uninvited."

I must have looked so immune and deaf to his rebukes that Kichka, too, was offended on his account.

"He can't see or hear a thing," she said. "He's head over heels in love like a schoolboy, that beauty has scrambled his brain."

"That's why I'm talking to him, to get his brains back in his head before it's too late." Stoyan signaled to Kichka to leave, and when we were alone, he put his hand on my shoulder. "Tell me as your brother and as a man, how far have you gotten with that girl? You need to realize in time that this question doesn't concern just you personally, but all of us, so we've got to decide it together. I can see you can trip up, that you've tripped up already, by letting Pashov's daughter come here to our place. What are your relations with her?"

"Ethereal."

"What do you mean, 'ethereal'? Are you mocking me? How long have you been seeing her?"

"Since an hour ago."

I told him the whole truth. My meeting with Nusha on the bus had been a chance crossing of paths. Our true meeting had happened an hour earlier. For several days I had been yearning for her, I was sure that she had been yearning for me, the two of us had been striving toward each other and now we had met. Stoyan knew I was telling him the truth, and precisely because he knew this, he grew even more alarmed. He was not lacking in insight – since I had known the girl only so recently, yet was so head over heels, it meant that this was no laughing matter, what we were dealing with was blind passion, which would not end without consequences if it was not nipped in the bud. But Stoyan loved me and was afraid that if he "cut short" my passion for the girl with one slice of the knife, he would be committing an assault of sorts not only on my very heart, but also on our brotherly love, and perhaps upon our whole life up until that point. He had likely also taken into account that my impending departure would play the role of the knife between Nusha and me, so after his fiery and unrestrained rebukes, he quieted down and even tried to justify my passion.

"We've all been blinded by women. You just need to get healthy, the rest will work itself out."

Two customers came into the tailor shop, Stoyan lit the lamp and started chatting with them, while I went outside, passed through the garden, and from there headed toward the fields. I wanted to get some fresh air and to think about how to resolve the question of my relations with Nusha. I was brimming with the feeling that my life had been transformed down to its foundations, I was illuminated by the happy insight that she had come to me, led by a pure outpouring of love, and that she would never leave. And now I would have to drive her away from me, once and for all, at that. That's what it had come to, my happiness depended on or would depend on outside circumstances. Nusha's father had been accused of betraying our comrades. We had discussed this treachery many times with the few communists in the village, a person had even come from the regional committee to lay out the case to us. Like the author of a detective novel, he presented us with a mystery, which we would have to solve ourselves. There had been a crime, but who was the criminal? Unlike the author of a detective novel, however, the messenger from the regional committee did not know who had done it, as became clear. What he knew was what we also knew. In early February of 1943, the canvas cover of Petar Pashov's threshing machine had been stolen. My brother had been asked to find, if possible, enough canvas cloth to make a dozen windbreakers. Such cloth in such a quantity could not be found even on the market. The only way we could get ahold of it was to steal the canvas cover of the Barakovs' threshing machine. Stoyu Barakov was the wealthiest man in the village, he had a hundred acres of land, he also had a threshing machine. One of his three sons, the youngest, was a member of our youth communist league, and we assigned him the task of expropriating his father. It turned out that their threshing machine didn't have a cover, and Miho, that was the boy's name, pointed us toward Petar Pashov from the neighboring village of Zhitnitsa. Pashov and Barakov were in-laws, they had married the daughters of two sisters, but due to old grudges they didn't keep up family ties. Their children didn't even have anything to do with one another, only Miho hadn't given in to old prejudices and would go to the Pashovs to see his cousin Nusha. He was courting one of her schoolmates, he had visited her at her apartment in town, and whenever he would come and go to the city by bus, he would always stop by their place. In any case, Miho knew the Pashovs' house best and offered to steal the cover of their threshing machine himself if we gave him two helpers. We sent them by horse cart around midnight and by dawn the canvas cover was already at our place. As luck would have it, it started snowing just then, so the tracks on the road were covered up. But Miho Barakov got us good and worried. Once the two helpers had left, he stayed to give a report on the mission and warned us that we were in danger of the police coming to search for us very soon, since Petar Pashov had seen and recognized them. Or more precisely, he had seen and recognized Miho. While the other two were lugging the canvas toward the street, he had been standing by the side of the house watching, Petar Pashov had appeared right in front of him like a ghost, he needed only to reach out his hand and he could have grabbed him. He had tossed on a fur coat and was bareheaded, he said only "Aha!" and left. It crossed Miho's mind to tell him about the whole business, but the other man instantly disappeared back toward the house. From there several dogs were let loose, they descended on him from all sides, they set all the other dogs in the neighborhood barking too. Miho didn't tell the other two about his run-in with Petar Pashov so they wouldn't panic, but mainly so they wouldn't go to the police if the whole business some-how came to an investigation. If Petar Pashov reports to the authorities, Miho said, I'll deny that he saw me in his yard, and he can't prove it. Everyone knows that his son is a communist, and the suspicion will fall on him. Communists can't swipe something from the family of a commu-nist without him knowing about it. Petar Pashov will have to think good and hard about which is more precious to him: a canvas cover or his son. Besides, we ought to go easy on him. He's a wealthy man and we might need him again…

We were familiar with Miho Barakov's cold-bloodedness, which he had displayed more than once in similar situations, and now we were convinced that he wasn't lacking in quick wits, either. But nevertheless we were on guard around the clock. We cut the canvas into pieces and hid them in various places around the yard and garden, while at night we took up our posts. Stoyan worked until midnight in the tailor shop, where every night men would stop by to chat, after midnight I sat there and read until morning. The police could come looking for us at any time, but we imagined that they would surprise us at night, so we tied the dog to the gate to warn us in time if outsiders came into the yard. Petar Pashov's exclamation turned into a psychological puzzle for us. What did he mean to say with that "aha"? An expression of fright or astonishment that he had seen a stranger in his yard in the middle of the night, or had he wanted to wash his hands of the whole business, figuring that it was being done with the knowledge of his son: "Let's just pretend I didn't see you!" But no matter how we interpreted it, one thing was clear – we had made a mistake, one that could turn out to be fatal. Rather than trembling in uncertainty, we needed to inform him right away to what end we had taken the canvas and thus to head off any eventual desire on his part to report the theft to the authorities. Precisely because everyone knew that his son was a communist, he could report the theft of the canvas to the police to protect his son from any suspicion, no father would turn in his own son for theft, and theft for political ends, at that. However, we didn't think to warn him in time and thus left everything to his own conscience.

A week passed, and no one came looking for us, so we began taking the canvas out of its hiding places piece by piece. Over ten nights, Stoyan sewed ten windbreakers. It was a slow and difficult job, since the canvas was as hard as plywood, Stoyan didn't have the right needles and thread, so he had to look for them among his colleagues in the city. I was forced to extend my vacation as well, so I could keep watch around the house and help him. We waited for all outsiders to leave, covered up the window, and opened up the inside door that connected the tailor shop to the barn. We gathered up all the scraps in a bag so that we could, if need be, quickly carry them out through the barn and into the room, and from there – outside. Stoyan had filled these kinds of orders before and had experience in such matters. A few days before I left for Sofia, a man came to the house and carried off the windbreakers.

Two months after that incident, Miho Barakov and six other young men were arrested and convicted via the "fast-track" procedure, Miho got ten years in prison, and the others from three to four years. The police didn't come after my brother or the other two boys who had helped in the operation, nor did they call Petar Pashov as a witness in the case. During the initial investigation, just as at the trial, Miho Barakov tried to take the entire responsibility, declaring that he had stolen the canvas cover by himself and sold it to some stranger for five hundred leva. He needed that money to sew himself a suit, to buy shoes, a shirt, and other things a graduating high school senior, who in a few short months would be a full-fledged citizen, would need. His father categorically refused to give that much money to such a "good-for-nothing" who only jabbered on about communism and was digging his own family's grave. He had long been in conflict with his father and brothers due to his ideological convictions, but that was his personal business, nobody could tell him what ideas to believe. Even the law couldn't force beliefs on him, since according to the Bulgarian Constitution citizens are guaranteed freedom of conscience. The law could only punish those who organized armed resistance or threatened national security with other means of violence. He sympathized with the idea of communism as it was just and humane, but did not belong to any political organizations and had never tried to force his ideas on others in any way whatsoever. They showed him a canvas windbreaker found in a forest after a skirmish between the police and the partisans. On the inside of the windbreaker the name of Petar Pashov was written in large, printed letters. Miho answered that he found it only natural that the name of the owner would be printed on the canvas and did not take responsibility for the fact that the canvas had reached the partisans in the form of some windbreakers. At the market, everyone sells his wares to strangers and never knows where they might end up after they are in the buyer's hands. The examining magistrate agreed that this was exactly how the question of buying and selling stood, yet the question of the canvas stood slightly differently, and then he told him that Petar Pashov had personally told him the name of the thief. Otherwise how could the investigation have led precisely to him, if the thief's name and the place and date of the theft were unknown?

In the fall Miho told a comrade who had come to visit him at the prison about Petar Pashov's treachery and asked him to tell my brother and all the communists from our region to steer clear of him. He also made the conjecture that Petar Pashov had not been called as a witness to the case because the police knew that his son had gone abroad and it wasn't fitting to compromise both the son and the father. Under interrogation, however, Miho Barakov indignantly rejected the magistrate's claim as slander against Petar Pashov. Pashov was his relative, he had visited him many times, and for nothing in the world would he have given him over to the authorities, even if he had caught him red-handed with the canvas. At worst, he would have stopped him on the spot or complained to his father later, otherwise why would he have kept silent while watching a relative of his carry things out of his yard? In the same way, he rejected the accusation that he was a member of the communist youth organization. When searching his apartment, the police had found some scrap of paper with a list of names across from which were written various numbers. The names and numbers were not written in his handwriting and he protested that they were trying to frame him with some planted notes. The next day he was confronted face-to-face with the individuals whose names were on the list. There were twelve young men, three of whom were his schoolmates and the rest were manual laborers and clerks. Miho, of course, could not deny that he knew his schoolmates, but he denied having any illegal ties with them, while he claimed not to have ever seen the other nine young men. After a few days one of his schoolmates couldn't hold out under the beatings and confessed that he had given Miho a dozen leva a month without a receipt. He made regular payments, but he didn't know what the money being collected was for, while Miho never gave him any explanations. From then on it wasn't hard for the police to catch most of the communist youth league activists and throw them in prison.

This was the mystery we agonized over for months – who had put that list with the names of the twelve young men in Miho Barakov's apartment? Our suspicions fell, of course, on Petar Pashov. We were led to believe this both by Miho Barakov at his own trial, as well as by Lexy's sudden departure abroad. In the beginning, both my brother and I had certain doubts that Petar Pashov, like any villager, so far from the city and any political struggles, would know the names of those twelve young men whom he had never seen and would go to turn them in to the police. It also seemed unbelievable to us that Lexy, whom we knew as a noble person, even if a provocateur, would hand over such a thing to his father. However, we also didn't have any facts in Pashov's favor. Suspicion of him spread among the communists in the nearby villages and grew over time. When I returned from Sofia after graduating from the university, I realized that Stoyan also fully believed in his treachery and nothing could convince him otherwise. That evening after Nusha's visit, I walked around the fields until late, thinking that my happiness depended on solving the mystery of this betrayal. After finishing his work, Stoyan came over to me under the awning of the barn and wished me good night. I was riled up and told him about Lexy's letter, which had awakened such hope in me. But instead of intriguing him, this news had the opposite effect on him. The night was very light and I saw a smile appear on his face, and it was the smile of a person filled with malice, hatred, and vengefulness.

"Aha, the rats realize that their ship is sinking. On the one hand, they bet their daughter, on the other, they try to make their son out as a heroic antifascist. Except that it's a little late. No letters can help them now."

He went into the house, while his final words stayed with me, radiating coldness and hostility: "Go to sleep, tomorrow you've got to clear out." This staggered me, because for the first time in our life together he had not shown sympathy, but almost scorn, for me, and this when I found myself in such a difficult and hopeless situation. I was already a grown man, but I harbored a filial feeling toward him, left over from childhood, I had gotten used to considering him as my father and mother. When our father died, he had been sixteen and had become the head of the family. He had finished middle school and very much wanted to go to high school, but my father's death prevented this. But even if he hadn't died, our father would hardly have sent him to the city, since he had only three acres of land, two oxen, and a cow, which in our region of large landholders and estates was true destitution. Besides, at that time the villagers never took their eyes off the land and lived in a closed circle, filled with some wild antagonism toward the city and learned people. Back then, the only village youngster to break that taboo was Ivan Shibilev.

Stoyan didn't like agricultural work and even back then had started hatching plans to take up a different trade. He felt he had a calling for some other kind of work, but he himself couldn't decide what, and this tormented him. In the meantime Ivan Shibilev had "gotten his fill of studying" as the villagers would say, and had returned to the village. He was dressed ultramodern for that time – with a double-breasted striped suit coat and wide-legged pants, while on his head he wore a wide-brimmed black hat. He lived free as a bird, constantly in motion between the village and the city, restless and cheerful, always brimming with ideas and notions, you could say that every social and cultural undertaking was thought up by him. Like any theoretician, however, he left it to others to put his ideas into practice, business dealings were not particularly pleasant for him, which is why, before championing some idea, he always made sure to secure loyal like-minded partners. One of those was my brother, Stoyan. Ivan Shibilev had discovered that he had a lively intellect, and when he decided to found the community center, he assigned the management of the construction to him. Stoyan gathered together a group of young men and as soon as early spring they were making mud bricks at the village swamp. During summer the bricks dried and in the fall, when all the fieldwork was done, the building of the community center began. Building a freestanding structure was out of the question, since there was neither a foundation nor materials for it, so they built it onto the back of the old four-room schoolhouse. The young people dragged away what they could from their homes: beams, roof tiles, old door frames, doors, and by the first snow the building had a roof. From the outside it looked like a shed or a barn, but inside instead of tools or livestock there was a theatrical stage raised half a meter off the ground. The stage needed cloth for a curtain, the windows needed pinewood window frames, and the floor needed bricks, but there was no money and nobody who would donate. No one wanted to bankroll such an unprofitable and above all questionable enterprise. The local authorities even fined Ivan Shibilev and my brother for illegal construction on the condition that if the fine wasn't paid within a year, the brick building would be torn down.

Ivan Shibilev responded to this economic oppression very craftily. He gathered up a small sum from the young people and rather than paying off the fine with it at the town hall, he bought a secondhand gramophone. That musical contraption played the same role in the spiritual development of our young people at that time as the role disco music now plays for contemporary teenagers. The community center didn't have any windows yet, but the young men gathered there every night and listened to the gramophone. The musical repertoire was modest, two tangos and two foxtrots, all told, but they were enough to open up for those young people the path to new music and new dances, and hence to a new life as well. Ivan Shibilev, with his proverbial patience, taught the young men their first steps in the tango and foxtrot, just as nineteenth-century Bulgarian Revival-Era activists had taught the youth military drills, while they repaid him for his efforts with Revival-Era-worthy zeal. Holding hands in pairs, they dragged their rough leather sandals across the dirt floor, bowed and said "*merci*" after every dance, drenched with sweat and choking on clouds of dust. Just as in every new undertaking, the young men now, too, divided themselves into progressive and conservative factions, and now the progressives, albeit smaller in number, yet dedicated and bold, looked bravely ahead toward the bright future and overcame all manner of difficulties in the name of that future, while the conservative elements sniveled around outside by the windows and smiled skeptically. After a month or two, however, they, too, gave in to the new spirit of the times and one by one stepped inside the mud-brick salon and took on the roles of ladies and gentlemen. While the true ladies were left alone at their working bees, bored without their suitors and waiting in vain for the dogs in the yard to start barking. The new dances and tunes enjoyed unexpected popularity. The girls weren't allowed to go into the community center on their own, but it was enough for a few of them to peer through the window and hear some melody, and the working bees themselves became dance parties. The girls no longer knitted or spun, but rather danced the tango and the foxtrot until midnight, bounding in their socks upon the corn mats and rag rugs. In the end, the parents could not withstand the girls' spontaneous rush to break down the wall between the sexes and were forced to apply a moral principle tried and true throughout the ages, namely to give their daughters over to vice and in this way to overcome it. The mothers, of course, did not realize this consciously and imagined that when they were leading their daughters into the bosom of vice, they would protect them from it through strict supervision. They would sit on low three-legged stools and watch like hawks to make sure the girls and young men did not take any liberties while dragging their feet on the floor and kicking up a dust cloud. The dances were strictly regulated. The girls could only visit the community center accompanied by their mothers, they must keep at least an elbow's distance from their gentlemen, they could grasp only the fingers of their hands, and they weren't even allowed to look each other in the eye. Many more dance rules were introduced, all with the goal of preventing any sexual displays on the part of the young people, yet never-theless the first symptoms of the sexual revolution were apparent, even if for now they were expressed only in the squeezing of hands to the point of rawness and the mutually blazing fire in their eyes.

The village authorities soon capitulated before this universal cult of the community center and not only did they waive the fine for illegal con-struction, they even released funds to finish the building. Plasterers and woodworkers were found, as were wooden boards for the stage, bricks for the floor, and chairs for the auditorium. The next year, the town hall also gave the community center two and half acres of fields from the village land fund, which the young people worked voluntarily. The profits from these fields went to outfitting the community center. Cloth was bought for the stage curtain, as well as a kerosene lamp, a stove, and most impor-tantly, a brand-new gramophone with many records – in short, the whole community center was completely modernized and reconstructed, and this created auspicious conditions for the perfecting of the old dances and the learning of new ones. The new dances, however, also required mod-ernized clothing. For example, you couldn't dance a waltz in breeches, puttees, with a fur hat on your head, and after the dance bow to your lady and tell her *"merci."* The new clothing imposed itself like a command that could not be abolished and was the cause for the rise of the new fashion.

First out of all the young men in the village, again following Ivan Shibilev's example, my brother, Stoyan, ditched the traditional full-bottomed breeches and padded jacket and donned a suit coat and pants, topped off with a cloth cap on his head. He and Ivan Shibilev took a roll of homespun cloth dyed with walnut leaves from our place and took it to a tailor who knew how to sew city clothes. Mother sold a basket of eggs and a few other things, gave the money to my brother, and he brought home his new suit. On Easter Sunday itself, when the whole village gathered on the square to dance the traditional folk dances, Ivan Shibilev and a few other young men came to our place, went into the room, and my brother put on his new suit in solemn silence. Ivan Shibilev looked him over from all sides and gave a short but prophetic speech: "This is not a homespun suit, boys!" he said, putting his hand on my brother's shoulder. "This is the armor of progress, which will withstand the bullets of spiritual poverty, baseness, and idiocy. The old-fashioned breeches, leggings, clogs, fur caps, and all those signs of stinking retrogradism will hurl themselves at us, foaming at the mouth, but we will withstand their abuse and curses and very soon our struggle for progress and happiness for young people will be crowned with success. Be bold, comrades!"

The young men didn't understand any of this melodramatic speech, but listened with the solemn stiffness of those being initiated into some sacred conspiracy. All of them were dressed in the attributes of stinking retrogradism, they felt a century behind my brother and all signs indicated that they would be following his example in the very near future. After this solemn act of getting dressed, which was in fact a baptism into the new fashion, they led my brother out to the dance. I was an eleven-year-old boy then, but I could already appreciate the significance of this crucial moment in the history of the village, and I joined my brother's cortege. The young men were walking close on either side of him, as if guarding him from an act of aggression. And so they reached the dance.

Easter was celebrated with particular splendor for three whole days, and to use contemporary terminology, we could say that this holiday was a fashion show of spring-summer collections. The young people, as was to be expected after the long Lenten fast, looked forward to the holiday with particular impatience. Until Easter no weddings or any kind of entertainment were allowed, so in the long winter nights girls had nothing to keep them busy besides their wardrobes. They wove cloth, embroidered blouses, knitted socks and vests, sewed new clothing for the men, and all that had to be put on display over the course of three days. On the first day, the young people went out in their most humble, almost everyday clothing, only some eye-catching head scarf, belt, or ribbon might hint at the next day's apparel. On the second day, new elements of that attire appeared, while on the third day, they brought out everything that had been sewn, embroidered, and dyed with imagination, aesthetic taste, and improvisation.

Early in the afternoon the young brides, unmarried girls, and bachelors came out of their homes, walking as if on eggshells, clean-shaven, pomaded, made up, their petticoats gleaming like glass, from beneath which delicate lace hung down to the ground, in brightly colored aprons with fluffy fringe, head scarves and shawls over braids that hung down to their knees, in bright tunics and striped sleeves, necklaces of beads and gold coins, new breeches with woolen braiding, red sashes, and flat-bottomed fur hats, white puttees with crisscrossed laces of black goat hair, violet padded jackets and vests. A little later the mothers and fathers came out, as well as mothers- and fathers-in-law, and they, too, walked – especially the wealthier among them – with an irresistible dignity, forming a circle around the dance ostensibly to chat about their own business, but really in order to more precisely observe, compare, and judge the young people on their dancing, their attire, and their behavior.

Tradition, as is always the case with those who are doomed, did not suspect that the homespun suit, which was standing there so solitary and anxious before her eyes, was a Trojan horse, from whose womb very soon would leap forth the fanaticized adherents of the new fashion who would attack her fortress from within. For now Tradition was invulnerable behind the thick walls of her ignorance, and was not even offended by the bold challenge of the homespun suit, she was satisfied to confer upon it a mocking smile and sarcastic slurs. The young people went past it and even though they did not admire it, they also did not make fun of it, but in the curiosity with which they inspected it a more watchful eye could discover the seed of a forthcoming defection from the old fashion. Only the young Gagauz men showed a rough lack of restraint, they looked at Stoyan's homespun suit point-blank as if he were a scarecrow, tried to tear off the buttons, giggled and talked amongst themselves in Turkish. They were a group of around twenty young men from a neighboring village, a bastion of old-fashioned prejudices and ignorance, which our folks derisively called Gagauzland. During the holidays, they had a tradition of touring around the neighboring villages like a troupe of folk dancers, who in passing just might kidnap one of the local girls. They arrived in carts or on horseback, stayed with acquaintances or in the fields, and went to the dance. They brought two of their own flute players with huge, loud flutes that sounded like the horns of Jericho. They were all handsome, husky young men with pointy Astrakhan hats, purple jackets, and black breeches decorated with woolen braid, above his right ear each of them had stuck a bouquet or a drake's tail feather bent like a comma. Unlike our men, they were shod in knee-high boots, from the top of which spilled triangular bits of lace knitted from brightly colored thread, beneath each of their sashes the handle of a pistol peeked out, while out of every boot glinted a knife hilt made of white bone. They talked to the local villagers in broken Bulgarian and our folks made fun of them using their own phrases: "nice horse go fast," "field very big," "I want eat," and so on. The phrase "up cut, down split" had attained particular popularity, spoken by a Gagauz who had wanted to praise his watermelons, which were so crisp and juicy that you only had to press your knife to the top and they would split down to the bottom on their own.

The Gagauz were famous for their bravado, for their beautiful horses, and especially for their ability to perform the *tropanka*, or stomping dance. With their undeniable artistry for performing this dance, they managed to overcome the barrier of centuries-old intervillage antagonism and win the admiration of the surrounding villages. In every square in the villages nearby, there was always one circle known as the "Gagauz's threshing floor," there was one in our village square too, where the dances were held. In that circle they performed their famous *tropanka* two or three times a year, and performed it such that no grass ever grew there. Their flute players stood shoulder to shoulder in the center of the circle, while the dancers, tightly holding each other's belts, began slowly and lightly, then they lowered their heads forward like rams, gathered tightly in next to one another, narrowed the circle taking squatting steps forward until their hats pressed in on the flute players, and began to stomp their boots on the ground so furiously that the whole square shook, while the people watched them enraptured, captivated by their primitive strength and passion. After they had performed their hit number, the guests would leave with shouts and gunshots, and the dust from their carts would still be hanging over the road when it was found that they had managed to make off with one of the local girls. It was precisely these hulking young men who displayed the sharpest dislike toward my brother's urban garb and threatened that if he didn't take it off, during their next visit they would strip him naked in the middle of the dance, and would tie the scraps of his suit on a stake in the melon fields. And so my brother, Stoyan, lit the first spark from which the war between the Old and New Fashions blazed up.

The Old Fashion barricaded itself behind the walls of Tradition's centuries-old bastion and from there pointed its cannons at the enemy; its barrels spewed a fire of curses, threats, and Old Testament dogma. The champions of the New Fashion walked on ahead empty-handed, their only weapon was their fanatical belief in victory. Each time they stormed Tradition's walls, their cry was not the usual "hurrah," but rather "down with conformity," they were ready to block the barrels of their enemies' cannons with their own bodies. None of them knew what the slogan "down with conformity" meant – it had been casually tossed out by Ivan Shibilev – but this slogan inspired them precisely because it was unfamiliar and new. The Old Fashion was waging a positional, defensive war, and no one has ever won that kind of war, especially if it is being waged in the name of a cause that has outlived its time. After a mere few months of siege, Tradition waved the white flag and capitulated once and for all.

This war had not only its moral and material cost, but also took human victims. Three fathers died of heart attacks, several young people were left crippled after intrafamilial civil wars, while one girl, in a sign of protest against her parents who would not let her cut her hair, left home, hired herself out as a servant in the city, and from there fell into disrepute. As was to be expected, the conquerors began mercilessly taking out retribution on the conquered, all of her external attributes were tossed out from the ravaged bastion of Tradition and replaced with heretofore unseen high-heeled shoes, gauzy stockings, flannelette, voile scarves, silk for the young ladies, and shoes made of buckskin or *juft*, cloth caps, bowler hats, English herringbone cloth, stripes and cheviot, double-breasted coats, and for young men, pants with legs as wide as a priest's sleeves. The women cut off their braids to bob their hair, and threw such a quantity of hair on the trash heap that Buchenwald's future executioners could have kept a whole industry going on it. Looms, heddles, carding combs, and spindles were one by one tossed into attics due to competition from factory-made fabrics. And if anyone had tried after just half a year to bring back the old fashions, everyone would have laughed at him.

Leading the charge in these reforms was my brother, Stoyan. Indeed, the idea for the reform had come from Ivan Shibilev, but, as we already mentioned, urged on by some inner restlessness, he was constantly shuttling from the village to nearby cities and didn't succeed in – and perhaps was incapable of – putting into practice a single one of his ideas. While he was roaming who knows where and why, Stoyan had taken charge of all the civic and educational activity in the village. Like Kemal Atatürk, whom he loved to quote, he believed that if people changed their outward appearance, they would change their lives as well, but since he didn't have the power like Atatürk to issue a decree banning fezzes and *shalwars*, he decided to carry out this reform in the most democratic way – from the ground up, and, of course, above all to set a personal example. After being the first young man to don a modern suit, he also became the first tailor in the village to sew modern men's clothing. In our times, as I'm making these notes, fashion has a lot of theoreticians. According to their ideological and aesthetic viewpoints, all of them "treat" fashion in different ways, but wherever they might search for its ideological roots, in society's socioeconomic relations or in the morals of the individual, no matter how they explain the phenomenon, no one denies that it is above all a mania for newness, and a fear of being démodé. People believe that clothing makes them more beautiful or even better people, even though in ancient times they had already invented the saying, "You may greet a man according to the clothes he wears, but you bid him goodbye according to the manners he has shown." This belief has changed into vanity, and vanity is easy to manipulate, it succumbs to mass culture and mass taste. It is precisely this tendency toward imitation – which is perhaps a kind of curiosity, a curiosity which brought irrevocable misfortune to our biblical forefathers – that has allowed even madmen or eccentrics to make some item of clothing fashionable. Such cases exist in the history of fashion. For a young man with an eighth-grade education and a sharp mind like my brother, it was not hard to understand this peculiarity of the mass psyche and to use it as a weapon in the war against the social system in place at that time.

As I look back at them now, Stoyan's efforts to transform society and his belief that he could do so through a change in clothing make me smile at his youthful naïveté. But that night, as I was lying under the awning of the barn, surprised and disconcerted by his harsh and merciless attitude toward me, I found a certain hope in just such memories, I wanted to see him as he had been at that time, gentle, compassionate, and selflessly devoted to the common good. I fondly recalled how we had lived with love and concern for each other. Being orphaned and destitute had drawn us so close and made us such equals that I didn't call him *bati*, or "older brother," as was expected, but rather by his name, even though he was six years older. He had finished middle school with straight As in three different villages, because at that time middle school, which sometimes included every grade, sometimes not, was only offered in certain villages depending on the number of students. Every autumn Stoyan would find out which villages had which middle school grades and would go there on the mare, only on the worst winter days would he spend the night there. Without taking into account our family's dire situation, he started harrying my mother, an illiterate and sickly woman, to send him to study in the city. A most oppressive atmosphere settled over our family; on the one hand, our mother's illness grew increasingly incurable, on the other, Stoyan fell into a deep melancholy, as fragile youthful souls so easily do. When our mother died, he was out of his head with grief, he stroked my hair, comforted me, and wouldn't let me in to see the dead woman so that I wouldn't be frightened. I suspect that during these difficult years he gathered in his heart a great hatred for and bitterness toward that way of life, toward material and spiritual poverty, and this determined his lifelong political outlook. After our mother's death, as sometimes happens when one finds oneself looking into the abyss of a terrible impasse, a quick change came over him, his despair and gloomy outlook on the future transformed into physical and spiritual energy. You have to study, he would tell me, since I didn't manage to, you'll study as long as you can and I'll help you as much as I can to escape from this misery so you can live a different life! He would speak to me as if he were talking about himself, as if he would be living a "different life," he identified with me, and was most sincerely ready to dedicate and sacrifice himself. And when I started studying and entered into the world of science, art, and history, I never anywhere found a more beautiful example of brotherly love, devotion, and obligingness than Stoyan's love for me.

Given the poverty he lived in, Stoyan could only from time to time send me a little wood, a boiled chicken, some beans, potatoes, and a bit of flour, but in any case, I didn't need anything more. Life was cheap in those times, morals were strict and frugal, people showed a noble condescendence to poverty, the town hall gave me a certificate of hardship so I didn't have to pay school fees. I didn't pay rent for an apartment, either. I lived under the veranda of a house, which was once a storage space for wood and odds and ends, but which had been refashioned into a living space, whitewashed and outfitted with a bed, a table, and a small cylindrical stove. Upstairs in two rooms lived an elderly, ailing woman who had long been widowed, and so as not to be all alone, she rented out the room to high school students. She didn't charge rent, however; after school I would bring fresh water from the school fountain, I would shop for her, buy her medicines from the pharmacy, in the winter I would chop wood. If Stoyan managed to send me some food, I would give it to the old woman to cook and then I would eat lunch and dinner with her. The rest of the time I ate at Bay Micho's diner. His requirements were not particularly complicated or strict – all you can eat in exchange for washing dishes when I had free time or was hungry. Petty clerks and villagers on market days ate at the diner. On the counter there was a large notebook to which a chemical pencil was tied with string; the clerks wrote down their lunches and dinners in the notebook and paid at the end of the month. I, too, wrote my lunches and dinners in that notebook when I didn't have time to wash dishes. I shopped for my landlady at the shop in the same way; there, too, was a notebook with a chemical pencil and the shopkeeper wrote down the purchases for the whole month with complete trust in his clients. Those years were the heyday of credit, of discounts, and of mutual trust between seller and buyer, thanks to which many of us poor kids from villages and cities managed to graduate from high schools and universities. Later, when the crisis of the war years struck, those same establishments put up signs: "Respect to all, credit to none!" – the official expression of the vanished trust between shopkeepers and customers. At that time I was studying in Sofia, and thanks to the experience I had gained in the provinces, I was able to enter the highest gastronomic circles. I worked as a waiter in the most celebrated restaurants, but I was "under a microscope" – every time I was late or made a mistake, they docked my wages.

The support Stoyan gave me was above all moral and for precisely this reason it was invaluable. For that time and for him, a young man of nineteen, oppressed by unenlightened ignorance and destitution, this support was tantamount to an act of heroism. With his lively intellect and his native intelligence, he had recognized my bent for books, which over time turned into a painful obsession, and for my sake he deprived himself of the joys of youth. He lived alone in the village, without the coziness of a family of his own, without a soul mate ("I won't get married until you finish high school!"), he worked alone in the field and was forced to do all the housework himself, to do the laundry and knead and bake bread. Despite this, during vacations I found the house spick-and-span, as if some woman had had a hand in it, while he himself was tidy, clean, and cheerful, joyfully affectionate now he was seeing me again, he would hug me tightly, pressing me to his chest. Our time together during vacations was the greatest holiday for both of us, we shared all the thoughts and feelings that had moved us during the months we had been apart, we discussed political events, I told him about books I had read and brought them for him to read.

During my second Christmas vacation, I came home to find a tailor shop and a tailor. Our house was a very old Tatar house, dug into the ground and built of woven sticks, there were two little rooms with a cattle barn attached. Stoyan had walled off part of the barn with bricks, taking away living space from the two oxen and the cow, and had opened a door and a window out onto the street. At the counter, standing on a stool, Master Stamo was cutting cloth – the same tailor who had made my first school uniform. Master Stamo had been working in the neighboring Gagauz village, but Stoyan had learned that he knew how to sew city clothes and had taken me to him. Back then I had been a little afraid of Stamo, and I was on tenterhooks all the while he was taking my measurements. He was a dwarf, no more than three feet tall, with the head of a normal man and his face a cobweb of wrinkles, on his back and chest he had enormous humps, such that his head stood between them like the head of a turtle jutting out of the opening of its shell. As he later told us, he had been born in Tulca, Romania. He had learned his trade from his father, a famous master tailor, but also a very enlightened man. He rebelled against the Romanian authorities, they tossed him into prison and he never came home again. Stamo's sister was married in another city, and his mother had passed away. He left Tulca, worked in various towns, moving ever farther south with the goal of getting closer to Bulgaria. Finally he settled in a little village on the border and waited for an opportune time to cross over. Bulgarians would secretly come to the village to visit their relatives, he met one such man, paid him what was due, and one night the man carried him over the border in a sack.

Like every enterprise, the tailor shop, too, had a company sign hung between the eaves and the upper sill of the door, the likes of which only Ivan Shibilev was capable of composing and writing out in large, colorful letters: "Au Bon Marché." There was also such a shop sign on the main street in the city, and although there it suggested provincial pretentiousness, here hung on the Tatar hovel, sunk amidst the brambles and knee-deep mud, it looked like an absurd joke. In this joke, however, lay hidden the ambition and boldness which also filled Stoyan. Master Stamo had sewn him a new suit of cheviot, he looked inwardly and outwardly transformed, ecstatic and cheerful as a man finally standing on the cusp of a dream that was coming true. I was infected by his enthusiasm as well, I was glad that he had discovered his calling, I was happy that I could now love him more than anyone in the world without the pangs of conscience I had felt until then, due to the fact that thanks to him, I was happier than he was. I spent every day of my vacation in the tailor's shop, I tried to help him, I lit the coals outside for the iron, brought wood for the stove, swept, and the rest of the time I read aloud the newspapers, magazines, and books I had brought from the city. Outside, either snow was falling gently or a blizzard was howling, but inside it was warm, food for lunch or dinner was bubbling on the stove, Master Stamo, standing on his stool, would trace a pattern on the cloth with chalk or a piece of homemade soap, and after that Stoyan would take the enormous, heavy pair of scissors and cut it.

In the evenings, Master Stamo would stay in the tailor shop to finish up some work or to go to sleep, while Stoyan and I would go down to the community center. From the very founding of the center, Stoyan had been its irremovable chairman, he felt at home there, he would stay late dealing with financial or educational issues, put together programs for the youth parties, or dole out roles for an upcoming theatrical performance. If Ivan Shibilev happened to be absent from the village, Stoyan would direct the plays, make up the actors, and play the leading – and most often female – roles. The girls' parents forbid them from playing parts in the "*teatro*," while the schoolteachers went back to their hometowns during vacations, thus we were forced to cut down the number of female roles. But still, we couldn't cut out all the female roles, so we would leave at least two – Stoyan would play one, and I would play the other. My beard hadn't grown in yet, but I had the bristly beginnings of a moustache, so I had to start shaving before my time. Stoyan also shaved off his moustache, and during the theater season, the two of us became women. We rehearsed our parts in falsetto voices, we learned to spin wool on a spindle, to walk, laugh, and cry like women, before the performance we slathered our faces with pomades and powders, put on dresses, on our heads we wore ladies' hats or kerchiefs, depending on what the role called for. I don't remember the names of the characters we transformed in to anymore, nor can I recall the plots of the plays themselves (*Yonchev's Inns*, *The Tatar Khan*, *Sonny Boy*), but I still remember the sense of compromised dignity I felt walking out onstage and the effort it took to speak in falsetto for two hours, which made my throat ache for weeks. What's worse is that the village wiseacres had changed our names to the female versions – Ilka and Stoyanka – and called us the Kralev Sisters. Stoyan was already a grown man, but he didn't think he was undermining his manly dignity by playing female roles. There's no such thing as degrading and shameful work when you're doing it for the good of the people, he would say, they may be laughing at us and reproaching us today, but tomorrow they'll realize what we were doing and praise us.

What he was saying was true, of course, but nonetheless I felt great relief in regards to my theatrical activities when he married Kichka. She was one of those girls the village called "brash" or "mouthy," but in my brother's opinion she was "forward-thinking." She was barely eighteen, petite, and still delicate in a childlike way, but she was energetic, handy, inventive, and practical in a womanly way. She turned out to be quite the housekeeper and in only a few months she had turned the old Tatar dump into a cozy home. Stoyan had already managed to take upon himself all the educational and political activity in the village, he gave lectures about the cooperative movement, about the Soviet kolkhoz system, about the exploitative nature of the capitalist economy, no worse than any modern lecturer could do, he enjoyed a reputation as a learned man not only in our village, but in the neighboring villages as well. He could have married a wealthier or more beautiful girl, but even back then he looked upon marriage from a class point of view, and as he confessed to me later, out of all the girls, only Kichka possessed the true qualities needed for a wife and comrade in life. Just as he was the first among the young men to don a suit coat and trousers, so she was the first of the girls to wear city clothing; just as the young men went to him to sew their new clothes, so the girls went to her for patterns for skirts and blouses. Kichka wasn't beautiful, but she dressed with taste, wore her hair in a bob like the schoolteachers, and like them said "please," "*merci*," and "pardon me" – polite words that had yet to enter the village youngsters' vocabulary. She had only finished one year of middle school, but like my brother she was inquisitive, following his example she would read a book now and then, she liked to be "in style," she taught herself good manners, and among the girls in the village at that time, she stood out as an intelligent, flirtatious, and graceful young lady, whom outsiders took for a schoolteacher or guest from the city. All of this lent her some charm and softened the sharpness of her small, bird-like face, which in moments of excitement became sweet, expressive, and even pretty, it also exonerated her from her conscious superiority over the other girls in the village, whom she treated with affectionate condescension, while laughing at them behind their backs. Stoyan was not annoyed by her self-confidence, since he thought it was unconscious and that it expressed the positive sides of her character – forthrightness, decisiveness, and a willingness to help others however she could. He was happy that he had bound himself to a woman whose outlook on life coincided completely with his own, even before they were married. Kichka eloped with him, not like the other girls who snuck away in the dead of night, but in broad daylight. She gathered up her dowry in a bundle and told her parents that she was going to Stoyan Kralev's to become his wife. They didn't believe her, because they didn't believe that without matchmakers, without maidenly bashfulness and dignity, she would go and throw herself into the arms of some man during the Lenten fast, and all this before her older sister had been married off. But Kichka did it, bravely ignoring the religious and worldly conventions of the times, and in doing so showed she was worthy of her future husband. A few days later they wanted to get married officially, but Father Encho advised them to wait until after Lent. Stoyan and Kichka knew weddings were not allowed during Lent; they took advantage of the opportunity to declare church weddings as religious prejudice and started living together unmarried. No one had permitted themselves such boldness as long as the village had existed, and not only Kichka's family but everyone was against them. With their illegal cohabitation, they profaned matrimony as blessed by God and tradition and set an example of flagrant debauchery; the priest threatened to expel them from the church. The three of us thought it over carefully and decided that at the moment, the conditions were not conducive to free civil marriage and we had best not scandalize public opinion because of a formality that might undermine the authority Stoyan had already won among the young and old.

Kichka very soon was heading the women's movement in the village, which initially expressed itself through imposing the new fashion, new dances at parties, and the recruitment of women for theatrical activities. *Boryana* was the first play in which the female roles were played by women, it enjoyed great success and was performed three times. In this play, Kichka debuted and established herself as the number one actress in the village. Ivan Shibilev's directing helped with this too. It turned out that during his frequent and mysterious disappearances from the village, he had joined various theater troupes in the nearby cities and from him for the first time we heard words and concepts such as "directing," "makeup," "mise-en-scène," "interpretation," "set," "prompter," and "intermission." During his brief experience with these troupes, Ivan Shibilev had managed to make off with some props and costumes, such as makeup, wigs, moustaches, and beards, which transformed our actors such that people could no longer recognize them. In our earlier plays, we had disguised ourselves with white and black wool, we stuck it to our beards, moustaches, and eyebrows with watermelon treacle, but the treacle would soften in the warmth of the salon, our beards and moustaches would fall off, or as soon as they started to come unstuck, the actors would take them off and put them in their pockets. There were some slow-witted actors who froze up, picked their beards up off the floor, and tried to stick them on again in the little room backstage, stopping the performance for several minutes. The actors were semiliterate young men and couldn't learn their roles from a written text. At rehearsals, my brother and I read aloud all the parts to each person individually, until they learned them by heart, and if they forgot some word during the performances, they fell silent like mutes and looked at our lips.

For this reason, Ivan Shibilev, after outfitting us with props, introduced a new personage to our performances – the prompter. The job of the prompter had to be filled by a literate person, so we turned to the schoolteacher, Pesho. Who knows why, but he despised the *teatro* and thought that all these parties, new dances, and fashions were corrupting the youth. Like most teachers at that time, he was as strict and demanding as a field marshal and never let a single violation go unpunished. When at last after much pleading he agreed to become the prompter, his first and only condition was that "we listen to him." For him, the whole village was a school, and all the people his students, thus for him the job of prompter was also part of his teacherly duties. Even when the roles were first being handed out, he would announce to the actors that by the third rehearsal they had to know their lines by heart, or… "they would be punished." Because he was a longtime teacher and mentor, and the most authoritative individual in the village, no one would ever dare talk back to him, we didn't dare talk back to him either. We had all been his students and remembered his supple dogwood switch that with a single blow turned your palms into puffy donuts. In any case, the troupe of actors had undergone a complete change. Like many other things in the village, studying had also become fashionable. We had one girl and four boys in high school who replaced the semiliterate young men onstage. And then our theater went full steam ahead. The number of high school students increased every year, as did the number of intelligent actors. Very often during one vacation we would stage three plays, we began touring to the neighboring villages as well.

No matter how often I go to the theater or watch a play on television, I always remember our performances in the mud-brick hall of the community center. It was not theater, of course, but "enlightenment activity," as naïve and ridiculous as a children's game, but perhaps precisely because of this it was truly the people's theater. The audience, not jaded like today's by its knowledge of theater and of all possible dramaturgical schools, never for an instant distanced itself from what it was watching, but became one with the life onstage and took part in it. One woman who got thirsty during a performance jumped up onstage, dipped a mug in the cauldron, and when she didn't find water in it, went over to Boryana and said: "For shame, Boryana, what time is it girl, and you still haven't gone to fetch the water?"

Another woman, who was sitting close to the stage, peeked at the wealthy Lord Marko's feast table and turned to the public: "Take a look at that, people, he calls himself a lord, but his table's full of nothing but empty plates and dry crusts of bread!"

There were also cases of direct interference in the performance on the part of the audience. In one play a murder was to take place. The plans had been laid in the first act, and in the second, Stoyan, who was playing the killer, was supposed to stick his knife in his opponent's back. He was waiting for him by the window, and when footsteps and his enemy's voice could be heard from outside, he hid behind the door and took his knife out of his belt. The door opened, and on the doorstep stood Neycho, who was to be killed. At that same moment, his father, Bay Ivan Geshev, leapt onstage, shouted at his son to run, grabbed the knife out of Stoyan's hand, and turned it against him: "Start marching to town hall or I'll stick it to you!"

Stoyan was taken aback and didn't know what to do, while Bay Ivan Geshev was holding the knife to his chest and hollering: "You low-down dirty scoundrel! I'll take you to court for trying to kill my son! You say he stole your money! My son doesn't touch another man's property. That floozy you're foolin' around with, she's the one who stole it, go after her!"

Pesho the schoolteacher was also dumbfounded by this incursion onto the stage. He was sitting in his prompter's seat in the corner, wrapped up in the curtain as if in a cocoon, so the audience couldn't see him, but he didn't do anything, as if he thought that the play contained such a scene that he had not noticed before and which hadn't been rehearsed. Relieved that the murder had been headed off, the audience was now impatiently waiting to see how Bay Ivan Geshev would deal with the culprit, without suspecting that his appearance onstage had been self-initiated. All of this went on for only two or three minutes, but for theatrical time a pause of this sort is catastrophic. In the end, Pesho the schoolteacher saved the day.

We signaled to him to patch things up, he promised Bay Ivan Geshev that he would testify in court in his favor, took the knife out of his hands, and hustled him into the dressing room.

We, of course, used the magical power that theater had over the villagers as a means of raising their class consciousness. We boldly reworked every play, cutting or changing the lines so as to load it full of socialist content, exaggerating the class strife. Onstage, the rich or wealthier characters in every play were called bloodsuckers, exploiters, and class enemies of the poor people, we propagandized for cooperatives and the Soviet kolkhozes, for equality between the sexes, we mocked religion and bourgeois morality, we rejected all the customs of that time. Actually, Stoyan was doing all the work, I helped him out with the literary material, which comrades from the city supplied me with. He would read or retell these materials to the villagers, explaining international politics to them, arguing with them, exposing his ideological enemies. I knew all this because he wrote me every week, informing me of village news in the greatest detail. I remember with what joy and enthusiasm he would tell me which lectures he had given before the young and the old in the community center, what questions had been asked, how most of them had accepted the idea of the Soviet kolkhozes and a couple of dozen people had already joined the party. By then I knew that my brother's true calling wasn't the tailor's trade but public service. For every injustice perpetrated by the local authorities – the giving of land to landless villagers, the imposition of fines or collection of various taxes – he always stood on the side of the injured party, and since he was better read and informed than the authorities themselves, in most cases he succeeded in imposing his opinion. Not a single public event took place or was called off without his opinion being taken into account, whether it was the building of a fountain, a school, or a highway, such that even though he was young and not authorized by any authorities whatsoever, he became the center of all events in the village. He was ready at all times to drop his personal business and not to sleep for nights on end so as to write lectures, learn parts for plays, look for lodgings for teachers, organize parties and raffles, sew uniforms for free for poor students, and even act as an adviser to families dividing up land.

Nevertheless, my brother's public activity in those years was peaceful, educational activity in comparison to the strenuous work that awaited him after the declaration of the German-Soviet war. The day the war was declared coincided with a great event in the life of our family – Kichka gave birth to a baby girl. In the morning an old woman had gone into her room to midwife for her, while my brother and I hung around in the yard waiting for the child to be born. From time to time, the old woman would appear on the doorstep and make us bring her warm water from the cauldron, which was simmering over the hearth in the other room, or she would ask for some clothing or a handful of wool and then we would hear Kichka's groaning. Stoyan was shocked and frightened, he was pacing back and forth around the yard, not taking his eyes off the door to the room. And so hours passed, it was noon, but still the old woman hadn't come out to tell us whether Kichka had given birth. At one point she opened the window of the room and once again disappeared back inside. Master Stamo came out of the tailor shop, stripped down to his shirtsleeves, and started crawling around the yard like a turtle. His humps were more pronounced than ever and they pressed on his throat, suffocating him. The heat was intolerable, the chickens were dozing in the shade of the apricot tree with open beaks and spread wings, the pig was panting in the pen. Master Stamo sat down under the awning of the barn, leaned his back hump against the post, and closed his eyes. After a short while we heard whispering, we turned to him and realized that he was telling us not to bake in the sun but to come into the shade. From the open window we heard Kichka give a single sharp cry that was not repeated. A sinister silence fell, the three of us stood as if petrified, oppressed by the majesty of a mystery that was taking place in the room, but what was that mystery – birth or death? The rooster, which had been lying among the hens, his beak hanging open from the heat, got up, shook off the dust, flapped his wings, and crowed. His clear, polyphonic voice resounded in the silence as loud as a shot and so absurdly that we jumped and turned toward him. The rooster cocked his head, fixed us with one eye, and stretched his neck, with his flaming red coxcomb on his head and steely spurs on his feet. He stood still and kept watching us with his cold eye, and we shuddered from superstitious fear, as if some unclean force stood before us, incarnated as a rooster.

"War with Russia!" someone said in a breathless voice.

"It's a girl!" the old woman cried at the same time from the doorstep. "May she live a long life, Stoyan, she's your spitting image!"

My brother ran toward the house, but when he reached the threshold, he stopped and turned toward Acho (the attendant from the community center) and asked: "What war?"

"Germany and Russia are going to fight," Acho said. "I heard it just now on the radio. Them Deutschers invaded and have already gotten a heck of a ways into Russia."

The midwife showed us the baby from the doorstep, but wouldn't let us in to see Kichka. She called out from the bed, saying she was all right, and immediately fell asleep. Acho was still standing in the yard, as if awaiting some orders from Stoyan. We sent him away and went into the garden, sat down amidst the lush alfalfa, and Stoyan said: "Now how's that for a coincidence! On one and the same day, my child is born and fascist Germany attacks the Soviet Union."

This declaration of war came as no surprise to me, because I had quite extensive information about Germany's intentions. I had already lived in Sofia as a student for one full year, and I had even known from unofficial sources that toward the middle of April Churchill had sent Stalin a message informing him that German forces were gathering on the border of the Soviet Union. Stoyan and I had spoken many times about the inevitability of such a war, yet still he was surprised, taken aback, and bewildered. He also didn't want to believe the radio report that the German Army in the very first days of the campaign had gotten a couple of hundred miles into Soviet territory. After the evening news we went back to the community center and listened to Soviet radio stations in the dark. They confirmed the report we had heard on our radio and talked about the Soviet troops' strategic retreat. I translated literally, but Stoyan questioned my knowledge of Russian, thinking I had translated incorrectly.

"It can't be!" he kept saying over and over like an incantation.

In my absence he might have fallen into despair like many others, but when we were together I never noticed in him even the slightest doubt regarding the outcome of the war. During the first days he was restless and anxious, he slept very little and worked a lot, and with great internal tension he managed to keep calm in front of other people. It was agonizing to listen to reports of German successes together with the whole village, and I sometimes stayed home, I couldn't bear the rebukes and taunts of the villagers to whom we had spoken so enthusiastically about the might, grandeur, and invincibility of the Soviet Union. Stoyan never missed a day in front of the radio, smiling calmly and even condescendingly like a person listening to some pompous palaver.

This war captured the interest of villagers from our far-flung region and awakened political passions in them. The successes of the "Deutschers" in Europe and even their entrance into our country had not made any particular impression on them, who knows why. But now most of the men left their fields at noon and stopped by to hear the news, while in the evening the community center was full of people. The secret of the Soviet Union, which had formerly prevented them from making comments, now came to light – if such a huge nation, with so many millions of people, could not stop a nation three times smaller, it was clear that under the Bolsheviks there was no order and discipline, instead just a jumble of hungry kolk-hozniks who ran away or surrendered; the Bolsheviks only had common pots of porridge and common women, there was only one pair of pants for every two people, so when one was wearing them, the other had to sit at home in his underwear.

The propaganda in the newspapers and on the radio was picturesque and easily graspable by the common folk, everyone knew the refrain by the rhymester who would sing out the news accompanied by guitar:

> *Rome, Berlin, and Tokyo*
> *each one true to the fight*
> *we will see a new world order*
> *thanks to the Axis might!*

In the fall, before I left for Sofia, Stoyan wanted to gather together all the communists to explain the political situation to them, but only two men came to the tailor shop. The rest openly and frankly declared that they didn't want to be considered communists anymore. "Leave off about that party, for Pete's sake, there ain't a shred left of Russia, and you still want to blabber on to us about communism!" I left Stoyan feeling lonely. Everything he had achieved with his sociopolitical campaign collapsed in a few months. The men and youth who earlier had openly showed him their gratitude, respect, and trust, now avoided talking to him and even made sport of him with his "invincible Russia." Stoyan was bitter, but not despairing. Before a year's gone by, he said to me as we parted, all those who skedaddled will come crawling back to us. That's how it is with a simple man, he only believes in something when he sees it in black and white...

I didn't sleep the whole night and could hardly wait until dawn. Kichka had left my suitcase in the little room the previous day, I quietly opened the door and went inside to get it. As I was leaving I saw Stoyan on the veranda. He told me I could've slept a bit longer, the man with the cart would be coming to get me in about an hour, plus I needed to eat breakfast before setting out. I told him that I had decided to stay in the village and cure myself. Since it was dangerous to live with people, I would go to Noseless Anani, whom I had spoken with a few days earlier. The sanatorium didn't give me a more certain guarantee of recovering than a separate room at Anani's, where I would live apart from people in peace and quiet.

"At the sanatorium, you'll be under the constant care of doctors and have all the right conditions for getting well," Stoyan said after hearing me out.

"According to the doctors, the first condition for getting well is peace, and I'll only feel peaceful when I'm here. You shouldn't take that away from me."

I grabbed my suitcase and set out to leave. Stoyan caught up with me in the yard and blocked my way. He rightly assumed that I was offended by our conversation about Nusha the previous evening and that I had decided to slip out of the house without taking advantage of his offers to help. He begged me not to be childish and to take the money he'd set aside for me. He couldn't stop me, but he couldn't leave me alone, either. We went out into the street, I started off toward the neighborhood farthest away, while he set out alongside me, confused and tormented. The sun still hadn't come up, but people were pottering about the yards and streets. The first sheaves of barley had ripened a few days earlier and most people were going out to reap. We neared Anani's house, but Stoyan still didn't believe that I was going to live under one roof with him. The whole village was revolted by the man and no one dared even set foot in his yard, but I went in. Stoyan, now totally dumbfounded, stopped at the gate. At that moment Anani came into view, coming from the house with a sack on his shoulder and a sickle in his hand.

"The house's o'en, go on in!"

Despite our agreement, it seems he had not believed I would set foot in his house. Pleasantly surprised, but also nervous that I might change my mind when I saw him up close, he turned his head aside and rushed past us like a man pursued. He had no nose, nor any lips, so he couldn't pronounce certain consonants. His face was flat and covered with a handkerchief from below his eyes to his chin, he had tucked the ends of the handkerchief under his hat at the back of his head. Between his eyebrows, where the base of his nose should have been, a small hole gaped like a tiny abyss. From beneath the kerchief the contours of his teeth and cheekbones stood out, one imagined his face as a half-naked skull and felt horror and disgust, since the handkerchief was wet with spit and secretions. Anani had caught syphilis during his army days and since then had lived exiled by his family and strangers alike. He knew people were disgusted by him, so he himself avoided them. In the fields, he worked apart from his brothers, they on one end, he on the other. They left his food far from the common table and he ate alone, with his back turned to the others. He drew water from the well only at night, he grazed his horses apart from the other horse herds, he didn't come out amidst the crowds on holidays, and no one ever went to see him. His house was one of the oldest, if not the oldest, in the village, but far from the most dilapidated. It had three rooms and a wooden veranda on the front, it was whitewashed, the door and window frames were painted blue, while the foundations were made of brownish-black local dirt. With its drooping eaves, concave walls, and jutting transverse beams, it looked like a centenarian grandmother who was just skin and bones, yet still hardy, tidy, and welcoming.

As children, we had been afraid to pass by this house. A certain Milan Manasev had lived there with his wife, he was from another village and was a horse thief, a dark and dangerous character in the minds of our sedate locals. One morning Milan Manasev and his wife were found slaughtered, likely by Romanian smugglers they had dealings with. After their death the house was abandoned and turned into that mysterious place which exists in every village. It was inhabited by all the mysterious forces from folk superstition – *karakondzhuli* (bogeyman-like satyrs), *samodivi* (wood nymphs), and all manner of evil spirits – whom many people had seen with their own two eyes. They had also seen both Manasev and his wife standing on the roof of the house at night, or dancing a round dance in the yard, dressed in white clothing, following villagers through the streets at night, or slaughtering livestock left forgotten in the fields. Later Anani had moved into the house to atone in solitude for the sins of his youth, while I went to him to await my death.

The cart Stoyan had hired to drive me to the bus loaded up my luggage instead and brought it to my new home. A little table with wobbly legs, a wooden bed, a blanket, a gas lamp, and books. There were many of them, hundreds of tomes, wrapped in paper and tied with string. While I was studying in high school and at the university, my main concern had been to acquire more books. Whatever money Stoyan had managed to send me during those lean years, whatever I had earned on my own in restaurants and other places, I had spent it all on books. We arranged my things in the room then went out on the veranda. Stoyan had been silent the whole time, depressed and bitter about my decision to stay here, he was still silent now. I felt a coughing fit rising in my chest. Already back in Sofia I had found a shallow metal box which I carried in the pocket of my jacket, I turned aside and spit blood into it. The cough was deep, coming from the very bottom of my lungs, and with every straining cough I saw stars. When everything was over, I hid the little box in my pocket and then I saw that Stoyan was crying. He was standing in profile, as if watching something over the tops of the trees, taut as a string from the effort of controlling himself. Tears gushed from his eyes, gathering in large drops under his chin and falling on his chest. His hands were clenched in fists and his whole body was shaking with tension. I felt guilty for causing him suffering, but I could not change my decision. At the same time, I felt somehow proud and elated because I was seeing him cry for the first time, and his tears were a man's tears, bursting from the depth of his brotherly heart. We took our leave silently. He turned around, passed behind me, and went out into the yard.

From that day on, everyone in the village knew I was sick with consumption and started looking upon me as doomed. Wherever I turned up, were it the community center or on the street, my presence made people anxious, while the children didn't dare approach me. I was the first and only college graduate in the village and just as earlier they had simple-heartedly shown me respect, now in the same way they showed me pity. The poor boy, what a waste, I heard them whispering behind my back, since TB's gotten ahold of him, he's done for! But I didn't feel so doomed and exiled from the world. Ever since the doctors had discovered the cavity in my lung, I knew I was going to die and death was the only thing I thought about. I thought about it especially during the days and nights when I started to seclude myself in my room. As soon as they found out I was sick, my comrades ceased assigning me tasks, they gathered up money and decided to send me to a sanatorium for those ill with tuberculosis. I refused to go and not only did I refuse, I ran away from the village. It seems that I had resigned myself to death or had become apathetic, only a single aspiration lived in my heart – to go back to the village and die there. This aspiration likely fed on my fear of meeting death among strangers, without receiving any final comfort from my nearest and dearest. Or it was an atavism found in some animals which, with their last ounce of strength, drag themselves to their lairs, so as to die where they had begun their lives, to unite the end with the beginning.

Whatever it was, resignation or apathy, in any case I had gotten used to thinking about death as a law of nature that did not spare any single living creature. I philosophized, loading my consciousness with all sorts of arguments in favor of that natural law so as to console myself that everything mortal was doomed to die. In this war millions of young people like myself had died and were dying on battlefields, who was I to cry out, I thought to myself, why should I writhe like a worm in the face of the inevitable? What difference did it make when I died, now or in ten or even one hundred years? The idea was to get used to the thought that whenever death did come, I would fear it again. Of course, with this sophistry I did not completely succeed in overcoming my fear, but at least I managed, as far as I could tell, to stand face-to-face with the inevitable without faint-heartedness and sniveling.

From the books I had read, I had understood that even the most insight-ful authors did not manage to fully express in words their human thoughts and feelings. There was always something for my imagination to add after reading, and this was likely the case with all readers. The word is power-less to fully express the complex and elusive movements of the heart and mind, they can only be experienced and reflected upon. Since this is the case, how could I express with my impoverished speech what I felt after my encounter with Nusha? I was filled and overflowing with her, that's what it was. She was my new life, my reincarnation. All my sophistic jab-bering about resignation to death disappeared immediately like so much smoke. A rebellion against nature itself and its primordial laws welled up inside me. Is not Mother Nature a blind force that creates so as to destroy? I could not resign myself to her amorality, my will to live erupted like a volcano, burning up with its lava my despair and resignation. In the morn-ing I did exercises, I walked in the fields for hours, I ate like a wolf. Stoyan had secured hearty food for me – honey, butter, fresh meat – and Kichka cooked for me. Every day I ate lunch and dinner at their place under the awning of the barn, I also had food at home. After lunch and dinner I would go to the community center to listen to the news. The authorities had long since placed a seal on the radio dial so we could not change the station, but the omnipresent Ivan Shibilev made short work of that.

After the official news, when the others went home, Stoyan, a few others, and I would stay in the community center, Ivan Shibilev would take off the back panel of the radio, fiddle around with some mechanisms, and find a Soviet radio station, usually Moscow. Even from the local radio station it was clear that the Germans were retreating in panic on all fronts in the east and west, but we wanted to hear the Russian language, the Kremlin's clock striking the hour, and Levitan's solemn voice. We got chills when that voice announced that in only five days Soviet troops had pushed back the enemy's lines of defense more than five hundred kilometers, freeing more than a thousand villages. We imagined the Soviet Army as a living avalanche destroying any resistance in its path, we could not contain our joy and ecstasy and broke into "Shiroka strana moya rodnaya" or some other Soviet song.

After leaving the community center, Stoyan always walked me back to Anani's house. From the very first evening I noticed that as we walked, his high spirits fell abruptly, as it were. He was silent or talked about inconsequential things, as if only minutes earlier we had not been rejoicing over the victorious advance of the Soviet Army and been singing songs. Obviously, Anani's house reminded him every time of my absolute refusal to go to a sanatorium and that darkened his mood. However, I could also sense that he still hoped that loneliness and cohabitation with the noseless man would depress me and drive me from the house. Before we would say good night, he would stand in front of me for a minute and then I could see his eyes glittering in the dark, I could hear him stifling a deep sigh in his chest. I had the feeling that my improved mood gladdened him on the one hand, while on the other it troubled and irritated him, since he saw it as an expression of flippancy. He wanted to ask me something but didn't dare. He himself seemed to realize that his questions would be unpleasant for me, and he had promised not to disturb my peace. It was not hard to guess what he wanted to know – how long would I stay in that hellhole and had I seen Nusha Pashova? If he had asked, I would have answered him that I had come to this hellhole not to await my death, as I wrote above, but to wait until I recovered, and that I hadn't seen Nusha, but that I was waiting for her always, both in my dreams and while awake. But he kept silent and thus for the first time the secret of unshared thoughts and feelings settled between us.

Paging through these notes, I see that I have used the word "insight" several times in the sense of an infallible premonition almost like clairvoyance. After she had come to our home, Nusha and I had not made plans to meet, or at least I didn't remember due to the obliviousness I had fallen into during our meeting, but I expected her every day. I didn't bother to think how she would get here on her own and whether her desire to talk to me in the future was as strong since she had found out that I was sick with tuberculosis. I had become a medium, I communicated with her at all times, I saw her incarnated in everything around me – in the sunflowers, in the clouds, which, as soon as I looked at them, took on her shape. I was so afraid that if she went looking for me at home, my brother and sister-in-law would insult her terribly and throw her out of the house, that I went walking through the fields every day so as to meet her outside the village. I strolled before lunch and in the late afternoon, as these were the times most convenient for her to visit me, and only in the western part of the village fields, where the road to Zhitnitsa passed. Here the summer crops had been sown – sunflowers, corn, and melons – and there were no people, because they were all reaping on the other side of the village land. I would walk amidst the crops, reach a small wood, rest for a bit, then walk back. In this way I watched the road between the two villages for a whole week. On the eighth day late in the afternoon, when I was already on my way back to the village, I heard a bell behind me. I looked back – Nusha was riding a bike. She was wearing a white shirt and had a wide-brimmed straw hat on her head.

I remember almost all the details of our second meeting. Nusha had not expected to see me in the fields and had almost passed me by. She only recognized me when I called out to her, she made some exclamation and her face flushed bright red. The bicycle brakes squeaked abruptly, she reeled to the side and put one foot on the ground. My sudden appearance was like a miracle to her and she couldn't seem to believe her eyes. These were her first words: "I can't believe my eyes."

"If you had looked for me at home, you wouldn't have found me," I said. "I don't live there anymore."

"I for my part have cut off all my hair," she said, taking the straw hat off her head. "Mama was really mad at me, she said I looked like a coquette from the city. Do I really look so ridiculous?" She glanced toward a nearby tumulus and her face took on an ecstatic expression, as if something endlessly tempting was standing before her. "Do you know that I've never climbed a grave mound? There are ancient grave mounds in all the village fields around here, only ours doesn't have one. Do you want to climb up and see the view from on top?"

Nusha left her bicycle in the bushes and set off on the narrow path toward the tumulus. She ran on ahead of me, waving her straw hat, and I felt a gentle puff of wind, saturated with the scent of blossoming sunflowers, I watched how her dark-brown hair fractured the sun's gleaming reflections and hung free about her shoulders. The grave mound was no more than twenty yards high, but on the plain it looked as imposing as a small mountain, grown over with wild multicolored grasses and bushes, hiding in its virginal womb the historic secrets of our land. On its top was a little clearing with lush grass and a small pyramid of rotting beams, the remains of an earlier triangular tower. We climbed up the pyramid and looked in all directions. In the distance the air was translucent and motionless, all the neighboring villages could be seen, the distant circumference of the horizon could also be seen, where the ashen blue of the sky and the land touched in a thin, straight line. The evening wind blew from the west, as always at that time of day, curling the verdant expanse into silvery waves and immersing us in the illusion of a sea. But it was not an illusion. I truly felt and saw the grave mound rocking like a ship, and that rocking filled my soul with a sweet vertigo.

Nusha said she was dizzy and climbed down. I followed her down, and we sat in the lush grass facing the village. It could be seen from one end to the other, sunk in the greenery of the yards, fenced off by brambly hedges and large, unhewn stones. The houses seemed to be playing hide-and-seek in that greenery, some peeked out with one eye, others showed their chimneys or a bit of their gray, old-fashioned roof tiles, only the school and the church stood at full height from the village square and looked at the world with open, light-orange faces. Here and there a thin stream of smoke curled up from a chimney, and this showed that the old women had begun cooking supper for the harvesters, who in an hour or two would come back from the fields. Nusha was sitting next to me as young girls sit, her skirt stretched over her legs to the ankles and her arms tucked under her knees, her gaze roamed in the distance and she rocked gently from side to side, as children do when they're thinking of something that is all their own and lovely. I had a lovely feeling as well, everything around was lovely as never before. Nusha's face glowed with a quiet happiness, a smile threatened to blossom on her lips at any moment, and then she laughed as if to herself in a thin, ringing voice, which filled all of nature and wrenched forth from her like a soft echo.

"I'll come to see how you're settling in to your new place and I'll bring you a present," she said as she laughed. "You might not like it, but I'll give it to you anyway…"

"My landlord will scare you," I said. "You'll be disgusted by him."

I told her about Anani and his isolation, but she didn't seem to hear me and continued her line of thought.

"But before that, you need to come visit us. Mom and Dad send their greetings and told me to invite you to visit. You know, Daddy is really worried about Lexy, he can't believe that he is alive."

We talked about Lexy until the sun went down. For some girls, their ideal model of a man is their brother or father, whom they adore. This adoration is likely due to various reasons of a physiological or other nature, but one such reason might be that these girls, who have not yet become women, are excessively sheltered, they haven't looked beyond the circle of their family so they discover the male principle first of all in men among their close blood relatives. Nusha was such a girl, she idolized her brother to such an extent that it was as if he was immune to life's ups and downs, she believed that he was alive and well and sooner or later would return, crowned with the glory of a legendary hero. Her brother was a myth and a legend to her, and she was pained even by the fact that her father harbored some doubts about her brother's fate. She talked about her brother as if he had gone to the city to take care of some business and would be back today or tomorrow.

"Do you believe that he's alive?" she asked me, just as she had asked me during our first meeting by the church fence.

"I do," I told her.

And this was the truth – the truth of the love that fully united me with her being and did not allow me to think differently than she did. Besides, I, too, had been enchanted by Lexy's personality, I, too, idolized him as did his sister, but in her absence, I wondered why he had left incognito to go abroad just as I wondered whether her father was the one who betrayed our comrades. My happiness depended solely on solving this puzzle, and every puzzle gives rise to doubt. Just as every doubt in turn succumbs to the most unfounded arguments, until it transforms into a form of self-torture. I'm not sure whether my brother understood that, but from the very start he began trying to fill me with doubts about Nusha's intentions, since he believed that she was throwing herself at me due to some impure calculations on the part of her family. At first he was more condescending, he advised me not to get mixed up with women at all ("I thought you wanted peace and quiet?"), because it was harmful to my health, until one evening he openly attacked me and accused me of being a renegade.

Nusha came to visit me that same day. It just so happened that Anani was at home too, and we spoke for the first time, if you don't count our conversation about my coming to live with him, which took place in the field and in the dark, at that. He was coming back from the field, I jumped up into his cart behind him, asked him if he would rent me a room, he agreed and that was that. Since I had become his tenant, however, he had been avoiding me. In the morning he got up before dawn, while I was sleeping, and went out to the fields, while in the evening I came back when he was already asleep. Sometimes there was a light in his window, but as soon as he heard me in the yard, he turned out the lamp and lay low. I nevertheless managed to observe him. In the morning he hitched up the cart and before going out to the fields he got a barrel of water, watered the vegetable garden, weeded, or did some pressing housework. Even though he assumed I was sleeping at that time, he still walked on tiptoe, ready to dart into the barn or somewhere behind the house if I were to appear at the window or come out into the yard. But I slept very lightly or didn't sleep at all, I still couldn't get used to my new living situation, I would read until my eyes ached and doze off with a book in my hand. No matter how carefully he crept out of his room, I heard his footsteps on the veranda and on the stairs, which were beneath my window, I got up just as carefully from my bed and watched him. In the first few days I hid in the farthest corner of the room, because I was afraid he would notice me, I didn't dare look at him from up close. At the same time, I felt pangs of conscience about this man who had upended his previous way of life for me, I was upset that I couldn't express my gratitude to him for taking me in under his roof. I couldn't overcome my revulsion toward him, he knew it and despite that tiptoed around in his own home as to assure peace and quiet for an unfamiliar and infectiously ill person.

I had to get over my revulsion at all costs, otherwise I would make his life even harder. I started hiding in the front corner near the window, so I could watch him from a yard away when he was coming up or down the stairs. My efforts to get close to him became an obsession. I was constantly listening for his footsteps and would rush to take up my place in the corner by the window, deliberately waiting for him to appear. I was curious to peek into his room, but an enormous padlock invariably hung from the door. He forgot to lock it only once and I snuck into his room. Judging by the neatness of the yard and the house's exterior, I hadn't expected to find the stinking den of a recluse, yet I was nevertheless surprised by its tidiness and coziness. Bluish-white walls, a floor spread with a layer of red clay and covered with colorful rag rugs, a wooden bed with flowers and figures carved into the head- and footboards, a pine trunk in the corner, above the trunk shelves with dishes – in short, a picture out of a children's magazine showing the interior of a typical village home. (Back then I didn't yet know that Anani spent his spare time woodcarving.) Three pictures hung on the wall behind glass in wooden frames – three portraits of Anani in his army uniform. In two photos he was with friends, in one he was alone, a close shot from the waist up. I recognized him by his forehead and his eyes, which were the same even now, the wide, square forehead, dark eyes slightly squinted and slanted toward his nose. Those eyes, which had turned into two sanctuaries of hermetic solitude, in those years had gazed out with the boldness of hope. In place of that repulsive nothingness that the handkerchief now hid, he had had a straight Roman nose, a long, high-cheekboned face, a thin moustache, shapely lips pressed tightly together, and a slightly dimpled chin. I noticed something else, which actually struck me the most. Between the stove and the back wall, there was a little round table covered by a blue tablecloth with white stripes, and on top of the tablecloth there were five bowls, five wooden spoons, and five forks of tarnished nickel. In front of each of the five place settings around the table stood low four-legged stools. One place setting and one stool showed signs of long years of use. Did that mean that throughout his years of loneliness, Anani had lived with an imaginary family made up of a wife and three children, with whom he ate lunch and dinner every day? Didn't other people in the village do the same thing, setting out plates of food for children who had died young, hadn't our mother set an extra place at the table even after our father's death? Anani had been living in an invented reality; wasn't I, too, living with the illusion that I was healthy, that Nusha loved me, and that we would soon be married and have a family and children?

After that, I had another image of Anani, an inner picture of a young soldier with a Roman nose and high cheekbones, who had become a forty-year-old man not resigned to his misfortune and who had managed to turn it into a meaningful life of hard work. How this small miracle occurred in me, by the power of suggestion or due to excessive empathy, to this day I still cannot explain. But the truth is that I managed to subject myself to visual and spiritual deception, I managed to replace Anani's actual physical appearance with my internal image of him and to talk to him like any other person. On that day he had stayed at home to rest or to finish up some housework, but as of three o'clock he still had not shown himself outside, perhaps because I was in my room. A meeting of communist and Fatherland Front members, to be held in the woods, had been scheduled for that evening, and I needed to give a report about the political situation. The Soviet Army had reached the Bulgarian border with Romania and we had received instructions to be ready to seize power. I had already scribbled out my report when I heard Anani come out of his room. I went out as well and met him on the veranda. He froze for a moment and wanted to slip down the stairs, but I stood in front of him.

"Bay Anani," I said. "It'll soon be a month since I've been living here, but we never seem to find time to see each other and talk."

He stepped toward the veranda railing and turned his shoulder toward me.

"Lotsa 'ork, you know, out in the 'ields e'ery day..."

We talked about the harvest and lots of other things, we talked about the war as well, because he was interested to know how far the Russians had gotten. We stood shoulder to shoulder and no matter how many times I turned toward him, he turned his head the other direction so I wouldn't look him in the face. He was nervous, I could hear his breath catching, he felt the ends of his handkerchief to make sure they were still tucked under his hat, his fingers were trembling. That's how Nusha found us. She had come through the garden gate and suddenly stepped out from behind the house. Anani saw her first because he was looking in that direction the whole time, he pushed me aside and hid in his room.

"See how I found you?" Nusha was saying, pushing her bike along with one hand and holding a cardboard box in the other. "Since you didn't come to see us, I came to you. Like in that saying about Mohammed and the mountain."

"Please, I never promised," I said, going down to her in the yard.

"You didn't promise, but you didn't say no, either. And now here's your present!" While I untied the string around the box, Nusha smiled as if she had gotten up to some mischief and was now counting on my indulgence. "You won't laugh, right, you promise?"

Me, laugh at her? Good God! Even now I am moved at the thought of that present. In the box was a dark-brown shaggy teddy bear with black eyes and a blue ribbon around its neck. There was no doubt about it, I was touched and my heart melted, as always in her presence, and I probably exaggerated the significance of that gift to the level of a symbol, but back then I thought that through this bear she was giving me the purity of her childhood. While she, in the most touching way, didn't realize that, she was looking at me with her warm, hazelnut eyes and telling me that her father had bought her that bear when she was eight, she had played with it until a few years ago, and now, "I don't know why," it had occurred to her to give it to me. "You're not insulted by this joke, are you?"

Stoyan surprised us in the early evening as we were sitting at the end of the yard. He didn't come in to us, but called to me from the gate and hid behind the hedge, thus making it clear that he didn't want to talk to Nusha. Never before had I felt so pathetic and guilty, as if caught at the scene of a crime. I hadn't promised Stoyan that I wouldn't see Nusha, yet I still felt guilty in his eyes. And not only in his, but in my own eyes as well. Now this terrible thought crossed my mind – that I felt guilty for loving Nusha. Why, I asked myself, and I couldn't answer. I hadn't thought about it, plus my nerves were frayed to the extreme and I couldn't control myself. I crossed the yard weak in the knees and went out into the street. Stoyan had fallen into some quiet rage. His nose had gone white, and there seemed to be a white circle around his mouth and that circle was smiling. Everything around us was sunk in elderberry and wormwood, their heavy poisonous scents invoked desolation and grief. But Stoyan was smiling with his pale lips and unrelentingly fixing me with his narrowed eyes.

"The meeting tonight is called off."

At lunch we had discussed my report point by point, and besides, calling off the meeting was impossible. There was no way to tell everyone, since they were scattered among the fields. I realized he was lying to me and told him so. He reached out and grabbed the bear, which I had forgotten in my hands. He turned it around, looking at it from all sides and tossed it into the elderberry thicket with a gesture of disgust.

"There'll be a meeting tonight, but you won't be going. The comrades are afraid of you, since you're making love to Petar Pashov's daughter."

That was a lie too. I was sure that none of the communists had said anything of the sort, unless he himself had suggested it to one of them, to have an ace up his sleeve against me. He had come to discuss the report one more time or was just passing along the street by chance, and when he had seen Nusha, he had taken advantage of the situation to distance himself from me or at least to scare me.

"Since you won't let me come to the meeting, I won't insist."

What else could I say?

"It's a well-known fact that you'd rather stay with your lady visitor here. It's not me but the comrades who don't want you, they're afraid you'll give us away to Pashov. The fascists are at their most merciless now, since they see that the end is near, and they're killing without judge or jury, all they need is a reason to suspect you. Since they know you aim to become his son-in-law, folks are afraid you'll let some of our business slip in front of him and he'll turn us over to the police. Everyone knows he's a traitor, and they figure if we had partisans in these parts, they would've liquidated him by now. He won't get off the hook later, either, but who can guarantee that he'll keep silent until then? You can't guarantee it either." Stoyan was whispering, but his whisper was so maliciously loud and echoed so painfully in my brain that it seemed to me that it could be heard throughout the entire village. "He just might keep quiet, to save his skin, but only under the condition of marrying into our family. He's hoping we'll hush up his treachery. So tell me, does that young lady know you're sick with TB?"

"Of course she knows."

"Now that's exactly what I wanted you to tell me, dearest brother, exactly that!" Stoyan said, and a diabolical smile twisted his face, which was burning as if from fever. "You've taught me everything, whatever I know in this world I learned from you. You've got my most sincere brotherly gratitude now and forever and ever, amen, as the priest would say. I don't dare try to teach you anything, but I'll ask you, I'll just ask you, what girl would want to join her life to a sick man? Why, and for how long? You think your Nusha doesn't know about her father's sins? Not only does she know, but she's been instructed in detail to keep up her affair with you. If you recover, you'll recover no sooner than a year and a half from now, that's what the doctors say, isn't it? The war'll be over in a few months, not more, and we'll start building a new life, and folks like Petar Pashov will just go on living their lives, safe and sound. It's not surprising they'd try to think up some contributions to the cause. Isn't their son a communist? Yes, he's a communist, but where is he? If he's the great communist they make him out to be, what government would give him a passport to go abroad and why would they give it to him? But if you don't recover... what I'm trying to say... Sorry, I'm speaking to you for the last time and I'm obliged to say everything, absolutely everything. If you don't recover, it won't be any sooner than a year and a half, and things still come out all right for the Pashovs... I'm trying to say that if you die, you'll die because of that woman, because of her you didn't go get treatment and stayed here in this hellhole. So let's say that one day you get married and start living together, what will people say then? Those Kralevs have been talking about class war since who knows when, and now they've taken a rich man's daughter into their family, the daughter of an ideological enemy and a traitor, at that. How will you face the world then? Everything we've achieved over all these years, you'll destroy it because of one woman, you'll disgrace your ideals and your honor as a communist. Go ahead, go on over to Petar Pashov, and warn him to watch out, and just throw us to the wolves. Maybe you've already let him in on some of our secrets..."

Stoyan had grown hysterical and said much more than I can remember now, all of it feverish and rambling, he repeated the same things over and over, begged, threatened, and prophesied my ignoble end as a turncoat. When he finally left, I found the bear in the bushes and went back into the yard, but didn't find Nusha there. Had she heard what my brother was saying and run away for good, or had she not dared to call out to me before she left? I went back to my room and didn't come out for two days and two nights. I lay there, trying to read, thinking things over. Those were some of the worst days of my life. Just at the thought that I would never see Nusha again, my heart burst with pain, but I shouldn't see her again. I couldn't even tell her the real reason for our parting, because her father might take advantage of that. Whenever I thought about him and his son, I always told myself that I shouldn't let prejudice get the best of me. I was a future lawyer or judge and I knew that I needed to judge myself and others with blindfolded eyes. I knew that every person to a greater or lesser extent was swayed by the power of suggestion, and I strained my will to guard myself against this weakness. Even back in high school our psychology teacher had done experiments with us to show us that people were influenced by suggestion. Once he had us sniff a test tube filled with some liquid. Thirty people – thirty different smells. But the test tube was filled with pure water.

From the brief conversation I had had with Petar Pashov, what had made the strongest impression was his question in regards to his son's letter: "What if he wrote it looking down the barrel of some gun?" Of course, even if he did know, he wouldn't tell me why and how his son had left to go abroad, but why did he assume that Lexy had been forced to write that letter, and in German no less? Could he have been hinting that Lexy, as a very important party functionary, had somehow been kidnapped and his captors had forced him to write that letter in order to compromise him and at the same time to warn his family (perhaps similar letters had been sent to his comrades-in-arms as well)? But his departure abroad could also have been organized by the party, so that he could take up some important job there. The question was why had he left and whom was he serving? He could be either an agent provocateur, or he could be working for Soviet intelligence. This was known only to the ones he was serving, while we were left but with doubts, which could destroy his family. As far as Lexy's father was concerned, the case seemed more clear-cut. As a wealthy villager, he hated the communists with good reason, and for the same reasons he fought against them. But had he betrayed them and if he had, would he dare use his daughter as a pawn, as my brother claimed, to save himself when the time came? Why not? Feminine charm had always played a leading role in the history of espionage, it had been used to fool men everywhere, and few were able to resist it. Perhaps I am one such fool too? I loved Nusha, but did she love me so selflessly and devotedly? I needed to make an unbiased judgment about her, I told myself, to suppress my feelings and see her true face. She treated me like a healthy man; not in a single word, glance, or gesture of hers had I caught any pity or fear of my illness. She also wasn't curious as to why I had left my home, how my life was at the noseless man's place, and how I felt. I didn't want to remind her of my illness in any way whatsoever, and if I tried to do it, she changed the subject and distracted me with another topic. That might be due to her love for me, but it could also be deliberate. Rumor certainly reproached her for taking up with a sick man, and she justified this by not believing it. Her parents were not opposed to our relationship and even encouraged her – at our every meeting she relayed their invitation to come visit. How could they allow her to come visit me on her own? She was "educated" and likely enjoyed a certain independence, but still, for villagers like them it was difficult to ignore the biases of the times. Many of the villagers had remarked to me that "Miss Nusha was coming at my beck and call." Perhaps that was precisely her parents' goal – to get word of our relations around and to tie me down with public opinion.

Whatever it was, I had to break things off with Nusha or at least curtail my relations with her for some time, until her father's situation was cleared up. Otherwise I risked sullying not only my brother's name and all his deeds, but I also risked trampling my own convictions. The poet had said "the world is watching us now"* and I could say of my brother and myself that now not only the village, but the whole region, was "watching us." We had taught people communist morals, we had preached that the communist was obliged to deprive himself of everything personal and to devote his strength and feelings to the revolution. And the revolution was imminent.

On the third day I came out of my room, passed through the garden gate, and set out for Zhitnitsa. I went to do what my brother most feared. I was going to Petar Pashov to let him in on one of our secrets, namely that the communists considered him a traitor, and thus to try to find out the truth about the man from himself. My heart rebelled with a terrible force against every logical argument concerning his guilt and powerfully led me onward. I realized that perhaps I was committing a crime, that I shouldn't trust my heart, since it was a blind, unknown force, it could crown a man with supreme happiness, but it could also lead him into the depths of hell. But I didn't turn back. I was risking everything, but I had to find out who Peter Pashov and his son, Alexander Pashov, were.

I had just stepped out of the gate when Nusha appeared in front of me on her bike. She was so pleasantly surprised at our meeting that she didn't notice the state I was in, and as soon as she got off her bike, she started telling me a dream she had had. She had dreamed of me in black clothes, coming down a hill and disappearing into some red abyss. Black and red meant something good, so some kind of happiness was in store for me and she had been coming to tell me. My heart quivered with joy at seeing her, but at the same time I wondered how she could have decided to come see me, after we had parted a few days ago without saying goodbye and without agreeing on a new meeting. Had she heard what my brother was saying and in spite of that had come, or did she think he had had something confidential to tell me connected to our party business? In any case, she had slunk off as if thrown out and any young lady in her place would have shown a certain pride. Or perhaps she "didn't have time" for such considerations?

Perhaps it was because I had to break it off with her for good, or at least temporarily, but to me it seemed that she had never before looked so lovely. She was dressed in a navy-blue blouse with white spots and a light skirt, her short hair was tousled like a mischievous boy's, her face, which was tanned, was radiant with some inner light. While she was telling me her dream, I wondered how to send her away and realized that I did not have the strength to do so. *Yes,* I thought to myself, *she truly did foresee my state in her dream, I really have fallen into the "red" abyss of love, where I was overcome by pangs of conscience over my lost honor.* If it turned out that she was being put up to it and, as my brother claimed, that she was trying to save her father and brother from the people's punishment through amorous games, then I deserved an even more severe punishment. Thus even if she was playing some unconscious role and even if she did sincerely love me, I had to break off our relations until her father's situation was clarified. The previous night Radio Moscow had reported that the Third Ukrainian Front had surrounded German units in the Iasi-Chisinau region. No matter how the war developed, the Soviet Army would be here in Bulgaria within a month at the latest, and in that time Nusha's father's fate would be decided. I had thought of secretly contacting him and telling him he was being accused of betrayal. If he really was a traitor, he would take preventative measures and that would be proof of his guilt.

The sun was already setting and that dusky toil- and heat-exhausted August silence, with its restful scent of ripe fruit, threshed hay, and near and distant noises, had settled over the village. A threshing machine rumbled mutedly from the upper part of the village, a light-golden cloud of hay dust wafted over the yards and gardens, smoke slowly and solemnly rose from the chimneys, at first thick and white, then ethereally blue as if from a pipe, from the fields came the jangling of carts, sparrows twittered in the thick, heat-scorched foliage of the orchard trees. All of that, both the noises and the scents, fused into a single tired sigh from the workday, which in an hour would be sitting at the table, and after that would give itself over to a short-lived, deep, and sweet summer sleep. Would I, too, close my eyes in sleep, or would I sit in bed with a book in my hand, or would I wander through the garden and the fields until morning, as I had been doing for weeks now? For whole nights I had pondered what to do about Nusha and her father, the time had come to act, yet I had neither the strength nor the desire for it. Would I not be committing a sacrilege against my heart, against Nusha's innocence, and even against nature itself, so still in this wonderful moment of contemplation, if I insisted upon a separation, against which my whole being rebelled?

Perhaps everything between us would have finished by the garden gate or somewhere along the road if my landlord Anani had not appeared, coming from the fields. He was still disconcerted by me, and when he saw Nusha, he stopped his cart for a moment, then turned down another road in order to enter his yard through the other gate. I asked Nusha to come inside, so as to give him the opportunity to finish his work in peace. Our previous meetings had always been outside, in the yard or the field, now Nusha came into my room for the first time. My furnishings – insofar as there were any furnishings to speak of – were extremely modest: a rag rug on the dirt floor, a table, a few chairs, a bed, and two large shelves of books, which Anani had quickly fixed up after I had moved in.

"You have so many books! My brother has books too, but not this many," Nusha said, looking at the books with her head cocked to one side so as to be able to read the titles. "Ah, there's *Anna Karenina*! I wanted to read it a few years ago even, but Lexy said I was too young and hid the book. Please give it to me to read. I'll give it back in a few days. Can I look at it?"

"Of course, why don't you sit down?"

Nusha took the book, sat down at the table, and started looking through it.

Now I had to tell her about our impending separation.

"Nusha, the day before yesterday I went to a doctor in the city and he insisted that I go to a sanatorium in the mountains. Otherwise there's a risk that my sickness will get worse and other cavities will open up. If I can't get into any sanatorium, I need to isolate myself completely and not meet up with anyone. You know that the local people, when they're sick with tuberculosis, they build huts in the woods and live there alone. I may be forced to isolate myself in the woods too."

As if to confirm what I had said, a spasm rose up in my lungs, I barely managed to take the little metal box out of my pocket, I turned my back to Nusha and spit into it. When I recovered from my coughing fit and turned toward her again, she had stood up from her chair and was looking at me with shining, unmoving eyes. Her suntanned face had turned a brownish pale, her hand had frozen on top of the book on the table. The evening burst in through the window in cold waves along with the dying, gentle glow of the sunset, out in the yard a bluish sphere of twilight settled along the fence, objects lost their outlines and colors and fused into dark blotches.

"When will you go?" Nusha asked.

"Perhaps tomorrow or the next day."

"Have you gotten ready?"

"I don't have all that much to get ready."

Nusha walked around the table and stepped over to me, and I could see that she was shaking as if with fever, while her eyes were shining ever more strongly and drily.

"I'll come with you!" she said. "I'll get a room next to yours and…"

"But how, Nusha? That's impossible."

"What, don't you want me to go with you? Tell me, please just tell me."
But she didn't give me a chance to tell her in any case, but went on talking
as if delirious. "I'll tell Mom and Dad this very night that I'm going with
you to the sanatorium to help you. They'll let me go, they'll definitely
let me go, they won't try to stop me. And they'll give me money. They
are good people, they love you and know you need to go get treatment.
But I have to be there with you, don't I, to help you get better as soon as
possible. I know you're going to recover, but I want to be closer to you. I
won't bother you. If you don't want to see me, you'll leave notes by the
door telling me what you need and I'll leave it for you in the same way."

While telling me this, she kept pressing against me ever more closely,
while I backed away. I could see she was not in her right mind and did not
realize what she was doing, I stepped back and put out my hands as a barrier between us. As always, I was afraid of infecting her, but she took my
hands in hers and squeezed them so tightly that I could feel the strength
in her fingers, warm and as hard as pincers.

"If you don't get better… If you don't get better, I won't go on living!
Do you know that, do you?"

We sat down on my bed and spent almost an hour holding hands like
that, then I took her back to her village. I rode the bike, while she sat in
my arms. We kept silent the whole way, as if we knew that even the most
beautiful words could not express what had happened between us. I left
her by the garden gate and went back to my village on foot. Even when
we parted we didn't say anything about my impending departure or about
our next meeting, as if we had become one mind and one body and there
was no need to share our thoughts and desires aloud.

The next day I hardly waited for evening to fall before starting out for
Nusha's village. I had decided to go to their place, even though she had
not invited me, but she had also set out toward mine, so we met halfway.

How I looked in the people's eyes, at that intense time at the end of the harvest and the beginning of threshing, on the eve of political events such as the entrance of the Soviet Army into Bulgaria, I found out later from friends – and of course, from my brother. In his eyes, I naturally looked like the most pathetic individual ever, for whose sake he was "burning with shame" in front of other people and especially the communists. I realized that precisely at that tense time when the political fate of not only the party and the people, but perhaps of the whole world as well, was being decided, I should not give myself over to my personal feelings to such an extent, to say nothing of having a love affair with the daughter of our eventual enemy. Sometimes I thought that the people among whom I lived found something selfish and indecent in my love, so devoted and beautiful, but still, at the end of the day, I ignored all considerations and set out for Nusha's village or waited for her at home. No more was said about my going to a sanatorium, even though another cavity opened up in my lungs at that time.

Only when Bagryanov's government resigned and the advance units of the Third Ukrainian Front reached the Bulgarian border at Silistra did I remember the danger threatening Nusha's father. I had read fiction and political literature about the revolution in Russia and I knew what it meant to be a person accused of treachery by the revolution. At the height of the chaos, the first days were lawless, there was no investigation or trials for the guilty and suspected. Not only those who had been, but those who would be, enemies of the revolution were condemned to death. If it turned out that Nusha's brother had worked against us too, the same doom would loom over their family as well.

The first thing that occurred to me was to go to Varna, where the trial against the twelve youth communist league members had been held, and to acquaint myself with the case. I didn't want to alarm Nusha and her family, but still I had managed to learn from my conversations with her that her father had not even been called as a claimant in the case, that he didn't know who had stolen his canvas threshing machine cover, he hadn't reported anything about it to anyone, nor had he known that the canvas had fallen into the hands of the partisans. It was most likely that Lexy had arranged for it to be "stolen," but it was more believable that someone had stolen it for money. Speaking of money, I had asked Nusha how much money Lexy's stay in Switzerland had cost and she replied that her father had not sent money because he didn't know his address, and that his stay abroad was a painful mystery for their family, even though they were sure that Lexy had been sent there by the party. That and several other facts gave me grounds to believe that Lexy was "hiding" abroad and was working for our intelligence, and that his father was not and could not be a traitor, even if he didn't share his son's convictions. The most indisputable fact concerning Petar Pashov's innocence was that his daughter was in intimate relations with me, which could cost her her life, or at least a bout of tuberculosis. According to people in the village, our relationship was based on my despair and her sheer lunacy, and Nusha never talked about how her parents explained and allowed this relationship.

I left for Varna to look at the case of the twelve young men and to convince myself fully that Nusha's father had been slandered or was the victim of a misunderstanding. The only person who could help me get my hands on the court archives was my fellow student and friend, Metodi Savov, with whom I had graduated from law school a year earlier. Metko's father, Georgi Savov, was one of the most prominent lawyers in our region and had a large clientele. From Metko I knew that his father was a Social Democrat who, as far as I could recall, had later gone over to the Communist Party. Georgi Savov had defended almost all the defendants accused under the Law for the Defense of the Nation, but inexplicably he hadn't taken part in the trial against the twelve young men. It turned out that Petar Pashov had been his client for many years. He also knew

Lexy, who had come to his practice on some errands for his father. When I briefly told him the story about the stolen canvas cover, the lawyer was astonished that Pashov hadn't been called into court as a claimant or witness, since he had seen and recognized the thief and, what was more inexplicable, especially after he had told the investigating institutions the name of the thief.

The three of us long mulled over what to do and the lawyer suggested, before we looked over the case, that we meet and talk to Miho Barakov and find out from him why, despite his testimony in court, he had told his comrades that Petar Pashov was a traitor. Was it true, or had other interested parties spread that rumor? We asked the prosecution for permission to visit Miho Barakov in prison, they put us off for two days and in the end refused our request. The reasons for this refusal were likely the events that were developing with mind-boggling speed and the general confusion. Muraviev's government had taken power and had published a declaration of full neutrality. Moshanov was authorized to hold negotiations for a truce with representatives of England and the United States. Rumors ran through town that partisan detachments were nearing the city. It was said that ships and planes from the Soviet maritime front were sinking German ships, which were fleeing toward the Bosphorus and the Dardanelles.

I spent those days waiting for permission to visit the prison with Nusha's former landlords. I had told her that I was going to the doctor for a day or two, and she gave me a letter so I wouldn't have to wander around looking for a hotel. The elderly couple joyfully welcomed me, and after we chatted a bit, I realized how much they loved Nusha and her brother, who had also lived with them during his high school years. In the afternoon we went to the courthouse and asked to see the case, but here again our request was refused. Savov went to the chief justice of the court and to the prosecutor, but in vain – access to the archives was strictly forbidden. We could only get to them through an insider and that insider was the examining magistrate on the case. While Miho Barakov had denied in court that Pashov had betrayed him, the examining magistrate had declared that Pashov had told him the name of the person who had stolen his canvas cover. We had to find out whether the magistrate really had identified Pashov as a witness to the crime. Savov found out the name and address of the examining magistrate from his colleague who had defended the twelve young communists, but refused to go see him. They were not on good terms, and he was sure that Marchinkov, that was the magistrate's name, would not let him anywhere near the archives and would not tell us anything of what interested us. Now all representatives of the justice system and especially examining magistrates on political cases were awaiting the impending events very uneasily for obvious reasons and didn't want to give any explanations whatsoever about their work, especially where political trials were concerned. If someone nevertheless managed to get in touch with Magistrate Marchinkov, it should not be a lawyer who had defended communists in the past or individuals tried under the Law for the Defense of the Nation. For this reason Savov refused to deal with Marchinkov and it was up to me to take on this task.

I went to his home three times and never managed to find him there. An old woman sent me to his office, from there they sent me back to his home. It was clear that he was hiding or had already skipped town, and that meant that very many and very serious transgressions weighed on his conscience. A hellish heat came pouring down on the city, the asphalt stuck to the soles of my shoes, I was about to drop from exhaustion, I was hungry, too. In the Sea Garden, I had already eaten the food I had brought from the village, and I didn't dare ask Metko to borrow some money, nor could I eat lunch and dinner at Nusha's landlords'. In the evening I came back late when they were already sleeping, and in the morning I went out early, turning down the breakfast they offered me. I had borrowed a bit of money from Anani, of that I only had two leva left, besides what I needed for the return trip, to buy bread and a kilo of tomatoes. And so it was until the evening of the third day. I was completely exhausted from the heat, plus I had a temperature, but rather than going back to my lodgings, I went to look for Marchinkov one more time. My persistence could not help but impress him, if he hadn't yet skipped town or was hiding at his home. I was sure that he had been watching me from somewhere or listening in on my conversations with the old woman, whom I invariably and very politely asked to inform Mr. Marchinkov that I wanted to tell him something of great importance to himself. My appearance and behavior must have inspired a certain confidence, and he finally agreed to see me. He led me into a room with high and long unpainted walls, with creaking floorboards and drawn curtains. A lightbulb without a lamp shade hung from the ceiling, barely lighting up the middle of the room.

The dingy ambience filled me with doubts whether I was finally talking to the person I had so persistently sought. I had imagined the home of a magistrate, a lawyer by education, if not swimming in luxury, at least clean and cozy. It crossed my mind that perhaps he was pretending to be poor by receiving me in such a room, but he himself resembled the room. I had interned at the court and had seen many magistrates and had formed a rather different idea about that class of people, to put it broadly – more physically imposing and more dignified. This man was around fifty, of average height and thin, almost skin and bones, with thinning, close-cropped hair, with a dry face and a sharply hooked nose such that his face looked as if made out of cartilage. But his ears were even more eye-catching, as they were disproportionately large for his head, and bent forward, dry and translucent like the wings of a bat. He knew that he had the biggest ears if not in the whole country, then in the whole city, he knew what a shocking impression they made on others, and for this reason he was sitting in front of me in half profile, as he likely sat in front of all his interlocutors. But his eyes were large as well, dark and warm, and they peered at me from beneath the shelter of his brow bone like two intelligent creatures. And his hands, which he was holding in front of himself in his lap, small, white, and covered with jutting veins, looked somehow smart, gentle, and cautious.

"How can I be of assistance to you?" he asked once we were sitting across from each other under the weak light of the lamp.

I introduced myself and told him all the most important things – my first name and surname, where I was born, my education – and in the end I added that we could be mutually helpful to each other if we spoke clearly and openly. Political events were developing so quickly that we needed to spare all unnecessary considerations and save every minute.

"Yes, go on." His eyes, those warm and intelligent creatures, were on guard under the shelter of his brow bone.

I had been thinking for so long of what questions I would ask him and the tone I would take with him that now I didn't know where to start. The thought that the impending conversation with this man could be life changing for Nusha's father and for our happiness kept me in a state of constant, ever-growing anxiety and strained my nerves to the very limit. I was exhausted by the day's heat, and hungry, too, on top of everything. That he had so long and so persistently refused to meet with me meant that a good outcome of our conversation depended largely on my questions and comportment. In my desire to have a frank conversation with him, however, I said that I was a communist and had connections to all the party leaders in the district. That, it seemed, sounded to him like a threat or at least a condition for the following conversation. His white hands, which were lying in his lap, twitched nervously, and it seemed to me that he was holding some object in his palms. With my appearance and with my feverish restlessness I probably looked like an impatient, vengeful fanatic come to settle the score with him, and now not only his eyes but he himself was on guard.

"I'm interested in the case of the twelve young men from last year. You were the examining magistrate on the case, were you not?"

"What more specifically are you interested in?"

"Why you didn't call the main witness Petar Pashov into court?"

"Pashov?"

"Do you remember the name? He was precisely the one from whom Miho Barakov stole the canvas, and that theft was the reason the criminal case was brought against him. Petar Pashov personally told you the name of the thief, who was arrested after the investigation established that Miho Barakov had stolen the canvas under the party's orders."

Marchinkov fell silent and his gaze seemed to fall on an old cabinet behind me. It crossed my mind that someone could be hidden in that cabinet, who could come to his aid if necessary and act as a witness to our conversation. But that person, likely the magistrate's official executioner, could rough me up as well, since I had so carelessly declared that I had connections to party leaders. They could torture me to find out their names and to liquidate them before the Soviet Army entered Bulgaria. I didn't know a single party leader, of course, I had said it to give myself more gravitas and to imply that I was speaking in the name of people who tomorrow might show certain lenience toward him, should that be necessary. But did I really know what kind of person the magistrate was? Many people like him acted in various ways in the face of the impending events. As I found out later, some fell into complete despair, others fled abroad, yet others tried to cover their tracks by destroying documents, witnesses, and those whom they expected to seek revenge. Many such thoughts went through my head as he sat there silently. I was gripped by the fear that I of my own free will had stumbled into his trap, from which I would not escape unpunished, if only for the fact that I was trying to put him in the role of the one being investigated, and at a moment when time was still on his side, at that. The Soviet Army had reached our border, but it might not cross it today or tomorrow as we expected, it could delay crossing for a month for tactical reasons. Marchinkov and others like him had a certain chance to act as they saw fit.

"Are you this... Pashov's son, or some other relative?"

"I told you who and what I am. Here is my ID card. I should have shown it to you in the very beginning."

"There's no need. I did not lead the investigation on that case, sir."

"But at the court..."

"Yes, at the court they told you I had led it. But only in the beginning. Due to certain considerations I had to turn the investigation over to another. I cannot tell you his name, you can find it out from the court."

"In that case, Mr. Marchinkov, I beg you to forgive me for disturbing you. What a shame that you did not lead the investigation. I have the feeling that you would have informed me fully on the questions that interest me. Now that I know you had no part in the case, I can tell you that I am not interceding for a communist, but for a nonparty, yet not guilty, person – Petar Pashov. He is a wealthy villager, he is not involved in politics, but he was slandered and his innocence must be proven at all costs."

"I understand," Marchinkov said, and got up.

I got up and saw that there was nothing in his delicate white hands, or he had managed to hide whatever it was in his pockets. He went ahead to open the door for me and it was then I felt my strength leave me and my knees give way. I fell backward and if I had not grabbed the chair, I would have fallen onto the floor.

"Allow me to rest for a minute," I said. "I feel unwell."

"You are sick, you are covered with sweat."

"I am sick and exhausted and hungry."

"Rest a bit!" Marchinkov said. "I'll be back in a moment." A few minutes later he came back with a small wooden tray upon which he had placed two rolls, a glass of yogurt, and a chunk of cheese. "Eat, get your strength up, don't worry. And take off your suit coat, why are you wearing a coat in this heat? Are you ill with tuberculosis?"

"Yes, how did you know?"

"My brother had it once... So, you say... that Petar Pashov was slandered. Before I handed the case of the twelve young men over to my colleague, there was some question of a Pashov, from Zhitnitsa, I believe."

"Yes, that's the one."

"His son had left for Switzerland, right? Do you know him?"

"Yes, we're friends."

"And because of that friendship you have come to try to save his father, despite the terrible condition you're in?"

"Not only because of friendship."

"You were the one who declared that we needed to speak openly."

"Of course. I'm in love with his sister."

"And does she return your feelings?"

"Oh, yes! Her parents know of our relationship as well and will allow us to marry when I recover."

"I'm very happy for you, Mr. Kralev."

While we were talking, I was eating. I realized that it was indecent of me to take food from hands that were possibly stained with the blood of innocent people, but I couldn't stand the hunger. In the meantime he had entered into his role as investigator and seemed to be taking advantage of my physical and spiritual weakness, and was calmly "wringing me dry." I had no will to resist, nor did I exercise even the most ordinary caution. I asked myself why I was confessing such intimate things to him, yet I told him that I wanted to save my love and my happiness. Later, when I recalled that meeting, I bitterly felt that I had not shown the necessary pride, but on the other hand, whatever I may have told the investigator, I subconsciously gave him to understand that he was dealing with a person who could not and should not be taken lightly. He likely understood very well that he was dealing with a sick and agitated person who was in no condition to pretend, thus my weakness turned out to be useful. As far as he had heard from his colleague who had led the investigation, as well as from other clerks at the court, the name of Petar Pashov had not figured in the investigation, as he had not accused anyone of stealing the canvas. This story was made up, most likely by the main defendant Miho Barakov for some unknown reasons...

"My dear young colleague, this seems unbelievable to you, does it not?" he said, when he saw my bewilderment and disbelief. "I would be willing to bet that you take it as a deception on the part of the enemy with the intent to sow unrest among your ranks. Fine, you should have warned Petar Pashov, your future father-in-law, that you were setting out to save his honor and his life. But you did not tell him of your intentions because you were afraid that he might truly be mixed up in this business and might take some measure to erase the proof of his treachery. Am I wrong in my assumption?"

"Unfortunately, no," I said. "But despite that I still want you to show me the case. Only then will I fully believe you."

"I have no reason to lie to you, Mr. Kralev. I am an expert and believe me if you will, but I have never toyed with the facts. You are a lawyer and you know the place and the significance of a criminal case. The sentence depends on my investigation – that is, the trial is prepared based on the investigation. Perhaps it is precisely because of this that you suspect that I could have altered the facts, whether due to bribes or to political convictions. I've never had need for bribes, I'm fairly well off in the material sense, and as far as my political convictions are concerned – I don't belong to any party. I'm not a fascist nor a communist. Political ideas usurp one's will and conscience and urge one toward transgressions. Yet I am not a sterile person, either. I, too, serve an idea, and it is the idea of discovering all the traces of a crime. In and of itself, this search is not only science, it is also an art to which I have dedicated myself ever since my youth. If one day you decide to dedicate yourself to investigative work, and as a calling at that, you will understand what I am saying. It is a passion, the creation of a novel far more interesting than those that are written. I have tried to stand between the extremes, to judge people's actions as impartially as possible. The final result of a case, however, depends on the skill and conscience of the prosecutors, judges, and lawyers, who do not always deal conscientiously with the facts I give them. This is what happened in the case you are interested in. Initially the investigation was assigned to me. I was just getting a handle on the case when the chief prosecutor and a few people from the police began to put pressure on me. I announced that I would not allow anyone to meddle in my work. A few days later they reassigned the case to another colleague, who was young, ambitious, and above all, a fascist. He was instructed by the relevant institutions to construct the case such that the trial would strike several blows. Namely – to smash the communist youth league, to make Petar Pashov a sacrificial victim by opposing him and his son, whom the police suspected of being an important communist. He had gone to Switzerland to study, but the police didn't know exactly why. And finally, they wanted to reestablish the government's prestige.

"The reversal on the Eastern Front made a strong impression on people's political consciousness. Some were disillusioned by fascism, others oriented themselves toward Russia, while still others, communists and their sympathizers, turned to direct subversive action, partisan units grew in number and size. The government was looking for an opportunity to frighten its political opponents and that case presented itself. Or rather the government orchestrated the case so as to show that its positions were strong and unshakable despite the crisis on the Eastern Front and that it wouldn't hesitate to sentence even trifling antigovernmental acts like giving a few leva in support of the communist movement. That was the reason for so much buzz around the case, and that's why so many sentences were handed down.

"From what I've said thus far you can probably guess why Miho Barakov spread the rumor that Petar Pashov was a traitor. From the information I managed to gather about his family, I understood that his father is an experienced political player and all-around daredevil. His son, the youngest one, actively "joined" the antifascist struggle after the disaster at Stalingrad. There is no way the wealthiest man in the village could not have realized, just as all the others like him did, that the tragedy at Stalingrad had decided the war in favor of the Russians, hence a bit of political insurance wouldn't hurt. The Bolsheviks are coming here, but we've got a communist in the family, who was interrogated and thrown into prison by the fascist government. For some time now I've noticed that most people are looking for a way to make nice with the communists, by whatever means. Fear of the Bolsheviks is making people their followers and they are willing to take certain risks. But the Barakov case has a more distant and certain aim. The younger Pashov has been compromised by his father and even if, despite this, he is named to some important post, he'll be forced to show a certain leniency toward others' mistakes.

"Besides that, their son was beaten while being interrogated after his arrest, in spite of which he took all the responsibility on himself. What fault of his is it if one of the kids couldn't hold out under torture and gave away his comrades? As far as I understood from my colleague, who came to consult with me about some questions during the investigation, your hero Barakov left that list with the twelve names in his apartment in a place where it would easily be found by the authorities. The names were written out by some semiliterate servant woman of his landlords. Despite being a fascist (he fled the city the day before yesterday) and endlessly ambitious, my colleague was nevertheless seriously concerned by the machinations they forced him to introduce into the investigation and came to consult with me. I told him what I thought, but since he'd already joined the dance, he had to pay the fiddler, and as became clear later, he couldn't stand up to the authorities' pressure. He also told me that your hero had been made up during the investigation to look beaten and during the trials faked injuries from the beating he had supposedly taken."

The next day Marchinkov gave me a copy of the twelve's sentence, we said goodbye and I immediately went to Miho's former landlords, from whom I found out the name and address of their former servant. Her name was Marga. I found her at her home in the Levski neighborhood. She was sitting with her husband in the little garden in front of their tiny house, lighting a fire in the hearth. Both her face and her body were somehow deformed. Her husband was blind, but he was very skillfully peeling potatoes, cutting them, and putting them in a pot. The reason for my visit was the greetings I was bringing from Miho Barakov. I told them that Miho's brother had opened a cloth store and needed a servant. The pay was good, the work was only until noon, but the servant needed to know how to write well enough to write down the clients' names. I was lying through my teeth, as they say, because I was afraid that if I told her the truth she would get scared and send me away. I have no idea what I would have told her if, taking into consideration the impending events, she had thought to ask me how Miho's brother was opening a store when all the other shopkeepers were closing up their shutters and wondering where to hide. But I didn't know how else to wrench a line or two of handwriting out of her.

The blind man sat there silently peeling potatoes, while she got up and went into the house. *Wouldn't you know,* I thought to myself while waiting for her to come back, *until now the fate of Pashov and his family depended on two big ears, now it depends on one freakish woman.*

"Well sure I know how to write," she said when she came back with a bottle of cooking oil and sat down by the fire. "I finished the second grade, plus Miho taught me to read and write, didn't he. Our poor old Miho was a good boy, but he went and landed himself in jail with that crazy business of his. He lived all by his lonesome in that shed, and I cleaned for him, washed and ironed his clothes for him. Now and then he'd tell me: "Auntie Marga, why don't I teach you to write a little prettier, so when I become a big-time communist, I'll make you a boss somewhere." I told her that she really could become a boss somewhere, only that now I needed to see whether she really could write neatly. I gave her my notebook, she set it on a stool and started writing the names I dictated to her. They were the names of the twelve young men. When she got to the fifth name, she stopped to think. I was scared that she would remember the names Miho had dictated to her, so I took my notebook and told her that I liked her handwriting and that Miho's brother would come looking for her in a week or so. She wanted to treat me to some rosehip jam, but I refused. I said goodbye and went out onto the street.

I took the bus that same afternoon and by the evening I was in Nusha's village. Nusha had been waiting for me for three days, she was waiting for me now. She had thought something bad had happened to me, and had been ready to come looking for me the next day. Sometimes life is so generous with its grief and joys that it makes your heart want to burst. On the bus I read in the paper that the Soviet Union had declared war on Bulgaria, which meant that Soviet troops would be crossing our border any minute now. I also brought the copy of the sentence which showed that Nusha's father had been slandered and that now he was not in any danger. While I recounted all my trials and tribulations trying to fight that slanderous accusation, he listened to me so calmly that I even felt to some extent unjustified in the efforts I had made to save his life. Nusha and her mother listened to my story with great agitation, they were stunned by Miho's act.

"Well, I saw that the rag, the canvas, I mean, was missing only at harvesttime when the machine operator said we ought to get it ready for threshing," Pashov said. "It never even crossed my mind to go looking for it or to go all the way to the city to report it to the police. My brother-in-law wanted to serve me up as a sacrifice to the communists, so hopefully they'd forgive his sins from back in '23."

And he told us of the fate of the village teacher from that time. He had been close with Pashov's father, since they had been in the army together and later were even sent to war together. Around the events of 1923 the teacher disappeared for a while and when he came back, he wanted Pashov's father to hide him at his home. The teacher was from central Bulgaria, he had led a band at the time of the uprising and now the police were looking for him all over the country. His father took him in, but a week later a man came to the teacher with a letter. When he read the letter, the teacher asked to be moved to some other place right away, or if they didn't have anyone they trusted, to take him to the Romanian border one night. His father fixed up the cellar under the barn and promised to hide him from the police as long as was necessary, but the teacher insisted on moving.

Petar Pashov had suggested to his father that he take the teacher to Stoyu Barakov in our village. They were brothers-in-law, relatives, he could trust him. He agreed from the very start and swore on his honor to keep the secret. Pashov would stop by to see the teacher and to leave him fresh clothes and something to eat. Once the teacher asked him to take a letter to someone. He went to Varna, delivered the letter to the address indicated, and brought back the answer. The teacher read the letter and asked the elder Pashov to come and see him. When he came back home, the elder Pashov said that the teacher had to leave for Varna the following Wednesday, and from there he would go to the Soviet Union. When Pashov went on Wednesday evening to pick him up and take him by cart to Varna, Stoyu Barakov began wailing and beating himself around the head. The teacher had disappeared. He had gone out the previous evening as always to stroll around the garden and hadn't come back. Pashov believed him, he didn't know his brother-in-law was a member of the Democratic

Union Party, which was in power at the time. A month passed after the incident and he was elected mayor. Shortly thereafter he bought fifty acres of municipal land for a song and got another fifty for free on top of that and became the richest man in the village.

Years later the senior municipal policeman told Pashov, when they started talking about those times, that Stoyu Barakov had betrayed the teacher to the authorities. He had come to the town hall and told the police superintendent, who happened to be there, how and when to catch him. That very night Bay Doncho received orders to arrest the teacher and bring him to the city. When he found out about this business, the elder Pashov was sick with grief. "A fine job the two of us did, we threw the man to the wolves and now we don't know if he's alive or dead!" He spoke this way until the end of his life, because his conscience was gnawing at him, and he swore never to set foot in Barakov's house and never to admit any of his family into his home.

"I don't know what the investigator's aim was, but he explained Barakov's politics to you very well," Petar Pashov added. "Back in the day he threatened that if we raised a stink about the teacher, he would tell the authorities who had hidden him in their home. He also used to say that communists like my son belonged behind bars, but when he saw which way the wind was blowing, he made his own son a communist. Both to wash away his own shame from back then, but also to put a black mark on my son's name by means of my treachery. You did well to uncover his machinations, but in the end, everything will depend on Lexy. But where he is, whether he's alive, and when he'll come back, the Lord only knows…"

A wave of worry and sorrow spread over his face, while his wife crossed herself and her eyes filled with tears. I wanted to console them so I said that according to investigator Marchinkov, who could be trusted, the police consider Lexy a very important communist who is "hidden" or planted somewhere abroad, and since the police have confirmed it, that meant Lexy would be coming back right after the Soviet troops entered Bulgaria. We talked for a long time after that and in the evening I got up to leave, but Nusha and her parents would not let me go for anything in the world and suggested that I sleep at their house. I refused to stay, but I dozed off during dinner. I only remember Nusha and her mother grabbing me under the arms and leading me somewhere, I heard a soft voice telling me "here, here."

At noon I looked for my brother in the community center, where he went every day to listen to the news. We hadn't seen each other in more than a month. I didn't dare go to their home, as Kichka was afraid I would infect their daughter, nor had they come looking for me. For some time after I had left the house, Kichka had kept making food for me and leaving it under the awning of the barn, where I ate lunch and dinner alone. When my relations with my brother deteriorated, I stopped eating at their place. Kichka sent me food via a neighbor, but I sent it back. I also sent back the money my brother sent me via other people. I gave them to understand that I was not taking any charity from them. My brother also sent me a letter, in which he begged me to take his money and go to a sanatorium. I knew that he was suffering both because of my illness and because of my love for Nusha, who, in his opinion, had driven me to ruin both as a man and as a communist, "right now, when all our hopes have almost come true." That's what he wrote me in his letter. But "right now" I was the happiest person in the world. Perhaps I had only a short time left to live, but I was happy. My love for Nusha, threatened by the impending events, had been saved once and for all. My brotherly love had been saved as well, without which both my and Stoyan's lives would be miserable. Now I was bringing him that salvation in a green folder with hard covers, upon which was written *Copy of the Sentence in Criminal Case such-and-such.* This document would clear up the misunderstandings between us and once again open our hearts to each other.

The radio announced the government's decision to break all diplomatic ties to Germany and to declare war on Bulgaria's former ally. They also announced that the government had issued a decree giving amnesty to political prisoners. After the news, I asked my brother to step outside as I had something exceptionally important to tell him. He was so surprised that he stopped and fell silent for a full minute, then something like a smile flashed across his face.

"Did somebody whisper it to you in the city or there?"

He nodded toward the west, where Nusha's village lay. I told him that "there" had no part in this matter and that nevertheless they had been slandered. Now his smile expressed disappointment. So that's what it is, this exceptionally important thing that I had to tell him – a new and useless attempt to clear the Pashovs' name. But when he read the copy of the sentence, he was stunned. We were sitting in Anani's yard, in the shade of the walnut tree. He had gone very pale and large beads of sweat formed on his brow. I took the folder from him and then he said: "It's terrible, what's written there… if it's true."

"Do you doubt it?"

"Could that investigator have falsified the copy of the sentence? At this point they're capable of anything and everything to save their own skins."

I told him that he could go to the city tomorrow himself to compare the copy of the sentence with the original, since the investigator was at our disposal. I also told him about Stoyu Barakov's treachery in 1923, which could be confirmed by the senior municipal police officer from that time, Bay Doncho. This earlier betrayal was the cause of the present one. Barakov had been warned by the police that the younger Pashov was an important communist agent, and likely following the police's instructions, he had taken advantage of the case of the stolen canvas to compromise the father in the communists' eyes. Barakov joined the Agrarian Party, while his youngest son got in with the youth communist league. The party's political program was long since common knowledge – after the victory, it would rule together with the agrarians and other parties. If Alexander Pashov returned alive and well, he could seek revenge for the betrayal of the teacher in 1923, but his father would also have turned Miho Barakov over to the fascist police. In the worst case scenario, the two families would now be quits – the fathers both committed political crimes, while the sons are active communists. Let bygones be bygones…

We sat there talking until late in the afternoon. No matter how indisputable my evidence of Pashov's innocence and of the Barakovs' guilt was, my brother somehow couldn't quite accept it wholeheartedly. It seemed unbelievable to him that "on my own initiative," and as sick as I was, I had managed to wrench this evidence from some fascist investigator. My efforts in and of themselves led him to believe that I hadn't conducted this investigation from a desire to uncover the truth, but rather because I was biased toward the Pashovs. Even if that was the case, there was no reason to doubt this truth, yet he doubted it. He had to act quickly, but he still couldn't decide on any definite action. I had read and told him about the complicated and contradictory paths the Russian socialist revolution had taken, about the dramatic interweaving of many, many human destinies, yet it was hard for him to accept that in our struggle, too, not everything was going smoothly and in a single direction. His notion of complex political battles, of people, and of the world as a whole were quite limited. Besides that, he was mistrustful and suspicious. He understood the conspiratorial system the party had taught him only in terms of cautiousness, and this prevented him from acting independently in a given set of circumstances.

"The investigator was right in explaining to you that more-or-less cautious people do everything they can to adapt themselves to circumstances," he said. "Since the Barakovs have done it, why shouldn't the Pashovs do it too? No one knows for certain who the younger Pashov is serving. If Miho Barakov has committed treachery right under our noses and we didn't realize it, how are we supposed to know what your friend is up to in some foreign country?"

What could I do in these circumstances? I was drained from exhaustion and stress, I was spitting up more blood than usual, but my brother would not even put me in touch with the party's regional committee. He was afraid that the committee would order Miho to be isolated from his comrades in prison and he would realize he'd been unmasked (if he really was a traitor), and the police would try to erase all traces of him. Either they would liquidate him, so he wouldn't fall into our hands after getting out of prison, or they would liquidate those of us who they suspected of unmasking him. That could be the two of us, for example, since the investigator had revealed Miho's treachery to us. Thus we could turn the copy of the sentence over to the committee only if we were absolutely sure that Soviet troops would be coming across the border the next day. But whether they would cross the border tomorrow or in a month, that was something nobody could guarantee. Just two days would be enough for the police to carry out a pogrom on all the communists in our region…

They had already announced on the radio that German troops had retreated to Yugoslavia, thus the Soviet Army had no reason to wait at our border twiddling their thumbs since they knew that in Bulgaria they would not face any resistance. But even that fact seemed unconvincing to my brother. To prove to him that his caution was unnecessary, that very night I seized power myself. It was the sixth of September. I went to the mayor, Bay Yanko, explained the political situation to him and asked him to give me the key to the town hall. He was a shrewd man and immediately agreed.

"But afterward you'll say you came at me with a weapon in hand. Because it's shameful to turn over power just like that. I'll be a laughing-stock…"

He gave me two old rifles, a revolver, and the village seal, and after that we acted out a small comedic skit. I put him "under arrest" in the neighboring room and wrote the new government's first proclamation in the name of the people:

> *We beseech the village inhabitants, upon hearing the signal of the schoolhouse bell, to come out onto the square in front of the town hall to meet the Soviet soldiers with bread and salt! Chairman of the Fatherland Front.*

I scrawled out an illegible signature, stamped the village mayor's seal on it, and went to put the proclamation up on the community center door. The young people I met there finished off the rest of the job themselves. They started ringing the schoolhouse bell and spread the news through-out the village. In half an hour, the people started gathering in front of the town hall. Stoyan arrived as well, surprised and excited, but when I told him what was going on, he called me off to the side and started scolding me, accusing me of playing games that could end up being very costly for us, and that on the eve of the great event itself, no less. I turned over the village seal and the weapons to him as a symbol of power, he outfitted three men with the rifles and the revolver and told the rest of the young men to arm themselves with whatever they could and to spend the night guarding the village. He, of course, did not fail to inform them that Soviet troops had not yet crossed the border and that I had taken it upon myself to announce their arrival, for which the police could slaughter us like lambs, being as defenseless as we were.

The young men were not the least bit fazed and went to carry out their military mission. The celebration marking the establishment of the new village government could not be put off. The square in front of the town hall slowly filled up with people, the youngsters brought out the gramophone from the community center and started dancing.

People from the nearest houses brought out wine and brandy, bagpipes and flutes started squealing, and the older folks joined in a traditional round dance. Stoyan went to set up guards around the village and came back only when people were already going home. We locked up the town hall and went our separate ways in silence. The establishment of the Fatherland Front government, which we had so long been awaiting, had not been celebrated with speeches and solemn ceremonies, but like an average, ordinary party.

The big celebration happened on September 9, and even then it was not so much due to the arrival of the Soviet troops as to the return of Miho Barakov. Unfortunately, the Soviet Army units did not pass through our village on the Ninth. They announced on the radio that they would pass through Dobrich, and the most impatient among us, led by Stoyan, of course, set out for the city by cart and horse at the crack of dawn. I, too, was burning with desire to go with them, but I didn't have the strength even to get into the cart, I was suffocating from a coughing fit and almost collapsed on the ground. I hadn't slept during the night in anticipation of the Soviet troops and had spent the whole week under great strain. Not a drop of rain had fallen the whole summer, a drought had gripped the plains, the dusty, scorched air was searing my rotted lungs.

In the evening, I got out of bed and went to the demonstration that had been called in front of the town hall. It was a full moon. The square was awash in white light and from afar you could see how people were arriving from all corners of the village, but despite this, two kerosene lamps had been hung over the town hall's door. Those who had gone to Dobrich to meet the Soviet troops excitedly described what they had seen and heard, shots rang out somewhere in the village, lots of people had been drinking and now they were already singing and had started up a round dance. And now Stoyan climbed up the stairs to the landing under the light of the lamps. I think that was the happiest day of his life. He was so ecstatic and filled with inspiration that he was shaking like a leaf, tears glittered in his eyes. This is a historic day for our people, he was saying, raising up his arm, fascism has finally been smashed and killed and communism has brought its great justice to us!...

After he finished his speech, he went down into the crowd and came over to me. He congratulated me on the new government and hugged me, pressing me to his chest. He held me in his embrace for a whole minute, without saying a word. I felt his flaming face next to mine, I could hear him breathing deeply and sobbing. I was happy at that moment, as I had been in my childhood when, coming back from the field in the late evening, he would pick me up in his arms and carry me home. But I could not say anything either. I was sobbing too.

In the morning I didn't feel well, but around noon I went out to get some fresh air. On the way home from my stroll, I passed by the tavern and sat down to rest on its veranda and that's when I saw a dozen cauldrons of mutton soup boiling in front of the Barakovs' house. Tables and chairs were set up by the cauldrons, along with several barrels of wine and brandy. At that time people hadn't seen such abundance in one place and the most tempted among them were already hovering around the cauldrons. Prisoners had been freed on September 8, but Miho Barakov had stayed in the city for two days to be on hand at the formation of the new People's Militia. The elder Barakov had made sure that his son's return would be celebrated as triumphantly and noisily as if he were rising from the dead. As we found out later, he had invited some influential people from Dobrich, he had also brought in musicians from there. Let the people eat, they're the ones my son risked his life for, he told everyone he met on the street and invited them to the feast. The previous day he had been appointed chairman of the village soviet, and now, with a vest on over a shirt with rolled-up sleeves, with a straw boater hat on his head and

a thin bamboo cane in his hand, he was shuttling with inimitable dignity
between his home and the town hall to see whether his son hadn't called
on the telephone to give more information about his arrival. He stopped
every minute, took a silver watch from his vest pocket, and held it far from
his eyes in order to read it.

I went back to my room and lay down. I slept, read, ate a bit, then
picked up my book again. At two o'clock I heard a car horn honking. A
car crossed the part of the square visible from my window, kicking up
a huge trail of dust. I soon heard shots ring out and cheers of "hooray."
Miho Barakov's triumphant welcome back home had begun. The sound
of the brass band hung over the village until late in the evening, along with
speeches and drunken shouts.

Before going out to the field, Anani had made me chicken soup, and
Auntie Tanka Dzhelebova visited me as well. Her sons had been having
trouble in high school, so during vacations I would tutor them in certain
subjects. Every time I went to their house, which was clean and cozy, I felt
a sort of solemnity on account of my visit; everyone in the family who did
not have work to do listened to my lesson with careful attention. Bay Kiro
Dzhelebov treated me with great respect, he loved asking me about all
sorts of things, he often wanted to borrow books as well. Because of this,
we grew close, and when I got sick, Auntie Tanka came once or twice a
week to check up on me. In her opinion, the best cure for any disease was
hearty food, so every time she came she brought me butter, eggs, honey,
a boiled chicken, or *banitsa*.

My brother came the next day in the afternoon. He was revolted by
Anani and was afraid of being infected by my illness, so he had never
before come into my room. This unexpected visit meant he had been
watching me. I hadn't shown my face in the village for a whole day, so
he had assumed that I had gone to the city to turn over the evidence of

the Barakovs' treachery, and now he was coming to see whether I was at home. My suspicions were confirmed when he asked for the file as soon as he stepped through the door.

"Give me the copy of the sentence for safekeeping! Your nerves are shot from your sickness, I'm afraid you'll get us all into trouble if you show it to somebody now."

"Somebody? That would be the party's regional committee."

"So you've decided to cut all ties, all the ties that have bound us as brothers until now!" Stoyan said, and began pacing back and forth across the room. His hands were clasped behind his back and I could see his palms were pressed together so hard they were almost bleeding. "Our lives are in danger! Yes, it's true!... And you want to turn some documents over to some committee. Listen to me, and listen well, so maybe you'll finally get your head screwed on straight again." He stopped in front of me and went on more quietly: "Last night two men came to our place well past midnight. One was around forty, the other couldn't have been more than twenty. They made me take part in the liquidation of an enemy of the people. Those scum have to be slaughtered down to the last man, they said. With no trial, no nothing. The revolution demands blood so it can reach deeply into the people's consciousness. The revolution demands revenge for every crime against the people, they said. Every tear the people have shed must be paid for with a human life. Did you hear that? With a human life! So that the people understand that the revolution has come in the name of their happiness. I told them that I couldn't lay a finger on another man. I couldn't kill a man for anything in the world, no matter who he was. You'll only be there as a lookout, they said, you won't have to shoot. But I still refused. They spent two long hours trying to convince me, but I kept refusing. In no uncertain terms. Since that's how it is, that's how it is, they said. You're a party secretary, you want everything handed to you on a silver platter. We'll draw our own conclusions from this. And not a word about this to anyone, or else this guy's gonna get involved –

and the older one showed me his pistol. If Miho is a traitor, he surely has gotten wind that we have something that could unmask him, and so he sent those people to test me. Otherwise why would they try to force me to kill somebody? The first thing he did on getting out of jail was to cover up his tracks by destroying the court records of his sentencing and liquidating the people involved in the case. That's why he came back yesterday, and not on the eighth when the prisoners were released. Perhaps he found out from the magistrate Marchinkov that you have a copy of his sentencing? If that's the case, we need to be careful…"

My brother left deeply upset. As I was seeing him off, my landlord Anani appeared, coming from the fields. I asked him to drive me to Zhitnitsa and he turned the cart around. I quickly got dressed, took the folder with the copy of the sentence, and got in the cart. The bus passed through Zhitnitsa at five o'clock, so I would reach the city when it was still light and be able to give the sentence to the committee. As soon as I reached Zhitnitsa, a villager I knew told me that Petar Pashov had been killed that morning.

I found Nusha and her mother prostrate with grief. They were dressed in black, with black kerchiefs on their heads, beneath which their faces looked translucently yellow, as if carved from wax. Nusha first saw me on the veranda, she ran toward me and pressed her head to my chest, without a moan or a word. She stood in my embrace, quiet and mute, while I had no idea what to say to her or how to comfort her. The women bustling around the house or coming in from outside were looking at us curiously and whispering, from the room where the dead man lay, the monotonous and oppressive wailing of the lamenters could be heard. Nusha's mother came up from the kitchen, where the rattling of dishes could be heard, and stood before us, with one hand pressed to her lips, and the other on my shoulder.

"We were waiting for one to come back alive, my son, but instead the other came back dead!" she said, stifling her sobs and glancing at Nusha.

"Tell her not to let this ruin her, tell her not to let it gnaw at her. Whatever happened, happened, it was God's will."

She was called down to the kitchen, while Nusha and I went into the room where the dead man lay. Elderly women were sitting around the coffin, speaking in whispers. When they saw Nusha and me, they fell silent, even the lamenters fell silent, and then one of the women whispered: "Her fiancé, got consumption." The coffin made of rough pine boards had been laid on a long table and was so piled with flowers that only Petar Pashov's face could be seen, clear, expressionless, and as calm as eternity. Nusha stood on the other side of the coffin, as thin and delicate as the very incarnation of gentle, inconsolable grief.

After the funeral I stayed at Nusha's place. Both she and her mother begged me not to leave them alone so soon. I spent the night at their house and in the morning hopped over to the city to give a copy of the sentence to the party's regional committee. I asked for an urgent meeting with the first secretary, telling the young man who was meeting visitors that I had to tell him about a murder that had been committed that morning. I whispered it in the young man's ear to intrigue him so he would let me in to the secretary more quickly. People were constantly going in and out of the reception room, always looking for the first secretary. Georgiev, that was the first secretary's name, called me in about half an hour later. I introduced myself and it turned out we were indirectly acquainted. Some years ago he had come to our house to see my brother on party business. Pashov's murder didn't seem to faze him particularly, or at least that's how it seemed to me. He thought for a moment and asked whether he wasn't the traitor involved in the smashing of the youth communist organization or his relative. I confirmed that he was the very "traitor" in question, and Georgiev got up and held out his hand: "He should have been sent before the People's Court."

I told him everything from beginning to end. The previous day, early in the morning, Petar Pashov had been called to the telephone to talk to Atanas Mirov from the neighboring village of Senovo. Atanas was a fellow student of Pashov's son, Alexander, and had graduated from medical school this year as an internist. He had a letter from Alexander, but hadn't been able to deliver it, since he had twisted his ankle, but he didn't want to send it via anyone else, so when Pashov found some free time, he should come and pick it up. The elder Pashov asked where he had seen his son, and he answered he had seen him in Sofia, but Alexander could not come to the village at the moment because he was extremely busy. The father set out for Senovo immediately and on the way was shot in the back twice. Accidental passersby found him about an hour later. Georgiev was so intrigued that he asked his assistant not to let anyone in until he called for him. For more than an hour, I told him the whole story, also reading passages from the sentence. In the end, Georgiev said our meeting needed to remain a complete secret, he advised me to go back to the village right away, to say hello to my brother from him, and under no circumstances were we to change our behavior toward Miho Barakov and his family. I left for the village that very day, but before departing I couldn't resist the temptation of checking whether the magistrate Marchinkov was alive and well. The old woman who had met me a week earlier recognized me immediately. She was very concerned and anxious and said that he had not come home for three days. She was his aunt and didn't know anything more about his whereabouts.

That evening I again stayed at Nusha's. It was sowing time and there was no one to take up the work. I hired a man to look after the livestock, I also found people to sow at least half the land designated for the autumn sowing, which had been left unsown. I took charge of their taxes and expenses and little by little I became something like the head of the household. The two women were in need of protection against both certain local communists as well as riffraff who thought that class equality – which they had had no inkling of yesterday – should come about the first day after the revolution. In these interregnum days of lawlessness, lots of old grudges were being dredged up along with the excitement, many gave free reign to their wildest urges and took revenge on their personal enemies in the name of the party and the people. They splattered the walls of the house with slogans and threats, stole from the yard and fields, at night they banged on the doors and condemned Nusha for her moral dissipation and called her a bourgeois whore. They meant our "illegal" relationship – but it was platonic.

Love came to me without youthful passion, when I was twenty-six years old and perhaps incurably ill. It came with the force and inevitability of a supernatural phenomenon and no one could extinguish it in my heart in any way. Nusha knew I was doomed, since all those sick with tuberculosis from the village had died, but still she wouldn't hear a word about us parting. Even if she did believe that I would recover, there is no way she could not have known that associating with me could cost her her life. She was so unaware of the risk she was putting herself at that I fell into despair over her lack of caution and felt like a calloused egoist. My love could become a crime if I did not keep my distance from her. I always told her this when we met, but she would cry and say that she was ready to take whatever strict hygienic measures were necessary, but she wanted to see me at least twice a week. To protect our love from rumors and people's disgust, we needed to get married, but in my state that was impossible. We could only announce our engagement, and that is what we did. Being engaged did not require us to live under a single roof, I visited them once or twice a week, and even then only with great caution…

Toward the end of '46 the campaign to found a collective farm began. We were so inspired that we didn't stop to think about the difficulties awaiting us from then on. We believed that since we wanted to build a more just life for the people, they would unanimously and voluntarily follow our lead. I had read about the difficulties in founding the Soviet kolkhozes, I had also told Stoyan what I had read, but to the both of us these difficulties seemed completely simple to overcome given the state of things here – in Bulgaria, we were moving toward collectivization almost a quarter-century later, thus our Bulgarian village had to be ripe for a revolutionary reform. Stoyan gave himself over completely to this campaign as the revivalists had dedicated themselves to freeing Bulgaria from the Ottoman Empire. He had lost weight from lack of sleep and sustenance, but I had never before seen him so energetic and sure of the future.

In the meantime a miracle had occurred. Toward the end of that same year I was already healthy. The strange thing was that I started feeling better and better after Nusha and I had gotten engaged. I wasn't spitting up blood, I wasn't feverish, I wasn't sweating, and little by little I was regaining my strength. I went to the city for an X-ray and the doctor was surprised. My lungs, as he put it, had patched themselves up – something that happened only rarely in those sick with tuberculosis. With what impatience and joy did I get off the bus and go to Nusha's house! As soon as I was through the door I called out that I was completely cured, and Nusha threw herself into my arms.

My relationship with Stoyan improved, but not to the point where we could live together again. He was very nervous when I told him I had given the copy of the sentence to the first secretary of the party's regional committee, but Pashov's murder had startled him as well. After Pashov, the former municipal police officer was killed, the magistrate Marchinkov also disappeared, along with the original sentence. As was found out later, these two or three murders (the third was that of Marchinkov, about whose fate nothing yet was known) had been committed in a single twenty-four-hour period, hence, if we had informed the committee on time, they could have put Miho Barakov under surveillance. At first my brother felt guilty for not putting me in touch with the party's underground regional committee, but then he began to wonder whether someone else had taken action on Miho Barakov's account, after he had somehow found out that the new government suspected him. Marchinkov, since it was not known whether he had been liquidated or arrested, could have been that someone.

Despite these events, Stoyan gave me to understand that a full restoration of our brotherly relations in the end depended on the situation of the younger Pashov, Alexander. If he had really worked for the communists abroad, why hadn't he come back right after September 9? If the opposite turned out to be the case, then the Barakovs were absolutely within their rights to take revenge on his father. And what would I do in that case? Would I marry his sister, as I had already promised her, or would I break off the engagement? And if I didn't break it off, I would have to go live with a family in which both the father and the son were traitors. No, there was no way they were traitors. With my own eyes I had read the case files of the trial against the twelve young communists and was convinced that the elder Pashov had been slandered. Lexy couldn't be a traitor either, but why hadn't he come back or at least contacted his family? I never doubted him for a minute, yet nevertheless, I remembered Devetakov's notes that I'd found amidst his books. Devetakov wrote that he had seen Lexy in a Zurich hotel, but Lexy had pretended not to recognize him and had passed him by. Lexy would never have passed by a person for whom he felt such great respect unless some exceptional circumstances required it of him. Devetakov with good reason had presumed just as we had that Lexy was working in espionage, but did that really give him the right to doubt his political convictions? "You have to be ready to expect anything from a person."

My brother and I sought the answers to these questions together. However, no matter how much we racked our brains, we could not solve the mystery of Alexander Pashov. Our only hope was that he had "infiltrated" some foreign espionage agency and was waiting to be exposed so he could go home and contact his family. Fate had given me my life back, why shouldn't it give me Lexy and brotherly love back as well? Nevertheless, fate turned out not to be so generous to me – after I recovered, Nusha fell ill with tuberculosis. Just as I, at the beginning of my illness, had refused to go get treatment at a sanatorium, she, too, categorically refused to leave her home. Both her mother and I, as well as the doctor, urged her in vain to go, she preferred to live alone in a hut in the woods, but she would not part from us. There could be no doubt that I had infected her. I had not been vigilant enough in my efforts to protect her and this tormented me terribly. Snow fell and the weather grew cold, but I went every day or every other day to her village to visit her, just as she had visited me when I was sick. My heart shriveled with pain as I saw her growing paler and coughing up blood more and more often, but she didn't seem to be worried about her illness, since she, like me, would overcome it and recover. She believed this, and I believed it too, but there came the time when she no longer had the strength to move. I took her in my arms, carried her over to the open window, and held her in my lap. She had become a little girl with a pale, tiny face and delicate hands covered with a lacy network of veins, which made them look touchingly exquisite.

"I'm not going to get better," she would say with an indifference that showed that her thirst for life had died out. "Until recently I had some hope, but now I have no hopes for anything. Last night I dreamed of Lexy again. He was holding a wedding crown, he wanted to put it on my head, but I pulled away and he laughed. If I were healthy, we would get married, wouldn't we? What would I have looked like as a bride? Mama has put together such a dowry for my wedding. Now she'll have to give it to my cousin. That's what I told her, and she started crying."

"Don't hurry to give away your dowry, because I won't marry you if you come with nothing," I would reply. "I have nothing of my own, and if you come with no dowry, how will we get by?"

"We just weren't fated to be together, you and I, my dearest fiancé. Oof, I need to lie down, all my strength is gone. I can't breathe. Help me get to the bed!"

I grabbed her by the shoulders and she, slowly and hesitantly, like a baby taking its first steps, walked toward the bed. She lay down on the blanket, closed her eyes, and drifted off. Her mother appeared at the window and called me outside. She wanted me to get a bucket of water from the well, I brought the water and asked her to make up a bed for me in Lexy's room, where I had been sleeping until now.

"Go home, my son!" she said. "Come and eat now, then go home to sleep. Get some rest, then you'll come back tomorrow. My sister and I will stay here with Nusha."

Early the next day, before noon, a villager from Zhitnitsa came. He climbed out of his cart, opened the gate to the yard, and started toward the house. I happened to be on the veranda and from the expression on his face, I realized that the worst had come to pass. Nusha didn't experience the miracle I had had the year before. Her tuberculosis was a fast-moving case and it took her life in less than a year. It seems that her mother had foreseen the end, which is why she had sent me home to rest and gather my strength. I spent the following night with Nusha. Around nine o'clock in the evening, when the others had left and it was just the three of us – Nusha's mother, her aunt, and myself – I asked the two women to go rest in the other room. They were worn out from exhaustion and grief, her mother in particular could hardly stay on her feet. They went into the other room and seemed to fall asleep, while I was left alone with Nusha. She was lying on the same table where her deceased father had lain two years ago, her coffin, too, was made of the same roughly hewn pine boards. I was sitting next to her, looking at her and thinking that I never would have expected to sit next to a dead person and feel a strange sort of peace. It seems my feelings were blunted from stress and pain, I was gripped by a spiritual desolation, yet my mind was working as usual, perhaps it was even sharper and quicker. For example, I was thinking that in the final words spoken to us by our dearest one, we must find some deep, ambiguous meaning or enigma, which, after their death, we must puzzle out and interpret as a legacy. This is what literature leads us to expect, but I nevertheless found that the final words Nusha had said to me were so simple and insignificant in comparison to the feelings we felt for each other: "Help me reach the bed!" No matter how much I tortured myself, I could not find any particular meaning in those words. Then I remembered Devetakov's notes, which I had found in his books. He wrote that death made life meaningless. When I was sick, I had known that I was doomed, and if I had had some hope, it was only one percent. Despite that, I didn't think about death, I didn't believe that I would die. I believed it in my mind, but not with my heart. I sometimes fell into deep, agonizing despair, but my thirst for life was so strong that it conquered the despair. Some inner force was pushing me onward toward the future and I forgot that death was inevitable. If I were to fall now into a similar despairing state, I surely would not survive.

But that night, as I was watching over the dead Nusha, I truly believed that death made life meaningless. What did it matter that Nusha was nineteen years old, beautiful, innocent, filled with light and joy, that she looked upon the world with angelic eyes, with selflessness and love? What did it matter that with her love she had perhaps brought me back to life, while she herself fell victim to her love's excess? What was the use of all these feelings and romantic yearnings, these hopes, these sufferings and joys, since they had to disappear once and for all? The phenomenon of death stood before me like a painful puzzle and I could not make sense of it. I could not understand how her eyes, which only last night had warmed my soul with a single glance, and filled me with happiness and faith, had now had their light extinguished forever; how her voice, so ringing that it pierced my whole soul, had now fallen silent; how her lips, from which I had heard so many tender things, had now gone cold and not a word nor a smile would ever come from them again.

While I was looking at her face, deep within myself I could not accept that she was dead. Despite death's cruel obviousness, in my heart a small seed of hope sprouted that Nusha was not dead, that it was impossible that she was dead. *Could she have fallen into a coma?* I thought, *and how could I check?* I looked for a mirror in the room to hold before her lips, but couldn't find one, I took the candle from her hands, blew it out and set it on a plate. I wanted to check her pulse, but then it seemed to me that her temple was throbbing, while her face took on a gentle rosiness. Her eyelashes slowly opened, she rose up from beneath the flowers and sat in the coffin. She looked all around and then fixed me with a puzzled smile.

"What am I doing in this coffin? You didn't think that I'd died? Good God!... I was just really tired and fell asleep. Don't look at me so scared like that! I just fell asleep, and you prepared me for burial."

"Yes, we thought you were dead, Nusha. For half a day you didn't give any signs of life. But I didn't believe you were dead, Nusha. I just wanted to check your pulse and you woke up."

"Oh, I love you so much!" she said. "I've never told you before how much I love you, have I? More than anything in the world. More than anything in the world... Please, take me in your arms. I want you to carry me around the room a bit."

I carried her around the room, and she pressed her sweet little face to mine and seemed to drift off. Oh God, oh God, she said at one point, but that was not her voice, but her mother's. I had fallen asleep with my head lying by the coffin, her mother was standing next to me, saying:

"Oh God, oh God, my sister and I fell asleep, and when I came in here I saw that you had dozed off too. Oh my son, what anguish has come down on us!"

I had not promised never to forget Nusha, but it so happened that even now, twenty-five years after her death, I am living with her memory. In the first years after her death I could even imagine someday getting married and having a family. Later, when the pain had dulled a bit, this thought passed through my head, especially on lonely days, but my memories of Nusha were so fresh that I saw her as if alive between me and the woman with whom in my imagination I could replace her in my heart. Our relationship had remained platonic, I hadn't even dared to kiss her on the lips, so as not to infect her with my illness, yet she had been ready to follow a doomed man until his dying breath. No, I could not fool myself, as well as some other woman, especially if she turned out to be good and honorable...

In the autumn of the following year, the collective farm fell apart. The impoverished collective hadn't inspired my confidence and I shared this with my brother, which became grounds for our relationship to become strained once again. I insisted that he shouldn't rush to found another collective, since the poor villagers didn't possess enough land or good livestock or tools. When one hundred paupers band together, they don't become rich, unless they have something that gives them an advantage over the private farmers, for example, machines. With shrewd foresight, Stoyu Barakov had already sold his threshing machine, seeder, harvester, and tractor around the Ninth, and now the collective farmers worked using antediluvian plows, seeded by hand, and threshed with threshing boards. There were not any common barns yet and everyone wanted to work with his own livestock and look after it at home. I kept the collective's books and saw that the situation was catastrophic – a day's labor came out to eighteen cents in the money of that time and the co-op members survived by payments in kind. In the days when the collective fell apart, Stoyan happened to be in Sofia taking courses. When he got back, there was no longer any collective, all the members had taken their livestock and their tools back home. The common property remained only on the books, over which I had racked my brains whole nights at a time. Things were in a complete jumble, which took us months to untangle.

Stoyan had come back from the city via the bus to Zhitnitsa and from there had walked home on foot. It was around ten o'clock at night when he entered the party clubhouse. He saw that the light was on, so he stopped by. I had kept him constantly informed about the state of the co-op, about all the failures that were piling up day by day over the course of a year and a half, he himself knew everything, but when I told him that the people had ransacked the inventory and made off with the tools and livestock, he became hysterical. He shouted only: "Why did you let that happen?" His face went pale, he was shaking, his legs gave way, he sat down on the floor and began kicking like an angry child and screaming himself hoarse. I was stunned, I tried to pull him to his feet, but he lay down on his back, started kicking again and shouting even more loudly: "They'll all bring it back, they've signed membership declarations, they're obligated to come back!" He went on like this for several minutes, then he went silent and got up. His face was bathed in tears and, so that I couldn't see, he turned his back to me and shouted: "To put so much into something and everything just goes to hell! Why? Because we didn't put the screws on them, we didn't show the necessary harshness. First thing tomorrow we start working on reestablishing the collective!"

And indeed, the very next day everything capable of propagandizing a return to the collective farm was called to heel: elderly men and women, young men and girls, children and teachers. Ivan Shibilev (if he was in the village), Kichka, Mona Koynova, the teachers, and I held rallies and performances several times, we also held parties and working bees. Stoyu Barakov also joined the propaganda efforts. Circumstances had worked out such that he was forced to hand over his land with a smile on his face. Who knows what kind of tremor was shaking him inwardly, but outwardly he looked happy that his son's ideas were finally being put into practice. He was talkative, he took the floor at every meeting, inviting the people to join the collective farm. *What an ironic twist of fate*, I thought to myself, while listening to his long-winded, tiresome speeches. The most prominent enemy of the new government and a criminal was preaching socialism and acting as a benefactor for the future cooperative farm because he was giving the most land. The former co-op members met us in their homes anxious and guilty, they hemmed and hawed, complained of their poverty, but they wouldn't hear a word about rejoining the collective. "We've already gotten burned by the co-op, let others join it now, and when we see that it's good, we'll join up too" – that's what they all said, as if taking the words right out of each other's mouths. They were dejected from the arguments and losses when the co-op fell apart, and in that state, it was better if we left them alone, at least for a while, all the more so because we failed in our mission, and it was precisely their loss.

But my brother was inexorable and inexhaustible. During the day, he would go around to houses, while in the evening he would call meetings. I would listen to him speak, and every time I was astonished by his will, energy, and enthusiasm. Only an incorrigible idealist with pure and strong impulses in his soul could so stubbornly defend the rightness of his deeds, without sparing his efforts, nerves, and health. But at the same time, he began losing patience and growing anxious. They called him in to the party's regional committee once or twice a week, and after every return from there he would be even more impatient. The committee had declared autumn as the final deadline for the reestablishment of the cooperative farm, they wanted to send their own representative to the village to help him, which to him meant that they doubted his organizational abilities. The committee was constantly suggesting to him that he had to use a firmer hand, that he wouldn't attract the hesitating villagers into the co-op with words alone, to say nothing of those who were outright opposed. He was forced constantly to dog them, to wrangle with them, and to put up with their hardheadedness and ignorance, and this filled him with disappointment and rage. "Why are these wretched folks giving us such a hard time?" he would ask sometimes in despair. "Why do they growl at us like a dog, as if we're trying to take the bone out of its mouth? Why do they resist and not understand that all this is being done for their own good, and for their children's future? No, I don't have any strength left to argue with them. I can see it in their eyes, they're afraid of me and hate me. I'd best go to the committee and say that I can't do the task that's been assigned to me. That they should appoint another party secretary or send a representative. I, too, need to sleep soundly for at least one night..."

This is how he would bemoan the situation in moments of exhaustion, but shortly thereafter, abashed at his own chickenheartedness, he would claim that the co-op would be founded not by whining and giving up in the face of difficulties, but by firmness and perseverance. If we waited for those lacking class consciousness to awaken, or for the opposition members to hand over their property to the cooperative farm themselves, we'd be waiting until the second coming. Nothing's going to get done with prayers, but with plows. That's why we're revolutionaries – to go before the others and to show them the way for a hundred years to come! This also determined his attitude toward the villagers – the attitude of an adult toward youngsters who needed their ears boxed when they didn't listen or fathom their own futures. Only that sometimes he didn't merely "box" the ears of the disobedient, but rather stretched them to the point of tearing them right off.

At that time almost all the families sent their children to study in the cities, but to be accepted into high schools or the university, they had to present so-called Fatherland Front certificates attesting their political trustworthiness. I issued these certificates in my capacity as chairman of the Fatherland Front organization, but my brother began using them as a means of coercion against those parents who refused to join the co-op. Many of the young people were denied an education or finished their education after a few years' interruption. The first young man to suffer in this way was Kuncho, who later became an associate professor in the Department of Physics and Mathematics. It turned out that as a first-year student in high school, he had been a *brannik*, a member of the fascist youth league, for half a year. The *branniks* championed a Greater Bulgaria that stretched from "the Danube to the Aegean Sea," but it wasn't their patriotic ideals that might cause a young boy from the village to fall into their ranks. Before September 9, the communist youth league, the legionnaires, and the *branniks* all competed to recruit "cadres" from among the newly arrived students. Those village youths who found themselves in the city without a prior political orientation often ended up in an absolutely unsuitable organization. This was the case with Kuncho as well. We would never have found out about his *brannik* past if he himself had not later talked about his political ignorance. My brother, however, took advantage of his openness and blacklisted him. Kuncho's father dug in his heels, spent three whole years outside the cooperative farm, and Kuncho entered the university three years later than he should have.

My brother found many other ways of putting the screws to people when they didn't want to join the co-op. One of the surest means for putting pressure on one of the wealthier villagers was to declare him a kulak. These wealthy villagers had about twenty-five acres of land each and had never used hired hands, but when necessary had practiced *medzhiya* – two or three families would join together to finish some fieldwork more quickly. The kulak had been declared the most notorious enemy of the people and socialism, and we never missed a chance to mock and stigmatize him in our speeches, propaganda campaigns, and theatrical performances. He was an agent of imperialism, a fascist and a warmonger, a die-hard opposition member and instigator, he would kill communists in the dead of night, burn down houses, and poison the co-op's animals, he hindered the building of the new life in any way he could. The kulak was constantly being written about in the papers and being talked about on the radio, he was depicted in caricatures and posters as a bloodsucker. In short, the kulak turned into a bogeyman, that evil spirit from children's fairy tales, only now adults were the ones afraid of him. There was no place for him in the village; so as to render him harmless, he and his family had to be resettled in some distant corner of the country or locked up in a labor camp. My brother kept several people in constant fear of such a fate, one of whom was Iliya Dragiev.

Iliya Dragiev had twenty acres of land and six children, each one smaller than the next. He had promised Stoyan that he would sign the membership declaration, but when he came to the party clubhouse, he lost his nerve. Stoyan took him to task for not keeping his word, but the other man told him that he'd already gotten burned by the co-op once and if he joined again, his children would die of starvation. Since he had managed to feed them thus far, he would be able to keep feeding them – he had two oxen, two cows, thirty sheep, plus a well in his yard.

Iliya left, and Stoyan ordered two young men to watch for when Iliya wasn't at home, then to board up his well and to seal it with a big padlock. During the big droughts in these parts, that well was a true oasis in the summer, because all the houses in the upper neighborhood drew from it when the water in the other three wells in the town square had dried up. The young men waited until Iliya was out in the fields and then boarded over and locked up the well. That evening he smashed the padlock and tore off the boards in order to water his livestock, but during the night someone dropped a dog in the well and left a note. The whole village bristled with anger. It was a dry autumn and people were drawing up sand from the bottom of the wells. They insisted that the two young men be punished, but they denied throwing a dog in the well. They had boarded it up under orders from the party secretary, but they hadn't thrown a dog in. The young men weren't lying. Some of the opponents of the co-op and my brother's personal enemies had taken advantage of the situation to make him look bad in front of the village, and just a few days after this incident someone shot at him. Around midnight, as he was going back home, three bullets whizzed past his head. The would-be killer was standing behind a fence where it could not easily be leapt over – in case my brother hadn't been hit and decided to try to chase the shooter. And that's exactly what happened. One of the bullets only nicked the batting of his left shoulder. Stoyan pulled himself together in time, fired his own gun, and wanted to give chase, but by the time he found a place where he could jump the fence, the gunman had already disappeared into the darkness.

In the morning we inspected the place and found no clues. Stoyan informed the police, and Miho Barakov, as if he had been expecting just such a case, immediately arrived with an investigator, along with two young men from the intelligence services. Miho Barakov ordered that several families be searched. I refused to be present during the search, and I advised my brother to do the same, declaring that it was unnecessary and indiscreet to sow unrest among the people right now, when they were not calm by any means. But Miho Barakov said that since we as claimants had called him in, we definitely must be present during the searches. People were horrified when the investigator and his assistants most unceremoniously started rummaging about in their homes, turning everything topsy-turvy and digging around in trunks and other places which outsiders' eyes should not see and strange hands should not touch. The women were wailing as if to raise the dead, the children started bawling too, it set off an uproar throughout the whole village. Weapons were not found and each of the suspects had an airtight alibi. This was Miho Barakov's new blow below the belt to us. A very quick and well-calculated blow.

But that was not the end of this whole business. First and foremost among the suspects had been, of course, Iliya Dragiev. His innocence did not need any proving. During the search of his home the man met us, flustered by the "high-ranking" guests, and started plying us with brandy despite the early hour. His children, the oldest sixteen and the youngest merely an infant, were half naked, still unwashed and snot-nosed, they had just gotten up from beneath the rugs they slept under and were scrambling around the room. They piled into one corner, huddled together like frightened animals, and watched us with shyness and curiosity. The room smelled of stale air and piss, the lady of the house, slovenly dressed, yellow and bony, hid her bosom as best she could with the swaddling of the baby she was nursing, and also stared at us from under her brow with curiosity and hostility. They asked Iliya whether he had any weapons and he said he did. He left the room, dug around beneath the eaves of the barn and pulled out a rusty barrel revolver.

"It was my father's way back when and it's been rusted out since then. As a child he would give it to me to play with, then I gave it to my boys as a toy."

The investigator took the revolver, tried to spin the barrel, and returned it to him. His assistants began searching through the pee-scented rugs, rifled through the linen trunk, poked around in the barn and the sheep pen, but didn't find anything. And then, goaded by some devil, Iliya turned to my brother and said, wagging his finger at him: "So, Mr. Secretary, since you're a party fellow, do you think you've got God by the balls? You want everyone to dance to your tune, as if the village is your birthright. The head of the police here is one of our boys, I'll tell him. You boarded up my well, locked it up with a padlock, and in the end tossed a live dog inside, 'cause I didn't want to join the co-op again. You left my children, the animals, and the whole neighborhood without water. We heard they shot at you last night. Why bother shootin' that guy and be forced to do time the rest of your life for it? Send him to court, but the court don't catch the likes of him, that's why he's ridin' roughshod over all of us. Since the court ain't gonna catch him, he oughta take one right there in the kisser. To open his eyes so he can see that there are people living in this village."

Iliya uttered all this in a single breath in a squeaky voice that kept catching, with clenched fists, flushed from indignation and overexcitement, while tears gushed from his big round blue eyes. He was one of those people who wouldn't hurt a fly, on top of that he was pudgy and flabby as if deboned, his raised fists provoked patronizing smiles. He had probably taken courage from the presence of the chief of police, who was "one of our boys," to tell someone off for the first time in his life. That same night, as if Iliya Dragiev's threat was being carried out, unknown assailants attacked my brother right in front of his home, as he was opening the gate to go into the yard. He tripped over something (a stretched-out rope), fell flat on his face, and his attackers hurled themselves on him. They tied his hands and gagged his mouth and started pummeling him with their fists. Luckily, the neighbor had come out on his veranda with a windproof lantern to go to the barn, because he was waiting for his cow to calve, heard someone groaning in the dark, and thus saved my brother. His enemies were quick and resourceful, they were able to gauge the psychological moment and to cover up their tracks. After they had thrown the dog in the well and shot at him the night before, the last thing my brother was expecting was for them to attack him the next night as well, and especially right after he had walked the chief of the police back to his father's home. My brother had no doubts about Iliya Dragiev's innocence, but to counter the compromising story of the dog in the well, he started accusing him of having thrown the dog into his own well so as to make the new government look bad in front of the village. The enemies of the co-op, who had thrown the dog in the well, took Iliya under their wing and he unwittingly joined their ranks. My brother had no choice but to force Iliya to join the co-op "voluntarily" somehow and thus to put an end to this unpleasant business. As I found out later, he threatened Iliya that he would denounce him as a kulak, but before that he decided to put him through another ordeal.

At that time a campaign to kill off dogs had been launched in the village. Economic want was cited as the reason behind this grisly campaign – there was a ration system in place and food needed to be saved. How many dogs each villager had was common knowledge, and the chairman of the village soviet, Stoyu Barakov, gave an order to leave only one dog per yard and for the rest to be killed. There were hundreds of extra dogs and since the soviet didn't have that many bullets on hand, they were slaughtered with a knife. This job was assigned to the Gypsy, Mato. His guillotine was a simple structure: a post driven into the ground with a hole drilled through it about a yard off the ground. Mato drew the dog's leash through the hole in the pole and pulled on it. The dog would rise up on its hind legs, exposing its chest, and Mato would drive the knife into its heart.

I had gone to Orlovo on business and on my way back I took a shortcut through the fields to the north of the village. My path led me right by the place where they were slaughtering the dogs – a meadow surrounded on all sides by thistles, in the center of which jutted up the canine guillotine. Lined up one next to the other on both sides of the road were thirty or more dead dogs. I was shocked by the sight and hurried to go back the other way when someone called my name. I looked through the brambles – in the meadow stood the blood-covered canine guillotine, and next to it was Iliya Dragiev. I went closer and saw that he was holding the leash of a large speckled dog. At the edge of the clearing Mato the Gypsy was sitting on a stump, smoking a cigarette rolled from newspaper like a man who had finished some important work and was now resting with satisfaction. He was smiling with his big, yellowed teeth and looking from the two knives stuck into the ground on either side of him to Iliya and back, shaking his head ironically: "He ain't got the balls! He can't stick it to him. Softie! He's been standin' here since Lord knows when and he can't do it."

"Who me? Just you watch! It's no problem to put this mutt under the knife!" Iliya cried, pulling the dog's leash through the hole and yanking him upright. The dog's head was looking upward and it was standing on its hind legs, its tongue was hanging out and it was choking. The Gypsy got up off the stump and held out the knife, Iliya didn't take it, he looked at the ground around the post, which was drenched in blood and covered with swarms of bluish-green flies, and let the dog go. He was shaking as if with a fever and his teeth were chattering, his pale face was slick with sweat. The autumn sun was beating down, it was hot and stuffy in the clearing ringed by thistles on all sides, it smelled of blood and dog feces. Grinning from ear to ear, the Gypsy was looking at Iliya, shaking his tousled, sweat-slicked head, then he took the knife and stepped toward the dog.

"Hey, Gypsy!" Iliya shouted, standing in front of him. "Don't you dare put your filthy hands on my dog! I'll rub you out like nobody's business. I'll kill the dog all by myself. I've raised it from a pup, I'll take its life by myself." The man was fussing around the dog as if he had lost his mind, now pulling on its leash to raise it on its hind legs, now letting it go again and smacking himself on the forehead. "How can I take your life, Rex! Tell me how! I don't have the heart for it, nor can I lift a hand on you." Finally he let the dog go and yelled: "I'll sign your declaration, why not?

Plenty of folks have signed and not died, it won't be the death of me, either! Ilko, come give me a declaration! This time I'll sign, to save my children's lives…"

As we walked toward the village, he told me how he had met with my brother several times one-on-one and Stoyan had given him the job of killing all the dogs instead of Mato the Gypsy. First your own dog, then all the others. If he didn't do it, Stoyan would denounce him as a kulak, since he had hired children to herd his lambs, and then he would send him to a labor camp for insulting a party secretary, and there's no getting out of a labor camp. He would rot away in there and his children would be left fatherless…

My brother wasn't at the club when we got there. I gave Iliya the declaration, he signed it and left. I was still under the depressing impression left by the canine guillotine and started rebuking my brother as soon as he came through the door. He saw the signed declaration, deftly tucked it away in the cupboard, and only then sat down across from me. I had not guessed he was so hard-hearted, and I told him this. I also told him that for some time now I had been wondering how it was possible for two brothers like us, who had grown up together in dire poverty, not to know each other by now. I thought he would be hurt by my reproaches, but he kept silent, his face taking on a strange expression of sorrow and resignation.

"Yes, yes, I think there is something to it," he said, looking me in the eye. "But why not?… Why shouldn't we know each other? Perhaps you don't know me, but I know you. Years ago, when we were striving toward our big goal, you were charging straight ahead like an arrow. Now you're different. You look to the side, you have your doubts, you hesitate. Yes, what we dreamed of several years ago doesn't match entirely what we have now. We thought and believed that as soon as we took power, the people would rush into the new life whistling and singing. But it didn't quite turn out like that. It turned out that not everybody thought like us. The struggles, the hesitations, the suffering began. But how could it be otherwise? You told me yourself many times that taking away private property is the biggest event in the history of mankind. That history has seen everything: hundred-year wars, and the change of epochs, revolution, the obliteration and creation of states, and what have you, but the confiscation of private property is happening for the first time. Twenty years ago in the Soviet Union, and now here in Bulgaria. This is the biggest revolution, all the others were some kind of reform, rebellions and nothing more. Our revolution has turned life on its head in order to completely renew it. Those are your words, my dearest brother, I'm quoting you. Since we're advancing toward a complete renewal of life, how can we not run into some difficulties? We didn't expect them to be quite this daunting, but since they've come crashing down on our heads we need to overcome them. You accuse me of using violence. Aren't you mistaken when you call my vigilance to overcome the difficulties on the path to the new life 'violence'? Fine, let's say my vigilance is violence. But why am I 'using force'? For myself, for my own benefit, or for the common good, the people's benefit? You feel sorry for folks because they're suffering. But why are they suffering? They're suffering over their pitiful little strip of land, over their mangy livestock, over what's 'theirs.' Isn't private property the root cause of all of mankind's suffering? I don't mean to be throwing your own words back in your face, but you taught me that, too. You've read me books on that question…"

Stoyan got up and started pacing around the room. His steps were slow and measured, as if on the edge of an abyss, and from time to time he would stretch his neck, as if the collar of his shirt were too tight. This tic showed that he could not suppress the storm welling up inside him, and that it would soon burst forth with all its force. To head off this storm, I got up to leave, but he caught up with me at the door and grabbed my shoulder: "Before you go, tell me how we're going to reach our goal –

socialism. We've discussed this question a hundred times, but I still haven't understood which tactics you're suggesting. Since you don't approve of mine, that means you must have your own tactics. I'm listening, lay it on me."

I told him that it was both out of place and mistaken to speak of tactics in this case. The good we want to do for the people comes from the soul, and not from some set of tactics. Tactics are a strategic notion, a skill or resourcefulness to win a war, attain riches, win a contest, etc., thus they cannot give rise to goodness. Goodness is a moral category and is not the result either of laws or of ideas that come to a man from the outside, but from his essence, like water from a spring...

He was standing before me strained and concentrated to the utmost, as if afraid to miss even a single sound, internal tension blazed in his eyes. But now, across his face, which had been frozen like a mask, ran a quiver of liveliness and that was a sign that he had guessed or he imagined that he had guessed my thoughts, even though I myself didn't understand completely what exactly I wanted to tell him. We had spoken many times about the question of "tactics," as he understood it, and I always got confused and never managed to express myself clearly and definitively. It was a question of carrying out in deed the revolutionary tasks the party had assigned to us, and on this question we had differing opinions. He rejected my opinion and in most cases never even heard me out. He interrupted me now again. He stretched out his right hand toward me like a sword, while his eyes flashed demonically.

"I get it, I get it! Just as I thought – the old tactic of waiting and whining. Of liberalism and mercy. Even though you know very well that every revolution is made by a smaller or larger group of like-minded people called a 'party,' which is in this case our communist party. The party leads the majority onward, while to the majority it always seems that the party is moving far faster than necessary. That's what revolution is. Whatever words you want to use to define it, that's what it is – organizing the people and leading them onward toward something new and better for them, through difficulties, through suffering, and if need be, through blood. And you reproach me that I'm thin-skinned, painfully touchy and vengeful, that I don't let anyone who dares insult me go unpunished. That's how the party's authority must be defended, so that a speck of dust does not fall on it. The party is never wrong, therefore it follows that the party secretary, when working under its instructions, is never wrong either. I am a soldier for the party and whatever it orders me to do, I do it. Now it wants me to reestablish the co-op at any price (at any price!) and I am obliged to act such that it is reestablished, even if I have to pay for it with my life. That's why I want to recommend that you…"

He didn't finish his thought, because blood spurted from his nose, wetting his moustache and dripping down onto the floor. I made him sit down in the chair, tilt his head back, and plug his nose with a handkerchief. He bled for a long time, he felt so weak that I had to walk him home. For the first time in four years I was to enter my childhood home and I was excited, but Kichka didn't even invite me inside. She was worried and wanted to take my brother to a doctor in the city, but he refused and went to lie down. In the morning I stopped by to see him. Kichka met me in the yard and wouldn't allow me to talk to him, so as not to upset him. He had been raving in his sleep all night, saying that Iliya Dragiev had been crying like a baby because he wasn't able to kill some dog. What dog? What were we fighting about again, what had I been picking an argument with him about? Are his troubles with other people not enough that I had to go poisoning him with mine as well? Glaring at me with hostility, Kichka told me quite a few home truths and I realized that Stoyan had shared all our arguments with her, which she called "rows," and that these rows weighed on his conscience and caused him to doubt his work. Why don't you just go your separate ways, since you can't seem to see eye to eye, she told me in the end. You're healthy already, you're a bachelor, find yourself a job in the city, either as a lawyer or a judge, get married and settle down. The way things are going with you and your brother, you'll be at each other's throats before long and will be the laughingstock of the village.

Kichka couldn't hide her feelings and for me it wasn't hard to guess that Stoyan had shared with her his desire to send me far away from the village, but he hadn't dared to tell me so she saved him that bit of unpleasantness. I had also thought of starting work in the city, but because of my illness, and later also because of events in the village, I hadn't made up my mind to leave. I had been the bookkeeper for the collective farm, I had been a teacher for one year, I also acted as a legal consultant for some time to the newly founded Machine and Tractor Station. It seemed to me that I could be useful at this moment when everyone was suffering, when a new era was being born with so much pain and torment. And perhaps I would've stayed for a long time in the village if it hadn't been for that paradoxical story of Ivan Shibilev being sent to a labor camp. Indeed, what bigger paradox than that – my brother expelling from the party organization the person who had founded it before the Ninth. Another paradox came as a result of the first – the political criminal and murderer Miho Barakov, in his capacity as the regional chief of police, taking advantage of how my brother had depicted Ivan Shibilev to the party's regional committee, sent Ivan Shibilev to a labor camp. The person who had wasted his talents in service to the party at a time when, instead of high art, the party needed propaganda and posters; a person who, through all the ups and downs of his outlandish and wild life, had never stopped serving the party, not even for a second. And yet another paradox – my brother denounced or threatened to denounce as kulaks villagers who had nothing to do with kulaks, while the only real kulak in the village, the political criminal Stoyu Barakov, was not only living in freedom, but he was also chairman of the village soviet, representing and exercising the people's power. Four years had passed since the crimes of the younger and elder Barakov had been discovered, but the party's regional committee still had not undertaken any action to unmask them. I had gone there several times to ask how long we would tolerate these wolves in sheep's clothing and they always answered me, with a finger to the lips, that I must keep what we knew about them an absolute secret. They didn't give any other explanations, but it was clear that the Barakovs' fate depended on Alexander Pashov's return, which in and of itself would be the best proof that he had worked for us while abroad and that his father had been sacrificed in vain. But unfortunately, Pashov still had not returned, while his mother had no news of him at all.

None of this would have happened if my brother hadn't taken party discipline as dogma and if he had showed a certain independence in his decisions. I very often thought of the question that the late Mihail Devetakov had asked, thinking about revolutions: Is it possible to achieve a humane end through inhumane means? At the time, when we had been talking with Devetakov, as he himself noted, this question did not exist for Lexy Pashov and me. For us back then, the impending revolution was the most long-awaited, historically magnificent, and humane event, and we had never thought of how it would be put into practice. But when it came, the question of what means to use to "impose" it here in Bulgaria became for me the most confounded question. The people were suffering, caught between two epochs. Few believed that the capitalist countries would declare war on us and bring the old times back. Most people realized that the revolution wasn't going to pass them by, but still they couldn't part with their property. Some elderly people had burst into tears in front of me. They pounded their heads with their fists, asking: "What can we do? There's no way forward, no way back!" Two died of heart attacks, while another hung himself. He voluntarily signed the co-op membership declaration and when he got back home, he went straight into the barn and hung himself.

During this hard time, I was often overcome with doubt and despair, it seemed to me that my one-time ideals had been exploited in practice, and it was then precisely that I would try to answer Devetakov's terrible question. I remembered visiting Devetakov's estate, first with Lexy Pashov, then in the following years on my own, and under the influence of the memory of that noble man, I mentally agreed with him, that a humane end cannot be reached through inhumane means. And what's more, man changes very slowly, if he does not stay constant, and only little by little – one millimeter per century or perhaps not even that much. Devetakov spoke of these things only rarely, perhaps so as not to bore me with his philosophizing or, as is more likely, to break down the age barrier between us. And indeed, the greater my reverence for his person was, the more free I felt before him. He expressed his thoughts in a soft, unusually pleasant voice, without imposing them, as if they had just occurred to him that minute and as if there was nothing of value in them. It always seemed to me as I listened to him that he was suppressing a thought: "Feel free to ignore what I just said." I always left the estate filled with spiritual bliss, my heart caressed by a gentle melancholic longing for another, different, unattainable world.

But no matter how enchanted I may have been by Devetakov's charm, deep down I felt resistance to some of his philosophical beliefs. This resistance, cowardly and fragile, was fed by my age and the environment I had been born into and grown up in. I was twenty-some years old, my lust for life was so insatiable that I didn't give in to despair even when I got sick and knew that I was doomed to death. Only once did I believe that death made life meaningless, and then only for a short time, when Nusha passed away and I felt endlessly alone. The energy of youth, which filled my whole being, rebelled against the despair of Devetakov, who was exhausted by knowledge and who had discovered the meaninglessness of being. Now, as I am approaching fifty, I understand the disconsolate cries of that despairing wise man, while back then it seemed to me that he was reciting aphorisms out of a surplus of reason, while I chalked up his suicide to incurable melancholy.

I sensed that Devetakov had fallen victim to a tragic lack of belief, and this strengthened my spirit, it gave me the strength to analyze impartially my brother's actions. Despite our tense arguments, which estranged us for years at a time, deep in my heart I nursed forgiveness for him, because he possessed more virtues than vices. If in our youth we experienced some happiness, that was our readiness to sacrifice ourselves for everyone suffering around the world, and they were the poor and underprivileged classes. At that time my brother had been for me a model of the ideal young man and not only for me, but for all the young people in our region. Empathetic, honest, and hardworking, he hated every kind of despotic behavior and lived with the illusion that all people in the world had equal rights. The difficulties he faced in his work were many and only a person like him, with inexhaustible energy, devotion, and faith in the work of socialism, could overcome them. He worked under orders from "up above" and the mistakes and distortions he committed were not his, or not his alone, but due to the "party line," to working methods at the time of collectivization. The instructions from the party's regional committee demanded he act with a "firm hand," and my brother understood these instructions just as all responsible party workers did. As they say, power had a finger in this business as well. It is complicated and difficult to trace and explain the influence of power on people, but it is indisputable that no one in this world has resisted its temptations, especially if this power is absolute. Those who exercise absolute power are obligated to work for the good of society, while society for its part is obligated to submit. And perhaps in the submission of the many to the single individual, power reveals its feminine seduction and turns into vanity and becomes second nature.

My brother, too, was going down that inevitable path. As I found out later from Ivan Shibilev himself, he had denounced my brother for his displays of despotism and with his inherent frankness had not spared him a single truth, without any intention of belittling him, but "just like that, as to one of my own." Ivan Shibilev hadn't picked the right moment, since at that time my brother had already become a powerful figure. The co-op had stabilized a bit and daily wages had risen from a few cents to a lev and a half. The time of sleepless nights, doubts, and hostile conflicts was over and my brother had gained some assurance and self-confidence. Little by little he had taken the village business into his own hands and without him nothing could be decided and no initiative whatsoever could be undertaken, both in the public as well as in the personal life of the people. Party propaganda glorified Stalin to the rank of a deity, placing him above everyone and everything, he was proclaimed omnipresent and omnipotent, artists competed to praise and immortalize him. To imitate him in our work, to temper our will like steel in the struggle against our ideological enemies, was for us a sacred party duty and a source of joy. But my brother started imitating him outwardly as well. A portrait of Stalin in his cap, his jacket buttoned up to the top and with the fingers of his hand tucked between the buttons, was hanging in the party club. My brother, it seems, had discovered in his own face a similarity to the face of Stalin, and as soon as he grew the same moustache, he looked strikingly like him. We frequently went to the cinema in the city and in both the newsreels and in the feature films themselves you could always see and hear the weighty stateliness with which this strong character moved around his office, how he spoke slowly and deliberately, without the gestures or emotions of mere mortals, how he expressed his great thoughts with the fewest words possible, and sometimes only with "yes" or "no."

My brother's imitation of Stalin was, of course, foolish and ridiculous, but the leaders of the party's regional committee looked upon his resemblance to Stalin as a personal service to socialism or even as a type of predestination and over time also began to respect him as a figure. They praised his organizational abilities, were more lenient with him than with the other village party secretaries, and promised in time to promote him to a more important position in the city. This could not have failed to inspire his self-confidence as a powerful figure, as mentioned above, and which became the cause for his conflict with Ivan Shibilev. Incidentally, this conflict shows that a strong character is magnanimous, he does not abuse the power he holds, he can handle the opinion, taste, and thoughts of others, while a weak character is not sure of his own cause and for this reason defends and imposes it with suspicion, pettiness, and brutality.

My brother didn't think twice about slandering one of his comrades before the party's regional committee only because he had "insulted" him, and thus helped throw an innocent man into a labor camp. First of all, he meddled in my intimate relations with Nusha, tried to nip my feelings for her in the bud, and as a result of this meddling her father, the former municipal police officer, investigator Marchinkov, and who knows how many others lost their lives. My situation was really quite complicated because of the unclear political standing of Alexander Pashov and because of the Barakovs' intrigues, thus my brother's hesitation and caution against acting quickly and decisively is to some extent justified. But the case of Ivan Shibilev, as well as with many others before him, showed that he had begun to play lord and master of others' fates, not on any public grounds, but due to personal considerations, and that he was no longer merely overstepping his rights, but had given himself over to

despotism. Since I knew that many other party officials like him were trying to infringe upon people's innermost feelings, to dig into their hearts
with their dirty hands and to manipulate them to their liking, I kept wondering how, with these people, deprived of their individuality and their
rights, we would create the most democratic society in the world, in which
man could be the true master of his labor, of the state, and of his own
freedom. My brother was indirectly guilty for Mona's death as well, and
I told him so. I also told him that he was blinded by his plebeian lust for
power and was making himself into a tyrant, while he had long since
stopped giving a rip about the people, in whose name he was speaking and
acting. He was enraged and ordered me to leave the village immediately,
so as not to hinder him with my rotten highbrow liberalism. If I didn't do
it, then something unpleasant might happen to me as well…

  Several days later I went to say goodbye to Nusha's mother. Every week
I stopped by to see her and to ask whether she had any news of Lexy. She
had adopted one of her sister's daughters and lived with her family. She
was shrunken by the years, but wiry and intelligent, while her eyes, dark
and moist, gave off a youthful glint. With those eyes, Lexy's eyes, she, too,
asked me from afar whether I had news from him and from the expression
on my face she could guess that I didn't. In good weather I would find her
in the yard or in the garden, but now I didn't see her anywhere. Before
I could knock on the kitchen door, it opened and Lexy was standing in
front of me. As happens in such cases, the two of us stared at each other
in surprise for a moment, then embraced. Later, when we were sitting
upstairs in his room, where I had spent so many nights and experienced
so much happiness and anguish, he told me about the highly secret work
he had been doing abroad over the past eight years…

PART FIVE:

KIRO "UP YOURS" DZHELEBOV

KIRO DZHELEBOV RECEIVED this unseemly nickname when he was still young and had started to live apart from his brothers. His house was built of hewn stone, had two stories, and like all the new houses at that time, it had an orange-colored façade with white molding around the windows and a wooden veranda with stone steps. It differed from the other houses only in that instead of being a barn for cattle, the lower floor was outfitted for living. At the time this domestic reform was met with mockery and even reproach from the older homeowners, but subsequently it turned out to be sensible and useful. A barn on the lower floor had a certain advantage during the winter, when the farmer could go down to feed and tend his cattle in his underwear, but the stench of manure and piss, as well as the various vermin, turned the whole house into a barn. Kiro Dzhelebov built his barns and outbuildings in the upper end of the garden, walled them off with a high adobe fence, and while in the neighboring yards dung piles towered like ancient Thracian burial mounds in which the pigs and chickens wallowed, his yard was as grassy and clean as a clearing in the woods.

Soon his home was recognized in the village as a model home. There was no sign to this effect on the front door, as can now be found on many of the doors in Bulgarian cities, indicating that our folks keep their homes neat and tidy only if they are awarded some distinction for it, and that in homes lacking such a sign live cavemen in impenetrable stinking squalor. It was at that time that I first visited Kiro Dzhelebov's home. I was in second grade and sat next to his son Marko at school. The schoolteacher lived with them and one day she brought us to look at their house, yard, and garden, and in the afternoon assigned us an essay on the topic: "What did we see in Kiro Dzhelebov's yard?" It seems that I did not have the aesthetic gifts for seeing something worthy of admiration in that model home, I got an F on my essay, thus my first visit to the Dzhelebovs' was tied to my first literary failure. It turned out that Marko and I were in the same class in high school, too, we lived together, and during vacations I often went to their place and only then did I discover and appreciate his father's homeownerly virtues, as well as those of the whole family. The orchard with its whitewashed trees (the only ones in the village), the rows in the vegetable garden as straight as arrows, the fence with its wooden planks, the fresh and clean grass in the yard, the flower bed in front of the house, the well near the outbuildings with its ring of hewn stone, the outer gate with its roof of bright-red tiles, and everything you could see showed that the owner was not only hardworking, but also exacting to the point of precision. And there was another thing that could not be seen anywhere else in the village, if not in the whole region, and perhaps not in the whole country. At that time there was a wild pear tree in almost every field. In the shade of this tree, people would eat and rest during the summer heat, they would hang their babies' cradles from it, keep their water and tie their livestock there in its cool shadow – in short, the wild pear was the farmer's invaluable assistant, and in our region without forests it was revered as a sacred tree. It grew on its own and no one took care of it. In good times, it would bear fruit, people would gather it and make pear soup for the winter; in bad times, caterpillars would ravage it, leaving not a single leaf on its branches. Only Kiro Dzhelebov took care of the wild pears in his fields, just as he cared for the fruit trees in his yard – he pruned them in spring, whitewashed their trunks, trenched around them so they could absorb moisture, sprayed them with bluestone, and harvested fruit from them every year. By the way, it was by the pear trees that everyone in the village, as well as from the surrounding villages, knew which field was his or her own.

There were always schoolteachers living at the Dzhelebovs'. They came from various parts of the country, coming to our godforsaken village for a few years to get their start in life. Whoever arrived first in the fall, the mayor would send her to the Dzhelebovs, just as he sent official guests from the city to sleep there. One of these schoolteachers became the reason for which Kiro Dzhelebov became stuck with his new nickname. Like all our local folks, he, too, would curse more or less every other word, with or without cause, cussing out everything he laid eyes or hands on. And our curses, to put it modestly, are exquisite bits of literature and are so strikingly realistic that, as one joker who came to the village put it, when you hear them for the first time, you unwittingly scratch certain parts of your body.

The first schoolteacher to be boarded at the Dzhelebovs' was named Hortensia. For a long time we could not remember that strange name, which inspired in us such awe that even when we remembered it, we didn't dare to utter it, so as not to make it sound coarse and unharmonious from our lips. The schoolteachers were like exotic flowers among us and the village, which in the summer was sunk knee-deep in dust, and in the fall and winter, in mud and snow. Almost all of them were from cities and at first had such a hard time adjusting and coming to terms with our way of life that the villagers themselves, with their inborn feeling of superiority and hostility toward "city ladies with their dainty white hands," at once reproached and pitied them: "The poor things, why did they come here to get barked at by dogs and bitten up by fleas like us!" They didn't know that these girls were penniless and came to our village from far-flung regions to make a bit of money, to be able to have a home and family of their own, or to further their education. Hortensia, for example, spent three years with us, without going home during vacations, so as to save travel expenses, and in the fourth year wrote to us from Switzerland, where she had gone to study medicine. She was from Kyustendil and often told us about that big city that was so wondrous in our imaginations, as we had not seen mountains or crystal-clear rivers or mineral baths. Even now, when I happen to see the town of Kyustendil on the map, I always think of "Miz Hortensia," my first teacher, I see her cautiously wading through the deep, sticky mud, her overshoes completely sinking in it, how she skipped lightly and gracefully across the fields with us in a white blouse and a black skirt, petite and slender, with her hair cut boyishly *à la garçonne*, I can hear her calling our names in her gentle, flute-like voice, I can smell the scent of her clothes and hands, the aroma of flowers amid our fur caps and leather sandals stinking of manure and dust.

As Auntie Tanka later told us, the first morning the new teacher came running to her in tears, saying: "My dear landlady, I'm leaving! I beg your pardon, but I can't stay here with you any longer!"

"But why not, Miss Teacher? You just got here last night, and now you're wanting to leave. You didn't see a snake in our house, now did you?"

The teacher told her how she had finally fallen asleep around dawn, and that the landlord's voice had awakened her just a short while ago. She sat up in bed and saw him standing in front of the window of her room, and spoke such words to her that she could not possibly repeat them. Auntie Tanka couldn't imagine what the explanation for this could possibly be, and she was burning with shame in front of the girl. A grown man with three children going and saying such shameful things to a young girl, she couldn't get her mind around it. She found her husband in the cattle shed and hauled off and gave him a piece of her mind. When he heard what his wife was accusing him of, Kiro in his turn burned with shame and swore that he hadn't seen the teacher, much less talked to her. And he hadn't been peeping through her window, but had seen a mouse on her window ledge, one of those that infest the foundations of the house all summer and can be killed off neither by water nor by poison. It was just standing on the window ledge looking him in the eye, as if thumbing his nose at him.

Auntie Tanka immediately guessed what he had said to the mouse, warned him next time to keep his "dirty mouth" shut, and ran back to the girl to calm her down.

"So that's what it was, eh, Miss Teacher? Well, that's what our men around here say instead of 'good morning.' Your uncle Kiro saw a mouse and he was threatening it, and here you are all in tears..."

Knowing the indelibly artistic impression made by our curses, which my grandfather began teaching me even before I went to school, I can only imagine how unambiguous his threat must have sounded, addressed in the early morning to the schoolteacher's window: "Ooh, you dirty little tramp, just wait till I get my hands on you, I'll skewer you alive!"

From that day forward, Kiro Dzhelebov fell ill, as hardcore smokers or drug addicts fall ill when deprived of tobacco or drugs. This new girl, "as pretty as a picture," inspired such respect in him that he suddenly recognized the obscenity of his habit, felt deeply ashamed, and decided to root it out once and for all. But habit, as we know, is man's second nature, and it is stronger and truer than man's first nature. This second nature had been sprouting in his soul since the cradle and had set down such strong roots that only a sworn saint could have cured himself of it, at the price of a lifelong vow of silence. For Kiro Dzhelebov, this meant being reborn, and under the condition no less that the teacher would live with them in order to raise him from infancy. His abstention turned into true sickness, making him agitated, petty, and quarrelsome. He had to take the teacher into consideration even when she was at school, because it seemed to him that she would hear him and burst into tears from the shame and insult of it. Only in his sleep could he fully relish freedom of speech, and for whole nights he would spew such masterpieces of cursing that Auntie Tanka would listen in delight. But wouldn't you know, the situation became unbearable and Kiro Dzhelebov tried to fool his habit, just like a smoker tries to outwit his urge with an unlit cigarette, candies, or sunflower seeds. He started replacing real swears with more innocent cusses, for example, "son of a biscuit" and "why don't you you-know-what your whatchamacallit," but all this abstract you-know-whatting could not satisfy his urgent needs. Finally, after extended artistic setbacks, he found an expression that he felt was fully synonymous with one of our classic curses. This expression, similar to modern art, was filled from end to end with subtext, in other words, with it you could say what you wanted to say in an Aesopian way, but on the other hand, no one could reproach you for vulgarity or old-fashioned realism: "Up yours!"

The local wiseacres had been watching his literary efforts at close range and as soon as they heard this expression come out of his mouth twice, they immediately appended it to his name.

Nikolin Miyalkov and Salty Kalcho flashed by like ghosts and went on their way farther into the woods, while he stood near the dry stump and cleared away the snow around it. For years he had manned this blind and he had always hit something. A narrow clearing headed downhill and the game always ran along it as it was being pursued. He stood there well hidden by the dry stump, such that even the wild boar couldn't sense him and came within a dozen feet of him. Two years earlier he had killed a boar with enormous tusks (golden tusks, as he was later to find out) in this spot and had given them to Stoyan Kralev. The forest was small, but held a lot of game. Besides rabbits, in recent years deer had been breeding there, pheasants had been introduced, and with them came foxes. Two herds of wild boar had turned up from somewhere, after plundering the corn they stayed to winter in the Inferno near the pools made by the spring. In late autumn, the snipes swooped in, attracted by the humidity, huge flocks of wild doves flew in as well, and the forest became a small but rich reserve. For fowl, they hunted "in situ," but for larger game, they split into beaters and hunters. Their hunting party was small, six men all told, four of them would go through the woods, making noise, hollering and shooting, while the other four would wait in the blinds. Each time they would do only two battues, but they never came back empty-handed. They would gut the game under the old oak tree, divide the meat into equal parts, after that one of them would gather in his hat one object from each of them – a pocketknife, matches, a button, or some other thing – hand the hat to another who would place the objects on the pieces of meat. During this ceremony all the others would stand with their backs turned, and afterward everyone would take the piece of meat marked with his object. In this fair way they divided even the small game. If there was an extra pheasant, partridge, or wood pigeon left, they would draw lots for it as well, and only then would they sit down beneath the old oak to rest. They would take whatever they had, brandy or wine, out of their backpacks, drink a few rounds, and give themselves over to the pleasure of hunterly talk.

Sometimes, exalted by drink, they would shoot at targets. They would throw empty bottles up and try to hit them, they would fire at newspapers and hats, but most often they took the raven's nest as their target. As is well known, ravens are centenarian birds, and it seems that they build their houses for a century to come. The nest was firmly jammed . between several branches at the very top of the oak and had been there for years. The hunters only shot at it in the fall, when it was empty, and never managed to destroy it either with buckshot or slugs, as if it were woven from armored steel. All of them had some pleasant or unpleasant memory from the hours spent under the old oak. For example, when Kiro Dzhelebov killed the large boar, he made a mistake that could have cost Stoyan Kralev his life. They had just sat down to their first round when Kiro Dzhelebov bumped his rifle, which he had leaned against the oak, with his foot. It fell, and as it fell it fired right at Stoyan Kralev. It missed him by a hair and tore a strip out of the sleeve of his padded jacket. He touched his left arm, while Kiro Dzhelebov turned white as a sheet. They all jumped up alarmed, only Stoyan Kralev remained sitting and tried to cover his fear with a joke: "Death tugged at my sleeve and passed right on by. For now, it said, I'm pushing back your deadline."

Kiro Dzhelebov got ahold of himself, grabbed his rifle, and slammed it into the oak so hard that he was left holding the butt in his hands.

"Christ, I just about killed a man for nothing!" he cried, pounding his head with his fists.

While he was getting a new rifle butt made in the city, he still went hunting. He said that on hunting days he couldn't sit still at home, so he became a permanent beater for the hunting party, but, in fact, he was only serving Stoyan Kralev. He would head straight for his blind, shouting, yapping like a hunting dog, and driving game to him. After the hunt he would quickly skin and gut Stoyan Kralev's portion, and only then would he sit down to rest. And so it was for two whole hunting seasons. He also helped him with his vineyard, fashioned all sorts of chicken coops and birdcages for him, and finally began inviting him to his house, all under the pretense that it was a "sacrificial offering" to make up for the incident beneath the old oak. He didn't feel any guilt over that unpleasant incident, which really could have cost Stoyan Kralev his life, yet nevertheless he constantly tried to show that he was indebted to him due to his carelessness and that there had been no intended malice in that carelessness. The more repugnant this toadyism was to his own nature, the more he tormented himself with his efforts to play the role of Stoyan Kralev's friend, and the more he tried to prove this to him. Stoyan Kralev repaid him for his generosity only with a bare and simple "thanks." This bootlicking was not particularly pleasant to him, but he allowed it, since with this bootlicking Kiro Dzhelebov showed the village, albeit with a great delay, that he was to blame for the serious conflicts that had played out between the two of them. He had been waiting for more than fifteen years for that proud man to bow his head and drop from his shoulders his great burden of guilt, which the elderly people still remembered and which they could not forgive him for. Kiro Dzhelebov even now was thinking about the sad and insurmountable consequences of that guilt. Down in the Inferno, a thick whiteness had settled, while up above in the blind the blizzard was raging at fever pitch. And it seemed to him that this cold and impenetrable white nothingness was rocking and making his head spin. If I didn't know what a state he was in, I wouldn't have been able to explain why he had agreed to head to the woods at that time, especially since he was the only one of the group who didn't understand the meaning of the episode with the bottle, which Salty Kalcho refused to drink from and which made him burst out crying. For the others, this was no mystery, since they had all been at the wedding of Salty Kalcho's daughter. And as we shall see a bit later, all of them had some fateful connection to that event. But even if Kiro Dzhelebov had been at that terrible wedding, the incident at the tavern would hardly have reminded him of anything. He headed for the woods, not to hunt some wolves, not out of solidarity with the others, but, as he himself was aware, to chase away his own anguish.

A few days after I had arrived in the village, he met me on the street and very insistently invited me to his home. He looked truly happy to run in to me, because he told me that many times he had thought of me, just like that, just as sometimes you remember things from the past. He led me upstairs to the east room, where the schoolteachers had once lived. The room was clean and cozy, and, of course, was arranged completely differently than it had been years ago when I had been a regular visitor at their house. Where there had once been a wall rug, sewn from pieces of woolen cloth and embroidery with colorful thread, now stood a two-winged wardrobe, the wooden bed had been replaced by an iron one, on the wall in a single frame were numerous pictures of his two sons with their wives and children, in the corner between the two windows stood a large radio, on its chain next to the bed hung the silver watch with Arabic numerals that Marko and I had used throughout our school years. Back then he had told us that his grandfather had gotten it from his own father when he was young, thus the watch had worked flawlessly for more than a century. There, too, an icon of the Virgin Mary had been placed, drawn by Ivan Shibilev's skillful hand. Unlike all the icons I had seen in city churches, the young woman was painted in profile, with one large Egyptian eye, in a dark-blue robe and with a green halo around her head. With one arm she held Jesus in her lap, while with the other she offered him a bright-red bunch of grapes. Jesus was reaching out his little hand toward the grapes with the impatience of a hungry child, and it was clear that after that bunch he would want to eat yet another. The only sign of his divine providence was the equally green halo around his head, otherwise he looked like any local child – with rosy cheeks and a white shirt, since at that age they did not yet dress them in pants. Ivan Shibilev had likely painted the icon in the summertime in the shade of the outdoor kitchen, because the background was golden yellow like ripe wheat, and around the two figures he had painted all sorts of domestic birds and animals.

"Sit down, I'll be right back," my host said, and a minute later brought a bottle of wine, two glasses, and a plate of blood sausage from the other room. "Your auntie Tanka went to the store, she'll be back soon, but in the meantime we can raise our glasses. Try some of the sausage, I just slaughtered my pig the other day, it's fresh. Welcome and cheers!"

"This is fine wine, Uncle Kiro!" I said. "I haven't had any like this in quite some time."

"Where would you get any? All that store-bought stuff is sour as vinegar. This is my old wine, I haven't opened up this year's yet. Sure, I've got wine, but who is there to drink it? My sons have gone and scattered off to the cities, they never seem to find time to drop by here. Your auntie Tanka and I are left alone, we look after ourselves somehow or another. Some nights we may drink a glass apiece, and that's the end of it."

While he was saying this, he got up, looked out through the window to the street, and tears filled his eyes. He filled up the glasses and said: "May he rest in peace!"

"May he rest in peace? Who?"

"My heart is aching with grief, my boy! I haven't breathed a word to anyone, but I'll bare my soul to you now. I've considered you one of our own since way back when, because you and Marko went to school together and hung around together. Marko is no longer with us!"

Marko had emigrated to West Germany in '52. He was the first defector abroad from our region and his defection at that time made a staggering impression on all of us, while his family fell into serious disgrace. Kiro Dzhelebov and I had never talked about this. I could see that at every one of our meetings he wanted to share something about his son, but didn't dare to, while I, for my part, could never decide whether to ask about Marko, I didn't want to be rubbing salt in the wound. Only now was he giving me the opportunity to comfort him, and I told him that Marko might come back someday. As far as I knew, he hadn't given up his Bulgarian citizenship, he had not declared himself a "nonreturner," so if he wanted to, he could come back. He shook his head.

"Marko passed away."

He took a crumpled piece of paper out of his wallet and handed it to me. It was a telegram, written in Bulgarian in Latin letters and for the recipient's benefit the contents had been written between the lines in Bulgarian letters:

Marko died wait two days funeral Juta Annie Kiril.

I studied the telegram for a long time, pretending that I didn't understand the text very well in Latin letters and was trying to translate it letter for letter, to make sure there hadn't been some mistake. But Kiro Dzhelebov knew why I was sounding out the text and saved me the trouble of sharing the banal condolences offered in such situations.

"I got this two days ago. I went to the city to mail him a letter. To wish him a Happy New Year. There's a clerk at the city post office, a relative of your auntie Tanka's, when a letter comes from him she sets it aside and gives it to me directly. The local folks here would open it up and rake me over the coals. You've got a letter, the woman said, read it, then send what you're going to send. I sat down and read the letter. Marko wrote that he was sick. He'd been having pain in his chest for more than two years, now he was in the hospital and didn't know when he would get out. I read the letter and the woman called to me through the window. You just got a telegram as well, she said. It was clear she was trying to prepare me for the worst and that's exactly what it was. I hid the telegram and as of now, no one knows anything. I don't want them either to feel sorry for me or to rub their hands with glee. I haven't told his mother or his brothers. Let them think that he's alive and well. I will bury him in my heart all by myself, I'll be his priest, I'll be his grave. He had an unlucky fate. And now I'll never see his children. Their mother'll turn them into Germans by the time they're grown up. As of now, both of them know some Bulgarian. The older one is named after me – Kiril. He writes a real fine Bulgarian, as if he had gone to school here. Grandma and Grandpa, he writes, why don't you come visit us, we've got a car, we'll take you around everywhere. Marko always wanted to work the land and he was working the land there. Whether he himself earned it, or whether it was his wife's land, I don't know. He just wrote that he had a small estate of around twenty-five acres. Here he is in a picture that he sent us two years ago."

The color photo he handed me was taken such that the viewer could see very well as much of Marko's prosperity as possible. He and his wife were sitting on chairs in a yard awash with flowers and greenery, the children were sitting in front of them on the grass. Behind them their house with its veranda and pointed roof could be seen, beyond the house, under the eaves of some outbuilding stood a blue car and a small tractor the color of a tomato. Both children were dark like their father, while the mother was light blond, almost as white as an albino.

We heard footsteps on the stairs outside, my host grabbed the photo out of my hands and put it in the drawer of the table and signaled to me to keep what we had been talking about a secret. Auntie Tanka came in, saw me, and cried in her ringing voice: "Well, look who came to visit us! Good God, we had guests and here I was fiddling around in the village! I went to the store to get this and that, then I stopped by my sister Ivana's, as she's a little under the weather." She set what she had been carrying on the table and fixed her kerchief. "Now let me give you a proper welcome!"

She held out her hand, as the village women do in greeting, and I kissed it. I always reminded her of Marko, I could see the grief rising in her eyes, but she, like her husband, never spoke of him. I wanted to tell her that I was glad to see her so spry and healthy, but she stepped toward me, got up on her tiptoes and silently kissed my left shoulder. This simple woman's gentle gesture touched me, I put my arms around her head and gently stroked it, she let out a sob, covered her face with her hands, and tears sprang out from between her fingers.

"I dream of him every night! Dressed in white clothes, with red flowers in his hands…"

"Come on now, don't wail as if for the dead, it's downright sinful!" her husband scolded her. "Folks haven't come to visit to hear about your worries! Go get us something to eat."

"Fine, fine, fiiine," Auntie Tanka said with quiet reproach, and left the room. "We always have to keep silent, always keep silent. How hard your heart must be! Drink another round, I'll be right back with food."

"Women! It's just like them to bawl over anything and everything," Kiro Dzhelebov said as we sat back down at the table, as if he himself hadn't been crying just a few minutes earlier. "No one's eternal in this world. A man is born wrapped in a black sash and as long as he's alive he has to deal with all sorts of things. It's easy to deal with the good stuff, but with the bad, you've got to go out and meet it. Either you tackle it or it tackles you, but you can't live just sitting there with your hands in your pockets... Help yourself to some more sausage, we'll be eating in just a bit. The food is ready, Auntie Tanka cooked before she went out. Come on now, cheers! I told you, didn't I, that this is last year's wine, I'll open up this year's one of these days. This year the grapes were late, but sweet. Forty days I waited for the must to clear up, it was just bubbling away..."

It was not difficult to guess that he was talking to me about the vineyard, the wine, and other things so as to erase the traces of the sentimentality he had shown earlier. In just a single minute he had managed to give his face such a calm expression that if I hadn't read the message about Marko's death, I would have no idea of the anguish he was going through. Auntie Tanka soon set the table. She, like her husband, had managed to change the expression on her face, she was smiling, as befit a hospitable host, and was constantly urging me to help myself to everything.

"Why, you eat no more than a sparrow, my boy! Eat up, eat up!"

This lunch was a difficult ordeal for me, and as they say in the village of such cases, I had to carry all the food on my back. I swallowed with great effort and said whatever came to my head, but I couldn't shake the feeling that I was at a wake after a funeral and that I was a coconspirator in a terrible secret which Marko's mother had managed to uncover through the mysterious conjectures of her heart and only out of respect for me was she not giving free reign to her grief. In her husband's silence there was a desperate pride, and in my hypocrisy – a sacrilege against her deep and holy grief. At the very start of the lunch I had announced that I needed to get ready to travel, and as soon as lunch was over, I got up from the table. Auntie Tanka started bewailing the fact that she hadn't had time to get a gift ready for my trip back to Sofia, she hunted through the house and in the end thrust a few links of fresh flat sausage into my hands. I took my leave of her on the stairs, while Kiro Dzhelebov saw me out to the street.

"I beg your pardon for burdening you with our problems, but that's how it worked out," he said, holding out his hand to shake mine. "But if the weather turns bad and you can't travel, come down to the *horemag* Sunday morning, we'll be holding Holy Communion with the new wines."

I went back to the old house of my aunt, who still lived in the village. She had lit the iron stove, it was warm in the room, it smelled of fresh-split logs and herbs, while outside snowflakes were already swirling and a strong wind bent the branches of the trees. I lay down on the colorful cover of the bed and tried to read, but by the very first page I couldn't concentrate and set the book aside. I thought about Marko, deceased, and saw him at different ages, from a child until the day he had taken that photo with his family. I knew that we had been sitting side by side since first grade, but I remembered him from second grade, when Pesho the schoolteacher came into class one day with Miss Hortensia and lined us up along the wall for a checkup. It had to be the beginning of the school year, because I remember we all had brown stains on our hands and mouths from the unripe walnuts, while our newly shaved heads shone like tin-plated bowls. Pesho the schoolteacher ordered us to unbutton the collars of our shirts and to take off our left shoes and socks, took the pointer from the blackboard, and started off down the line. First of all he inspected our necks and ears for grime, then checked our collars for lice, and finally our hands and feet for untrimmed nails. For untrimmed nails and a grimy neck you got three switches to the palm, for lice – five. The more chick-enhearted among us started crying even before he wound up to strike, and hid their hands, but the inveterate defender of hygiene grabbed the crying children's hands, turned their palms up and delivered the necessary number of blows. He had been teaching since the school had opened, and in the village, from the children up to the grandmothers and grandfathers, there wasn't a single person who hadn't been beaten by him at least once. As the doyen of the teaching staff, he was given the honor of carrying out this execution and he carried it out so conscientiously and impeccably that Miss Hortensia burst into tears and left the room. In those days of campaigns against filthiness, especially at the beginning of the school year when we arrived at school straight from the fields as wild and headstrong as the livestock we had spent the summer with, in the classrooms you could hear screams like those during a police interrogation, after which we all ran home to our houses. Till late in the evening a fire would be burning in every yard, our mothers would strip us naked, delouse us, wash us, and scald our clothes in a cauldron.

I remember Marko from that day, perhaps because he alone out of all those singled out for punishment instead received praise. Pesho the schoolteacher scrutinized him for quite some time, surprised, and perhaps disappointed, that for the first time in his long years of teaching, he could not make use of his rights as executioner. He stripped him naked to the waist, inspected his clothes down to the last seam, but his unprecedented cleanliness was irrefutable and in the end he was forced to point him out as an example before the whole school. As a student, however, Marko did not stand out, he had neither failures nor great successes, with effort and diligence he passed from grade to grade with Cs and sometimes even Bs. Our friendship was not completely disinterested, but was nonethe-less mutually beneficial. I soon noticed that Marko would glance at my notebook and during recess he would ask me about the lesson for the next class. I would tell him what I knew, while he would return the favor however he could – sometimes by giving me an eraser or his pocketknife, which was linked to his pocket with a little chain. In late autumn and winter there were days and weeks when the village was sunk in mud and snow. Our fathers carried us to and from school on their backs. We brought our lunches in bags and at lunchtime we all ate at our desks. For lunch, Marko brought a piece of *banitsa*, a slice of grilled meat, a bit of sausage, butter or cheese, and I would start glancing at his feast, just as during class he glanced at my notebook. I was most interested in his bread, usually the heel of a big, fluffy loaf with a pinkish crust and soft as cotton. Because of that bread I began to put more systematic effort into Marko's education. I would test him on the following lesson, I helped him do his homework, while his menu became ever more varied and plentiful, he would place it on the middle of the desk and invite me to help myself, and so I would. Thus from a very early age I started selling my intellectual labor to satisfy my most vital material needs.

When the time came to go to high school, Kiro Dzhelebov himself suggested that Marko and I live together in an apartment. The boys are used to being together here, let them live together in the city as well, he said, but his offer was hardly the result of sentimental motives, especially since other boys, and wealthier ones at that, would also go to study at the high school. He was a fair to middling farmer, he showed a certain indulgence to our family, yet it seemed that he had valued the help I had given his son in primary school and hoped that I would "prop him up" in high school as well. In any case, they found us an apartment, bargained with the landlords so we could eat with them, discussed how much and which foodstuffs to deliver, then he and my brother left, and on that day Marko and I became high school students.

The city didn't seem to make much of an impression on Marko or at least it didn't change his way of life. Right after the very first day he wrapped all his textbooks and notebooks in blue paper, stuck labels on them, and arranged them in one corner of the cupboard; after dinner he looked over his lessons and went to bed. In the morning he got up an hour earlier than me and shined his shoes, brushed his clothes off, washed at the fountain in the yard, and then woke me up. And that's how it was for the five years we lived together. Marko didn't demonstrate any particular talents in high school, either, and never budged a bit from his C average. Like a good parent who gives equal attention to each of his children, he equally distributed his efforts over all his subjects as if having weighed them on a pharmacist's scale; thus on his report cards and later on his high school diploma, his results were written in the form of a column of Cs. This column of Cs was like a chain made of identical links and gave the impression of mediocrity, but also of proverbial persistence and spiritual resolve. His father, who was otherwise ambitious and demanding in his work, did not go after his son to try for better grades. When you set your mind to some task, he would say, it gets going on its own and sooner or later brings you success.

During the vacations and especially the summer vacations, Marko spent more time in the fields than at home, dressed like the illiterate village boys, in a simple shirt, leather sandals, and a straw hat on his head. They had around fifteen acres of "well-tended fields" and he, like his father, felt himself to be the true master of this land. In the last year of high school, his younger brother also came to study with us, and his youngest brother had finished middle school, so the family had four fully capable workers. Kiro Dzhelebov could rely on any one of them, even the youngest, who was not yet strong enough for the hoe or the scythe, yet who could look after the livestock no worse than adult farmers. In the fields Kiro Dzhelebov would reap in the center to keep the rows straight, while his sons would work to his left, both stripped to the waist "city style," tanned and as husky as grown men. If rain hadn't fallen the previous day, the three of them would stay to sleep in the fields. They would eat supper in the dark, spread sheaves of wheat beneath the pear tree, and immediately fall asleep. The youngest, Dimcho, would go to graze the horses in the Inferno and would sleep there with the other horse herders, and in the morning he and his mother would bring food to the fields. Kiro Dzhelebov would wake up several times during the night, he would check to see how the boys were sleeping, would guess what time it was by looking at the stars, and would lie down again, but he always slept with one eye open. He would have vague dreams and at the same time he would hear the sounds of the night, he would catch the scent of the grasses, the wheat, and the land. And that's how he would pass the night until the first hoarse and sleepy rooster's crow came from the village. He would get up quietly, so as not to wake the boys, who were sleeping soundly with their eyes tightly shut, and would go to the other end of the field to pull up grass to bind the sheaves. In the east, the dark blue of the sky would be growing ever paler, spilling over into purple, pink, and finally golden yellow. During that time he would be twisting grass into rope and as soon as he went to put it under the pear tree, the boys would hear his footsteps and would jump to their feet like soldiers at attention. Sleep a while longer, it's still early, he would say to them, but the boys were already splashing their faces with water from the jug and grabbing their scythes. In the first few days of the harvest their hands got blisters and bled, in the morning they could hardly open their fingers, but instead of complaining they joked that they had become delicate city ladies. They had been used to working hard since they were children and patriarchally revered their parents, who suffered so much deprivation on their account. At home, in the fields, or wherever they were, as soon as their mother or father appeared they were on their feet, they never reached out for food at the table before their parents did, and did not take any liberties in their presence. Kiro Dzhelebov did not bore them with lectures about the benefits of hard work, since he was convinced that a person would not fritter away whatever strength and ability he was given. They, for their part, never asked him for money or clothing, because they knew he would give each of them what they needed when the time was right. Consanguine solidarity made them trust one another and they had no memories of any arguments or spats within the family.

They would have reaped a row or even two by the time the sun was up. An ethereal twilight hung over the field, tiny droplets of dew glittered on the ears of wheat, the quails tried to outsing one another right at the boys' feet. The three of them hurried to finish before the heat and worked in silence, while behind them the sheaves of wheat stacked up, as neat and orderly as skeins of wool. And when the sun rose a bit in the sky, now shrunken and red-hot with fury, their cart would appear on the road. The youngest brother, Dimcho, would be driving the horses, while their mother would be sitting in the middle of the cart making sure the pots of food didn't spill. She, too, got up at the first rooster's crow and set about lighting the stove, milking the cow and buffalo, then driving them out to meet the cowherd, feeding the chickens, and finally making food for the fields. By the time the men got back to the pear tree, by the time they washed up, she would have spread a tablecloth in the shade and arranged the dishes she had cooked at the crack of dawn: chicken stew, yogurt, *banitsa*, cucumbers, wild plum compote or water with grated garlic, sugar, and vinegar to slake their thirst, all of it in pans, in earthenware dishes and pots, wrapped in white strips of cloth or covered over with pumpkin leaves. The boys ate like wolves, she would peck at the food, just enough so as not to be sitting there twiddling her thumbs, and she never took her eyes off them, as she had no other chance to get her fill of watching them. In the morning they got up early, in the evening they came back when it was dark, and before she knew it the summer would turn to autumn rain and they would be putting on their school uniforms and leaving for the city.

"Why are you sitting off to the side there? What, did you cook just for us?" Kiro Dzhelebov would say, as he saw her barely pecking at the food like an uninvited guest.

"Don't bother with me, you eat up, eat your fill, 'cause reaping is the hardest bit of fieldwork, you need your strength," she would answer. "While I was cooking, I tried a bit of this, a bit of that, and got filled up before I knew it."

All three of them were the spitting image of their father, dark with bristly black hair and bluish-green eyes, as hardworking and adept as he was. She caressed them in her mind and in her dreams, otherwise she didn't dare touch them. Even the youngest didn't allow any cuddling, he would frown, ashamed that the older boys might think he was still a child. One after another they passed: reaping, threshing, stacking, the Assumption with the first baskets of grapes, and before you knew it on September 14 early in the morning several carts would be driving the students off to Varna, Dobrich, Provadia. Kiro Dzhelebov was now sending off three students, two to Varna and the youngest to the Model Estate Institute near Ruse.

The events of September 9, 1944, found Marko and me doing our mandatory army service. He was serving in Varna, I was in Shumen. When we were discharged, the village was so stirred up that we could hardly recognize it. Our folks had been telling us regularly in letters everything that was going on, yet still we were surprised by the changes that had occurred and above all by the irrepressible political passions. Before September 9, only a few of the students had talked openly about their political convictions and two of them had landed in prison, several adults were known to be communists or Bulgarian Agrarian Union supporters, but now everyone had joined some kind of party. There were socialists and Zveno adherents, there were also radicals who had earlier not even heard of these parties, much less been familiar with their political platforms. They held meetings at their clubs, made decisions, accepted or expelled members, fought amongst themselves, and fought with the supporters of the other parties. Many skeletons were dragged out of the closet, old scores were settled, so much so that an outsider might have thought that our villagers were charging at each other with bayonets bared in a massive free-for-all. Later it became clear, however, that our local folks were not so socially and class-conscious so as to wish to slaughter one another. All this political hysteria was due to their fear of the cooperative farm. Many believed that if they didn't join the communist party, but rather some other party, then the nationalization of land would somehow pass them by. Since the communist party made its own members join a common farm, let them do it with their land, landowners from other parties would keep working their land as they had until now. To protect themselves in this way, in many families fathers, sons, and brothers were members of different parties; they sold land or signed it over to heirs so they would owe less in state delivery quotas and fewer taxes.

Kiro Dzhelebov was one of the few, if not the only person in the village, who steered clear of all political parties. If he was called to the pan-village meeting, he never refused to go, he would listen to what was said from start to finish and then he would go home. There were a dozen people who had to be handled more carefully due to their authority in the villagers' eyes. It was thought that if they dug in their heels and refused to join the co-op as founders from the very beginning, they would make the others lose their nerve, and vice versa – if they joined, they would drag the others along after them. Stoyan Kralev ordered us to speak to these people almost allegorically on the question of collectivization, we needed ever so gently to "finagle" them, to flatter them and convince them that as good farmers in the co-op, they would also enjoy great respect. Kiro Dzhelebov had given us no reason to put him in the category of "tough nuts to crack," he had never shown even the slightest hint, but his pensive attitude toward the events of those days of general overexcitement led us all to believe that it would be hard for him to decide to join the co-op or that perhaps he would never come to that decision. At the same time, however, all of us expected from him some pleasant surprise, namely that after thinking it over and considering the circumstances better than the others had, one day, perhaps the last day, or even at the last minute of the meeting in which the co-op would be founded, he would rise up from the back row in the hall, where he always sat, and silently submit his application to join. With these divergent feelings toward him, Stoyan Kralev gave me very detailed instructions to finagle him ever so gently and to win him over to our side at all costs.

"I don't need to tell you what kind of man he is, you know him best. They're your people, you know how to talk to them, get to work!"

Stoyan Kralev assigned me this task with a sense of certainty that obliged me, and the very next day I found an excuse to stop by to see Kiro Dzhelebov. Everyone knew that we young propagandizers considered the number of people each of us got to join the co-op as a matter of prestige, and that propagandizing itself had its romantic side for us. Our local folks, so divided in their support of various political parties and so suspicious of one another, unexpectedly showed a united front against us, yet we ourselves turned into phantoms and found holes through which we slipped into their homes. We found ourselves in various situations, most of them unpleasant, some sent us away with kind words, others threw us out with curses and set their dogs on us, they stymied us with questions that Marx himself wouldn't have been able to answer, they laid traps for us. We responded to all this with the patience of missionaries inducted into the great mystery and set out with unprecedented self-abnegation to share this mystery with the poor of spirit; we knew our jaws should never stop flapping at top speed under any circumstances. For the "village masses," in other words, everyone but the dozen people mentioned earlier, Stoyan Kralev gave us clear and firm instructions. "Once you've got your hands on him, don't let him go until he softens up. Wherever you meet him – on the street, in the fields, in the tavern – you'll tell him the advantages of collective farming over private farming, about the exploitation by the estate-holders and kulaks, and most of all about the prosperity of the Soviet kolkhoz members. Keep the declaration in your pocket – if he says 'yes,' give it to him to sign!" And we carried out his instructions with the greatest enthusiasm and delight. Everything that we had read and heard about the Soviet kolkhozes we retold to the villagers so graphically and with such inspiration it was as if we ourselves had become grain producers, stockbreeders, and machine operators. And so as not to leave the slightest hint of doubt in their mistrustful souls, at the end we flung before them the final and most shattering argument for the prosperity of the kolkhoz workers, precisely that the kolkhoz members at the end of the year take only a small part of their remuneration, because this small part is so large that it is enough to satisfy all their needs. What's more, the kolkhoz member can use as much as he wants of the common property. That means if somebody feels like slaughtering ten chickens today, he can go ahead and slaughter them and nobody will stop him, but he wouldn't do it anyway, he wouldn't cause harm to his comrades, because he is a conscious Soviet man, the new man, and so on and so forth.

Kiro Dzhelebov was shoveling manure in his backyard. Stripped down to his shirtsleeves and shod in old galoshes, with his pant legs rolled up, he was jabbing the metal pitchfork into the thick pulpy mash and throwing it into an oxcart. Steam was rising from the dung heap and the astringent scent of aged manure hung in the air, several chickens were right at his feet, getting in his way, and every time he lifted the pitchfork they lunged forward greedily to peck at the worms. He carefully pushed them aside, scolding them like mischievous, gluttonous children: "Don't poke around in there, you'll be skewered on my pitchfork before you can say boo! You're pecking around with those busy beaks of yours and still there's no filling you up. Shoo, get out of my way!"

Absorbed in his work, he only saw me when he heard the garden gate creak, he stuck the pitchfork into the dung heap and came to meet me.

"I won't shake your hand," he said, "because my hands aren't clean, but it's sure good to see you! I was thinking to take a little manure to the fields near the grove. This year I planted it with sunflowers, but on one end they didn't grow worth a darn. I said to myself, the place is on a slope, and the rains have washed away the soil, so why don't I toss down a cartload or two of manure? Come on inside, your auntie Tanka will treat us to a bunch of grapes or the like."

At that moment Auntie Tanka came out onto the veranda, saw me, and invited me into the house. I told her I had just stopped by for a bit on my way to somewhere else, but in the next few days I would come to visit them properly. She started hanging braids of onion and garlic under the eaves of the veranda, while her husband and I stayed by the dunghill. I asked him if he had gotten a letter from Marko, who had been a student in Sofia for two months, I asked him about his other sons as well. He said Marko wrote regularly, that he was doing fine, he was living with another young man from a village near Plovdiv. He had enrolled in agronomy. Before leaving for Sofia, he had thought to study at the polytechnical institute, but when he got there he decided to sign up for the agronomy department. Well, since he wants agronomy, let him study agronomy, that's his business. We sent him a little package the other day with this and that so he can eat a square meal now and then, since the food in Sofia was a bit scarce. Anyo was slogging away in his military service, and Dimcho would graduate from the Model Estate Institute this year, God willing.

While he was telling me about his sons in a few short phrases, as one gives short reports to outsiders, Kiro Dzhelebov unwittingly took up the pitchfork, and while tossing manure into the cart, he started talking about the chickens, who were pecking for worms at his feet: "I don't know if you've noticed, but the chicken is as greedy as a goat. If you leave a goat to graze all day, it'll never get full, while a chicken will keep pecking away with its beak from morning till night like a sewing machine. From the looks of it, its throat isn't even the size of your hand, but there's no filling it. Especially this one here, the red one, a Stara Zagora breed, it's always got its eye on the grain. The Rhode Island breed eats less, but grows bigger. Whatever it pecks up goes straight to its back. The Plymouth Rock is the same. Whereas the Leghorn is better for laying eggs. It more or less lays eggs year-round, and every day at that. Only you've got to feed it milk sops and mix in a little chicken feed or sunflower. They don't lay eggs well on corn or other grains. A chicken's a chicken, but it still wants things just so. But at any rate, a chicken is soil's worst enemy. Let it rove around the garden for a week, who knows what it does to the soil, but if you don't fertilize afterward with manure, you can kiss next year's crop goodbye."

After this short but exhaustive lecture on poultry farming, Kiro Dzhelebov brought over the oxbow that had been leaning against the cattle shed and set about putting it on the cart shaft, I wished him a good day and left. I hadn't been expecting to have any particular success in my mission, because I knew the first meeting was only the beginning, yet I still had the feeling that it would keep getting harder and harder for me to meet up with him. It seemed to me that I would insult his dignity if I set about trying to convince him to turn his life upside down by giving up private property in the same way as I had been convincing the other farmers. I could go see Salty Kalcho, for example, whenever I wanted to, or I could stop him in the street. At first he flat out refused to hear about "that there durn co-op," but gradually he got drawn into the conversation and when I managed to convince him (and I always managed to convince him) that on the common farm all the fieldwork would be done with machines, he would simple-heartedly exclaim: "Well, that sounds mighty fine!" However, as soon as I handed him the membership declaration to sign, he would reply: "That'll happen when the time is right, it'll happen, don't you worry!" And he really did become a founding member of the cooperative farm. I saw Zhendo Ivanov several times a day, because our two families essentially shared the same yard, which was symbolically divided by a rotting, thorny hedge. For many years, I, like everyone in the village, didn't know why they called him "the Bandit," especially since he was a respectable and hardworking farmer. Clearly his christener had heard a little something about his biography during his younger years, but since Zhendo came from a different village and had never once showed his "bandit" character, we all thought he had been given this nickname by mistake. Only a few days before the wolf hunt did I find out why the local folks called him "the Bandit." I had "stopped by" his place, we had a few drinks as is only fitting, and fell into a long and involved conversation. The wall across from me had an open cupboard built into it, in which had been placed some kitchen utensils and, among them, a rusty revolver. I picked up this antique to look at it and then Zhendo told me his story, which we already know. Whether what he told me was true in its details, whether he wasn't attributing others' feats to his own name so as to sound more interesting – that doesn't really matter much. The important thing is that even if he had made up the story from beginning to end, he told it as his own and insisted that I believe every word of it. All signs indicated that he had decided suddenly and unexpectedly, even to himself, to reveal his life's "secret," which he had for years been hiding "under his tongue." This is precisely what made the strongest impression on me. Much later it occurred to me that he had told me his life story only a few days before the wolf hunt, and I found in his confession a tragic omen.

Nikolin Miyalkov and four more of my "parishioners" signed membership declarations without dramatic agonizing, only Nikola Denev repeated one and the same question during every conversation of ours: "So, we'll plow up the dividing lines and all the little fields will become one big field, is that right?" Yes! "And we'll drive all the livestock into a common barn, is that right?" Yes, we will. "And we'll work together like one big family?" One night he disappeared with his wife and two children without telling anyone. He had three acres of land which he left to the future farm and kicked off the wave of migration to the cities. "Is that right?"

My work with these people was not easy, my determination to undermine the foundations of their patriarchal way of life led them to keep their distance from me, they were worked up and curious, they asked, argued, rejected, and threw me out or else like sick men sought me out to give them relief. ("You're one of our boys, well educated, I'm joining the co-op on your word, if you're fooling me, sonny boy, you'll be the one to blame!") In a word, they let me get close to them. With Kiro Dzhelebov it was like knocking on an open door. I wouldn't have been surprised if he refused to join the co-op, because he wouldn't be the only one in the village refusing. What was painful about the situation was that he wouldn't let me get close to him. The simplest thing to do would have been to ask him: Uncle Kiro, so on and so forth, what are your intentions regarding the cooperative farm? But I couldn't do it. I was quite young, and my pride must have been too young and painfully sensitive for me to try to propagandize him, simply to risk him looking me in the eye and saying: "So that's why you've been hanging around me – trying to teach me what to do." Not only did my pride prevent me from "teaching" him, I also felt for him the feeling which they call "respect" and which is hard to explain.

Even Stoyan Kralev felt it, in the beginning, and it's no coincidence that he himself didn't deal with him directly, but rather sent me to "sound him out," and very carefully at that. "Sounding him out," however, did not mean showing him that his way of life heretofore had been incorrect and depraved from the point of view of the new times and that everything he had built and looked after – his land, livestock, equipment – which bore the traces of his heart and soul, must be handed over to the cooperative farm today or tomorrow at the latest, just like that, suddenly, as if it had never been his.

I had promised to come visit him and so I went, but again on my way elsewhere and just for a few minutes "because I'm busy with the upcoming meeting for founding the collective farm." And other times, when I ran into him by chance, I was always saying that I couldn't come visit him because from morning till night we were "rushing around" finishing tasks for the meeting, in the hopes that he would show some interest in such an important event, but he would always say: "Well, fine, when you're free, stop by our place, Marko sends his greetings!" I wondered whether he didn't realize that he was doomed as a private farmer, and if he did realize it, how he could keep his composure, when all around him life was roaring like the sea. Indeed, at that time he seemed like some sort of Gulliver, looking down from his gigantic height at the hundreds of little dwarves crawling around at his feet, stirred up by some worry of theirs, and he was being careful not to step on them. I also wondered whether he hoped that this common fate would pass him by, and if so, what his belief was based on. Stoyan Kralev, for his part, began asking me ever more often what was going on with "my man" and I would reply that my man was hesitating and still couldn't make a decision. That's how they are, Stoyan Kralev would say, citing the canons of class theory, they've got to moan and groan before they crawl out of their petty bourgeois shell.

Don't leave him too much time to philosophize over it, work him over good and hard so he doesn't think the party will be tickling him with a feather his whole life...

I, however, didn't know whether Kiro Dzhelebov was hesitating, or whether he even had an opinion about the future co-op at all. People wrongly believed that he and I were "close" and "on good terms." Even our families hadn't grown close, as one might have expected. Auntie Tanka would stop by our house now and then "to see what they would be sending to the schoolboys," my mother would stop by their place in the same way. They were always promising to have a nice, long visit and they never quite got around to doing it. Kiro Dzhelebov had only once come to our house, for fifteen minutes, he and my father talked about our school business and he even declined to drink a glass of brandy. Both he and his wife were sitting as if on guard, as if they didn't dare touch the objects around them, so as not to get dirty. They scorned our impoverished furnishings or didn't want to worry us with their presence, since they noticed that my parents were indeed worried by their visit. Otherwise, Kiro Dzhelebov frequently came to our place, but only to the gate, he would put whatever my parents had prepared for me into the cart and take it to the city. In our apartment in the city, too, he was always "just passing through," he would leave whatever he had brought and set out for the village again as soon as the horses were rested.

Every family lives by its own laws and habits, has its own secrets, plans, and contradictions. In the village, however, these soon come to light; naïveté and curiosity are so closely entwined that people can't manage to hide their personal lives behind impenetrable walls, there even the dogs "talk," and the villagers understand their language very well. Everything was known about the Dzhelebov family, just as everything was known about every family, but, in fact, nothing was known. I mean about the internal life of their family, where the outside eye and the outside ear cannot penetrate. No one had heard them "raising their voices" to one another or admonishing one another, or seen them exchanging meaningful glances, and it was difficult for people to imagine that like every family, they, too, had hours when they would gather together to discuss important family issues and to make plans for the future. Both their working and personal relations were so smooth, calm, and harmonious that it seemed like all of them, young and old alike, were equally wise, they understood one another as if by telepathy and didn't need to advise one another. They were also not secretive, as they had nothing to hide from outsiders, but rather were reserved and concentrated on their work. Their reaction to the tempestuous political events during the war and especially during the revolution was every bit as reserved, they didn't take sides, so you couldn't figure out how they saw these events. Everyone in the family managed to maintain their self-control, holding to a strict neutrality when it came to the outside world and not giving in to political passions.

I ran into Kiro Dzhelebov on the day the cooperative farm fell apart. This was the saddest day in the new history of the village. At first everything went relatively smoothly, people recognized their own livestock, untied them from the mangers, and drove them to their homes, but when it came to the sheep and the equipment, arguments and rows broke out. Every farmer had put a mark on his sheep's ears by which he could pick them out from the common neighborhood herd. Each of these herds was made up of a dozen or so households and each of the marks was different. The cooperative farm had gathered sheep from eighty households, many of the marks coincided, and the owners argued over which sheep belonged to whom, each of them wanting to take the better ones. Many sheep had died, but there were also many lambs from the spring and this was cause for even greater disorder when the property was being divvied up. The same thing happened with the equipment. One man's cart was damaged so he took someone else's, while another had his plowshare switched on his plow, while yet another took someone else's horse collars, and before we knew it the taking back of property turned into looting. Many were at each other's throats and even came to blows, the women were screaming and cursing frantically, the dogs were barking. It had been raining since morning and the dust had turned to mud, on top of everything the church bell started tolling to announce a death and its protracted sounds floated over the village like an omen. The situation came to a head right before our eyes, several collective farms in the vicinity had fallen apart, half of our members had long since submitted requests to leave the co-op. And yet we were surprised, it seemed to us that something unexpected had happened, as disasters that are no one's fault tend to happen. Nothing could head it off and those of us who had made such efforts to establish the co-op now watched crestfallen as the people, muddy and wet, tore into the co-op's corpse like vultures and scampered back to their dens with chunks of its flesh.

So on that black day in the late afternoon, as I was going home, Kiro Dzhelebov caught up with me on the street, greeted me, and started walking alongside me. I returned his greeting without looking at him, so as not to see on his face the gloating malice that was written on all the private farmers' faces. I felt awkward even about those unspoken conversations with which I had intended to win him over to our side. I was in such despair about this defeat that I could not disguise the state I was in, and this made me touchy. For example, I thought that he could have gone home by another street or have waited for me to go on ahead and not shown me his face on this day of all days. We walked for several minutes without talking, but I could sense what he wanted to tell me with his silence: "We all knew that your co-op would fall apart, only you, it seems, didn't know this, and now you're upset." This infuriated me all the more and for the first time my heart quivered with hatred toward him. We reached the street where we had to part ways and he said: "The cooperative farm will work out, don't worry. Even as soon as next year, at that."

I stopped unwittingly and looked at him. His face showed no malice, but it didn't show sympathy or pity either. As always, this event, too, had passed by him without touching him and without even disturbing his everyday working habits. He was dressed in a short denim jacket and rubber sandals with his pant legs rolled up, he was carrying a hoe over his shoulder. While a hurricane had been raging in the village, he had gone to his fields or vineyard to tend to his work.

"There's no way it won't happen," he repeated. "Otherwise, what kind of revolution would it be! Only you should have waited a bit, let the people come round a bit. Now they're startled as if jerked out of a dream. They're watching with their eyes wide open, but they can't see what's going on around them. So chin up and take care of yourself!"

He turned right and walked off down the street.

"If you and other farmers like you had joined the co-op, it wouldn't have fallen apart!" I shouted after him.

He seemed to have been waiting for me to say those words, he took a few steps back and stopped. It was no longer drizzling, the clouds had broken up and the sunset was glimmering bluish-green. From the lower neighborhood protracted wailing for the dead could be heard, while on the muddy square behind us a man and a woman were pushing a shaftless cart and arguing about something.

"It's still early for me," Kiro Dzhelebov said.

"And will it still be too early for you next year?"

"I don't know. I've got two sons to put through school, in a year or two, it may be three. How can I support them on a salary of a few cents a day?"

And he continued back down the road. This was the conversation that I wasn't able to decide to have with him for more than a year. I had been worried for nothing that at his house I would be knocking on an open door. Just as I had assumed, he knew no less than we did that the collectivization of land was inevitable, thus over the course of a year, as he himself foresaw it, he would have to decide what to do. The year passed, the cooperative farm was established for a second time, and he still stayed out of it. They started consolidating blocks of land. Three-quarters of the farmers had joined, so the private farmers were pushed out to the edges of the village fields.

Kiro Dzhelebov began working someone else's land, and that land had been tended so poorly that he hardly managed to make his state quotas, which were calculated by acres of land and heads of livestock, and not based on what you had produced. Marko was in his sophomore year at the university, Anyo had just been discharged from the army and that same fall had enrolled at the University of Economics in Varna, while Dimcho started his army service. The two students spent most of their vacation on youth brigades and were only in the village for a few weeks. Kiro Dzhelebov was having an ever-harder time finishing the fieldwork and soon was forced to give half his land to the co-op. And if with his pride he managed to hide his mental state, his clothes clearly gave away that he was headed for financial ruin. I had long since noticed that he wore his sons' old shirts, and there were little patches here and there all over his clothing. Auntie Tanka, too, wore clothes faded from so much washing. I saw her more often. No matter how often I passed by their place, I always saw her in the garden or the yard, working on something, I would greet her and she would always invite me to stop in. She would treat me to a piece of fruit or something sweet, and while I was eating, she would sit on the edge of her chair, just enough to "rest her legs," and since even with her pride she couldn't manage to hide the family's impoverished circumstances, from her I found out how hard it was for them to make ends meet. "I've even become a merchant." She smiled and with simple-hearted frankness she told me how she and her husband had gone to the city to sell "this and that." Kiro had wrapped up the hubcaps of the cart in rags so they wouldn't rattle, they had snuck out the garden gate and had gone to the city on side roads. They had arrived there before dawn, Kiro stayed on the outskirts with the cart, while she had slipped through the vineyards and gone to her aunt's daughter, who worked at the post office and had sold cheese, butter, honey, and eggs to her acquaintances. They tucked away the money from such sales and every month they sent some of it to their sons.

"As long as we're alive and well, everything else will fall into place," she would say, while seeing me off to the front gate. "Marko will finish up next year, Anyo will graduate the following, and as for Dimcho, if he decides to go on with his studies, he'll be the only one left and we'll put him through school somehow too."

But not one of their sons managed to finish his education.

One day at the end of the summer of 1950, Stoyan Kralev ordered me to make a list of the families who would receive rations – sugar, women's head scarves, leather sandals, and a few more bare necessities. He often assigned me such written duties, I sat at the end of the table scratching things out with my pen, while he would do his other work or go out and about in the village. I had just finished the list when Ilko, Stoyan Kralev's brother, came into the club. He was the chairman of the Fatherland Front committee, he looked at the list and started reading a newspaper. Stoyan Kralev also looked over the list and gave me some instructions for the brigadiers. Then Kiro Dzhelebov came into the club. The door was open, he knocked on the door frame, took off his straw hat, and greeted us.

"Come on in, sit down," Stoyan Kralev invited him.

There were several chairs against the wall, Kiro Dzhelebov sat down obediently and put his straw hat on his knees. Stoyan Kralev leaned on his elbows, looked at him, and asked: "Well, how's the private sector going?"

"We're having a hard time."

"We're having a hard time, indeed, but we still won't give up on it," Stoyan Kralev said with a malicious smile.

Kiro Dzhelebov ran his hands over his head where the hat had flattened down his hair and kept silent. A few seconds passed and he turned to Ilko: "I came to get the notes for my sons."

"Just a moment, Bay Kiro."

Ilko got up and went over to the table. It had two drawers. One held the party's documents and stamp, while the other held the Fatherland Front's. Ilko reached toward his drawer, but Stoyan Kralev put his hand on the handle.

"First of all Comrade Dzhelebov and I are going to have a little chat, then we'll see about notes. We haven't spoken in years, we haven't looked each other in the eye, as if we didn't live in one and the same village."

Indeed, he would be speaking to Kiro Dzhelebov for the first time in several years. He got up, went around the table, and began pacing back and forth across the room. He walked slowly and his footsteps cut through the silence with a creaking circumspection. His brother, Ilko, had described him in detail and quite accurately, and I will allow myself to repeat from his description only the fact that in this case, as had already become his habit, Stoyan Kralev was imitating Stalin – as he had seen him in films. At the time we saw nothing funny about this, on the contrary, we felt a certain envy that he was able to transform himself into a personage that was so dear to us. We all lived, thought, and acted under the spell of that steely figure, we were in awe of his firmness and self-denial, while one episode from his life made a staggering impression on us – when the tsarist police flailed him with their whips, he sat calmly, reading a newspaper. In films, too, he was sparing with his words and gestures, the only thing he permitted himself was an ironic smile "under his moustache," thus his magnificence was adorned with an unusual cold-bloodedness in all circumstances. Stoyan Kralev, alas, did not possess this unconquerable strength of will. In cases such as the present one, he would start by speaking calmly and would even smile, but after only a few minutes he would turn into an affected and wildly gesticulating copy of his idol.

"Comrade Dzhelebov," he said, while smoothing down his moustache with his thumb and pacing back and forth with his hand stuffed between the buttons of his jacket, "there's a celebration on our street too. Our efforts have been crowned with success. The cooperative farm now exists. Without you and another thirty or so folks like you, who have each sunk their teeth into a bone and are gnawing on it like dogs in a backyard. But from now on there won't be any more bones. There won't be any black market, no petty trade in this and that, and no cold, hard cash in your purse. This fall – everyone must join the co-op! We can't have some building a house now, only to have others move into it tomorrow and make themselves at home. We can't have some plowing and sowing, only to have others gobble up the bread tomorrow. Private farming has come to an end! Our patience has come to an end! In such cases, the people have a saying: I'm talking to you, my daughter, so think hard, dear daughter-in-law. That means if the daughter-in-law is clever and honest, they don't need to tell her flat out what they want from her, she'll realize it herself. But our 'daughters-in-law' here are deaf and stupid toadies to kulaks. They don't understand hints, you've got to slap them in the face with it."

His gestures were growing larger and jerkier, his words harsher and more infuriated. Three brigadiers came into the club most likely to take the instructions I had written out for them, and when they saw what mood Stoyan Kralev was in, they silently stood in a line against the wall. Kiro Dzhelebov looked as if he had been caught in a sudden ambush in which they'd thrown mud in his face, so unexpected were the party secretary's words to him. We all knew his proud character, we knew that Stoyan Kralev's "raised voice" would offend his dignity, to say nothing of Kralev's comparing him to a dog, and they were clearly anxious on his account. But perhaps it was precisely his offended dignity that was fanning Stoyan Kralev's fury all the more.

"Hey, buddy, where do you think you are, hm? Blood is gushing from people's hearts, while not a single hair on your head has been touched. We all tiptoe around you, God forbid we disturb 'the good farmer's' peace and quiet. While he, that good fellow, is looking after his own personal interest, he's supporting two sons in college, and next year he'll send the third. Us co-op members, how do we support our sons and daughters?"

"Just one more year, at least till my oldest graduates!" Kiro Dzhelebov said.

"Not a year, I'm not even giving you a week!" Stoyan Kralev shouted. "If you don't submit your membership declaration to the co-op by tomorrow, you won't be getting any notes for your sons!"

Ilko conspiratorially winked at Kiro Dzhelebov: "When he gets over this, everything will be fine. Best go ahead and leave." Kiro Dzhelebov got up and left without saying a word. Stoyan Kralev interpreted this as an act of blind Dzhelebov pride and became even more enraged. No one had dared turn his back on him with such clear scorn and he could not control himself: "Up yours!" As he shouted this curse, Stoyan Kralev quickly turned to his brother and pointed at him: "You're the reason that wretch still hasn't joined the co-op and is muddying the waters. I would've long since put him in his place, but you? No! You protect him, you wouldn't let even a speck of dust settle on him. He's a good farmer, he's an honest man, you say. If he's such an honest man, why doesn't he come join all the other honest folks instead of staying with the enemies of the co-op? And you support him…"

"I'm not supporting him, but I don't have the right to force him, to say nothing of cursing at him. We've waited a few years for him, why don't we wait until spring? It'll be hard for him to support two students in the city as a co-op member. Our daily wage is still low, we've got no reason to hide that fact. And we can't help him, either. In a few years we'll give scholarships to students, but now we can't. Besides, Dzhelebov's son is studying agronomy, when he graduates he'll come work on our farm."

"You've always got your nose stuck in a book, but look what good it's done for your mind!"

Stoyan Kralev was staring at his brother without blinking, as if trying to hypnotize him, while at the same time out from under his moustache a rancorous smile appeared, like a weasel coming out from under a fence. For some time now they had constantly been at odds over various questions and word in the village was that they didn't even act like brothers anymore, and saw each other only on business. Until now, however, they hadn't quarreled so openly in front of outsiders, and this presaged a clash that would inevitably end with a rupture between them. The brigadiers and the other men who had come into the club felt awkward and wanted to leave, but Stoyan Kralev ordered them to stay because he had business to take care of with them. He clearly wished to make his argument with his brother public and said: "We're not divvying up our family inheritance, but talking about questions of principle, and there's no reason we should hide from the people. So now I'm asking, do you justify Kiro Dzhelebov's remaining outside the co-op on principled grounds? No! You're going to bat for him purely for personal reasons. When you were sick, his wife brought you a few bowls of honey and butter and now you can't thank them enough. And you misled me, too. You tied my hands for so many years with that charity of yours: 'Don't bother him, leave him alone to decide what to do on his own.' We saw what he does. His sons' higher education cost him just a few bowls of honey and butter, while for us – it's costing millions in losses. Our co-op fell apart because of him and others like him."

"You know my viewpoint on that question, it's pointless to argue anymore," Ilko said.

"Because you don't want to dirty up your dainty little hands! You spew your liberal drivel to pass as the good guy. We're the bad guys, because we force people to join the co-op. We make revolutions, while you sit around philosophizing about what's violence and what's not. Only a few short years ago you were saying morning, noon, and night that the truth is with the majority. With the majority! And that's a fact. The fact is that now seventy percent of the villagers are co-op members, that means they're the majority, the truth is on their side, reality about life is on their side. What does this truth oblige us to do? To totalize the co-op by the end of autumn, to not leave a single farmer outside it. Not a single one! That's right. So now you know my 'viewpoint' on that question, it's pointless to argue anymore. Brigadiers, stay here with me, the rest of you are free to go."

At the same time, Kiro Dzhelebov climbed up to the second story of his house and sat down on the veranda. He flopped down into an old chair and felt a sharp pain in his back. He had just been stepping over the threshold of the party club when something hit him right there, between the shoulder blades. He went to turn around to see who had hit him and why, but at the same moment he realized that Stoyan Kralev's curse had crashed down on his back like a heavy stone. His head was blazing with the effort of maintaining his self-control, so as not to go back to Stoyan Kralev and spit in his face. He felt dizzy, the ground was crumbling beneath his feet, the sun was rocking right above the upper edge of the village. He felt nauseous, the pain in his back pierced him like a knife. A tree was in the way right in front of his face and he recognized it – the old mulberry near the bend in the road – nausea welled up in him, he hugged the trunk of the mulberry tree and threw up. He realized he had given in to weakness and looked all around him to make sure no one was watching him. "I can't go all soft like this," he kept telling himself, "it's downright shameful! What had to happen has happened, it's not going to pass anyone by, it's not going to pass me by, either."

But bad luck always arrives early and catches us unprepared, even when we are expecting it. Kiro Dzhelebov knew that joining the co-op was inevitable, yet he turned out to be so unprepared for the event that it tore him out of his usual state. None of the village leaders had come to try to convince him, as they had with other private farmers, and this little by little had given him hope that the others' fate would somehow pass him by. A completely nonsensical hope, but don't we all know that we will die sooner or later, yet still don't believe it? Besides that, it seems Kiro Dzhelebov was betting on the fact that two of his sons were studying at the university. Actually, that was the only thing that explained the village leaders' loyal attitude toward him, and he believed they would leave him to work his land for another year or two, until his sons graduated. But now his turn had come and he lost his mental balance to such an extent that he didn't suspect even in the slightest that Stoyan Kralev would insult him so cruelly at that moment of extreme agitation, and then expect him to change his opinion the next day. The fear that man had inspired in him for some time now, even if indirectly, now suddenly came flooding over him and was like a shock, such that he couldn't find the strength to withstand it or to wait a few days at least, as Ilko had advised him. He went into the next room, where his sons kept their books on a small bookshelf, put the inkwell on the table, took a piece of graph paper, and started writing out his membership request to the co-op's administrative council.

I wish to be accepted as a member of the Stalin Labor-Coopera-tive Agrarian Farm. I have seven acres of land and the following equipment and livestock, which as of tomorrow, September 11, 1950, I will turn over to the cooperative farm: 1 horse cart, 1 oxcart, 2 horses, 2 oxen, 1 cow, 28 sheep, 2 plows, 2 pigs weighing 130 lbs each. I obligate myself to...

Here the quill got stuck on the paper and dripped a large blotch of ink over the next word. He grabbed the inkwell, poured it over the paper, and left it lying on its side. The ink spread black over part of what was written and ran from the paper onto the tablecloth.

There was no one home. His wife had gone out somewhere, and his sons were harvesting sunflowers. They had about a quarter-acre left and had told him that they wouldn't come home until they had finished harvesting it. They needed to leave for school in a few days, so they were looking to finish as much of the fieldwork as they could before then. This was the last thing he thought about the real world. He went out into the yard as if in a dream, passed through the garden, looked in at the birds, and then went under the awning of the summer kitchen. Various tools were lined up in the shed next to the oven so they would be close at hand, he took a spade and a hoe, put them over his shoulder, and went out through the garden gate. The sun had gone down, but a bright golden light was streaming from the sky, bathing the fields from end to end, the expanse echoed with the evening sounds of the village, the scent of lit hearths and the delicious aromas of food wafted through the air. Kiro Dzhelebov was walking in no particular direction through the unharvested cornfields, through the stubble fields and fallow land, he turned left and right and finally stopped in a melon patch that had already been harvested. He set the hoe down and started digging with the spade. The soil was crumbly and clean, the spade sank in up to its footrest and after fifteen minutes the pit was deep enough that when he stood in it, it reached his waist.

He reached out, grabbed the hoe, and started filling in the hole, first of all toward his back, scooping in as much as he could without turning around, then along his sides, and finally in front of himself. When he had buried himself up to his waist, he threw the hoe, then tossed away the spade as well, crossed his arms over his chest and stood like that, buried and motionless, as if he had finished some ordinary bit of fieldwork and now needed to rest.

Auntie Tanka came home as the sun was setting and went about cooking dinner. If she had looked toward the garden gate when she came into the yard, she would have seen her husband with the spade and the hoe over his shoulder heading toward the fields, but she hurried to put what she was carrying in the lower room and went to the summer kitchen. While the food was stewing over the fire, she milked the cow, penned up the chickens, and by that time it was completely dark. The men would come back from the field any minute and she set the table so they could eat dinner right away and then lie down to rest. The boys came back from the field, unhitched the horses, put them in the barn, and went to the well to wash up. The well's chain rang out with delicate glad tones and a moment later from beneath the earth came the rumble of the heavy wooden bucket as it plummeted down to the water. Auntie Tanka could hardly make out the boys' profiles in the twilight, but she knew that it was the middle boy, Anyo, who had let the empty bucket down so recklessly. Two of them quickly turned the crank on the well, set the full bucket on the stone ring, stripped down to the waist, and started pouring water over each other's heads. She could hear them snorting with satisfaction under the cool stream, they were talking, laughing, and slapping each other's backs.

"Come on, you'll catch cold!" Auntie Tanka shouted at them.

The boys dashed under the awning of the kitchen and simultaneously each took a towel from their mother's hands. They dried off, got dressed, and looked impatiently toward the dinner waiting on the table. They combed their hair, sat down on either side of the table, but didn't dare reach for the food without their father.

"Where's Dad?" Anyo asked.

"What, he isn't with you?" Auntie Tanka said. "Here I was thinking he had stayed in the barn with the livestock."

"When it was still light he went to the village to get our Fatherland Front notes from Ilko."

"Is that right? He must've gotten to talking to someone there. You go ahead and eat, don't wait for him this time, he might be late."

While the boys were eating voraciously, Auntie Tanka as always picked away at her plate like a guest, and was telling them how Aunt Ivana had knit Anyo's sweater. In the late afternoon she had gone to get it and Anyo needed to try it on now or tomorrow before they went out to the fields so if there was some problem it could be fixed. She wondered whether she hadn't forgotten to get them some food ready for their trip, she asked them, too, and so it went during the whole dinner. At one point they heard a noise coming from the gate, the three boys stopped eating and stared in that direction, listening.

"Now what could be holding that man up, for crying out loud!" Auntie Tanka said. "Could they have roped him in to some meeting?"

The black cauldron over the fire came to a boil, Auntie Tanka poured the water into a washbasin and soaked the dishes in it. A cow mooed from the neighboring yard, most likely forgotten out on the street, the night grew lighter with the stars and they could see all the way to the end of the garden. A cold breeze blew, the boys fell to talking about their upcoming departure, they were yawning and looking toward the gate. Auntie Tanka washed the dishes and set two plates on the table – one with food, the other with bread – covered them with a towel, and left her hand resting on the plate with bread.

"Just look what time it is and your father still isn't home!" she said quietly, looking toward the garden, which in the gleaming starlight appeared as if covered in a delicate frost. The boys turned to her and fell silent. She kept sitting there with her hand on the plate of bread, listening to the ghostly silence of the night.

"Well, go out and look for him in the village!"

The boys jumped up as one from the table and darted toward the street. Once they were out of sight, Auntie Tanka covered her mouth with her hand and rushed to the house. She dashed up the stairs in a single bound and peered into the three rooms: "Kiro, Kiro, are you here, did you fall asleep?" The beds were empty, but she ran her hand over them, then she got scared and went back out to the summer kitchen.

The boys soon returned out of breath. They had run to the *horemag*, to the town council building, to the party club and the store, everything was locked up, they only saw light coming from a single house. They stood there next to one another, shoulder to shoulder, not knowing what else to say to their mother.

"Dear God!" She sobbed and her face turned white as lime, lost its lively expression, and turned into an ugly mask foretelling horror.

"Oh no, oh no!" Marko said, with this exclamation confirming his mother's terrible suspicions.

The boys only now noticed that her kerchief had fallen down around her shoulders, and saw in this a sinister omen. A few more seconds passed in this stupor, then the mother took the lamp down from the beam and headed toward the house. She was walking with an even, heavy step, and the yellow light did not flicker in her hand. Her sons followed her, as perhaps people had once followed their priestess in a midnight ritual procession. While they covered the thirty or so steps to the house, they could sense their mother transforming and becoming the head of the family, ready to lead in case of a misfortune, just as her husband had led them until now.

"We'll look for him," she said as they went into the middle room, as if sharing a family secret between four walls. "Find the lantern and light it!"

She wanted to say something more, but the ink stain on the paper caught her eye with its dark sheen. Her sons also noticed it. Marko cautiously righted the upset inkwell and went to the other side of the table to read what was written. Anyo tried to read it upside down, and their mother, her arms firmly crossed beneath her chest, looked from one to the other, to see which of the two of them would first read out loud what was written.

"A membership request to the administrative council of the cooperative farm," Marko said. "But it's not finished. He wrote a few sentences and then stopped. He accidentally spilled the inkwell on the paper and left it for tomorrow to rewrite it."

Their father's request reminded them of a suicide note, left unfinished in a fit of deranged impatience to put an end to one's life; the overturned inkwell indisputably bore witness to his mental state when he had written "I obligate myself to..." and when he had realized precisely the nature of the obligation to the cooperative farm that he was taking upon himself. This phrase was the border between two lives, a fateful border that he had been unable to cross, but his sons believed that they knew their father's character as well as they knew their own and did not suppose that he would have paid for the entrance to the cooperative farm with his life. No one had pressured him until now, and it was unthinkable that someone would have pressured him precisely this afternoon, and so brutally that he would have been forced to sit down and write out his membership request. There had long been talk in the village about "totalizing" the farm – in other words, making absolutely everyone join – and their father had joked ever more often that since the bear was dancing in their neighbor's yard, it would soon be dancing in theirs as well. The full collectivization of the land was already a fact that one could dispute, but which one could not escape. Insofar as they had talked about their impending entrance into the co-op (and that had been only rarely), they had not noticed resistance or concern in their father, as if he had taken this event as the fate of the times, which no one could or even should resist. The question had arisen of putting off "this business" as long as they could, until they finished their education, and "from then on, we, too, will go where all the others have gone." Thus what was written on the piece of paper remained a mystery, and the boys did not connect it with their father's disappearance, if he had even disappeared at all. In a few days the harvested sunflower field would need to be plowed up and they suspected he had gone to the neighboring village to get the plowshares he had given to the blacksmith there to sharpen. But their mother, like every wife and mother, suspected the worst. Her face changed its shape and expression, and while her sons were discussing various conjectures, her whole being was concentrated on the outdoors and her pricked-up ears caught even the softest noises of the night. And then a howl resounded, loud and ominous, as if the dog were standing on the doorstep. The woman shuddered, a dark atavistic sob tore from her heart with a sinister foreboding, her hand rose to her forehead and made the sign of the cross. The dog's howl sounded again, even more drawn out and sinister, again filling the room with an ominous portent.

"We forgot to unchain him," Marko said. "I'll go let him off."

"Take the lantern," their mother said.

They let the dog off the chain and he dashed around the yard with happy whimpering and from there headed toward the street. The three of them stepped toward the sheep pen. Auntie Tanka went in first with the lantern in her hand, she held it high over her head and looked at the ceiling from one end to the other. They went into the barns and the lower rooms of the house, they searched every corner of the yard and went into the garden. Auntie Tanka always walked in the lead with the lantern in her hand, looking at every tree and every bush, and her sons followed her. When they reached the fence, two men were suddenly standing before them, asking what they were doing out in the garden at that time of night.

True to the Dzhelebov custom of keeping their family business a secret, the three boys fell silent, it seemed absurd and shameful to admit that they were looking for their lost father, but they couldn't come up with another reason, either. The men beyond the fence were silent too. They were from the night watch and this wandering about in the garden in the dead of night seemed suspicious to them. Many of the private farmers made illegal threshing floors, slaughtered their livestock, or buried grain underground, and the night watch had to make sure they weren't committing any violations.

"Auntie Tanka, what are you doing here?" one of the watchmen asked again.

"Iliycho, is that you?"

"It's me, Auntie Tanka."

"What are we doing, you ask? Look, the sun is about to rise and your Uncle Kiro still hasn't come home. We thought perhaps he'd taken ill and fallen somewhere here in the yard."

Iliycho was one of the brigadiers who happened to be in the club when Stoyan Kralev had raked over the coals first Kiro Dzhelebov, then his own brother.

"Well, I just saw him this afternoon at the party club. He had come to ask for some notes, but the party secretary was giving him a hard time."

"About what?"

"About those notes he wanted for the boys. When you join the co-op, he says, then you'll get 'em."

"And what did Kiro say?"

"He didn't say anything. He just got up and walked out."

Auntie Tanka and the boys went back home, while Iliycho and the other watchman set out to make the rounds of the streets. Within a few hours, the whole village knew that Kiro Dzhelebov had disappeared from his home.

But at that time Kiro Dzhelebov was walking with an old man along some elevated ground scattered with big round rocks and grown over with strange trees, bushes, and flowers. The trees were heavy with so much and such varied fruit that he couldn't take his eyes off them, while the scent of the flowers filled him with bliss. From both sides of the path, playful little streams trickled down, birds with golden plumage strolled around the meadows, down at the foot of the elevation sparkled a river of clear blue water. Kiro Dzhelebov was looking at this heretofore unseen wonder and at the same time trying to recognize the old man. He was looking askance at him and it seemed to him that it was the old priest, Father Encho, who had put on his gold-laced sticharion as if he had just come from celebrating a service. But Father Encho did not have such white and luxurious hair as that which was hanging in soft waves around the old man's shoulders, and besides, he limped with one leg and was a chatterbox, they could not have walked together for so long without him starting to talk. Kiro Dzhelebov tried to get ahead of him to see his whole face, but all his efforts to move his feet forward met with some invisible barrier. When he again tried to recognize the old man, his profile transformed into that of Stoyan Kralev with a slightly hooked nose, a hard graying moustache, and a chin that jutted forward, beneath which the collars of his homespun jacket could be seen. The slope they were walking up also changed, just like the old man's face – now it was a bare meadow, strewn with round gray rocks, now it was some fantastical garden. When they reached the peak of the slope, Kiro Dzhelebov realized that they were at the Crag – a desolate place with a deep, dry ravine, at the end of the village lands. He looked back and saw that the dry rocky path was strewn with little bunches of colorful flowers in the form of human footsteps, and those were the old man's footsteps.

"Well, did you recognize who I am?" the old man finally said.

"I did," Kiro Dzhelebov said, stunned by fear and delight. "You are God!"

"Well, lookee here how he recognized his good old God!" The old man smiled. "And your good old God has come to help you. To see what's weighing on your soul."

They were standing across from each other and Kiro Dzhelebov could look him in the face. A hoary-headed old man's face, yet unusual, giving off a radiance that Kiro Dzhelebov felt in his soul, and his soul rejoiced, intoxicated by some sweet bliss. *God, God,* he thought to himself, and didn't know how to express his delight and joy. *God has come down to me, he has never come down to any person before, only to me.*

"Do you believe in me?" God asked him.

"I believe, God, I believe!" Kiro Dzhelebov replied, and heard his voice resounding like an echo in the rocky wasteland.

"Now we'll see about that," God said. He drew a large knife out of the sleeve of his robe and handed it to him. "You will be saved from all suffering. Your property will be yours, and from your hands it will pass into your sons' and grandsons' hands. But you must prove your faith in me."

Kiro Dzhelebov took the knife, looked God in the eye, and noticed that one of his eyes was bluish-green, moist and bleary like Father Encho's eyes, while the other was dark brown with a sharp glitter like the eyes of Stoyan Kralev. And his face had transformed into two faces, one half into the face of Father Encho, the other half into the face of Stoyan Kralev.

"I'll prove it, God!" When he said that, Kiro Dzhelebov sensed that internally he was shaken by God's strange incarnation, but yet also in awe of his grandeur and omnipotence.

"Sacrifice him!" God said.

"Sacrifice who?"

"That one! Your firstborn!"

Kiro Dzhelebov glanced aside and saw his three sons standing next to one another in a line, they had come straight from the fields in their work clothes, with smiling, sunburned faces. In front of them lay a large oak stump, hewn with hundreds of cuts from the blade of an axe, the same stump he chopped wood on in the winter. Marko stepped away from his brothers, lay down on his back, and put his head on the stump. His neck stretched and his veins were standing out such that along them the steady beating of his heart could be seen.

"I can't, he is the dearest to me!" Kiro Dzhelebov cried.

"Then I can't save you," God said. "Decide for yourself!"

"Slaughter me! Kill me, since you need a life sacrificed."

"I don't need your life," God said.

Kiro Dzhelebov got scared that perhaps God would make him slaughter his son and threw the knife aside as hard as he could. The knife flashed in the air, landed on a large rock, and gave out a loud sound like the ringing of a bell. Other sounds followed this, clear and fast, as if the church bell was ringing to sound the alarm. *There must be a fire*, he thought, and wanted to head to the village and saw that he was in the middle of the field, buried up to his waist in the earth, alone and helpless, yet he didn't ask what he was doing there, nor was he frightened by his isolation. The conversation with God repeated itself many times (he would have to kill now his eldest son, now his middle son, now his youngest son, and about each one he would say that he was dearest to him), it happened simultaneously at the Crag amid the large gray rocks and here, in the harvested melon field, where he could see amid the scorched stems tiny little melons, some whole, others split from overripeness, still others squashed by a cart's tires. The sun was beating right on his face, he bowed his head to shade it with the rim of his straw hat and then he saw the whole field before him, sparkling with the morning dew, he heard the rattling of a cart racing down the soft roads. He was tormented by thirst and his right hand stretched for hours toward one little melon, as large as a fist, split from being overripe, with red flesh and black seeds, his head flopped down onto the ground and he again sank into a dream or a faint.

The ringing of the church bell had not been a hallucination. Early in the morning they had told Stoyan Kralev about Kiro Dzhelebov's disappearance and he ordered them to ring the church bell. The people gathered in front of the church and Stoyan Kralev asked all of them to check their yards and gardens for him, and then also their fields. The missing man might have been killed and tossed in some yard to cover up the traces, he could have fallen somewhere in the fields from a heart attack, he might have ended his own life, thus people peeked with fear into the hidden corners of their yards and gardens. On the third day, he was accidentally found by a young man. In the morning he was late getting to the fields, so he went straight through the village lands and came across him. He first saw the spade and the hoe, then a few meters from them a man chopped in half at the waist. The young man was so frightened of this corpse chopped in half that he rushed back to the village and started shouting in the streets: "There's a man chopped in half in the Barakovs' melon patch!" He couldn't explain who the person was and he hadn't even thought that it might have been Kiro Dzhelebov, for whom they had been searching for two days, but everyone was sure that it was Kiro Dzhelebov and the tragic news of his death spread through the village in less than half an hour.

Kiro Dzhelebov's family was already dressed in mourning, but when they told Auntie Tanka that they had found her husband's body, she, who knows why, did not let the sexton ring the church bell. "Let's bring him home first, then we'll ring it." She also did not allow her sons to take part in carrying his corpse home, so as not to be upset at seeing him disfigured. She sent someone to call Aunt Ivana (the same one who had knitted sweaters for her sons), the two of them climbed into the cart and set out for the Barakovs' melon patch. When the cart reached the fields and started across them, men and children flocked in from all sides and set off after her. The old woman drove the horses, while Auntie Tanka sat behind her, and they did not exchange so much as a word the whole way. Soon the cart turned off the path and entered the melon patch. Someone was standing at the other end of the patch and as soon as he saw or heard the cart, he started toward it, running and waving his arms. The sun was behind him so they couldn't recognize him, nor could they hear what he was yelling. Only Auntie Tanka, it seems, heard him or guessed what he was yelling and jumped down from the cart as it was still in motion.

"Good God, oh my God!" she cried, clasping her hands to her chest, and to the amazement of everyone watching her, there was a hint of joy in her voice. "Oh, oh!" She sighed, standing with her head bowed forward, as a person exhales when a heavy weight has been lifted and he feels the aching sweetness of having been freed of the burden. The man coming toward her was no longer running, he wasn't waving or yelling, but still no one could recognize him, while Auntie Tanka's face lit up with a bright radiance, just as the earth brightens on a cloudy day when the sun finds a chink in the clouds. As soon as the man's silhouette had appeared at the other end of the field, she seemed to have guessed by the movement of his arms and by his gait that he wanted to give her some comforting news. And that's how it turned out.

"He's not chopped in half, he's not chopped in half," the man shouted when he was within fifty feet of them. "He's buried up to his waist and he's looking around, but not talking." It was Grandpa Pondyo. He lived at the edge of the village, and as he explained later, the young man had first told him about the murdered man and he had immediately come to see with his own two eyes what the situation was. "He won't speak, but he's alive. I was just saying to myself that I needed to unbury him, when I saw…"

The crowd raced to the other end of the field and in a few minutes they had started digging out Kiro Dzhelebov. He was lying on his chest, his head flopped down on his arms, as a man lets his head rest on a pillow in a deep sleep, his face was stretched taut in a deathly yellowish dryness, only his eyelids opened from time to time and moisture flashed in his eyeballs.

Several days later (and for years afterward), when he came to, he would try to explain the state he had fallen into, and he would remember only the image of his wife, blurred and disjointed in colorful blotches; how despite this he recognized her well, he felt the urge to tell her something, but he couldn't do it; how he sensed the silence around himself and in this silence he heard only the slight crunching of the spade in the dirt; how his body was freed from the heavy stiffness and was being carried toward the heads of the horses, and after that lifted over the cart, and all of this was an unbelievable mix of colors, voices, people, and objects, unclear and painful, yet at the same time familiar and close. He also felt a strong sense of shame, especially in front of his sons, that he had allowed himself to lose his will and his reason, and so that they wouldn't think he was mentally ill, he often found reasons to laugh at himself: "Well, I sure pulled a stunt, boys, just like a dog out in the fields. I turned out to have a few screws loose, so now folks have someone to laugh at!"

His sons didn't think that his suicide attempt was the result of mental illness, but due to a momentary nervous breakdown, which was expressed so strongly because for years on end he had been withstanding the tempestuous events in the village with his legendary reserve. They had long since understood that their father was painfully proud, and it was from this pride that he spoke almost like a communist about the necessity to do away with private property to show that he understood the times as well as anyone else, while, in fact, hiding the wholehearted attachment to his property that ran in his blood. Inwardly his sons had given up that property, and in this lay the seed of a tacit discrepancy with their father, imposed by the unrelenting reality that they knew and now understood even better than he did. They would never express this openly because of their innate reverence for and filial piety toward him, and now also due to his unprecedented readiness to sacrifice himself for them, just as they would never even hint to him that precisely because of this self-

sacrifice, he was ruining their futures. Thus they lived in deeply camou-
flaged duplicity, fearing that their father might sense this and again lose
his mental balance. For his part, Kiro Dzhelebov also realized that he was
destroying his sons' future and often said that there was no two ways
about it anymore, he needed to join the co-op if they invited him, but
neither did he go to submit a request for membership, nor did anyone
from the co-op come to invite him. After his suicide attempt, the co-op
leaders didn't dare disturb him, and Stoyan Kralev, too, had ordered them
to leave him to "get over it," without, of course, giving his sons proof of
political reliability.

Kiro Dzhelebov was completely recovered after two weeks, like a man
who had spent nearly sixty hours from the waist down in a cast of soil, and
went to work with his sons. As always, the three of them went out to the
fields before dawn and returned after dark, but they didn't feel the same
sense of satisfaction with the work as before. Uncertainty hung over the
family and no one dared to mention it, plus they had given up half their
land, so the fieldwork was done very quickly. They harvested the corn,
plowed, sowed the autumn crops, and went back to the village. Whatever
work there was around the yard, they finished it as well and were left with
nothing to do. The autumn rains came as well. Long days dragged on, the
streets were swollen with mud, the whole village retreated to dry ground.
The three young men went to bed and got up early out of habit and the
whole day they mooned around the house empty-handed.

In November the rains stopped and Marko left for Sofia. He wanted to
see if he could somehow sign up for the semester without a certificate of
political reliability, he knew students who had studied without such notes.
If he didn't manage to enroll, he would return for the holidays. After a
dozen days, they got a letter from him. He wrote that he had moved back
into his old apartment, had been going to lectures, and hoped that one of
his professors would help him. About a week later, they got another letter

from him. He asked his father to stop sending him money. The lectures this semester were repeats of the lectures from the previous three years, he was only required to go to them twice a week, while the rest of the time he was working in an office and earning a salary. "Plus, there's nothing for me to do in the village until spring, two workers there are enough," Marko wrote by the by. But Kiro Dzhelebov stopped on that sentence, read it several times, and gave the letter to Anyo so he could read it too.

"What is your brother trying to say?"

"What do you mean, 'what'!" Anyo replied. "As far as I understand him, he wants to say that if he can't figure things out with his studying, he'll work as a clerk so he won't be wasting his time."

"Well, that's true…"

Kiro Dzhelebov understood very well what Marko was hinting at, yet he still wanted to hear the opinion of his younger son, to make completely sure. Marko wrote regularly every ten days, but didn't mention anything about his studies, even though his father asked him about them in every letter. And so it was until the first day of spring. They had eaten lunch and while Auntie Tanka was clearing the table, Kiro Dzhelebov said to his son: "Boy, give me a sheet of paper and the inkwell! The time has come for the bear to dance in our yard as well!"

Auntie Tanka, who had been heading for the door, stopped for a moment, then went out of the room. Her face flushed scarlet, but she didn't even turn around toward her husband, so as to show him that she didn't attach any significance to what he had decided to do. Anyo had long been waiting for this moment, but he also acted as if his father were about to do something completely ordinary. He set the paper and the inkwell on the table and started to joke: "Dad, why don't you let me write the request? I can see your hands are shaking, we don't want you to go and knock over the inkwell on the paper like last time!"

"You mean to say you don't want the demons to get ahold of me again and for me to bury myself alive in the ground," Kiro Dzhelebov laughed, "that's not going to happen. In any case our land has been in the co-op for a year already, and we can't get by with these four acres of someone else's land. Last time I tipped over the inkwell because I was insulted. That scoundrel Stoyan Kralev cussed me out in front of a whole slew of people, it was enough to make me see red. Well, we all know it wasn't only the curse that made me go off the deep end. But whatever I tell you, you won't understand me. Back then I didn't talk to you very much about that business. No matter how dear to you that land is, it's not in your blood. Your eyes are turned elsewhere, you have other hopes. We've been saying that for as long as the world's been turning, for the first time private property is becoming common property. No, there was a time when people lived in a primitive social system. Isn't that how you and your brothers put it? Only that was a million years ago so it may as well not have been. So for the first time man has to give up what's his. To make everyone equal, so we'll all be good. For a long time now I've been thinking: What does equality have to do with goodness? There are poor and good people. There are rich and bad people. So goodness doesn't depend on how many shirts a man has on his back, but on something else. From now on they'll order people to be equal, so that means they're ordering them to be good as well. Let's hope they are! And I've been thinking something else as well. What is good for a man, and is the good man skillful and useful to others? Now that's the sort of thing I've been thinking to myself and getting myself all muddled up, I haven't got the brains to make sense of it. Anyway, grab the quill and write! We've got nowhere to retreat to anymore, so onward! We've got to dance to their tune."

Anyo wrote to his brother a week later:

> Today we drove the horses, the oxen, and the sheep into the common barn. Dad was appointed brigadier of the animal husbandry brigade. A boss from his very first day. I congratulated him, he chuckled and said if things kept going this way, he could

be chairman of the co-op by next year. Before going to turn in his membership request, he wanted Mom to pour out a cauldron of water so as to guarantee "smooth sailing," she told him to get lost, and he poured out the water himself and headed to the co-op office. You should have heard how he was joking about everything and about himself, how he had gotten carried away with philosophizing before he joined. He was talking about the history of society, about biblical legends and many other things. When we see each other, I'll tell you everything in more detail, just let me note here that until now we did not really know our father well. I suspect that he was soaking up everything you, Dimcho, and I talked about in his presence, just as children soak up what they hear from their parents. I also suspect that he has secretly been reading our books and textbooks. I'm worried that this "intellectual" outburst, as well as his desire to joke around as never before, may be due to some intense mental agitation that he is trying to hide. That's why I'm always looking to stay close to him. The day before yesterday they called a meeting to accept new members. It turned out that all the two dozen families who had not joined the co-op, as soon as they found out Dad had joined, immediately submitted membership requests too. I was at the meeting as well, only outside. I hung around the community center for almost an hour, and as soon as the meeting was over, I hurried and beat Dad home. I wanted to see how he looked and what he would say. We sat down to dinner and chatted about this and that – not a word was said about the co-op. Only when we were done eating did he tell Mom that from tomorrow onward we would go to the common field whistling and we'd come back whistling as well.

Now it is exactly midnight, but he is still not asleep, he's reading his Bible. For some time now he has started reading it *again every night. I looked – he left a scrap of newspaper where it tells about some Job or other. I don't know whether you've tried to read the Bible, I've tried and it immediately gave me a headache. I wonder how Dad can read those tiresome and ridiculous Bible stories for hours, he even knows a lot of them by heart. I can still hear him wandering around the room, going out into the yard and coming back. I don't dare go to bed before he's fallen asleep, I don't think Mom is sleeping either. We're a little bit afraid for him. Today, as we were driving the livestock to the co-op, he was joking again. He said that since a man can live without his parents and brothers, then living without his livestock should be no problem at all. I guess I'm feeling a little sad, too. The yard looks empty to me. Any other night, as you know, a sheep would be bleating, a horse would be whinnying, and now it's quiet, only the dog barks now and then. But what had to happen has happened, and now we won't have any more problems with our studies. If you're sick of pushing a pencil there, drop it, come back to the village and we'll do some day labor for the co-op, mostly to buck up Dad, while in the fall you'll go back to the university. Write Dad right away, you'll make him happy and calm him down. It wouldn't be bad for you to take some vacation and to come home. Come back, we all need to be with Dad right now.*

Marko wrote in early May from West Germany. He said that he had been sent there for a month for his work and that on the very first day he had met a really nice girl. They had grown close and she had invited him to her house. He was going to their place almost every day. The girl's father was a communist, he had spent a few years in a fascist concentration camp and wanted to send his daughter to Bulgaria to study Russian language and literature at any cost. The girl had suggested that they get engaged, so what could he do? He agreed. According to German custom, an engagement is not as binding as in Bulgaria. There any young man and woman who have been going out for at least a week announce themselves as engaged, so his engagement was practically a formality. If the girl came to study in Sofia, they could get married, but only if she agreed to live in Bulgaria. And so on.

The letter was brought by their neighbor who had gone to the post office in the city. The postal worker there, a relative of theirs, had likely been disconcerted by the stamps and postmarks belonging to the capitalist country from where the letter had come, and had therefore put it in a plain, local envelope, so that people in the village wouldn't see it. Anyo opened it, and even while he was reading it he realized that everything in it was a lie meant to temporarily fool the authorities and thus to delay and soften the blow on their family. Under the power of some strange, inexplicable premonition, he never doubted for a moment that his brother had taken a desperate and irreversible step that would turn out to be life changing for him and for their whole family. He could only not explain how and through which channels he had emigrated, whether he had done it in a fit of despair, just as his father had attempted suicide, or if he had thought everything out beforehand. To be completely sure of his defection, he wrote the very next day to Marko's landlady in Sofia, and she replied that "Comrade Marko Dzhelebov left the apartment a month ago, and before that he had not worked in any office, but on a construction site as an unskilled worker." Now their roles were reversed. Just as his father had pretended that by joining the co-op, nothing much had changed in his life, in the same way Anyo tried to cover up his brother's defection, and in the same way, no less: with jokes and made-up stories from his personal life.

It never crossed Kiro Dzhelebov's mind that his son might lie to him about anything whatsoever, and it seems he was not very familiar with the political situation at that time, either, so he believed in his son's business trip abroad and was more satisfied than concerned. ("Our folks here won't give him a simple note of reliability, whereas those folks in Sofia have sent him all the way to Germany on state business!") But an engagement with a faraway and unknown girl seemed to him a naïve and light-minded move.

"Their customs there may be different than ours," he mulled it over, "but an engagement is still an engagement. Once you get engaged to a girl, you have to bring her back to your house or stay at her place. Otherwise how can you just take your hat and up and go?"

"Marko has experience with this stuff, it's not his first time," Anyo said. "He's a ladies' man."

"How so, a ladies' man?"

Kiro Dzhelebov had no inkling of his sons' personal lives, since they had grown up and become men far away from him, but he had always thought that despite the temptations of the urban setting, they would live as chastely as the adults in the village. The closer Marko came to graduating from the university, the more often Kiro Dzhelebov spoke with his wife about his settling down, they tried to guess which girl he would marry and when, and believed that when he found a girl, he would tell them and, as was only proper, ask for their blessing. Thus they imagined their sons' marriages village-style and didn't even stop to think that while they were studying, they might become mixed up in "that nonsense with women," and that they might unbeknownst to them get engaged and unengaged. This is why Kiro Dzhelebov felt somehow offended by the news that Marko was a "ladies' man."

"Well, he had lots of girlfriends. He'd go with one for a while, then dump her, then take up with another. They were always throwing themselves at him!"

"Well now, just think what kinds of women he was getting mixed up with! And this one there, this German, she must have thrown herself at him too."

"I don't know, but I'm sure that he'll dump her and come back by himself. He doesn't let himself get tied down too easily."

"Humph! Let's hope that's true! Go to the post office in the city tomorrow and see if there's a letter from him."

"Why would he write us another letter? His business trip'll be done in two weeks, he'll write from Sofia. But if you insist, I'll go."

Their conversations about Marko's engagement began and ended in one and the same way, and Anyo was amazed that his father, who otherwise was a sagacious person, did not notice this and continued to believe in the letter, even though he felt increasingly bitter at Marko's thoughtlessness. In his opinion this engagement was a betrayal of the family's tradition of mutual trust and agreement on all questions. For the first time, one member of the family had decided something so important "on his own," and perhaps precisely because it was the first time, this filled him with indignation and concern for the future. And even though he condemned Marko's "ladies' man" ways, his only hope lay therein – since he didn't let himself get too tangled up with girls (brothers knew each other's secrets!), he would tell her a simple *auf Wiedersehen* and that would be that.

Anyo was convinced that his brother's defection would become known very soon, in a month at the latest, as the relevant government bodies were waiting for the end of his "business trip" to pass, but he continued to keep up the illusion in front of his parents, while trying to prepare himself little by little for the awful truth. Marko wrote a second letter in which he reported that after the engagement the marriage itself would very soon have to follow. She was a nice, pretty girl, she had come to love him, and his conscience wouldn't allow him to leave her "high and dry," especially since the question of her coming to study in Sofia was already settled. After the marriage, he would have to stay in Germany "for a month or so," but he had informed his employers of this in time and had gotten their permission. This letter also had no return address. Anyo hid it and thus sowed yet another lie in the family, more sinister and destructive than any other lie, since it was a betrayal of a sacred parental hope. If his father hadn't looked upon the whole business so naïvely, and his mother, too, alongside him ("Whatever Kiro says!"), they would all have borne the brunt of this misfortune together, and for him it would have been somehow easier. But here an inevitable question kept popping into his head: "What if Dad has guessed that Marko has defected and is playing naïve for the sake of the rest of us? What if he has already taken the blow and his heart is broken, but continues smiling so as to shield us from the intense shock? He has already shown that he is capable of such a supreme sacrifice for our sake. But how can I find out whether he has already come face-to-face with the inevitable, and how will he react when this becomes known to all of us?"

These days were some of the most difficult, if not the most difficult, of his life. At first, it was as if the "technical" side of his brother's defection interested him the most, he strained his mind to imagine how and where his brother had crossed the border, what documents he had traveled with, where and how he was living now – in short, he had the feeling that he had begun reading some adventure novel, agonizing yet nevertheless fascinating. But the more he thought about the consequences of this defection, the stronger and more contradictory became his feelings, tearing apart his soul, the future looked ever more hopeless to him. He was especially tormented by the mystery of his own presentiment – how had he, from the very first moment, believed that his brother had defected, without having any direct proof? What unknown force had made him believe this so unreservedly? Had he suspected it even before, when the conflict arose between their family and the village leaders? Or had he suspected that he himself was capable of defecting, if the circumstances were propitious, as they had been for Marko? *No, I would never for anything in the world decide to leave my parents and brothers*, he thought to himself honestly and sincerely. *Perhaps it's due to cowardice, but still, I would never decide to defect, no matter what happened in life. But how did Marko decide to take that fateful step, our stable, good, reasonable Marko, who weighed his every word, his every intention! How could he not miss us terribly, how could he have written us off forever, pushed us out of his heart as if we were dead?* This is precisely what tormented him the most cruelly – why and how had Marko, their blood brother and son, decided to follow a destiny different from theirs, full of uncertainties, full of sorrow and loneliness, and perhaps even lifelong suffering? Perhaps he had become mentally deranged, or had he consciously decided on eternal exile?

Anyo constantly sought and failed to find in his memory cases when his brother, albeit only with a word or a hint, had expressed his intention to defect from Bulgaria. Indeed, in the last few years their family had lived in worry and want, they had had to pinch and scrape so they could study, but even in the darkest days, even when they denied them the right to continue studying at the university, Marko did not rail against Stoyan Kralev with any particular passion, nor against the party's system as a whole. He was unhappy, of course, but not hopeless. "By now we should have convinced Dad to join the co-op," he would say. "No matter how hard it is for him to do it, there's no other choice. And we would have gotten by somehow, like poor students always have. But we'll wait, in a year Dad will have joined." Anyo remembered from his life with his brother only mutual trust, warmth, and love, both between the two of them, as well as between everyone in the family. He also recalled that in his attempt at suicide for their sake (they were convinced that this was why he had done it), their father had shaken them down to the marrow and fused them in consanguineous unity as never before; his tragic attempt to bring about his own demise seemed to have inspired strength and confidence in them to stand shoulder to shoulder and to overcome all the ups and downs on their path. But Marko had torn apart and desecrated that unity. He had closed his eyes and hurled himself into the abyss of the unknown. Why? From weakness, from egotism, or from a desire for adventure?

Anyo realized with horror that an ever more insistent, unpleasant, and bad feeling toward his brother was creeping into his heart. *It's terrible for me to judge him*, he would think, while tormented by this feeling, *for deciding to take such an extreme step, he must have had insurmountable reasons that I don't know about. I shouldn't judge him, I shouldn't, that is base on my part, it is the equivalent of fratricide!* Yet in spite of his will, he judged him all the same. His empathy for Marko gave way to doubt and reproach, until he started blaming him as well. *Whatever the motives for his defection may have been*, he would think, *it was in fact egotism, cruelty, and betrayal. He knew the political situation in Bulgaria and he knew very well what consequences his defection to the capitalist camp would have for our family. He should have taken his brotherly share in our common fate and it wouldn't have been so terrible. Now look, Dad joined the co-op and in only a few months we would have been back studying at the university. In only a few months! Now Dimcho and I will never continue our education and who knows what paths fate will push us down. Isn't it egotism to save yourself through defection at the expense of four people, your full-blood brothers and parents at that? And will you really save yourself? What if you die an absurd death in foreign lands and cause our parents even more suffering?*

Every other day late in the afternoon, the postal carrier's horn could be heard. At that time Anyo would be in the field, hoeing corn on the co-op land with fifty women and girls. The bugle's hoarse sound carried from the village like a lonely bird exhausted from the heat, the girls would straighten up with their hoes in their hands and say in unison: "The post-man's here." They would start squawking like magpies, wondering aloud who was expecting a letter from whom, they would tease one another, laughing simple-heartedly and foolishly. Anyo knew he would not receive the letter he had long been wanting, yet every time he found himself waiting for the postman's horn to blow. His heart quivered with despondency and loneliness, he hated the exhausted women for their naïve conversations and jokes, his life seemed more boring, stupid, and pointless than ever, he felt a wild urge to run away wherever his feet would take him and to never come back. He worked more diligently than the others, he worked with a desperate fury, in the evenings he could not fall asleep until late, he was thinking about his brother, he was also thinking about the girl from whom he had not gotten a letter in a long time. Her name was Slava, they had been in the same year at university, they had sat next to each other and lived on the same street a few houses apart. They had already grown close in the first few days of the school year, because they walked to and from the university together. Their classmates from the very beginning had started looking on them as a couple. Anyo would grow flustered at their unambiguous hints, while she acted as if she had not heard them or did not want to hear them. She would sit next to Anyo during lectures or would always be close by him, as if sticking near to a relative or a friend from childhood. Indeed, it was the fact that they were neighbors and their classmates' attitude that made them grow close. If Slava happened to be absent from a lecture, they would ask Anyo about her and vice versa. Even Anyo's landlady found excuses to tell him that he and Slava were perfectly matched and that her parents "really liked him." Slava's father was a carpenter and worked in a shipbuilding yard, while her mother was a homemaker. They had a tidy brick house a story-and-a-half high with a vine arbor in front of it; under the trellis was a cement patio with a table and chairs. Once Slava and Anyo were talking through the gate and her father saw them. As soon as he caught sight of the older man, Anyo said goodbye and turned to leave, but her father called very casually after him: "Hey, boy, where are you running off to?"

"Oh no... please!"

"Why don't you get acquainted?" Slava said. "Dad, this is my classmate Anyo."

"I know him, we are neighbors, after all. Well, come on in, what are you waiting for?"

The autumn was still warm, they sat under the trellis, Slava's mother soon came to join them as well. She, too, had long known Anyo, because she had constantly seen him with her daughter going to and from lectures, so she, too, greeted him very warmly, almost as if he were a frequent guest of the family. Her father told them about some event at the shipyard, then he fell to talking with the mother about household concerns, while Slava and Anyo were left to chat about their studies. Anyo was shy and even though he frequently stopped by Slava's house after that, he never managed to relax around her parents. He was disconcerted by them and was afraid that if they found out about his feelings for Slava, they would be offended precisely because they had treated him as a trusted friend of the family; he didn't dare take advantage of their trust. For the same reason he was disconcerted by Slava herself and could never decide whether to hint at his feelings for her. She also acted unpretentious and natural around him, as if she considered him a trusted friend, and when she would ask him for some small favor, she would say: "Aren't you my little gentleman friend?" just as the older girls would patronizingly speak to the neighborhood boys when they had an intimate relationship with some other man. At the same time, Anyo was sure she didn't have a boyfriend, or if she did, he didn't live in Varna and would only come back during the holidays. This last possibility tormented him terribly and caused him to suffer bouts of suspicion and jealousy. He observed her very carefully and noticed that sometimes she was very distracted, especially during lectures. While he diligently took notes in every subject, she would sit there lost in her thoughts, looking off to the side and seeming to be daydreaming. "Hey, where are you?" he would ask her in a whisper, and she would nudge him in a special way with her elbow and both affectionately and angrily reply: "Leave me alone!" *But if she had a boyfriend who studies or works in another city,* Anyo wondered, *why would she go out and about only with me, wouldn't that be compromising in his eyes, even if she was only using me as a "little gentleman friend" so as not to go around the city by herself?*

Anyo was in love, but in love Dzhelebov-style, proudly, devotedly, and bashfully. He knew that in such cases the gentleman had to reveal his feelings to the lady first, yet his pride was every bit as strong as his love. If Slava were to be surprised by his confession, even if she only said that she would "think about it," he would have to run away from her once and for all, he wouldn't be able to bear only friendship. It was all or nothing. By and by, they were now going to the cinema together as well. She herself had invited him "to escort her," because she didn't feel comfortable going alone. Once (it was after Christmas vacation) they were watching a film about the war and in one brutal scene Slava grasped his hand and squeezed it in her palm. Anyo placed his other hand on top of hers: "Don't be scared!" The episodes on the screen went from calm and cheerful to horrifying and painful, and Slava's hand remained clasped in his until the end of the film. It was cold outside, a piercing February wind was blowing, the sidewalks were iced over like skating rinks. Slava's gloves were very thin, she kept her hands in the pockets of her overcoat, and if she slipped, she would not have been able to keep her balance. Anyo took her arm to keep her from falling, and so they walked all the way to the gate. Two more times it happened to be very cold when they went to the cinema, and both times they returned home arm in arm.

At the beginning of July they also started going to the beach several times a week. Slava would bring a piece of white cloth from home, Anyo would drive four stakes into the sand, stretch out the cloth, and thus make a shade. Exam period was beginning at that time, the two of them would lie in the shade and go over what they had studied the previous night. After an hour or an hour and a half, they would take a break, go running over the sand, and dive into the water. Then they would duck their heads under the makeshift "beach umbrella" again and take up their notes, quizzing each other, clarifying questions, and before they knew it, the exam period had ended successfully, they both had passed all their exams. The next day Anyo had to leave for the village. He had full room and board at his landlord's, thus he didn't have much baggage. He gathered up his things in a pasteboard suitcase, said goodbye to his landlords, and set out for the train station. On the corner, Slava was waiting for him with a bouquet of flowers, dressed festively and smiling. They walked slowly, discussing their recent exams, summer vacation, and the fall when they would once again go to lectures together. Anyo bought ice cream, they sat in the garden in front of the station and started licking at their cones like children.

"Will you write to me?" Anyo had been thinking about this since the morning and finally decided to ask her.

"Of course! Will you write to me?" Slava asked, and laughed at her naïve question.

"Of course I'll write to you. Only *you*'ll be going to the beach and you won't have time to read my letters," Anyo said, drawing out the word "you" suggestively.

"I don't think *I*'ll be going" (Slava even more distinctly uttered this phrase), "because Mom is going to the mineral baths for a whole month and everything at home is left in my hands." She looked at the station clock and got up. "You'll be late, you've only got ten minutes left."

Anyo brought his suitcase onto the train car and went down to the platform to her. She handed him the bouquet with her left hand while extending her right to him, such that the bouquet was between them. They stood there, holding hands, until the second bell. Anyo climbed into the train car and stuck his head out the window.

"Have a good trip and write me, please!" Slava said, giving him her hand and starting to cry. Her tears gushed out suddenly, running down her face. "Oof, how ridiculous I am!" she said, her face twisting foolishly from spasms of sobs.

"Don't cry!" To Anyo, this seemed to be the most tender thing he had ever said to her since they had met. "I'll write you tomorrow."

The train started off. Slava ran alongside the train, clutching his hand.

"Let go!" the conductor said from the steps of the train car.

Why did she burst out crying then? Anyo would ask himself, and would answer: *Out of capriciousness, or no, from pangs of conscience. She knew in advance that she would have to break things off with me, so here's a few crocodile tears for you, here's a few comforting words so you don't think me some flighty and ungrateful young lady! Because her letters, too, were written solely to console me: How are you, when are you coming back, aren't you bored in the village? Yes, the little gentlemen friends have to be given their lollipops so they won't get mad that the big girls already have their true gentlemen. And he's with her now, he's come back from somewhere for the summer and perhaps he will stay with her forever. It was all a sham, a way to kill time, and I believed that I was the only one in her life. At least it's good that I didn't fall to my knees in front of her and beg for her love. How she would have mocked me inwardly, how treacherously she would have played the hypocrite! But still, it's a good thing she stopped writing to me, it was nevertheless honorable from her side to stop leading me on!*

Anyo felt satisfaction in nursing this bitterness toward the girl and most of all toward himself for having fallen for her deception. In the loneliness of the night his pride suffered more than ever and he felt hatred for the girl and swore that if he ever met up with her again somehow and she tried to speak to him, he would turn his back on her with all the scorn he could muster, and perhaps he would even insult her. But when he was swinging the hoe, more or less the only man among dozens of women (this, too, seemed demeaning to him), memories pressed in on him and committed outrages against his consciousness with the clearest of details that he had not noticed at the time. At noon the heat became unbearable, no breeze blew, and the air quivered as if white-hot. After lunch the women lay down next to one another under the pear tree, they chattered for some time, then fell into a deep sleep with their kerchiefs pulled down, smelling of sweat, with dirty feet and cracked heels. Anyo lay on his belly far away from them, on the dried clods of earth, drenched in sweat, his bones aching and his head blazing. He would put his hands under his cheek and try to doze off, but the earth was burning beneath him like embers, big green flies swooped down on him as on carrion and stung him through his shirt, ants, with their slender bodies pinched in the middle and with enormous heads, crawled over his arms and legs, all manner of insects crawled only inches from his eyes. And perhaps because of the unbearable heat, Anyo could not entirely resist the memories, they transported him to the beach in front of the casino, under the white makeshift shade, where exactly a year ago at this time he and Slava had been studying for their exams. Neither of them could swim and she was always asking Anyo to hold her up with his arms as she floated on her back. She splashed around like a child and as soon as she swallowed water or her face got dunked in, she instinctively clutched at him like a drowning man, crying: "You're going to drown me!" Her body clung closely to his and with his skin he felt the slippery cold caress of her skin, her blue irises seemed to him to be growing wider not so much from panic as from a desire to play, to feel him even closer to her, which she could only permit herself to do in the water. He could only dive in the shallower water with his eyes open and would do so when she was looking away, to grab her by the leg and surprise her. These dives lasted only seconds, as long as he could hold his breath, but he would dive with pleasure, because he found himself in a different, wondrous world. The rays of sunlight were fractured into gentle fantastical hues in the water and made little golden circles on the sand, where thin reseda-colored seaweed swayed, adorned with multicolored microscopic shells; tiny frightened crabs would dart away and finally her body would appear, bathed in a translucent pink, unreal and yet so real and so long dreamed of that Anyo would cry out with all the air he had in his lungs: "I love you!"

This underwater confession was the first and most cherished of his life, but Slava could not hear it. Feeling something squeezing her ankle, she would let out a fake shriek and as soon as he appeared above the water, she would start splashing water in his face. When they returned to the shade and sat down to dry off, Slava would gather her long blond hair in her hands, turn to the side, and wring it out. The water would trickle through her fingers in thin rivulets onto the tawny skin of her shoulder, one stream would drip along her arm to the tip of her elbow and pour into the sand, while the other would run along her shoulder blade and slip beneath the strap of her bathing suit. And then Anyo, with deeply suppressed passion, would stare from very close up now at the downy golden hairs on the back of her neck, now at the mole on her left shoulder blade that would shift up and down with the movement of her arm. He would touch it cautiously with the tip of his finger and she would always say: "Hey, what do you think you're doing?"

"I thought it was an oyster shell."

Before lying down in the shade and getting to work on their lecture notes, she would shake out her hair so as to arrange it over her shoulders, and then invisible sprays emanating a sweet fragrance would envelop his face like an ephemeral caress, the only caress she could give him. At the memory of it, Anyo would be filled with magnanimity and tenderness and all his doubts and reproaches toward her would seem to him unfair and even cruel. *She could not be other than what she was, uncorrupted and inexperienced* – he thought with gentle fondness. *If I hadn't stayed in the village, in the future she would have been only with me. I broke it off with her, not she with me, and I didn't even dare explain to her why I was breaking it off. I was afraid that when she found out the reason, she would leave me. How could she marry a man denounced by the authorities and who wasn't even allowed to study at the university? I hemmed and hawed in my letters, I lied to her that I was sick, but I couldn't think up what I could be so sick from that I couldn't go to Varna at least once to see her. But I should have gone, to tell her the truth, and she would have decided whether she would stay with me given all the circumstances or not. But I was afraid that she wouldn't stay with a man with no future. I could sense it and that's how it turned out. From now on, I will never set foot in the university again. I will be either a hoer or a plowman at the co-op, or a worker in some factory. They wouldn't even let me become a village schoolteacher. Then why was I angry with the girl? Could she tie herself down to a worker or a villager? My future would be full of uncertainties. Actually, I have no future. It was taken away by my own dear brother!...*

One evening at the end of June, Anyo was sitting with his father under the awning of the summer kitchen, and his mother was getting supper. It had been a long time since they had eaten supper together, because they were working on different brigades and came home at different times. They would each eat whatever they found on the kitchen table and go to bed.

"Why don't you hop over to the post office in the city tomorrow, hm?" Kiro Dzhelebov said. "Marko must be back in Sofia by now."

Anyo had just washed up at the well and was combing his still-damp hair.

"He didn't come back and he's not coming back!" he said.

"What do you mean, 'he's not coming back'?"

"Just that, he's not coming back."

"Do you hear what you're saying?" Kiro Dzhelebov said.

"I hear very well and I'll say it again: Marko won't be coming back anymore, Marko is an emigrant. A Political emigrant, with a capital *P*! There's no girl, there's no engagement. Can you really not understand that he thought up that engagement to temporarily throw the authorities off the scent and to prepare us for the worst? He assumed that once we read his letter more carefully, we would guess what was what and little by little we'd swallow the bitter pill. Look what a considerate son and brother, how he cares about us! I'm not going to inform you of my defection up front and suddenly so you don't swallow your tongues or have a stroke. But I could immediately tell something was fishy. I mean, it's as plain as day. Who's going to send a person abroad, and to a capitalist country at that, when he doesn't even have a certificate of reliability and they won't even let him study at the university? I wrote to his landlady, too, I wanted to check nonetheless. And she wrote me that he hadn't been going to lectures, but had been working on some construction site. He'd been planning his defection even last year in the fall and until now he's been fooling us with these office jobs and business trips. Our clever and good firstborn son and brother is no longer with us to…"

"That's enough!" Kiro Dzhelebov cut him off.

As soon as Anyo started talking, Kiro Dzhelebov had pulled back against the backrest of his chair as if something had hit him in the chest, he was listening and didn't take his eyes off him. Auntie Tanka, as she was bending over the fire and stirring the sizzling frying pan, cried out, "Good Lord!" and also fixed her eyes on her son, without moving the whole time. *What am I doing,* Anyo thought, *up until this minute wasn't I wanting to spare them, to let them in on this whole business gradually, to prepare them for the worst. I was supposed to stretch Marko's story to unbelievable lengths, even when it was challenged by indisputable facts, I needed to swear that this wasn't and couldn't be the truth, that there must have been some misunderstanding, our brother and son would never have run away abroad, he would never stain the family name, bring shame upon his loved ones and hurl them into disgrace. But what am I saying now and why am I saying it? Just look, they're petrified from shock, there's not a drop of blood left in their faces, they are almost slain and I am twisting the knife to finish them off.* But at the same time, Anyo felt a wild urge to tell them the whole truth as he saw it, to deprive them of their final hope, to spit on all filial virtues. And that's what he did, clearly realizing all the while that he shouldn't be doing it.

"Just two more words and I'll stop," he said. "The girl Marko is engaged to is not a girl, but a foreign country he has 'taken to wife.' That's how we need to interpret it. (*And why am I making up these metaphors, why don't I just stop and say that I'm speaking this way out of nerves, out of exhaustion, out of boredom!*) Soon he'll marry the girl and have a family. He's trying to say that he'll be staying in Germany forever. I got a second letter from him which said that he would soon be getting married and would be 'staying there awhile.' I didn't read you the letter so as not to worry you. It's upstairs in the room, in the drawer of the table. But there's something else, too. What if our dear Marko has been recruited as an agent for some foreign intelligence service? (*Now I really shouldn't have said that, because it's a pure fabrication that just came to me now.*) Otherwise there's no way he could have crossed the border legally. He must have gone with a foreign passport, and later he'll have to pay dearly for that. And then he'll ruin every last one of us. I'm finished!"

Anyo got up from the table and headed out into the yard. When he reached the middle of it, he stopped and looked back at the kitchen. The butter had boiled over, spattering into the fire, the flames had set alight the pile of kindling next to the hearth and were licking at the dried bunches of savory hanging above it, the smell of burned grease filled the yard. His mother and father were still frozen to the spot, not seeing or sensing anything. Anyo went back, set the frying pan on the ground, and used the tongs to extinguish the kindling. Suddenly his bitterness was replaced by empathy for his parents, lately he had very often swung sharply from one state to another, thus going to extremes. Now his heart was breaking with pain and tenderness for his parents, especially his mother, who was still standing up, but looking as if she would slump to the ground at any moment. He put his arm around her shoulders, picked her up like a child, and gently sat her down.

"Mom, sit down! Whatever Marko has done, we'll face it and live through it. The important thing is that he's alive and well. Maybe things will be better for him there. If not, then no one will stop him from coming back. Some woman has turned his head, but as soon as he gets ahold of himself, he'll come back. I'm sure of it."

"And are you sure he's defected?" Kiro Dzhelebov said finally.

"Not entirely, but that's what I suppose…"

"Man supposes, God disposes, as the old folks say. Since you don't have any certain proof, you have no reason to slander your brother. And even if he did defect, he didn't do it to ruin all of us. He wasn't in his right mind, he had lost his will and reason. Otherwise he wouldn't have put his own head in the noose. None of us could betray his own, therefore your brother, too, would never run away from us."

They went to their rooms, but no one slept until the morning. Anyo was tormented by pangs of conscience for having accused his brother so harshly. His father's blind faith in Marko's innocence seemed to undermine his certainty that Marko had emigrated and burned all his bridges once and for all. Perhaps some influential person (say, the father or brother of one of his fellow students) had decided to trust him and had included him in some group business trip because he knew German well, thus Marko might really have gone abroad legally and really have gotten involved with some girl. If he were to marry the girl and start living with her either here or there, that would no longer be emigration, but marriage to a foreigner, and there were those kind of marriages all over the world, they existed here in Bulgaria as well. In any case, it was getting toward the end of June, and the local authorities still hadn't been informed of Marko's defection. Was it possible that in Sofia they didn't know about his stay abroad, or perhaps that they had sent him from there?

Kiro Dzhelebov and Auntie Tanka also weren't sleeping. She had long since had a premonition that Marko had defected, but she hadn't dared to share it directly with her husband, so as not to upset him like before and make him "pull some stunt again." If Anyo had foreseen his brother's defection out of fear for his own future, she had foreseen it out of fear of losing her son. Her instinct for preserving her family gave her the strength to stand firmly on both feet and to defend it to the bitter end against all ensuing misfortunes. She agreed with her husband that Marko "was not capable of such a thing," but at the same time she hinted to him to take it as their fate, which they would have to accept.

"Just so long as he's alive and well, leave the rest of it to God. He's not in another world, once time passes, just you wait and see, he'll be back before we know it. These countries won't be fighting forever, we might even find ourselves making matches with them after a while."

"You're talking as if you've already written him off," Kiro Dzhelebov said. "But I'm telling you again that Marko couldn't have run away. But who knows! You have to be ready to expect anything from a person..."

His unshakable faith in Marko came not from his reason, but from his blood. He believed blindly and wholeheartedly in the family's blood ties, just as his forefathers had believed in them, and that was the only consolation that could fortify him in the times ahead; even if he had defected, Marko hadn't run away out of light-mindedness and in his blood he would always remain with his own people. As a matter of fact, deep within himself he was unsure, he reproached Marko for having shown cowardice in spite of everything, but his conscience would not allow him to judge his son. *He was offended by the authorities*, he would think, *and with good reason, since they wouldn't let him finish his education and turned his life upside down. But the insult alone wasn't enough to shut his eyes. Here we're talking about a harsh shock to the soul. A shock to the very depths of his being that makes a man go right off his head. Like what happened to me last year. Why did I go to end my own life? Even now that whole business isn't fully clear to me. It was like I was split into two people. I realized very well that it was high time to join the co-op, and since it was, I should accept my situation and swallow Stoyan Kralev's insult. His lot can't be easy either, he might have jumped out of his own skin as well. That's what I was thinking, but my heart was being torn apart by rage and helplessness. How can somebody order me to hand over my property down to the last acre on such and such a day, and to insult me on top of everything, and I'm not able to defend my honor! Keep ahold of yourself, I kept telling myself, but I couldn't control myself, my whole body was shaking as if feverish, I felt nauseous and my legs were going out from under me. I was thinking what would happen to my sons from now on and since I knew that I couldn't help them with anything, I was seething with anguish and hatred. You'll have to sign that membership declaration, I kept telling myself, and to bring it to him right now and get this all over with. This business won't pass me over, if not now, it'll have to happen next year at the latest. I got away for a year or two because of my sons, but now it's clear that I won't be able to dodge it any longer. More or less everybody has joined the co-op, am I going to be the only one left sticking out like a sore thumb? I sat down to write my membership declaration, but as soon as I wrote two lines, my hand froze up. I couldn't go on, I couldn't swallow back my will and bow my head. I've got to bow my head, I kept telling myself, it's necessary. The times necessitate it. Fine, but why by force? In whose name are they trampling me like a worm, spitting in my face and grabbing at my property and my honor? In the name of goodness, they say. So why is this good for me, if they have to thrust it into my hands by force, good that's been forced on you is worse than evil. It's like in school — they beat and punish the children to teach them sense and reason, then when they grow up, every child becomes the person he was meant to be. The smart one is smart, the foolish one is foolish. But who knows, I would think on the other hand, maybe it really will be better under socialism than it is now. It hurts now, but tomorrow it won't, just like after an operation. Today they cut out a chunk of your living flesh, tomorrow you're healthy. But I wonder whether after today's operation things will be better for people? If it's not a success, some will die, others will be maimed for life.*

And that's how the two Kiros in me were fighting. One thought one way, the other, the opposite. After that, everything was like a dream. I knew that I shouldn't do it, but I did it. I wasn't wanting to end my own life, yet I was going off to do so. There was only one thought in my head: that only death would fix everything. Where that thought came from and why, I don't know, but I kept repeating it in my mind as I was digging the pit. I had often dreamed of being buried alive before and those dreams were agonizing. But now I was going to do it myself and I wasn't afraid. My heart was light and peaceful, I felt some sweet relief washing over me. And when I had buried myself to the waist, it crossed my mind that I might get scared and try to dig myself out, so I threw the spade and the hoe far away. I knew that no one would find me and save me now, and my soul felt so nice and calm. I wonder if Marko didn't have two souls in him, if he didn't throw some things far away from himself so that there was no way he could come back?

The blizzard blew in a vague, fractured cry that interrupted his thoughts. He stopped to listen, looked ahead, and saw Stoyan Kralev sunk up to his waist in snow. He recognized him by the earflaps of his hat, the ends of which could not be tied and which hung down on the sides like wings.

"Over here, over heeeere!"

Stoyan Kralev called out once more and, searching for a path, disappeared again behind the brush. And then Kiro Dzhelebov remembered, for the thousandth time already, but, as it seemed to him, with new details, their meeting by the barn that morning, when a terrible, insurmountable hatred for that man had suddenly flared up in his soul. He had hated him earlier as well, especially when he had deprived his sons of their education, but deep in his soul he had tried to justify him as an administrative figure who was carrying out orders from higher-ups, thus he didn't hate so much him personally but rather the party's policies as a whole.

That morning, after he hadn't slept a wink all night, he went to the horse barn even before the crack of dawn. They were housed in an abandoned shed at the edge of the village that had been refashioned into a barn. At the far end of the unfenced yard stood several carts. One was painted in bright colors, which made it look brand-new, and an old leather bench seat taken from a scrapped truck or some other vehicle had been mounted in its bed. Stoyan Kralev used it to drive around the fields, to go to the neighboring villages and sometimes even to the city. Kiro Dzhelebov noticed him only when he passed by the colorful cart – he had set his bag on the leather seat and was leaning against the cart rails.

"Good morning, I must be late," Kiro Dzhelebov said, and for some reason, his heart shrank at this unexpected meeting.

"You're not late, I'm early so as to catch the bus in Vladimirovo. They've called me in to the regional committee first thing this morning."

"I'll hitch it up right now," Kiro Dzhelebov said, and went into the barn.

He brought out the horse collars, then led out the horses and started hitching them up. Stoyan Kralev was still standing there, leaning against the cart rails, turned to the side and silent. When everything was ready for the trip, he spryly leapt into the driver's seat. As soon as they felt the reigns in his hand, the horses started off, but he stopped them and turned toward Kiro Dzhelebov.

"Well, look now, I almost forgot. Congratulations on your new daughter-in-law!"

"What new daughter-in-law?"

"There's no way you don't know that your son Marko has married a German girl?" Stoyan Kralev's clean-shaved face went pale, grew longer, and took on a repugnant expression.

"I don't know any such thing," Kiro Dzhelebov said, a strong spasm squeezing his throat.

"Well, if you don't know now, you'll find out."

Stoyan Kralev started up the horses but they soon stopped and Kiro Dzhelebov saw that the rotted gate was closed. He ran over, pulled open the gate, and stood behind it.

"This isn't the end of our little chat!" Stoyan Kralev said as the cart went through the gate.

On top of everything I had to open the gate for him like a servant, Kiro Dzhelebov thought; the spasm in his throat gripped him to the point of suffocation and a hot wave washed over his body. And it was precisely in that instant that he felt a terrible, staggering hatred for Stoyan Kralev, a hatred so strong and uncontrollable that he was scared of losing his will and reason and hurling himself at him. *I'll kill him,* he said to himself, and this thought wedged so firmly and permanently in his head that even now, as he stood in the blind, numb to the cold and the blizzard, with an aching relish he remembered even the smallest details of their meeting that morning. The sun had half appeared over the horizon, like half of a well-baked loaf of bread, beneath it the field glowed bluish, cold, and desolate, some bird darted forward, leaving a streak on the pinkish dawn, and as he went through the gate, Stoyan Kralev momentarily blocked the fiery half-sun with his body. The horse on the right kicked up a pebble and Kiro Dzhelebov noticed that the shoe on its left front hoof was missing. *The horse is barefooted, how did I not notice until now,* he thought, and his eyes passed over the tailgate of the cart, where Rayna Knyaginya* was painted with a green flag and a sword in her hand, then his gaze stopped on the back of Stoyan Kralev's head, where the hair was trimmed short and was almost covered by his cap of homespun wool. The horses broke into a trot and Kiro Dzhelebov watched Stoyan Kralev's back growing smaller and his bag, bulged like a stuffed sack, bouncing on the back seat. The cart hurtled toward a large flock of geese. One of the goslings fell beneath the horses' feet, tumbled around between the wheels and a moment later came out in the dust cloud unharmed, but scared and crying. Two of the adult geese immediately swooped down on it and started yelling and pecking at its back with their bills. Kiro Dzhelebov understood their language as well as he understood human speech, unwittingly he listened to the geese scolding the gosling: "Why don't you watch out, what were you day-dreaming about, you could've been crushed or maimed!" And they went on boxing its ears as they hustled it back to the flock. Then Kiro Dzhelebov looked back at the cart and saw how Mincho Naydenov, who was to drive Stoyan Kralev to the bus stop, jumped into the cart in motion and took up the reigns, while Stoyan Kralev moved to the leather back seat.

And everything turned out as Anyo had foreseen. The relevant state security agencies had read the letters from Germany or perhaps they had known about his defection from the very beginning, but in any case they waited for the deadline set by the defector himself for his return. News of his defection instantly swept through the village, and in a few days, through the whole region. To people of these parts, who were used to a sedentary life far from the tempestuous social events in the interior of the country, defection, of course, made a very strong, almost stagger-ing impression, and this circumstance in and of itself already isolated the Dzhelebov family and landed them in disgrace. Everyone avoided them, so as not to be accused of being in cahoots with them, especially since Kiro Dzhelebov and Anyo were put under investigation. They were asked whether they knew of the defector's plans in advance, what kinds of people he had been in contact with, had these people come to their home, and at the same time, they were constantly conducting searches of their house. There was no way the security agencies could not have known that when a person decides to defect abroad, given the political circumstances of the time, he would not share this even with his nearest and dearest, but they kept calling the two of them in, just as a lesson to the rest of the population. This went on for several months. Marko didn't write or his letters got lost somewhere. He finally wrote after about a year and announced that, in fact, he had only just now gotten married to Juta. Whether it was the same girl he had written about in his first letters or someone else, they never did find out, just as they never found out how he had managed to slip across the Bulgarian border. For a long time they didn't dare answer him because they knew their letters would be read, they were afraid of letting some inopportune word slip that would make their situation even more difficult. But Stoyan Kralev soon reminded them, under the most ostensibly pleasant of pretenses, not to forget their son, and in doing so confirmed that the letters coming and going were being counted, since the relevant security agencies still hoped to get their hands on some intelligence.

"Have you gotten any letters from Marko, have you written him?" Stoyan Kralev asked him once, when they happened to have been left alone for a few minutes after a meeting.

"When would we find time to write now?" Kiro Dzhelebov said. "We'll write during the winter."

"Come on, don't be that way, Kiro! Don't abandon the boy! He went astray, but maybe he'll regret it. Advise him to come back and to continue his education. Nobody'll do him any harm. Otherwise the shame of it will weigh on you your whole life."

"No one can shame me except myself," Kiro Dzhelebov said. "My son isn't a child, whatever he's done, he's done it himself, let him pay the piper. Since he doesn't answer for me, I don't answer for him, either. The other day he wrote that he'd gotten married, that his wife wanted to study in Sofia, but as far as I could tell from the letter, our folks here won't give her permission."

"That's not true!" Stoyan Kralev cut in, but then, realizing that with such a categorical statement he was only confirming that he was informed about the issue, he fell silent for a bit before going on. "Perhaps our folks here have dug in their heels a bit. After all, she is a foreigner, from a capitalist county, West Germany to boot. They've got to gather intelligence on what sort of person she is."

"Her father is a communist, he did time in fascist camps."

"Is that so? Well, that changes things entirely. Since her father is an active fighter against fascism, then there shouldn't be any obstacles to his daughter's coming to study and live in Bulgaria, and that means that Marko will come too. We've got to write to the Interior Ministry in Sofia to look into this question ASAP. What's the girl's name, what city does she live in?"

"The girl's name is Juta, but I don't know her last name or the city. It was written in German on the envelope and Anyo couldn't understand it, since he hasn't studied German. I'll give you the letters, send them wherever you need to send them to read the address."

Whenever they met (and this happened often in the fields or at the brig-adiers' meetings), Stoyan Kralev would inevitably bring up the defector. He knew that Marko wasn't coming back, but he kept asking about him to morally torment his father. The two of them had far tenser and more difficult conversations, especially in the first year after Marko's defection, when Stoyan Kralev threatened to kick him out of the co-op and send him to a labor camp. "I should have smashed your face in back in the day," Stoyan Kralev would say, shaking his fist under his nose, "and forced you into the co-op. If I'd done it, we wouldn't have to bother with this squabbling now. But certain people misled me, and plus I thought you were an honest man too. And here you were the lowest, dirtiest enemy of the people's power!" From time to time they searched the house as well. Unfamiliar plainclothes agents would come long after midnight and rush in to rummage through the house. They would turn everything upside down, then they would go into the empty barn, they would even slip into the henhouse, saying that they were searching for saboteurs.

This was the sorry state their youngest son, Dimcho, found his family in. Like every young man, he had developed certain habits in the army, where he had spent two years in a strictly limited world of obedience and state-enforced optimism, thus some time had to pass before he forgot them and adapted to life in the village. Under the influence of these habits, he brought to the family an irrepressible gust of cheerfulness, which is found in every young man deprived of freedom and the pleasures of civilian life for a long time. The very next day after his return he joined one of the co-op brigades and began working alongside the others, as assiduous as a soldier, inexhaustible, and accommodating to everyone. In the evenings, when the youth club was open, he would go straight there from the field, happy that he could spend the night out and about until as late as he wanted, and that he could go to bed without the bugle and evening inspections. In the army he had learned to smoke and drink a bit, so on days off he would visit the tavern with some of the younger men. During the New Year's holidays, the college and high school students would come back, and as always, this livened up the village greatly. Parties were organized at the community center, discussions and theatrical performances were held. Dimcho took part in these youthful initiatives and began to banter with the schoolgirls with the ferocity of a grown man who had not yet come into contact with a woman. He fell in love with every girl who paid attention to him, courting them with his soldierly lack of ceremony, and his fame as a skirt-chaser soon spread throughout the village. On the whole, Dimcho showed tendencies that in another time his parents would have judged as vices, but now no one reprimanded him. Everyone could see that he was intoxicated by the freedom of civilian life and had not yet truly realized the situation his family had fallen into, as well as the limitations facing his own future. His natural, youthful impulse to live life to the hilt to some extent filled the vacuum in the family, collapsing as it was under the weight of isolation and uncertainty as to what tomorrow would bring. Kiro Dzhelebov and Auntie Tanka even began to think, and since they thought it, they began to believe, that their youngest would grow attached to life in the village, would get married and stay with them. Let him horse around with the girls, let him drink and smoke a bit, as long as he doesn't start looking toward the city. Like his elder brother. Because Anyo already had one foot out of the village and they had resigned themselves to this. They tried to keep him there, yet they themselves realized that he couldn't and shouldn't stay in the village any longer.

Anyo was very depressed and lonely. While Dimcho was getting together with the village young people, Anyo would spend holidays and weekends in his room, rereading old books and textbooks, mentally returning to his short-lived student days. Since he knew that he would never again set foot in the university, he fell into a deep despair and this despair made him bitter and withdrawn. He couldn't find a common language even with his brother, and even though he was only three years older, he looked upon Dimcho as a mere kid who was still wet behind the ears. Dimcho could sense this and saw him as a snob who had gotten a taste of life at the university and who now was angry with the whole world. When they were together at lunch or dinner, the two of them would always find reasons to toss barbed, indecent comments at each other, while their father cringed with anguish. *What have we come to*, he would think, his heart heavy, *that my sons, who until yesterday lived together in love and harmony, now are at each other's throats at the dinner table in front of their parents!* He could sense that sooner or later some row would break out between them, undignified and shameful for brothers, spurred on by nothing but despair and the inability to deal with the current situation, which had turned their lives upside down and cut off their paths to the future. He didn't know how to guide them and in the end he himself suggested to Anyo that he look for work somewhere in the city.

Anyo had long been trying to get in touch with his friends from the army or some of his former fellow students whose addresses he happened to have saved. He asked them to help him find some kind of work. Of the eight people he wrote to, he managed to connect with only two of them. One – a veterinarian in Shumen – suggested he come there and "since you're a bachelor, we'll find you both a job and a place to live." The second was living and working in Stara Zagora as a dump truck driver. He and Anyo had taken auto mechanic courses together in the army and had gotten licenses to drive large vehicles. This friend wrote that they were hiring drivers, so he could come right away. Anyo decided to go there and in early April he left for Stara Zagora. A few weeks later he wrote to his family that he had started work and that for the time being he was living in a dormitory.

The Dzhelebovs' hopes rested with their youngest, but a year later, he, too, left them, and in the midst of a scandal at that. In the course of horsing around with the girls, Dimcho had grown close to the school-teacher Yanka Grasheva and had fallen in love with her. She was a local girl and after she had finished high school, she became a teacher at the elementary school. Their dates did not remain a secret and so as not to compromise the girl's reputation, one evening Dimcho went to her father to ask for her hand. The elder Grashev refused him as soon as he opened his mouth and announced that he had no daughter to marry off. Yanka advised Dimcho not to go to her father a second time, nor to send his parents, because her father had sworn not to allow them to get married. The two of them continued meeting in secret and looking for a way out of the situation. Dimcho thought of going to some city and finding work and a place to live, and then sending for her, but Yanka didn't want to be separated from him. Several months passed and they still didn't know what to do. Dimcho fully felt then the isolation his family was trapped in. He had felt it earlier as well in people's hints and especially in the co-op leadership's attitude toward him (he put in the most workdays in his brigade, yet at the end of every campaign, they always declared others as the most outstanding workers), but this unfairness hadn't offended him in the least. He was happy that he could work, and that after work he could meet Yanka at the youth club or the community center. After a few years

everything would be forgotten, he would tell Yanka, my brother did an
unreasonable thing, why should I have to pay for it with my happiness and
my future? Yanka shared everything with him and told him word-for-word
what had been said at home. Her father, her brother, and all their relatives
didn't want to become in-laws with the Dzhelebovs, because they were
all reactionaries, enemies of the authorities, spies, and their sons had no
future, and whoever joined their family must be like them.

Near the end of the school year Yanka went to the city for a teachers'
conference. Her brother drove her to the city by cart and they arranged
for him to come pick her up the next day, and he headed back to the
village. Yanka got on the train to Shumen and at noon got off at the village
of Nevsha. In this village lived their distant relatives Aunt Rusiika, her
mother's cousin, and her husband, Uncle Pasko. When she was young,
Yanka had gotten some sores on her legs and her mother had taken her
to the village to be treated by a famous healer. They stayed with Aunt
Rusiika and Uncle Pasko, went to the healer, who covered the sores with
salve and gave them some of it to use at home, and they should have left,
but their hosts kept them there a whole week. They had no children and
were overjoyed by Yanka, they carried her in their arms all day, pamper-
ing and indulging her and sending her home with lots of presents. Now
Yanka remembered these people and decided to drop in on them. She
told them she was going to Shumen for work and had decided to stop by
to see them on the way. The elderly couple was pleasantly surprised and
just as before was overjoyed to see her. In the late afternoon Yanka went
to leave, but they stood at the door and blocked her way. They talked until
midnight, quizzing her about her family, her work at the school, and, of
course, wouldn't they soon be invited to a wedding? Yanka begged them
to keep what she shared with them an absolute secret, the elderly couple
crossed their hearts, and she told them about her love affair with Dimcho.
While telling it, she burst into tears, the elderly couple burst into tears as

well, and in the end, they decided her fate: "Get the boy and come here to us! You'll get married and live here as long as you like, you've got a house here, you've got everything!"

As soon as the school year ended, Yanka and Dimcho disappeared from the village. The Grashevs were bristling with spite, they raised the alarm with the police and searched for their daughter at the Dzhelebovs. The elder Grashev, his son, and a policeman burst into their house, searched everywhere, and not finding the young people, turned upon Kiro Dzhelebov and his wife with curses and threats. Thus a new misfortune came crashing down on the family – their youngest son had left them as well. The Grashevs spread a rumor around the village that Dimcho had kidnapped their daughter, and since she didn't want to go with him, he had killed her and buried her body somewhere. Blinded by rage, they also spread the absurd rumor that in order to escape from the law, Dimcho had defected abroad and joined his older brother. The Dzhelebovs were now branded, anyone could hurl stones at them, people believed the rumors and even made up some of their own. Again the interrogations, threats, and forced visits to the village soviet began and went on for almost a month, until Dimcho and Yanka wrote to their families that they had gotten married and were living in a distant village.

And so the Dzhelebovs were left completely alone and lived like that for twelve years. Their strong blood would have its say – despite all the misfortunes that befell them, the two of them were healthy and never missed a day of work. Yet a day never passed in which they forgot their loneliness. Constant thoughts of their sons kept this loneliness in their hearts like an open wound. Of Marko, they knew only what he told them from time to time in his letters. They couldn't take his wife and children, whom they saw in photographs, as real live people. That's how they dreamed of them as well – as moving photographs, lacking flesh and blood, mute and colorless beings who stood in one place or moved within the small space of a postcard. Only Marko was alive among them, and he was as they had known him. In the pictures he was dressed differently, in an overcoat or a suit coat, in a sweater or a button-down shirt, but they mentally took these clothes off him and saw him as he had been dressed here. They could not imagine that he had changed, that he was living a different life among different people, they felt him close to them, yet at the same time so far away and inaccessible that perhaps they would never see him for the rest of their lives.

Anyo came to the village with his wife and little boy only once during those years, and all in all they visited him three times in Stara Zagora. His first marriage didn't work out and he got remarried. As they had come to understand, his first wife had turned out to be careless, inept, and barren at that, they stayed together for two years but couldn't get along. They knew his second wife, she seemed to them a tidy, good mother and wife. She had an office job, she had a house with a yard and Anyo lived with her. Her parents were elderly, her father was so senile that they had constantly to keep an eye out that he didn't leave the yard, yet he would nevertheless manage to slip out onto the street and head off wherever his feet led him. He couldn't remember his address, so he would stay wherever he happened to stop, and so Anyo would spend whole nights searching for him and would find him asleep in a ditch outside the city or in some park. He, it seems, did not like his son-in-law, he would shout at him for nothing and threaten to throw him out. Anyo tolerated him because he was sick and old and, most of all, for his wife's sake, with whom he lived in complete harmony. He had been working in an auto repair shop for several years, he also took on private jobs and made good money, yet his parents were still not at peace on his account. It seemed to them that he still hadn't come to accept the life fate had dealt him, and since they knew his implacable character, they worried that some petty disagreement would once again break up his family.

Dimcho and Yanka lived only a three-hour train ride away, but they never once came to the village. After they ran away, the Grashevs disowned their daughter, they wrote to her that they did not want to see her anymore, so she didn't dare visit them, and alongside her, Dimcho, too, did not come back to the village. Uncle Pasko passed away, while Aunt Rusiika was already well into her eighties. Until recently she had taken care of the children and the housework, but now she would sit all day on the window seat, as tidy, fluffy, and white as an angora cat, trying to knit with two pairs of glasses on her nose. Yanka had taken a few courses in Shumen and was now teaching at the middle school, while Dimcho, in the absence of a head agronomist in the village, had taken up that post for many years now. The two of them begged the elderly couple to come live with them, but the Dzhelebovs couldn't decide. The more keenly they felt their loneliness, the more firmly they were attached to the house where they had spent their youth and brought up their children.

"Ooooof!" He heard a voice and in a fleeting lull in the blizzard, he caught sight of Stoyan Kralev twenty steps away. "Who's there? Kiro, is that you?"

"It's me," Kiro Dzhelebov called.

"Man alive, I'm beat… Come on and help me, mate! Here…"

The blizzard enshrouded him once again and Kiro Dzhelebov remembered how years ago he had silently asked him for help, but hadn't even received sympathy. The campaign to dismantle Stalin's cult of personality had passed, Stoyan Kralev had been removed from his post as party secretary and had just been appointed chairman of the co-op. Four horses had died and the medical inspectors had established that they had been poisoned. As early as the previous evening Kiro Dzhelebov had noticed that the horses were sick, he went to inform the co-op chairman and to insist that they call a veterinarian from the city immediately. Stoyan Kralev had already gone to bed, he listened to him through the window and ordered him to stay with the horses until the morning. They sent for a veterinarian, but he arrived in the afternoon and found the horses dead. An investigation was launched and suspicion fell on Kiro Dzhelebov. The investigator not only did not interpret to his advantage the fact that he had warned the chairman in time about the sick horses, but even gave it the opposite reading, in the sense that sometimes a criminal himself reports the crime with the goal of securing an alibi. One of the horse grooms who was directly responsible for the dead horses had been gone the whole day, the other didn't know anything. Only Stoyan Kralev could help him or at least alleviate his situation with a word, and Kiro Dzhelebov asked him to give his opinion on the matter as well. Stoyan Kralev shrugged and kept silent during the whole interrogation. In the end the investigator let him go, but gave him to understand that the absence of evidence in no way meant that he was no longer under suspicion.

And that's how it was with every unpleasant situation that arose in the animal husbandry brigade. If something was stolen, if any illnesses spread, if the livestock was dying off due to no fault of anyone's or if the blame couldn't be proven – Kiro Dzhelebov had to answer for all these damages not only as a brigadier, but as the direct perpetrator. Out of inertia, people from the brigade blamed him for anything that went wrong, and some of his ill-wishers in the co-op took advantage of this. They sabotaged the co-op's work and then skillfully hid behind the permanent disgrace he had fallen into. For his part, Stoyan Kralev took advantage of a tried-and-true method – a disgraced man was more obedient and compliant, and could be used to carry out special jobs for the leadership. More than once in his presence Stoyan Kralev had said that certain people had gotten themselves into such a position that they had to watch very closely what the co-op members were doing, otherwise there was no way around it, they would be blamed or would be considered an accomplice to the guilty parties. *He wants to make me an informer on top of everything, to make me as low as dirt,*

Kiro Dzhelebov thought, and at every convenient opportunity asked to be sent out to the fields to work.

"Whatever else you might be, you're a good worker," Stoyan Kralev would say. "The animal husbandry brigade couldn't get along without you, so I'm not going to send you to another job. We value good workers, Dzhelebov, and we're not vindictive, as some people might think. We take an individual approach to every person and evaluate his qualities as a laborer regardless of whether he shows ideological weaknesses or not. It wouldn't have cost me anything to put you in your proper place when your son emigrated, but instead of that I appointed you as a brigadier. Now I can tell you in confidence that they removed me from my post as party secretary only because of your son, for poor watchfulness. Which means if I had kept a firm hand on people like you, I'd be in a different position now."

At such moments Kiro Dzhelebov felt that sharp spasm in his throat, which began strangling him and washing over his body in hot waves. He often fell into this state of intense, deranged animosity, especially in those first years after Marko's defection, but accidental circumstances always kept him from going to extremes. He could, of course, have killed Stoyan Kralev at any time, except that after getting so intensely agitated he would manage to overcome his hatred and even felt fear at such a possible murder. He would think over his situation calmly and find that it couldn't be otherwise, given the current political circumstances, and that only time would mitigate his guilt. *Relations between people will change, as they have already been changing, many things will be forgotten, hence it follows that I have to be patient and resigned.* When he thought things over calmly and soberly like this, he even freed Stoyan Kralev of any blame – he was just a tool of the higher-ups and acted as they ordered him to, just as his inferiors danced to his tune. Whoever instead might have been in his place as party secretary would have acted the same way, otherwise they would have gotten rid of him. Thus even he, the other party secretary, wouldn't be patting the back of a man who remained outside the co-op for so long and whose son, on top of everything, had committed a political crime. The only difference would be in their outward approach, but that was a question of character. Stoyan Kralev was hotheaded, he had no talent for demagoguery, whatever was on the tip of his tongue came out of his mouth. That's why they removed him from his post, he didn't have a way with people...

After so many and such stinging insults, which wounded his dignity and pride to the quick, Kiro Dzhelebov perhaps would not have sought and found peace in resignation through his own moral strength if he hadn't been drawing hope from the Bible as well. He had started peering into that book even in his younger years to see what his grandfather had written in it and what his father had later added. In the pages of their family chronicles, his grandfather Kiro had written in chemical pencil the names of all or almost all the people in their family, from his great-grandfather to his grandchildren, as well as the most important events in their lives. At the root of the large family tree stood a certain Angel, a braid maker and merchant who had lived somewhere in Thrace. After him came his two sons and his daughter, their sons and grandsons, one of whom was Grandpa Kiro, who had lived in Sliven in his younger years and from there had moved to Dobruja. Grandpa Kiro had written the date of his wedding to Grandma Grozda and the birthdates of his children. After him, the elder Marko Dzhelebov had written in blue ink the date of his wedding, the birthdates of his three sons, and the untimely deaths of his daughter and his wife. And finally – the wedding of his firstborn son, Kiro. Marko Dzhelebov died at the age of fifty-four of a heart attack while threshing, while lifting sheaves of wheat onto a stack. He was healthy until the last minute of his life, a strict and withdrawn person, he only let children get close to him, since, as he always said, only they were truly people. After his death, Kiro Dzhelebov moved into the house where they lived now, taking the Bible with him along with all the housewares, and several months later wrote Marko's birthdate in the family chronicle. After some time his middle brother had a daughter, while his youngest brother got married; he wrote these events there too, and thus he became the chronicler for his whole extended family. When reading over the names of his distant forefathers, he would unwittingly rack his brains to imagine their faces, voices, their clothes and their lives, he was overcome by a strange feeling when he stopped to think that the blood of these people was running in his veins. Judging from the short notes about each one of them, they were an implacable lot, with different inclinations and fates. Among them, there were craftsmen, merchants, priests, and teachers, one volunteer revolutionary fighter,* two army officers, one exile in Anatolia, one fighter in Hadzhi Dimitar and Karadzha's rebel band, there was also a young bride named Kirka "who killed herself with a sickle after being ravaged by Turks," while her brother Dimo took revenge for her by slaughtering an entire family of Turks, Atanas disappeared as a communist during the events of 1923, Grandma Mina had eighteen children, while some Mircho or other ended up in Russia and his grandchildren were now living there in the city of Nikolaev. The names of all these people had been passed down from generation to generation, so that they remained alive until this very day, and this itself was a kind of miracle. The name of that first great-grandfather Angel, borne by so many Angels, was now borne by Anyo, his other son, just like his brothers' sons and daughters bore the same names that were written in the family chronicle. He himself bore the name of the bride Kirka, who had lived in the dark days of Ottoman slavery and violence and who had preferred to kill herself rather than live defiled. He tried to imagine the dramatic fate of this young woman, as well as the fates of all the others, and in so doing he sank into the myster- ies of a sprawling two-centuries-old family that was scattered across the whole of Bulgaria and abroad, which had passed through countless ups and downs, through blood and fire, so as to live on today in him and his sons, in his brothers and their sons.

In his younger years, when he opened up the first pages of the Bible, Kiro Dzhelebov was surprised to find that there, too, the genealogy of a family was told, and that was the family of mankind. The very first stories about the creation of the world, about Adam and Eve and the flood, seemed to him as naïve as fairy tales for children, and he was curious as to whether this enormous book was filled only with such tales. And so he read about Abraham's family, about Sodom and Gomorrah, about how Sarah became the pharaoh's wife, and when he read the tempestuous, moving story of Joseph, he found himself in a world of horrors, struggles, suffering, and miracles, which he could no longer tear himself away from. For years on end he slowly entered into that world of vague and contradictory events, he would get confused and reread them, and at the same slow pace would make sense of them and separate out the truth from the legend. He didn't share with anyone what he had read, since his sons didn't show any interest in the book, they called it "Daddy's book," and he was not angry with them for their good-natured mockery. They were young and could not discover the truths about life in these parables and legends, just as he at their age could not discover them. There was even a time when he considered these writings to be an entertaining read or like the tales in *One Thousand and One Nights*. Because he had also read that book (one of the schoolteachers had given it to him), as well as the short retelling of the *Iliad*, which he had found in Marko's high school textbooks. The first of these two books had drawn him in with the endless vicissitudes of the plot, while he had not understood the latter due to the brief and dry presentation, and also due to his lack of familiarity with Greek mythology. He was to some extent a well-qualified reader. He alone of the villagers would pick up the newspapers and magazines at the community center, he had read many books belonging to the schoolteachers who had lived in his home, as well as his sons' old textbooks and books they had left behind, he also borrowed books from Ilko Kralev. However, no one besides his wife knew that during the long winter evenings he would read whatever he could get his hands on. He did not like to share with anyone what he had read, so as not to appear in the others' eyes as a person who had taken up a calling unnatural to him; what's more, his generation of villagers had long nursed an innate scorn for "bookish folks." This was why even his sons had no inkling of how inquisitive he was and how many books he had read. He listened carefully to what they said on various topics, just as he had listened to the schoolteachers, and thanks to the former and the latter he had learned to speak and write as properly as they did. As a child he had finished fourth grade and he still remembered the lessons, short stories, and poems they had studied, just as he remembered almost everything he had read.

Out of all the books he had come across, the Bible made the biggest impression on him. He was stunned by the fact that the life described in it from thousands of years ago fully resembled present-day life, only the names of the countries, cities, and people were different. Everywhere there were wars, poverty and misery, treachery and lies, violence and slavery, joy and happiness. *Why had mankind lived all these millennia, since nothing had changed in the least, not getting any worse or any better*, he would ask himself and then answer: *People seem to have merely reproduced in this world and nothing more.* He found himself liking some of the stories more and more and he would often reread them, the people they told about seemed to come alive before his eyes, as if he had met and talked to them. When he read about Joseph, he imagined as if seeing it in real life how his brothers threw him down a well, sold him into slavery, and lied to their father that he had been devoured by wild beasts, he also saw the lonely Ruth walking through the rich man's fields, gleaning wheat after the reapers had passed, just as he had seen poor women from the village gleaning wheat in the fields after the reaping was done, he also saw Job sitting on the dung heap in front of his house scraping the pus from his boils with a potsherd, he could hear his voice: "Let the day perish on which I was born! Have I not kept silent, have I done anyone wrong?" Over the years, when many misfortunes befell him, Kiro Dzhelebov would once again reread the stories about these and many other biblical figures and was comforted by their fate. All these innocents had suffered, yet they were not angry with anyone and did not seek revenge for their suffering, and in the end they were rewarded for their uncomplaining patience. And then he believed that patience and resignation were man's supreme virtues and that every evil deed gave rise to more evil. Whoever took revenge and killed, even if the law was on his side, thinking that he would be doing away with one evil, in fact had brought about yet another evil. In killing your brother's murderer, you bring about for his loved ones, who are innocent, the same evil that he brought about for your loved ones. Instead of ten, twenty people would suffer – the evil will have been avenged, but not eliminated.

This was how Kiro Dzhelebov managed to smother the hatred that had blazed up in his soul that morning in the yard outside the horse barn. But life constantly tempted him toward vengeance – either a new misfortune would occur at the co-op, for which they would suspect him and reproach him, or his sons would suffer some setback precisely because Stoyan Kralev and others like him had put the whole family in this miserable situation. And it always happened such that Stoyan Kralev as an official functionary would be the first to express his indignation and hatred toward him. The sharp spasm in his throat would begin to suffocate him, and the thought that everything could be made right with death would once again grip his mind. This thought had conquered him once and forced him to attempt suicide, he knew its strength and knew that if he let it overwhelm him again, this time he would inevitably commit murder. In hours of extreme agitation, this idea pushed him toward the crime, he was ready to commit it and only his strenuous struggle against it returned him to mental equilibrium. But the idea lived in him and was constantly eating away at him, and over the years it turned into an intense illness which was only waiting for a stimulus in order to cloud his reason and conquer his will. Like every sick man, he sought a cure for his illness and found it in resignation. But even resignation did not help him in decisive moments, and he resolved to swallow the bitterest of pills – self-abasement. Only this could act upon him as an antidote to his grueling desire for revenge and as we already know, he decided to turn his primordial enemy into a friend.

Stoyan Kralev interpreted Kiro Dzhelebov's desire for friendship as repentance for his unexpiated guilt and allowed him to grow close in the naïve belief that all opponents of the new life sooner or later realized the error of their ways, while for him this was a moral reward for his years-long efforts to win over such people to his cause. Stoyan Kralev arranged with the police to get Kiro Dzhelebov a hunting license and a rifle and accepted him into the village hunting party, and in so doing gave him to understand that he accepted his repentance and put an end to their former enmity. Stoyan Kralev, of course, did not feel guilty for this enmity and had no idea that Kiro Dzhelebov was committing outrages against his own pride out of fear that he would give in to his own hatred and kill him. Kiro Dzhelebov really did do everything he could to grow close to him and become tied to him, and even went so far as to turn into his servant, offering up his services himself, he did much work for him around the yard, invited him over, and would himself go to Stoyan Kralev's house now and then. Four or five years passed and no disputes cropped up between the two of them. In the beginning, Kiro Dzhelebov suffered from his own hypocrisy and could not sleep whole nights, especially when he learned that the village wiseacres had stuck him with a new nickname – "the Bodyguard" (of Stoyan Kralev, of course). On the other hand, however, he felt relief from his deadly passion for revenge, while his efforts at toadying up to Stoyan Kralev and playing the role of the repentant ever more strongly pushed his worries about his sons and life as a whole to the back burner. Thus with exorbitant efforts of the will, he managed to replace in his consciousness the thought of revenge with the virtue of resignation. Besides that, he discovered new features in Stoyan Kralev's character, which earlier he had not been able to or due to his bias had not been willing to see. He showed solidarity with his comrades in the hunting party, he patiently listened to the co-op members' criticism and advice, if the occasion permitted he would have a drink and make merry right alongside the others, and sometimes he would even criticize certain irregularities in the running of the village. Whether years ago his official position demanded that he act differently with people, or whether he was now pretending to be someone else, was not so important at the end of the day. What was important was that Kiro Dzhelebov had already tasted the fruits of his resignation. He and his wife worked at the co-op, they were healthy, their sons and their families were healthy, he went hunting on his days off, in the winter they would get together on holidays or at comradely gatherings – in short, after numerous misadventures, life had once again set off down a well-beaten path and his soul became more peaceful. *We only have one life, right? So we'll live it out, just so long as we're healthy,* he would think, remembering the old saying: "With patience, even water can be carried in a sieve."

He tried to take the news of Marko's death as a terrible twist of fate which could befall a man at any time, and decided to take on the anguish of this great misfortune alone. He hid the telegram from his wife, and while he was preparing her for the tragic news, he also asked their relative who worked at the city post office to keep it a secret. He purposely delayed his return to the village, so as not to find his wife at home; for several evenings she had been going to a neighborhood working bee. She had left his supper on the table, he set it aside, got the ink and the Bible, and opened it to the pages of the family chronicle. The original pages had long since been filled and he had glued in new pages from his sons' school notebooks. On them he had noted his joining of the co-op, Marko's defection, his other sons' weddings, and the birth dates of his grandchildren, the birth of a lamb with two heads, the big hailstorm two years earlier, and other important events connected to the life of the family. On the final page there were two blank lines and he wrote:

> *My eldest son, Marko Kirov Dzhelebov, died in Germany on December 20, 1965 May he rest in peace!*

He read what was written and anguish suddenly overcame him as if from an ambush, it pierced his heart and his breast so sharply that it stopped his breath, as if Marko's death had become real and irreversible only after he had written it in the family chronicle. He paced around the room, then opened the window and stuck his head outside for some fresh air. The wind had grown stronger, snowflakes whirled in the light from the window, he could hear the branches of the acacia tree creaking, a freezing, inescapable sorrow wafted in from the night. Kiro Dzhelebov sensed that he had never felt a more intense pain or stronger spiritual shock. As always in such states he realized that now, too, he must find the strength to bear his suffering, he tried to comfort himself with the simple and indisputable truth that death did not pick and choose, but took those it had marked beforehand. This time, too, he tried to find consolation in the Bible. He opened it to a page which he had marked with a scrap of paper the last time, and it was the story of Job. He started reading somewhere in the middle, but his consciousness was split, he was wondering why, in fact, Job had been punished with such suffering, and at the same time he was imagining Marko lying in a coffin in some hospital, alone in his death among foreign people in a foreign land. After that he saw him as a baby with his soft, elongated skull, kicking unswaddled in his crib, which had been hung right there on that hook in the ceiling, he remembered how, when Marko was three, he had gotten scared by the neighbor's dog and with a shriek had snuggled in his embrace and he had inhaled the intoxicating scent of a child's flesh, while feeling with his palm the fast beating of his little heart. *That flesh and that heart are now dead,* he thought to himself, while reading about Job's friends who asked why and how it was that innocent people were made to suffer. *One of his friends says that suffering is not always punishment for sins that have been committed and that sometimes God tests the faith of his most devoted mortals by subjecting them to the most harrowing trials. And God himself tells Job that he is tormenting himself in vain trying to discover the reasons for his suffering, because God's intentions cannot be fathomed, they are beyond human understanding.* This thought stunned him, because after many years he only now made sense of it. Until that minute he had not thought about the nature of God, out of habit he had taken him as an omnipresent and impersonal force that stood behind everything in the world. Now he saw him in the image of a hoary-headed old man, as he had once dreamed of him, an inaccessible, merciless despot who played with human fates with impunity and disposed of them however he saw fit. He remembered how he had led him to the Crag in his dream and had forced him to slaughter his firstborn son, just as he had forced Abraham to sacrifice his son. He had read that story many times as well, but only now did he make sense of it, too. The all-powerful God was not certain of his strength and his right to lord over people, and in order to impose his cult upon them, he stopped at nothing, even laying waste to whole nations. He was not even certain of those who were endlessly devoted to him, and he subjected them to the most terrible suffering, he wanted them to prove their faith with that which was dearest to them, with their flesh and blood. "What is this cruel, unappeasable, bloodthirsty God?" – Kiro Dzhelebov cried out, and for the first time, in a state of intense agitation, he did not realize he had fallen into a frenzy, he was talking to himself and pacing around the room from wall to wall. "People have made him up, because they realized they were weak and they needed someone to protect them and to rule them. Fine, but why did they think up such a God? He wants people to believe in him, but he himself doesn't believe in them, he asks for resignation, but himself takes revenge. They need to think up a new God, this one is godless! This one is only concerned with himself, with his own glory and power, while he derives the poor little people of their individuality, so they serve him and glorify him. Job, Abraham, and many others like them were robbed of their character, they aren't men at all, since they accept their suffering without complaint so as to appease his caprices. Abraham is a criminal, with a clean conscience he raised a knife to his son in order to prove his faith, but what is that faith that has to be proven with a crime? If he was a true father, he would have to sacrifice himself for his son or to take revenge for him. Yet he is ready to give away what is most sacred to him so as to pander to his God and to receive happiness, glory, and blessings from him. I, too, was like Job and the others; I, too, curled my tail between my legs in the face of my tormentor. He, too, demanded obedience and resignation from me, and constantly took revenge on me for others' sins. He's still taking revenge on me even now by pretending to have forgotten what evils he has done to my family. As if that wasn't enough, he has even 'forgiven' me for those evils, he 'forgives' me for having killed my son. He killed him! If he hadn't driven him to wander hungry in foreign lands, he wouldn't have come down with that sickness in his lungs. Who knows what hardships he had to pass through before he found his footing, what terrible worries he carried in his heart, what anguish he felt for us, for his brothers, for his home. And my other sons would have stayed here, they wouldn't have gone wandering to strange homes like apprentices, they wouldn't be ashamed to set foot in their home village. For so many years I spit in my own face, I turned myself into a bootlicker in people's eyes out of fear of washing away this shame. Out of fear alone, and nothing else. I thought up everything else, but deep down I knew that it was out of fear..."

The dog barked on the veranda, signaling that someone was coming, he soon heard footsteps on the stairs as well. Kiro Dzhelebov got ahold of himself and saw that he had left the window open and that the room had grown cold. He closed the window, put the Bible away, and bent down to put more wood in the stove. This is how Auntie Tanka found him, bent over the stove, still wearing his coat. He told her that he had sent Marko a New Year's telegram, that on his way back he had gotten delayed at the co-op office and had only now come home. While she was making up the bed, he ate, then drank a glass of wine and went to bed. When Auntie Tanka had cleared the table and lain down beside him, he was already asleep or had at least drifted off. A strange peacefulness came over him, as was to be expected after extreme spiritual agitation. He slept deeply, and in the morning awoke a bit later than usual and went to the co-op. After icing everything over in the night, the blizzard had grown stronger and covered everything in deep snowdrifts. He spent two days around the barns, he returned home for lunch, and after supper he went to bed. On the third day, Sunday, he filled two bottles with new wine, took a bit of roasted pork as an appetizer, and around ten o'clock went to the tavern. Despite the blizzard, all the vineyard owners arrived one by one, sat down, and started tasting the new wines. An hour later, when Ivan Shibilev suggested that the hunters set out on a wolf hunt, Kiro Dzhelebov didn't ask himself whether this was wise or wonder whether he should go out into the fields in such weather, he got up serenely with the other hunters and went home to get his rifle. Auntie Tanka had lit the oven in the room on the ground floor, she was working on something there and didn't hear him. He went upstairs, put on a pair of wool socks, grabbed his rifle and his cartridge belt, and went to leave, but then thought of something and returned from the doorway. He took the Bible out of the cupboard, took out the ink, and just as he was, with his rifle slung over his shoulder, he wrote in the margins of the last page of the family chronicle:

Kiro Dzhelebov killed Stoyan Kralev on December 24, 1965.

He tucked the Bible back into the cupboard and went out.

ENDNOTES

PAGE 10: An honorific title for an older man, coming from the Turkish *bey*.

PAGE 24: Gyuro Mihaylov – a Bulgarian soldier who died in a fire on Christmas Day in 1880, after refusing to abandon his post without orders, despite the encroaching blaze. He has become a symbol of loyalty and bravery – as well as foolhardiness.

PAGE 72: After a baby is born, Bulgarians traditionally do not merely dispose of the stump of umbilical cord, but rather bury or toss it in a carefully selected place, often the family home, believing that in doing so the person will be deeply tied to that place for their whole life.

PAGE 83: The September Uprising of 1923 was organized by the Bulgarian Communist Party (with backing from Comintern) to overthrow Alexander Tsankov's right-wing government, which itself had come to power through a coup d'état. The uprising was crushed and thousands of communists, anarchists, and agrarians were killed in the subsequent reprisals. During this period, Bulgaria was in a state of virtual civil war.

PAGE 108: Nikola Petkov (1893–1947) was one of the leaders of the Bulgarian Agrarian National Union. Although the Agrarians were initially allies of the Communists in the antifascist Fatherland Front movement established during World War Two, soon after the communist coup on September 9, 1944, Nikola Petkov became one of the leaders of the opposition, struggling to restore parliamentary democracy. The communists outlawed the opposition, while Petkov was accused of espionage, put on a show trial, and hanged in 1947, despite protests from Western nations.

PAGE 196: Russian for "Greetings, big brothers" – this phrase has historical significance, as Bulgarians also used it to welcome Russian troops who liberated them from the Ottoman Empire in the Russo-Turkish War of 1877–78.

PAGE 227: After the communist coup in Bulgaria, the new government set up People's Courts and tried hundreds of former politicians, as well as prominent business and military leaders. The victims included the country's three regents (who had had stewardship of the country on behalf of boy king Simeon II), eight royal advisers, twenty-two cabinet ministers, sixty-seven members of parliament, and forty-seven generals and other senior military officers. They were sentenced to death in a show trial in February of 1945, executed, and buried in mass graves.

PAGE 411: From a famous patriotic poem by Ivan Vazov, the patriarch of Bulgarian literature, about the battle of Bulgarian volunteer fighters against the Ottoman forces at Shipka Pass in 1877.

PAGE 555: A Bulgarian schoolteacher who sewed the flag for the April Uprising of 1876 against the Ottomans. The uprising was brutally suppressed, but ultimately contributed to Bulgaria's liberation, as public outrage over Ottoman brutality convinced the Great Powers to allow Russia to defeat Ottoman Turkey in the final Russo-Turkish war of 1877–78.

PAGE 569: Many Bulgarian irregulars volunteered to fight in the Russo-Turkish War of 1877–1878, which ultimately led to Bulgaria's liberation from the Ottoman Empire.

The translator Angela Rodel would like to thank the following people: Dr. Viktor Todorov, who served as linguistic editor, comparing every word of the English translation to the original and helping to track down obscure dialectal expressions; Ophelia Petrova, the author's widow, who generously gave her advice and support during the translation project; and Dr. Plamen Doinov, whose academic research on the reception of The Wolf Hunt *in Socialist Bulgaria was extremely enlightening.*